PART ONE

GLASSES

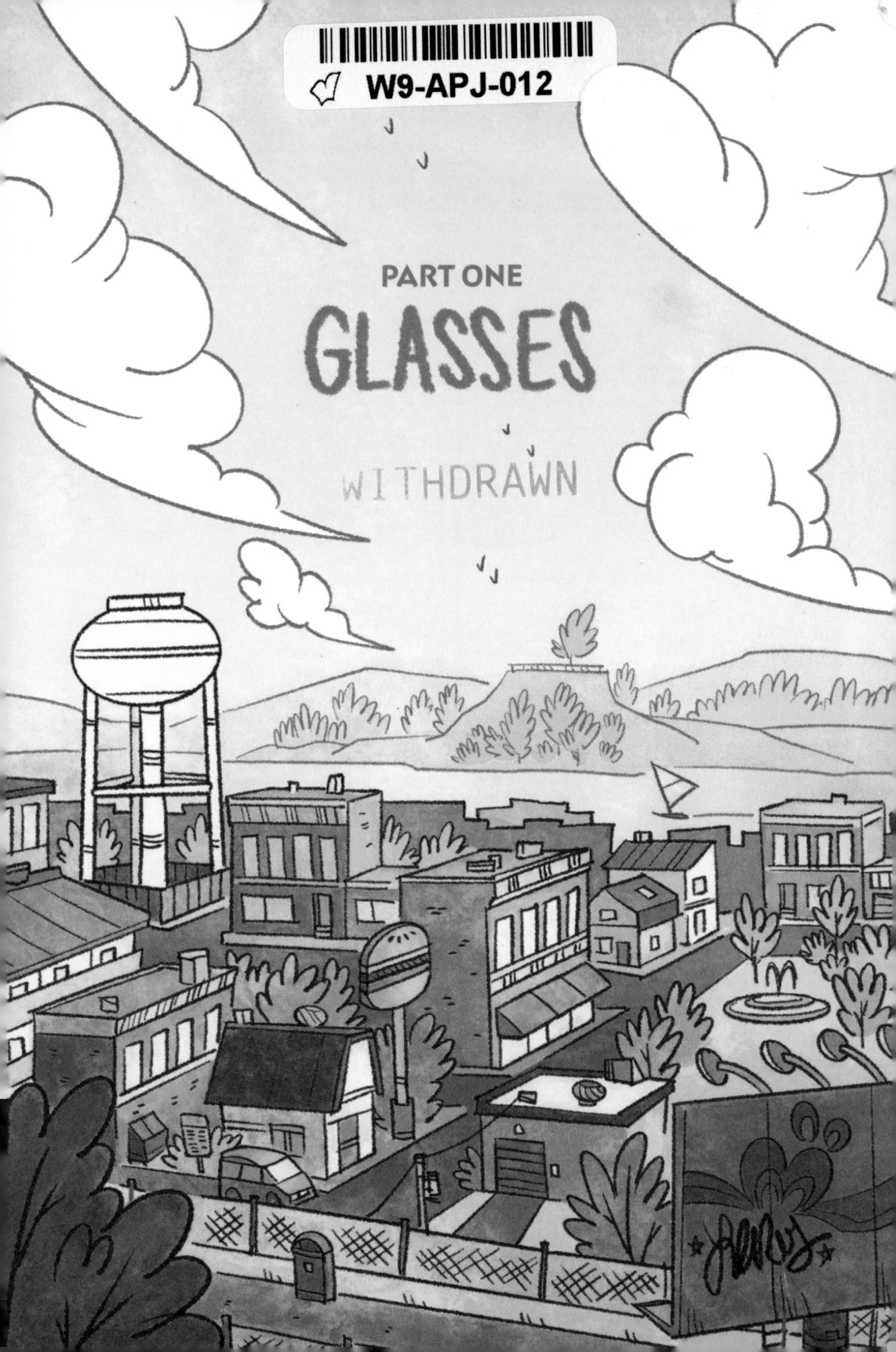

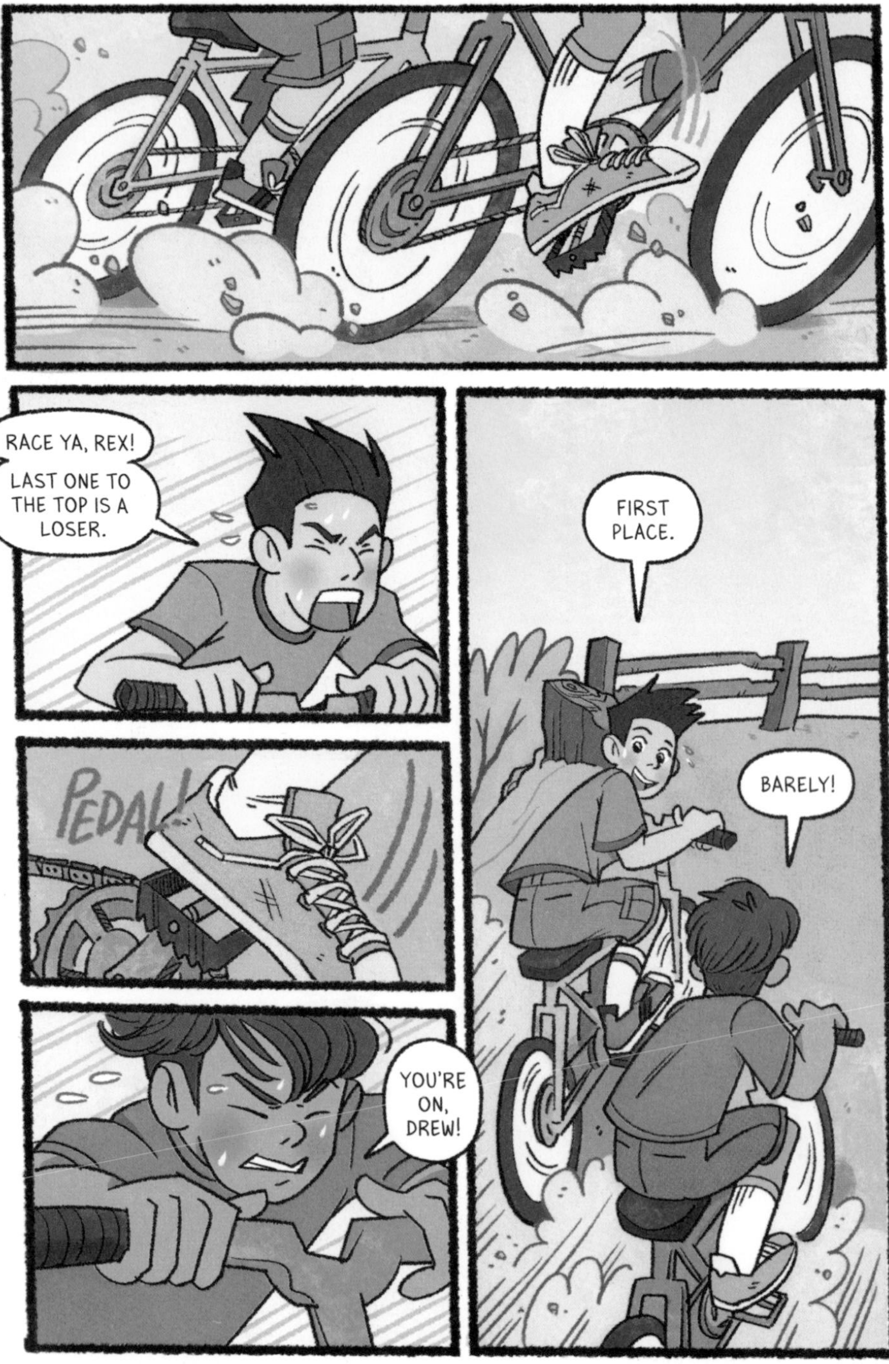
RACE YA, REX!
LAST ONE TO THE TOP IS A LOSER.
PEDAL!
YOU'RE ON, DREW!
FIRST PLACE.
BARELY!

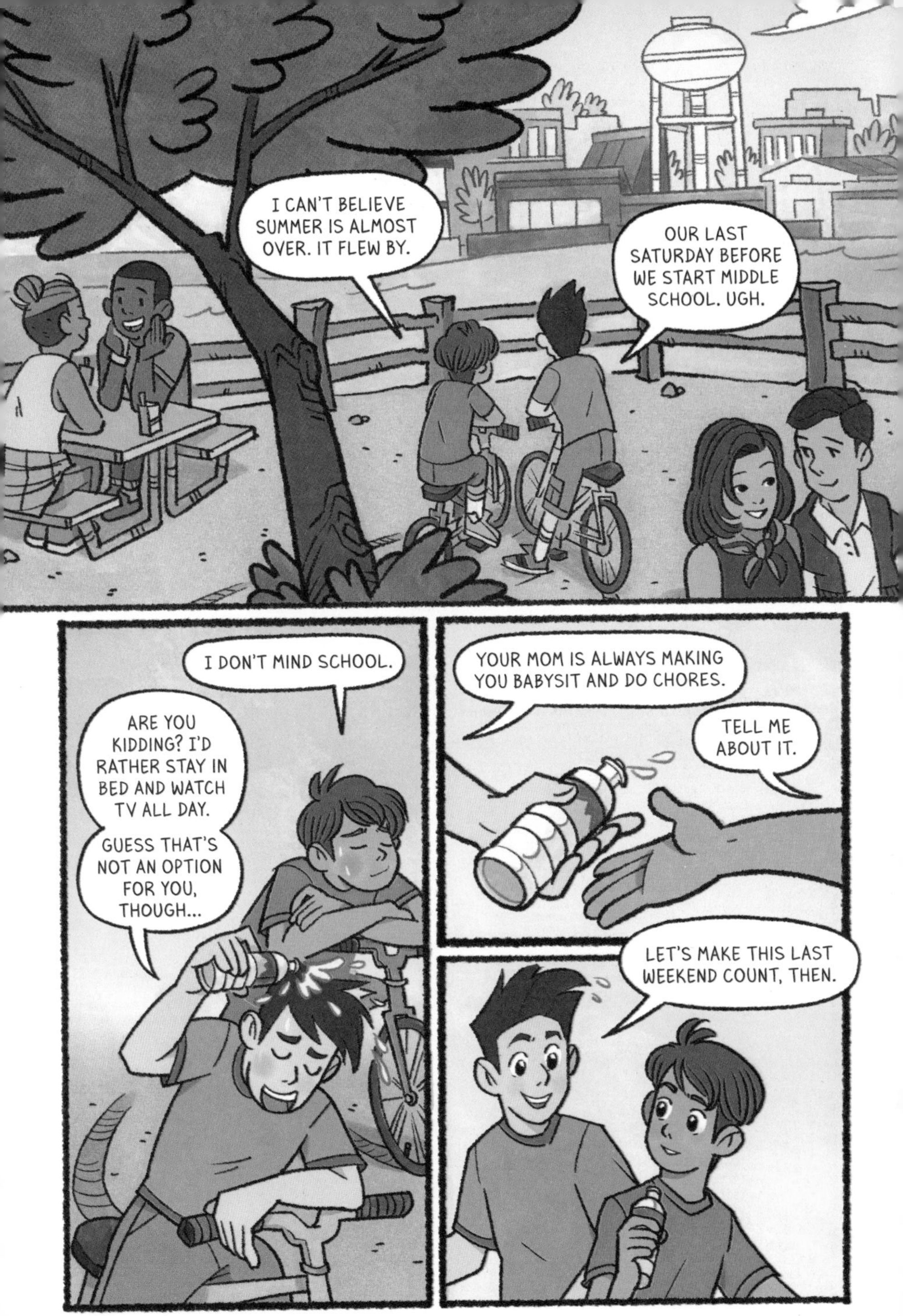
I CAN'T BELIEVE SUMMER IS ALMOST OVER. IT FLEW BY.
OUR LAST SATURDAY BEFORE WE START MIDDLE SCHOOL. UGH.
I DON'T MIND SCHOOL.
ARE YOU KIDDING? I'D RATHER STAY IN BED AND WATCH TV ALL DAY.
GUESS THAT'S NOT AN OPTION FOR YOU, THOUGH...
YOUR MOM IS ALWAYS MAKING YOU BABYSIT AND DO CHORES.
TELL ME ABOUT IT.
LET'S MAKE THIS LAST WEEKEND COUNT, THEN.

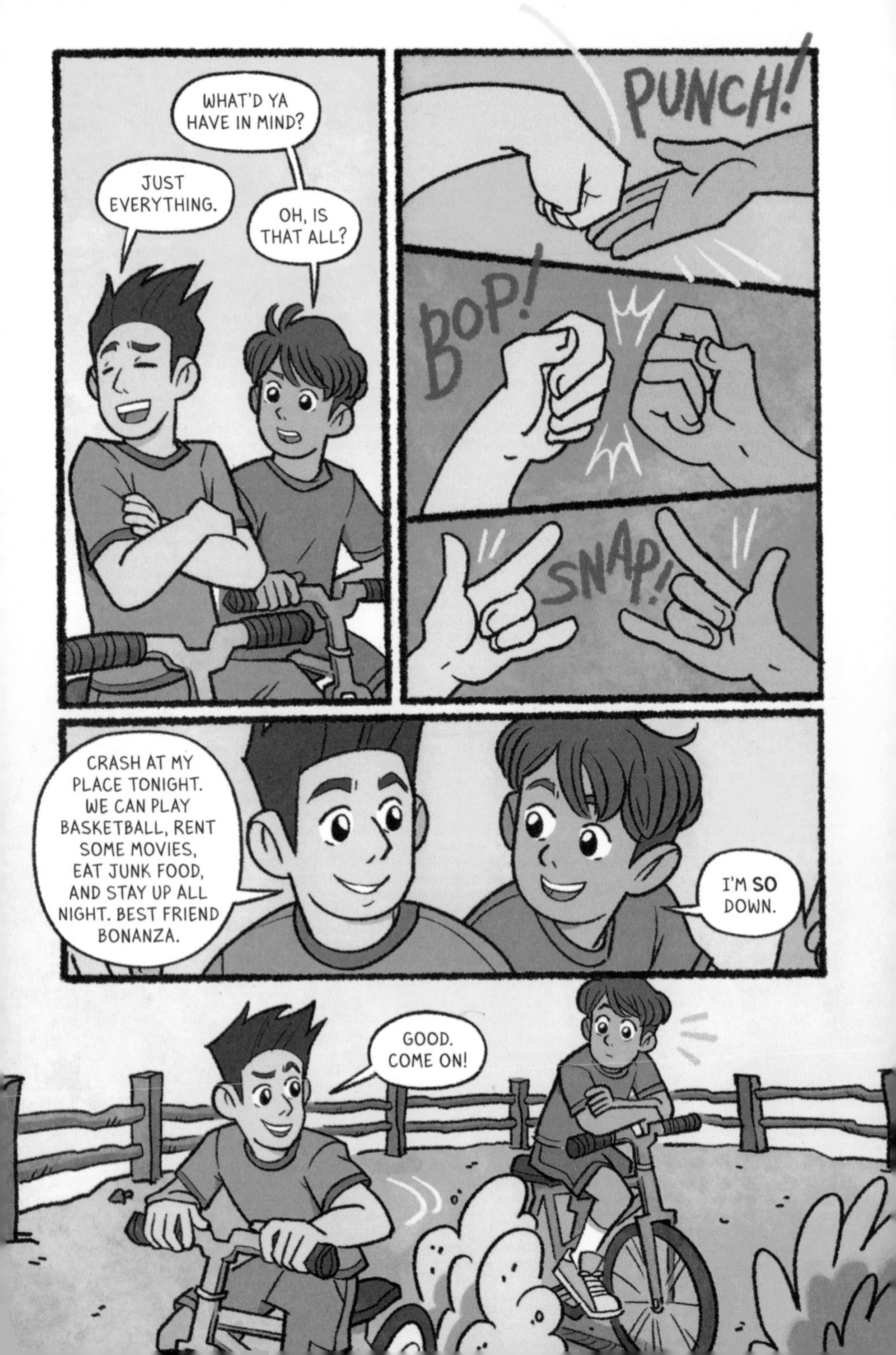
WHAT'D YA HAVE IN MIND?
JUST EVERYTHING.
OH, IS THAT ALL?
PUNCH!
BOP!
SNAP!
CRASH AT MY PLACE TONIGHT. WE CAN PLAY BASKETBALL, RENT SOME MOVIES, EAT JUNK FOOD, AND STAY UP ALL NIGHT. BEST FRIEND BONANZA.
I'M **SO** DOWN.
GOOD. COME ON!

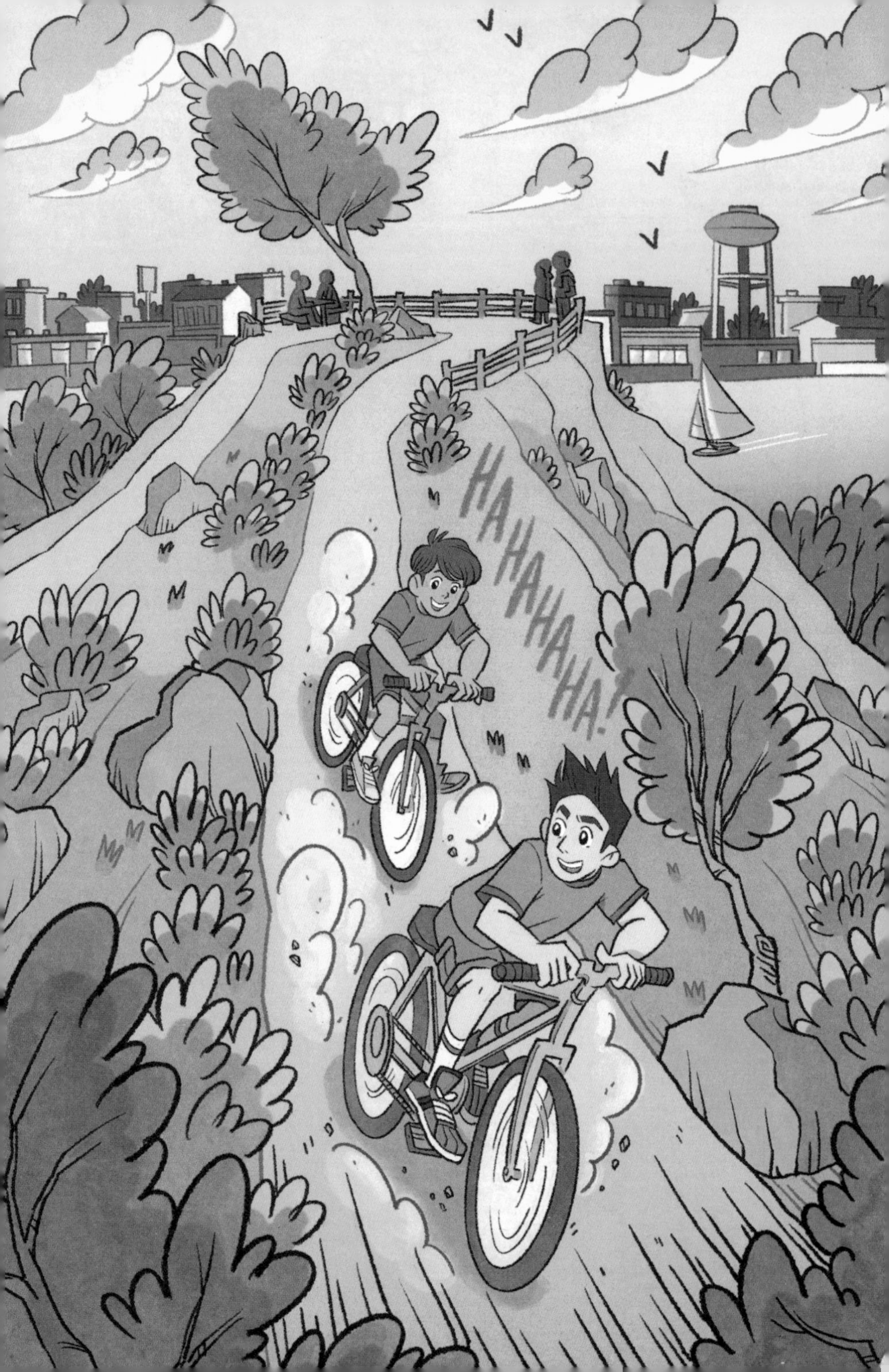
HAHAHAHAHA!

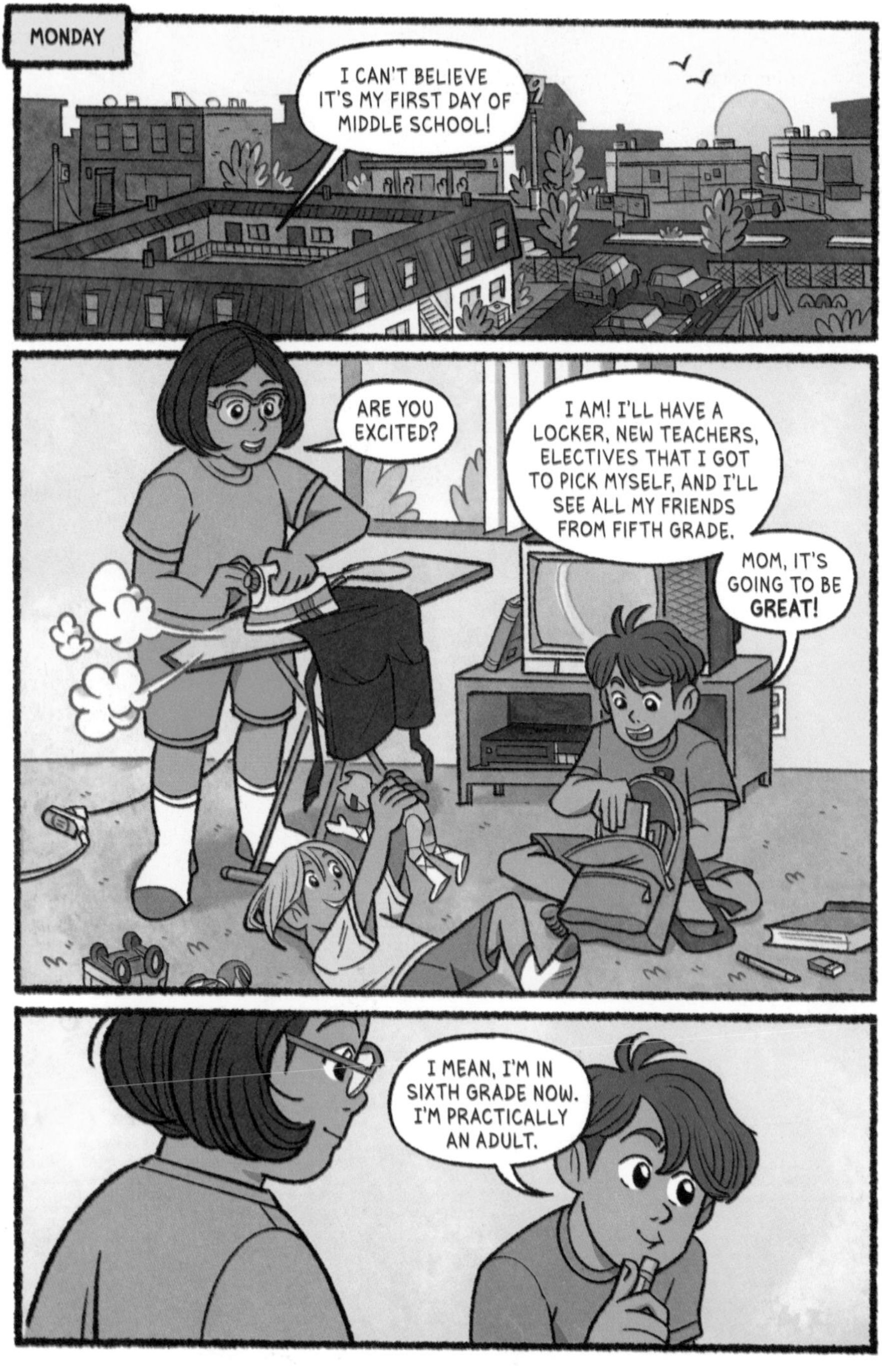
MONDAY
I CAN'T BELIEVE IT'S MY FIRST DAY OF MIDDLE SCHOOL!
ARE YOU EXCITED?
I AM! I'LL HAVE A LOCKER, NEW TEACHERS, ELECTIVES THAT I GOT TO PICK MYSELF, AND I'LL SEE ALL MY FRIENDS FROM FIFTH GRADE.
MOM, IT'S GOING TO BE **GREAT!**
I MEAN, I'M IN SIXTH GRADE NOW. I'M PRACTICALLY AN ADULT.

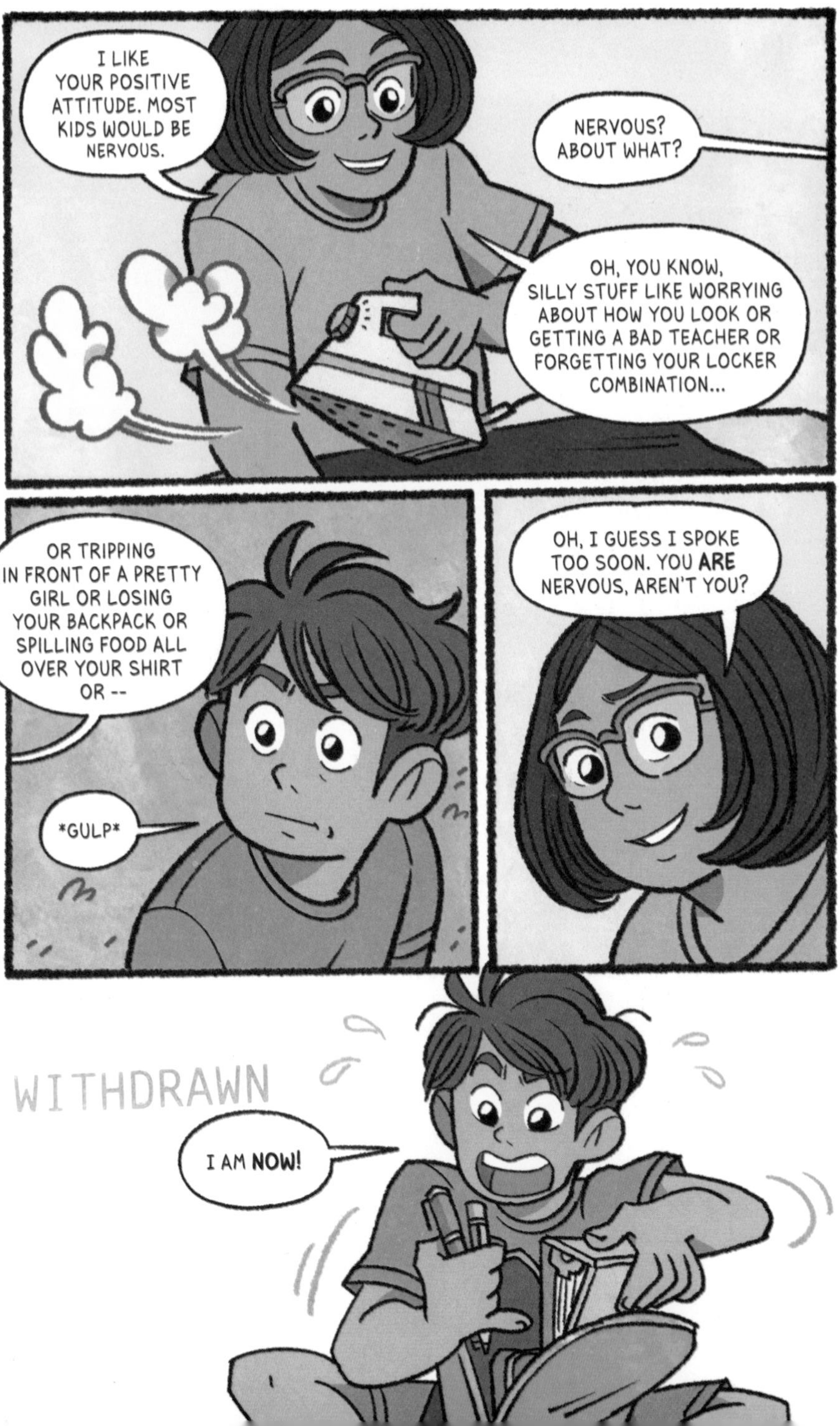
I LIKE YOUR POSITIVE ATTITUDE. MOST KIDS WOULD BE NERVOUS.
NERVOUS? ABOUT WHAT?
OH, YOU KNOW, SILLY STUFF LIKE WORRYING ABOUT HOW YOU LOOK OR GETTING A BAD TEACHER OR FORGETTING YOUR LOCKER COMBINATION...
OR TRIPPING IN FRONT OF A PRETTY GIRL OR LOSING YOUR BACKPACK OR SPILLING FOOD ALL OVER YOUR SHIRT OR --
GULP
OH, I GUESS I SPOKE TOO SOON. YOU **ARE** NERVOUS, AREN'T YOU?
I AM **NOW!**

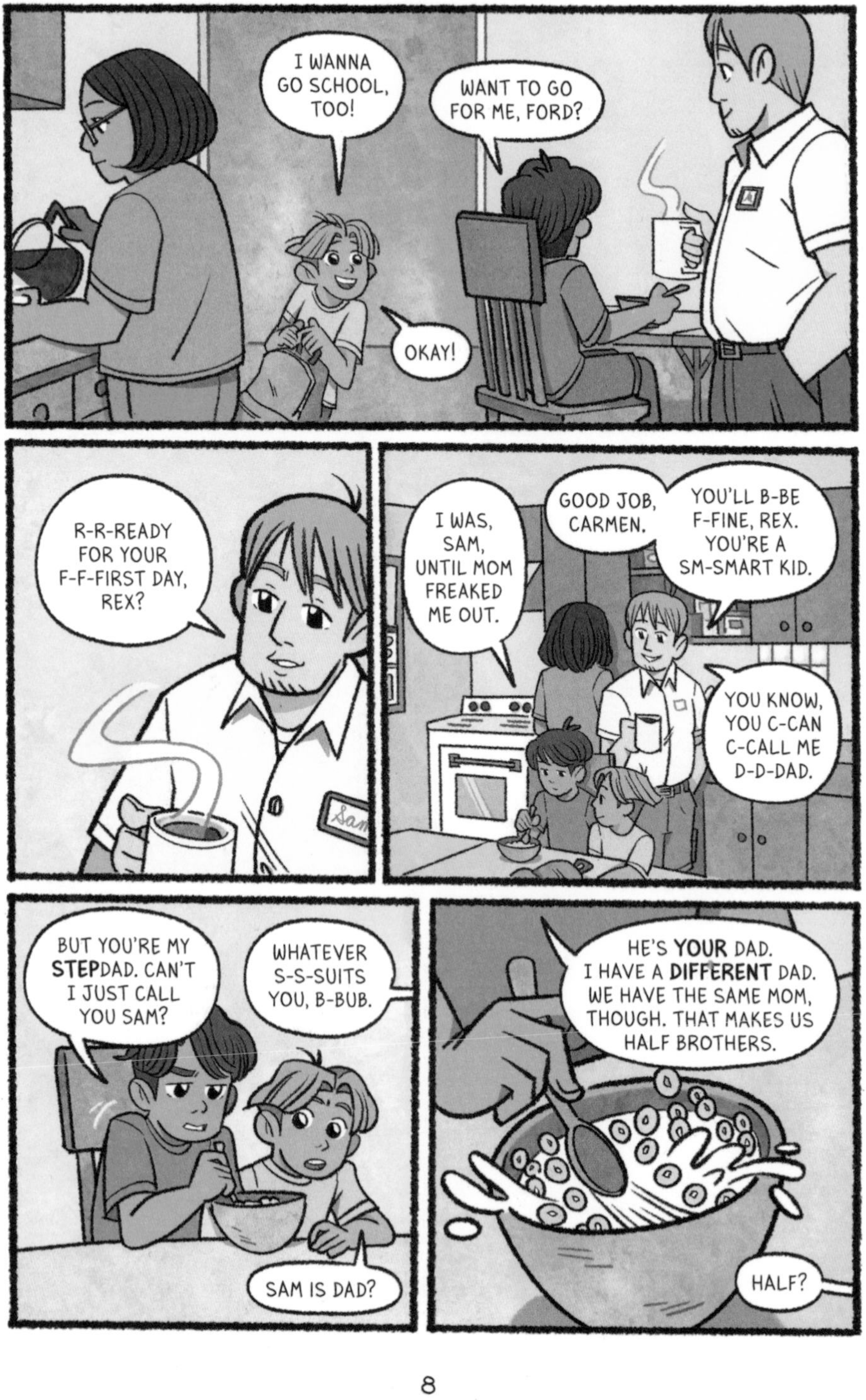
I WANNA GO SCHOOL, TOO!
WANT TO GO FOR ME, FORD?
OKAY!
R-R-READY FOR YOUR F-F-FIRST DAY, REX?
I WAS, SAM, UNTIL MOM FREAKED ME OUT.
GOOD JOB, CARMEN.
YOU'LL B-BE F-FINE, REX. YOU'RE A SM-SMART KID.
YOU KNOW, YOU C-CAN C-CALL ME D-D-DAD.
BUT YOU'RE MY **STEP**DAD. CAN'T I JUST CALL YOU SAM?
WHATEVER S-S-SUITS YOU, B-BUB.
SAM IS DAD?
HE'S **YOUR** DAD. I HAVE A **DIFFERENT** DAD. WE HAVE THE SAME MOM, THOUGH. THAT MAKES US HALF BROTHERS.
HALF?

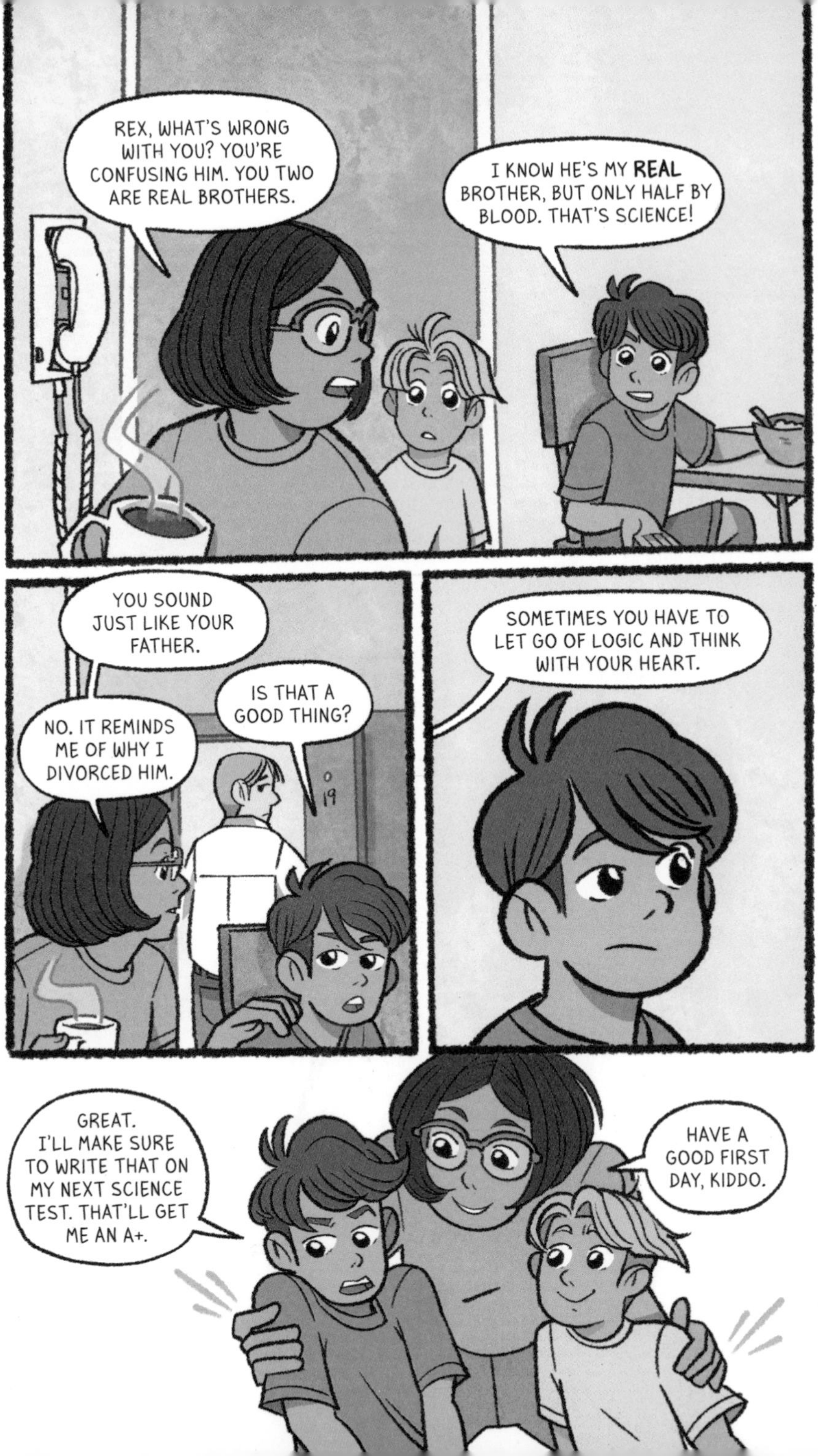
REX, WHAT'S WRONG WITH YOU? YOU'RE CONFUSING HIM. YOU TWO ARE REAL BROTHERS.
I KNOW HE'S MY **REAL** BROTHER, BUT ONLY HALF BY BLOOD. THAT'S SCIENCE!
YOU SOUND JUST LIKE YOUR FATHER.
IS THAT A GOOD THING?
NO. IT REMINDS ME OF WHY I DIVORCED HIM.
SOMETIMES YOU HAVE TO LET GO OF LOGIC AND THINK WITH YOUR HEART.
GREAT. I'LL MAKE SURE TO WRITE THAT ON MY NEXT SCIENCE TEST. THAT'LL GET ME AN A+.
HAVE A GOOD FIRST DAY, KIDDO.

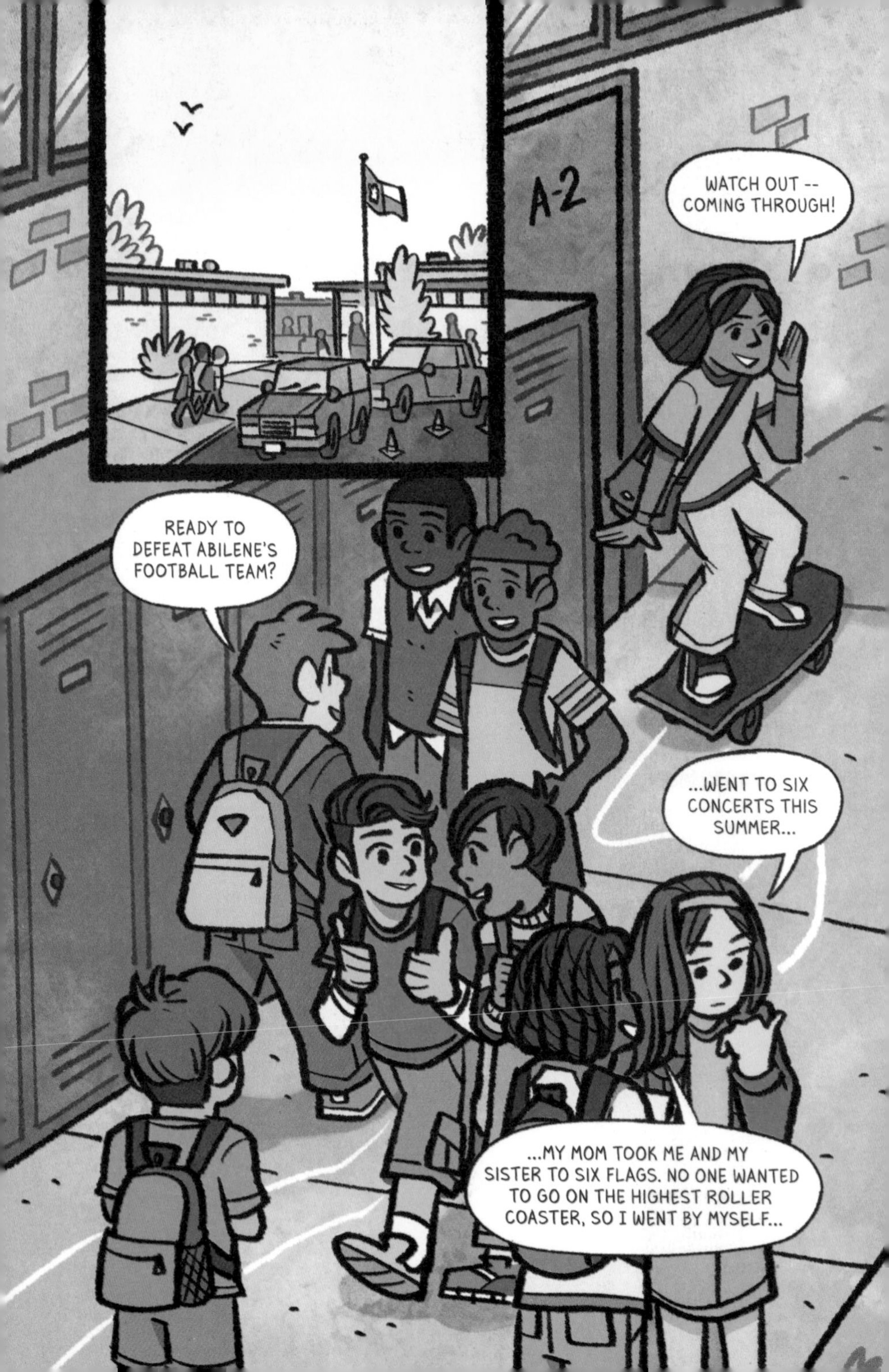
A-2
WATCH OUT -- COMING THROUGH!
READY TO DEFEAT ABILENE'S FOOTBALL TEAM?
...WENT TO SIX CONCERTS THIS SUMMER...
...MY MOM TOOK ME AND MY SISTER TO SIX FLAGS. NO ONE WANTED TO GO ON THE HIGHEST ROLLER COASTER, SO I WENT BY MYSELF...

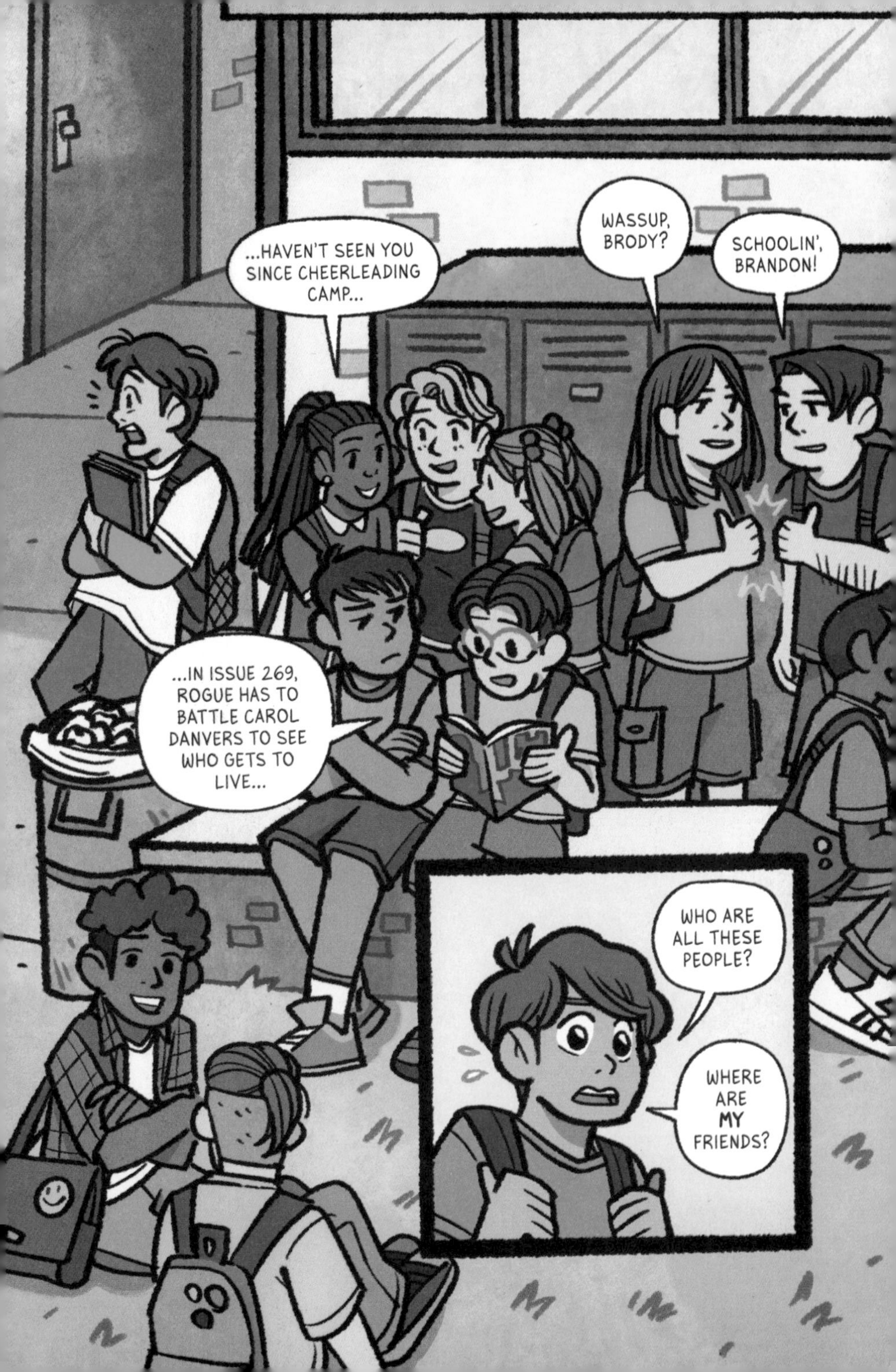
...HAVEN'T SEEN YOU SINCE CHEERLEADING CAMP...
WASSUP, BRODY?
SCHOOLIN', BRANDON!
...IN ISSUE 269, ROGUE HAS TO BATTLE CAROL DANVERS TO SEE WHO GETS TO LIVE...
WHO ARE ALL THESE PEOPLE?
WHERE ARE MY FRIENDS?

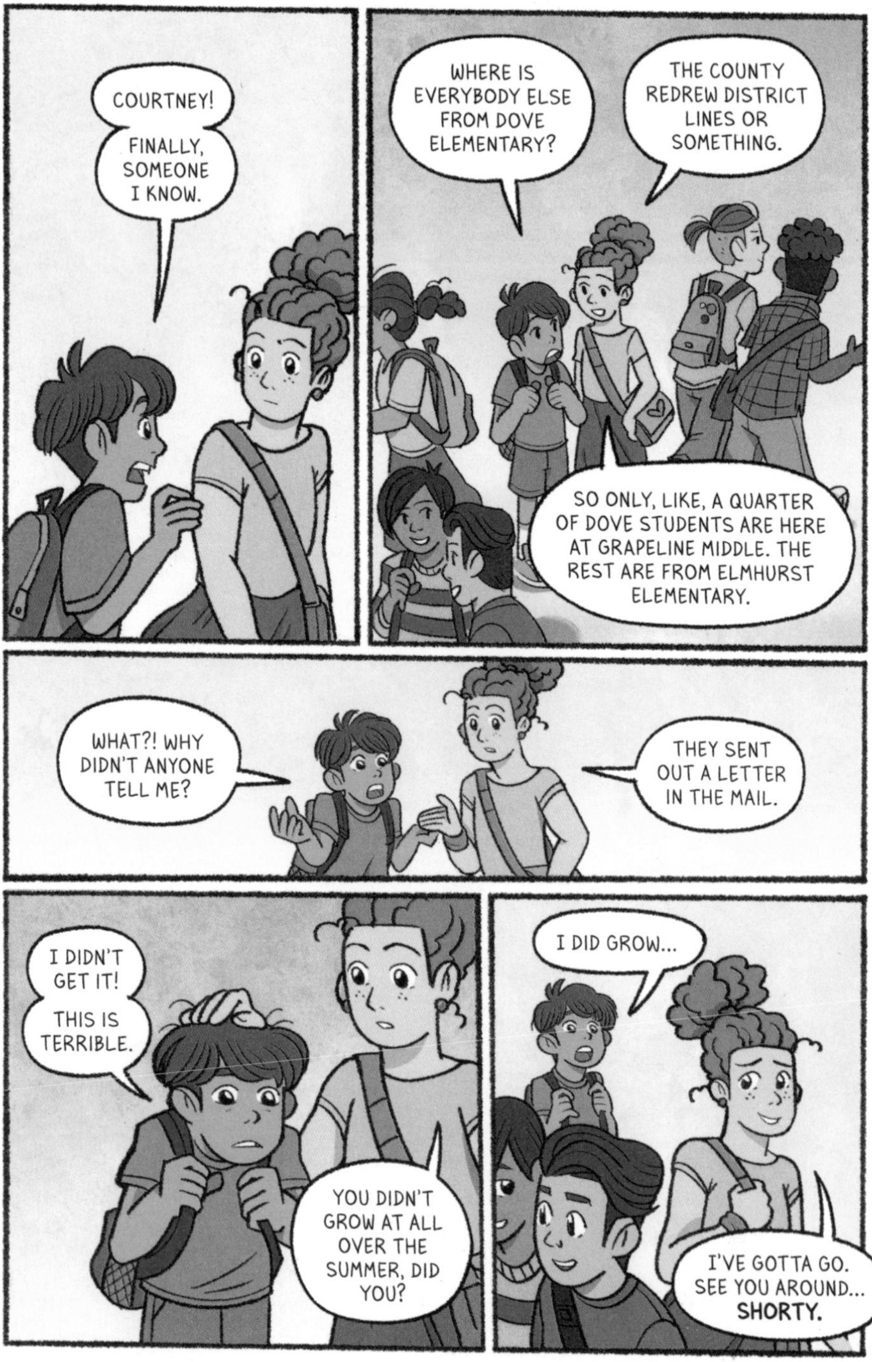
COURTNEY!
FINALLY, SOMEONE I KNOW.
WHERE IS EVERYBODY ELSE FROM DOVE ELEMENTARY?
THE COUNTY REDREW DISTRICT LINES OR SOMETHING.
SO ONLY, LIKE, A QUARTER OF DOVE STUDENTS ARE HERE AT GRAPELINE MIDDLE. THE REST ARE FROM ELMHURST ELEMENTARY.
WHAT?! WHY DIDN'T ANYONE TELL ME?
THEY SENT OUT A LETTER IN THE MAIL.
I DIDN'T GET IT!
THIS IS TERRIBLE.
YOU DIDN'T GROW AT ALL OVER THE SUMMER, DID YOU?
I DID GROW...
I'VE GOTTA GO. SEE YOU AROUND... **SHORTY.**

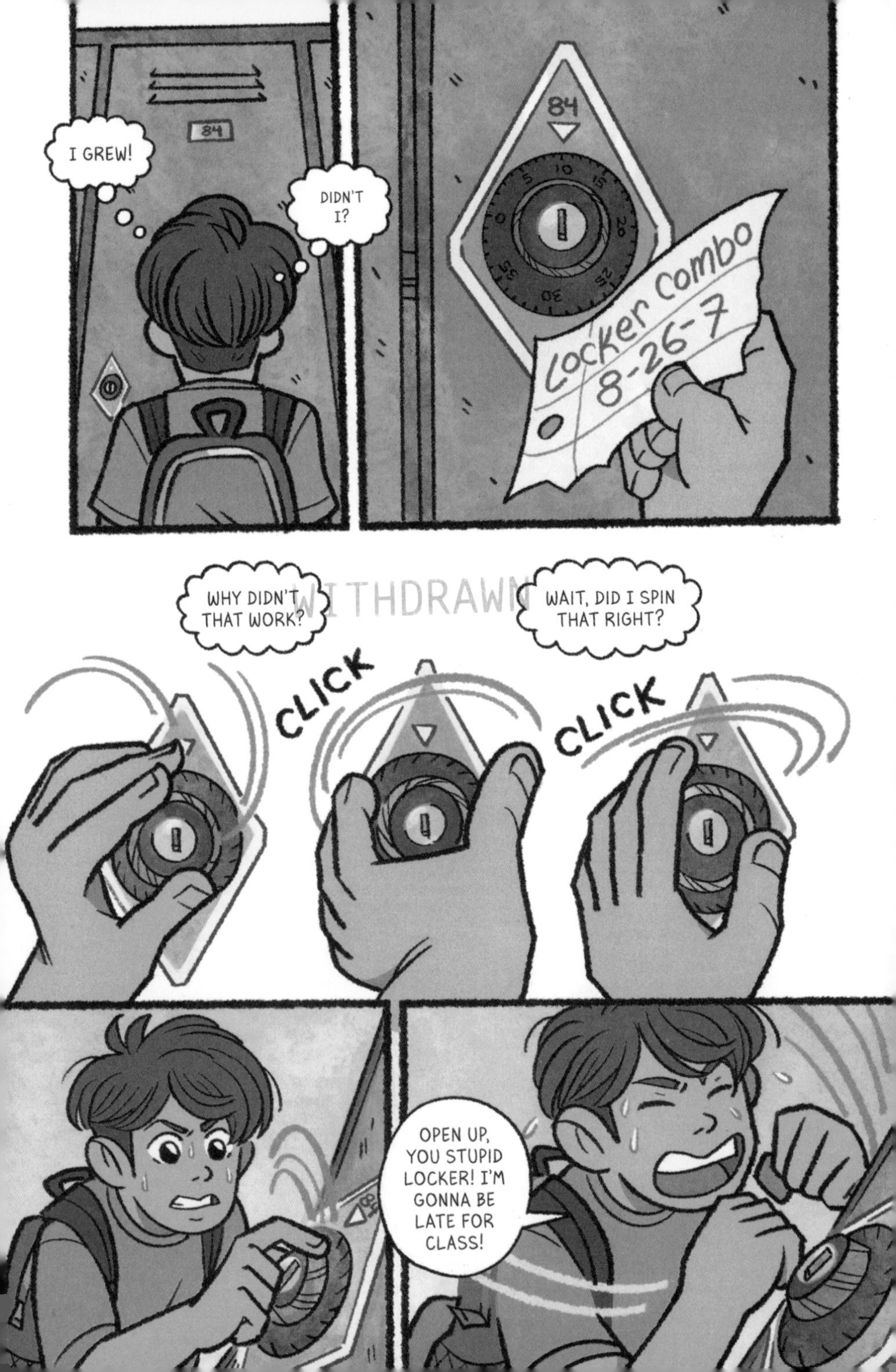
84
I GREW!
DIDN'T I?
84
Locker Combo
8-26-7
WHY DIDN'T THAT WORK?
WAIT, DID I SPIN THAT RIGHT?
CLICK
CLICK
OPEN UP, YOU STUPID LOCKER! I'M GONNA BE LATE FOR CLASS!

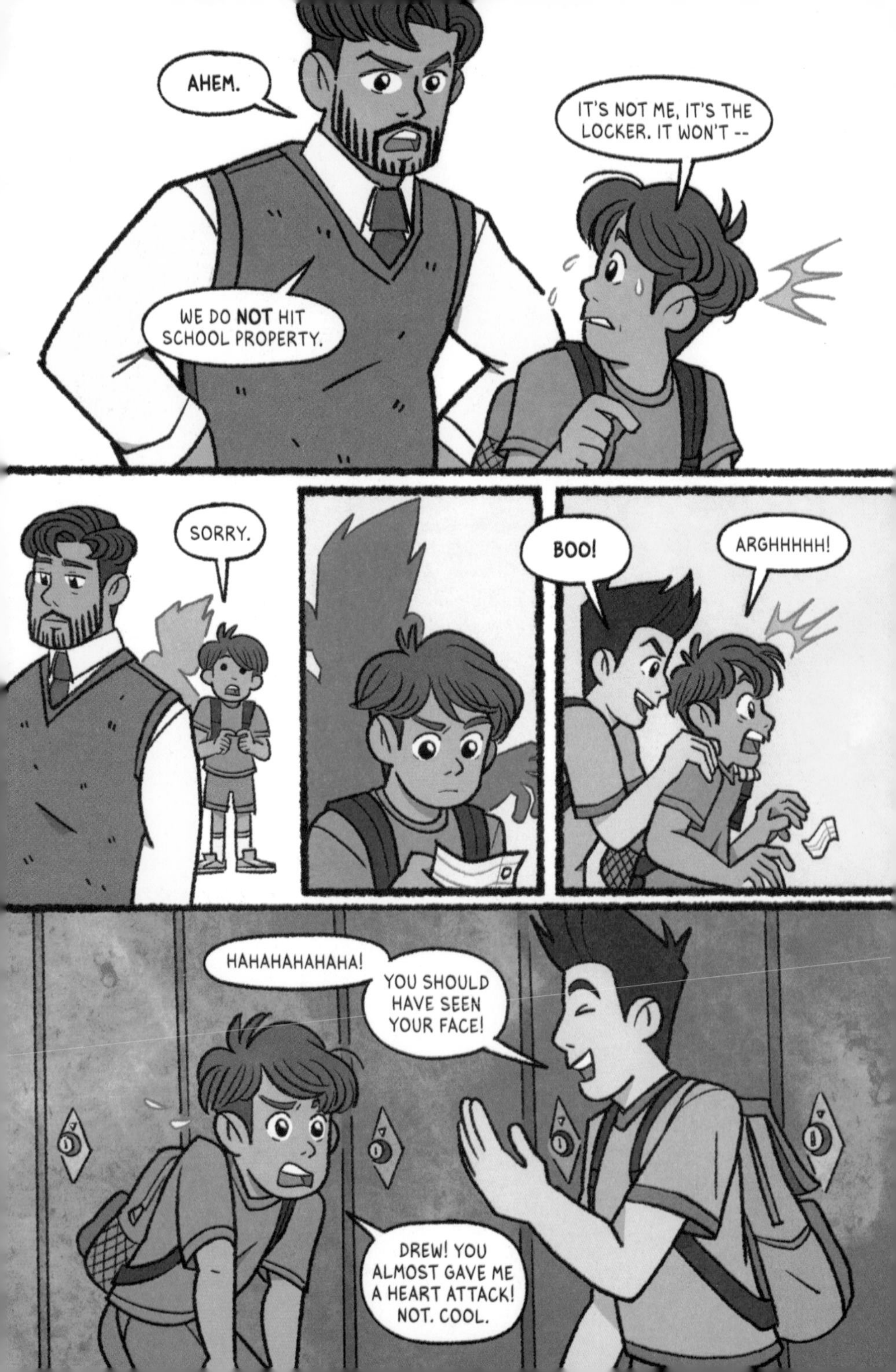
AHEM.
IT'S NOT ME, IT'S THE LOCKER. IT WON'T --
WE DO **NOT** HIT SCHOOL PROPERTY.
SORRY.
BOO!
ARGHHHHH!
HAHAHAHAHAHA!
YOU SHOULD HAVE SEEN YOUR FACE!
DREW! YOU ALMOST GAVE ME A HEART ATTACK! NOT. COOL.

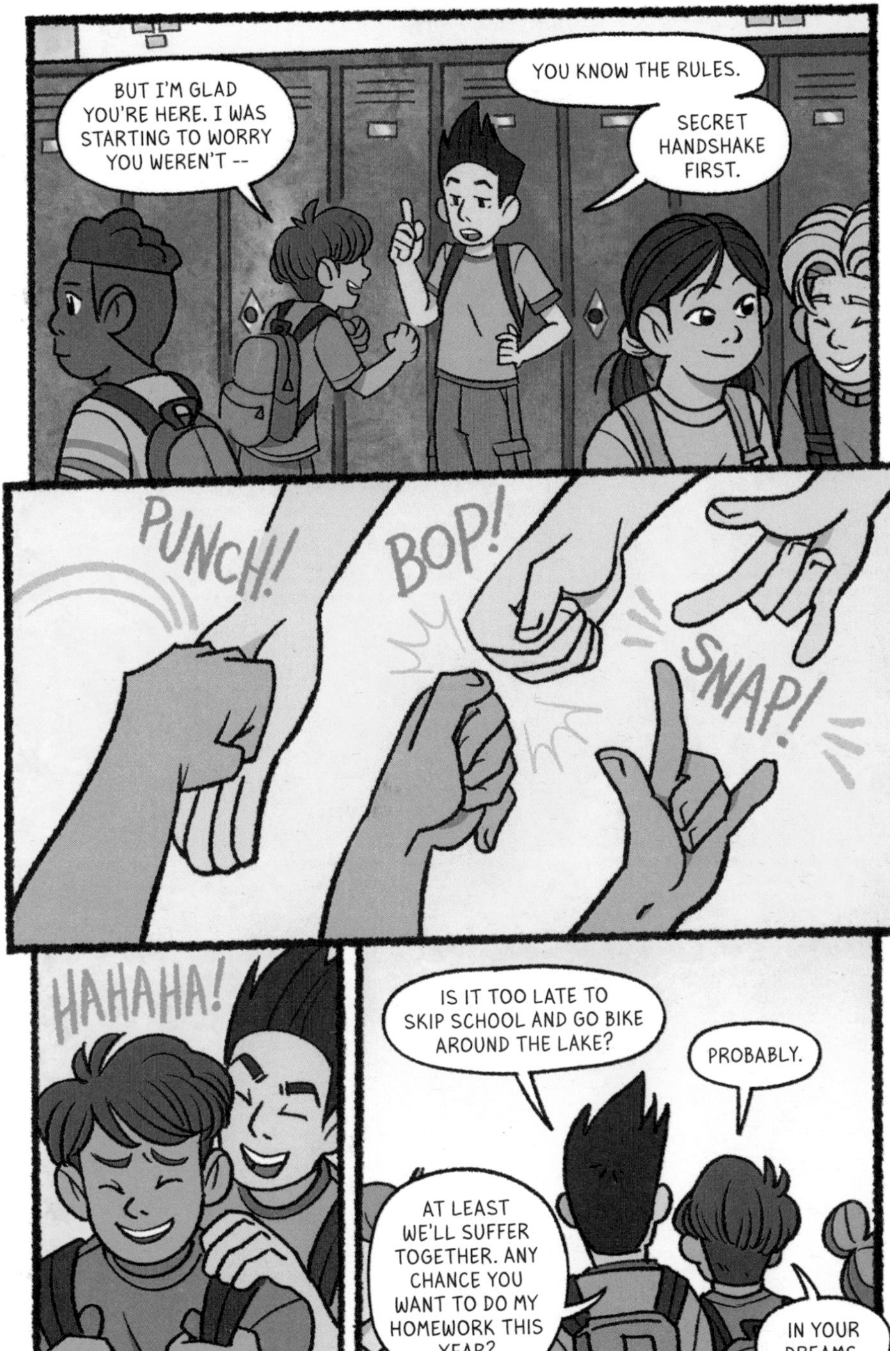

BUT I'M GLAD YOU'RE HERE. I WAS STARTING TO WORRY YOU WEREN'T --
YOU KNOW THE RULES.
SECRET HANDSHAKE FIRST.
PUNCH!
BOP!
SNAP!
HAHAHA!
IS IT TOO LATE TO SKIP SCHOOL AND GO BIKE AROUND THE LAKE?
PROBABLY.
AT LEAST WE'LL SUFFER TOGETHER. ANY CHANCE YOU WANT TO DO MY HOMEWORK THIS YEAR?
IN YOUR DREAMS.

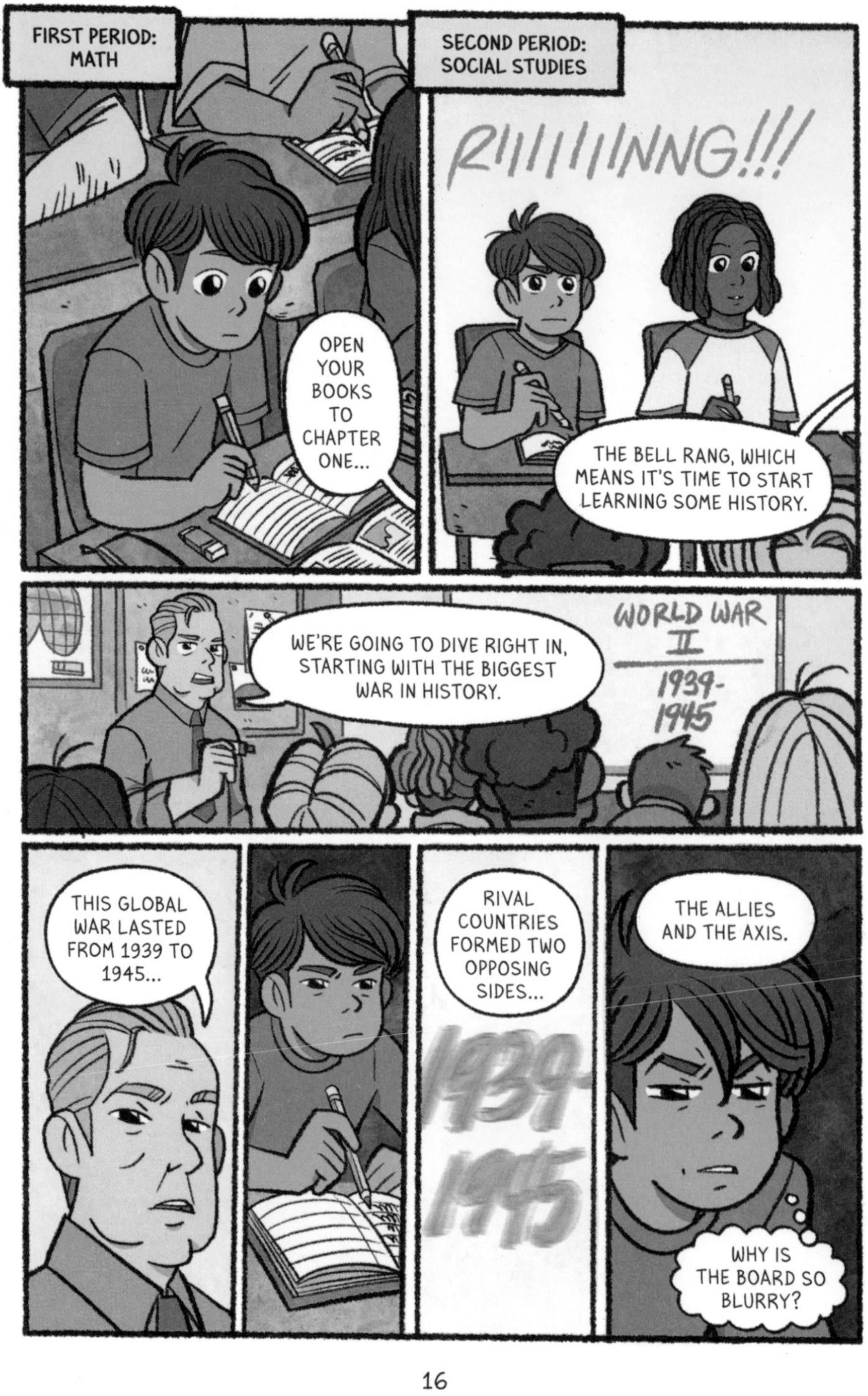
FIRST PERIOD: MATH
OPEN YOUR BOOKS TO CHAPTER ONE...
SECOND PERIOD: SOCIAL STUDIES
RIIIIIINNG!!!
THE BELL RANG, WHICH MEANS IT'S TIME TO START LEARNING SOME HISTORY.
WE'RE GOING TO DIVE RIGHT IN, STARTING WITH THE BIGGEST WAR IN HISTORY.
WORLD WAR II
1939-1945
THIS GLOBAL WAR LASTED FROM 1939 TO 1945...
RIVAL COUNTRIES FORMED TWO OPPOSING SIDES...
THE ALLIES AND THE AXIS.
WHY IS THE BOARD SO BLURRY?

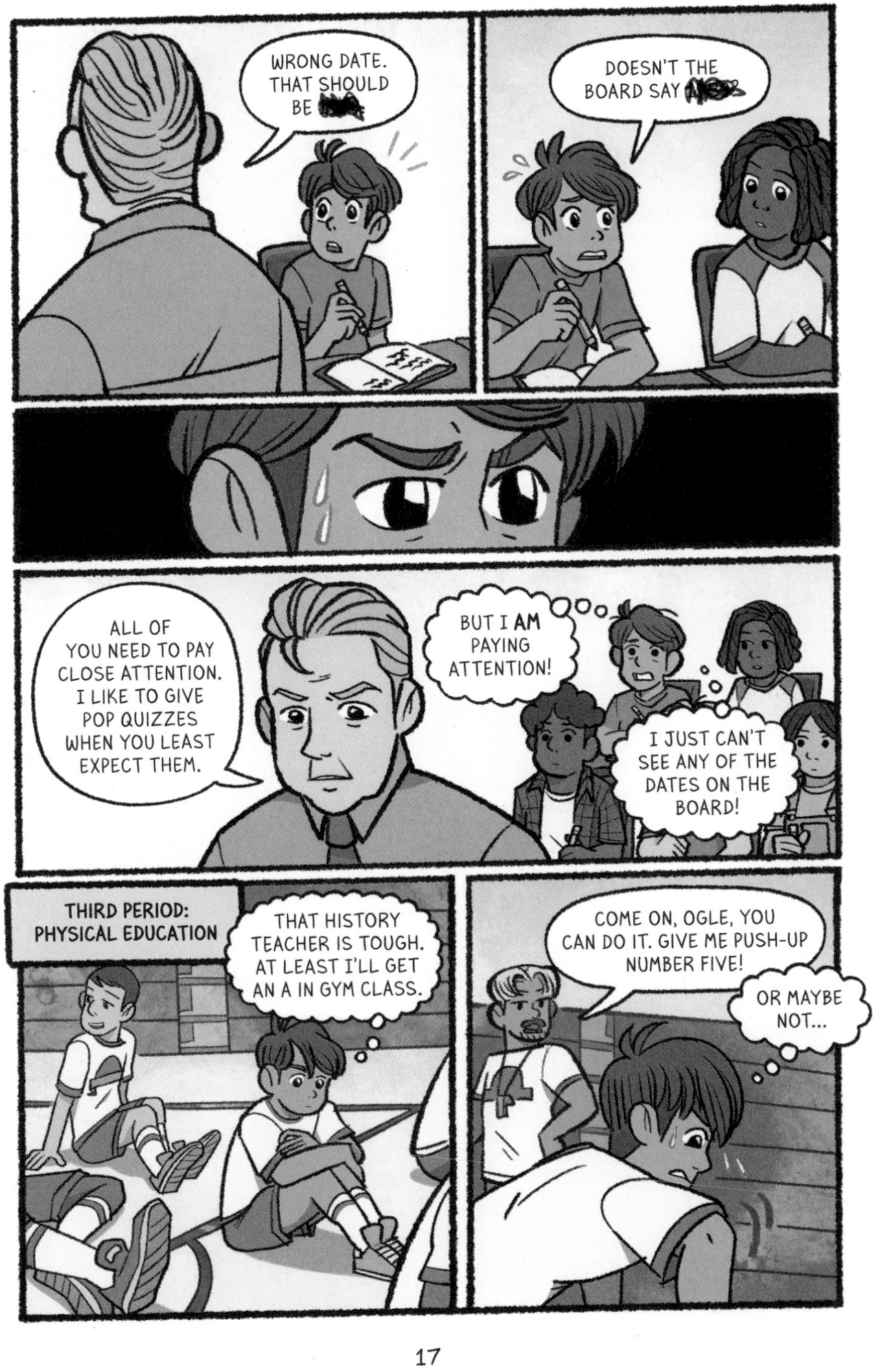
WRONG DATE. THAT SHOULD BE [redacted]
DOESN'T THE BOARD SAY [redacted]
ALL OF YOU NEED TO PAY CLOSE ATTENTION. I LIKE TO GIVE POP QUIZZES WHEN YOU LEAST EXPECT THEM.
BUT I **AM** PAYING ATTENTION!
I JUST CAN'T SEE ANY OF THE DATES ON THE BOARD!
THIRD PERIOD: PHYSICAL EDUCATION
THAT HISTORY TEACHER IS TOUGH. AT LEAST I'LL GET AN A IN GYM CLASS.
COME ON, OGLE, YOU CAN DO IT. GIVE ME PUSH-UP NUMBER FIVE!
OR MAYBE NOT...

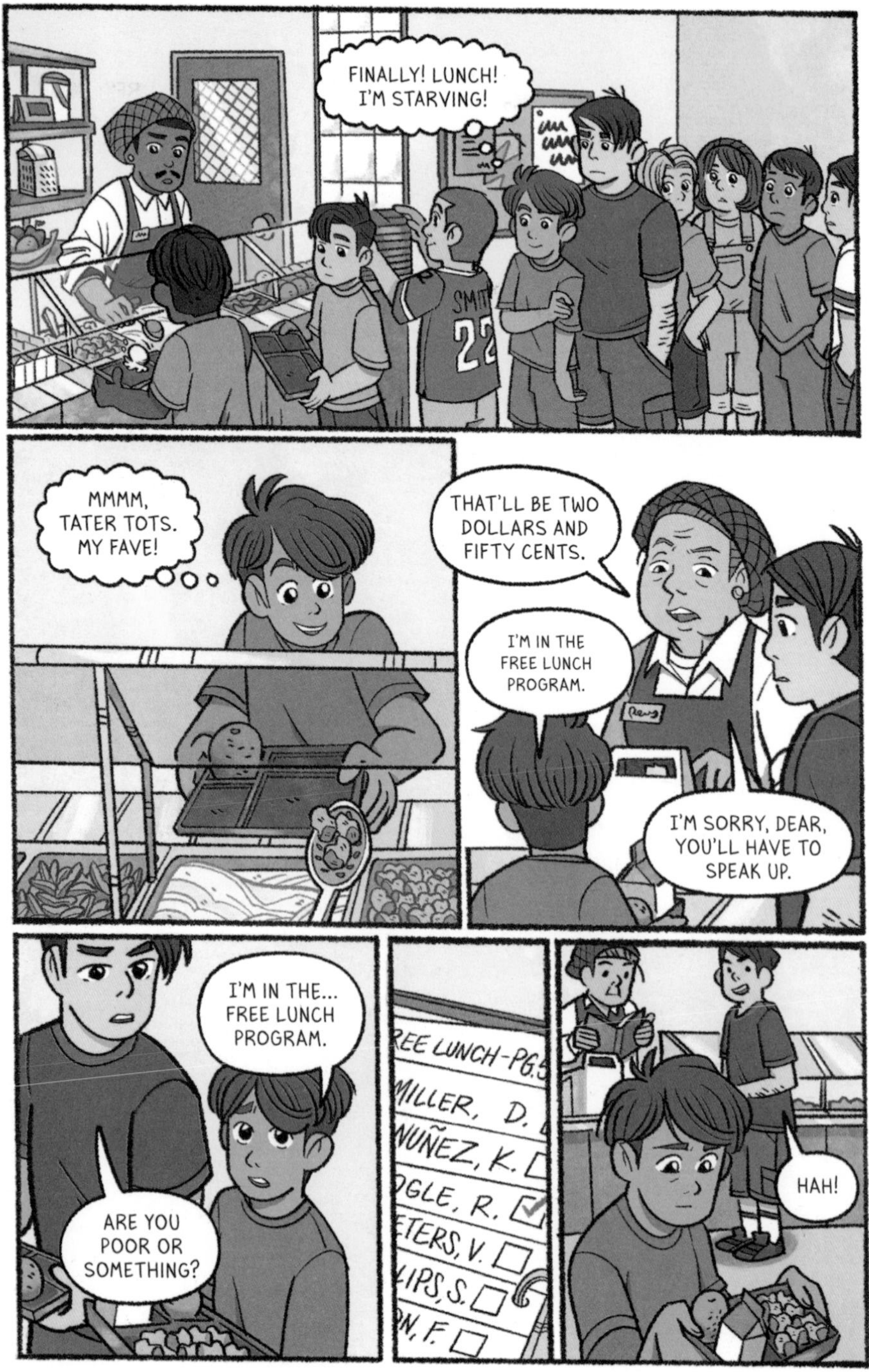
FINALLY! LUNCH! I'M STARVING!
MMMM, TATER TOTS. MY FAVE!
THAT'LL BE TWO DOLLARS AND FIFTY CENTS.
I'M IN THE FREE LUNCH PROGRAM.
I'M SORRY, DEAR, YOU'LL HAVE TO SPEAK UP.
I'M IN THE... FREE LUNCH PROGRAM.
ARE YOU POOR OR SOMETHING?
REE LUNCH-PG.5
MILLER, D.
NUÑEZ, K.
GLE, R.
ETERS, V.
IPS, S.
N, F.
HAH!

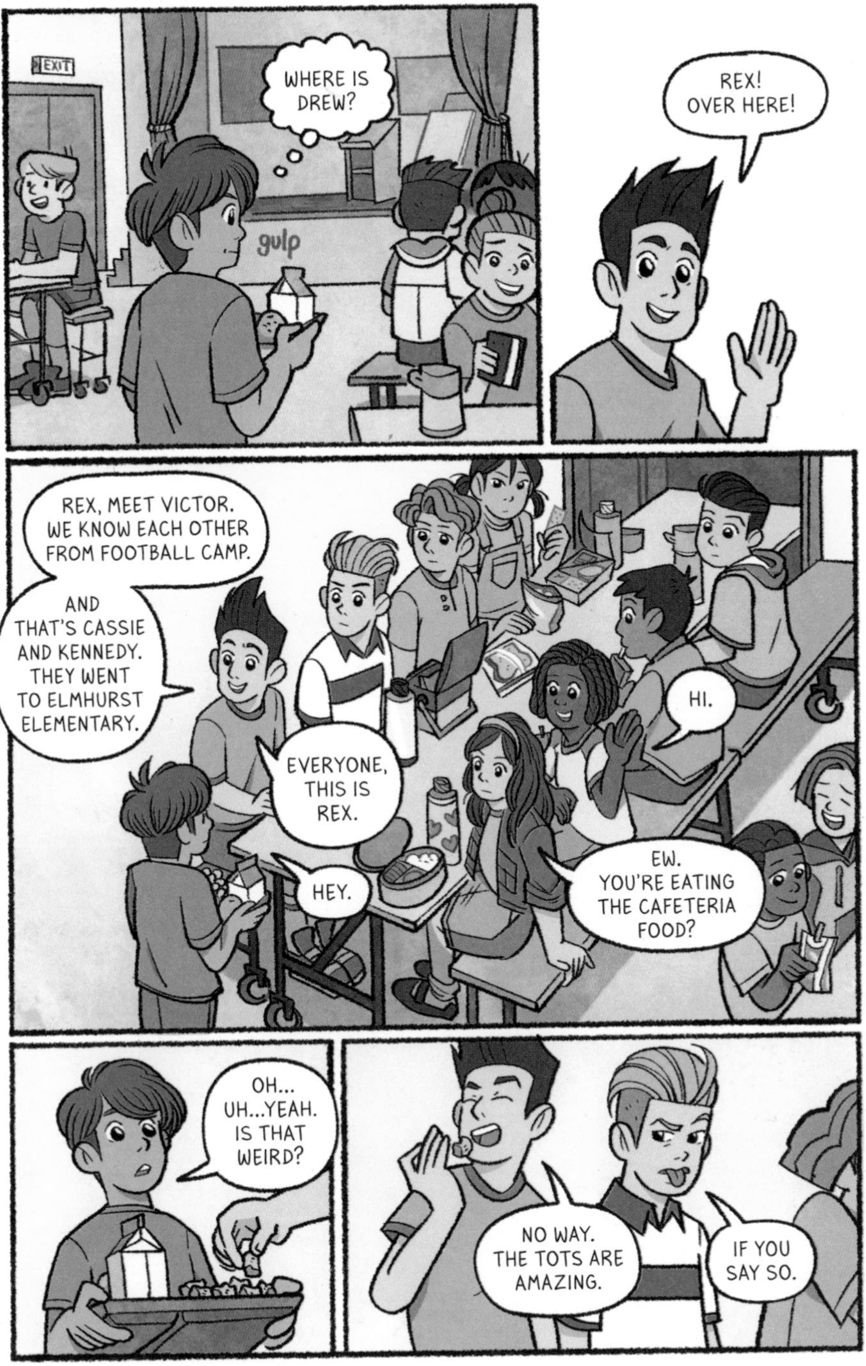
EXIT
WHERE IS DREW?
gulp
REX! OVER HERE!
REX, MEET VICTOR. WE KNOW EACH OTHER FROM FOOTBALL CAMP.
AND THAT'S CASSIE AND KENNEDY. THEY WENT TO ELMHURST ELEMENTARY.
EVERYONE, THIS IS REX.
HI.
HEY.
EW. YOU'RE EATING THE CAFETERIA FOOD?
OH... UH...YEAH. IS THAT WEIRD?
NO WAY. THE TOTS ARE AMAZING.
IF YOU SAY SO.

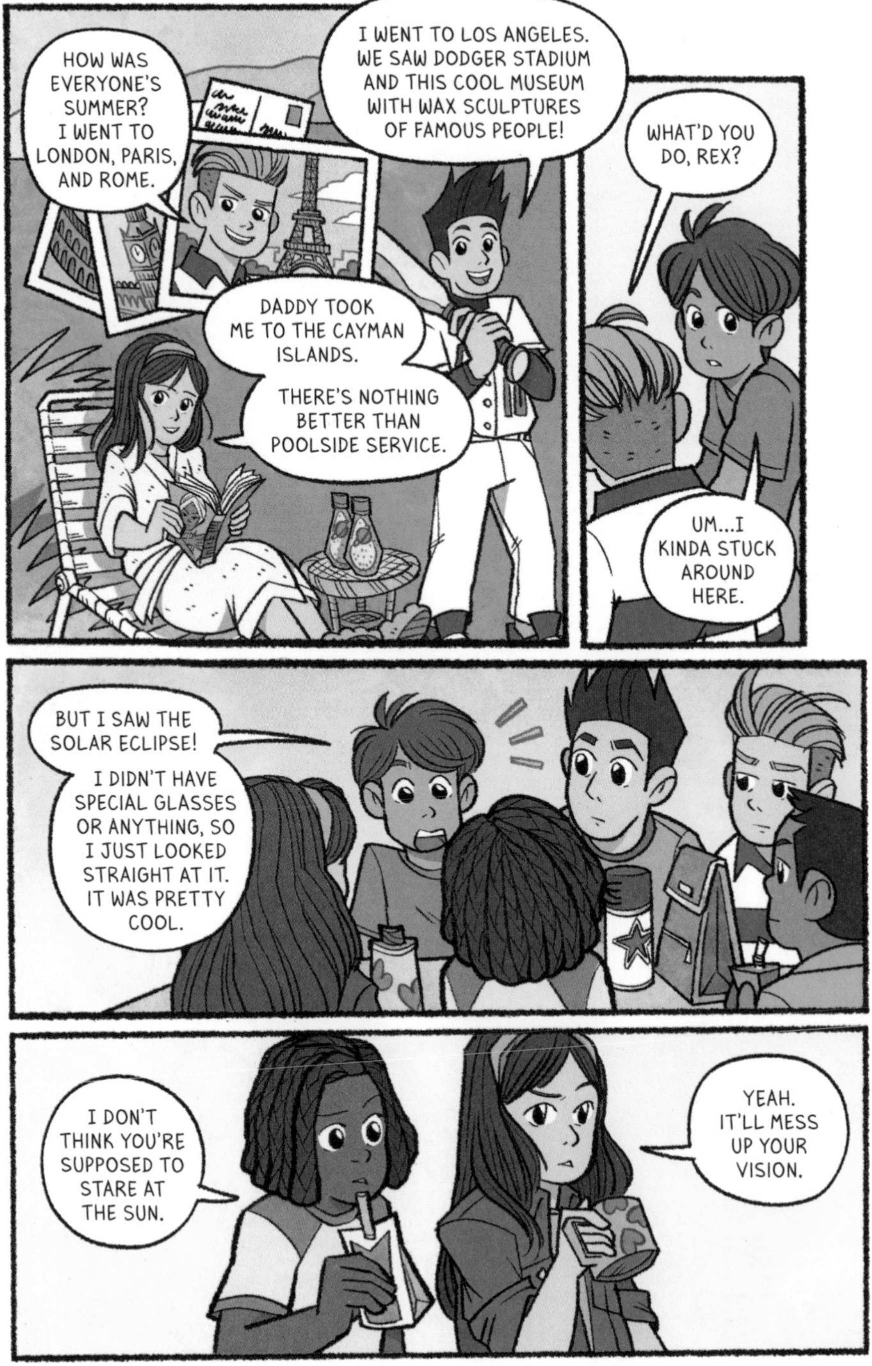
HOW WAS EVERYONE'S SUMMER? I WENT TO LONDON, PARIS, AND ROME.
I WENT TO LOS ANGELES. WE SAW DODGER STADIUM AND THIS COOL MUSEUM WITH WAX SCULPTURES OF FAMOUS PEOPLE!
DADDY TOOK ME TO THE CAYMAN ISLANDS.
THERE'S NOTHING BETTER THAN POOLSIDE SERVICE.
WHAT'D YOU DO, REX?
UM...I KINDA STUCK AROUND HERE.
BUT I SAW THE SOLAR ECLIPSE!
I DIDN'T HAVE SPECIAL GLASSES OR ANYTHING, SO I JUST LOOKED STRAIGHT AT IT. IT WAS PRETTY COOL.
I DON'T THINK YOU'RE SUPPOSED TO STARE AT THE SUN.
YEAH. IT'LL MESS UP YOUR VISION.

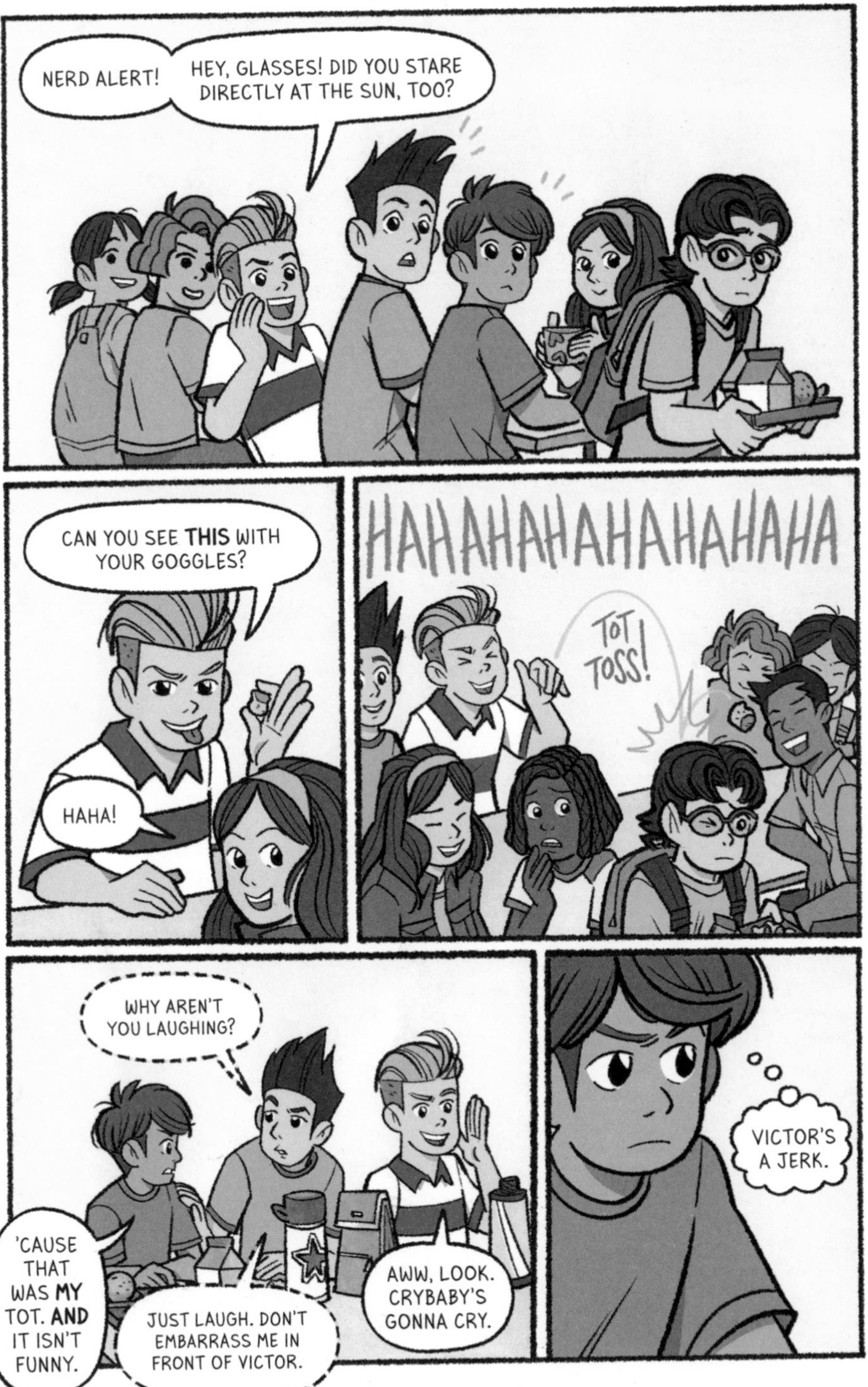
NERD ALERT!
HEY, GLASSES! DID YOU STARE DIRECTLY AT THE SUN, TOO?
CAN YOU SEE **THIS** WITH YOUR GOGGLES?
HAHA!
HAHAHAHAHAHAHAHA
TOT TOSS!
WHY AREN'T YOU LAUGHING?
'CAUSE THAT WAS **MY** TOT. **AND** IT ISN'T FUNNY.
JUST LAUGH. DON'T EMBARRASS ME IN FRONT OF VICTOR.
AWW, LOOK. CRYBABY'S GONNA CRY.
VICTOR'S A JERK.

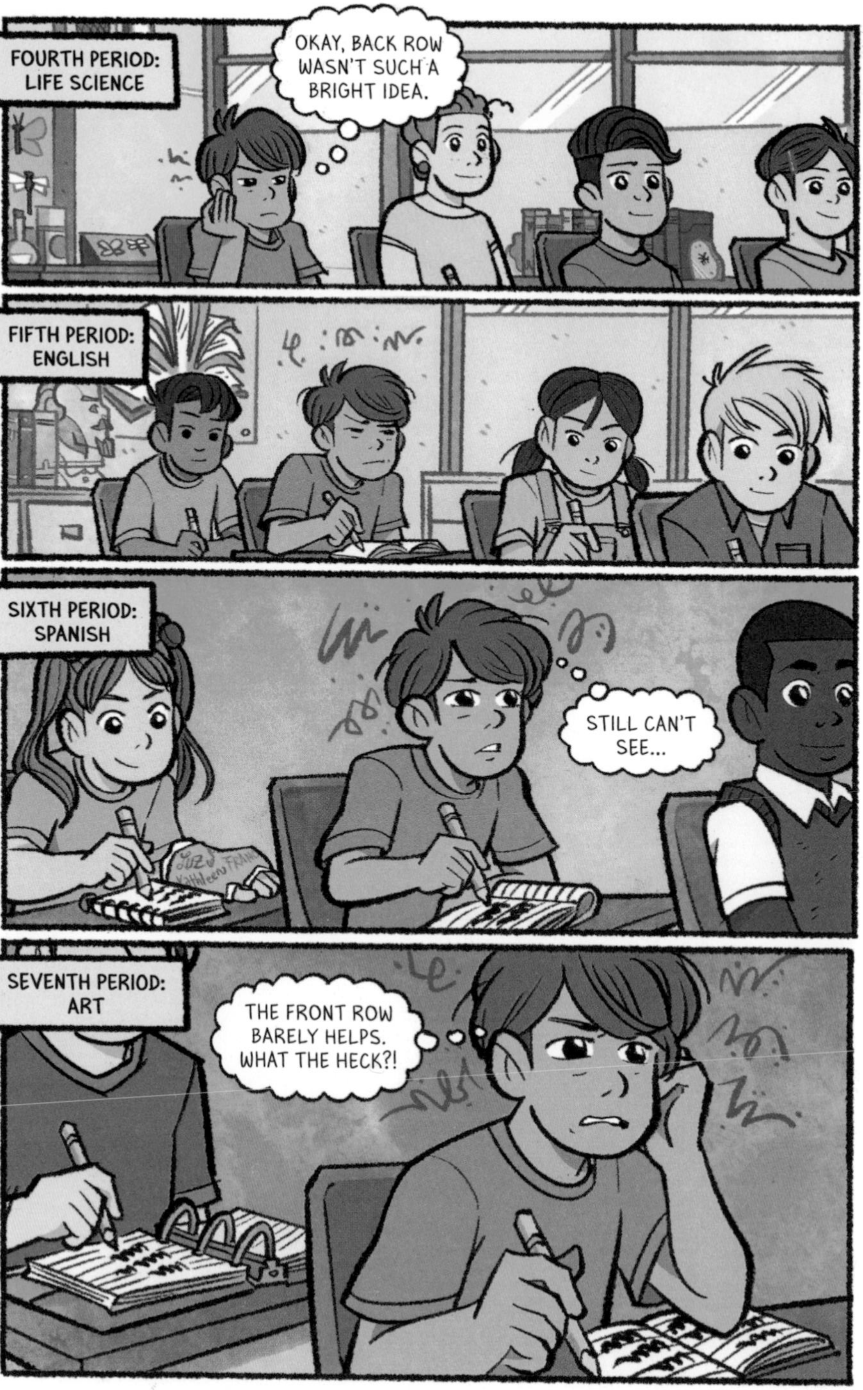
FOURTH PERIOD: LIFE SCIENCE
OKAY, BACK ROW WASN'T SUCH A BRIGHT IDEA.
FIFTH PERIOD: ENGLISH
SIXTH PERIOD: SPANISH
STILL CAN'T SEE...
SEVENTH PERIOD: ART
THE FRONT ROW BARELY HELPS. WHAT THE HECK?!

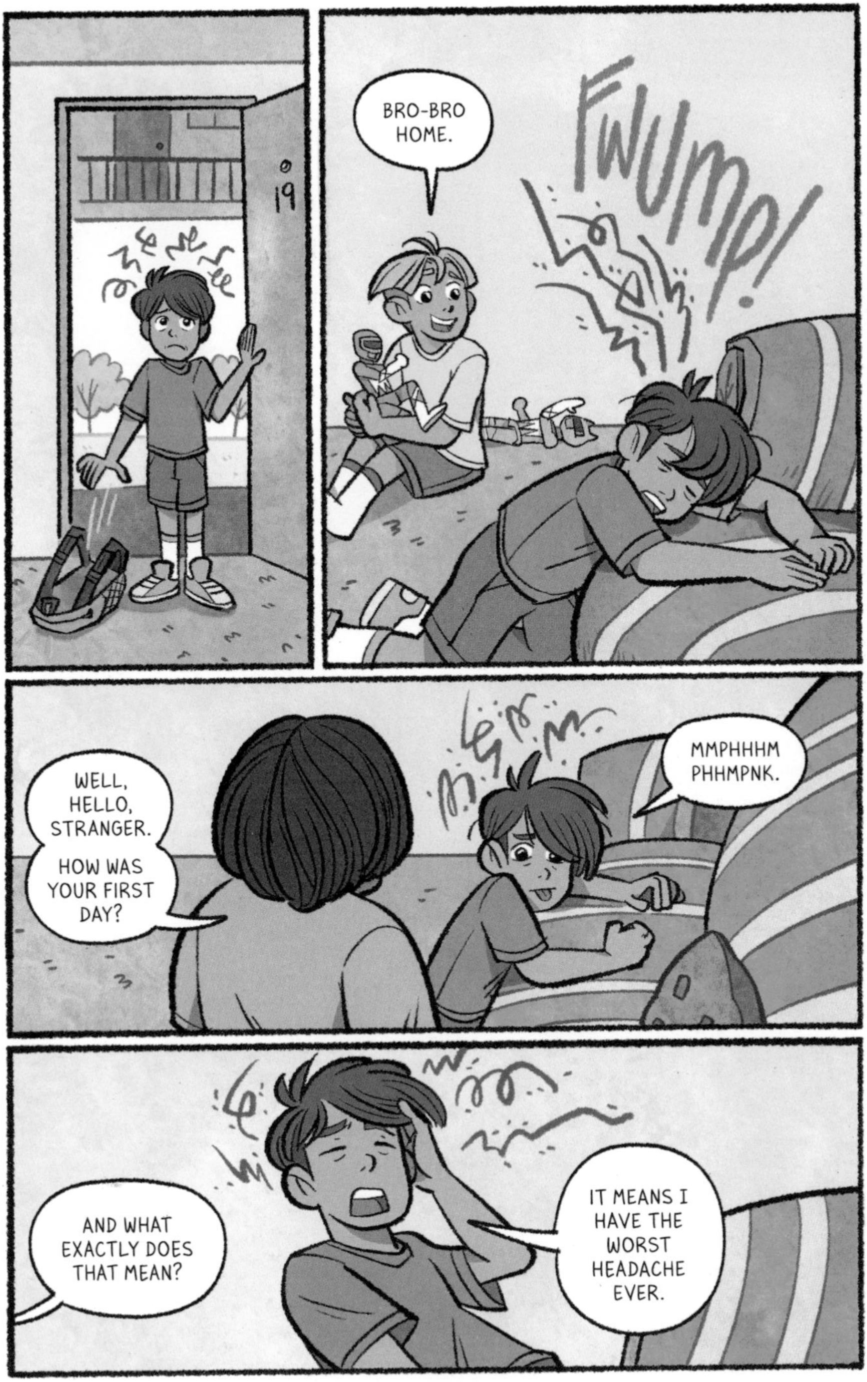

19
BRO-BRO HOME.
FWUMP!
WELL, HELLO, STRANGER.
HOW WAS YOUR FIRST DAY?
MMPHHHM PHHMPNK.
AND WHAT EXACTLY DOES THAT MEAN?
IT MEANS I HAVE THE WORST HEADACHE EVER.

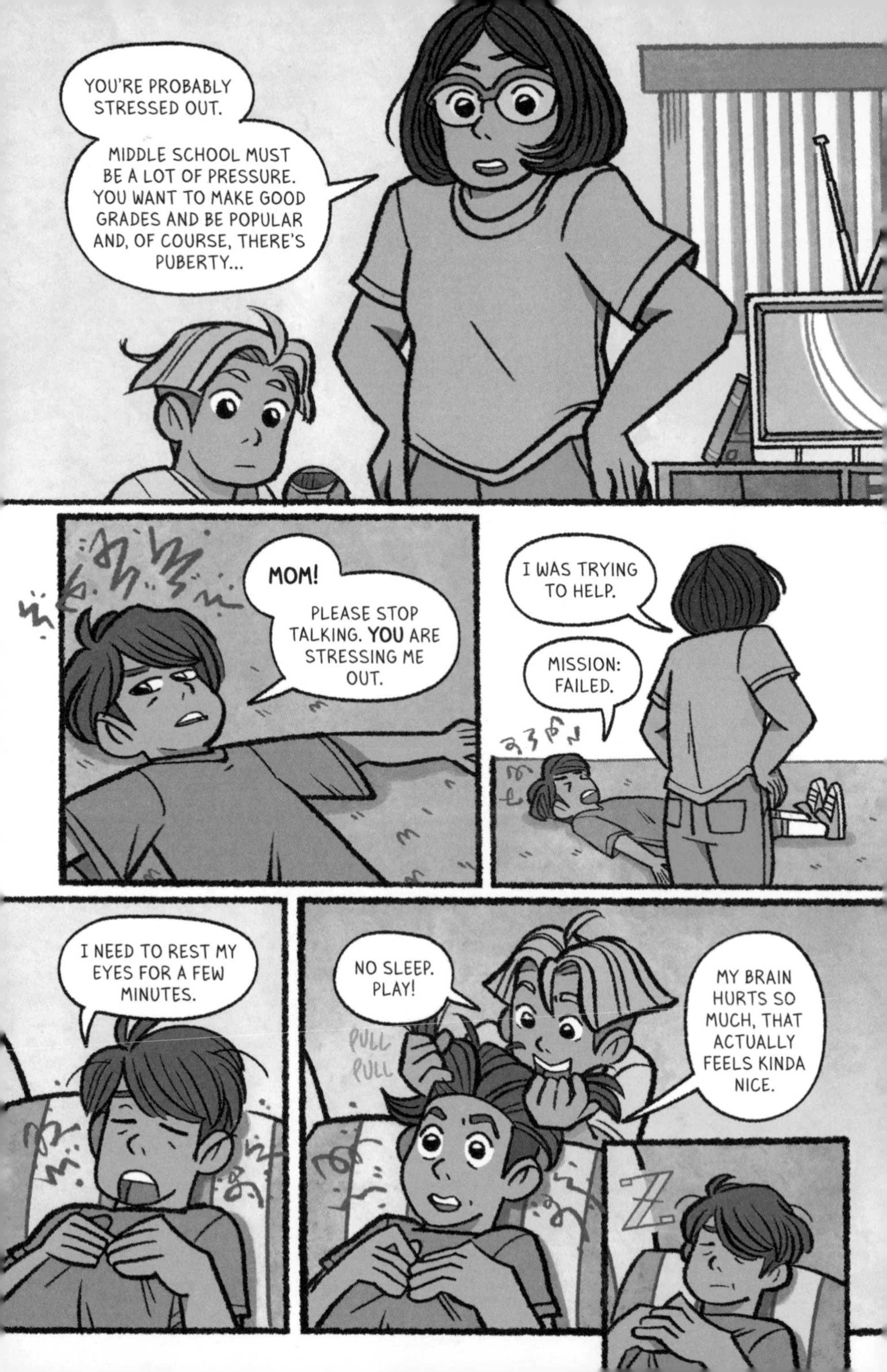
YOU'RE PROBABLY STRESSED OUT.
MIDDLE SCHOOL MUST BE A LOT OF PRESSURE. YOU WANT TO MAKE GOOD GRADES AND BE POPULAR AND, OF COURSE, THERE'S PUBERTY...
MOM!
PLEASE STOP TALKING. YOU ARE STRESSING ME OUT.
I WAS TRYING TO HELP.
MISSION: FAILED.
I NEED TO REST MY EYES FOR A FEW MINUTES.
NO SLEEP. PLAY!
PULL PULL
MY BRAIN HURTS SO MUCH, THAT ACTUALLY FEELS KINDA NICE.
Z

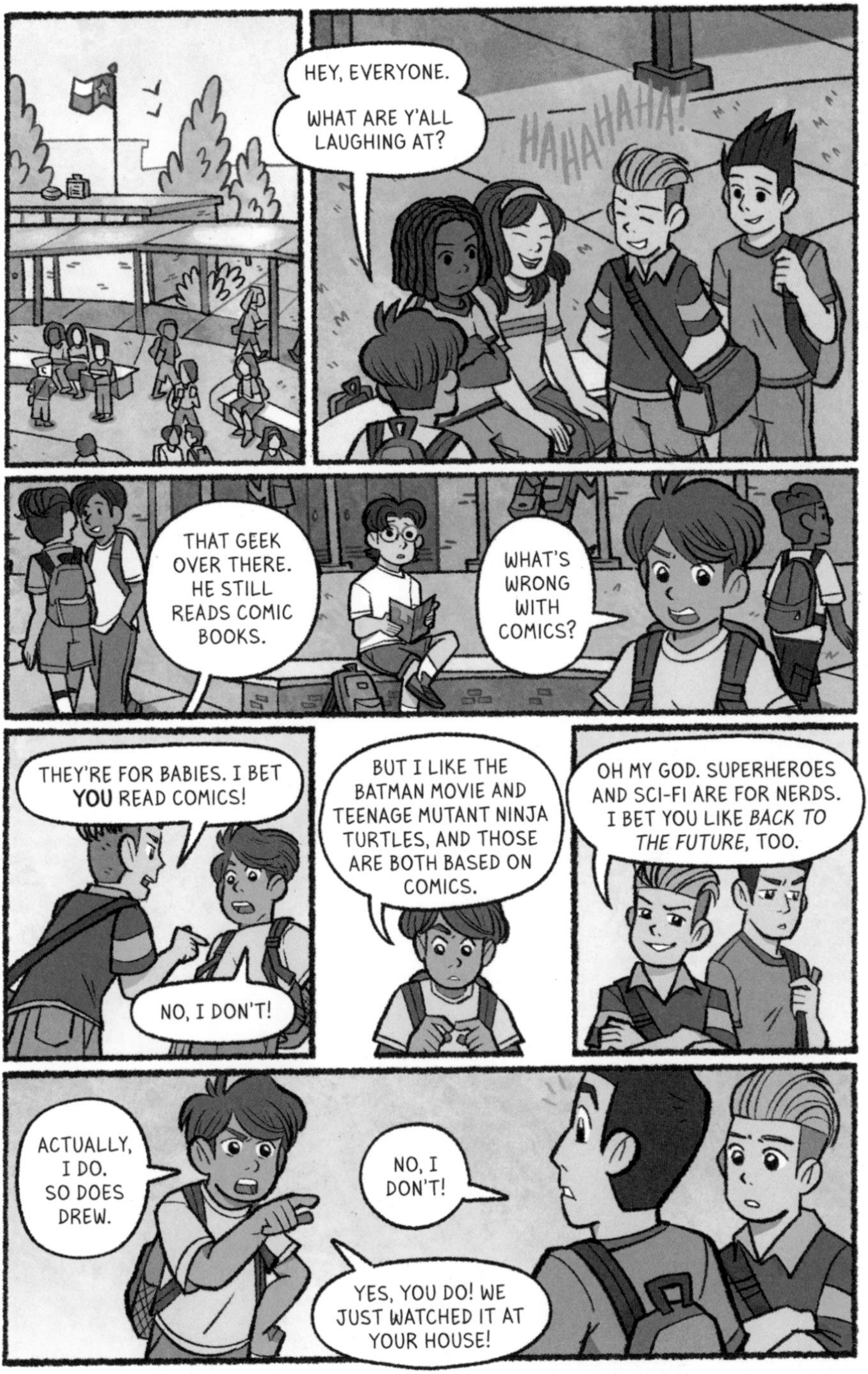
HEY, EVERYONE.
WHAT ARE Y'ALL LAUGHING AT?
HAHAHAHA!
THAT GEEK OVER THERE. HE STILL READS COMIC BOOKS.
WHAT'S WRONG WITH COMICS?
THEY'RE FOR BABIES. I BET **YOU** READ COMICS!
NO, I DON'T!
BUT I LIKE THE BATMAN MOVIE AND TEENAGE MUTANT NINJA TURTLES, AND THOSE ARE BOTH BASED ON COMICS.
OH MY GOD. SUPERHEROES AND SCI-FI ARE FOR NERDS. I BET YOU LIKE *BACK TO THE FUTURE*, TOO.
ACTUALLY, I DO. SO DOES DREW.
NO, I DON'T!
YES, YOU DO! WE JUST WATCHED IT AT YOUR HOUSE!

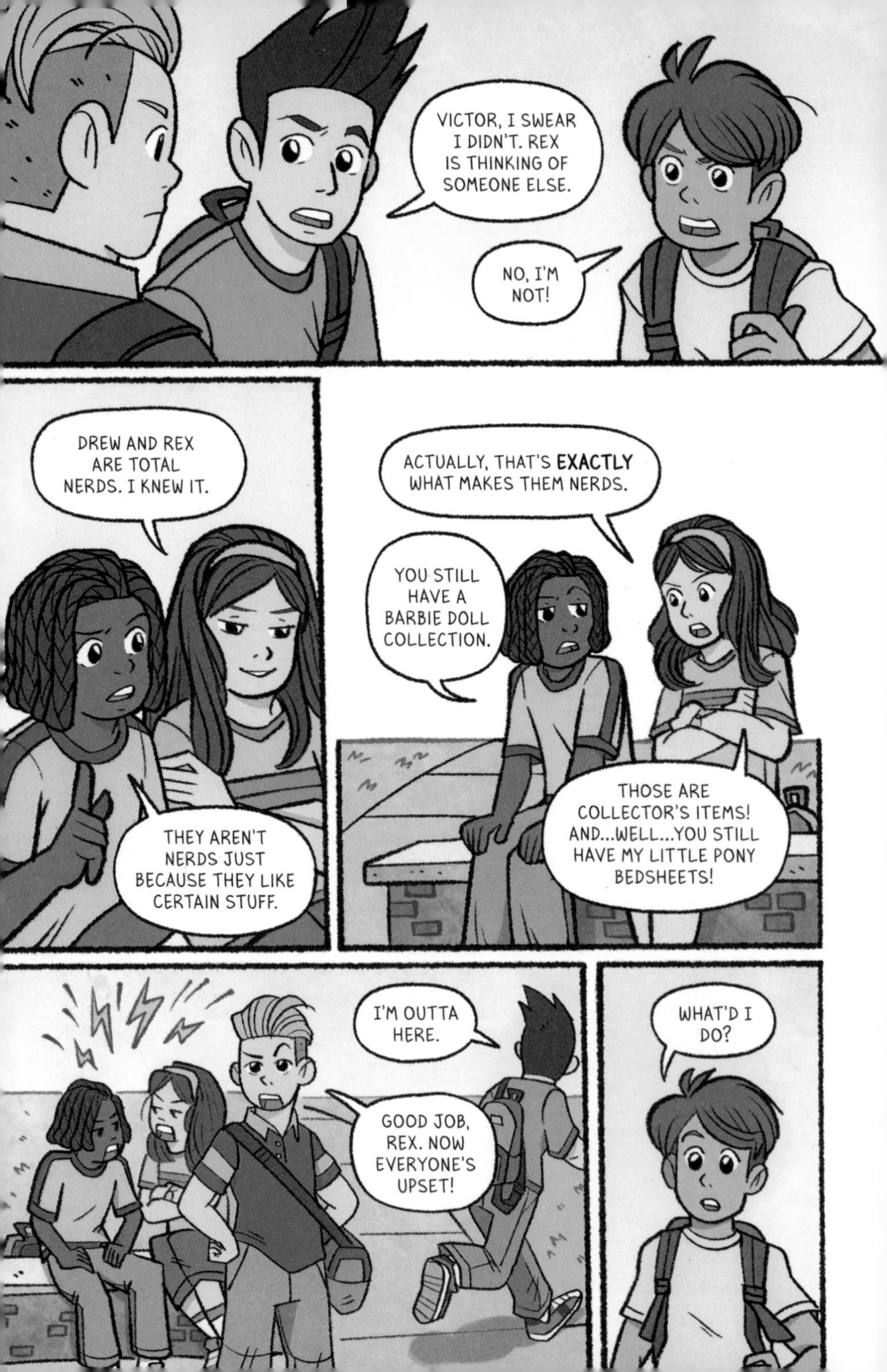
VICTOR, I SWEAR I DIDN'T. REX IS THINKING OF SOMEONE ELSE.
NO, I'M NOT!
DREW AND REX ARE TOTAL NERDS. I KNEW IT.
THEY AREN'T NERDS JUST BECAUSE THEY LIKE CERTAIN STUFF.
ACTUALLY, THAT'S **EXACTLY** WHAT MAKES THEM NERDS.
YOU STILL HAVE A BARBIE DOLL COLLECTION.
THOSE ARE COLLECTOR'S ITEMS! AND...WELL...YOU STILL HAVE MY LITTLE PONY BEDSHEETS!
I'M OUTTA HERE.
GOOD JOB, REX. NOW EVERYONE'S UPSET!
WHAT'D I DO?

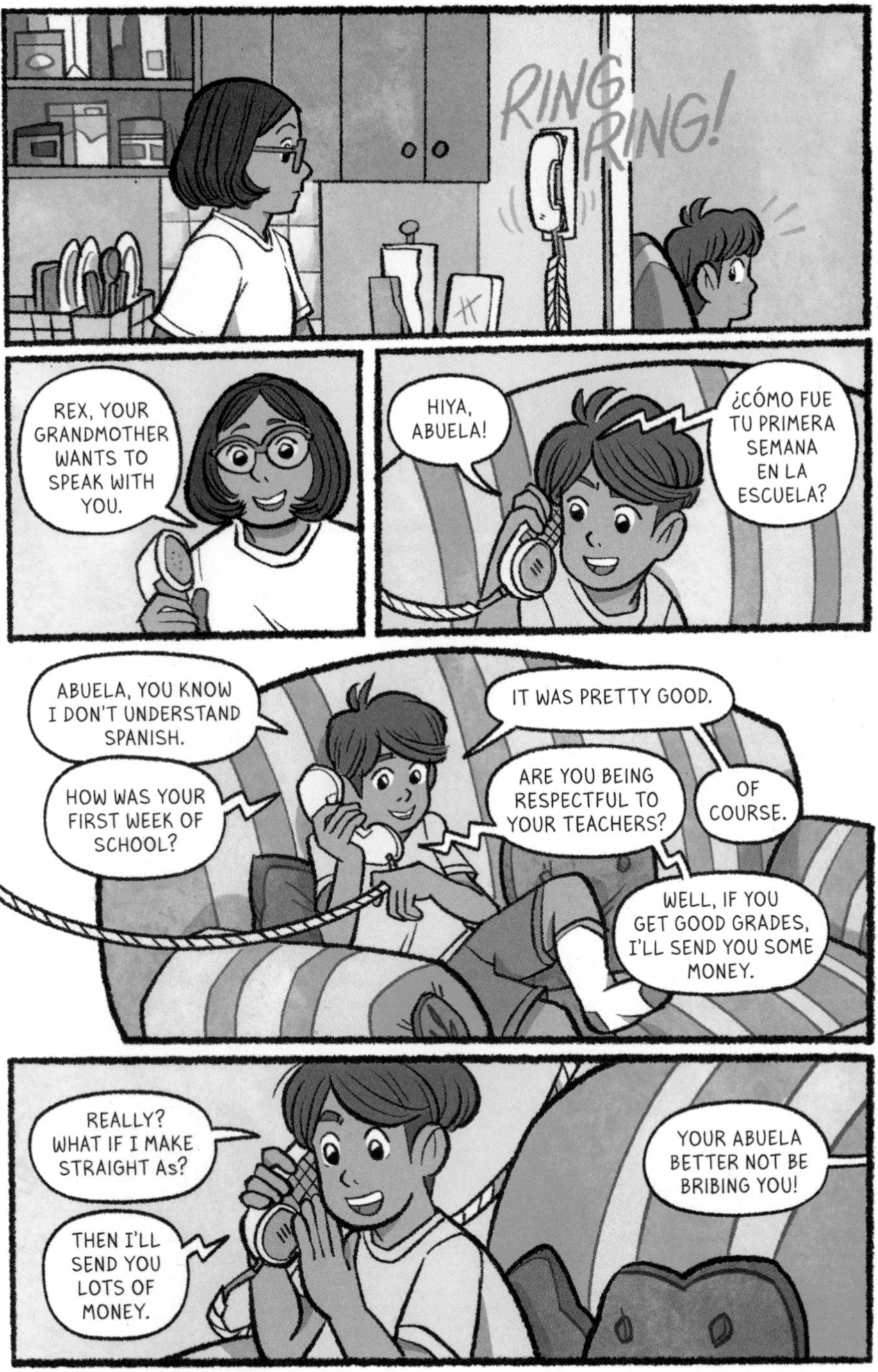
RING RING!
REX, YOUR GRANDMOTHER WANTS TO SPEAK WITH YOU.
HIYA, ABUELA!
¿CÓMO FUE TU PRIMERA SEMANA EN LA ESCUELA?
ABUELA, YOU KNOW I DON'T UNDERSTAND SPANISH.
HOW WAS YOUR FIRST WEEK OF SCHOOL?
IT WAS PRETTY GOOD.
ARE YOU BEING RESPECTFUL TO YOUR TEACHERS?
OF COURSE.
WELL, IF YOU GET GOOD GRADES, I'LL SEND YOU SOME MONEY.
REALLY? WHAT IF I MAKE STRAIGHT As?
THEN I'LL SEND YOU LOTS OF MONEY.
YOUR ABUELA BETTER NOT BE BRIBING YOU!

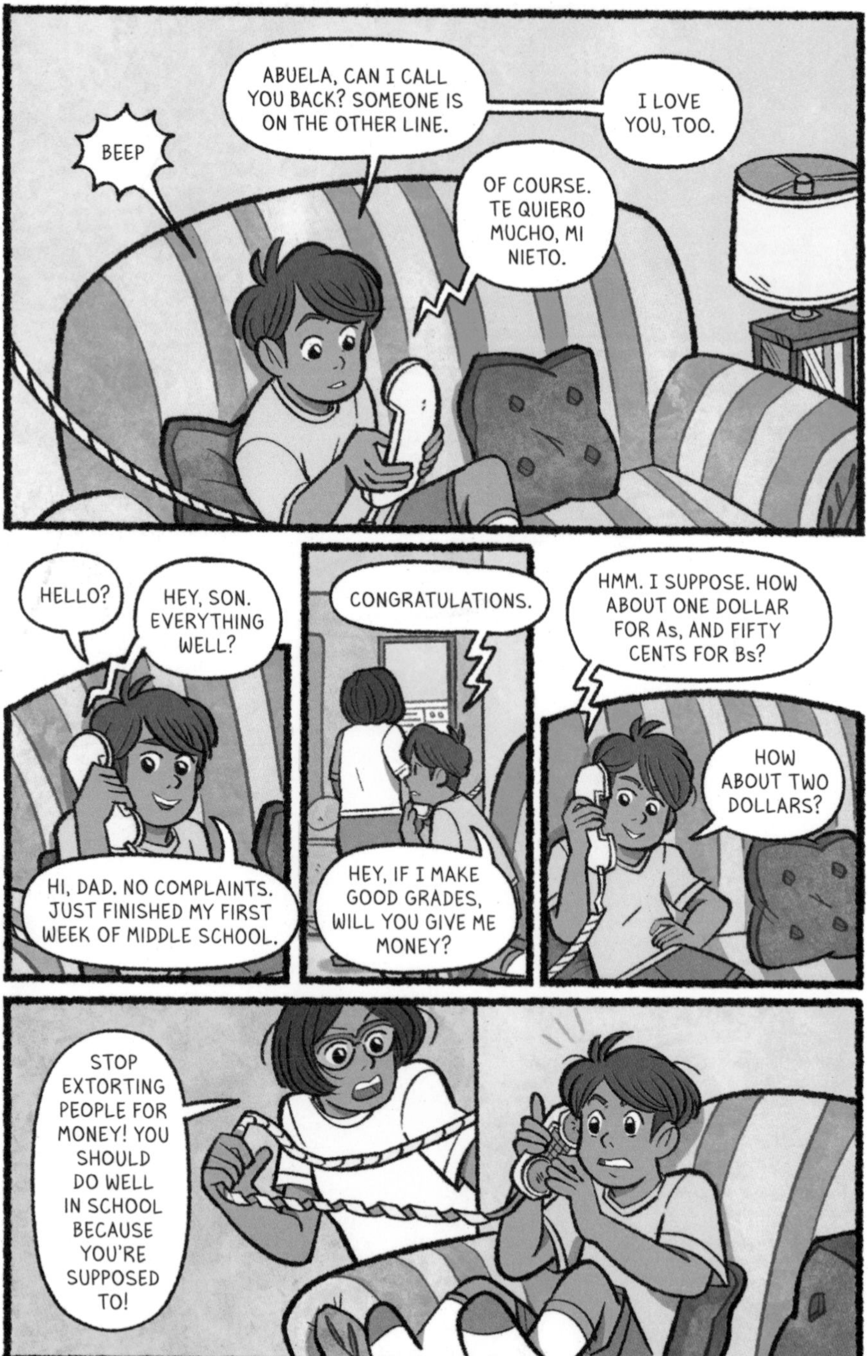
BEEP
ABUELA, CAN I CALL YOU BACK? SOMEONE IS ON THE OTHER LINE.
OF COURSE. TE QUIERO MUCHO, MI NIETO.
I LOVE YOU, TOO.
HELLO?
HEY, SON. EVERYTHING WELL?
HI, DAD. NO COMPLAINTS. JUST FINISHED MY FIRST WEEK OF MIDDLE SCHOOL.
CONGRATULATIONS.
HEY, IF I MAKE GOOD GRADES, WILL YOU GIVE ME MONEY?
HMM. I SUPPOSE. HOW ABOUT ONE DOLLAR FOR As, AND FIFTY CENTS FOR Bs?
HOW ABOUT TWO DOLLARS?
STOP EXTORTING PEOPLE FOR MONEY! YOU SHOULD DO WELL IN SCHOOL BECAUSE YOU'RE SUPPOSED TO!

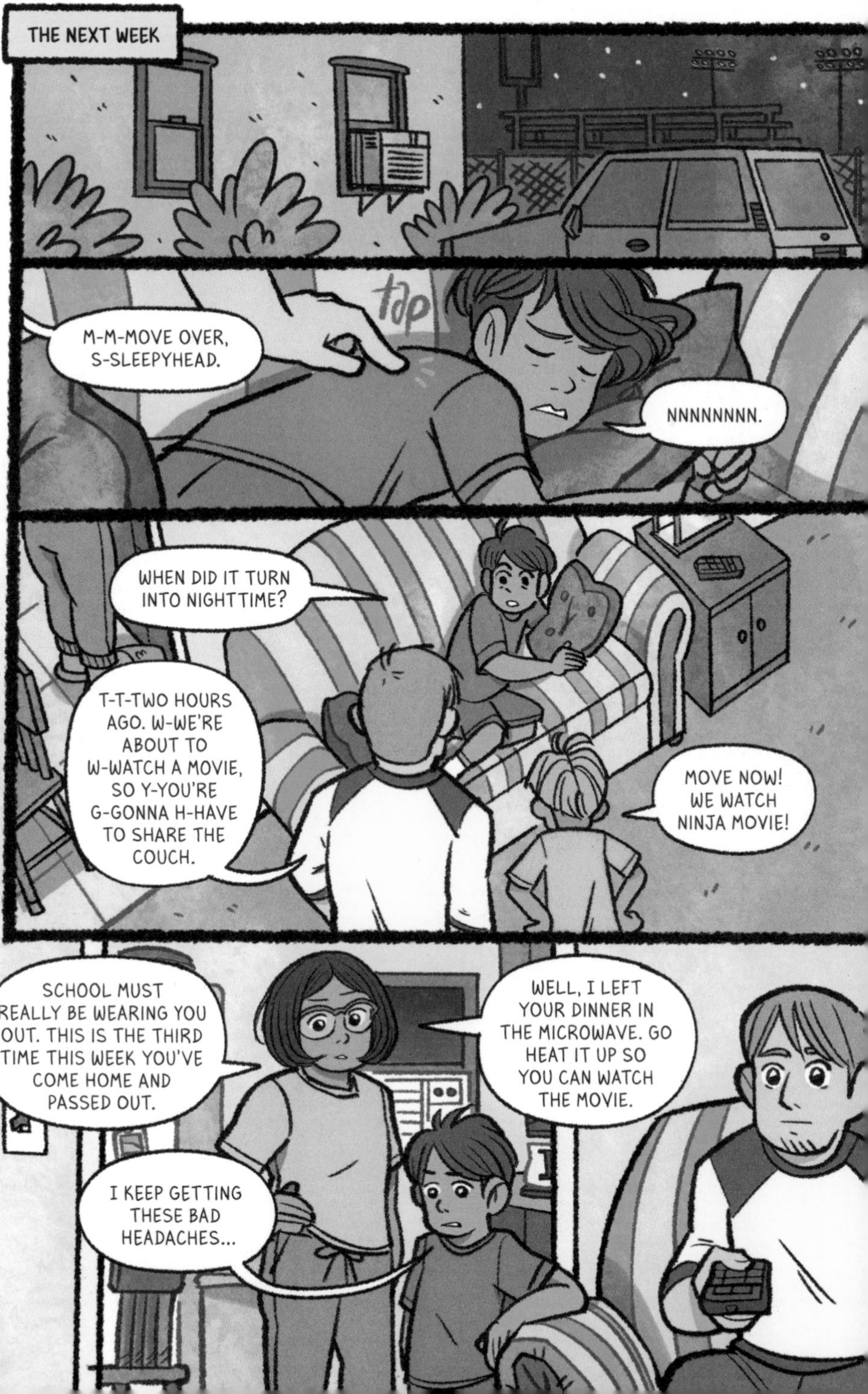
THE NEXT WEEK
tap
M-M-MOVE OVER, S-SLEEPYHEAD.
NNNNNNNN.
WHEN DID IT TURN INTO NIGHTTIME?
T-T-TWO HOURS AGO. W-WE'RE ABOUT TO W-WATCH A MOVIE, SO Y-YOU'RE G-GONNA H-HAVE TO SHARE THE COUCH.
MOVE NOW! WE WATCH NINJA MOVIE!
SCHOOL MUST REALLY BE WEARING YOU OUT. THIS IS THE THIRD TIME THIS WEEK YOU'VE COME HOME AND PASSED OUT.
WELL, I LEFT YOUR DINNER IN THE MICROWAVE. GO HEAT IT UP SO YOU CAN WATCH THE MOVIE.
I KEEP GETTING THESE BAD HEADACHES...

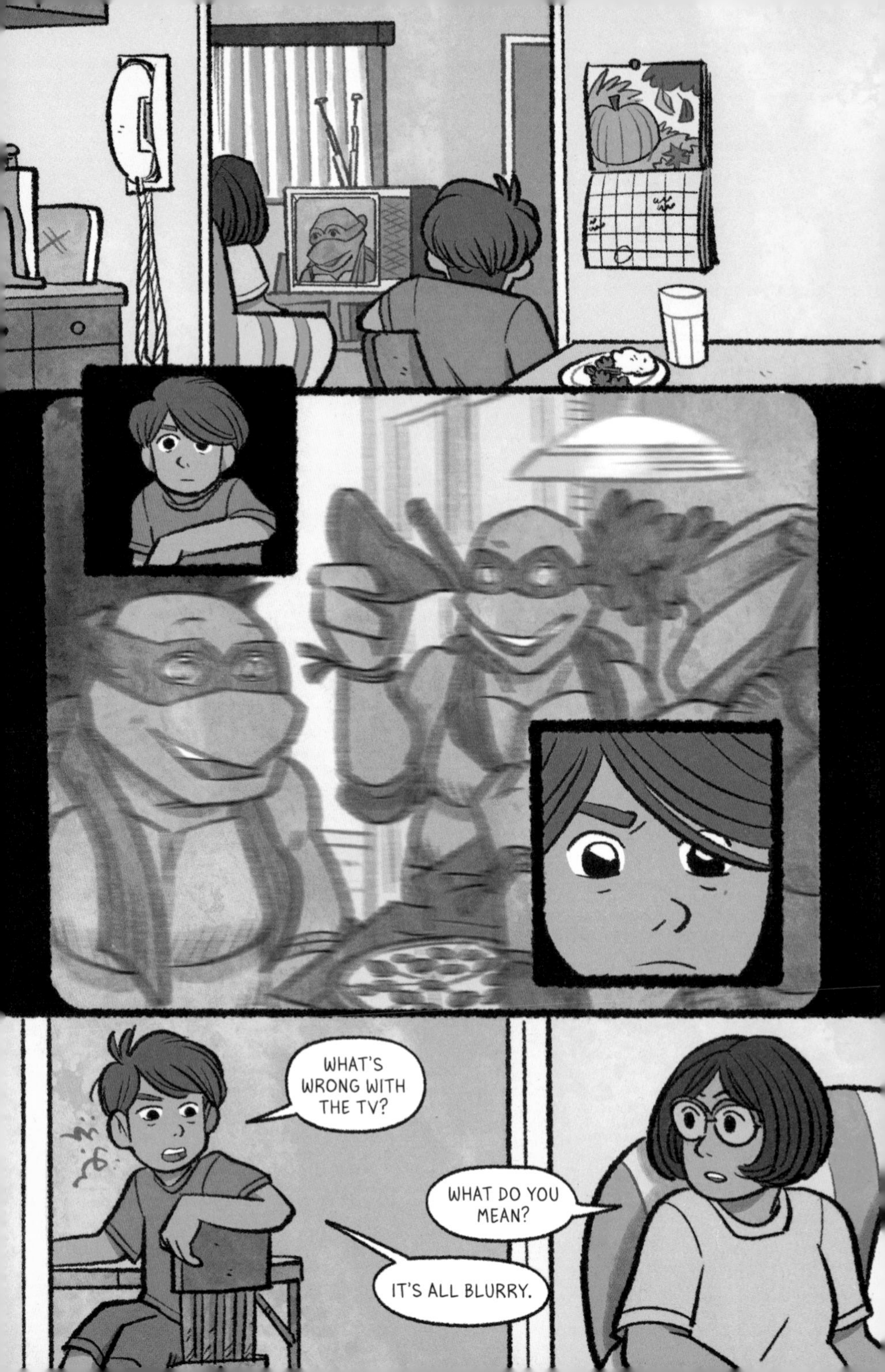
WHAT'S WRONG WITH THE TV?
WHAT DO YOU MEAN?
IT'S ALL BLURRY.

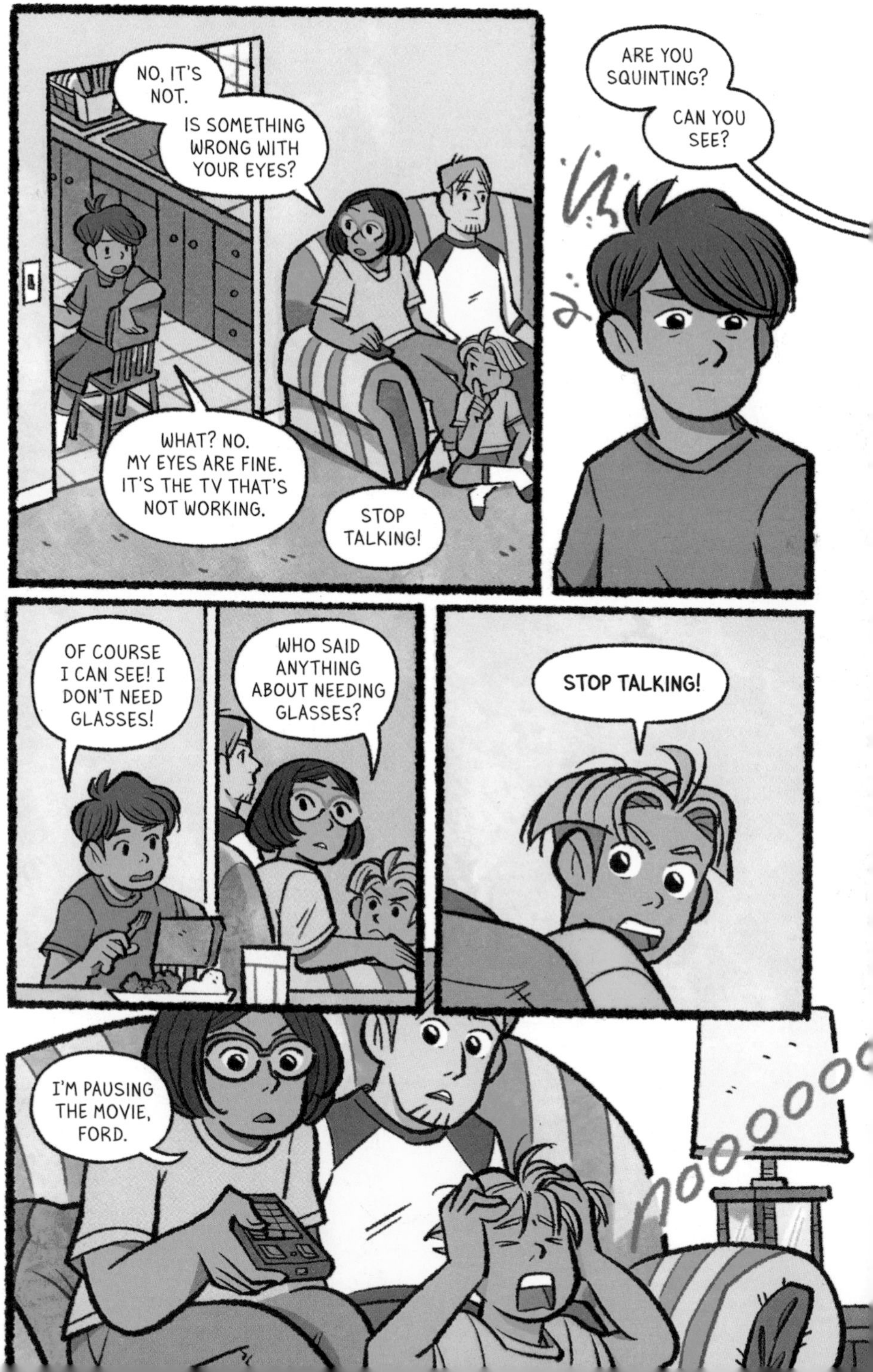
NO, IT'S NOT.
IS SOMETHING WRONG WITH YOUR EYES?
WHAT? NO. MY EYES ARE FINE. IT'S THE TV THAT'S NOT WORKING.
STOP TALKING!
ARE YOU SQUINTING?
CAN YOU SEE?
OF COURSE I CAN SEE! I DON'T NEED GLASSES!
WHO SAID ANYTHING ABOUT NEEDING GLASSES?
STOP TALKING!
I'M PAUSING THE MOVIE, FORD.
NOOOOOOO

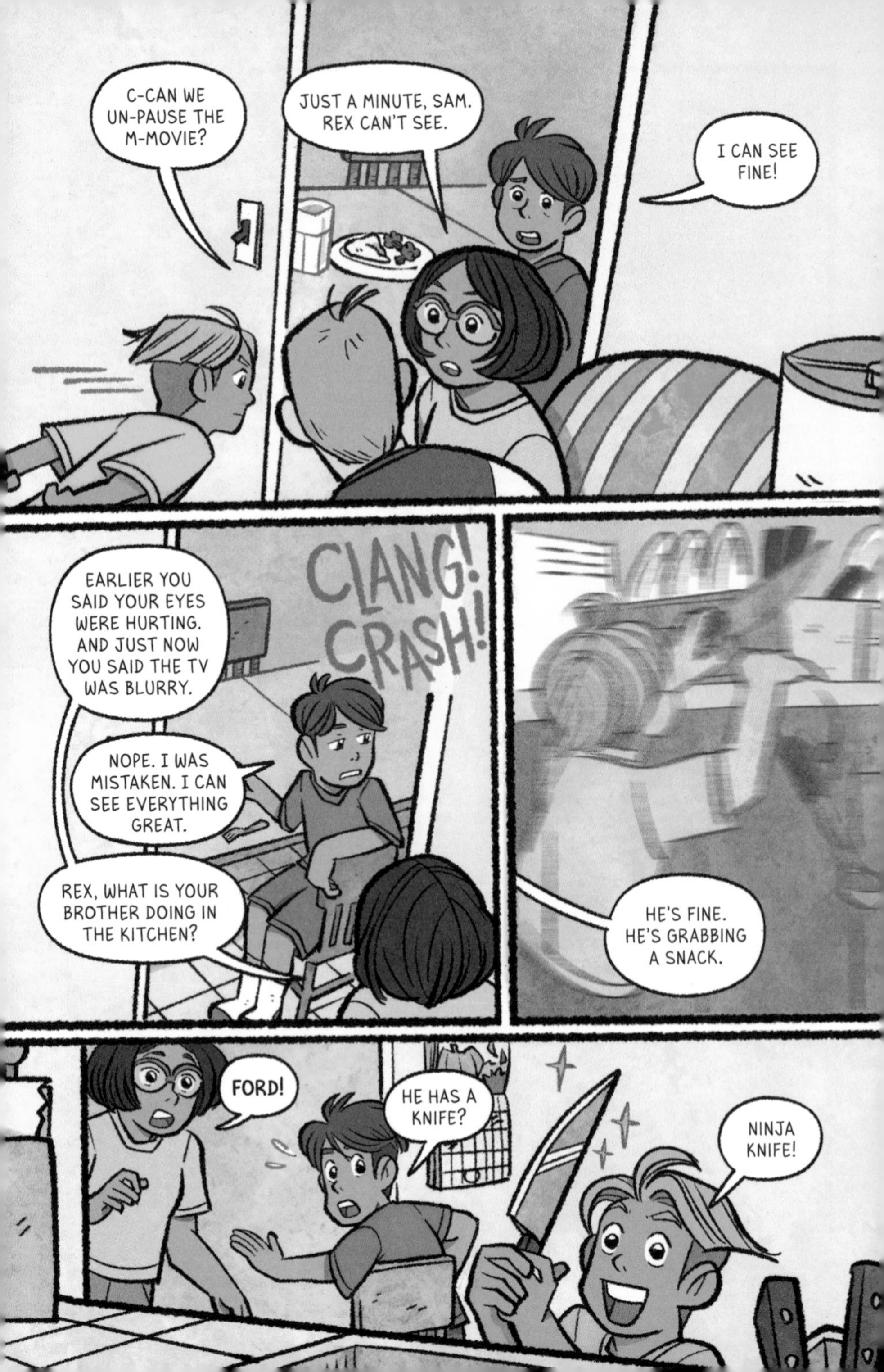
C-CAN WE UN-PAUSE THE M-MOVIE?
JUST A MINUTE, SAM. REX CAN'T SEE.
I CAN SEE FINE!
EARLIER YOU SAID YOUR EYES WERE HURTING. AND JUST NOW YOU SAID THE TV WAS BLURRY.
CLANG! CRASH!
NOPE. I WAS MISTAKEN. I CAN SEE EVERYTHING GREAT.
REX, WHAT IS YOUR BROTHER DOING IN THE KITCHEN?
HE'S FINE. HE'S GRABBING A SNACK.
FORD!
HE HAS A KNIFE?
NINJA KNIFE!

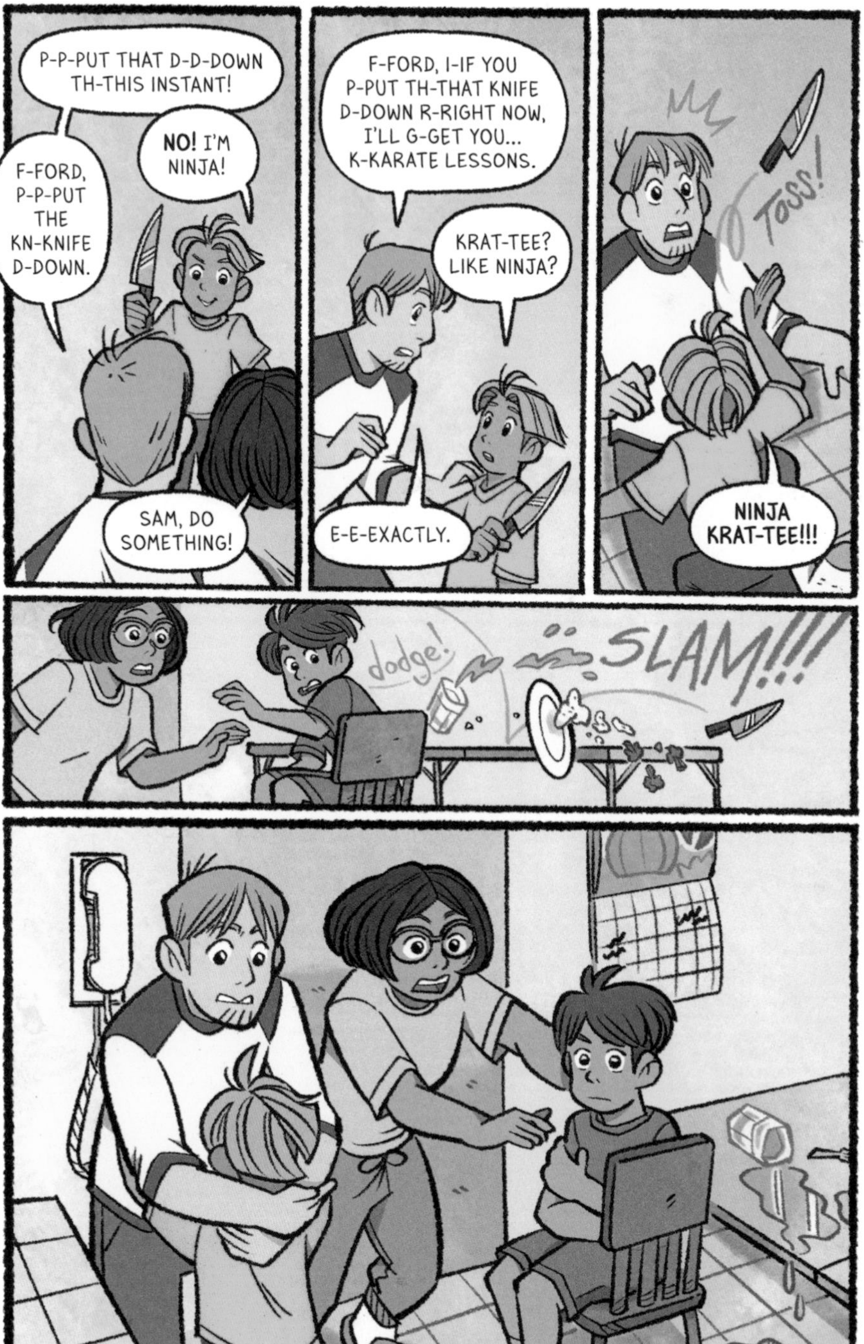
P-P-PUT THAT D-D-DOWN TH-THIS INSTANT!
F-FORD, P-P-PUT THE KN-KNIFE D-DOWN.
NO! I'M NINJA!
SAM, DO SOMETHING!
F-FORD, I-IF YOU P-PUT TH-THAT KNIFE D-DOWN R-RIGHT NOW, I'LL G-GET YOU... K-KARATE LESSONS.
KRAT-TEE? LIKE NINJA?
E-E-EXACTLY.
TOSS!
NINJA KRAT-TEE!!!
dodge!
SLAM!!!

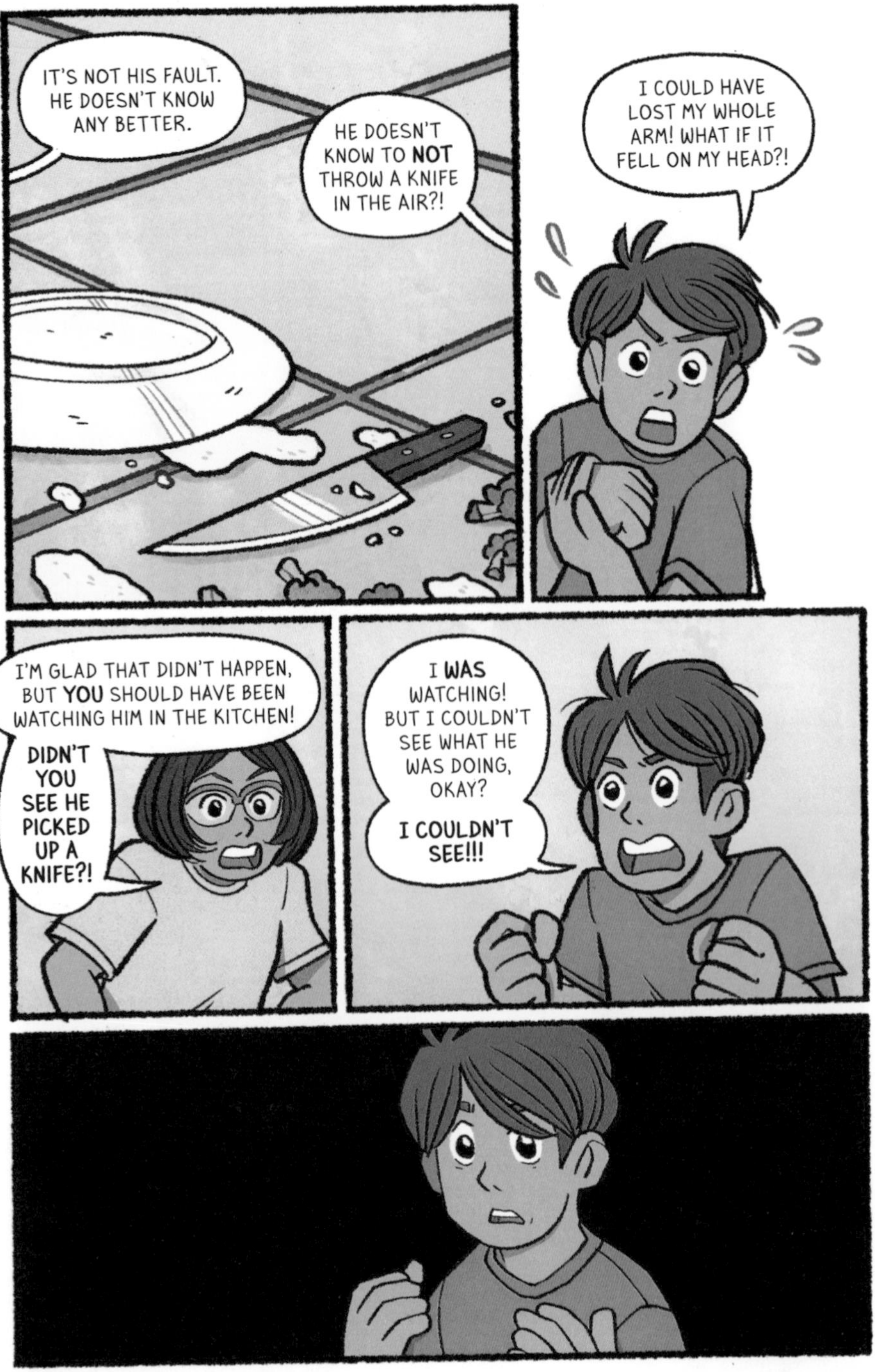
IT'S NOT HIS FAULT. HE DOESN'T KNOW ANY BETTER.
HE DOESN'T KNOW TO **NOT** THROW A KNIFE IN THE AIR?!
I COULD HAVE LOST MY WHOLE ARM! WHAT IF IT FELL ON MY HEAD?!
I'M GLAD THAT DIDN'T HAPPEN, BUT **YOU** SHOULD HAVE BEEN WATCHING HIM IN THE KITCHEN!
DIDN'T YOU SEE HE PICKED UP A KNIFE?!
I **WAS** WATCHING! BUT I COULDN'T SEE WHAT HE WAS DOING, OKAY?
I COULDN'T SEE!!!

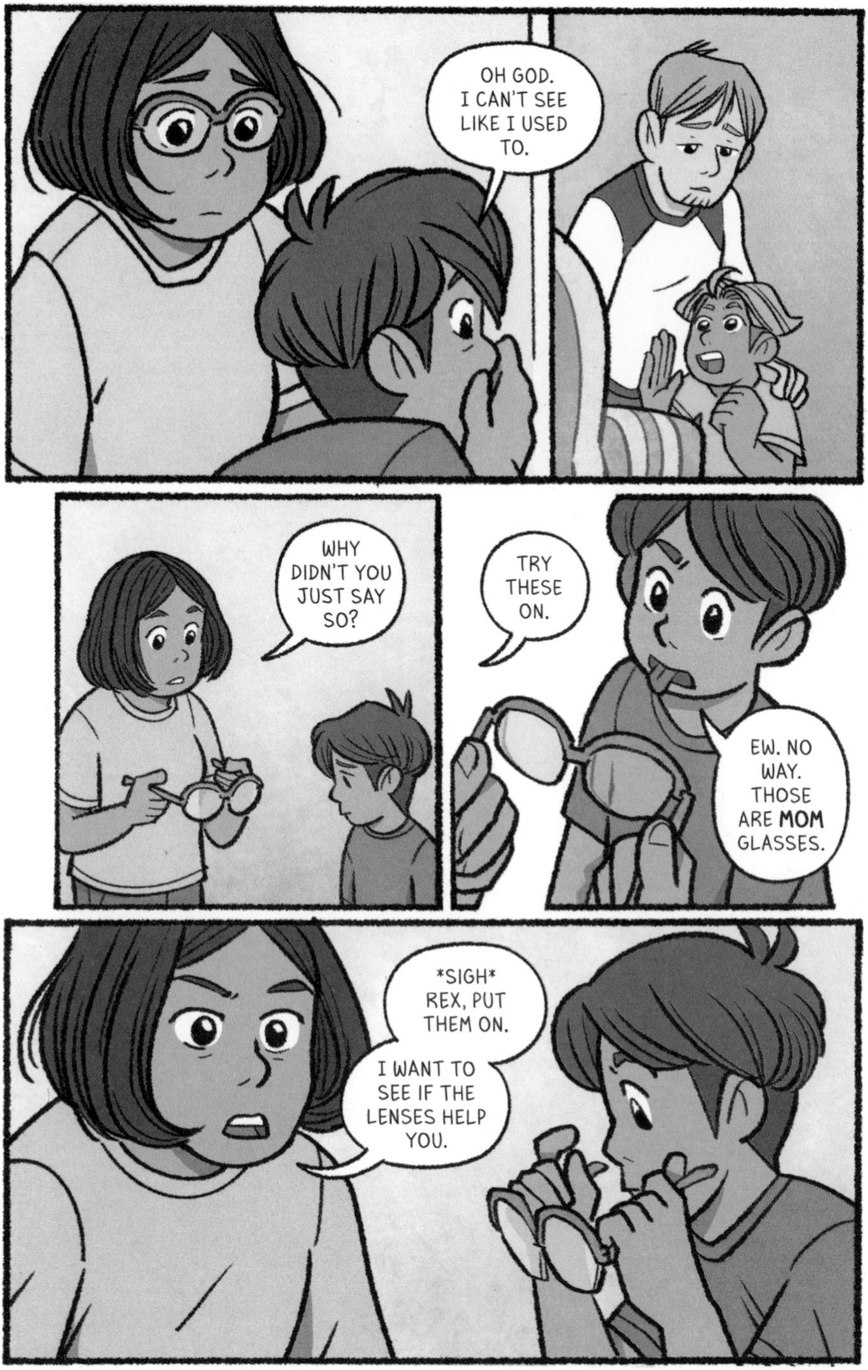
OH GOD. I CAN'T SEE LIKE I USED TO.
WHY DIDN'T YOU JUST SAY SO?
TRY THESE ON.
EW. NO WAY. THOSE ARE **MOM** GLASSES.
SIGH REX, PUT THEM ON.
I WANT TO SEE IF THE LENSES HELP YOU.

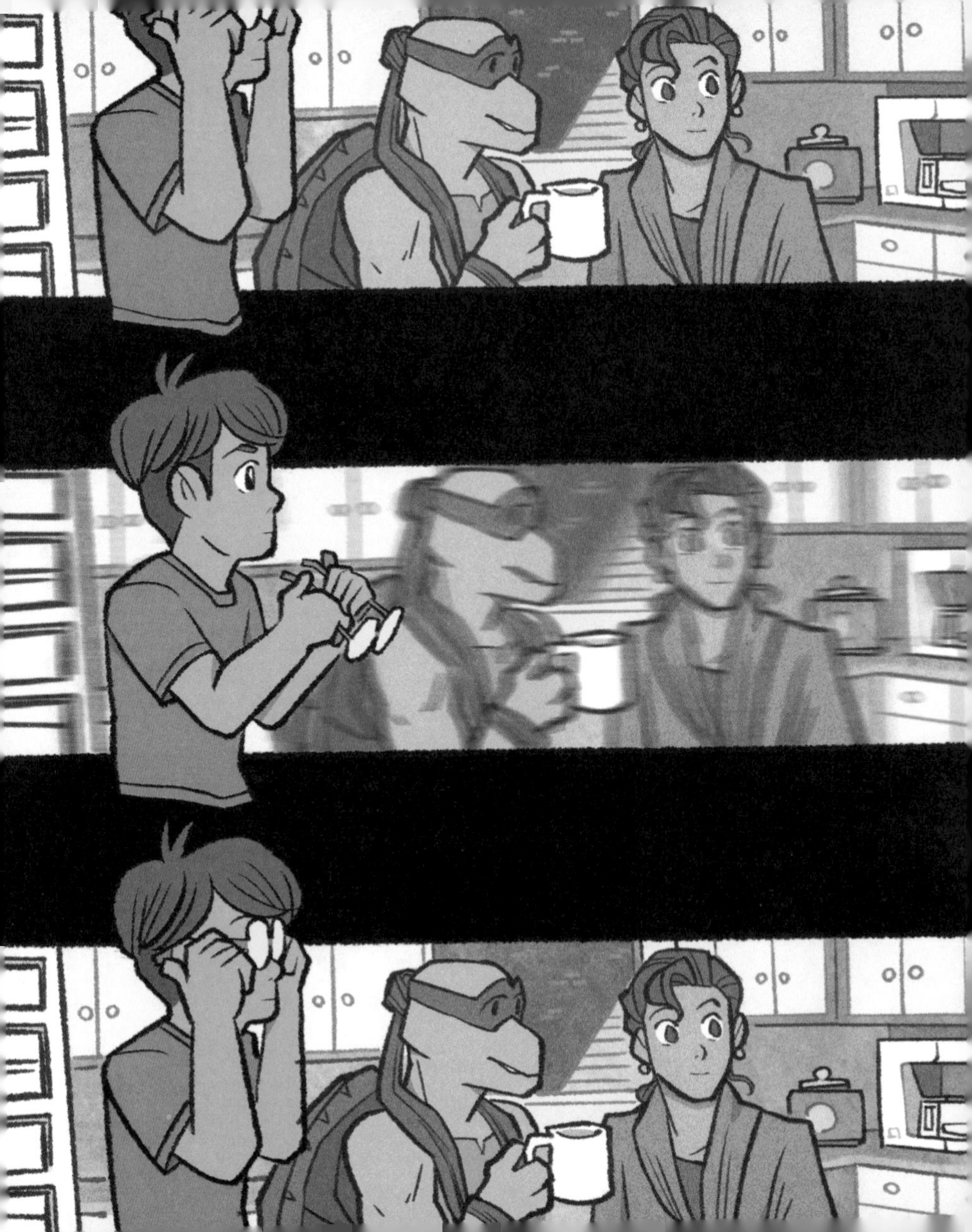

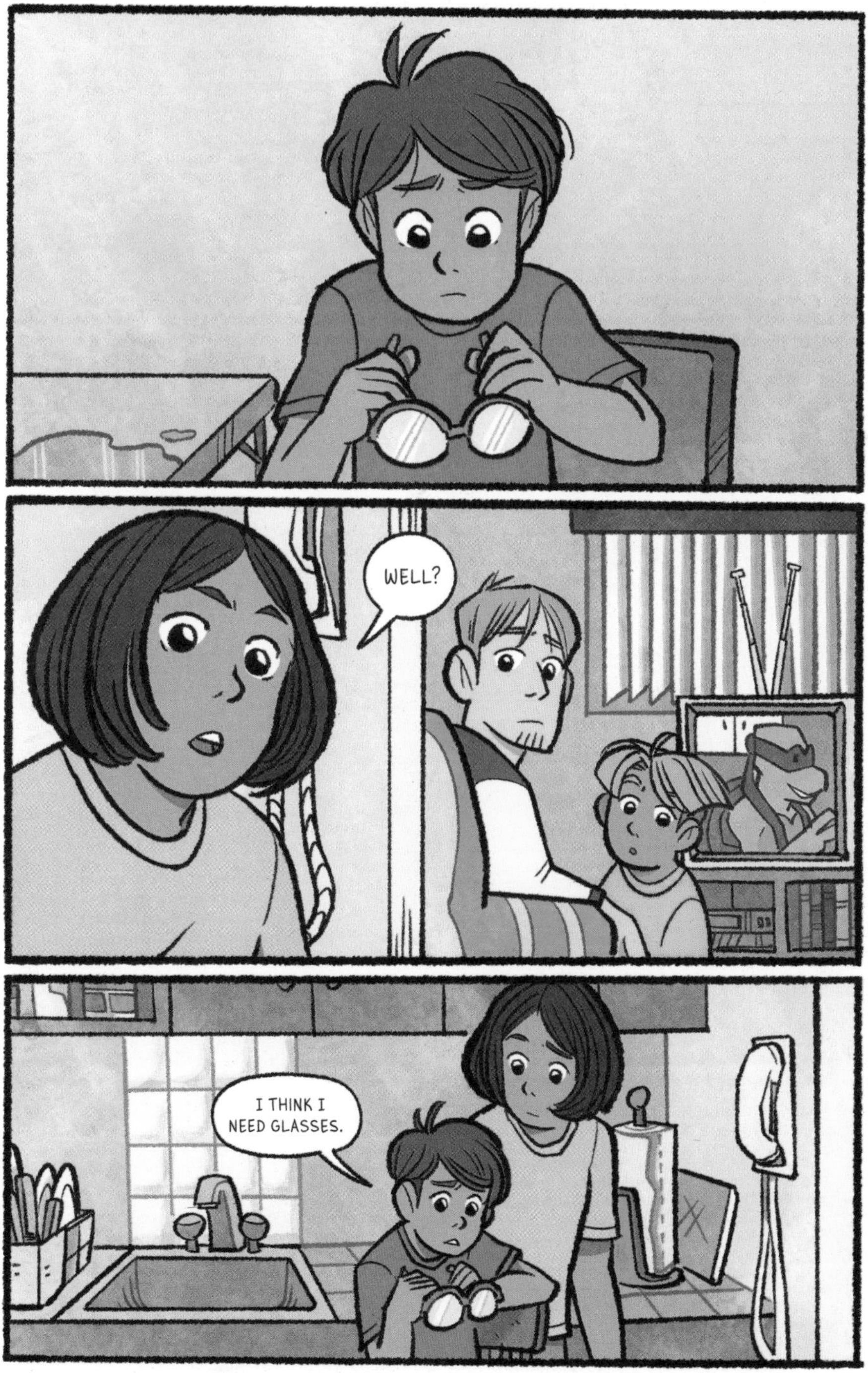
WELL?
I THINK I NEED GLASSES.

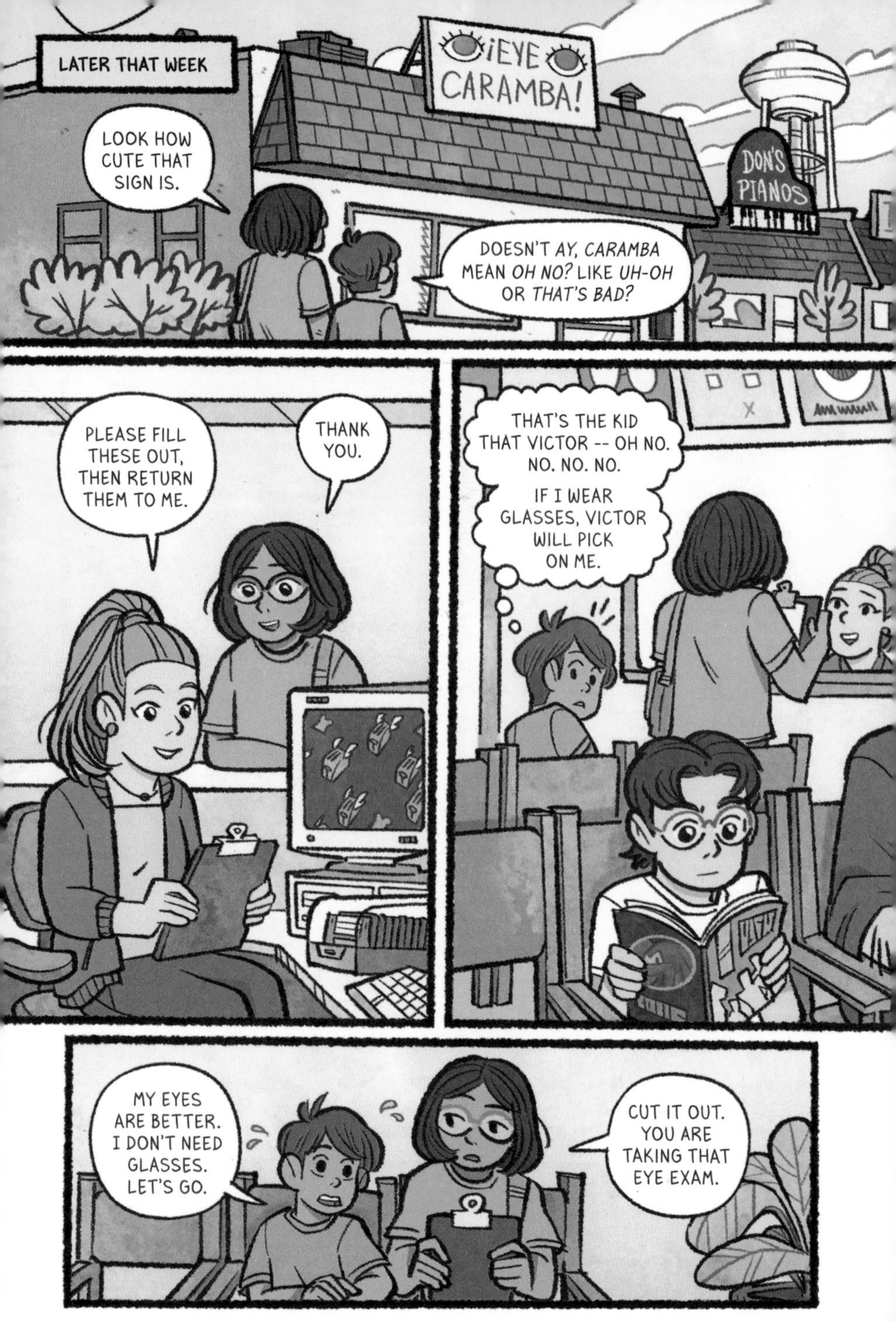
LATER THAT WEEK
¡EYE CARAMBA!
DON'S PIANOS
LOOK HOW CUTE THAT SIGN IS.
DOESN'T AY, CARAMBA MEAN OH NO? LIKE UH-OH OR THAT'S BAD?
PLEASE FILL THESE OUT, THEN RETURN THEM TO ME.
THANK YOU.
THAT'S THE KID THAT VICTOR -- OH NO. NO. NO. NO.
IF I WEAR GLASSES, VICTOR WILL PICK ON ME.
MY EYES ARE BETTER. I DON'T NEED GLASSES. LET'S GO.
CUT IT OUT. YOU ARE TAKING THAT EYE EXAM.

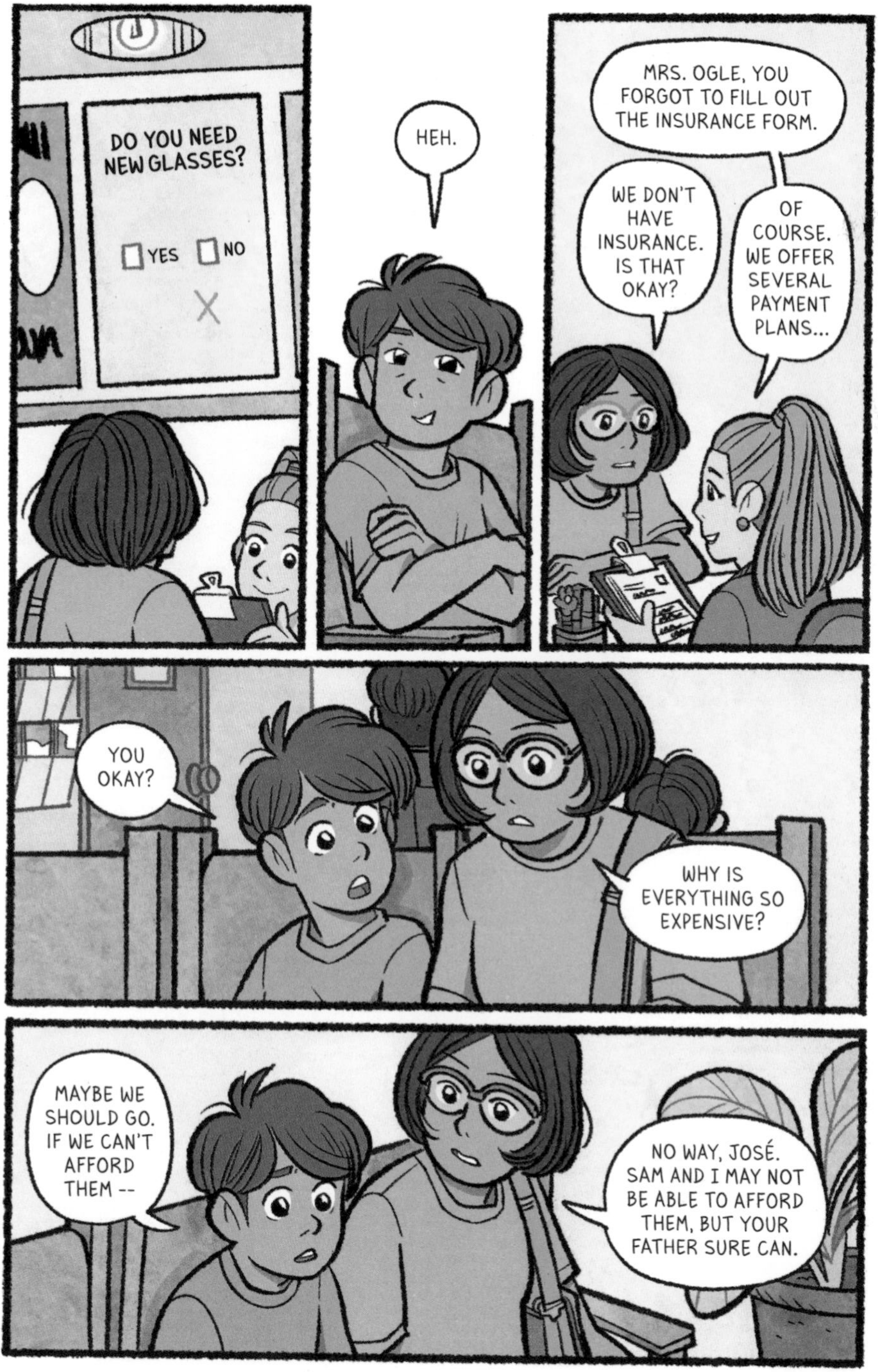
DO YOU NEED NEW GLASSES?
YES NO
HEH.
MRS. OGLE, YOU FORGOT TO FILL OUT THE INSURANCE FORM.
WE DON'T HAVE INSURANCE. IS THAT OKAY?
OF COURSE. WE OFFER SEVERAL PAYMENT PLANS...
YOU OKAY?
WHY IS EVERYTHING SO EXPENSIVE?
MAYBE WE SHOULD GO. IF WE CAN'T AFFORD THEM --
NO WAY, JOSÉ. SAM AND I MAY NOT BE ABLE TO AFFORD THEM, BUT YOUR FATHER SURE CAN.

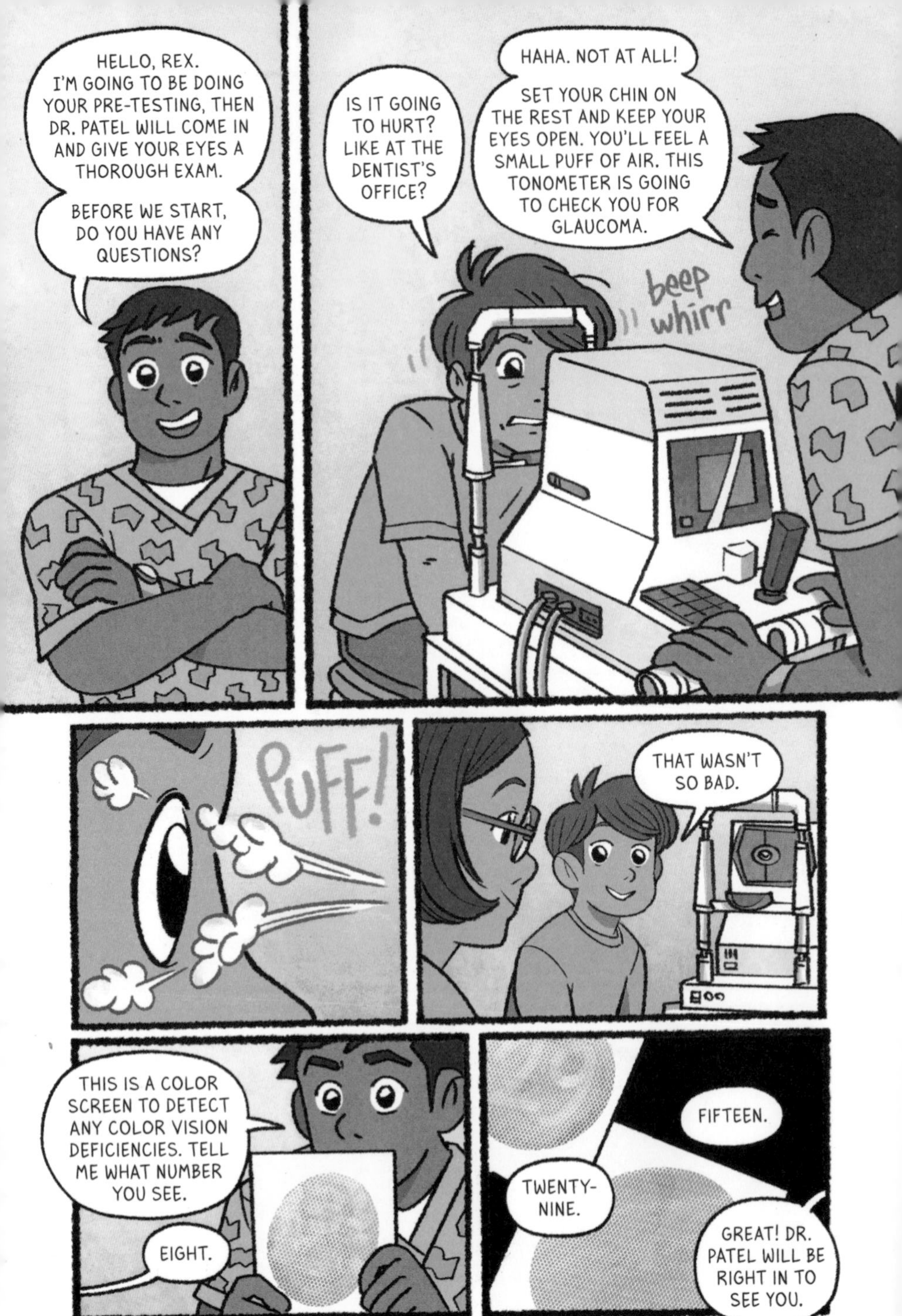
HELLO, REX. I'M GOING TO BE DOING YOUR PRE-TESTING, THEN DR. PATEL WILL COME IN AND GIVE YOUR EYES A THOROUGH EXAM.
BEFORE WE START, DO YOU HAVE ANY QUESTIONS?
IS IT GOING TO HURT? LIKE AT THE DENTIST'S OFFICE?
HAHA. NOT AT ALL!
SET YOUR CHIN ON THE REST AND KEEP YOUR EYES OPEN. YOU'LL FEEL A SMALL PUFF OF AIR. THIS TONOMETER IS GOING TO CHECK YOU FOR GLAUCOMA.
beep whirr
PUFF!
THAT WASN'T SO BAD.
THIS IS A COLOR SCREEN TO DETECT ANY COLOR VISION DEFICIENCIES. TELL ME WHAT NUMBER YOU SEE.
EIGHT.
FIFTEEN.
TWENTY-NINE.
GREAT! DR. PATEL WILL BE RIGHT IN TO SEE YOU.

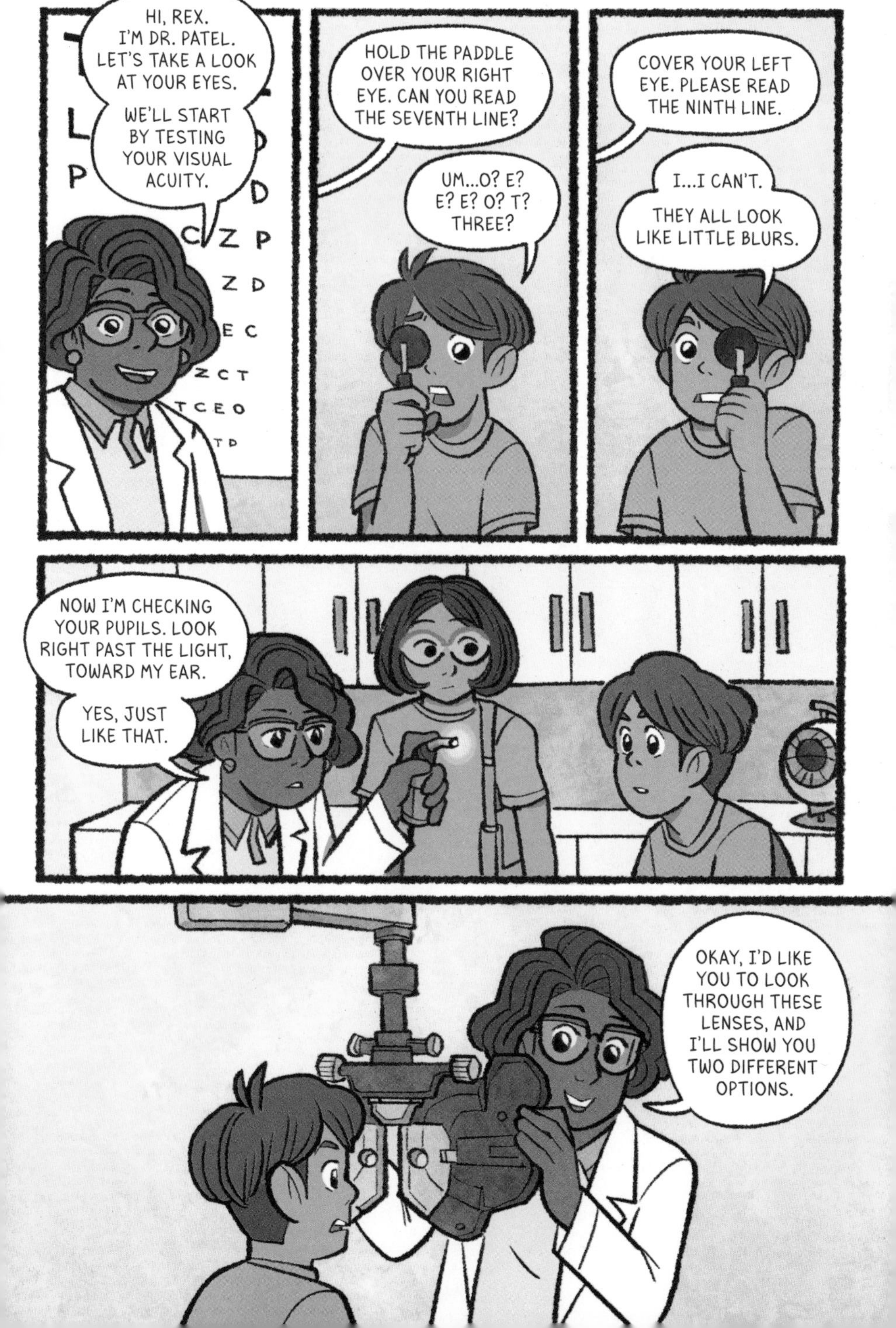
HI, REX. I'M DR. PATEL. LET'S TAKE A LOOK AT YOUR EYES.
WE'LL START BY TESTING YOUR VISUAL ACUITY.
HOLD THE PADDLE OVER YOUR RIGHT EYE. CAN YOU READ THE SEVENTH LINE?
UM...O? E? E? E? O? T? THREE?
COVER YOUR LEFT EYE. PLEASE READ THE NINTH LINE.
I...I CAN'T.
THEY ALL LOOK LIKE LITTLE BLURS.
NOW I'M CHECKING YOUR PUPILS. LOOK RIGHT PAST THE LIGHT, TOWARD MY EAR.
YES, JUST LIKE THAT.
OKAY, I'D LIKE YOU TO LOOK THROUGH THESE LENSES, AND I'LL SHOW YOU TWO DIFFERENT OPTIONS.

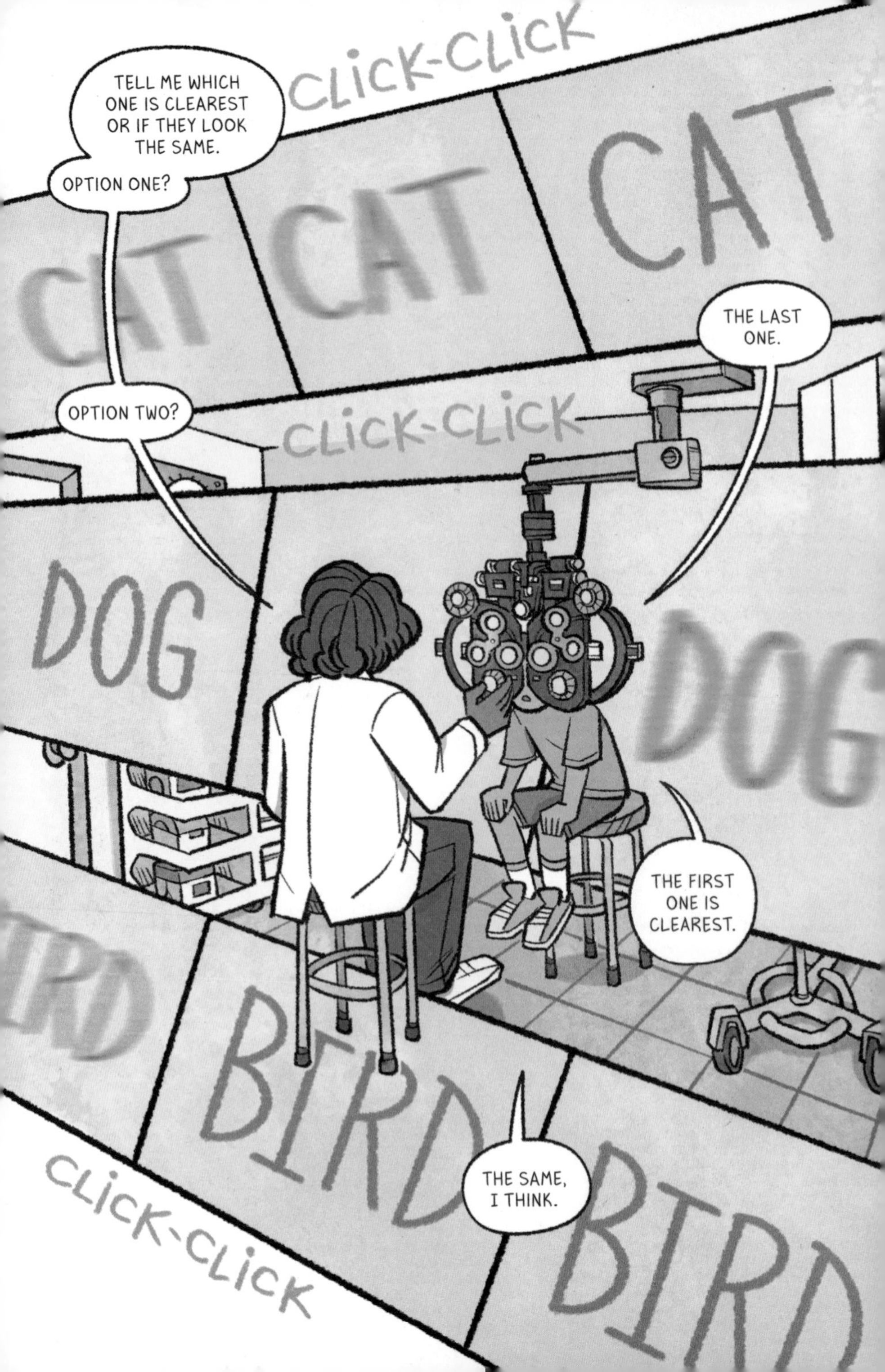
CLICK-CLICK
TELL ME WHICH ONE IS CLEAREST OR IF THEY LOOK THE SAME.
OPTION ONE?
CAT
CAT
CAT
OPTION TWO?
CLICK-CLICK
THE LAST ONE.
DOG
DOG
THE FIRST ONE IS CLEAREST.
BIRD
BIRD
THE SAME, I THINK.
CLICK-CLICK

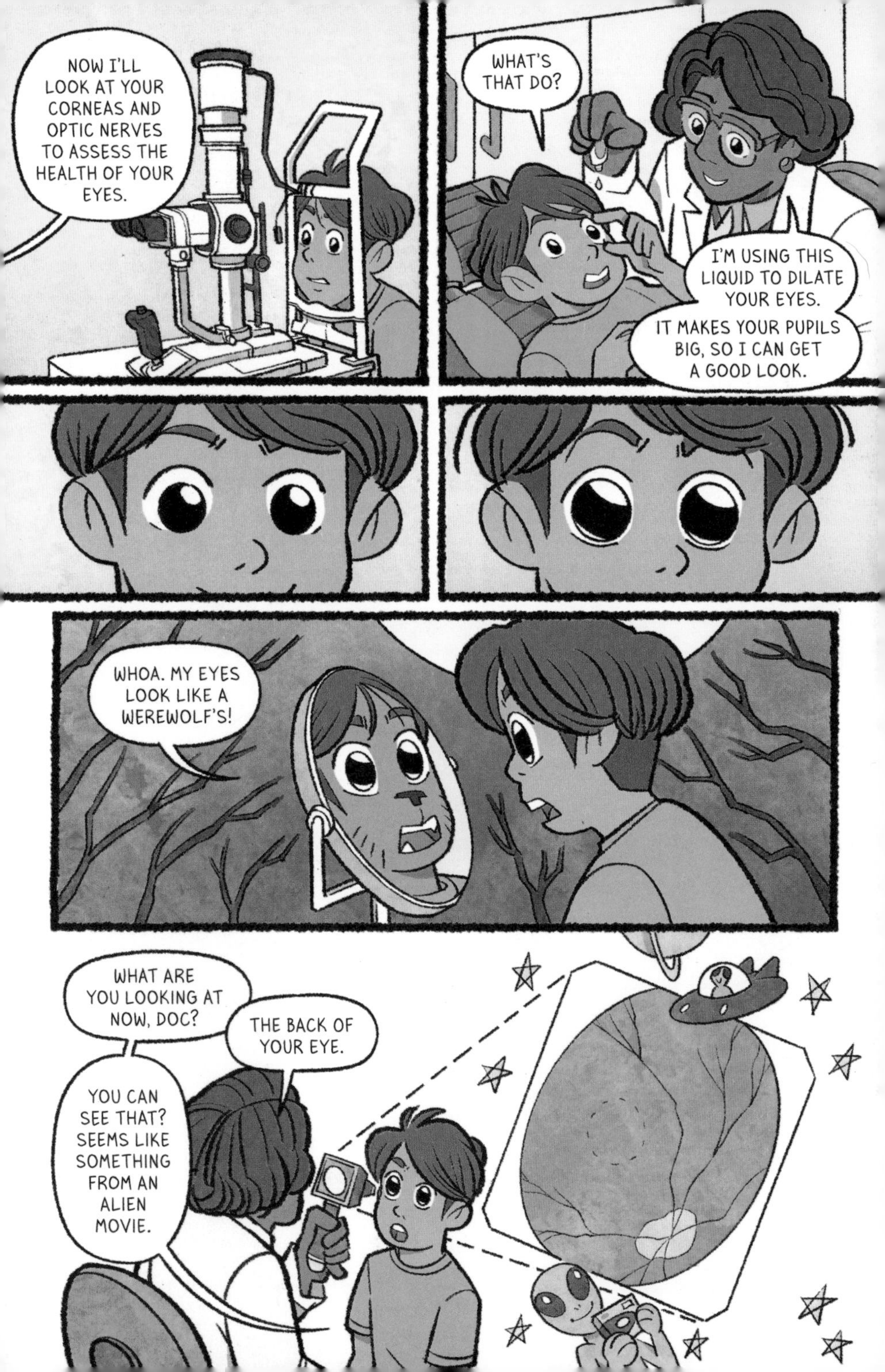
NOW I'LL LOOK AT YOUR CORNEAS AND OPTIC NERVES TO ASSESS THE HEALTH OF YOUR EYES.
WHAT'S THAT DO?
I'M USING THIS LIQUID TO DILATE YOUR EYES.
IT MAKES YOUR PUPILS BIG, SO I CAN GET A GOOD LOOK.
WHOA. MY EYES LOOK LIKE A WEREWOLF'S!
WHAT ARE YOU LOOKING AT NOW, DOC?
THE BACK OF YOUR EYE.
YOU CAN SEE THAT? SEEMS LIKE SOMETHING FROM AN ALIEN MOVIE.

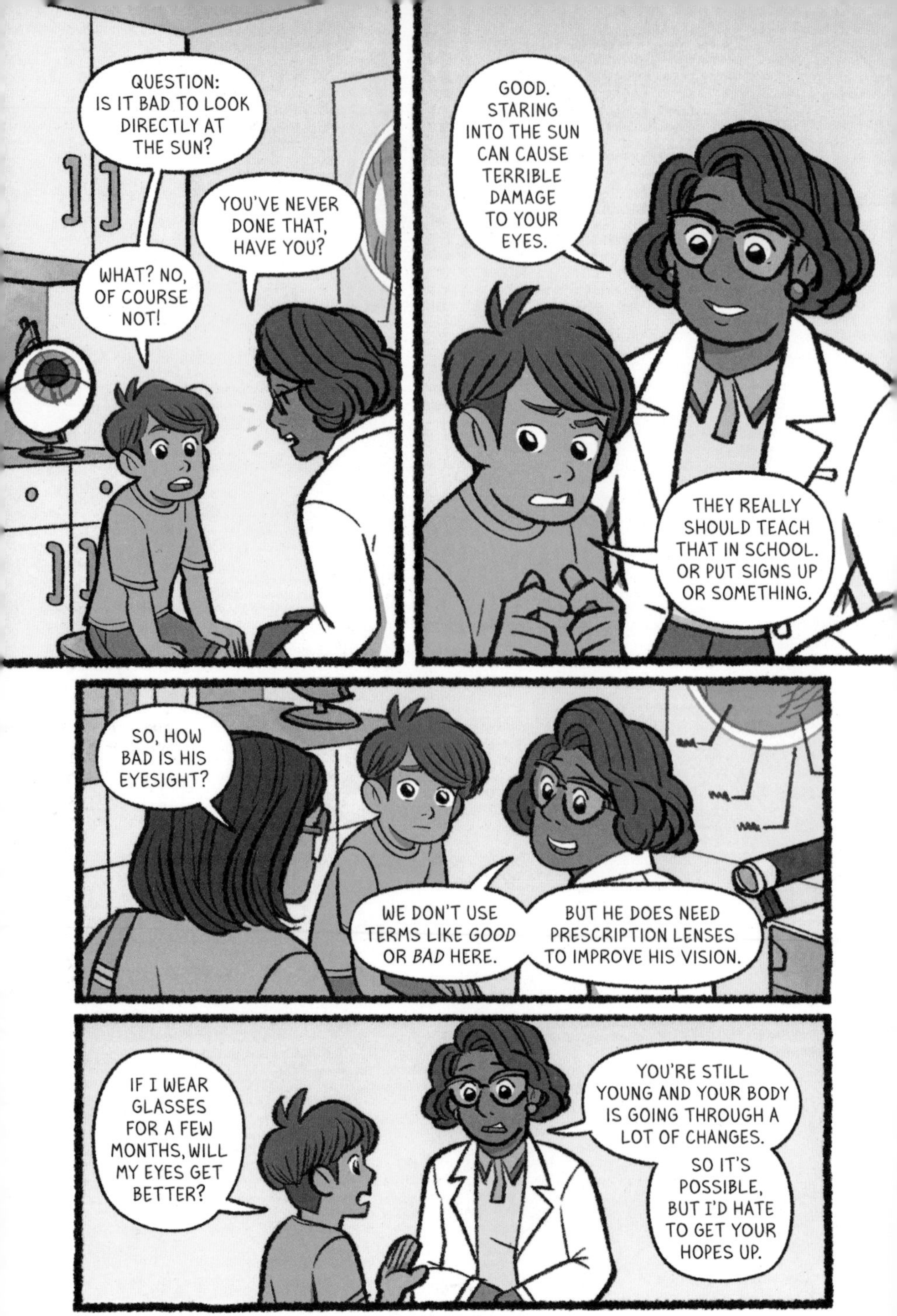
QUESTION: IS IT BAD TO LOOK DIRECTLY AT THE SUN?
YOU'VE NEVER DONE THAT, HAVE YOU?
WHAT? NO, OF COURSE NOT!
GOOD. STARING INTO THE SUN CAN CAUSE TERRIBLE DAMAGE TO YOUR EYES.
THEY REALLY SHOULD TEACH THAT IN SCHOOL. OR PUT SIGNS UP OR SOMETHING.
SO, HOW BAD IS HIS EYESIGHT?
WE DON'T USE TERMS LIKE *GOOD* OR *BAD* HERE.
BUT HE DOES NEED PRESCRIPTION LENSES TO IMPROVE HIS VISION.
IF I WEAR GLASSES FOR A FEW MONTHS, WILL MY EYES GET BETTER?
YOU'RE STILL YOUNG AND YOUR BODY IS GOING THROUGH A LOT OF CHANGES.
SO IT'S POSSIBLE, BUT I'D HATE TO GET YOUR HOPES UP.

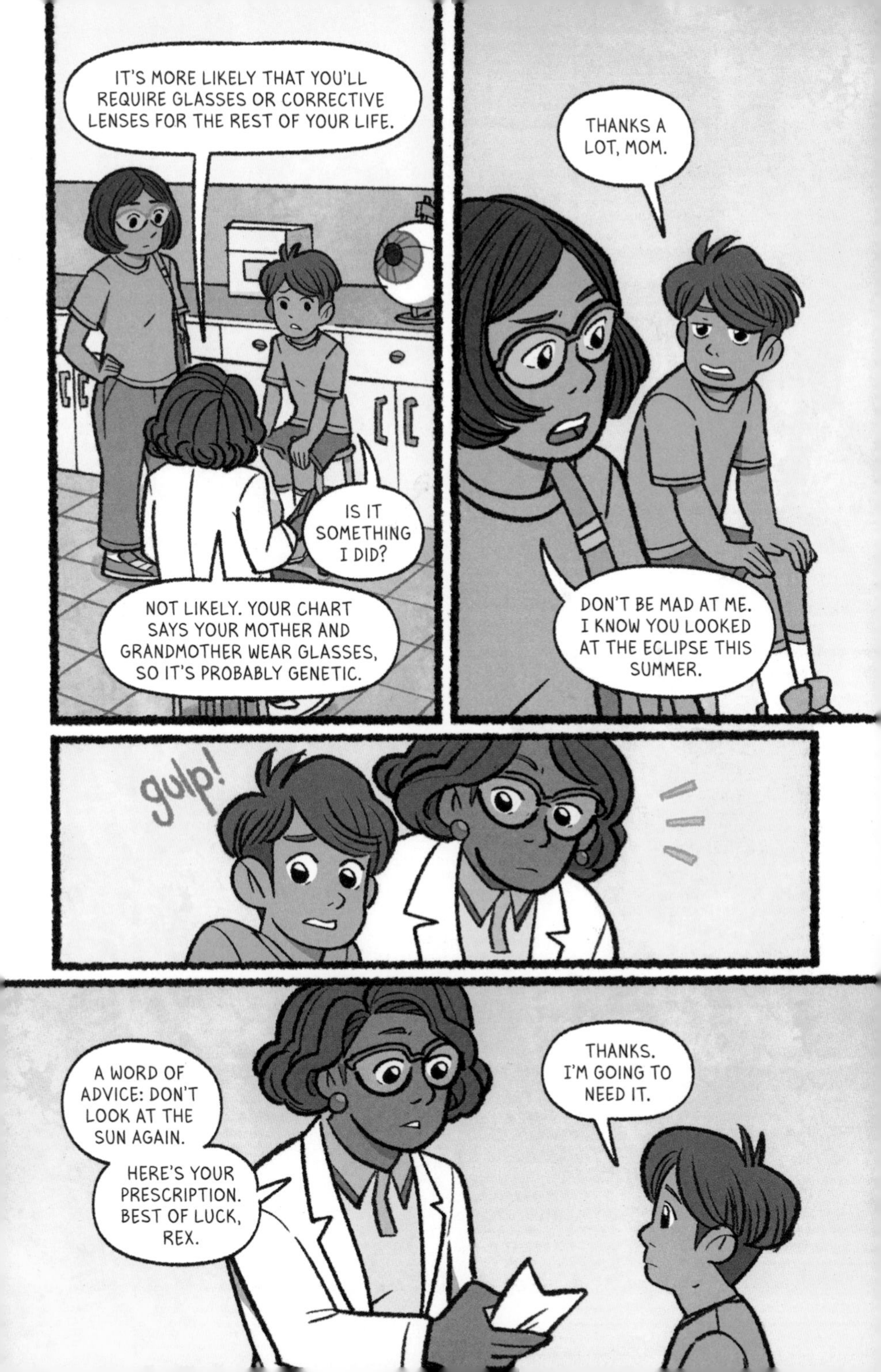
IT'S MORE LIKELY THAT YOU'LL REQUIRE GLASSES OR CORRECTIVE LENSES FOR THE REST OF YOUR LIFE.
IS IT SOMETHING I DID?
NOT LIKELY. YOUR CHART SAYS YOUR MOTHER AND GRANDMOTHER WEAR GLASSES, SO IT'S PROBABLY GENETIC.
THANKS A LOT, MOM.
DON'T BE MAD AT ME. I KNOW YOU LOOKED AT THE ECLIPSE THIS SUMMER.
gulp!
A WORD OF ADVICE: DON'T LOOK AT THE SUN AGAIN.
HERE'S YOUR PRESCRIPTION. BEST OF LUCK, REX.
THANKS. I'M GOING TO NEED IT.

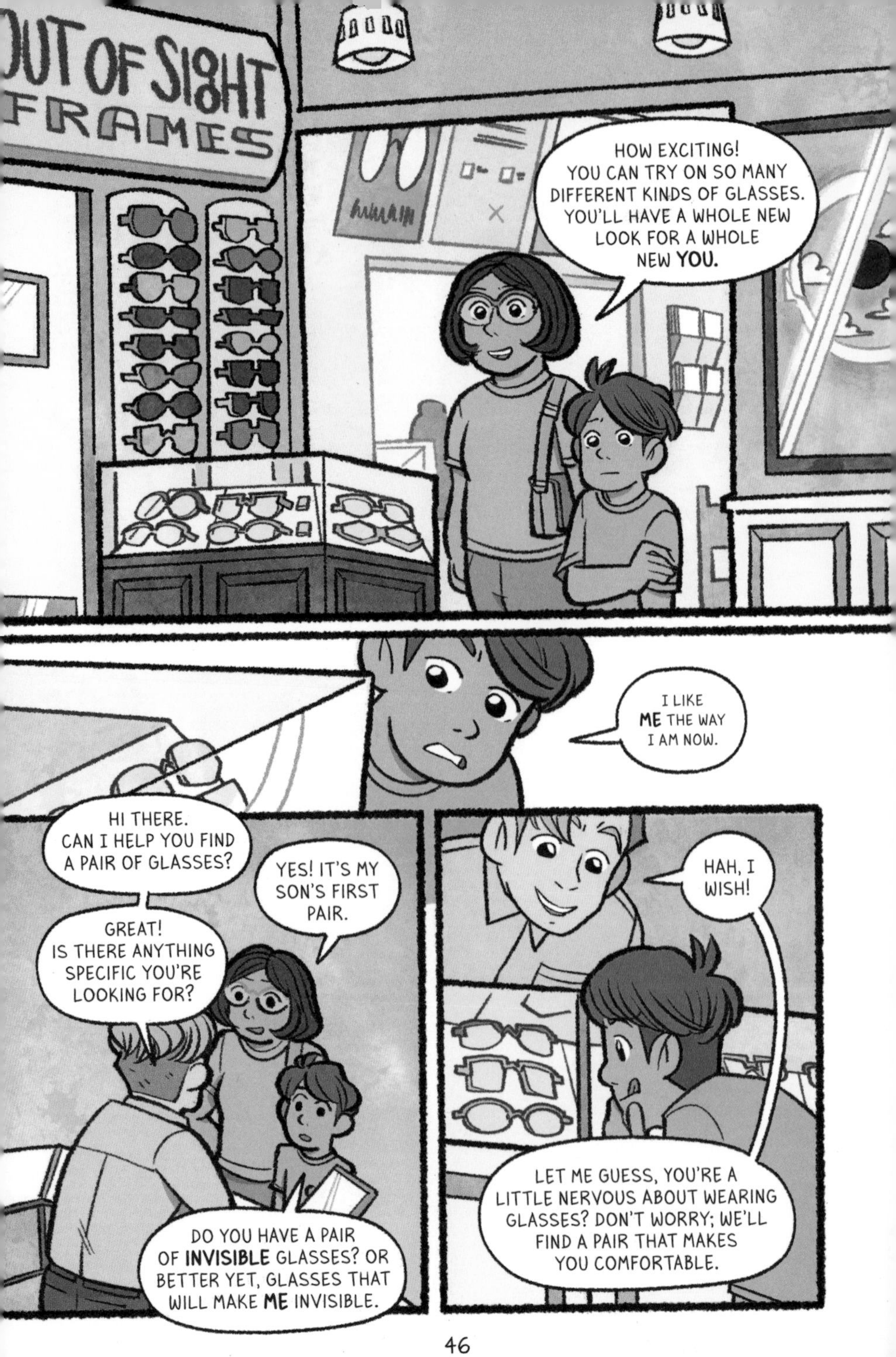
OUT OF SIGHT FRAMES
HOW EXCITING! YOU CAN TRY ON SO MANY DIFFERENT KINDS OF GLASSES. YOU'LL HAVE A WHOLE NEW LOOK FOR A WHOLE NEW **YOU.**
I LIKE **ME** THE WAY I AM NOW.
HI THERE. CAN I HELP YOU FIND A PAIR OF GLASSES?
YES! IT'S MY SON'S FIRST PAIR.
GREAT! IS THERE ANYTHING SPECIFIC YOU'RE LOOKING FOR?
DO YOU HAVE A PAIR OF **INVISIBLE** GLASSES? OR BETTER YET, GLASSES THAT WILL MAKE **ME** INVISIBLE.
HAH, I WISH!
LET ME GUESS, YOU'RE A LITTLE NERVOUS ABOUT WEARING GLASSES? DON'T WORRY; WE'LL FIND A PAIR THAT MAKES YOU COMFORTABLE.

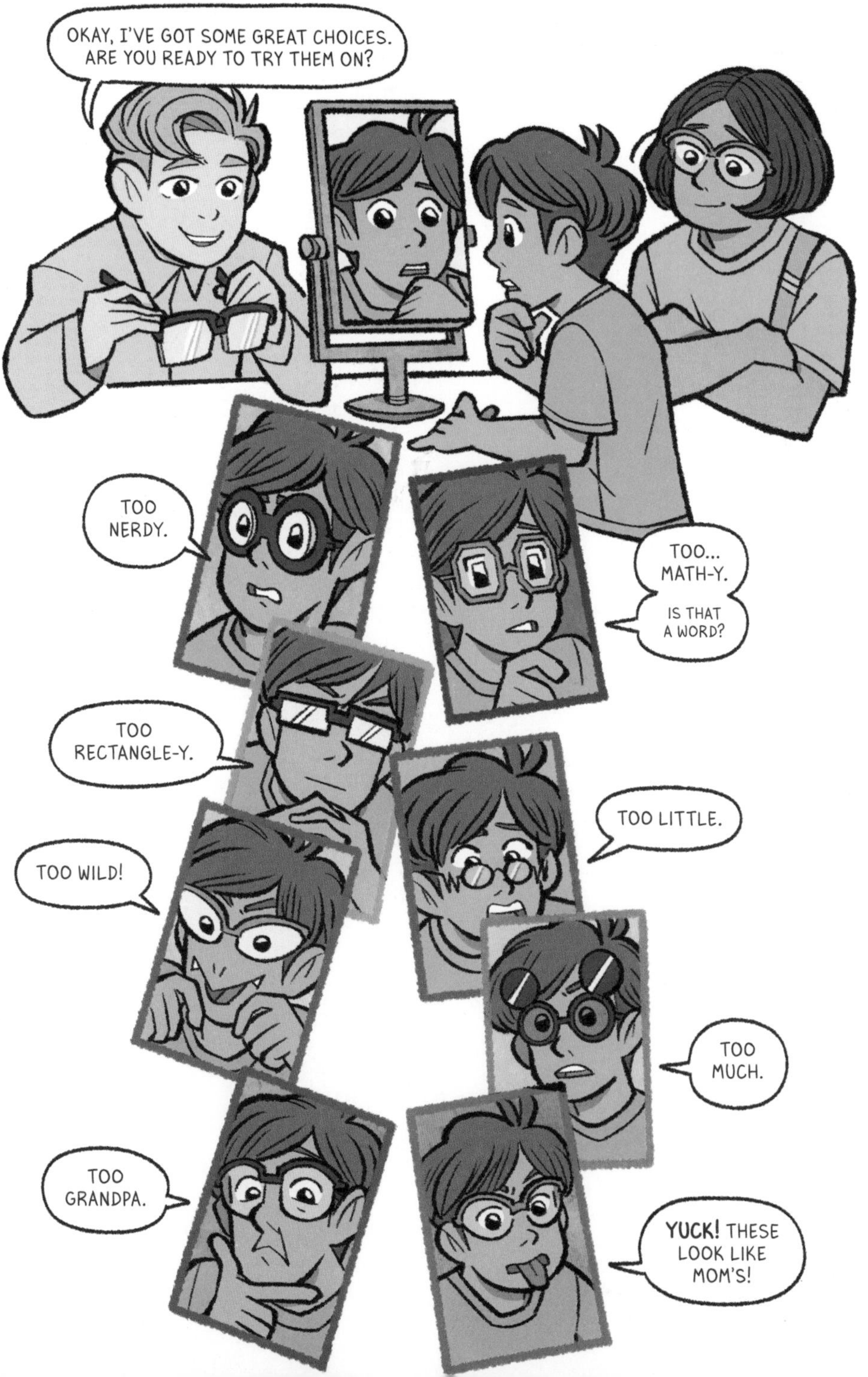
OKAY, I'VE GOT SOME GREAT CHOICES. ARE YOU READY TO TRY THEM ON?
TOO NERDY.
TOO... MATH-Y.
IS THAT A WORD?
TOO RECTANGLE-Y.
TOO LITTLE.
TOO WILD!
TOO MUCH.
TOO GRANDPA.
YUCK! THESE LOOK LIKE MOM'S!

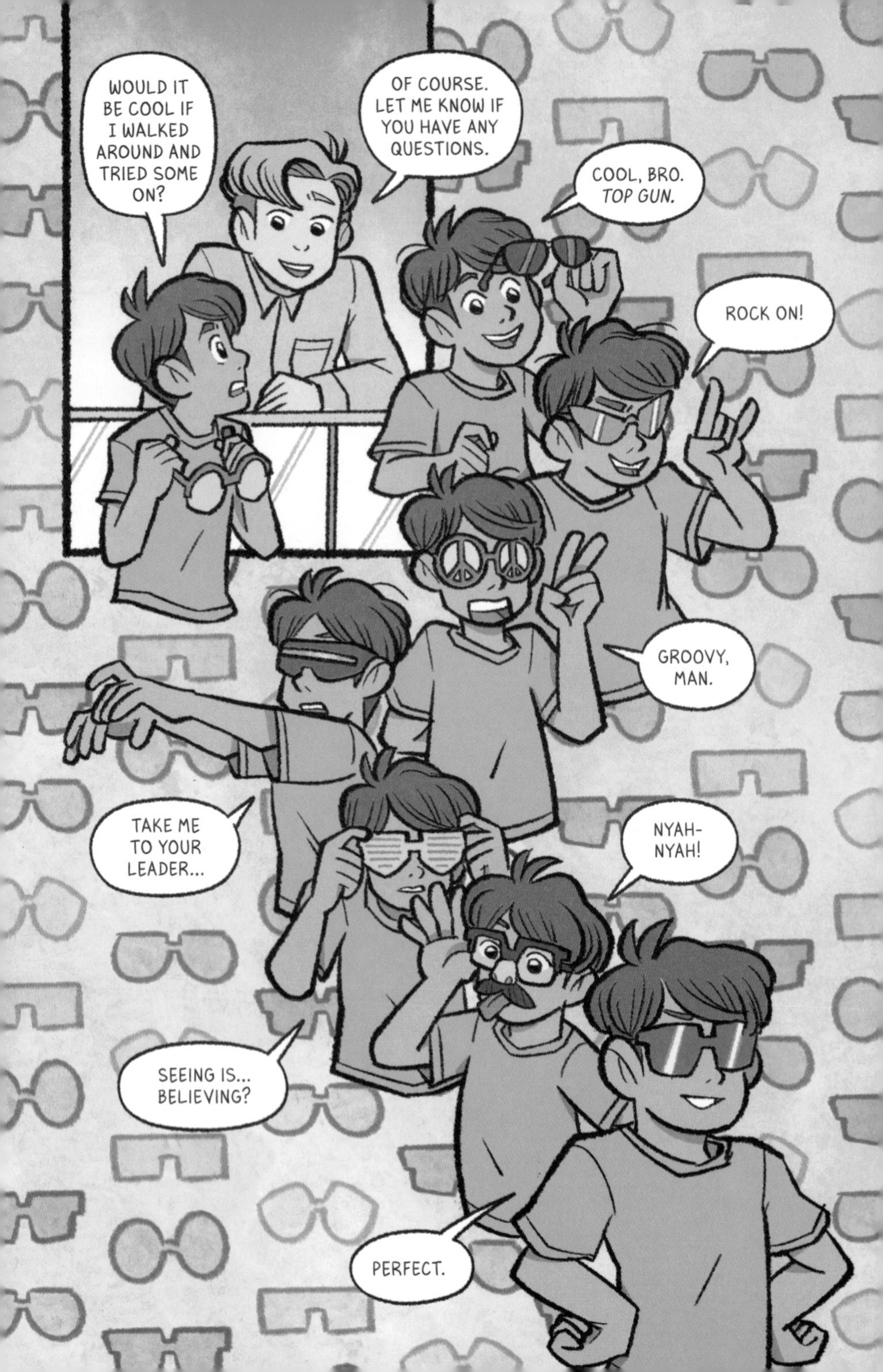
WOULD IT BE COOL IF I WALKED AROUND AND TRIED SOME ON?
OF COURSE. LET ME KNOW IF YOU HAVE ANY QUESTIONS.
COOL, BRO. *TOP GUN.*
ROCK ON!
GROOVY, MAN.
TAKE ME TO YOUR LEADER...
NYAH-NYAH!
SEEING IS... BELIEVING?
PERFECT.

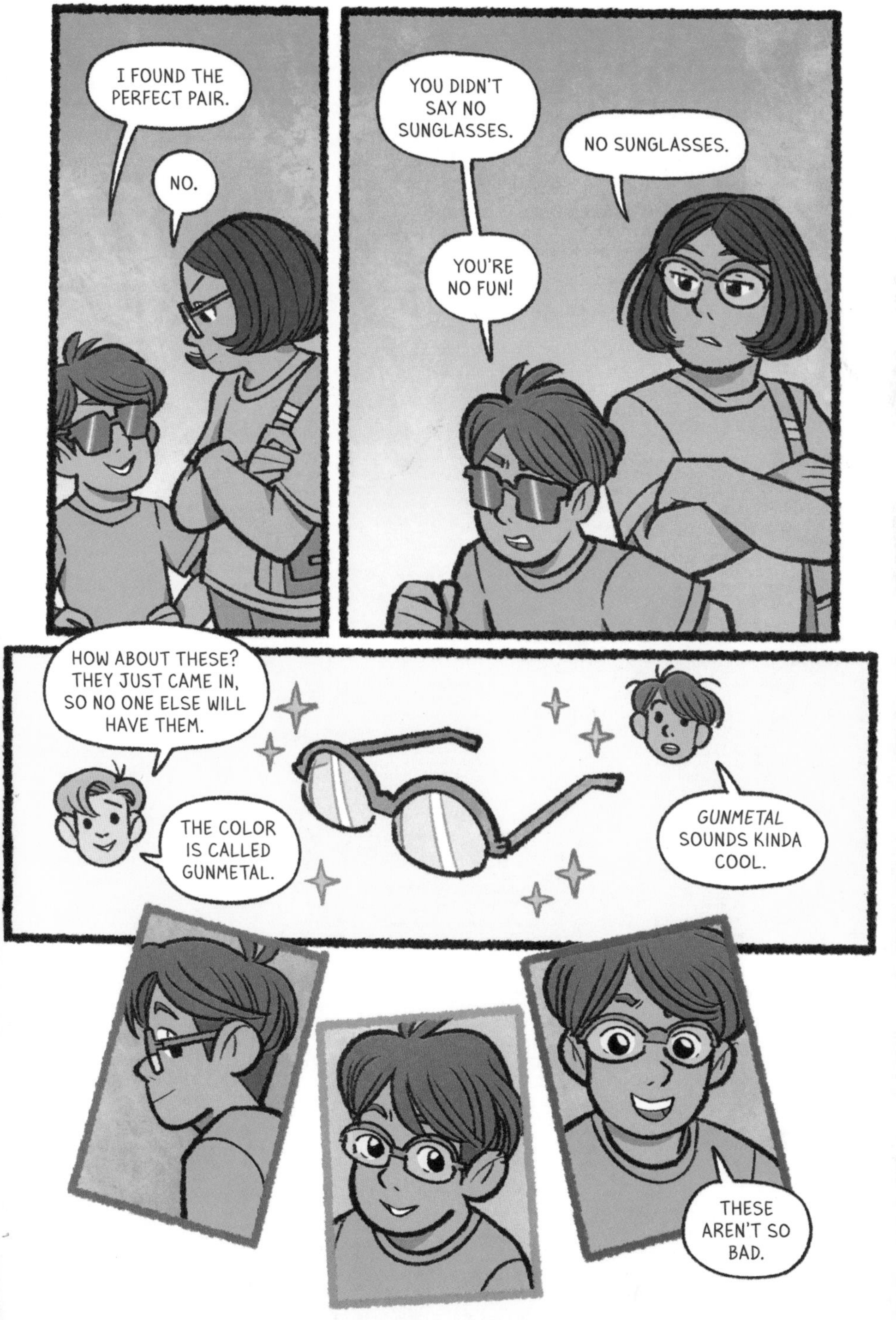
I FOUND THE PERFECT PAIR.
NO.
YOU DIDN'T SAY NO SUNGLASSES.
NO SUNGLASSES.
YOU'RE NO FUN!
HOW ABOUT THESE? THEY JUST CAME IN, SO NO ONE ELSE WILL HAVE THEM.
THE COLOR IS CALLED GUNMETAL.
GUNMETAL SOUNDS KINDA COOL.
THESE AREN'T SO BAD.

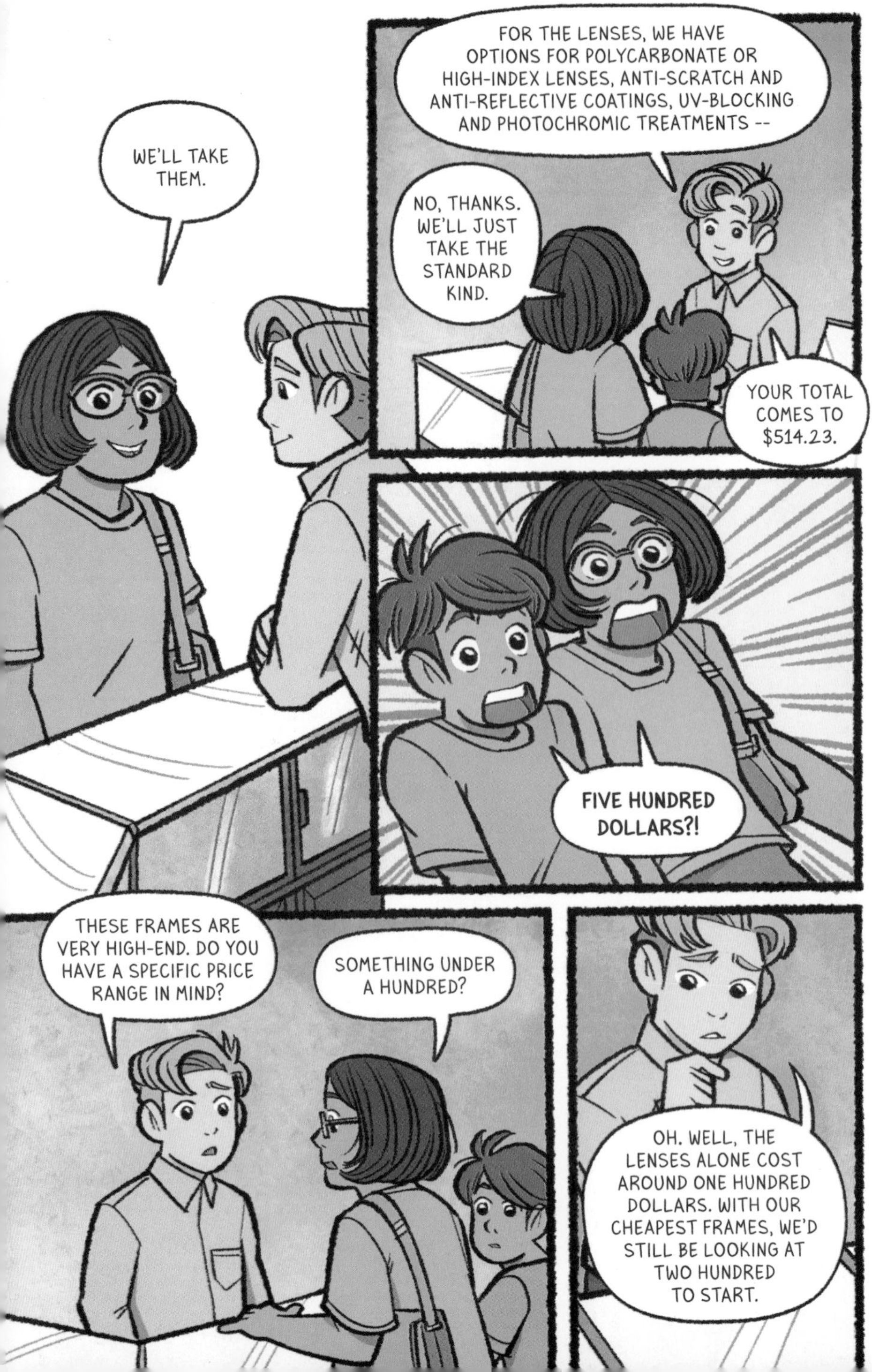
WE'LL TAKE THEM.
FOR THE LENSES, WE HAVE OPTIONS FOR POLYCARBONATE OR HIGH-INDEX LENSES, ANTI-SCRATCH AND ANTI-REFLECTIVE COATINGS, UV-BLOCKING AND PHOTOCHROMIC TREATMENTS --
NO, THANKS. WE'LL JUST TAKE THE STANDARD KIND.
YOUR TOTAL COMES TO $514.23.
FIVE HUNDRED DOLLARS?!
THESE FRAMES ARE VERY HIGH-END. DO YOU HAVE A SPECIFIC PRICE RANGE IN MIND?
SOMETHING UNDER A HUNDRED?
OH. WELL, THE LENSES ALONE COST AROUND ONE HUNDRED DOLLARS. WITH OUR CHEAPEST FRAMES, WE'D STILL BE LOOKING AT TWO HUNDRED TO START.

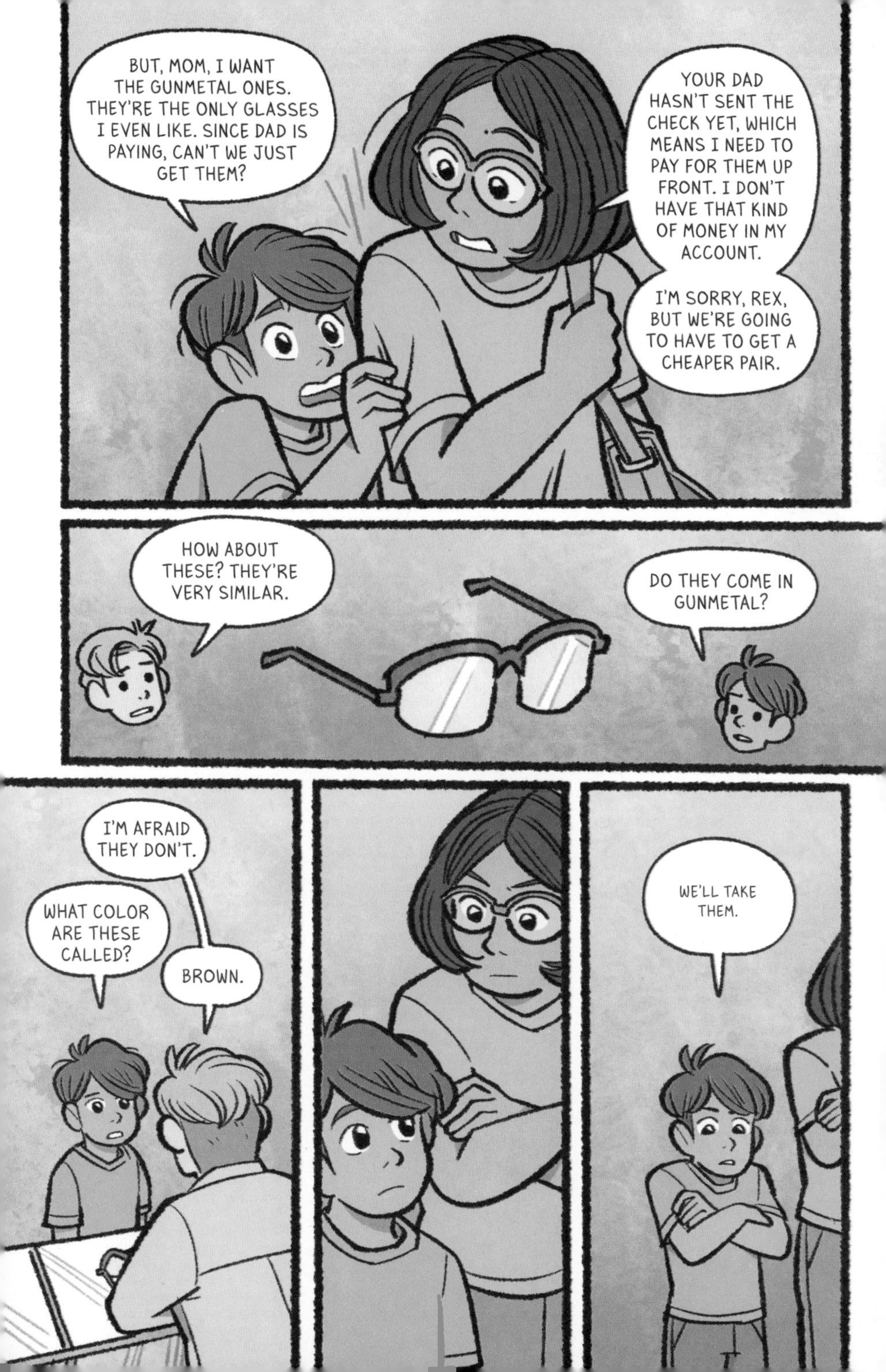
BUT, MOM, I WANT THE GUNMETAL ONES. THEY'RE THE ONLY GLASSES I EVEN LIKE. SINCE DAD IS PAYING, CAN'T WE JUST GET THEM?
YOUR DAD HASN'T SENT THE CHECK YET, WHICH MEANS I NEED TO PAY FOR THEM UP FRONT. I DON'T HAVE THAT KIND OF MONEY IN MY ACCOUNT.
I'M SORRY, REX, BUT WE'RE GOING TO HAVE TO GET A CHEAPER PAIR.
HOW ABOUT THESE? THEY'RE VERY SIMILAR.
DO THEY COME IN GUNMETAL?
I'M AFRAID THEY DON'T.
WHAT COLOR ARE THESE CALLED?
BROWN.
WE'LL TAKE THEM.

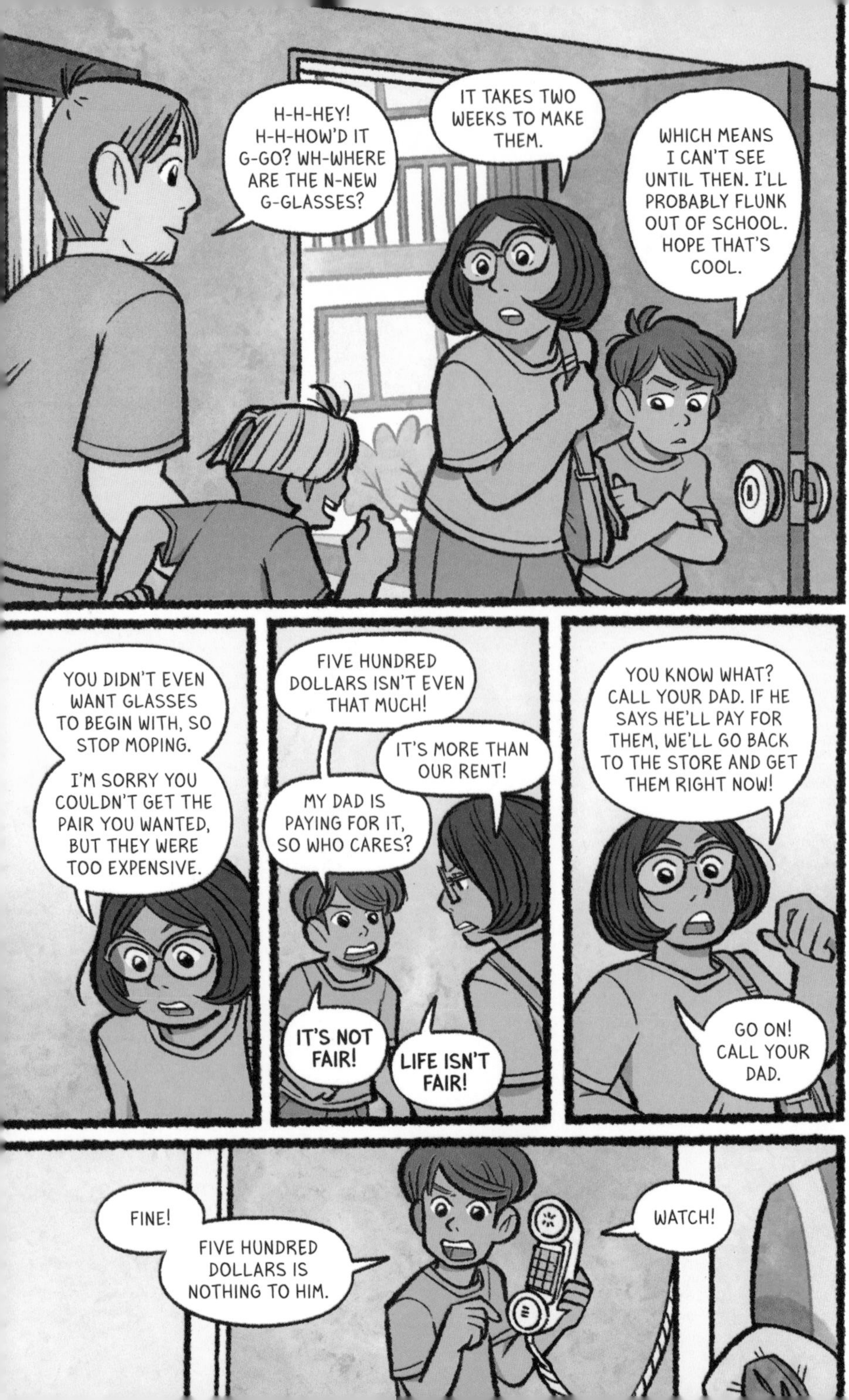
H-H-HEY! H-H-HOW'D IT G-GO? WH-WHERE ARE THE N-NEW G-GLASSES?
IT TAKES TWO WEEKS TO MAKE THEM.
WHICH MEANS I CAN'T SEE UNTIL THEN. I'LL PROBABLY FLUNK OUT OF SCHOOL. HOPE THAT'S COOL.
YOU DIDN'T EVEN WANT GLASSES TO BEGIN WITH, SO STOP MOPING.
I'M SORRY YOU COULDN'T GET THE PAIR YOU WANTED, BUT THEY WERE TOO EXPENSIVE.
FIVE HUNDRED DOLLARS ISN'T EVEN THAT MUCH!
IT'S MORE THAN OUR RENT!
MY DAD IS PAYING FOR IT, SO WHO CARES?
IT'S NOT FAIR!
LIFE ISN'T FAIR!
YOU KNOW WHAT? CALL YOUR DAD. IF HE SAYS HE'LL PAY FOR THEM, WE'LL GO BACK TO THE STORE AND GET THEM RIGHT NOW!
GO ON! CALL YOUR DAD.
FINE!
FIVE HUNDRED DOLLARS IS NOTHING TO HIM.
WATCH!

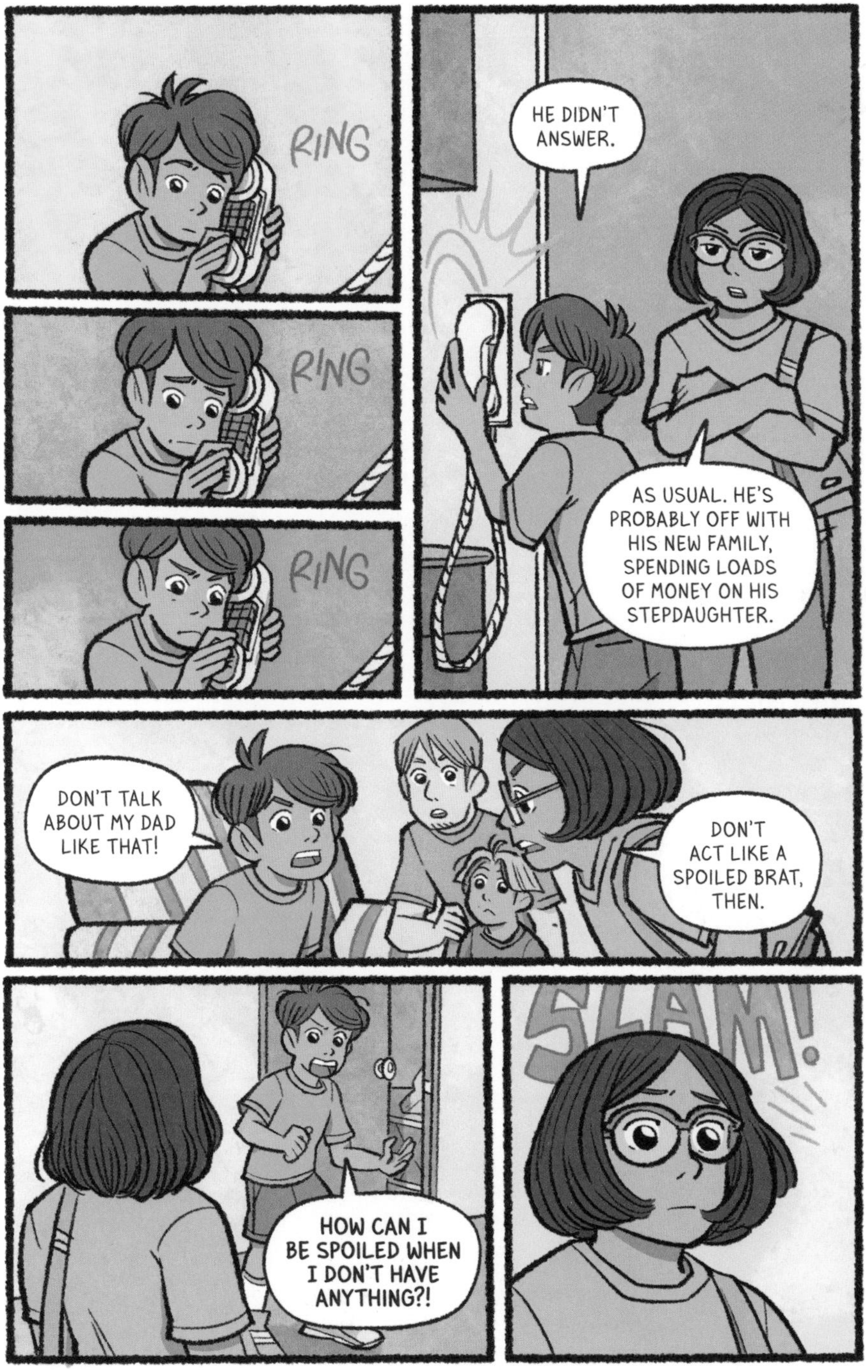
RING
RING
RING
HE DIDN'T ANSWER.
AS USUAL. HE'S PROBABLY OFF WITH HIS NEW FAMILY, SPENDING LOADS OF MONEY ON HIS STEPDAUGHTER.
DON'T TALK ABOUT MY DAD LIKE THAT!
DON'T ACT LIKE A SPOILED BRAT, THEN.
HOW CAN I BE SPOILED WHEN I DON'T HAVE ANYTHING?!
SLAM!

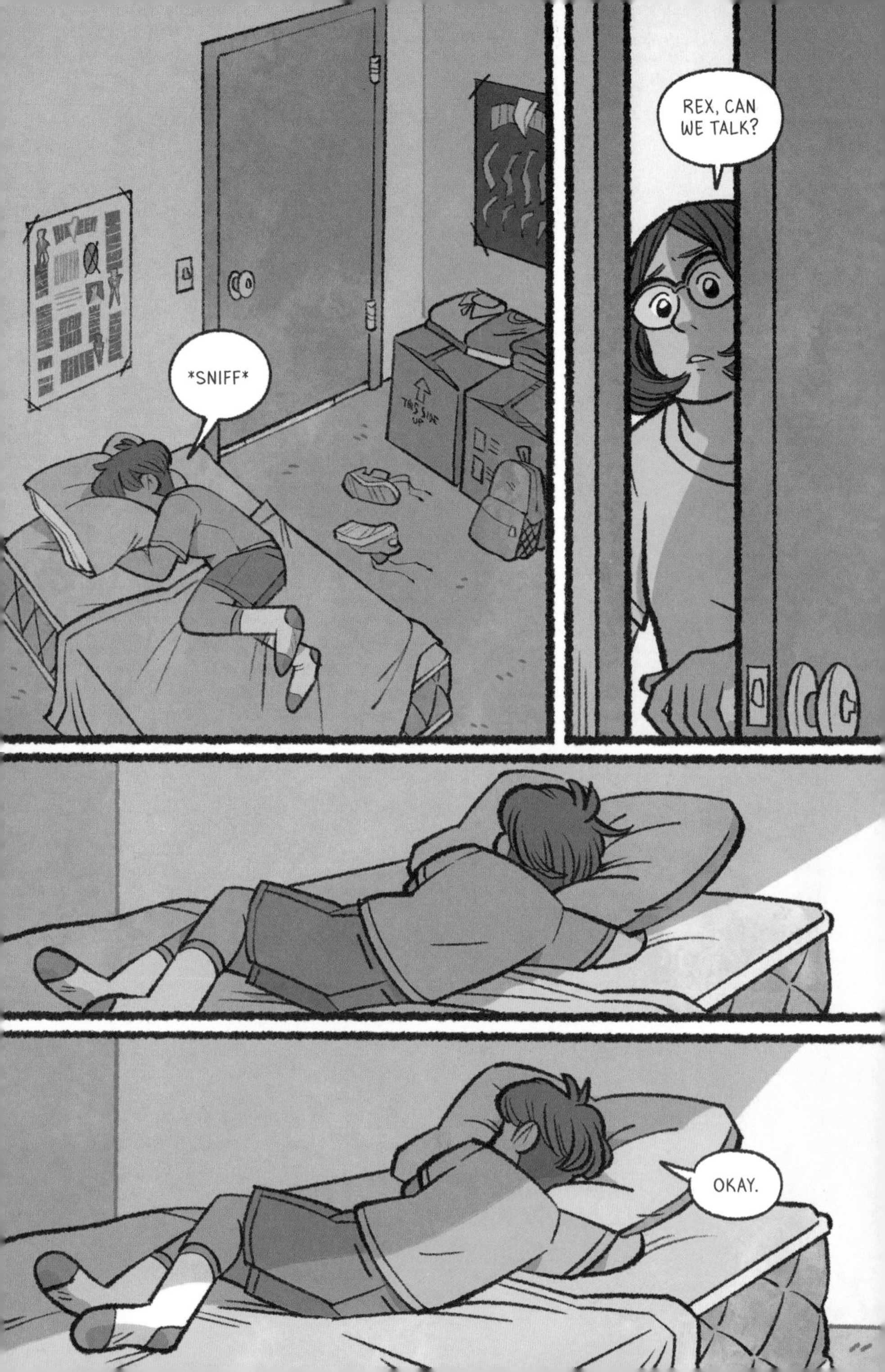
SNIFF
REX, CAN WE TALK?
OKAY.

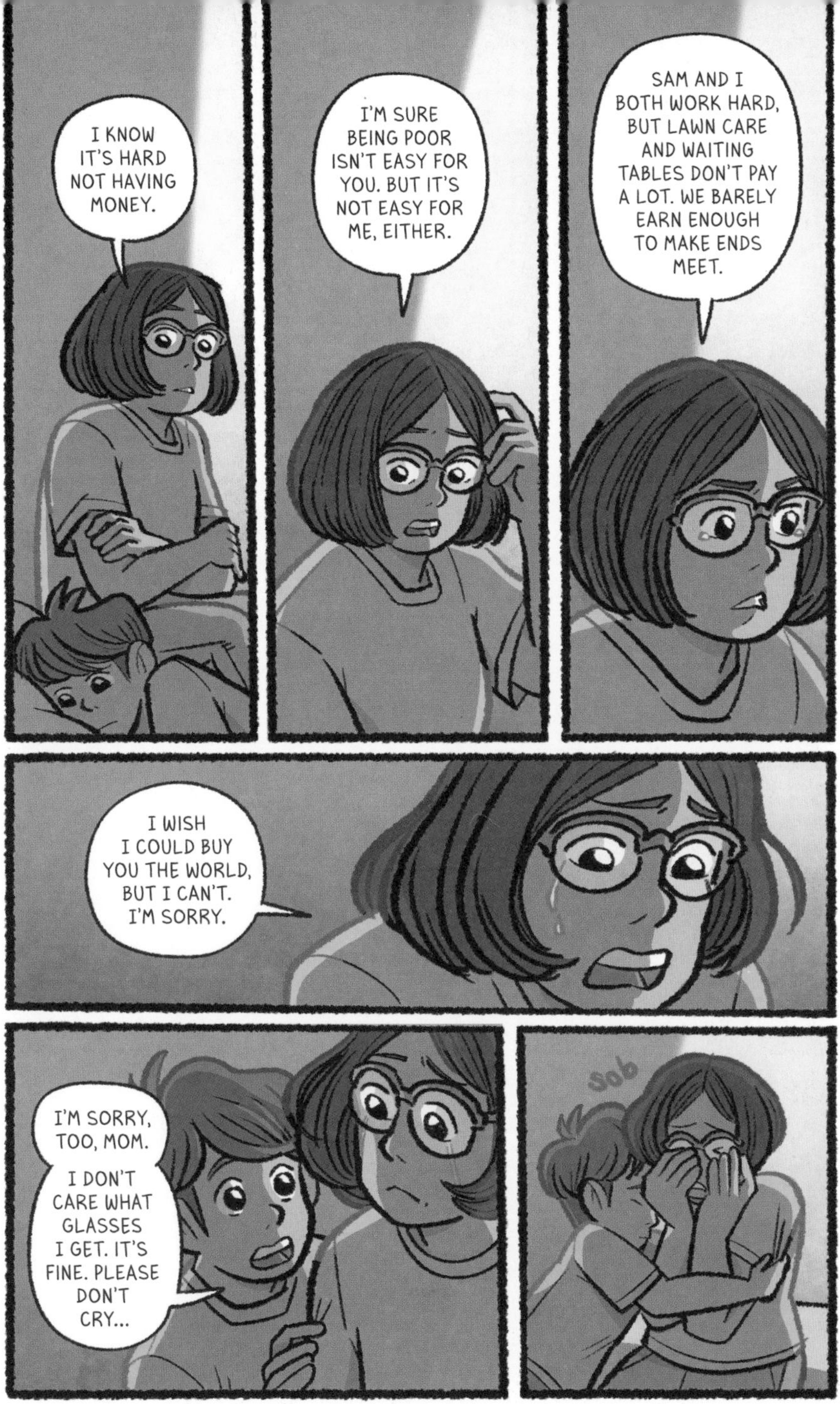
I KNOW IT'S HARD NOT HAVING MONEY.
I'M SURE BEING POOR ISN'T EASY FOR YOU. BUT IT'S NOT EASY FOR ME, EITHER.
SAM AND I BOTH WORK HARD, BUT LAWN CARE AND WAITING TABLES DON'T PAY A LOT. WE BARELY EARN ENOUGH TO MAKE ENDS MEET.
I WISH I COULD BUY YOU THE WORLD, BUT I CAN'T. I'M SORRY.
I'M SORRY, TOO, MOM.
I DON'T CARE WHAT GLASSES I GET. IT'S FINE. PLEASE DON'T CRY...
SOB

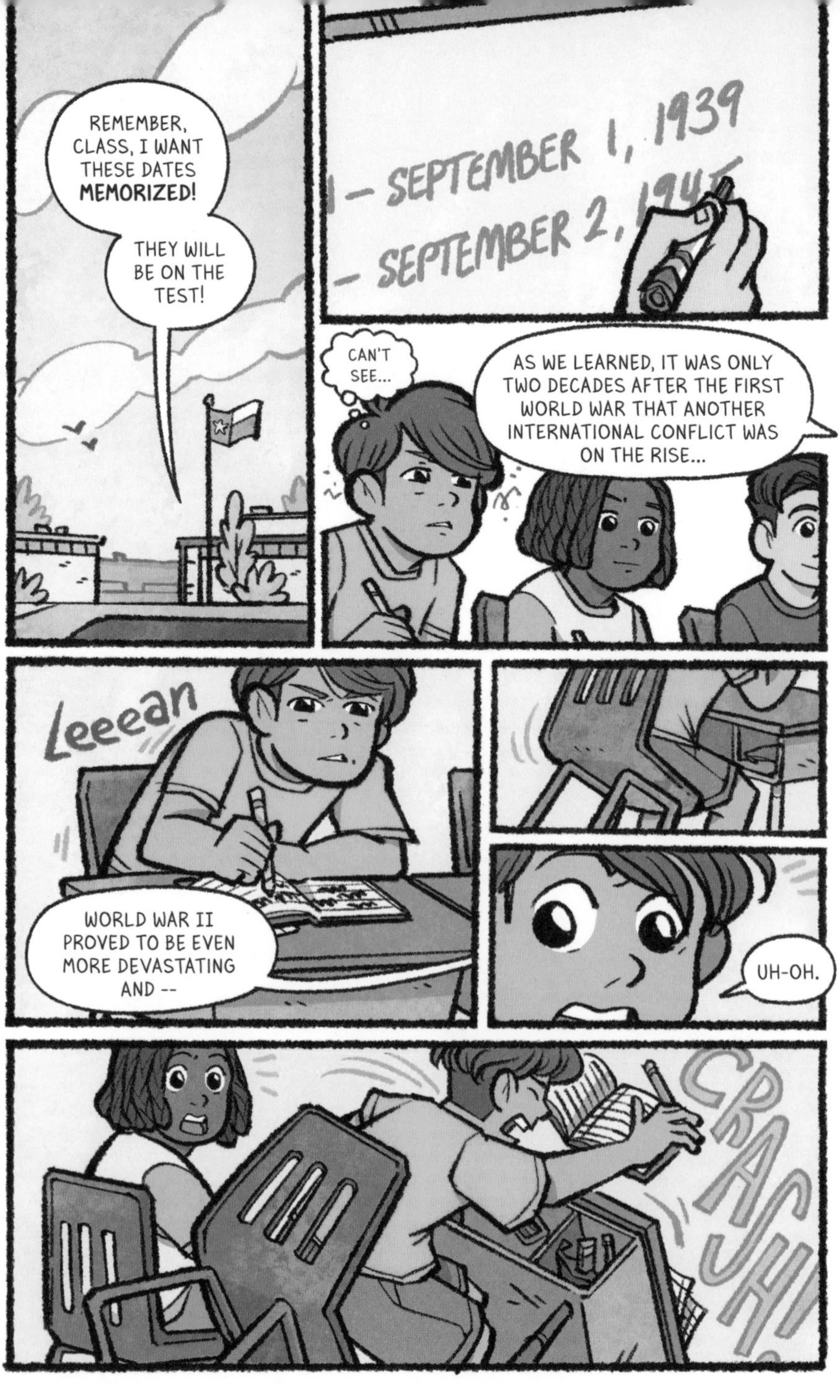
REMEMBER, CLASS, I WANT THESE DATES **MEMORIZED!**
THEY WILL BE ON THE TEST!
– SEPTEMBER 1, 1939
– SEPTEMBER 2, 1945
CAN'T SEE...
AS WE LEARNED, IT WAS ONLY TWO DECADES AFTER THE FIRST WORLD WAR THAT ANOTHER INTERNATIONAL CONFLICT WAS ON THE RISE...
Leeean
WORLD WAR II PROVED TO BE EVEN MORE DEVASTATING AND --
UH-OH.
CRASH

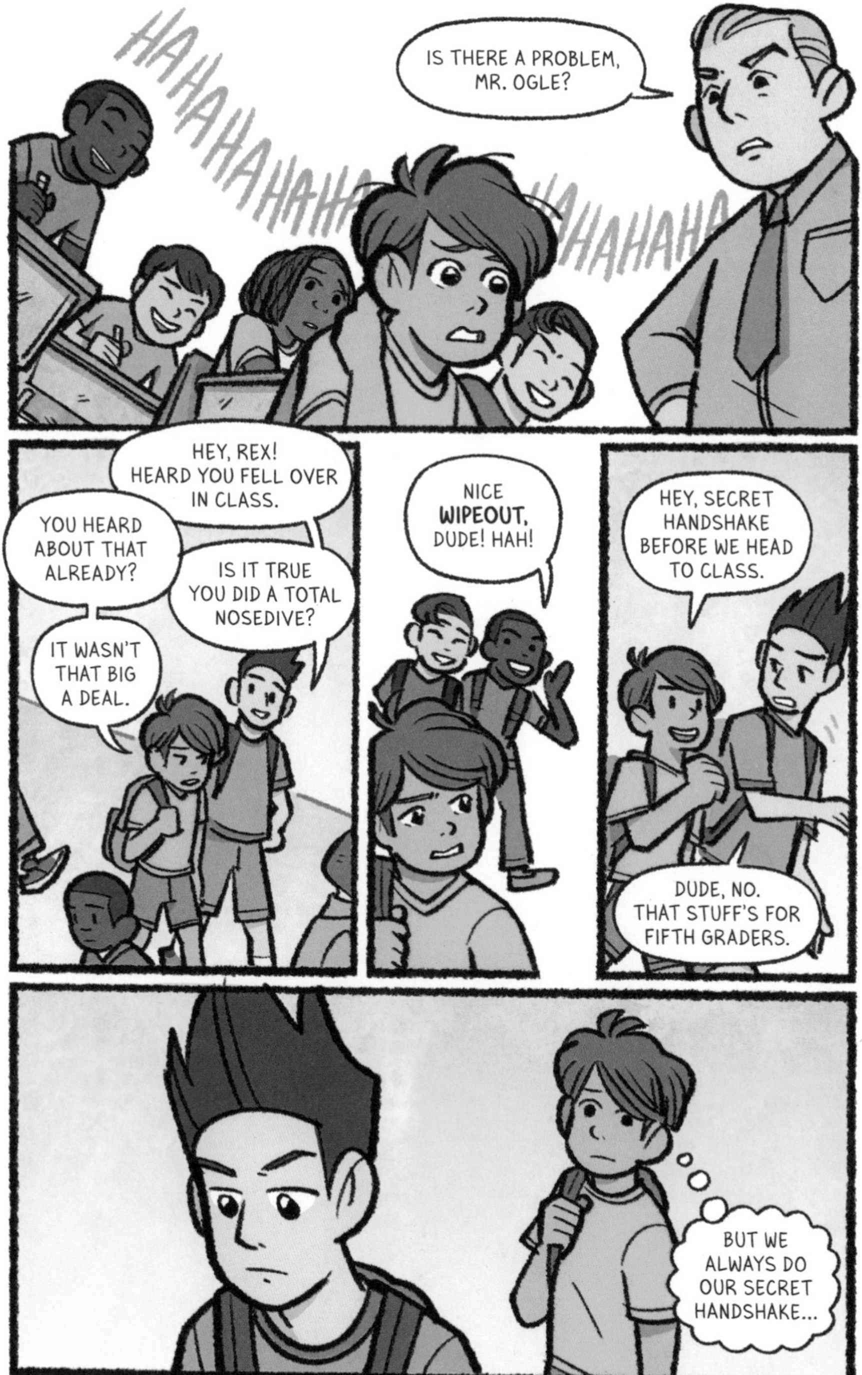
HAHAHAHAHA
HAHAHAHA
IS THERE A PROBLEM, MR. OGLE?
HEY, REX! HEARD YOU FELL OVER IN CLASS.
YOU HEARD ABOUT THAT ALREADY?
IS IT TRUE YOU DID A TOTAL NOSEDIVE?
IT WASN'T THAT BIG A DEAL.
NICE **WIPEOUT,** DUDE! HAH!
HEY, SECRET HANDSHAKE BEFORE WE HEAD TO CLASS.
DUDE, NO. THAT STUFF'S FOR FIFTH GRADERS.
BUT WE ALWAYS DO OUR SECRET HANDSHAKE...

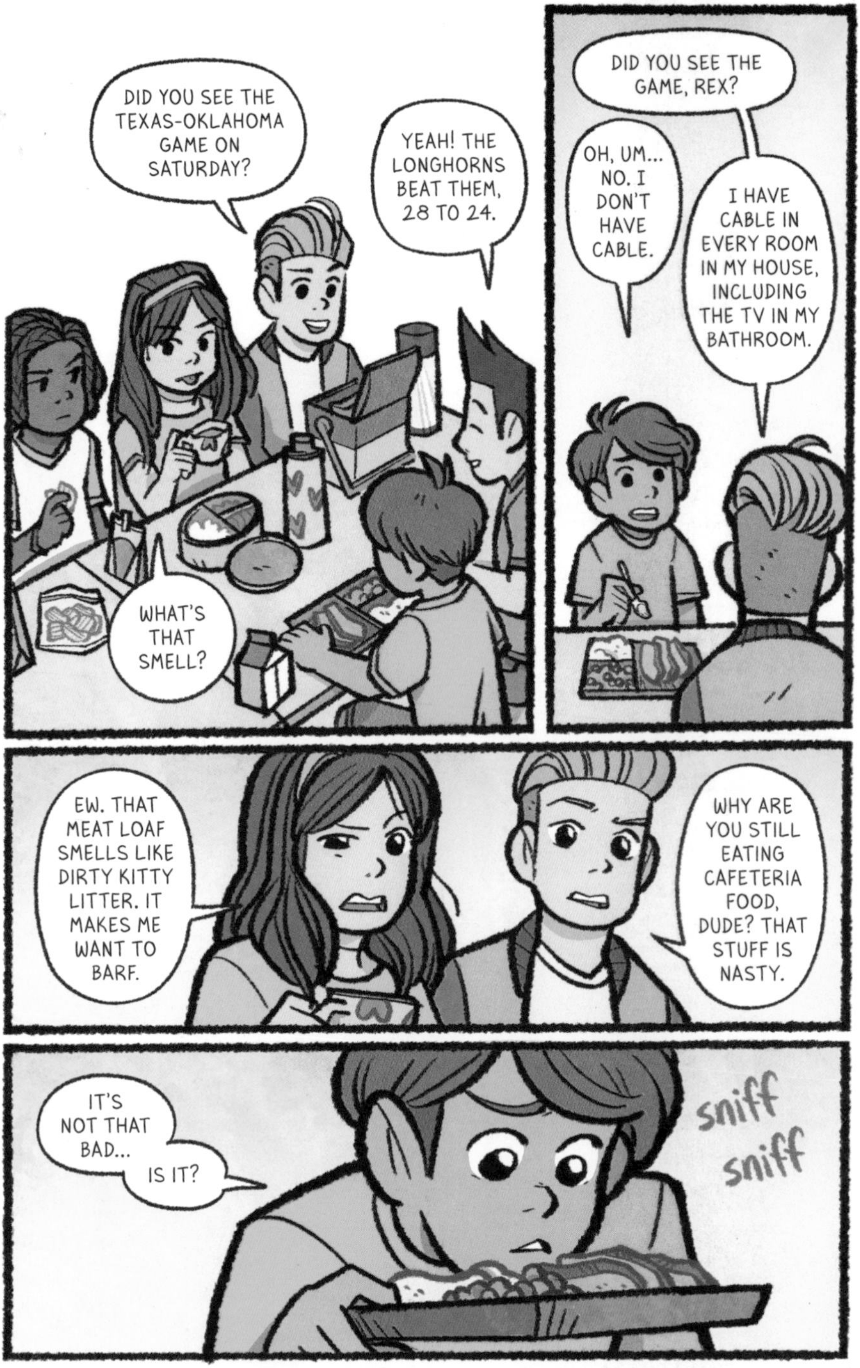
DID YOU SEE THE TEXAS-OKLAHOMA GAME ON SATURDAY?
YEAH! THE LONGHORNS BEAT THEM, 28 TO 24.
WHAT'S THAT SMELL?
DID YOU SEE THE GAME, REX?
OH, UM... NO. I DON'T HAVE CABLE.
I HAVE CABLE IN EVERY ROOM IN MY HOUSE, INCLUDING THE TV IN MY BATHROOM.
EW. THAT MEAT LOAF SMELLS LIKE DIRTY KITTY LITTER. IT MAKES ME WANT TO BARF.
WHY ARE YOU STILL EATING CAFETERIA FOOD, DUDE? THAT STUFF IS NASTY.
IT'S NOT THAT BAD...
IS IT?
sniff
sniff

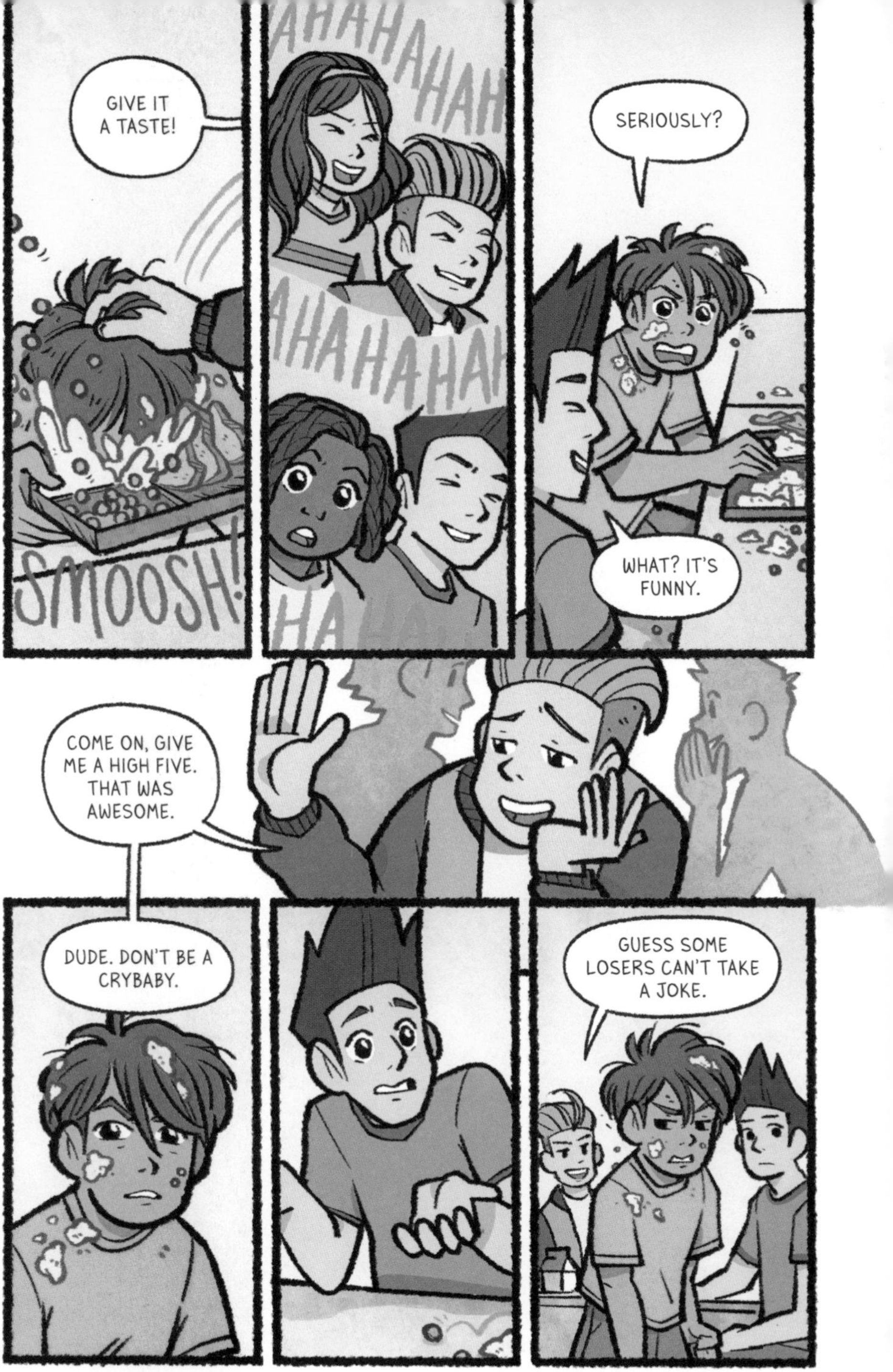
GIVE IT A TASTE!
SMOOSH!
HAHAHAHAH
HAHAHAHAH
SERIOUSLY?
WHAT? IT'S FUNNY.
COME ON, GIVE ME A HIGH FIVE. THAT WAS AWESOME.
DUDE. DON'T BE A CRYBABY.
GUESS SOME LOSERS CAN'T TAKE A JOKE.

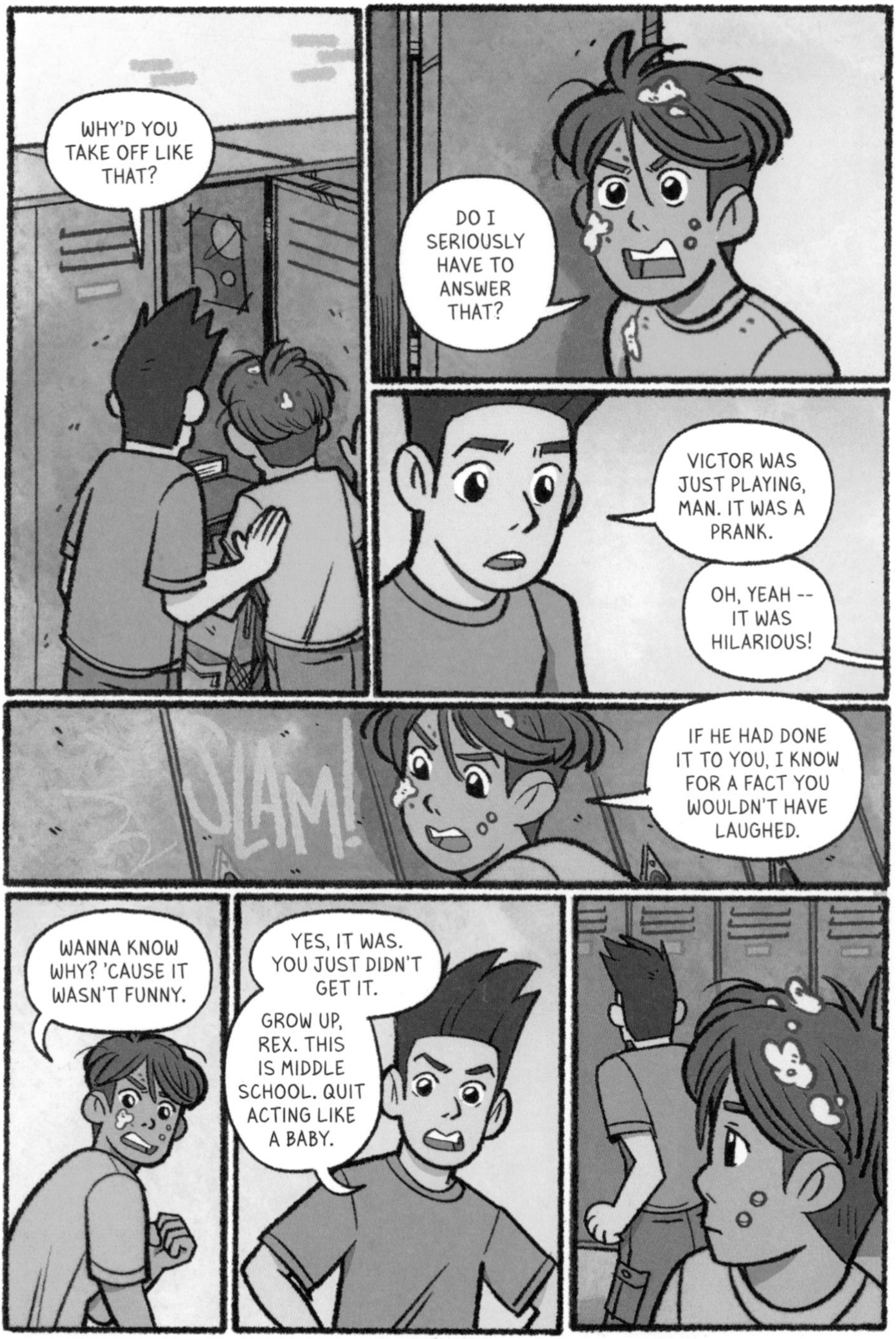
WHY'D YOU TAKE OFF LIKE THAT?
DO I SERIOUSLY HAVE TO ANSWER THAT?
VICTOR WAS JUST PLAYING, MAN. IT WAS A PRANK.
OH, YEAH -- IT WAS HILARIOUS!
SLAM!
IF HE HAD DONE IT TO YOU, I KNOW FOR A FACT YOU WOULDN'T HAVE LAUGHED.
WANNA KNOW WHY? 'CAUSE IT WASN'T FUNNY.
YES, IT WAS. YOU JUST DIDN'T GET IT.
GROW UP, REX. THIS IS MIDDLE SCHOOL. QUIT ACTING LIKE A BABY.

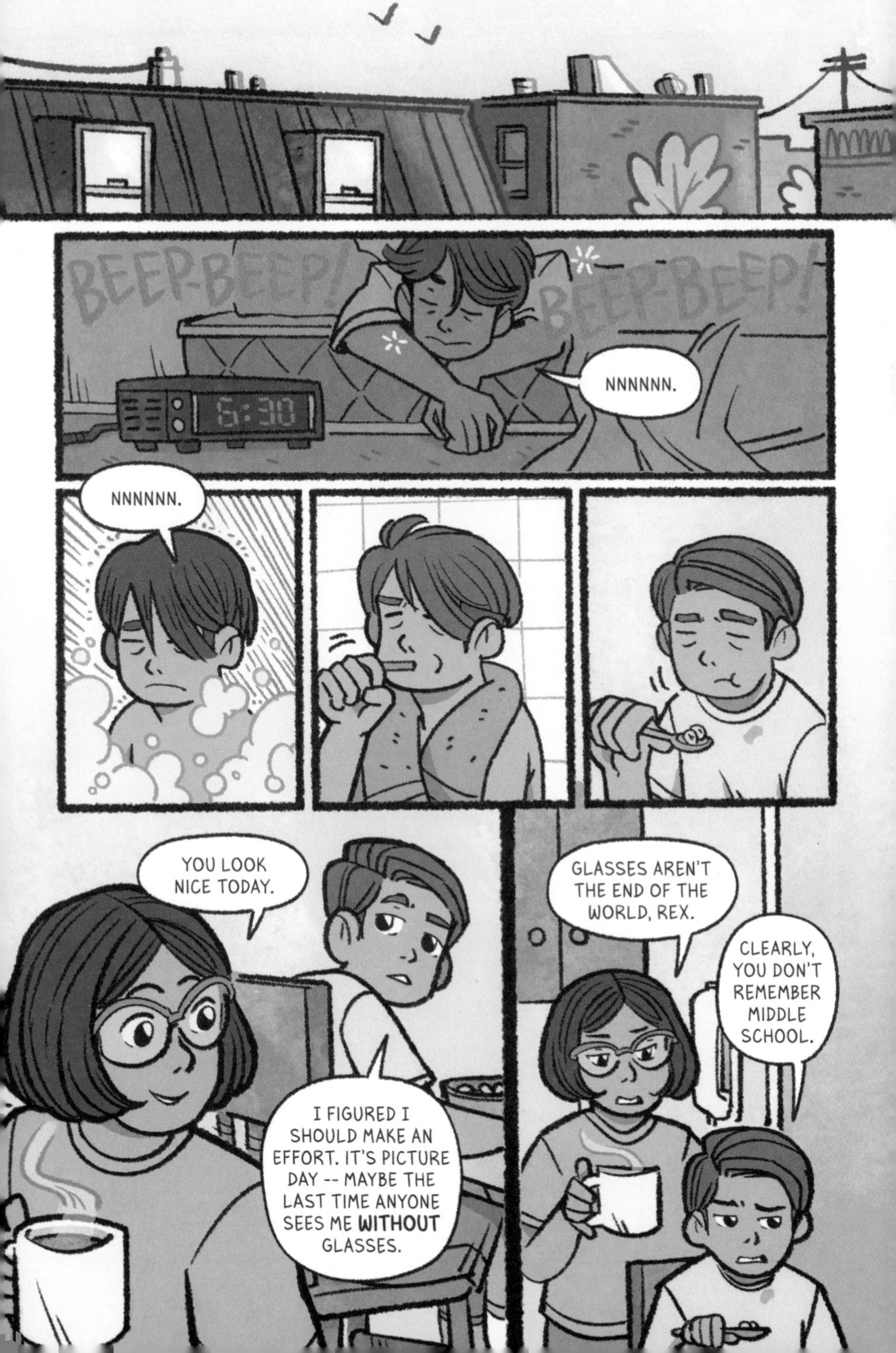
BEEP-BEEP!
BEEP-BEEP!
6:30
NNNNNN.
NNNNNN.
YOU LOOK NICE TODAY.
I FIGURED I SHOULD MAKE AN EFFORT. IT'S PICTURE DAY -- MAYBE THE LAST TIME ANYONE SEES ME **WITHOUT** GLASSES.
GLASSES AREN'T THE END OF THE WORLD, REX.
CLEARLY, YOU DON'T REMEMBER MIDDLE SCHOOL.

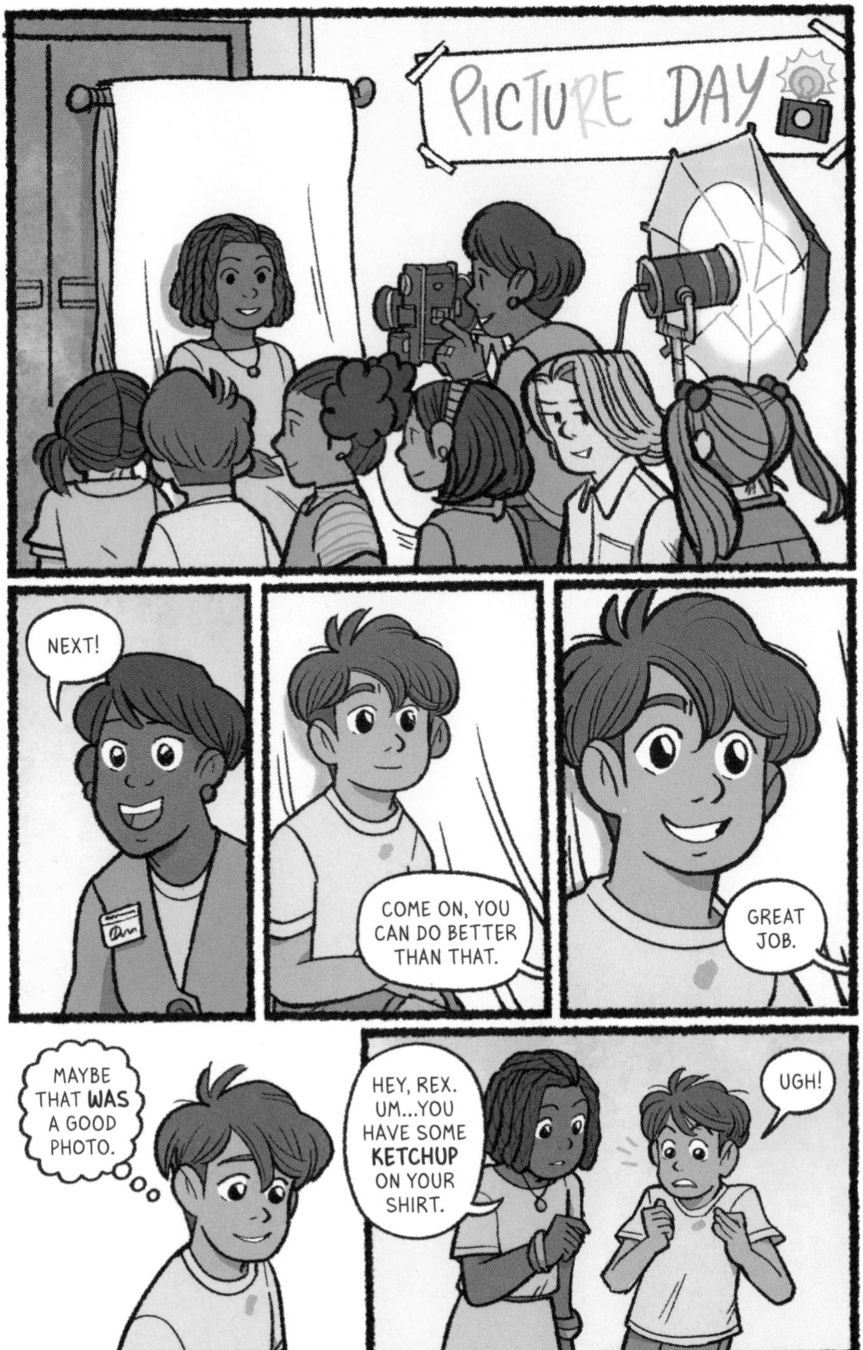
PICTURE DAY
NEXT!
COME ON, YOU CAN DO BETTER THAN THAT.
GREAT JOB.
MAYBE THAT **WAS** A GOOD PHOTO.
HEY, REX. UM...YOU HAVE SOME **KETCHUP** ON YOUR SHIRT.
UGH!

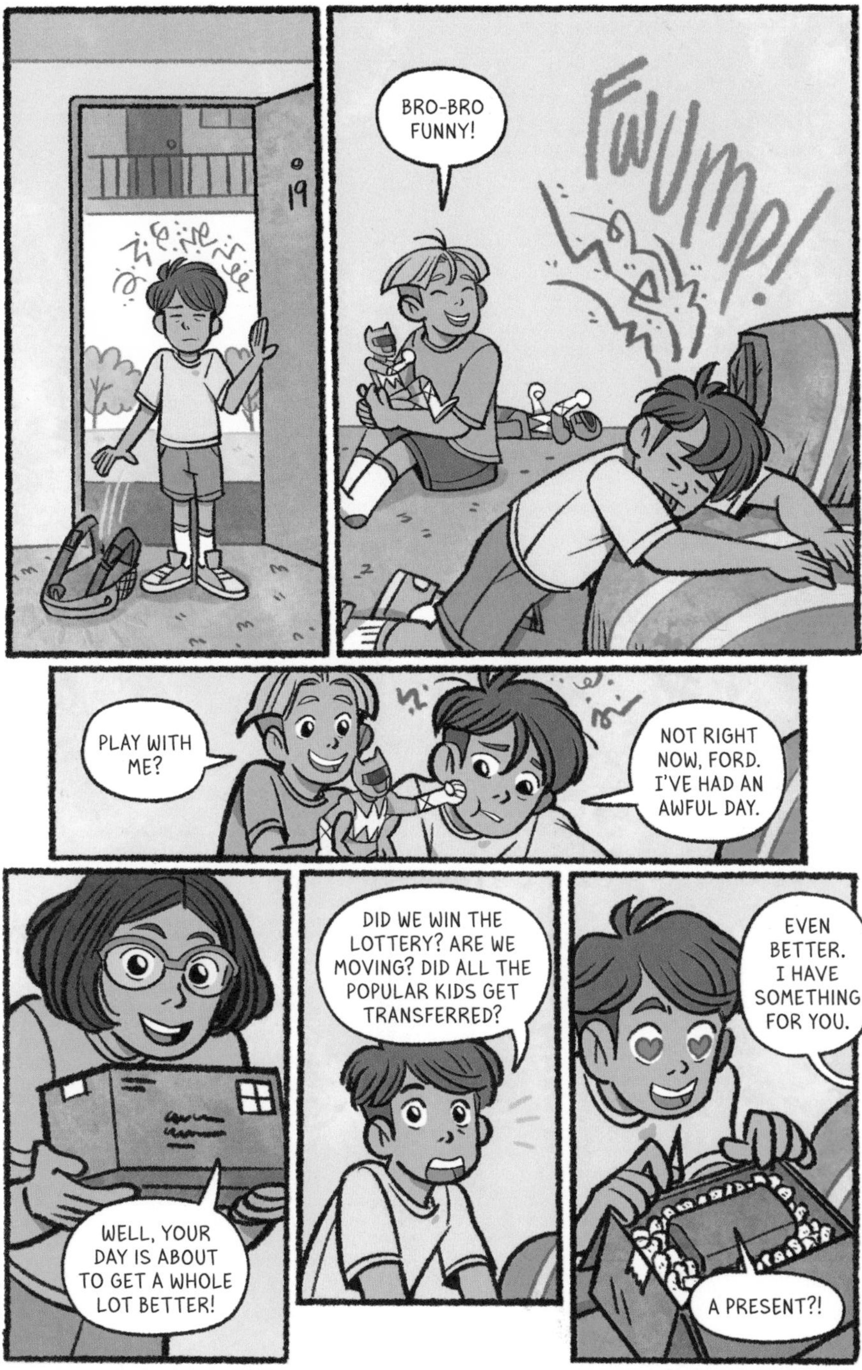
BRO-BRO FUNNY!
FWUMP!
PLAY WITH ME?
NOT RIGHT NOW, FORD. I'VE HAD AN AWFUL DAY.
WELL, YOUR DAY IS ABOUT TO GET A WHOLE LOT BETTER!
DID WE WIN THE LOTTERY? ARE WE MOVING? DID ALL THE POPULAR KIDS GET TRANSFERRED?
EVEN BETTER. I HAVE SOMETHING FOR YOU.
A PRESENT?!

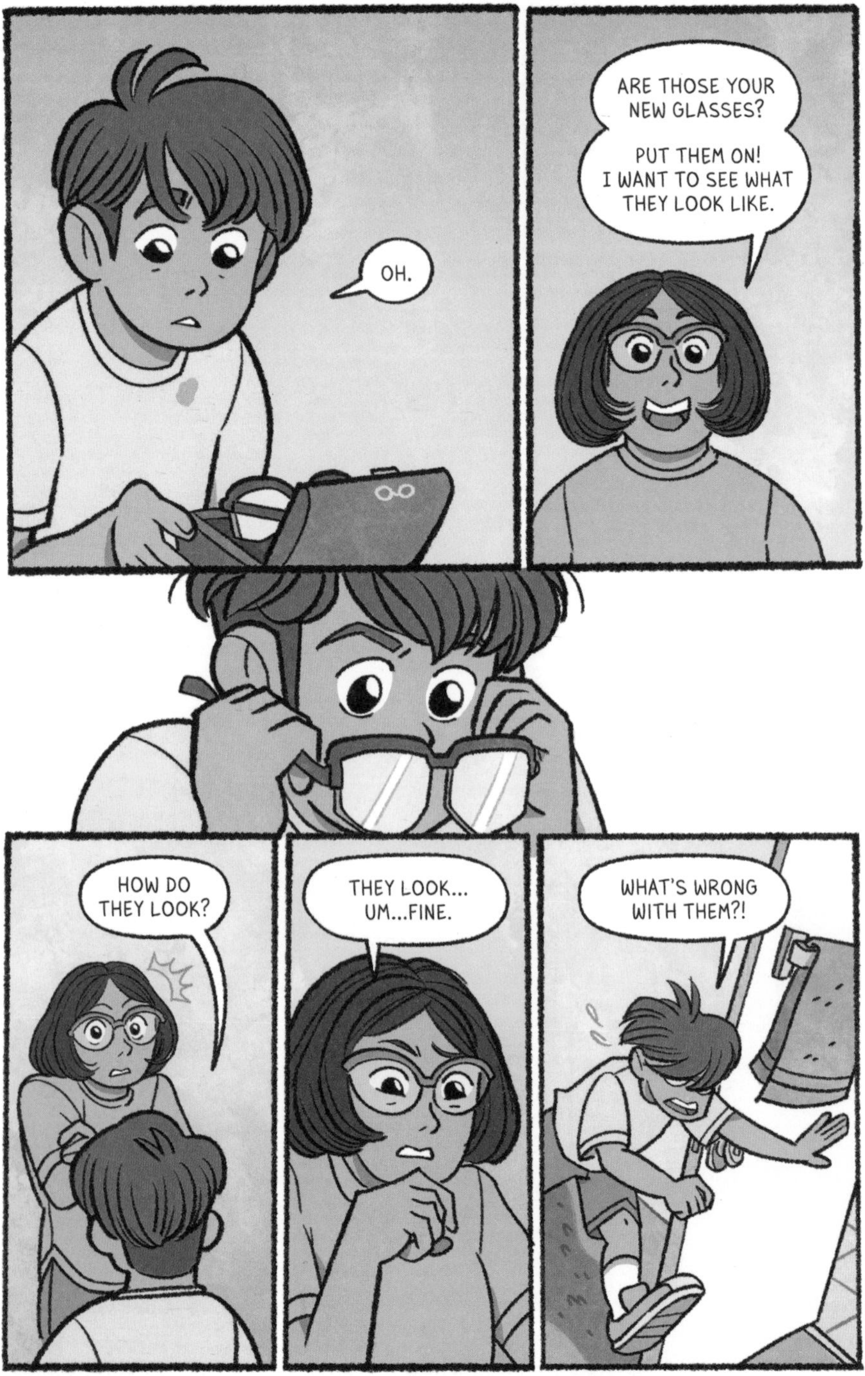
OH.
ARE THOSE YOUR NEW GLASSES?
PUT THEM ON! I WANT TO SEE WHAT THEY LOOK LIKE.
HOW DO THEY LOOK?
THEY LOOK... UM...FINE.
WHAT'S WRONG WITH THEM?!

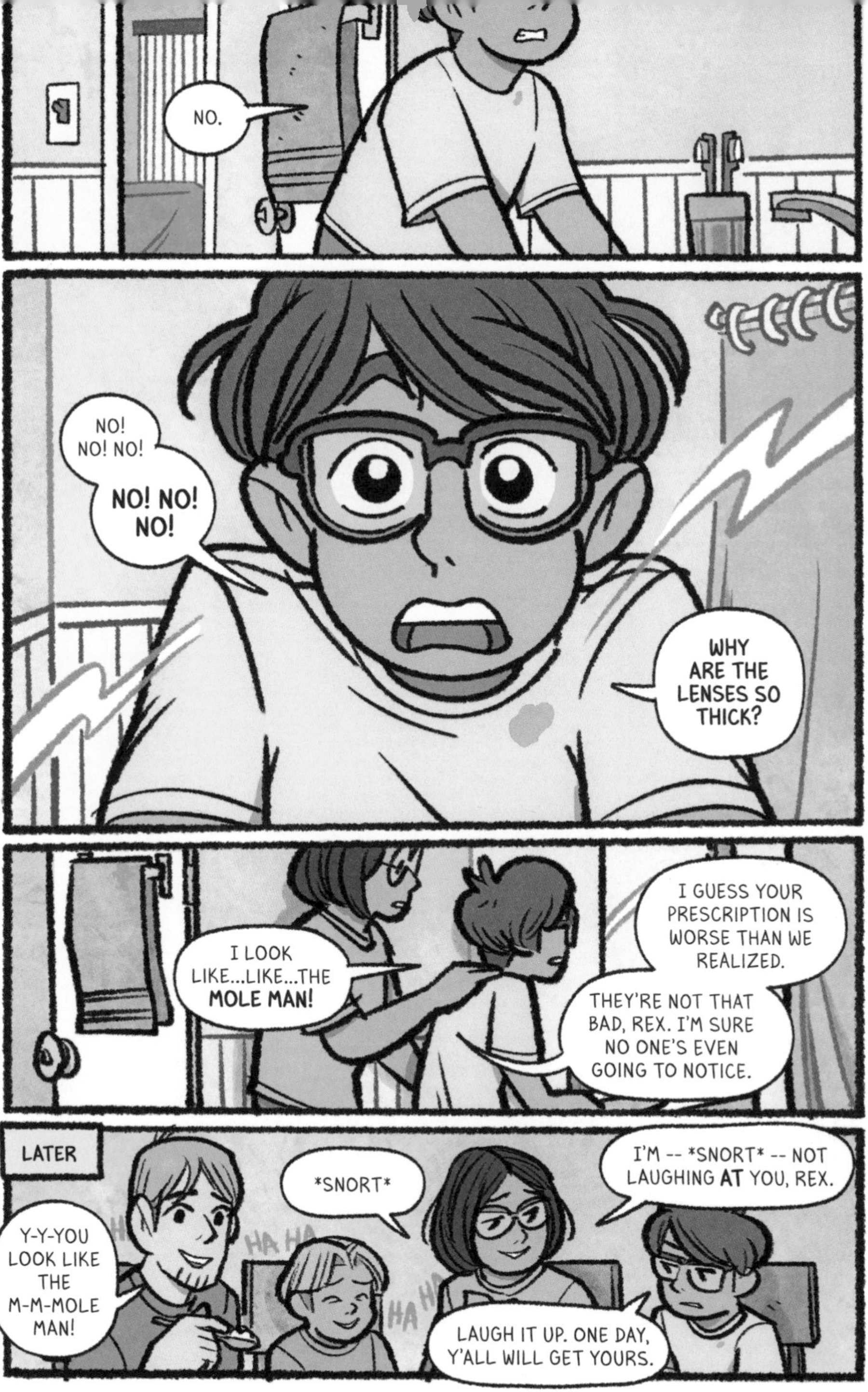
NO.
NO! NO! NO!
NO! NO! NO!
WHY ARE THE LENSES SO THICK?
I LOOK LIKE...LIKE...THE MOLE MAN!
I GUESS YOUR PRESCRIPTION IS WORSE THAN WE REALIZED.
THEY'RE NOT THAT BAD, REX. I'M SURE NO ONE'S EVEN GOING TO NOTICE.
LATER
Y-Y-YOU LOOK LIKE THE M-M-MOLE MAN!
HA HA
SNORT
I'M -- *SNORT* -- NOT LAUGHING AT YOU, REX.
LAUGH IT UP. ONE DAY, Y'ALL WILL GET YOURS.

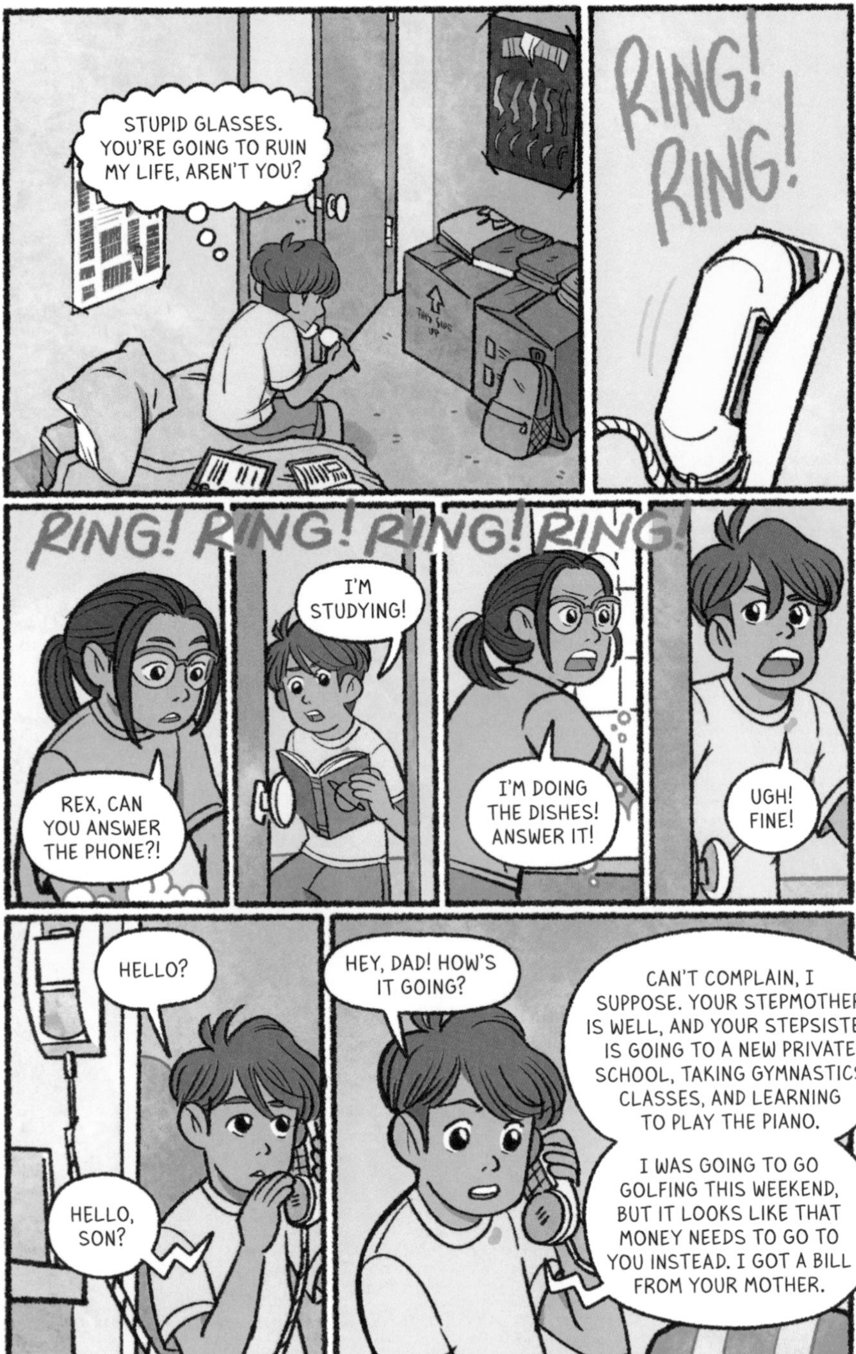
STUPID GLASSES. YOU'RE GOING TO RUIN MY LIFE, AREN'T YOU?
RING! RING!
RING! RING! RING! RING!
REX, CAN YOU ANSWER THE PHONE?!
I'M STUDYING!
I'M DOING THE DISHES! ANSWER IT!
UGH! FINE!
HELLO?
HELLO, SON?
HEY, DAD! HOW'S IT GOING?
CAN'T COMPLAIN, I SUPPOSE. YOUR STEPMOTHER IS WELL, AND YOUR STEPSISTER IS GOING TO A NEW PRIVATE SCHOOL, TAKING GYMNASTICS CLASSES, AND LEARNING TO PLAY THE PIANO.
I WAS GOING TO GO GOLFING THIS WEEKEND, BUT IT LOOKS LIKE THAT MONEY NEEDS TO GO TO YOU INSTEAD. I GOT A BILL FROM YOUR MOTHER.

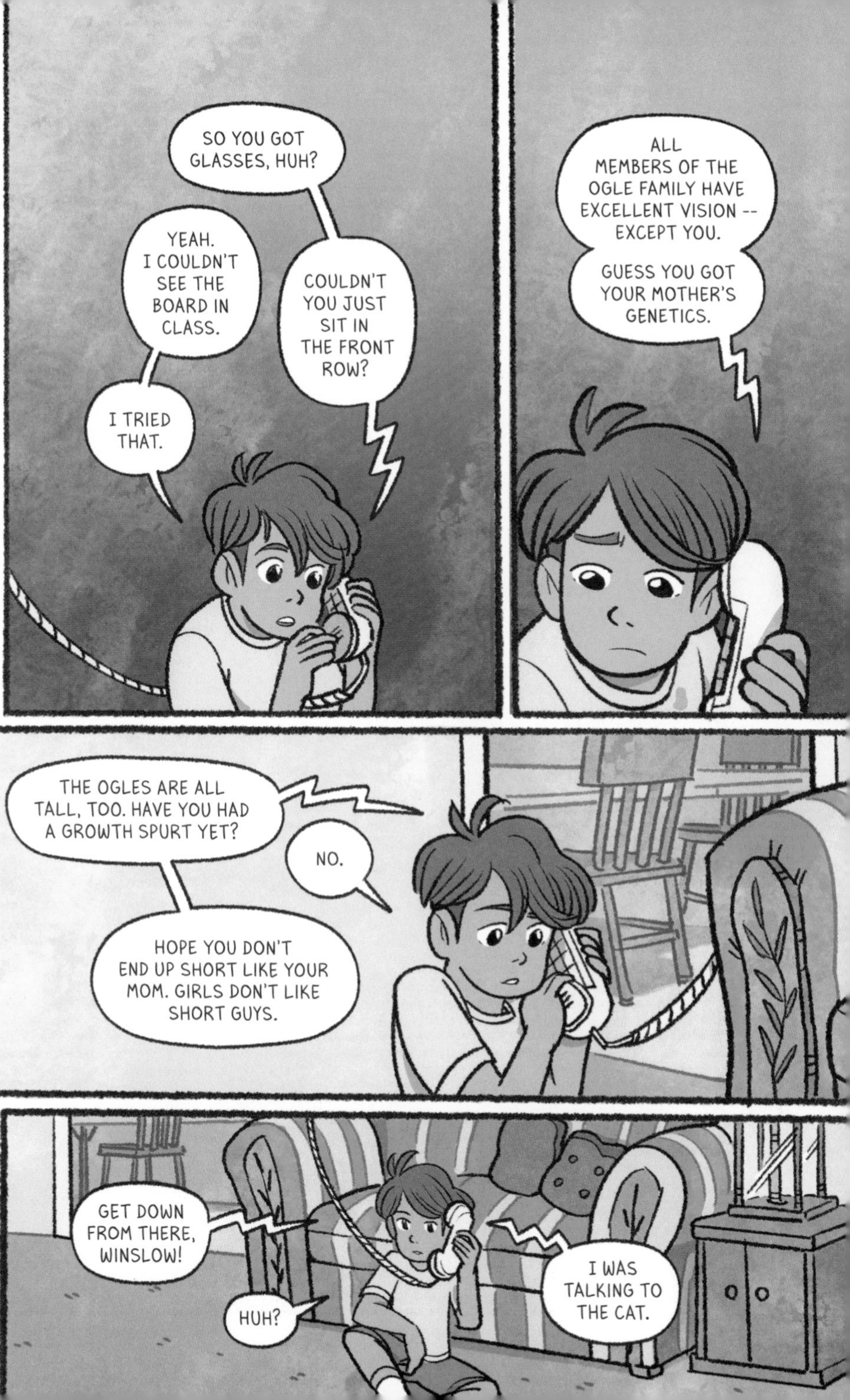
SO YOU GOT GLASSES, HUH?
YEAH. I COULDN'T SEE THE BOARD IN CLASS.
COULDN'T YOU JUST SIT IN THE FRONT ROW?
I TRIED THAT.
ALL MEMBERS OF THE OGLE FAMILY HAVE EXCELLENT VISION -- EXCEPT YOU.
GUESS YOU GOT YOUR MOTHER'S GENETICS.
THE OGLES ARE ALL TALL, TOO. HAVE YOU HAD A GROWTH SPURT YET?
NO.
HOPE YOU DON'T END UP SHORT LIKE YOUR MOM. GIRLS DON'T LIKE SHORT GUYS.
GET DOWN FROM THERE, WINSLOW!
HUH?
I WAS TALKING TO THE CAT.

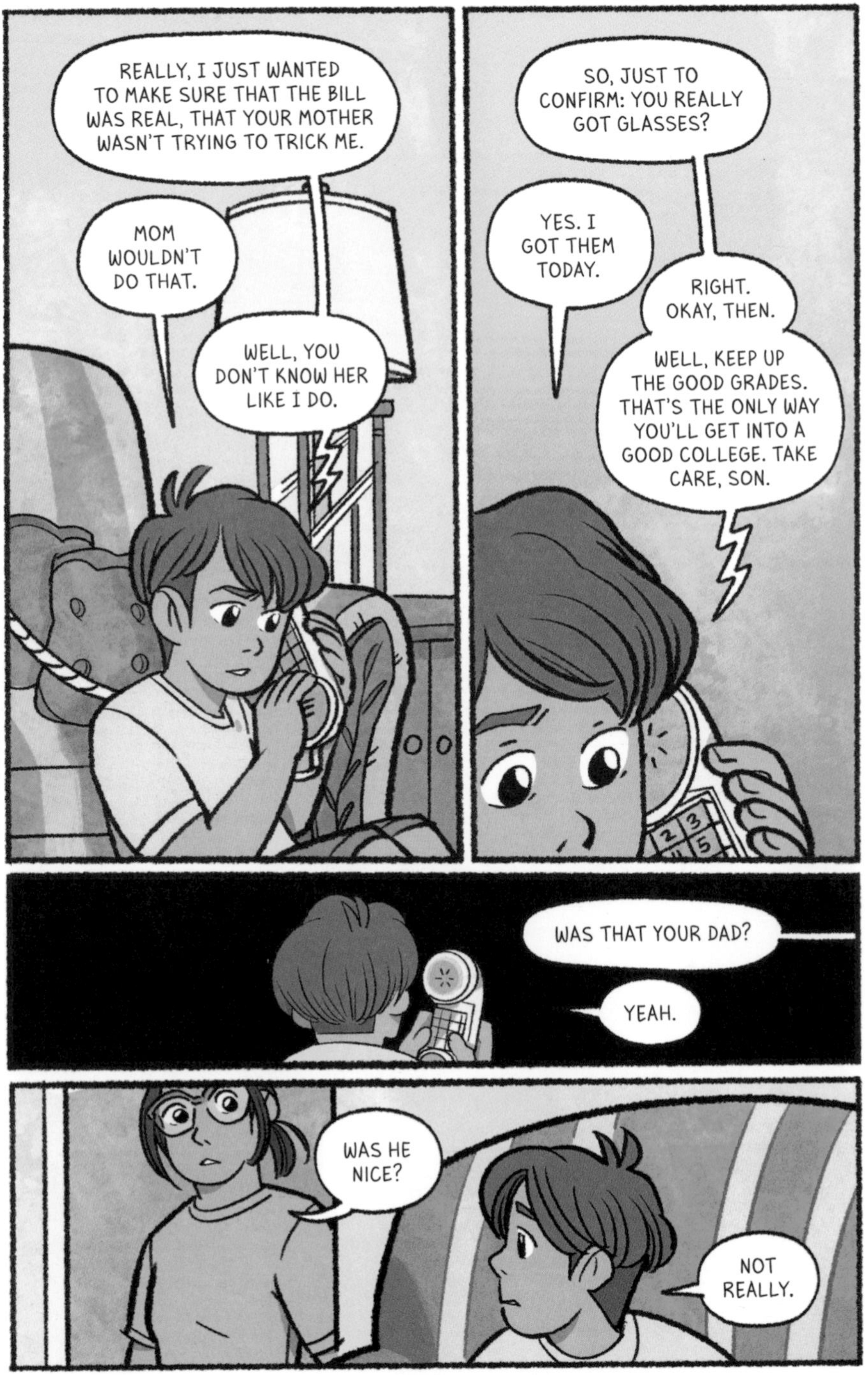
REALLY, I JUST WANTED TO MAKE SURE THAT THE BILL WAS REAL, THAT YOUR MOTHER WASN'T TRYING TO TRICK ME.
MOM WOULDN'T DO THAT.
WELL, YOU DON'T KNOW HER LIKE I DO.
SO, JUST TO CONFIRM: YOU REALLY GOT GLASSES?
YES. I GOT THEM TODAY.
RIGHT. OKAY, THEN.
WELL, KEEP UP THE GOOD GRADES. THAT'S THE ONLY WAY YOU'LL GET INTO A GOOD COLLEGE. TAKE CARE, SON.
WAS THAT YOUR DAD?
YEAH.
WAS HE NICE?
NOT REALLY.

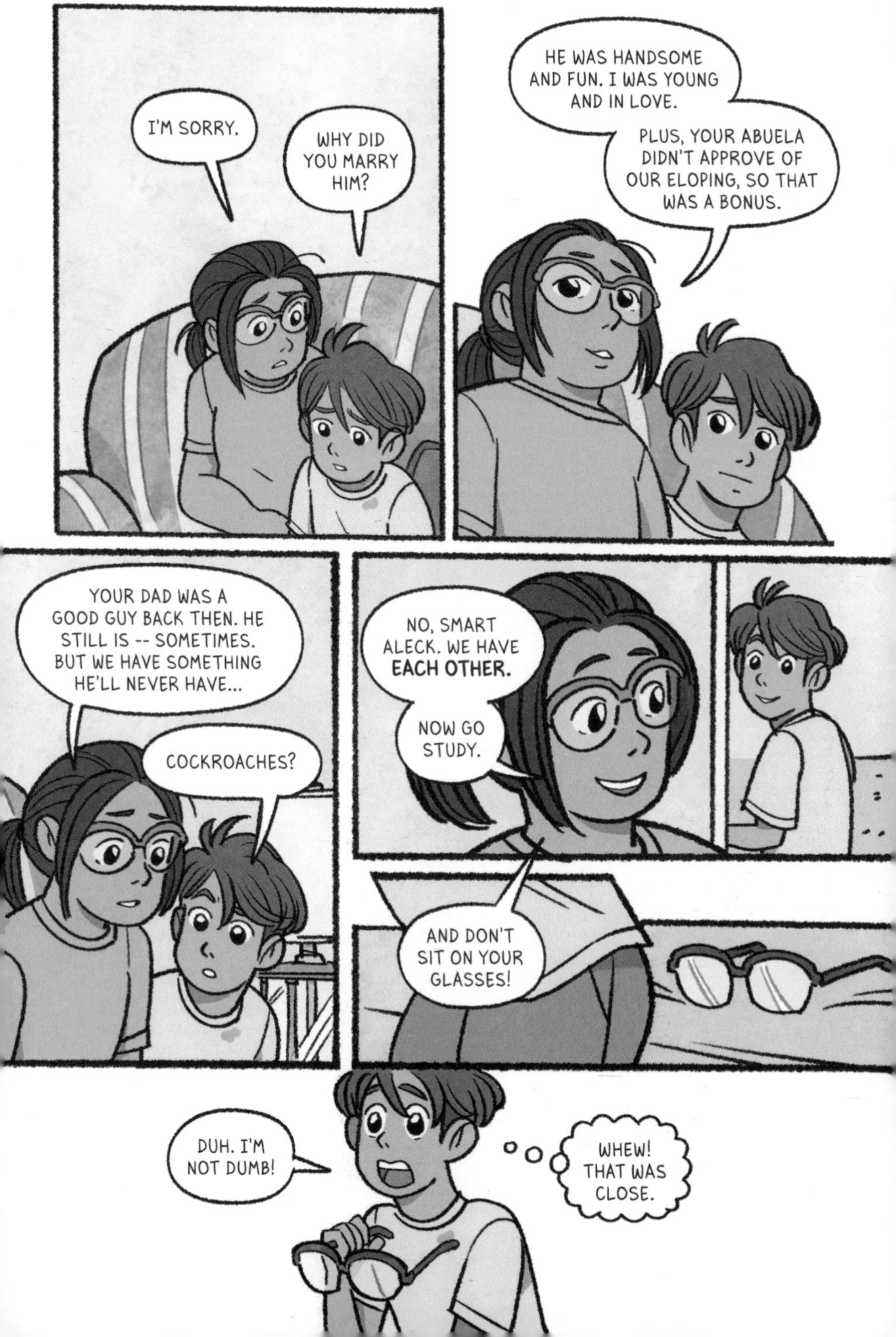
I'M SORRY.
WHY DID YOU MARRY HIM?
HE WAS HANDSOME AND FUN. I WAS YOUNG AND IN LOVE.
PLUS, YOUR ABUELA DIDN'T APPROVE OF OUR ELOPING, SO THAT WAS A BONUS.
YOUR DAD WAS A GOOD GUY BACK THEN. HE STILL IS -- SOMETIMES. BUT WE HAVE SOMETHING HE'LL NEVER HAVE...
COCKROACHES?
NO, SMART ALECK. WE HAVE **EACH OTHER.**
NOW GO STUDY.
AND DON'T SIT ON YOUR GLASSES!
DUH. I'M NOT DUMB!
WHEW! THAT WAS CLOSE.

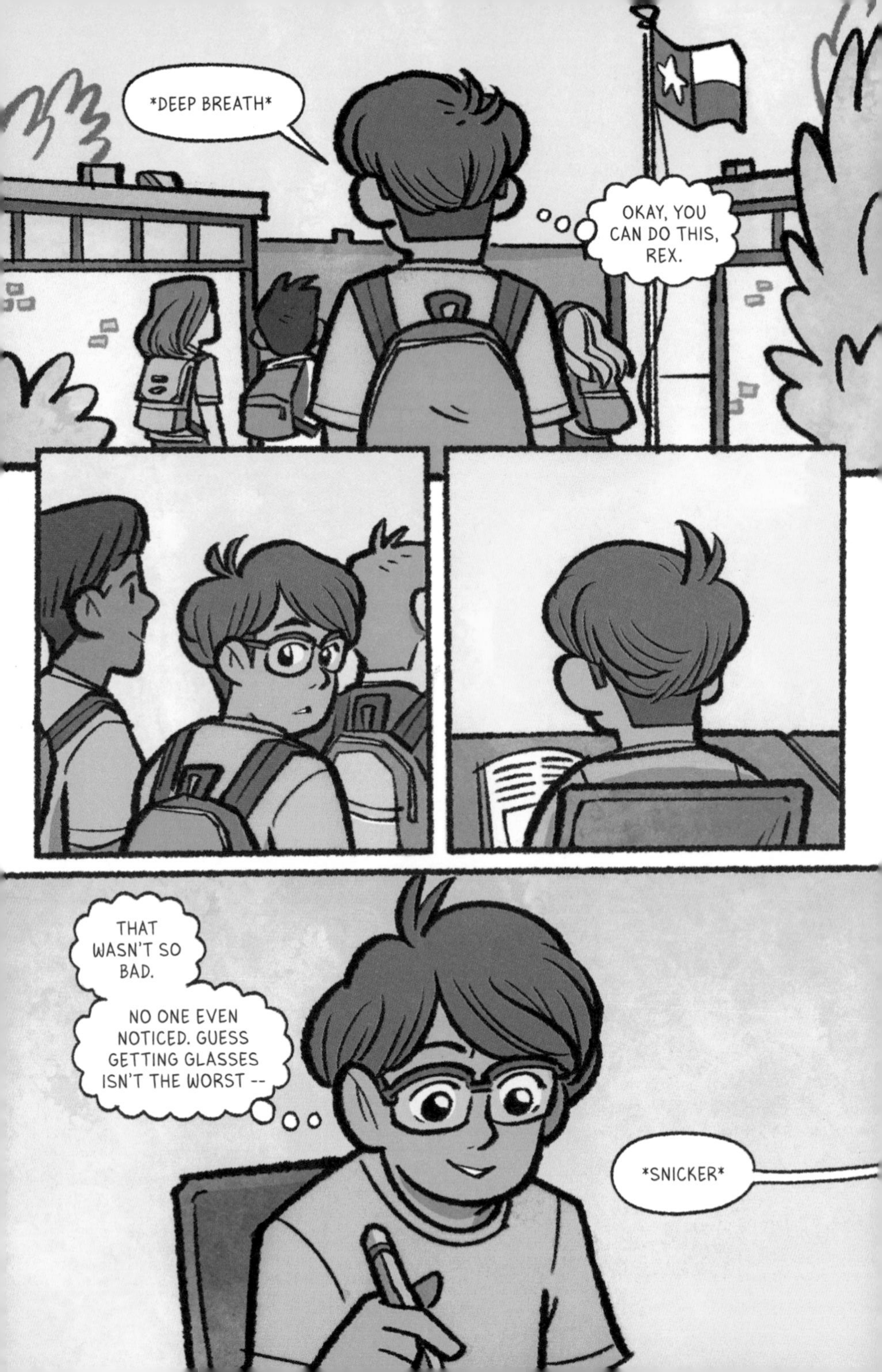
DEEP BREATH
OKAY, YOU CAN DO THIS, REX.
THAT WASN'T SO BAD.
NO ONE EVEN NOTICED. GUESS GETTING GLASSES ISN'T THE WORST --
SNICKER

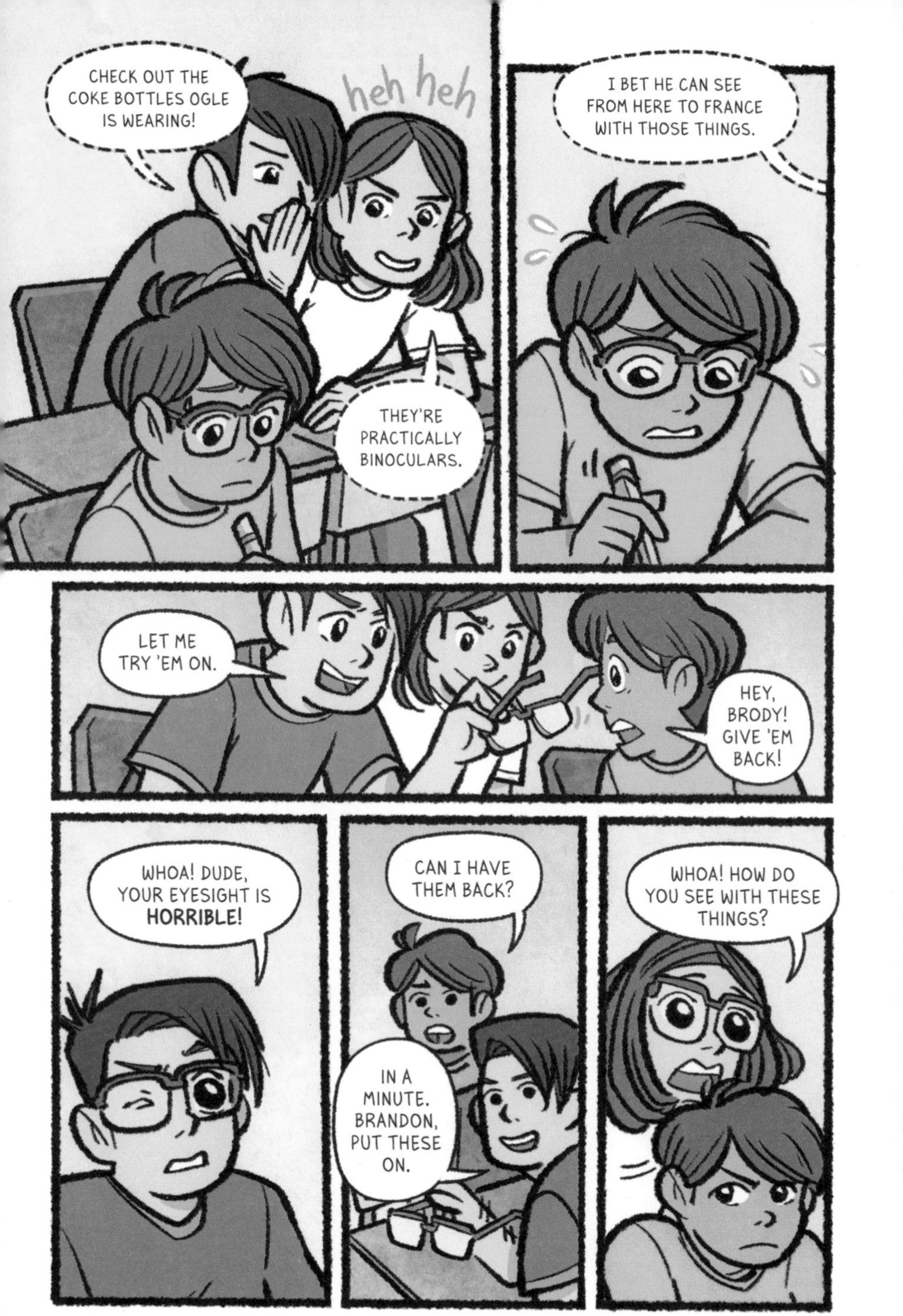
CHECK OUT THE COKE BOTTLES OGLE IS WEARING!
heh heh
THEY'RE PRACTICALLY BINOCULARS.
I BET HE CAN SEE FROM HERE TO FRANCE WITH THOSE THINGS.
LET ME TRY 'EM ON.
HEY, BRODY! GIVE 'EM BACK!
WHOA! DUDE, YOUR EYESIGHT IS **HORRIBLE!**
CAN I HAVE THEM BACK?
IN A MINUTE. BRANDON, PUT THESE ON.
WHOA! HOW DO YOU SEE WITH THESE THINGS?

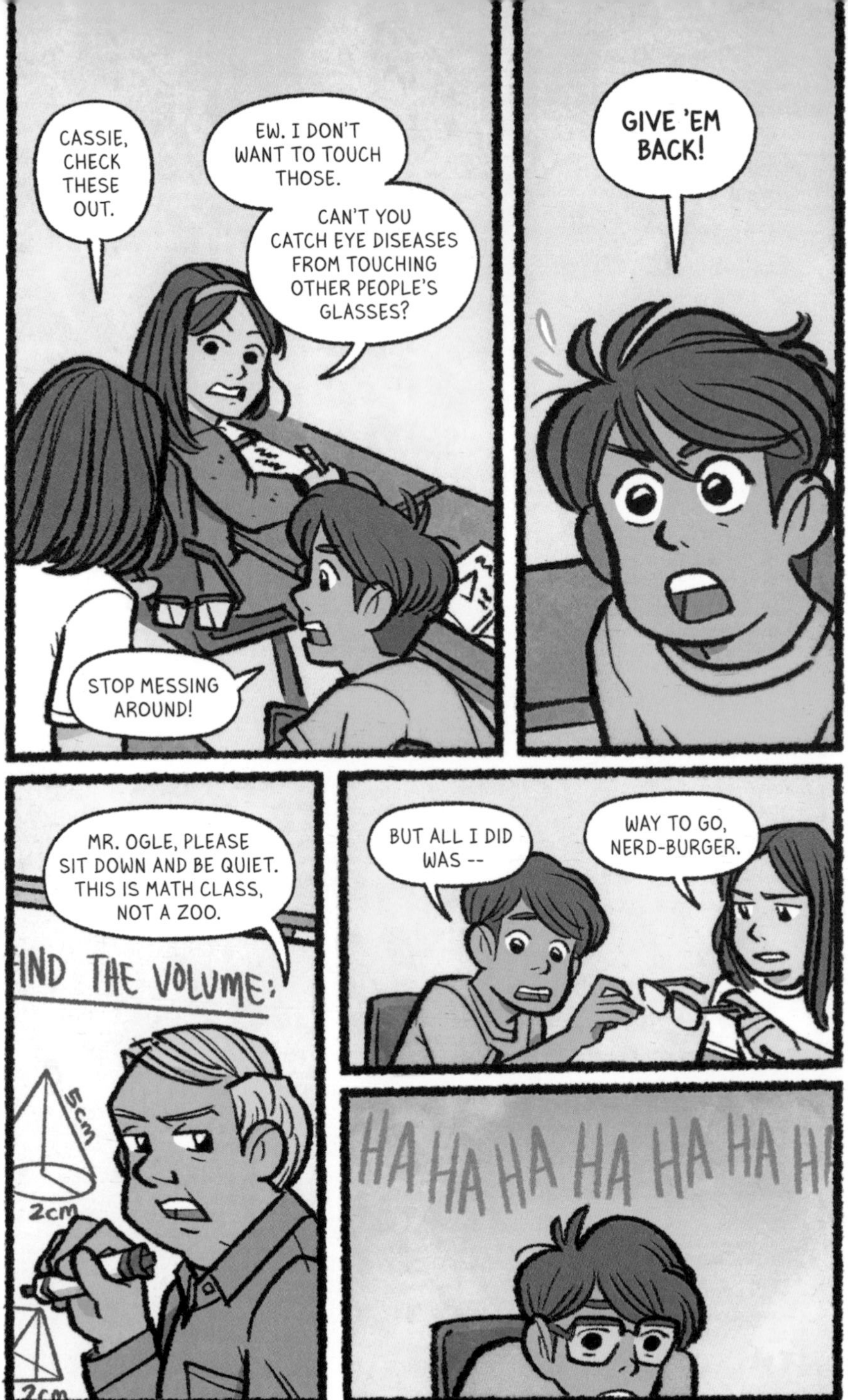
CASSIE, CHECK THESE OUT.
EW. I DON'T WANT TO TOUCH THOSE.
CAN'T YOU CATCH EYE DISEASES FROM TOUCHING OTHER PEOPLE'S GLASSES?
STOP MESSING AROUND!
GIVE 'EM BACK!
MR. OGLE, PLEASE SIT DOWN AND BE QUIET. THIS IS MATH CLASS, NOT A ZOO.
FIND THE VOLUME:
5cm
2cm
2cm
BUT ALL I DID WAS --
WAY TO GO, NERD-BURGER.
HA HA HA HA HA HA H

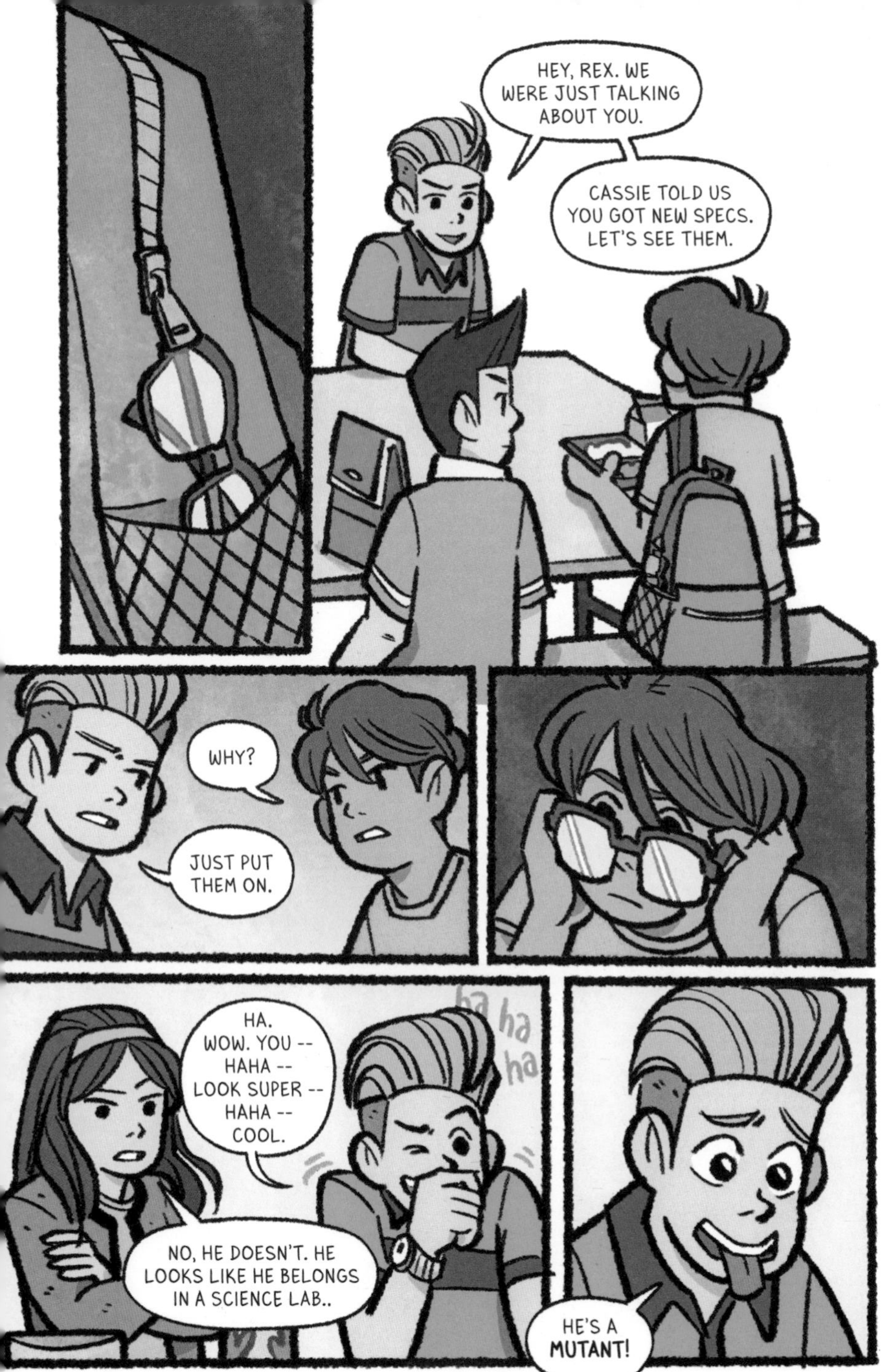
HEY, REX. WE WERE JUST TALKING ABOUT YOU.
CASSIE TOLD US YOU GOT NEW SPECS. LET'S SEE THEM.
WHY?
JUST PUT THEM ON.
HA. WOW. YOU -- HAHA -- LOOK SUPER -- HAHA -- COOL.
ha ha ha
NO, HE DOESN'T. HE LOOKS LIKE HE BELONGS IN A SCIENCE LAB..
HE'S A **MUTANT!**

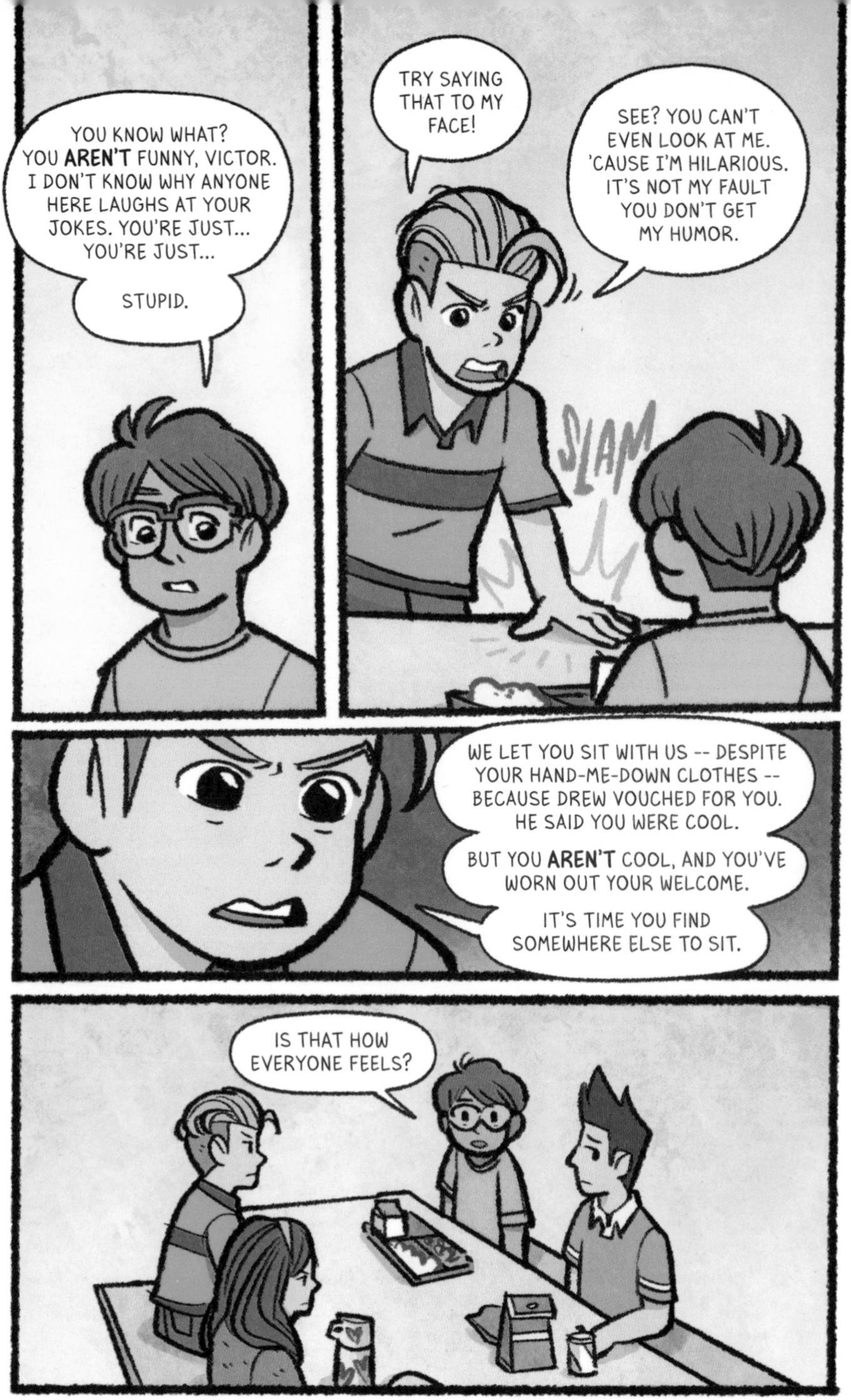
YOU KNOW WHAT? YOU **AREN'T** FUNNY, VICTOR. I DON'T KNOW WHY ANYONE HERE LAUGHS AT YOUR JOKES. YOU'RE JUST... YOU'RE JUST...
STUPID.
TRY SAYING THAT TO MY FACE!
SEE? YOU CAN'T EVEN LOOK AT ME. 'CAUSE I'M HILARIOUS. IT'S NOT MY FAULT YOU DON'T GET MY HUMOR.
SLAM
WE LET YOU SIT WITH US -- DESPITE YOUR HAND-ME-DOWN CLOTHES -- BECAUSE DREW VOUCHED FOR YOU. HE SAID YOU WERE COOL.
BUT YOU **AREN'T** COOL, AND YOU'VE WORN OUT YOUR WELCOME.
IT'S TIME YOU FIND SOMEWHERE ELSE TO SIT.
IS THAT HOW EVERYONE FEELS?

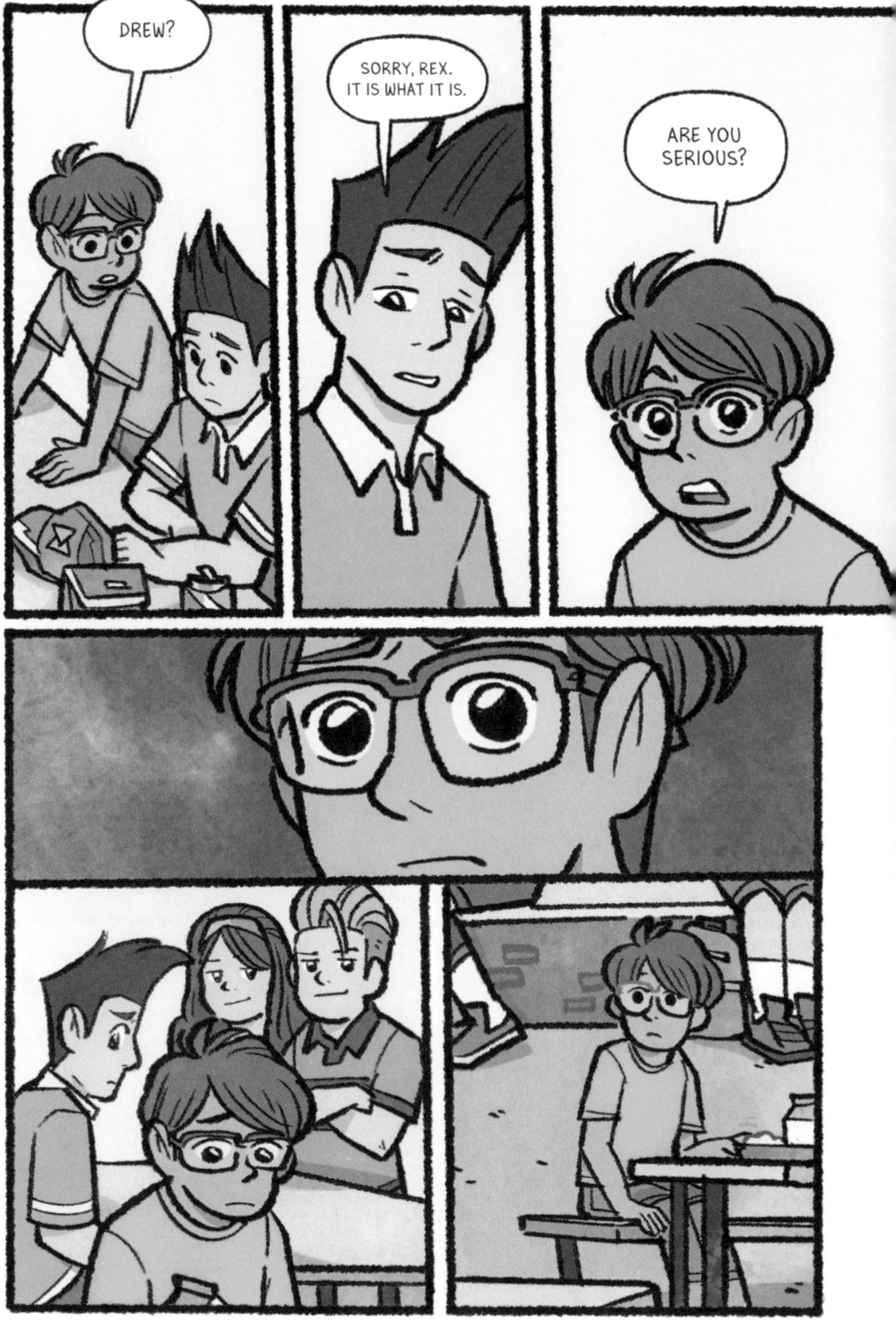
DREW?
SORRY, REX. IT IS WHAT IT IS.
ARE YOU SERIOUS?

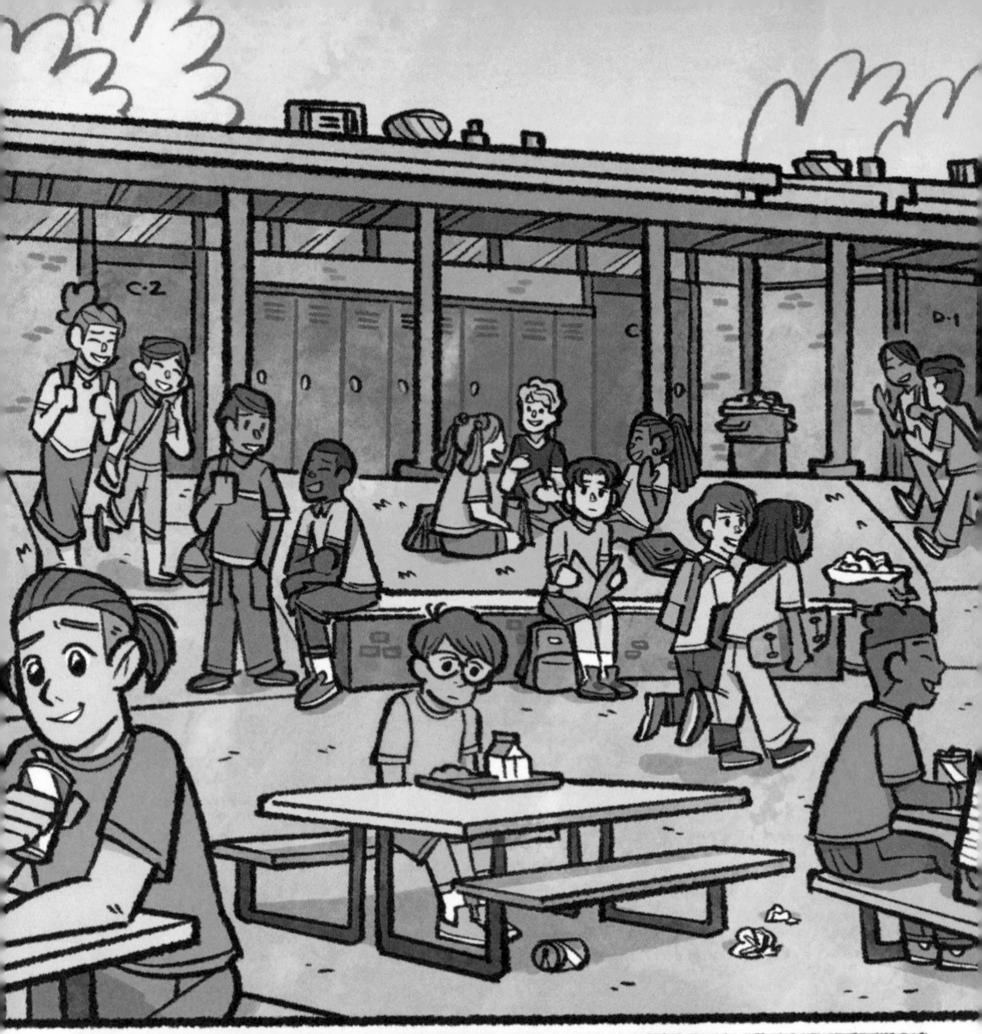
C-2
D-1

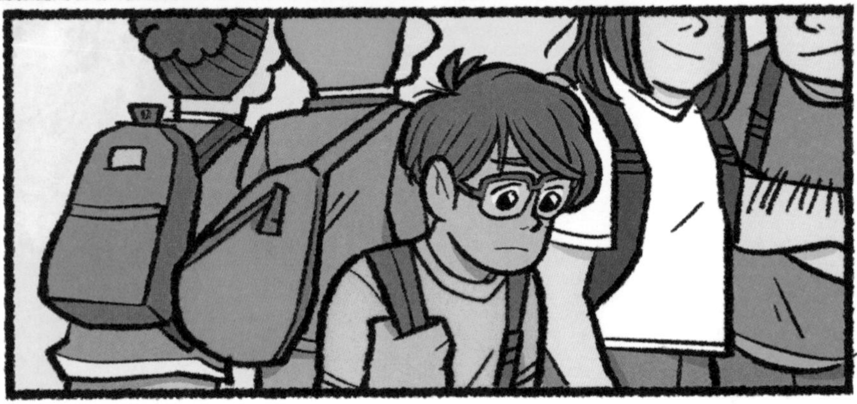

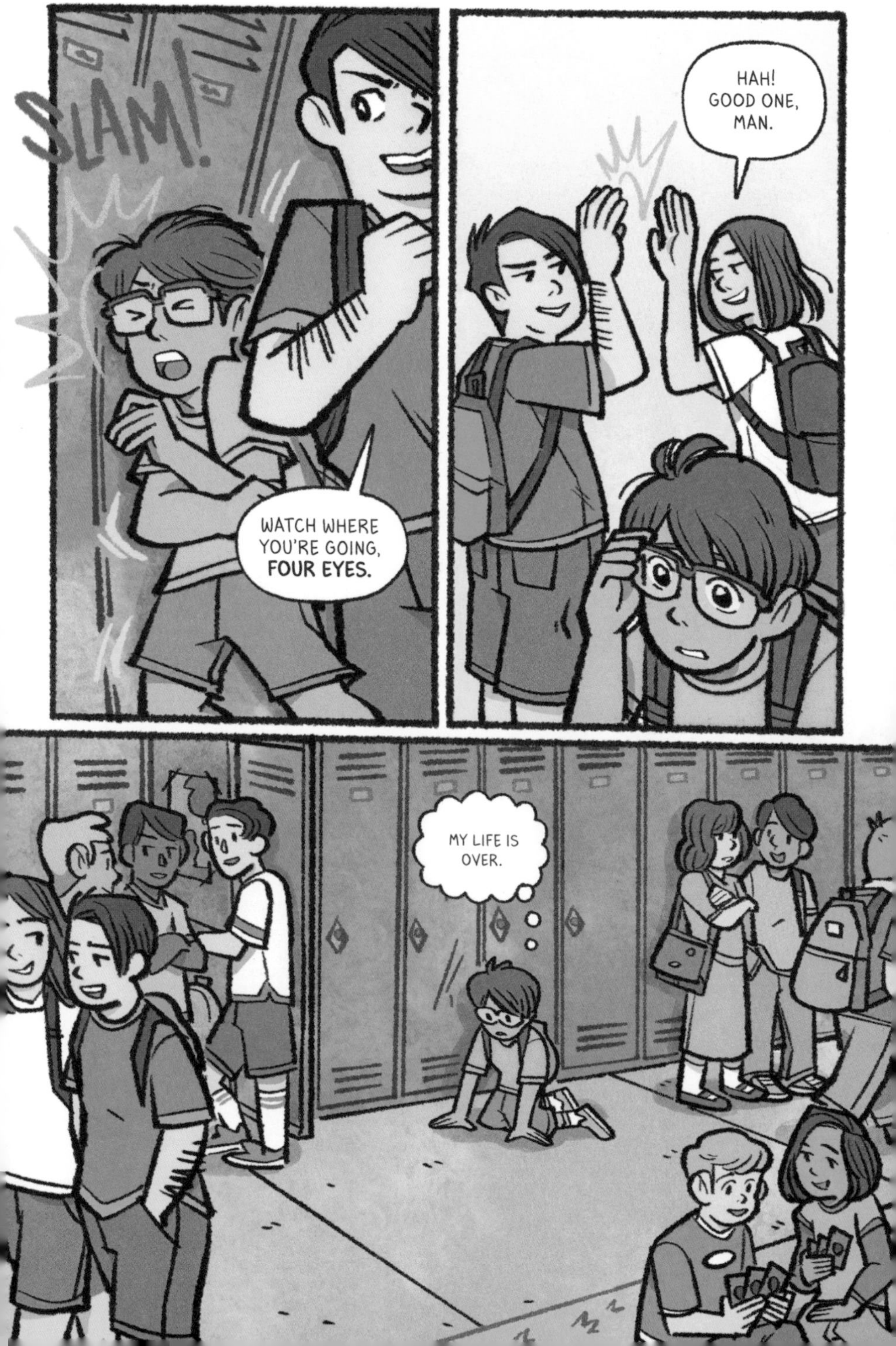
SLAM!
WATCH WHERE YOU'RE GOING, **FOUR EYES.**
HAH! GOOD ONE, MAN.
MY LIFE IS OVER.

PART TWO

BROKEN

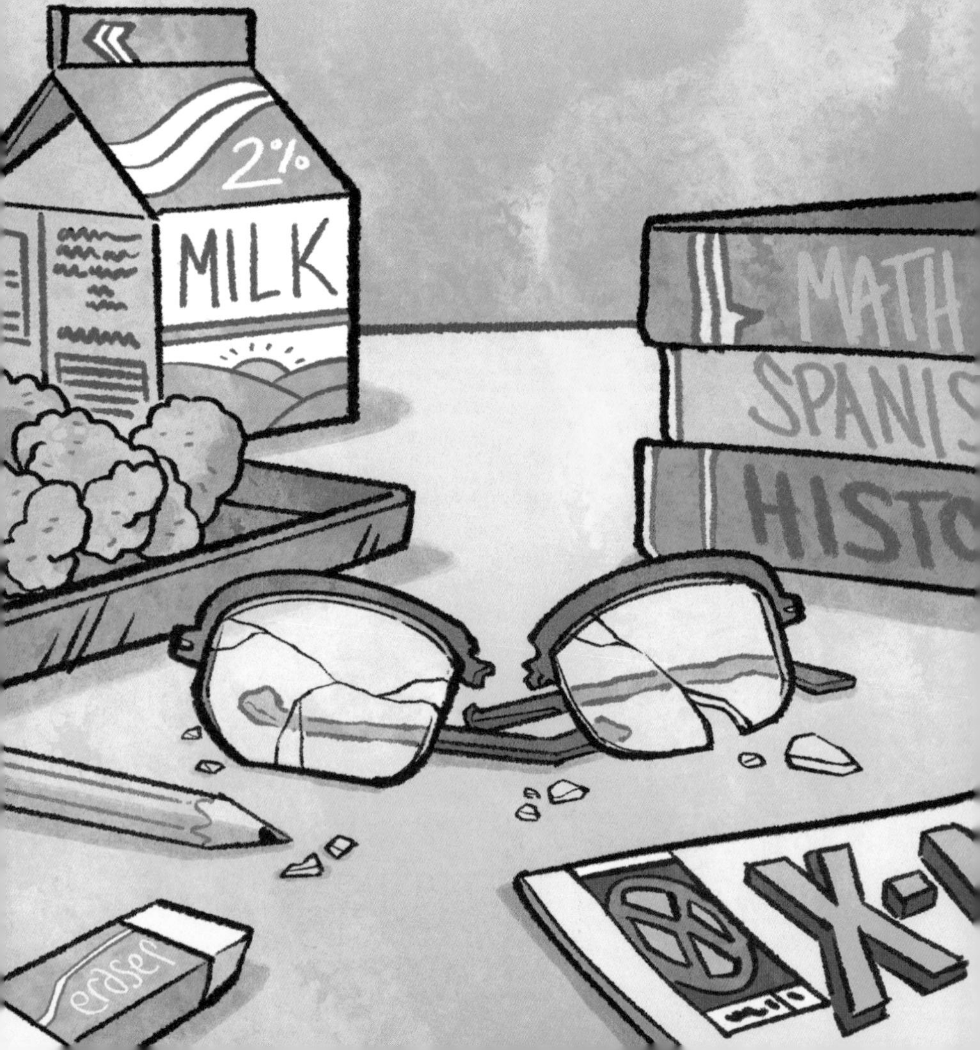

2%
MILK
MATH
SPANIS
HISTO
eraser

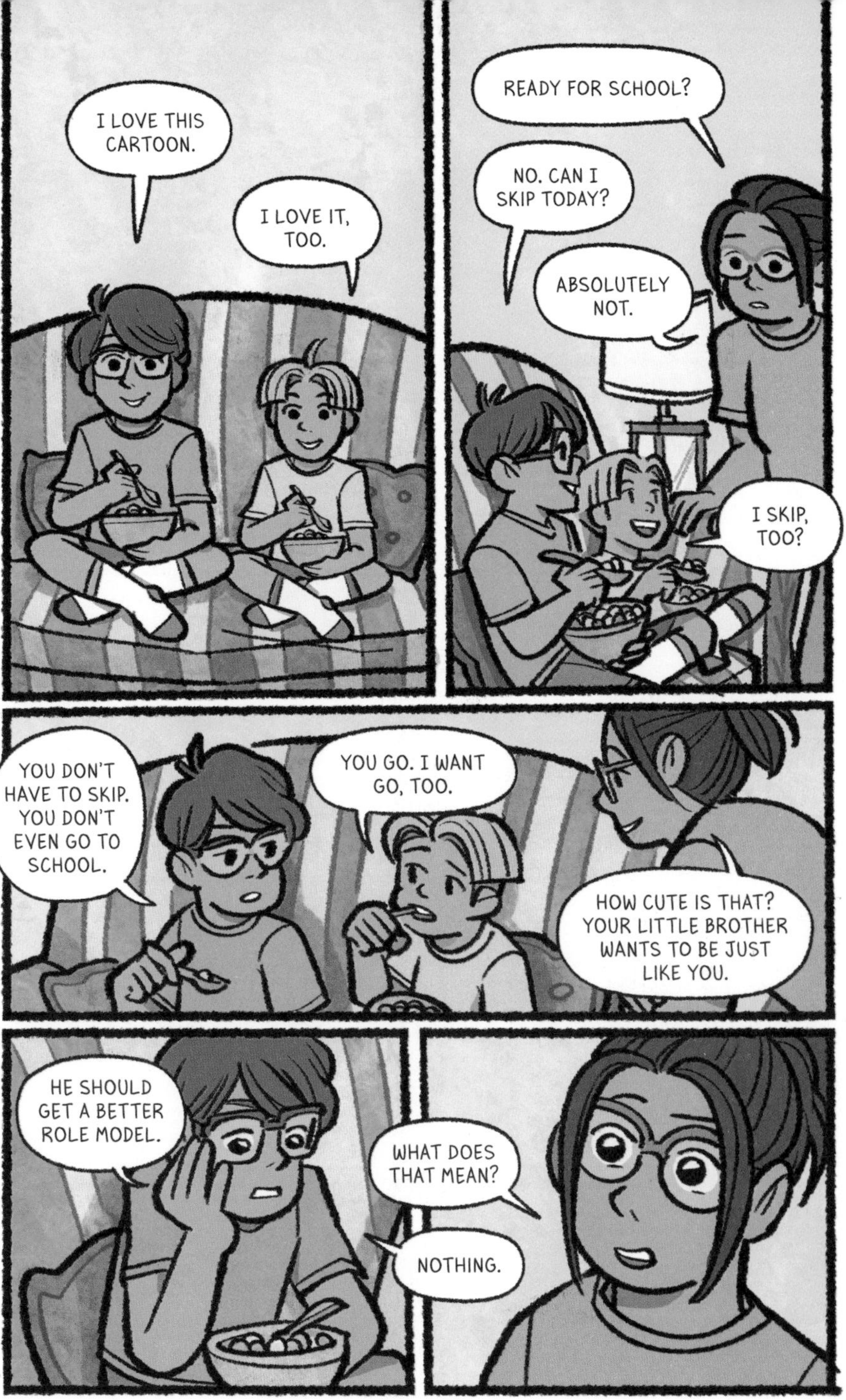
I LOVE THIS CARTOON.
I LOVE IT, TOO.
READY FOR SCHOOL?
NO. CAN I SKIP TODAY?
ABSOLUTELY NOT.
I SKIP, TOO?
YOU DON'T HAVE TO SKIP. YOU DON'T EVEN GO TO SCHOOL.
YOU GO. I WANT GO, TOO.
HOW CUTE IS THAT? YOUR LITTLE BROTHER WANTS TO BE JUST LIKE YOU.
HE SHOULD GET A BETTER ROLE MODEL.
WHAT DOES THAT MEAN?
NOTHING.

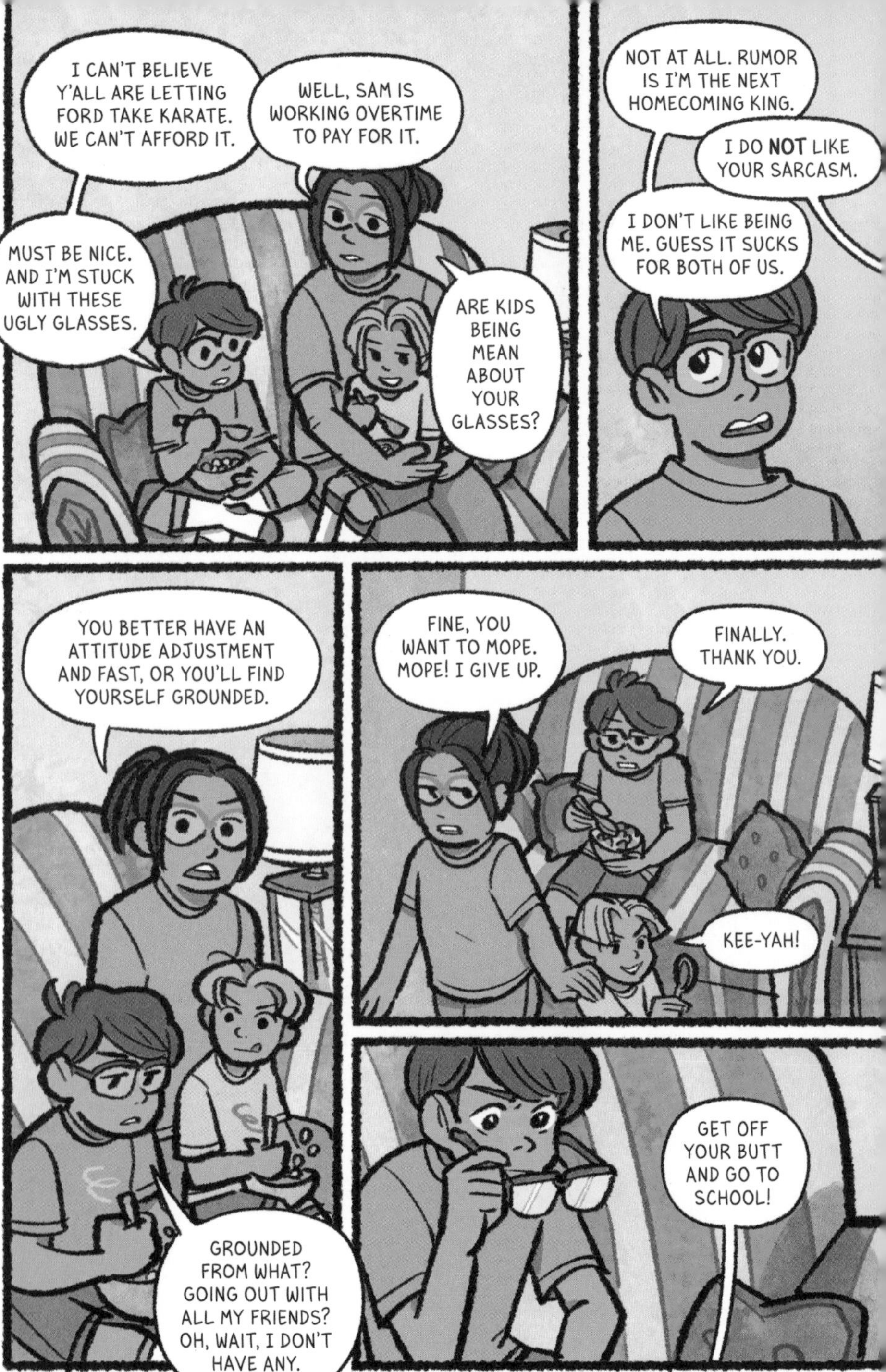
I CAN'T BELIEVE Y'ALL ARE LETTING FORD TAKE KARATE. WE CAN'T AFFORD IT.
WELL, SAM IS WORKING OVERTIME TO PAY FOR IT.
MUST BE NICE. AND I'M STUCK WITH THESE UGLY GLASSES.
ARE KIDS BEING MEAN ABOUT YOUR GLASSES?
NOT AT ALL. RUMOR IS I'M THE NEXT HOMECOMING KING.
I DO **NOT** LIKE YOUR SARCASM.
I DON'T LIKE BEING ME. GUESS IT SUCKS FOR BOTH OF US.
YOU BETTER HAVE AN ATTITUDE ADJUSTMENT AND FAST, OR YOU'LL FIND YOURSELF GROUNDED.
GROUNDED FROM WHAT? GOING OUT WITH ALL MY FRIENDS? OH, WAIT, I DON'T HAVE ANY.
FINE, YOU WANT TO MOPE. MOPE! I GIVE UP.
FINALLY. THANK YOU.
KEE-YAH!
GET OFF YOUR BUTT AND GO TO SCHOOL!

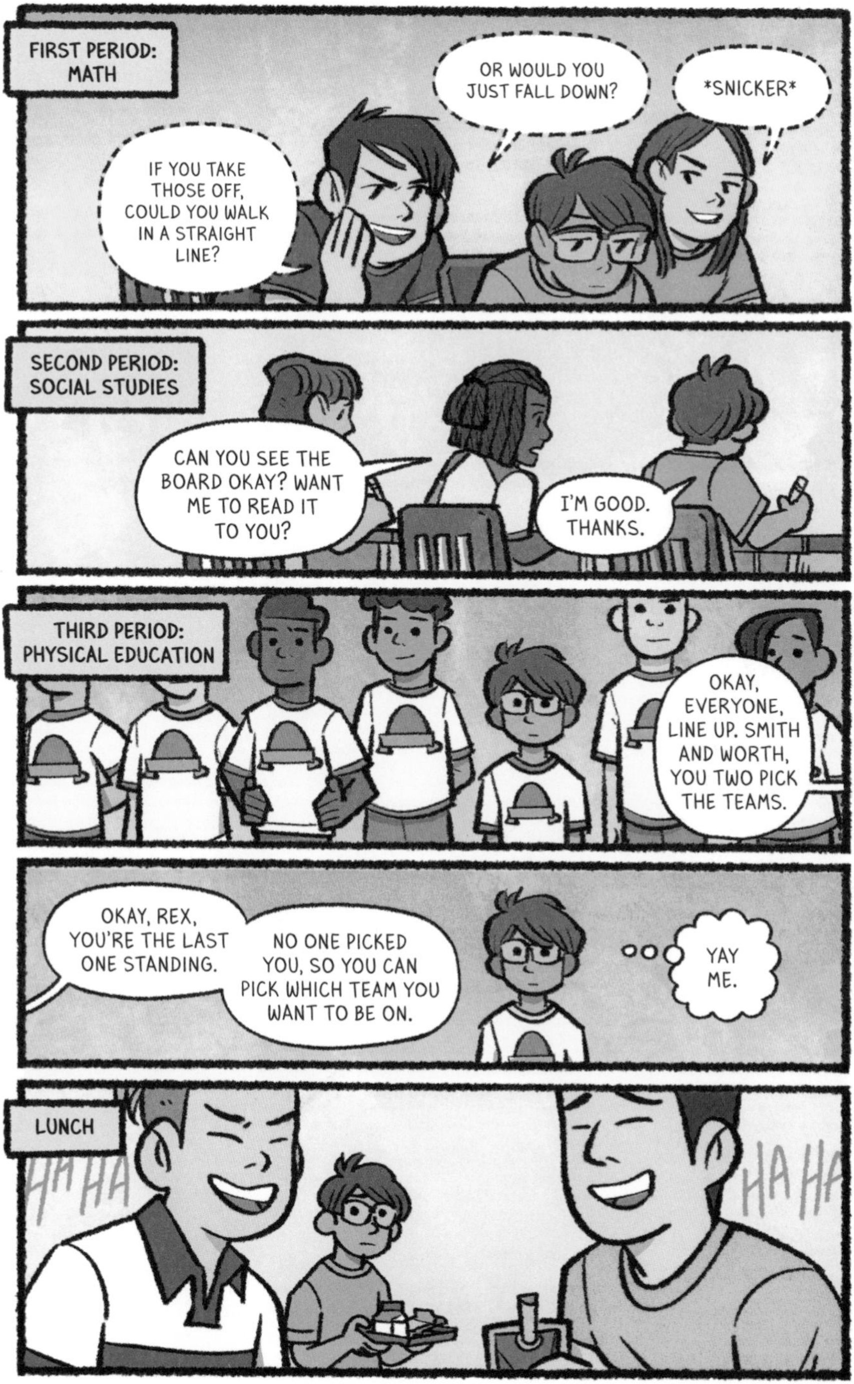
FIRST PERIOD: MATH
IF YOU TAKE THOSE OFF, COULD YOU WALK IN A STRAIGHT LINE?
OR WOULD YOU JUST FALL DOWN?
SNICKER
SECOND PERIOD: SOCIAL STUDIES
CAN YOU SEE THE BOARD OKAY? WANT ME TO READ IT TO YOU?
I'M GOOD. THANKS.
THIRD PERIOD: PHYSICAL EDUCATION
OKAY, EVERYONE, LINE UP. SMITH AND WORTH, YOU TWO PICK THE TEAMS.
OKAY, REX, YOU'RE THE LAST ONE STANDING.
NO ONE PICKED YOU, SO YOU CAN PICK WHICH TEAM YOU WANT TO BE ON.
YAY ME.
LUNCH
HA HA
HA HA

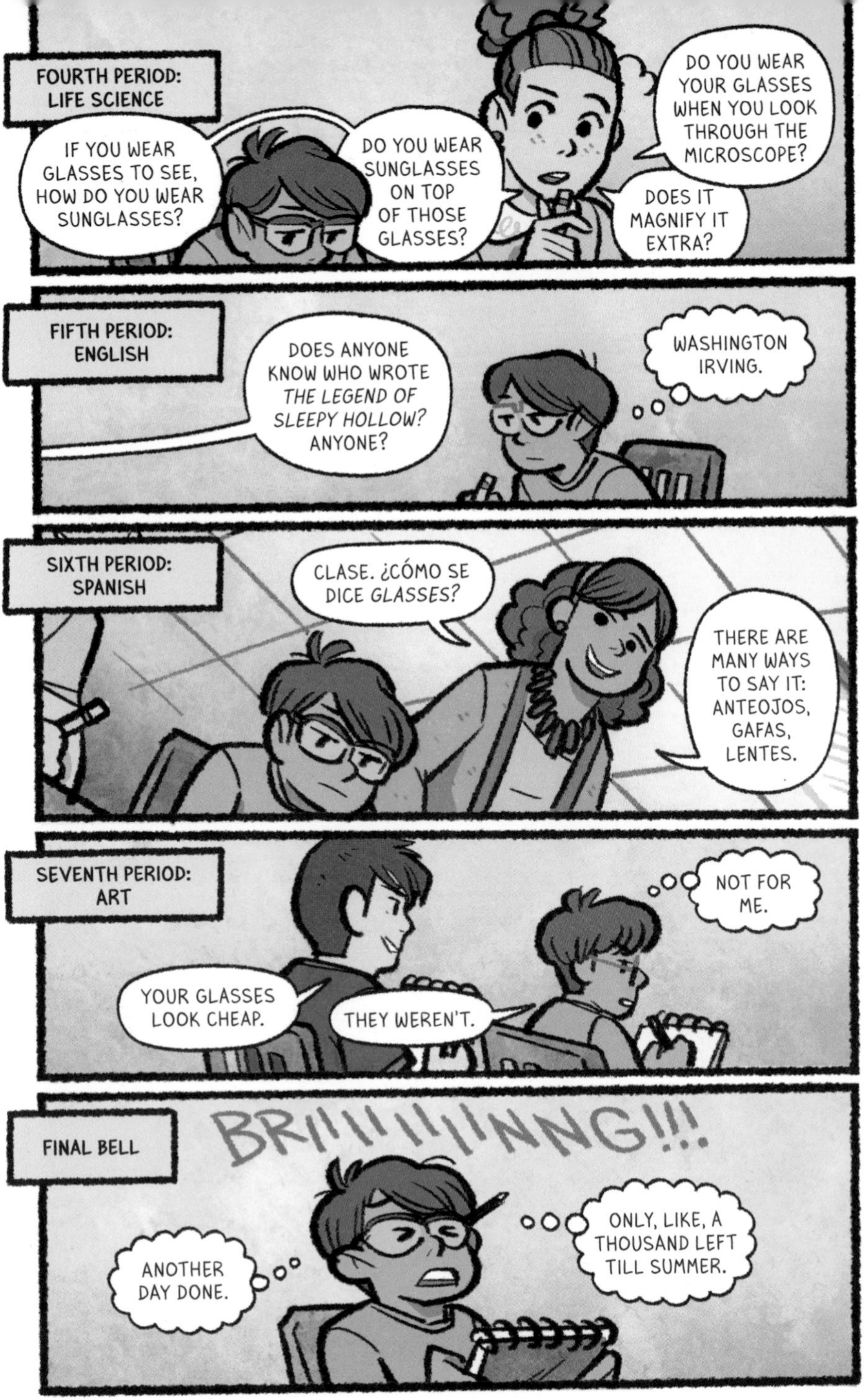
FOURTH PERIOD: LIFE SCIENCE
IF YOU WEAR GLASSES TO SEE, HOW DO YOU WEAR SUNGLASSES?
DO YOU WEAR SUNGLASSES ON TOP OF THOSE GLASSES?
DO YOU WEAR YOUR GLASSES WHEN YOU LOOK THROUGH THE MICROSCOPE?
DOES IT MAGNIFY IT EXTRA?
FIFTH PERIOD: ENGLISH
DOES ANYONE KNOW WHO WROTE *THE LEGEND OF SLEEPY HOLLOW?* ANYONE?
WASHINGTON IRVING.
SIXTH PERIOD: SPANISH
CLASE. ¿CÓMO SE DICE *GLASSES?*
THERE ARE MANY WAYS TO SAY IT: ANTEOJOS, GAFAS, LENTES.
SEVENTH PERIOD: ART
NOT FOR ME.
YOUR GLASSES LOOK CHEAP.
THEY WEREN'T.
FINAL BELL
BRIIIIIIIINNG!!!
ANOTHER DAY DONE.
ONLY, LIKE, A THOUSAND LEFT TILL SUMMER.

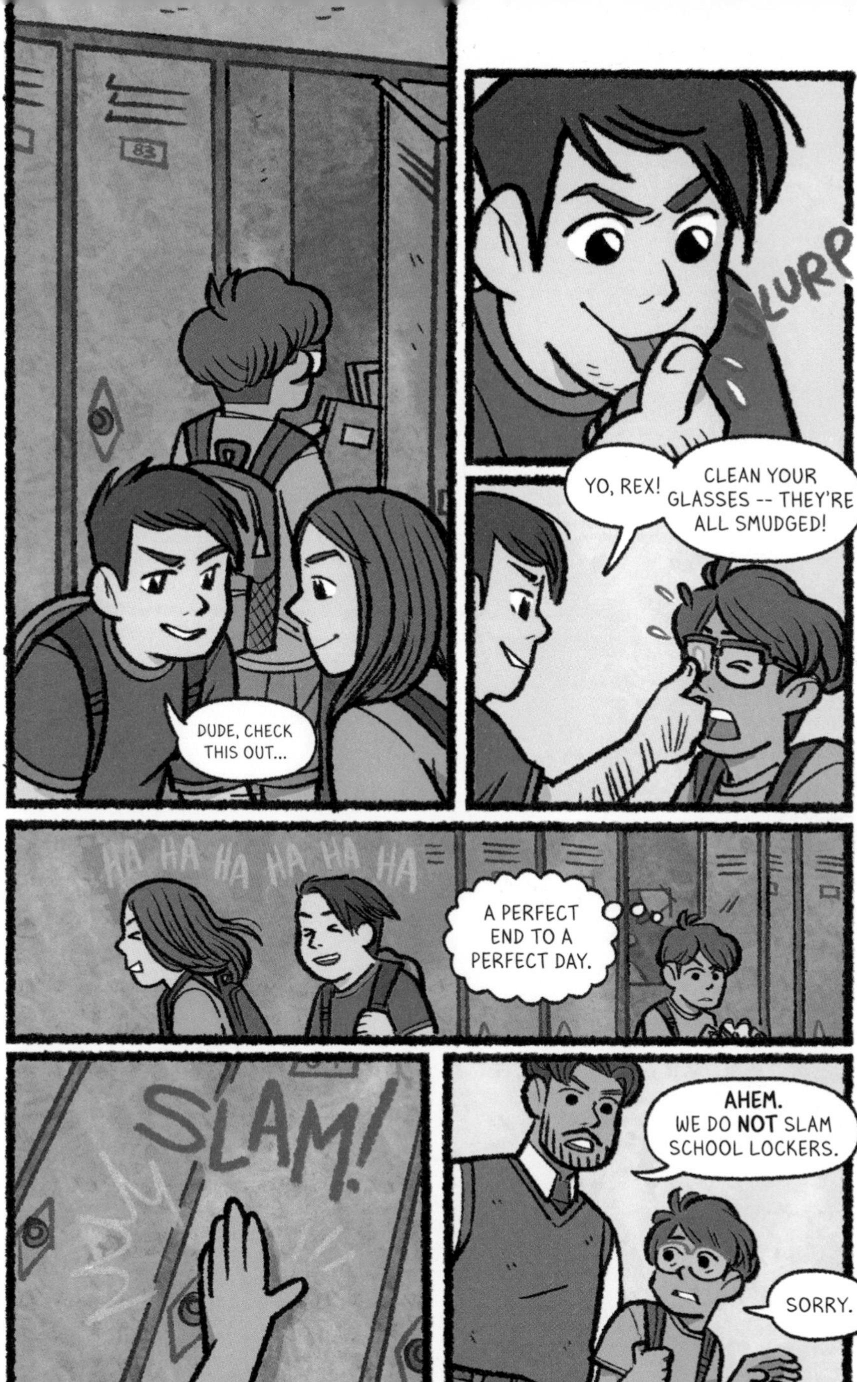
SLURP!
DUDE, CHECK THIS OUT...
YO, REX!
CLEAN YOUR GLASSES -- THEY'RE ALL SMUDGED!
HA HA HA HA HA HA
A PERFECT END TO A PERFECT DAY.
SLAM!
AHEM. WE DO **NOT** SLAM SCHOOL LOCKERS.
SORRY.

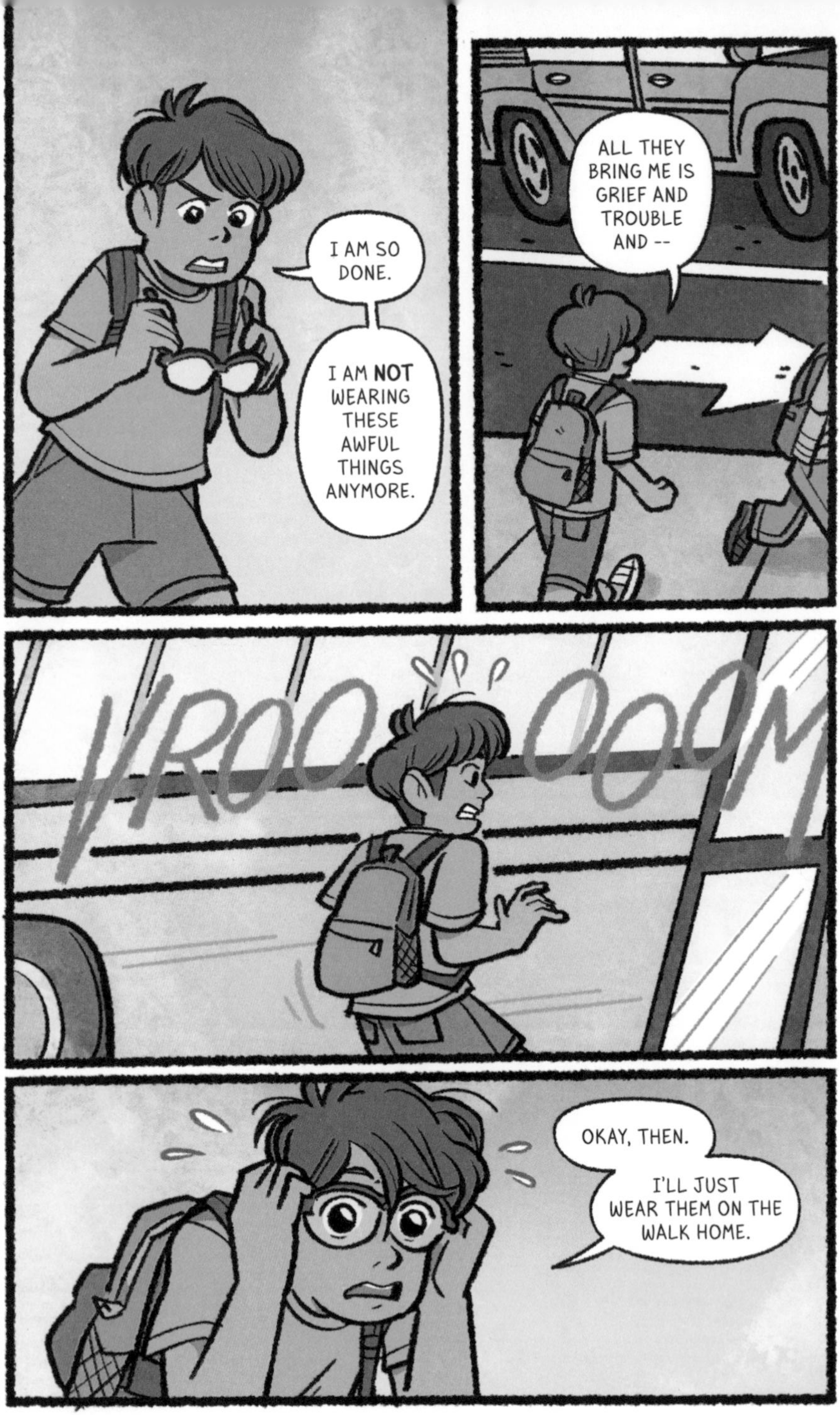
I AM SO DONE.
I AM **NOT** WEARING THESE AWFUL THINGS ANYMORE.
ALL THEY BRING ME IS GRIEF AND TROUBLE AND --
VROOOOOOM
OKAY, THEN.
I'LL JUST WEAR THEM ON THE WALK HOME.

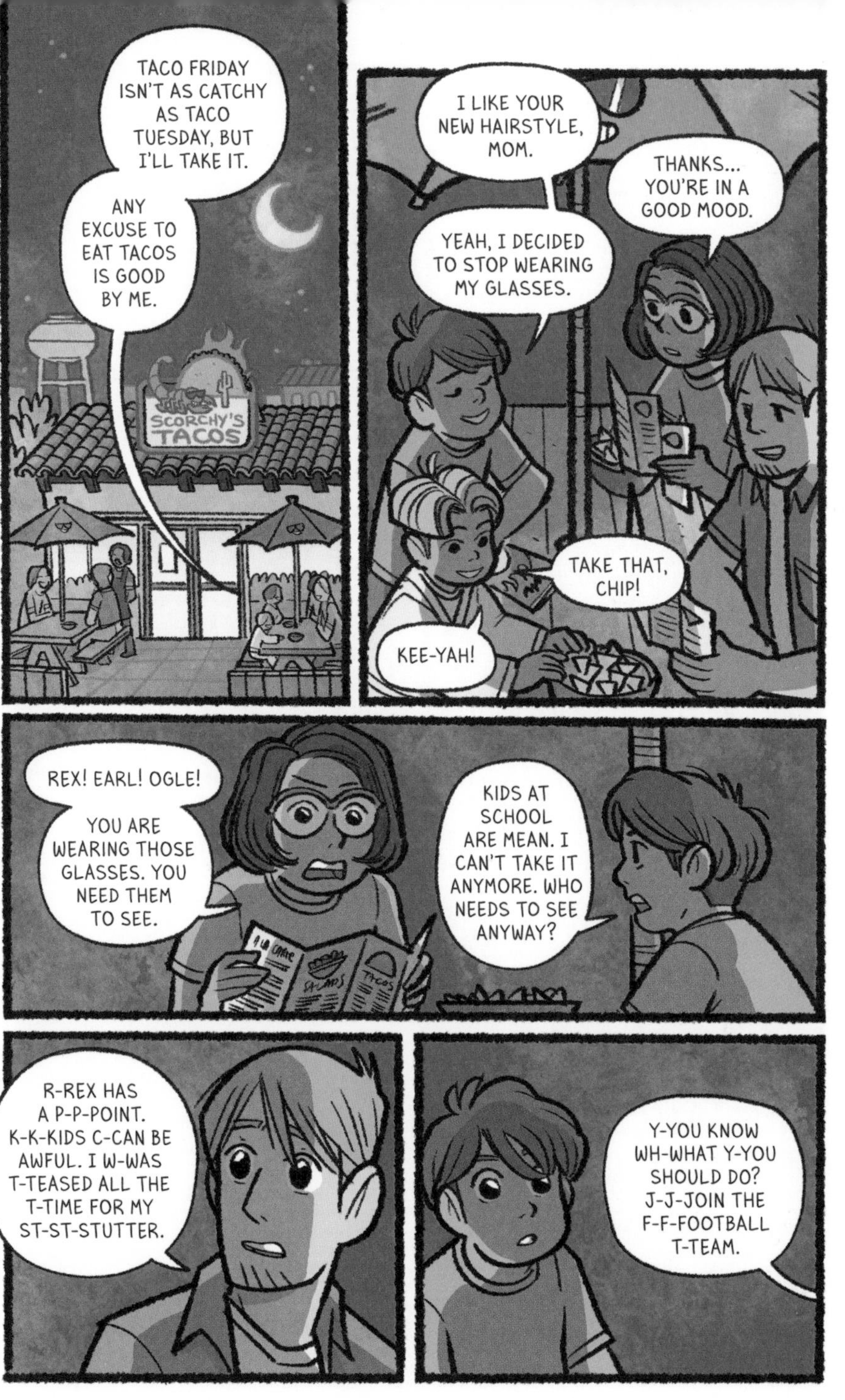
TACO FRIDAY ISN'T AS CATCHY AS TACO TUESDAY, BUT I'LL TAKE IT.
ANY EXCUSE TO EAT TACOS IS GOOD BY ME.
SCORCHY'S TACOS
I LIKE YOUR NEW HAIRSTYLE, MOM.
THANKS... YOU'RE IN A GOOD MOOD.
YEAH, I DECIDED TO STOP WEARING MY GLASSES.
TAKE THAT, CHIP!
KEE-YAH!
REX! EARL! OGLE!
YOU ARE WEARING THOSE GLASSES. YOU NEED THEM TO SEE.
KIDS AT SCHOOL ARE MEAN. I CAN'T TAKE IT ANYMORE. WHO NEEDS TO SEE ANYWAY?
R-REX HAS A P-P-POINT. K-K-KIDS C-CAN BE AWFUL. I W-WAS T-TEASED ALL THE T-TIME FOR MY ST-ST-STUTTER.
Y-YOU KNOW WH-WHAT Y-YOU SHOULD DO? J-J-JOIN THE F-F-FOOTBALL T-TEAM.

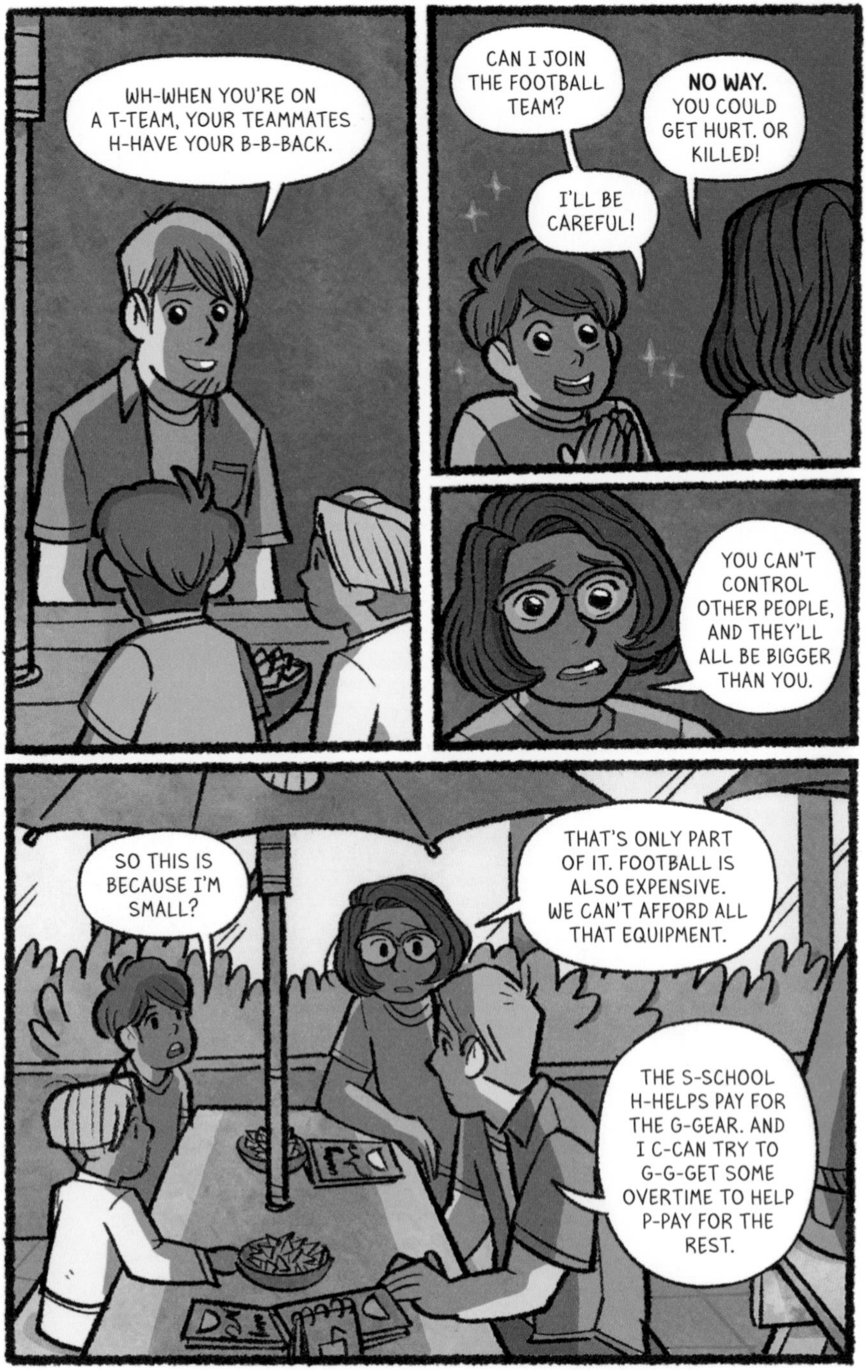
WH-WHEN YOU'RE ON A T-TEAM, YOUR TEAMMATES H-HAVE YOUR B-B-BACK.
CAN I JOIN THE FOOTBALL TEAM?
I'LL BE CAREFUL!
NO WAY. YOU COULD GET HURT. OR KILLED!
YOU CAN'T CONTROL OTHER PEOPLE, AND THEY'LL ALL BE BIGGER THAN YOU.
SO THIS IS BECAUSE I'M SMALL?
THAT'S ONLY PART OF IT. FOOTBALL IS ALSO EXPENSIVE. WE CAN'T AFFORD ALL THAT EQUIPMENT.
THE S-SCHOOL H-HELPS PAY FOR THE G-GEAR. AND I C-CAN TRY TO G-G-GET SOME OVERTIME TO HELP P-PAY FOR THE REST.

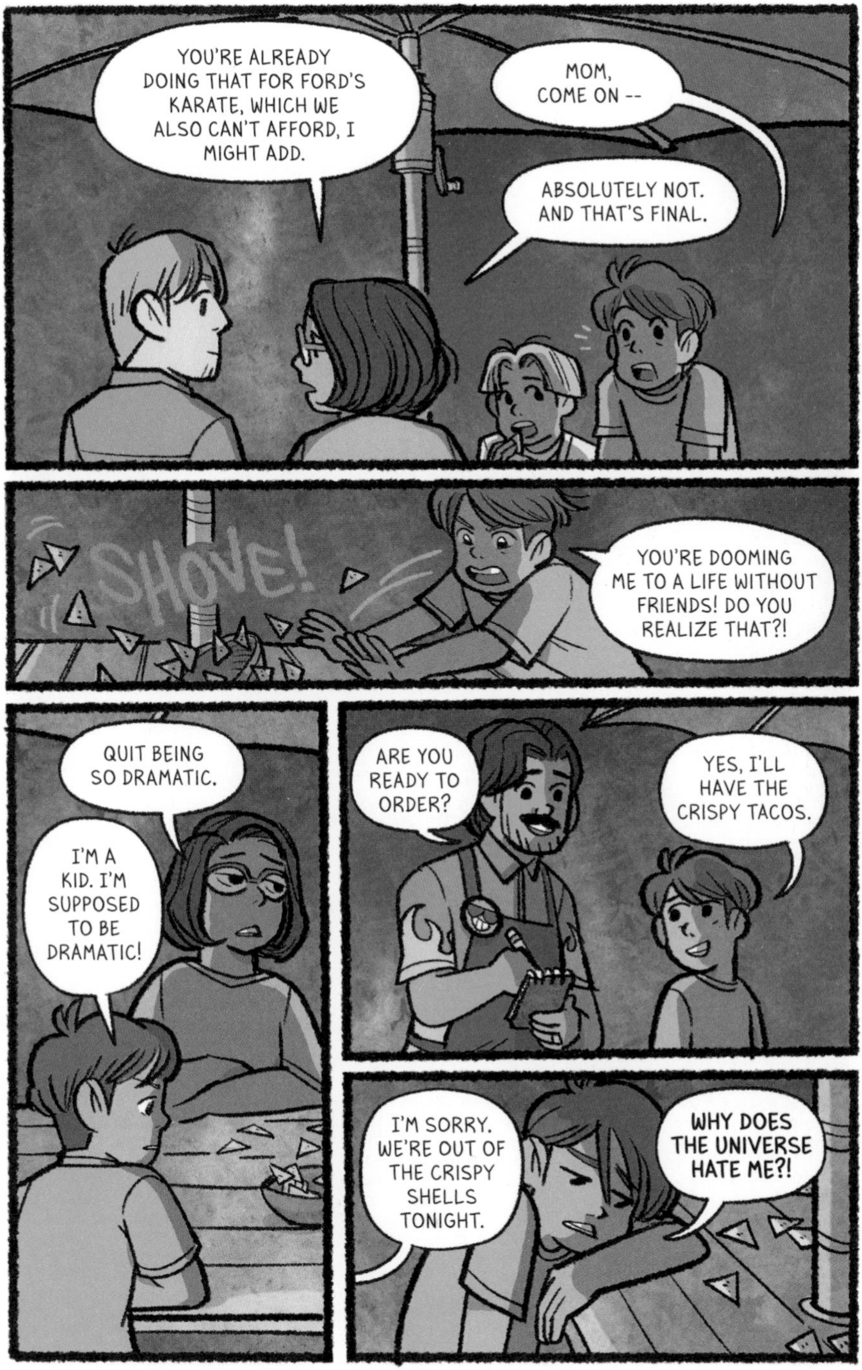
YOU'RE ALREADY DOING THAT FOR FORD'S KARATE, WHICH WE ALSO CAN'T AFFORD, I MIGHT ADD.
MOM, COME ON --
ABSOLUTELY NOT. AND THAT'S FINAL.
SHOVE!
YOU'RE DOOMING ME TO A LIFE WITHOUT FRIENDS! DO YOU REALIZE THAT?!
QUIT BEING SO DRAMATIC.
I'M A KID. I'M SUPPOSED TO BE DRAMATIC!
ARE YOU READY TO ORDER?
YES, I'LL HAVE THE CRISPY TACOS.
I'M SORRY. WE'RE OUT OF THE CRISPY SHELLS TONIGHT.
WHY DOES THE UNIVERSE HATE ME?!

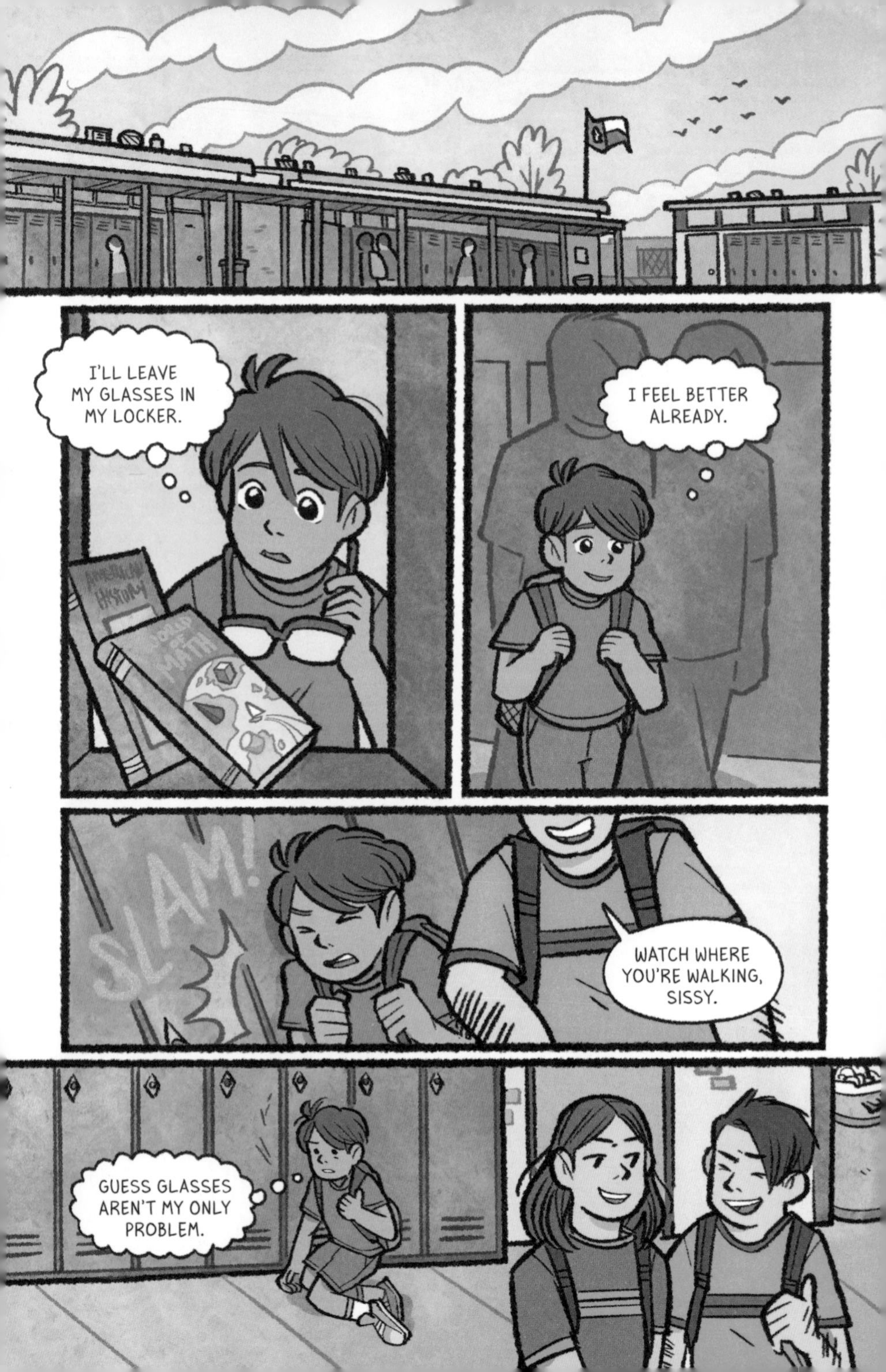
I'LL LEAVE MY GLASSES IN MY LOCKER.
AMERICAN HISTORY
WORLD OF MATH
I FEEL BETTER ALREADY.
SLAM!
WATCH WHERE YOU'RE WALKING, SISSY.
GUESS GLASSES AREN'T MY ONLY PROBLEM.

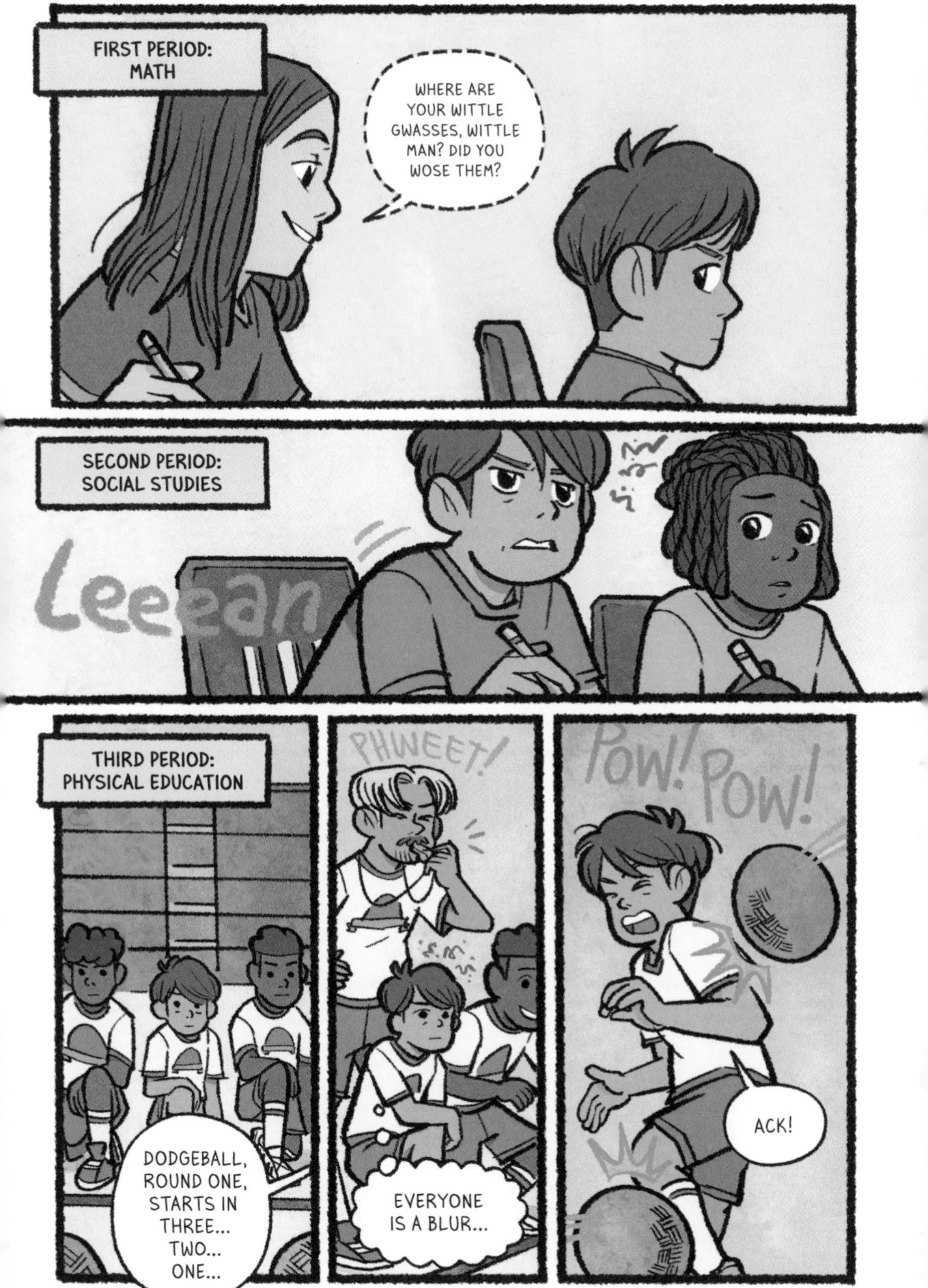
FIRST PERIOD: MATH
WHERE ARE YOUR WITTLE GWASSES, WITTLE MAN? DID YOU WOSE THEM?
SECOND PERIOD: SOCIAL STUDIES
Leeean
THIRD PERIOD: PHYSICAL EDUCATION
DODGEBALL, ROUND ONE, STARTS IN THREE... TWO... ONE...
PHWEET!
EVERYONE IS A BLUR...
POW! POW!
ACK!

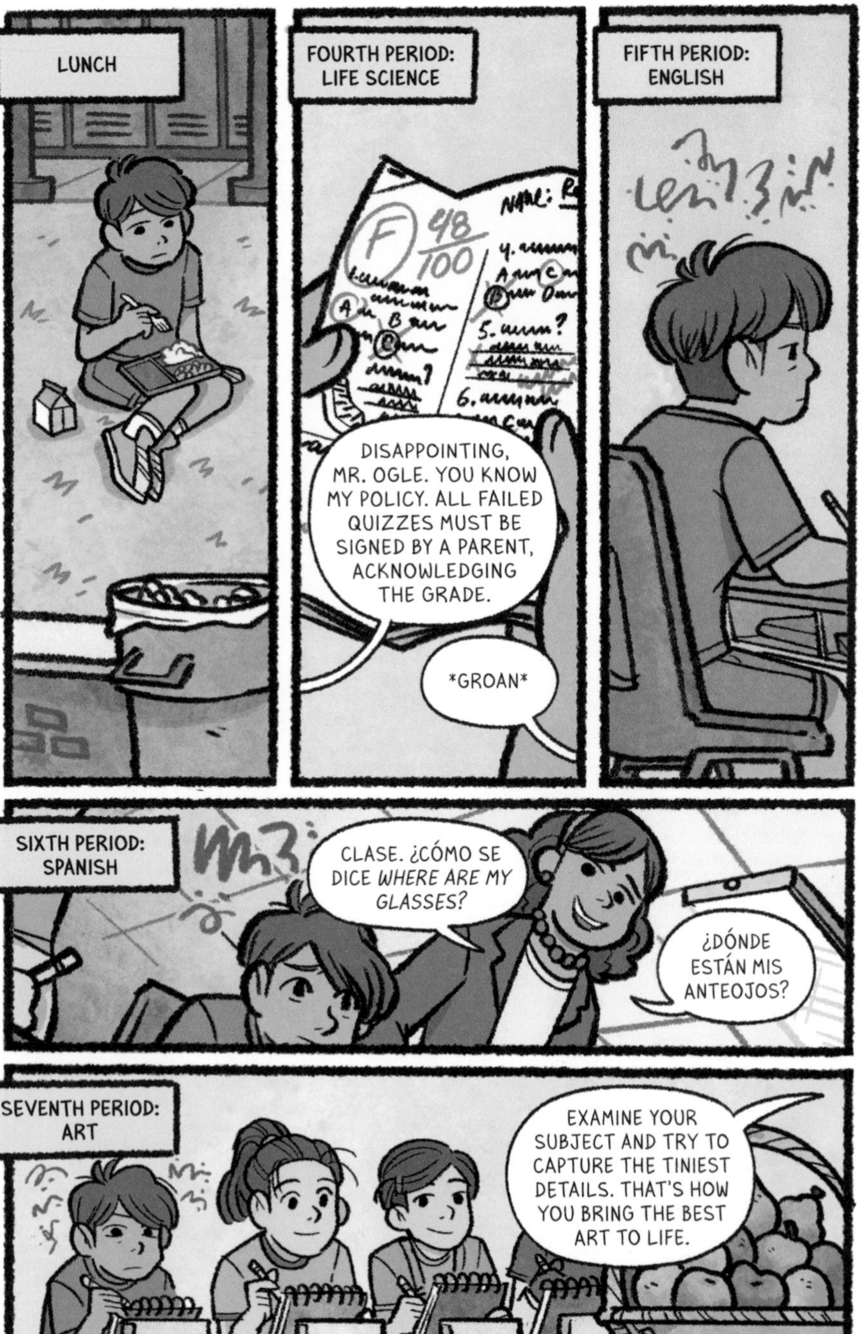

LUNCH
FOURTH PERIOD: LIFE SCIENCE
F 48/100
DISAPPOINTING, MR. OGLE. YOU KNOW MY POLICY. ALL FAILED QUIZZES MUST BE SIGNED BY A PARENT, ACKNOWLEDGING THE GRADE.
GROAN
FIFTH PERIOD: ENGLISH
SIXTH PERIOD: SPANISH
CLASE. ¿CÓMO SE DICE *WHERE ARE MY GLASSES?*
¿DÓNDE ESTÁN MIS ANTEOJOS?
SEVENTH PERIOD: ART
EXAMINE YOUR SUBJECT AND TRY TO CAPTURE THE TINIEST DETAILS. THAT'S HOW YOU BRING THE BEST ART TO LIFE.

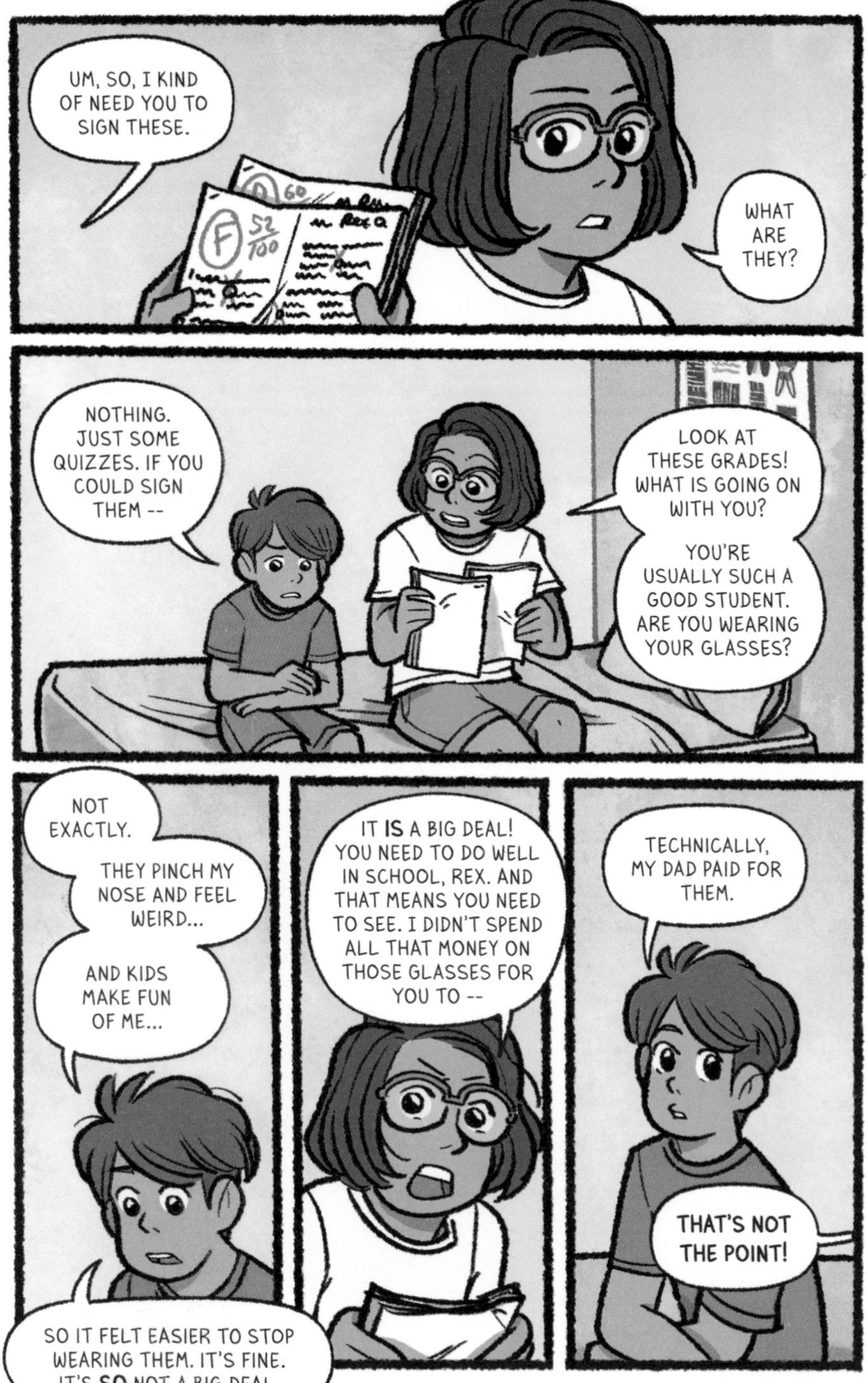
UM, SO, I KIND OF NEED YOU TO SIGN THESE.
WHAT ARE THEY?
NOTHING. JUST SOME QUIZZES. IF YOU COULD SIGN THEM --
LOOK AT THESE GRADES! WHAT IS GOING ON WITH YOU?
YOU'RE USUALLY SUCH A GOOD STUDENT. ARE YOU WEARING YOUR GLASSES?
NOT EXACTLY.
THEY PINCH MY NOSE AND FEEL WEIRD...
AND KIDS MAKE FUN OF ME...
SO IT FELT EASIER TO STOP WEARING THEM. IT'S FINE. IT'S **SO** NOT A BIG DEAL.
IT **IS** A BIG DEAL! YOU NEED TO DO WELL IN SCHOOL, REX. AND THAT MEANS YOU NEED TO SEE. I DIDN'T SPEND ALL THAT MONEY ON THOSE GLASSES FOR YOU TO --
TECHNICALLY, MY DAD PAID FOR THEM.
THAT'S NOT THE POINT!

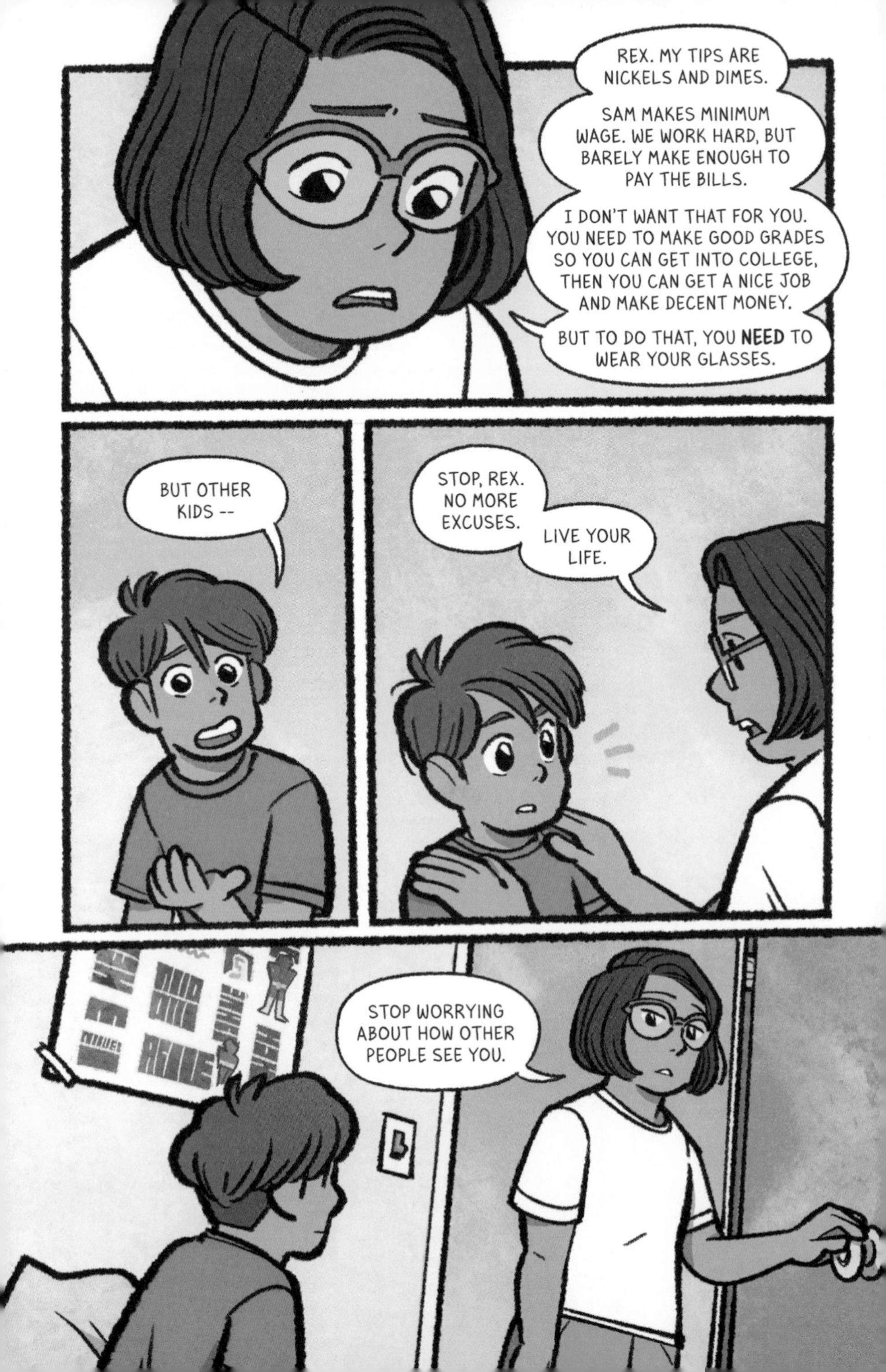
REX. MY TIPS ARE NICKELS AND DIMES.
SAM MAKES MINIMUM WAGE. WE WORK HARD, BUT BARELY MAKE ENOUGH TO PAY THE BILLS.
I DON'T WANT THAT FOR YOU. YOU NEED TO MAKE GOOD GRADES SO YOU CAN GET INTO COLLEGE, THEN YOU CAN GET A NICE JOB AND MAKE DECENT MONEY.
BUT TO DO THAT, YOU **NEED** TO WEAR YOUR GLASSES.
BUT OTHER KIDS --
STOP, REX. NO MORE EXCUSES.
LIVE YOUR LIFE.
STOP WORRYING ABOUT HOW OTHER PEOPLE SEE YOU.

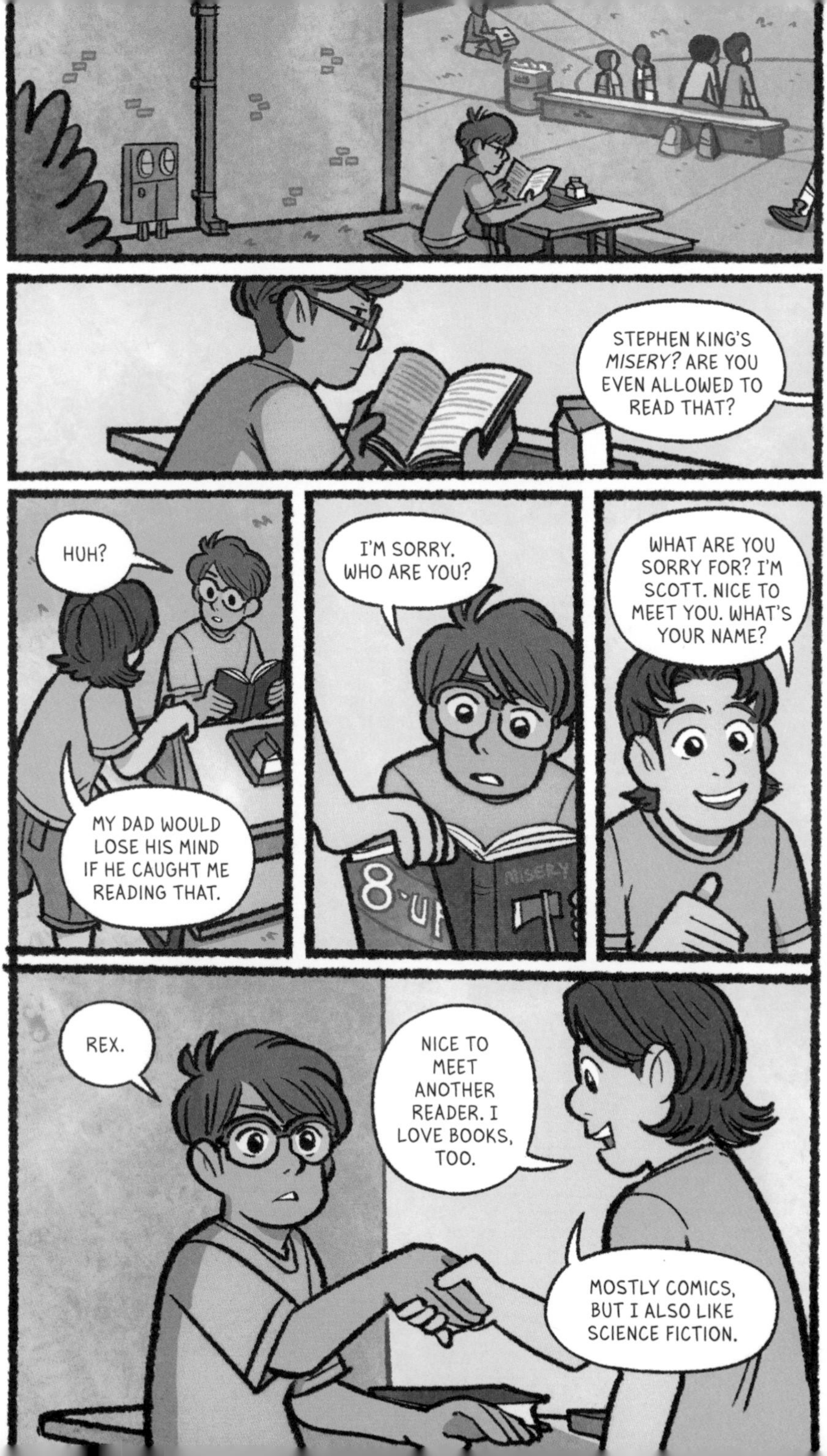
STEPHEN KING'S *MISERY*? ARE YOU EVEN ALLOWED TO READ THAT?
HUH?
MY DAD WOULD LOSE HIS MIND IF HE CAUGHT ME READING THAT.
I'M SORRY. WHO ARE YOU?
8-UP
MISERY
WHAT ARE YOU SORRY FOR? I'M SCOTT. NICE TO MEET YOU. WHAT'S YOUR NAME?
REX.
NICE TO MEET ANOTHER READER. I LOVE BOOKS, TOO.
MOSTLY COMICS, BUT I ALSO LIKE SCIENCE FICTION.

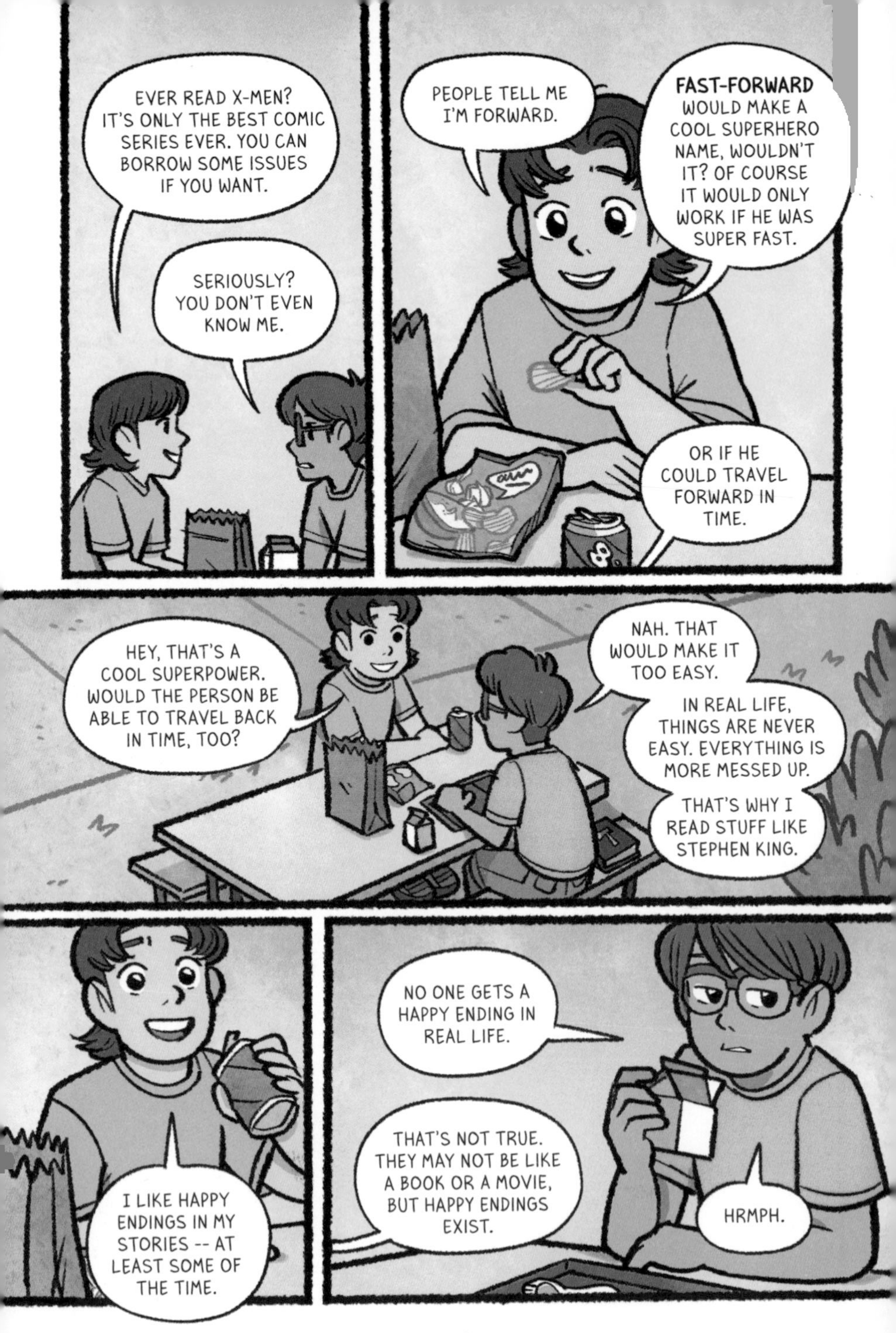
EVER READ X-MEN? IT'S ONLY THE BEST COMIC SERIES EVER. YOU CAN BORROW SOME ISSUES IF YOU WANT.
SERIOUSLY? YOU DON'T EVEN KNOW ME.
PEOPLE TELL ME I'M FORWARD.
FAST-FORWARD WOULD MAKE A COOL SUPERHERO NAME, WOULDN'T IT? OF COURSE IT WOULD ONLY WORK IF HE WAS SUPER FAST.
OR IF HE COULD TRAVEL FORWARD IN TIME.
HEY, THAT'S A COOL SUPERPOWER. WOULD THE PERSON BE ABLE TO TRAVEL BACK IN TIME, TOO?
NAH. THAT WOULD MAKE IT TOO EASY.
IN REAL LIFE, THINGS ARE NEVER EASY. EVERYTHING IS MORE MESSED UP.
THAT'S WHY I READ STUFF LIKE STEPHEN KING.
I LIKE HAPPY ENDINGS IN MY STORIES -- AT LEAST SOME OF THE TIME.
NO ONE GETS A HAPPY ENDING IN REAL LIFE.
THAT'S NOT TRUE. THEY MAY NOT BE LIKE A BOOK OR A MOVIE, BUT HAPPY ENDINGS EXIST.
HRMPH.

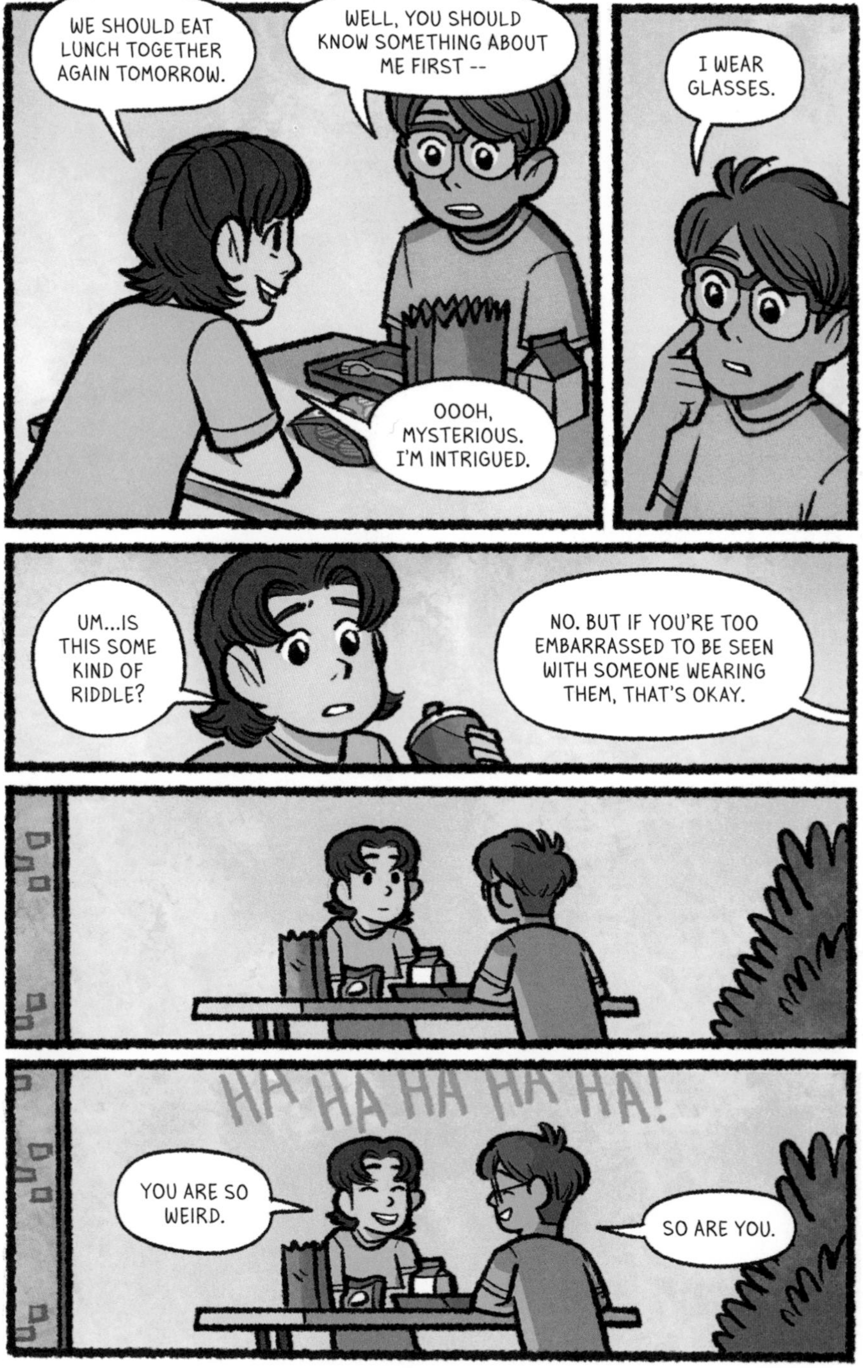

WE SHOULD EAT LUNCH TOGETHER AGAIN TOMORROW.
WELL, YOU SHOULD KNOW SOMETHING ABOUT ME FIRST --
OOOH, MYSTERIOUS. I'M INTRIGUED.
I WEAR GLASSES.
UM...IS THIS SOME KIND OF RIDDLE?
NO. BUT IF YOU'RE TOO EMBARRASSED TO BE SEEN WITH SOMEONE WEARING THEM, THAT'S OKAY.
HA HA HA HA HA!
YOU ARE SO WEIRD.
SO ARE YOU.

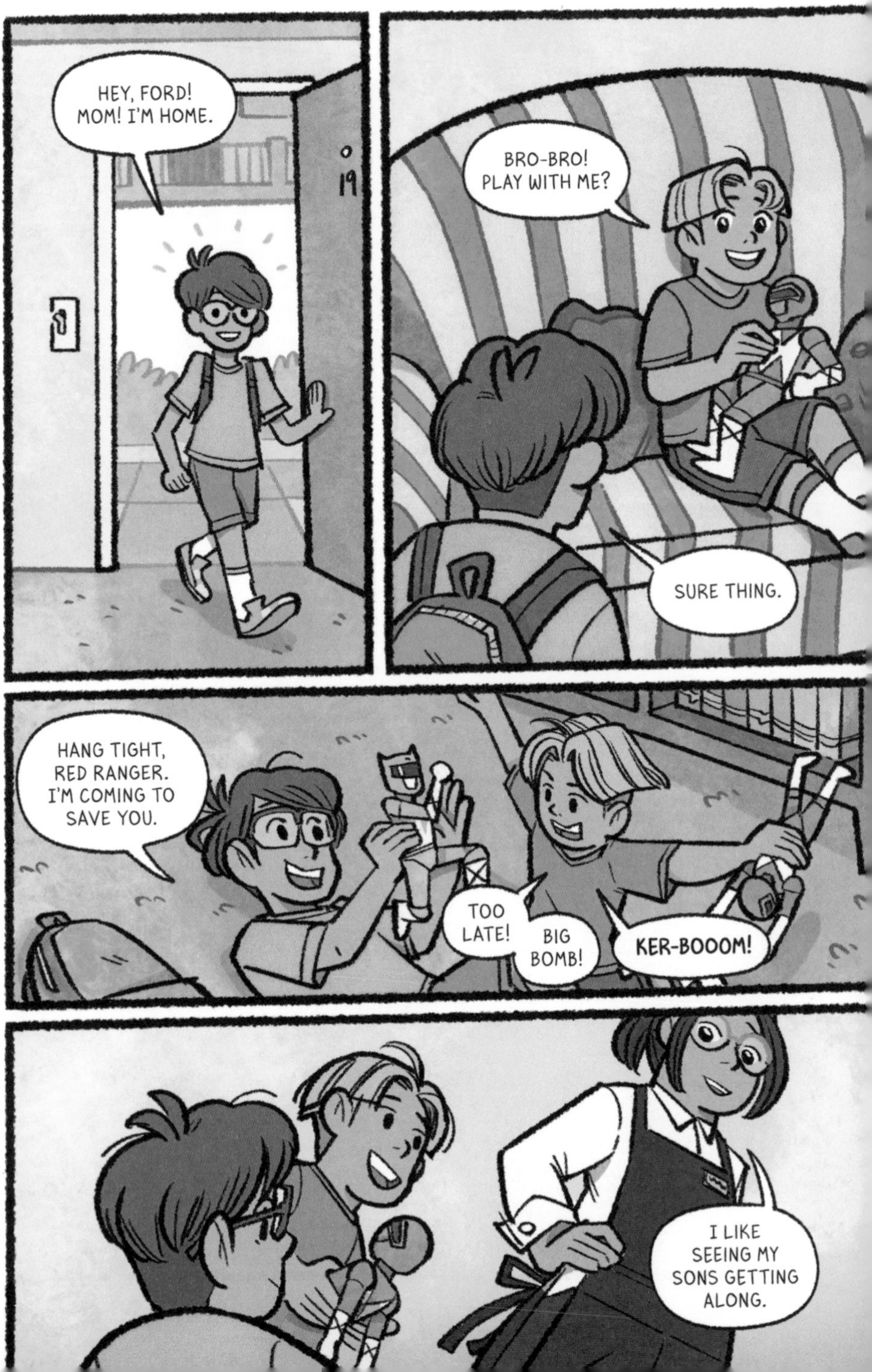
HEY, FORD! MOM! I'M HOME.
19
BRO-BRO! PLAY WITH ME?
SURE THING.
HANG TIGHT, RED RANGER. I'M COMING TO SAVE YOU.
TOO LATE!
BIG BOMB!
KER-BOOOM!
I LIKE SEEING MY SONS GETTING ALONG.

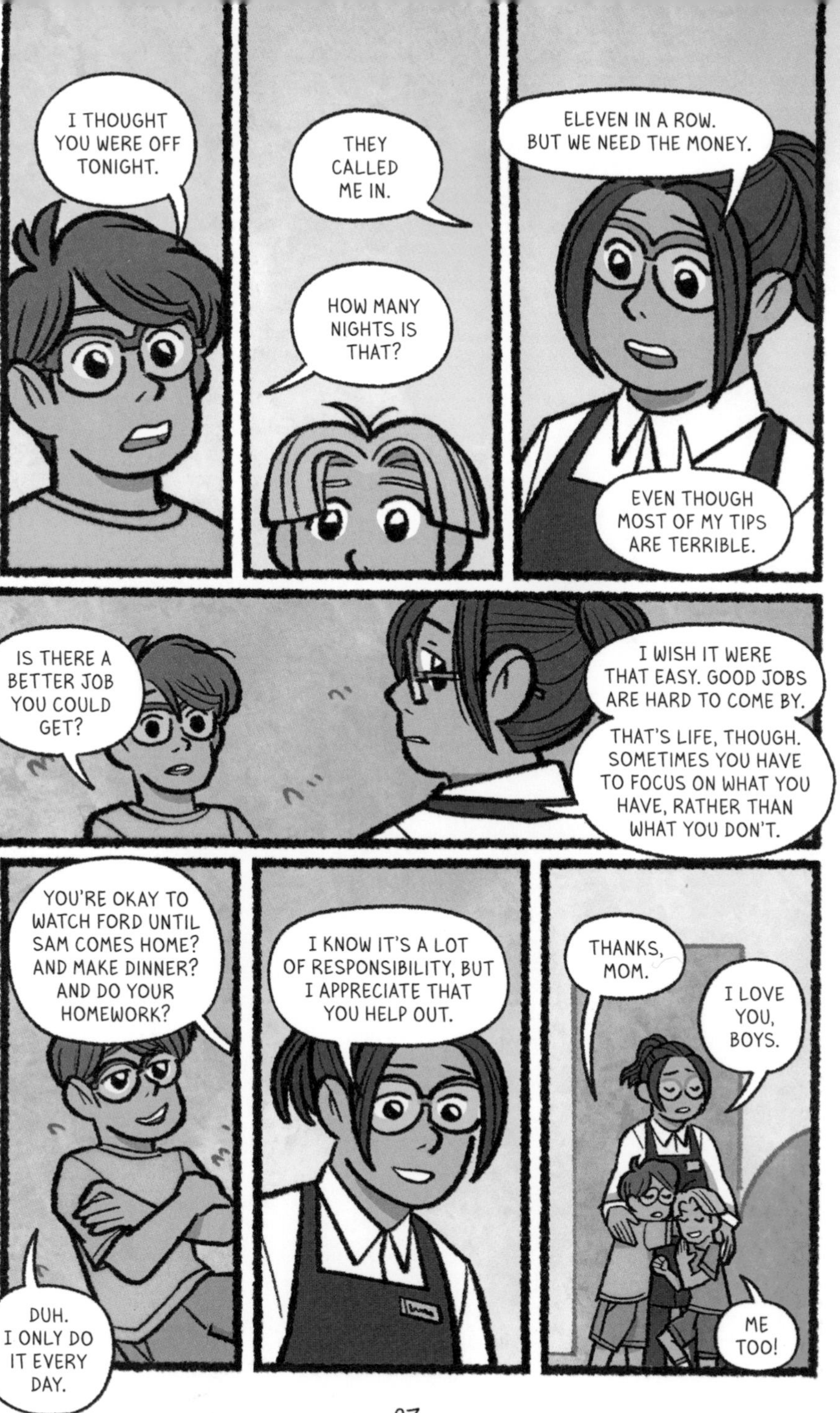
I THOUGHT YOU WERE OFF TONIGHT.
THEY CALLED ME IN.
HOW MANY NIGHTS IS THAT?
ELEVEN IN A ROW. BUT WE NEED THE MONEY.
EVEN THOUGH MOST OF MY TIPS ARE TERRIBLE.
IS THERE A BETTER JOB YOU COULD GET?
I WISH IT WERE THAT EASY. GOOD JOBS ARE HARD TO COME BY.
THAT'S LIFE, THOUGH. SOMETIMES YOU HAVE TO FOCUS ON WHAT YOU HAVE, RATHER THAN WHAT YOU DON'T.
YOU'RE OKAY TO WATCH FORD UNTIL SAM COMES HOME? AND MAKE DINNER? AND DO YOUR HOMEWORK?
DUH. I ONLY DO IT EVERY DAY.
I KNOW IT'S A LOT OF RESPONSIBILITY, BUT I APPRECIATE THAT YOU HELP OUT.
THANKS, MOM.
I LOVE YOU, BOYS.
ME TOO!

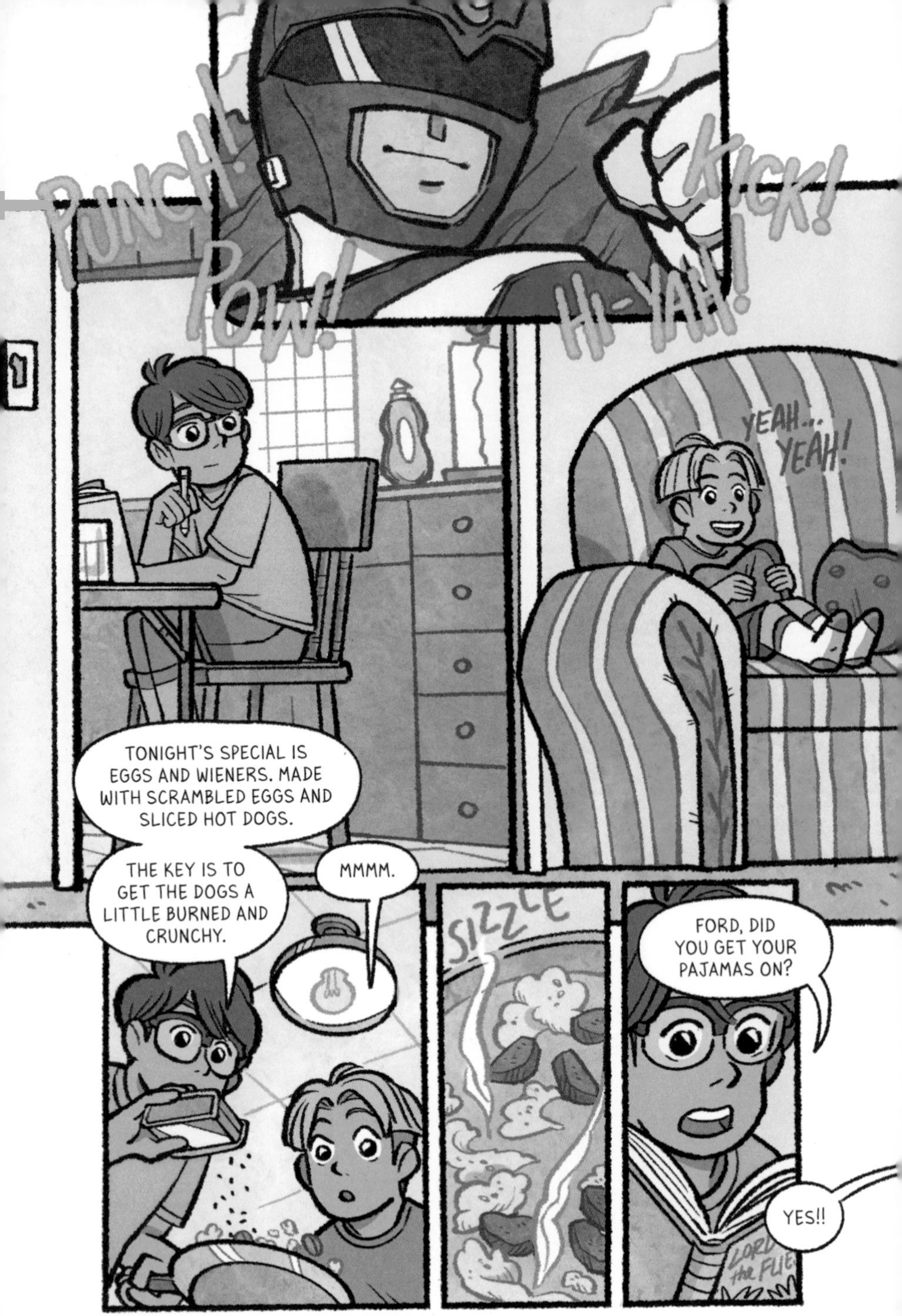
PUNCH!
POW!
KICK!
HI-YAH!
YEAH... YEAH!
TONIGHT'S SPECIAL IS EGGS AND WIENERS. MADE WITH SCRAMBLED EGGS AND SLICED HOT DOGS.
THE KEY IS TO GET THE DOGS A LITTLE BURNED AND CRUNCHY.
MMMM.
SIZZLE
FORD, DID YOU GET YOUR PAJAMAS ON?
YES!!

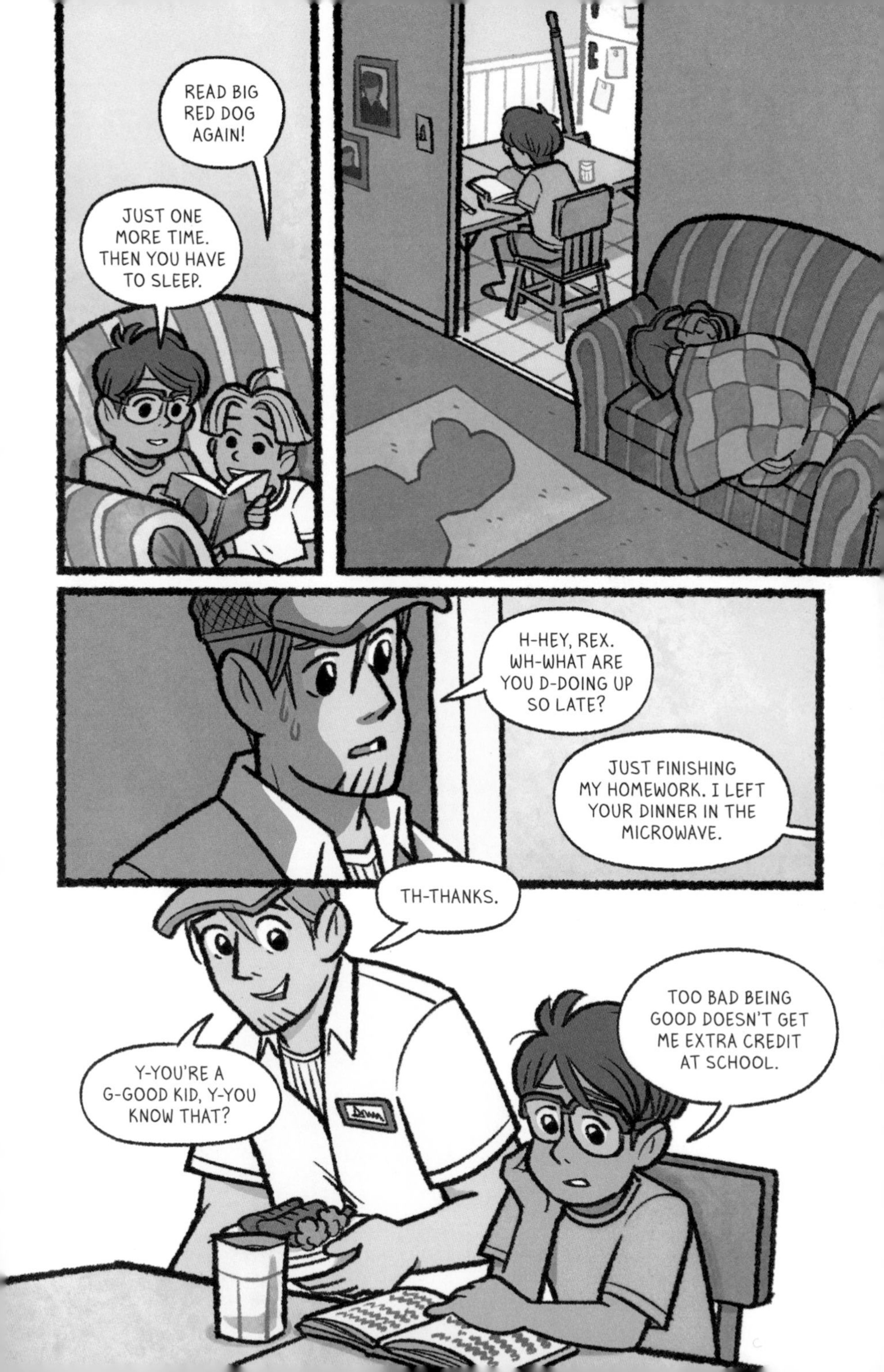
READ BIG RED DOG AGAIN!
JUST ONE MORE TIME. THEN YOU HAVE TO SLEEP.
H-HEY, REX. WH-WHAT ARE YOU D-DOING UP SO LATE?
JUST FINISHING MY HOMEWORK. I LEFT YOUR DINNER IN THE MICROWAVE.
TH-THANKS.
Y-YOU'RE A G-GOOD KID, Y-YOU KNOW THAT?
TOO BAD BEING GOOD DOESN'T GET ME EXTRA CREDIT AT SCHOOL.

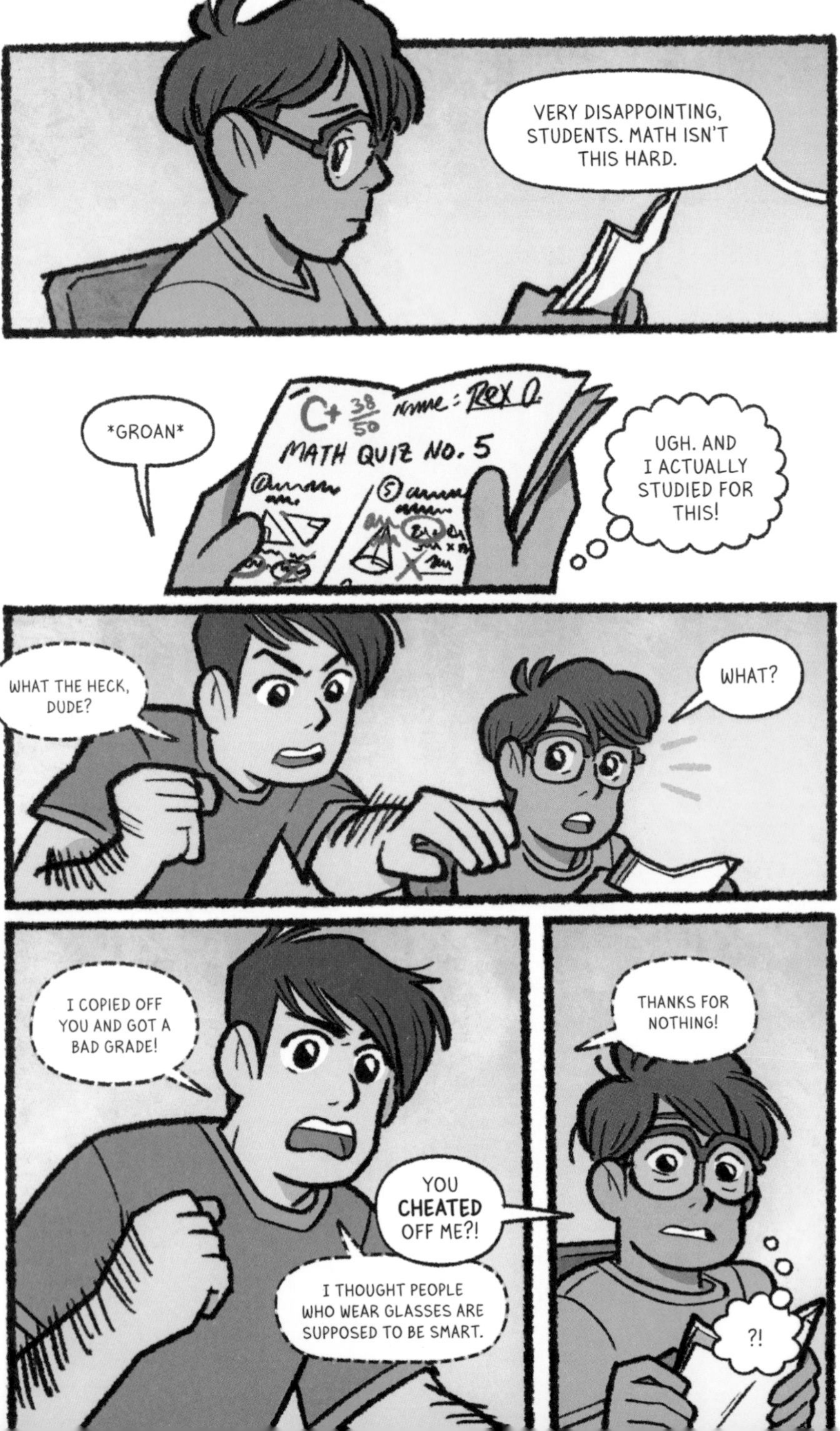
VERY DISAPPOINTING, STUDENTS. MATH ISN'T THIS HARD.
GROAN
C+ 38/50 name: Rex O.
MATH QUIZ NO. 5
UGH. AND I ACTUALLY STUDIED FOR THIS!
WHAT THE HECK, DUDE?
WHAT?
I COPIED OFF YOU AND GOT A BAD GRADE!
THANKS FOR NOTHING!
YOU **CHEATED** OFF ME?!
I THOUGHT PEOPLE WHO WEAR GLASSES ARE SUPPOSED TO BE SMART.
?!

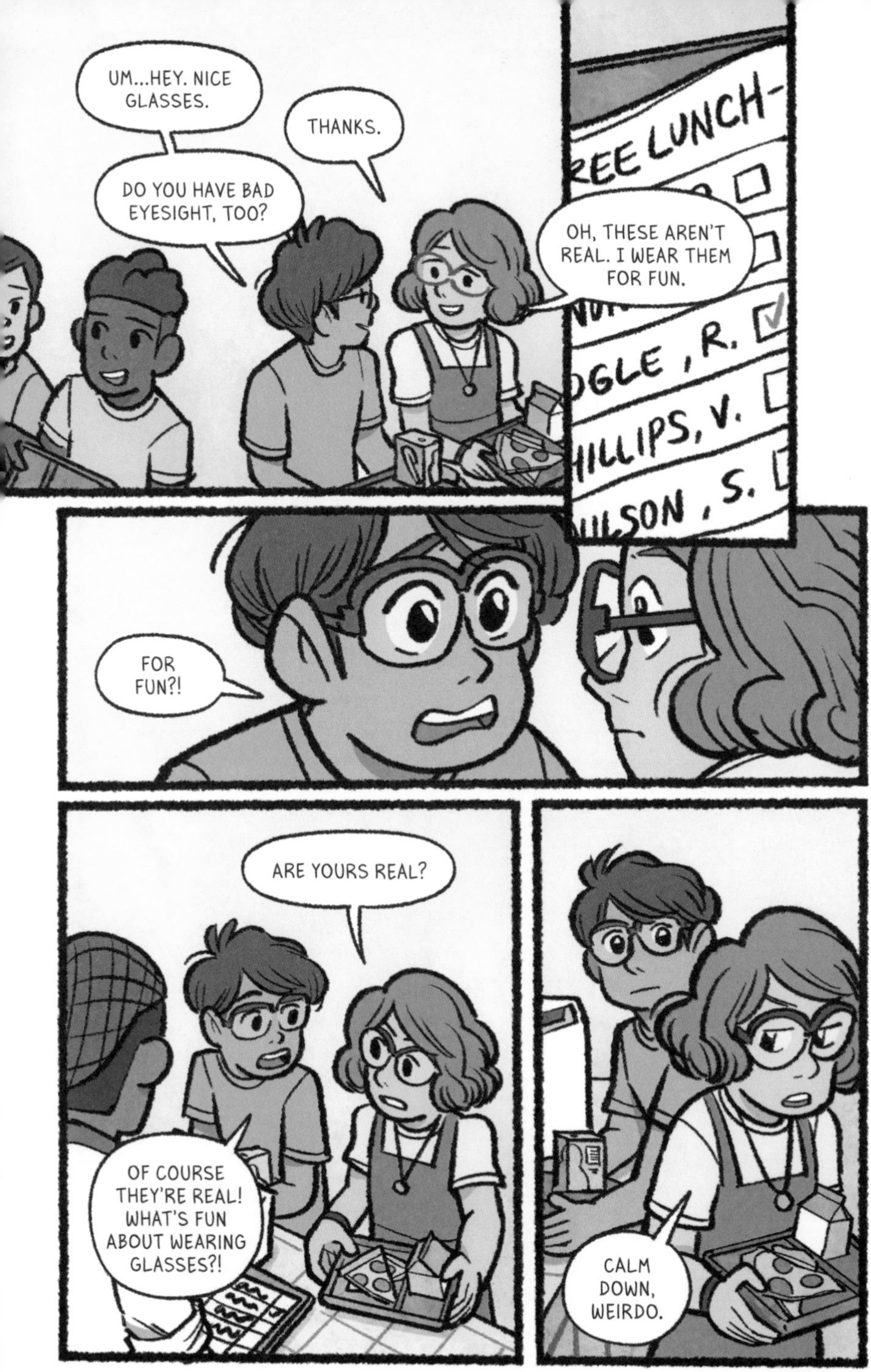
UM...HEY. NICE GLASSES.
THANKS.
DO YOU HAVE BAD EYESIGHT, TOO?
REE LUNCH-
OGLE, R.
HILLIPS, V.
ULSON, S.
OH, THESE AREN'T REAL. I WEAR THEM FOR FUN.
FOR FUN?!
ARE YOURS REAL?
OF COURSE THEY'RE REAL! WHAT'S FUN ABOUT WEARING GLASSES?!
CALM DOWN, WEIRDO.

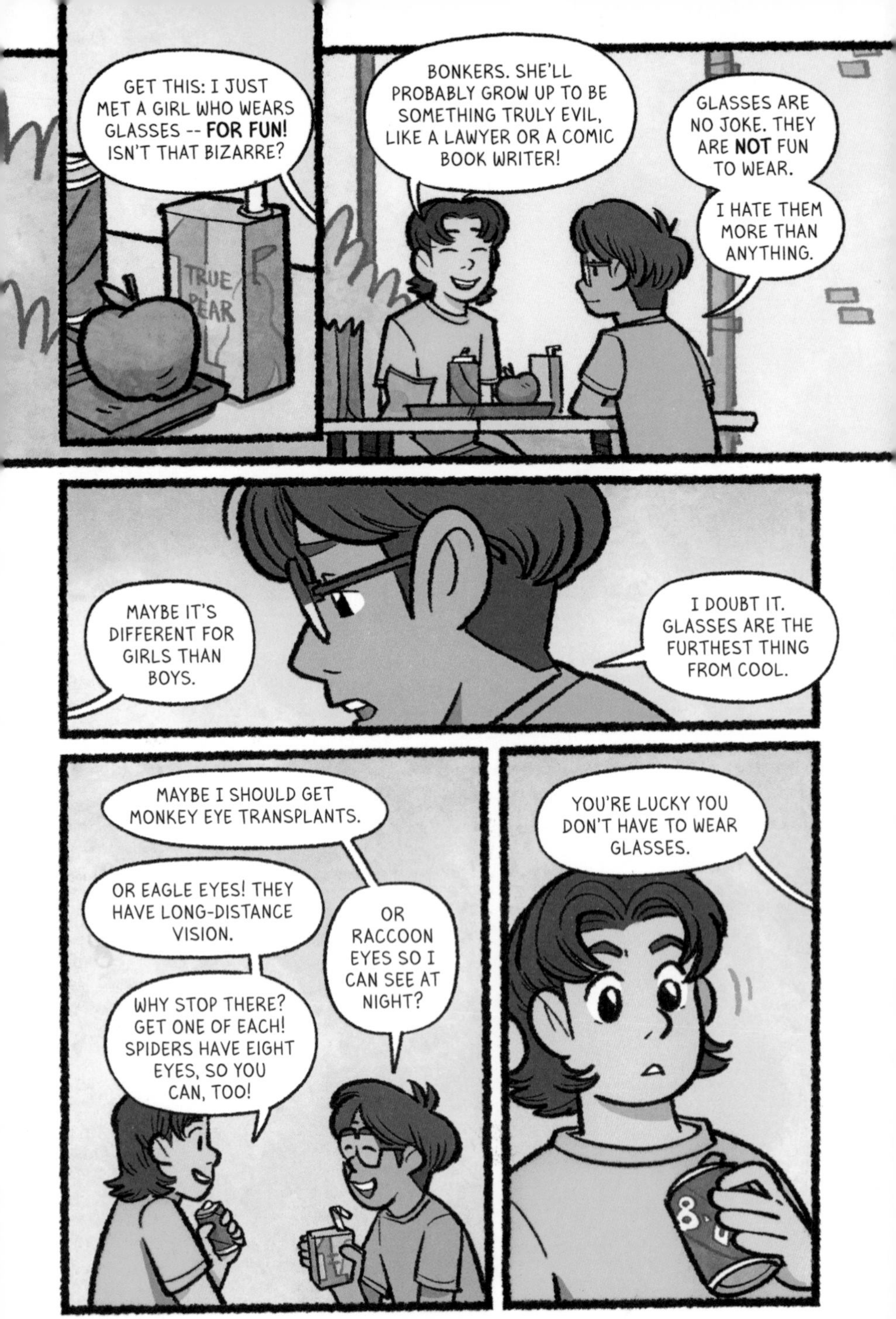
GET THIS: I JUST MET A GIRL WHO WEARS GLASSES -- **FOR FUN!** ISN'T THAT BIZARRE?
BONKERS. SHE'LL PROBABLY GROW UP TO BE SOMETHING TRULY EVIL, LIKE A LAWYER OR A COMIC BOOK WRITER!
GLASSES ARE NO JOKE. THEY ARE **NOT** FUN TO WEAR.
I HATE THEM MORE THAN ANYTHING.
TRUE PEAR
MAYBE IT'S DIFFERENT FOR GIRLS THAN BOYS.
I DOUBT IT. GLASSES ARE THE FURTHEST THING FROM COOL.
MAYBE I SHOULD GET MONKEY EYE TRANSPLANTS.
OR EAGLE EYES! THEY HAVE LONG-DISTANCE VISION.
OR RACCOON EYES SO I CAN SEE AT NIGHT?
WHY STOP THERE? GET ONE OF EACH! SPIDERS HAVE EIGHT EYES, SO YOU CAN, TOO!
YOU'RE LUCKY YOU DON'T HAVE TO WEAR GLASSES.

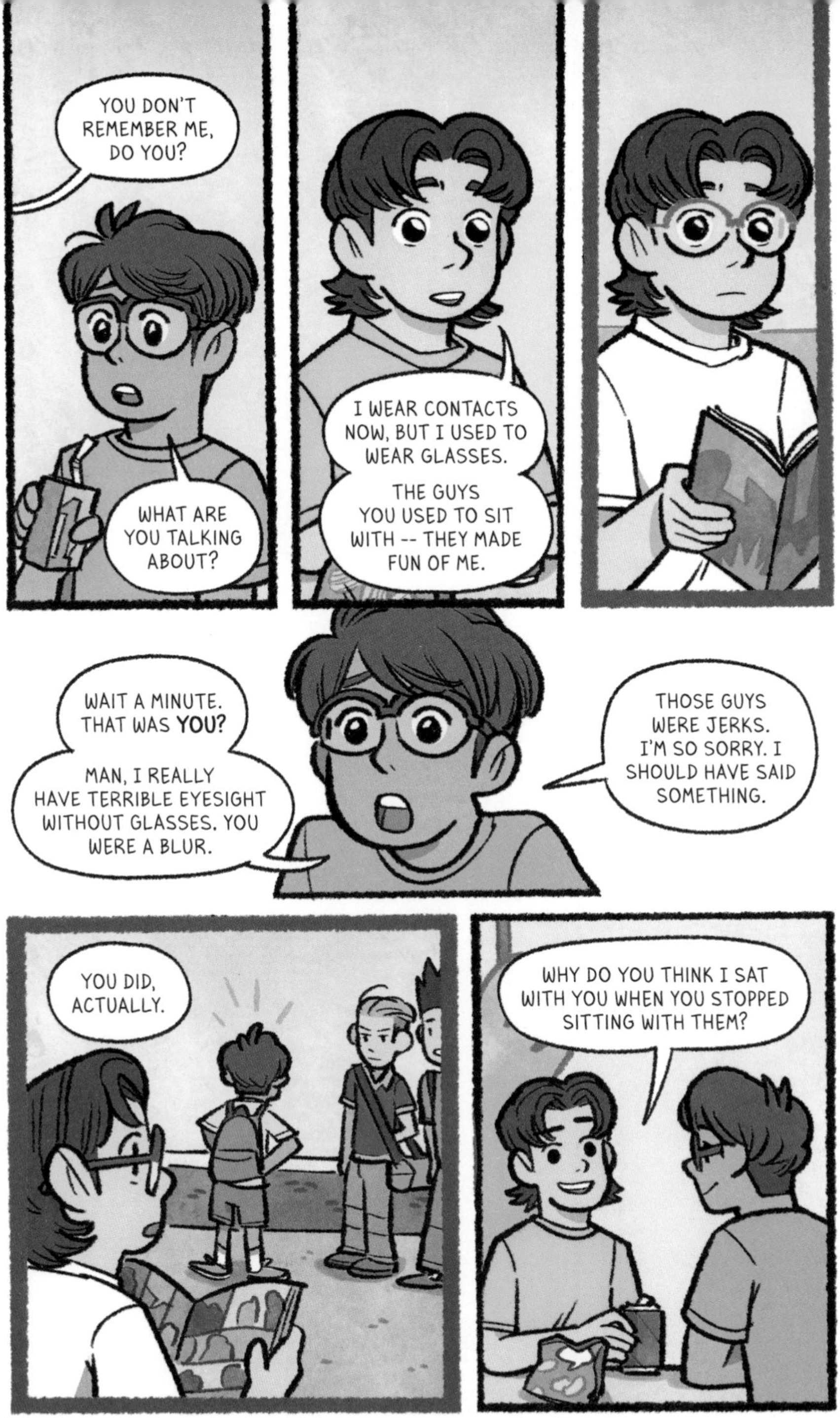
YOU DON'T REMEMBER ME, DO YOU?
WHAT ARE YOU TALKING ABOUT?
I WEAR CONTACTS NOW, BUT I USED TO WEAR GLASSES.
THE GUYS YOU USED TO SIT WITH -- THEY MADE FUN OF ME.
WAIT A MINUTE. THAT WAS **YOU?**
MAN, I REALLY HAVE TERRIBLE EYESIGHT WITHOUT GLASSES. YOU WERE A BLUR.
THOSE GUYS WERE JERKS. I'M SO SORRY. I SHOULD HAVE SAID SOMETHING.
YOU DID, ACTUALLY.
WHY DO YOU THINK I SAT WITH YOU WHEN YOU STOPPED SITTING WITH THEM?

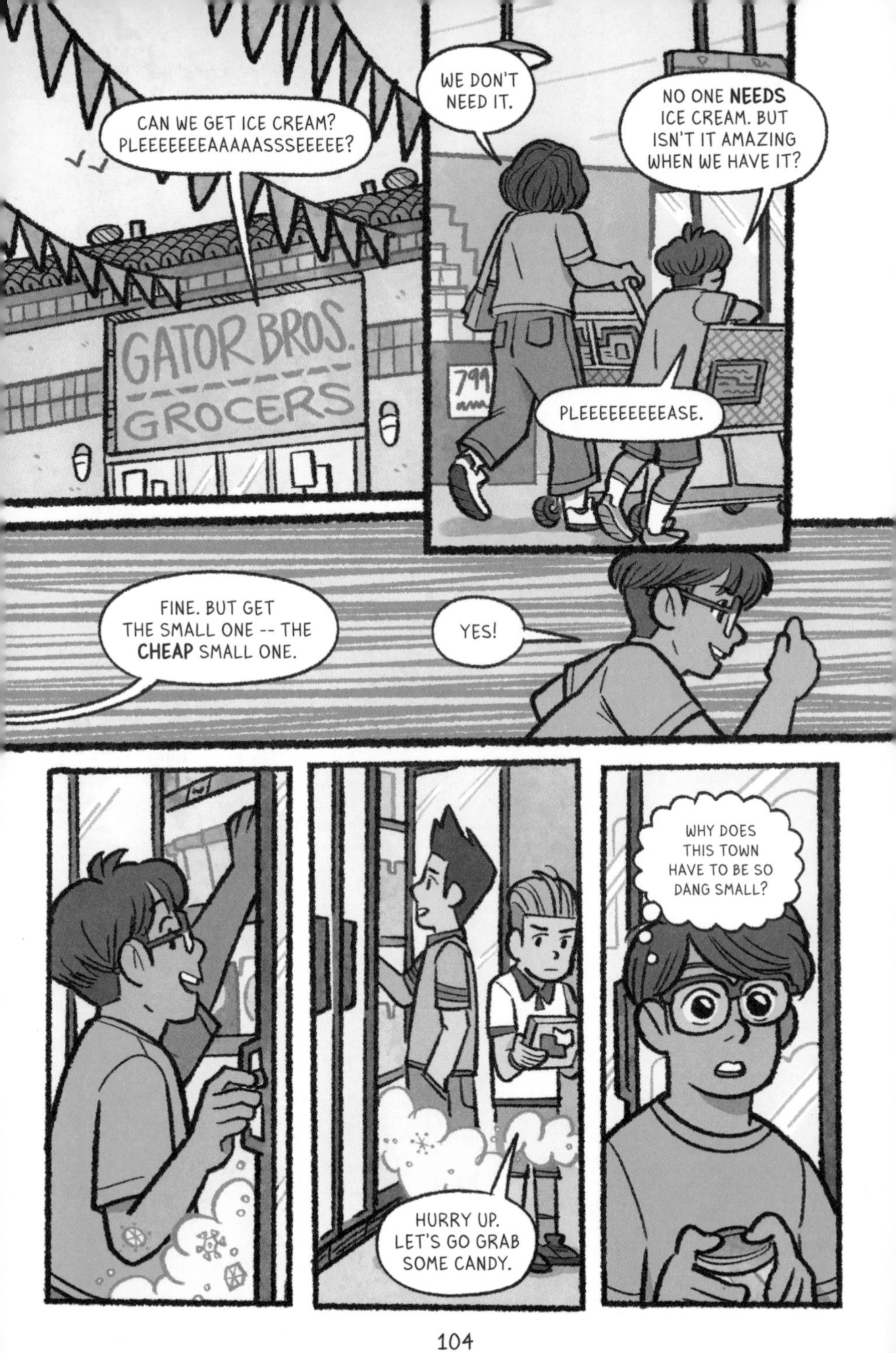
CAN WE GET ICE CREAM? PLEEEEEEEAAAAASSSEEEEE?
GATOR BROS. GROCERS
WE DON'T NEED IT.
NO ONE **NEEDS** ICE CREAM. BUT ISN'T IT AMAZING WHEN WE HAVE IT?
PLEEEEEEEEEASE.
FINE. BUT GET THE SMALL ONE -- THE **CHEAP** SMALL ONE.
YES!
WHY DOES THIS TOWN HAVE TO BE SO DANG SMALL?
HURRY UP. LET'S GO GRAB SOME CANDY.

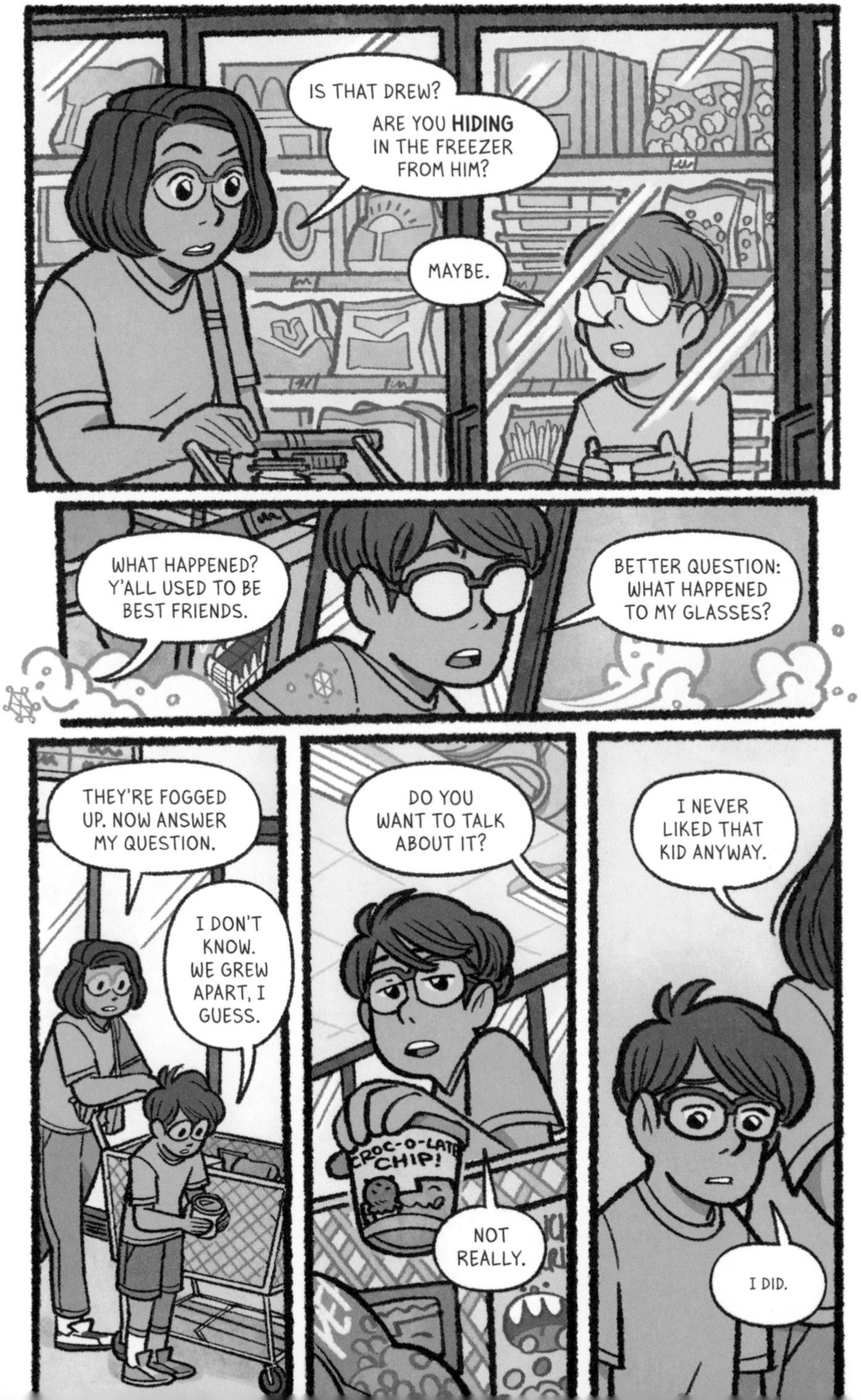
IS THAT DREW?
ARE YOU **HIDING** IN THE FREEZER FROM HIM?
MAYBE.
WHAT HAPPENED? Y'ALL USED TO BE BEST FRIENDS.
BETTER QUESTION: WHAT HAPPENED TO MY GLASSES?
THEY'RE FOGGED UP. NOW ANSWER MY QUESTION.
I DON'T KNOW. WE GREW APART, I GUESS.
DO YOU WANT TO TALK ABOUT IT?
CROC-O-LATE CHIP!
NOT REALLY.
I NEVER LIKED THAT KID ANYWAY.
I DID.

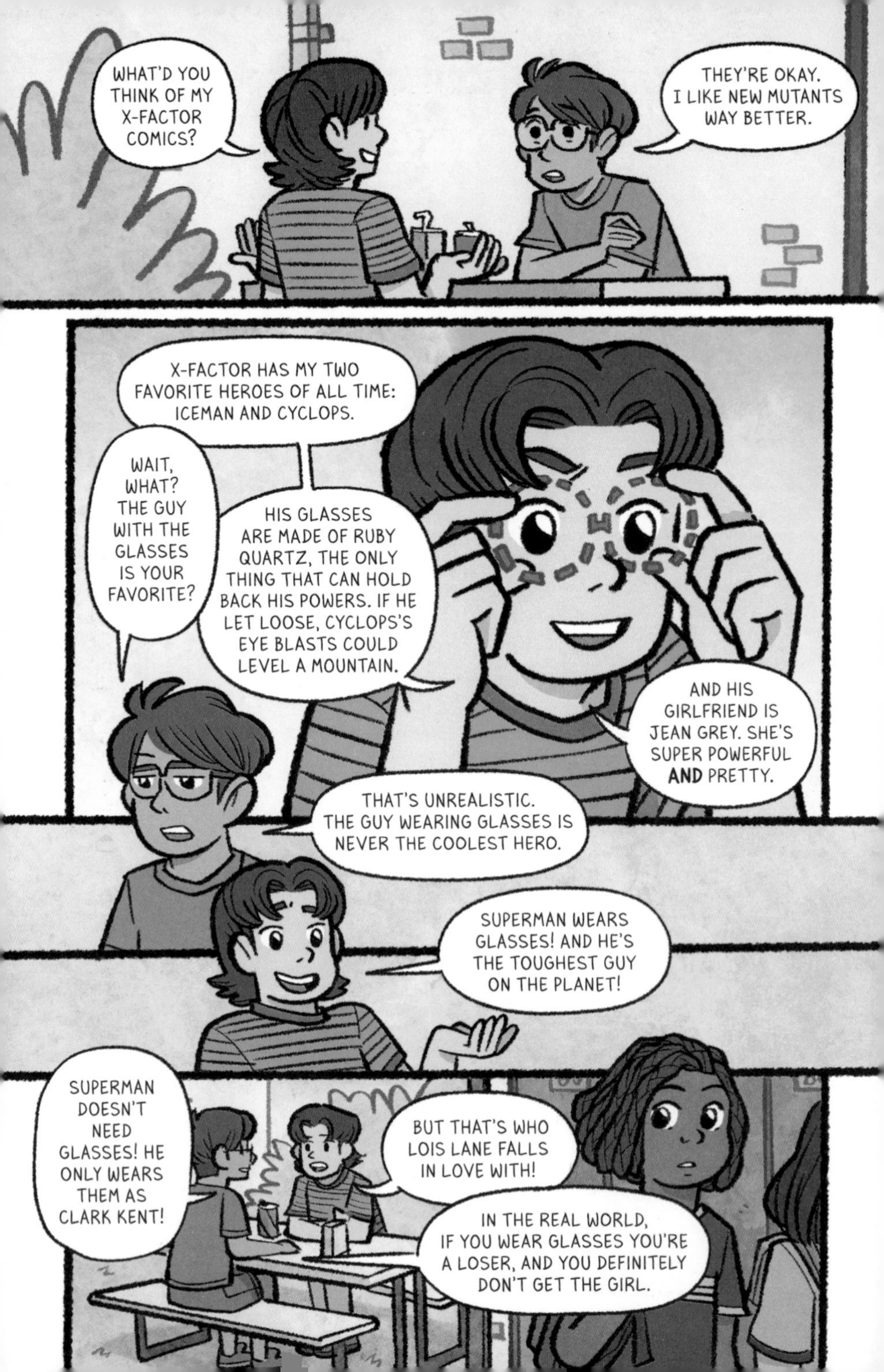
WHAT'D YOU THINK OF MY X-FACTOR COMICS?
THEY'RE OKAY. I LIKE NEW MUTANTS WAY BETTER.
X-FACTOR HAS MY TWO FAVORITE HEROES OF ALL TIME: ICEMAN AND CYCLOPS.
WAIT, WHAT? THE GUY WITH THE GLASSES IS YOUR FAVORITE?
HIS GLASSES ARE MADE OF RUBY QUARTZ, THE ONLY THING THAT CAN HOLD BACK HIS POWERS. IF HE LET LOOSE, CYCLOPS'S EYE BLASTS COULD LEVEL A MOUNTAIN.
AND HIS GIRLFRIEND IS JEAN GREY. SHE'S SUPER POWERFUL **AND** PRETTY.
THAT'S UNREALISTIC. THE GUY WEARING GLASSES IS NEVER THE COOLEST HERO.
SUPERMAN WEARS GLASSES! AND HE'S THE TOUGHEST GUY ON THE PLANET!
SUPERMAN DOESN'T NEED GLASSES! HE ONLY WEARS THEM AS CLARK KENT!
BUT THAT'S WHO LOIS LANE FALLS IN LOVE WITH!
IN THE REAL WORLD, IF YOU WEAR GLASSES YOU'RE A LOSER, AND YOU DEFINITELY DON'T GET THE GIRL.

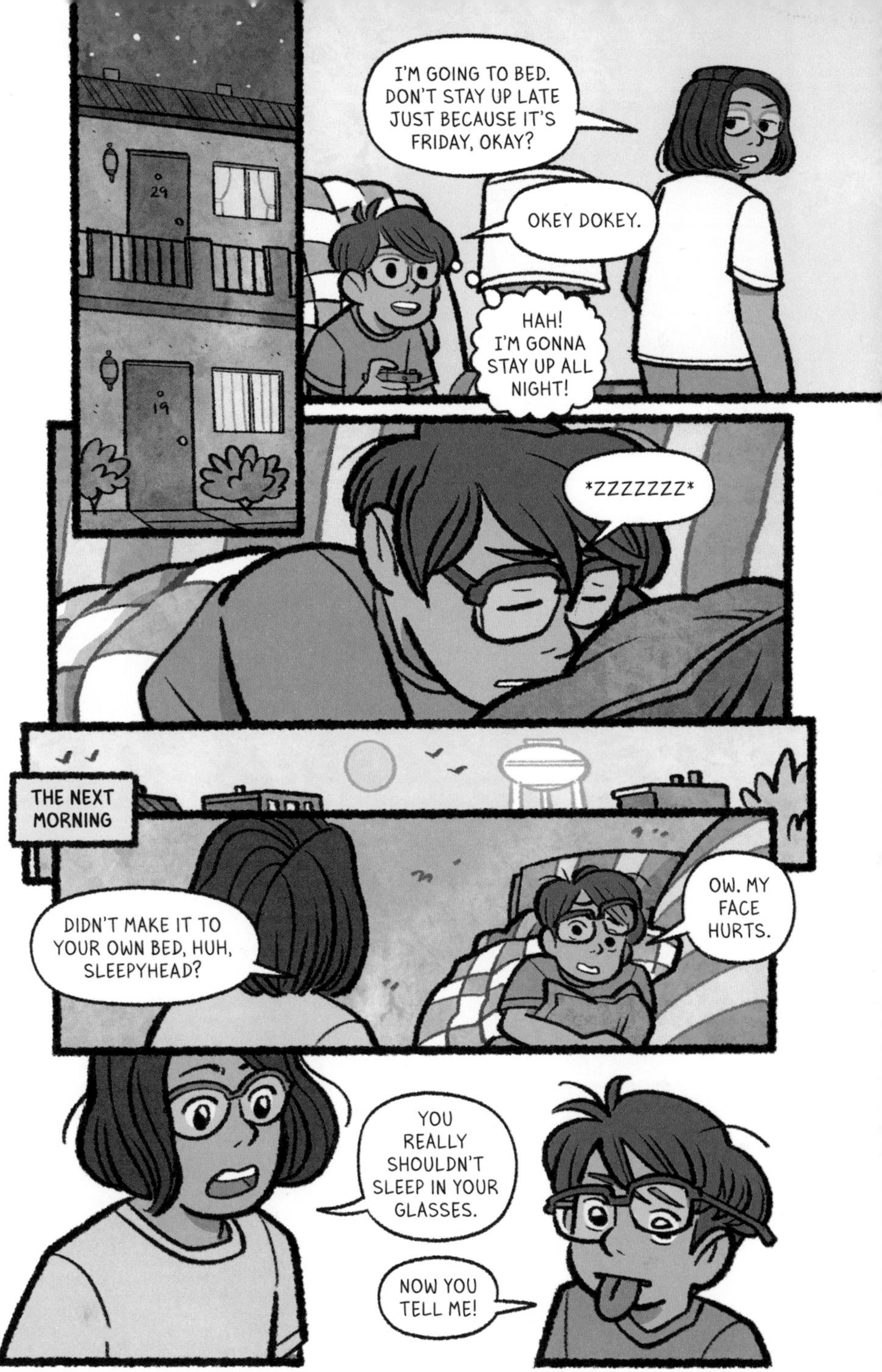
I'M GOING TO BED. DON'T STAY UP LATE JUST BECAUSE IT'S FRIDAY, OKAY?
OKEY DOKEY.
HAH! I'M GONNA STAY UP ALL NIGHT!
ZZZZZZZ
THE NEXT MORNING
DIDN'T MAKE IT TO YOUR OWN BED, HUH, SLEEPYHEAD?
OW. MY FACE HURTS.
YOU REALLY SHOULDN'T SLEEP IN YOUR GLASSES.
NOW YOU TELL ME!

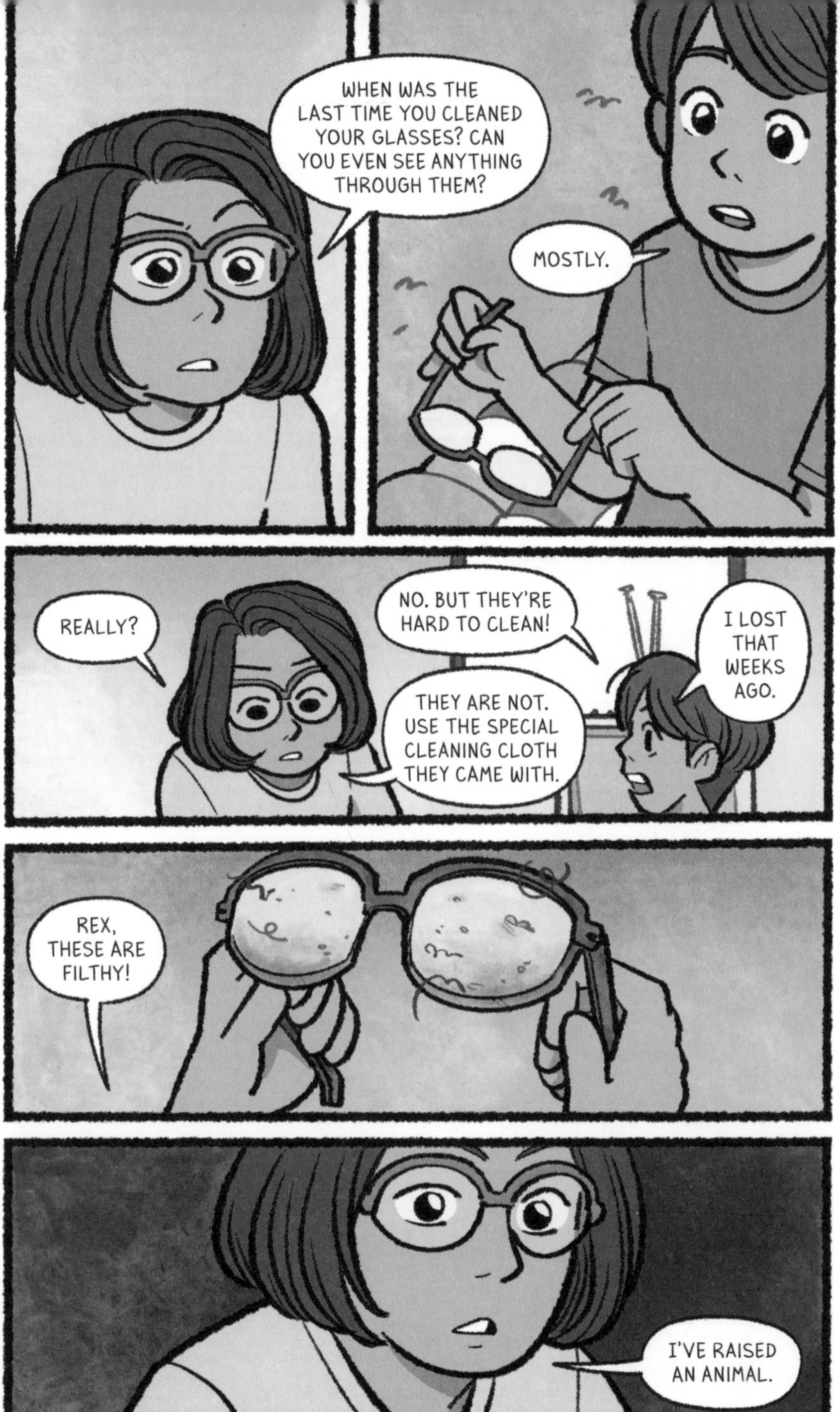
WHEN WAS THE LAST TIME YOU CLEANED YOUR GLASSES? CAN YOU EVEN SEE ANYTHING THROUGH THEM?
MOSTLY.
REALLY?
NO. BUT THEY'RE HARD TO CLEAN!
THEY ARE NOT. USE THE SPECIAL CLEANING CLOTH THEY CAME WITH.
I LOST THAT WEEKS AGO.
REX, THESE ARE FILTHY!
I'VE RAISED AN ANIMAL.

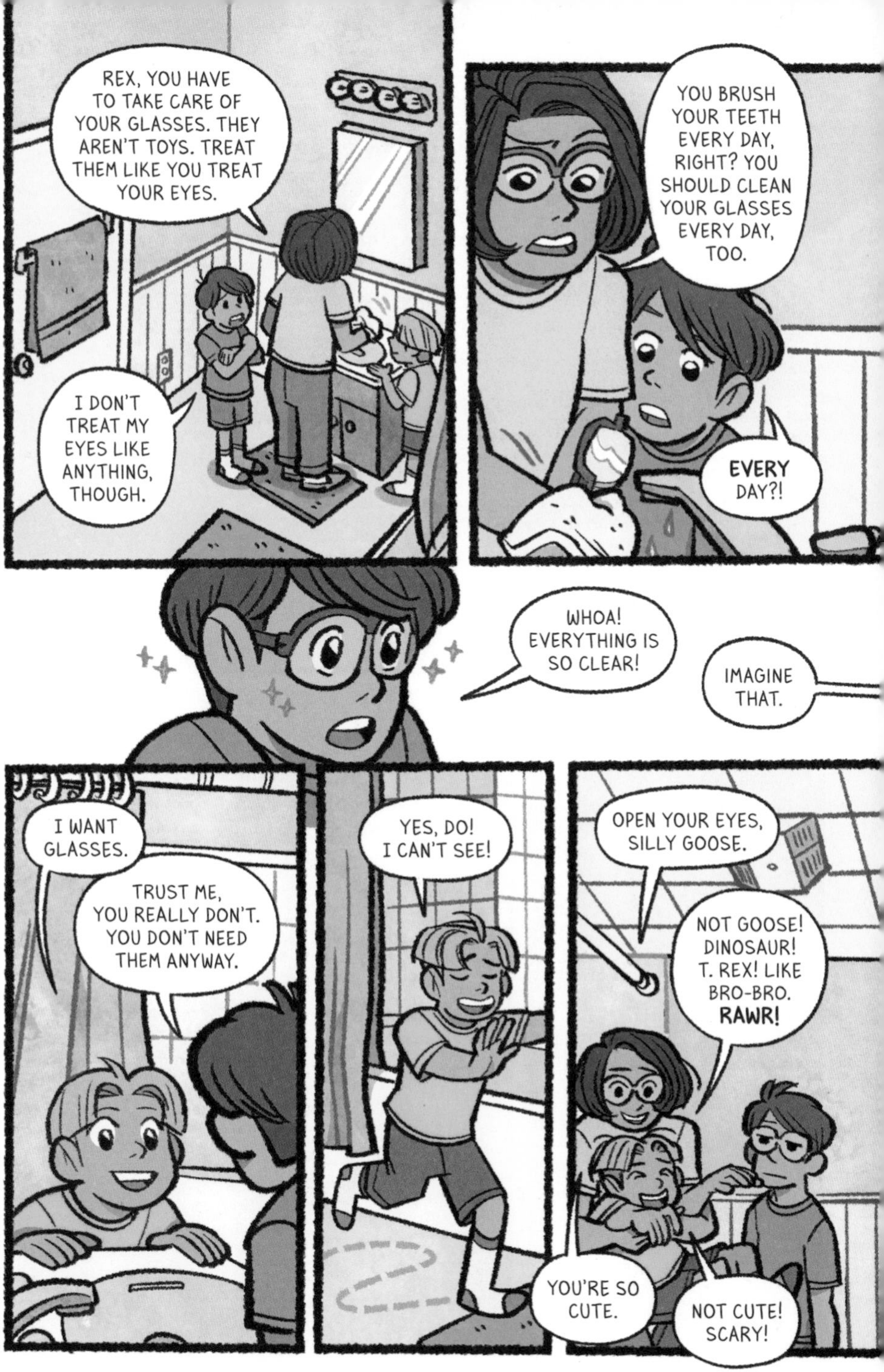
REX, YOU HAVE TO TAKE CARE OF YOUR GLASSES. THEY AREN'T TOYS. TREAT THEM LIKE YOU TREAT YOUR EYES.
I DON'T TREAT MY EYES LIKE ANYTHING, THOUGH.
YOU BRUSH YOUR TEETH EVERY DAY, RIGHT? YOU SHOULD CLEAN YOUR GLASSES EVERY DAY, TOO.
EVERY DAY?!
WHOA! EVERYTHING IS SO CLEAR!
IMAGINE THAT.
I WANT GLASSES.
TRUST ME, YOU REALLY DON'T. YOU DON'T NEED THEM ANYWAY.
YES, DO! I CAN'T SEE!
OPEN YOUR EYES, SILLY GOOSE.
NOT GOOSE! DINOSAUR! T. REX! LIKE BRO-BRO. **RAWR!**
YOU'RE SO CUTE.
NOT CUTE! SCARY!

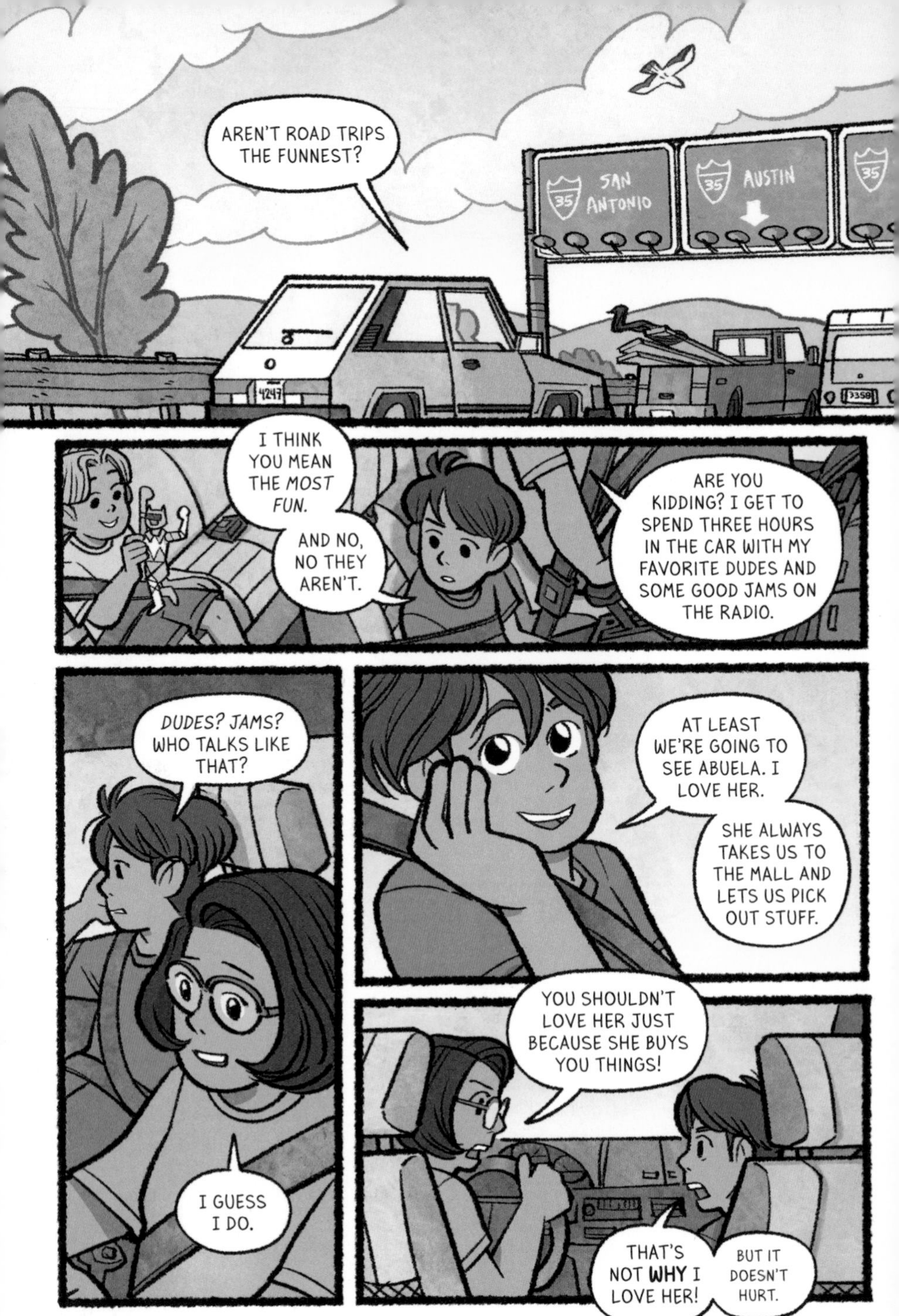
ARE'T ROAD TRIPS THE FUNNEST?
SAN ANTONIO
AUSTIN
35
I THINK YOU MEAN THE *MOST FUN.*
AND NO, NO THEY AREN'T.
ARE YOU KIDDING? I GET TO SPEND THREE HOURS IN THE CAR WITH MY FAVORITE DUDES AND SOME GOOD JAMS ON THE RADIO.
DUDES? JAMS? WHO TALKS LIKE THAT?
AT LEAST WE'RE GOING TO SEE ABUELA. I LOVE HER.
SHE ALWAYS TAKES US TO THE MALL AND LETS US PICK OUT STUFF.
I GUESS I DO.
YOU SHOULDN'T LOVE HER JUST BECAUSE SHE BUYS YOU THINGS!
THAT'S NOT **WHY** I LOVE HER!
BUT IT DOESN'T HURT.

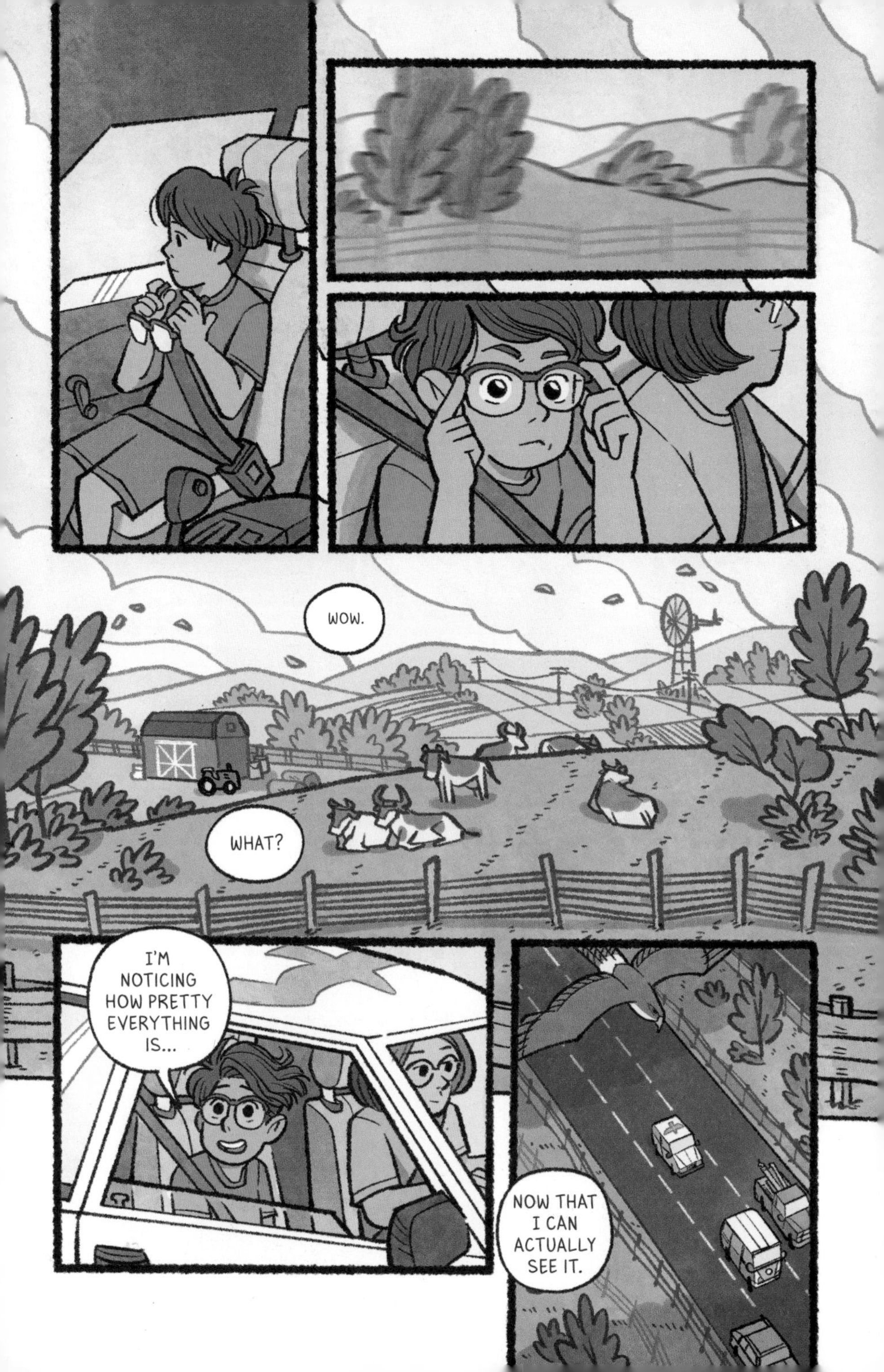
WOW.
WHAT?
I'M NOTICING HOW PRETTY EVERYTHING IS...
NOW THAT I CAN ACTUALLY SEE IT.

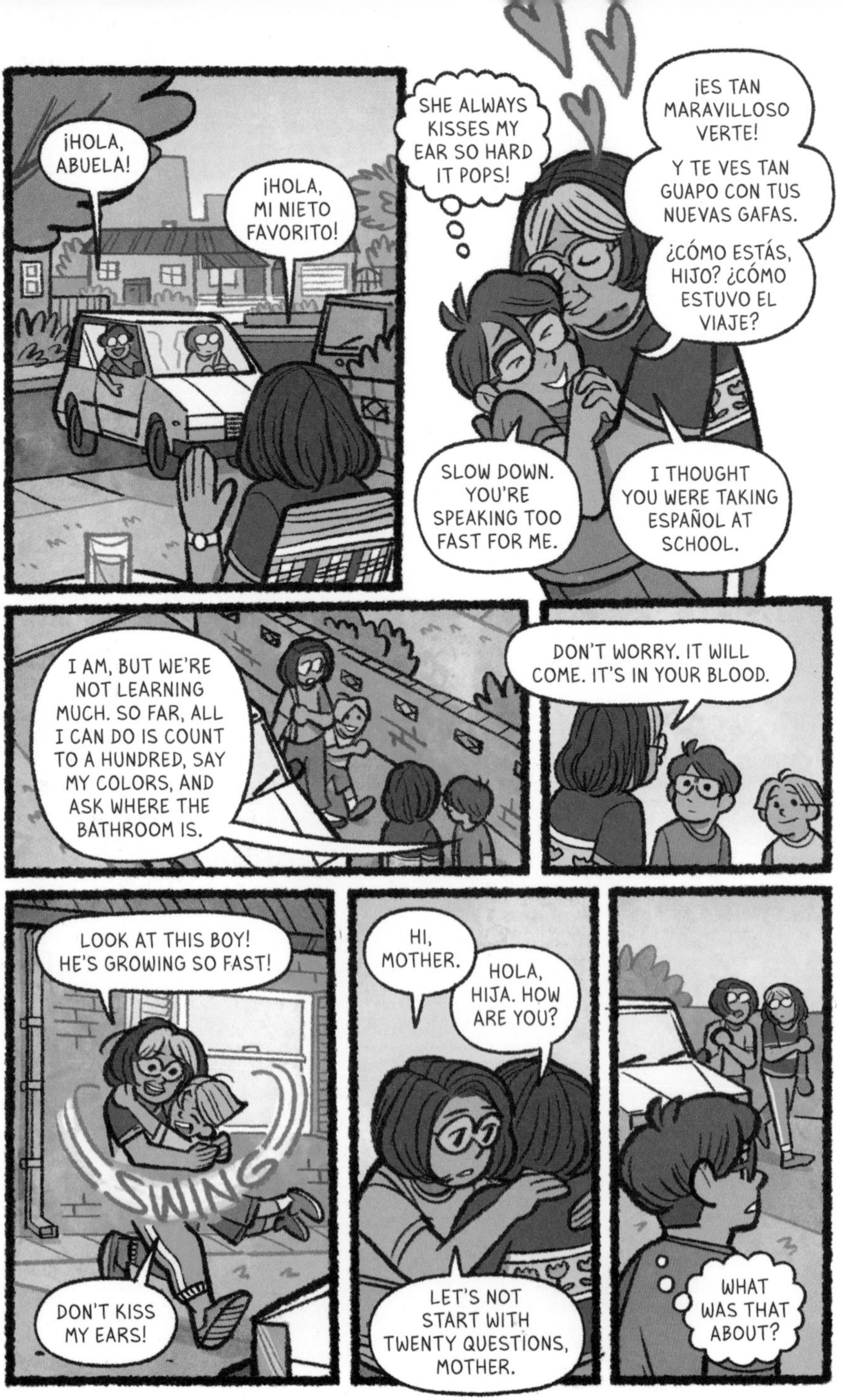

¡HOLA, ABUELA!
¡HOLA, MI NIETO FAVORITO!
SHE ALWAYS KISSES MY EAR SO HARD IT POPS!
¡ES TAN MARAVILLOSO VERTE!
Y TE VES TAN GUAPO CON TUS NUEVAS GAFAS.
¿CÓMO ESTÁS, HIJO? ¿CÓMO ESTUVO EL VIAJE?
SLOW DOWN. YOU'RE SPEAKING TOO FAST FOR ME.
I THOUGHT YOU WERE TAKING ESPAÑOL AT SCHOOL.
I AM, BUT WE'RE NOT LEARNING MUCH. SO FAR, ALL I CAN DO IS COUNT TO A HUNDRED, SAY MY COLORS, AND ASK WHERE THE BATHROOM IS.
DON'T WORRY. IT WILL COME. IT'S IN YOUR BLOOD.
LOOK AT THIS BOY! HE'S GROWING SO FAST!
SWING
DON'T KISS MY EARS!
HI, MOTHER.
HOLA, HIJA. HOW ARE YOU?
LET'S NOT START WITH TWENTY QUESTIONS, MOTHER.
WHAT WAS THAT ABOUT?

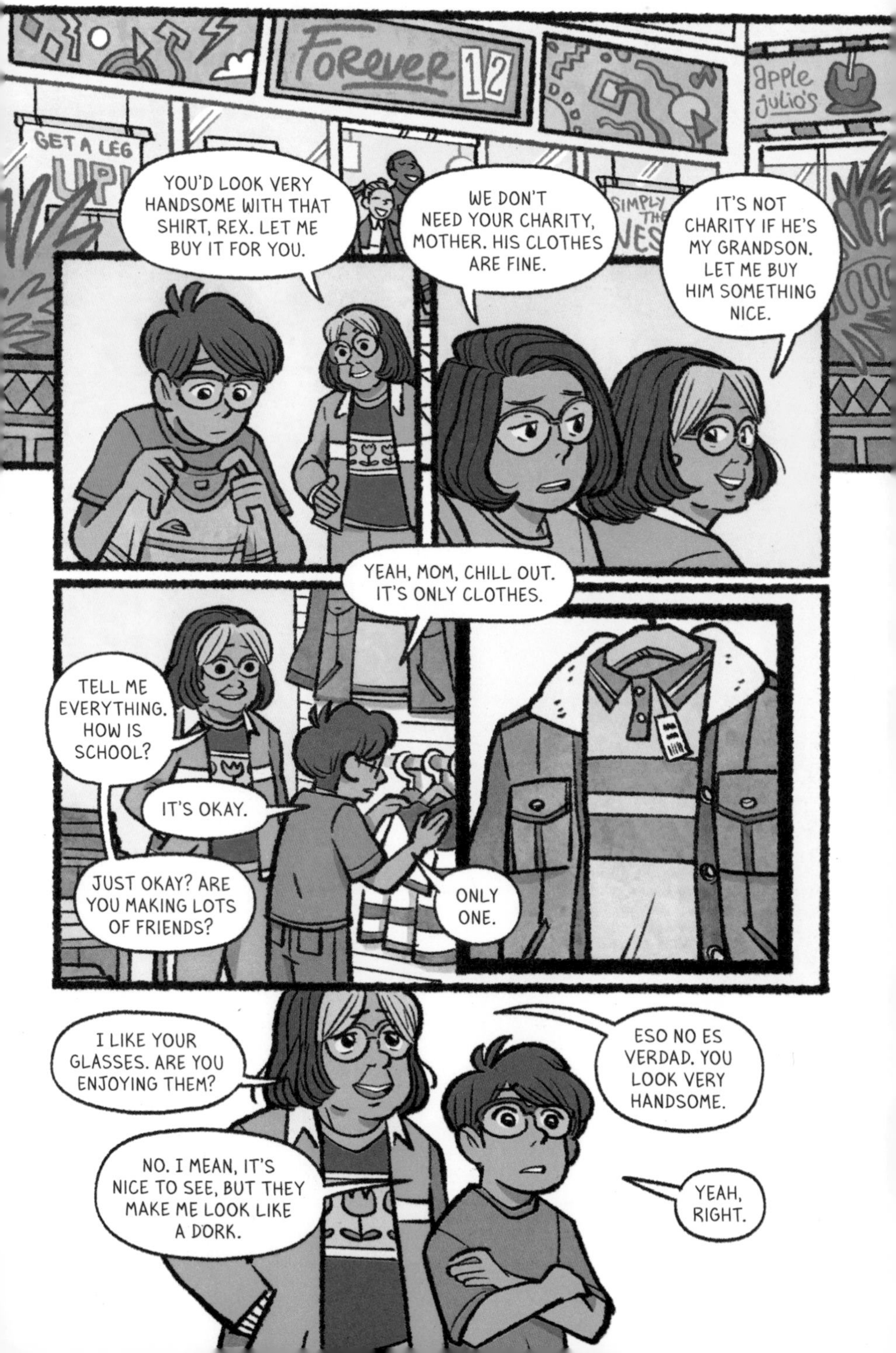
FOREVER 12
GET A LEG UP!
SIMPLY THE VEST
apple julio's
YOU'D LOOK VERY HANDSOME WITH THAT SHIRT, REX. LET ME BUY IT FOR YOU.
WE DON'T NEED YOUR CHARITY, MOTHER. HIS CLOTHES ARE FINE.
IT'S NOT CHARITY IF HE'S MY GRANDSON. LET ME BUY HIM SOMETHING NICE.
YEAH, MOM, CHILL OUT. IT'S ONLY CLOTHES.
TELL ME EVERYTHING. HOW IS SCHOOL?
IT'S OKAY.
JUST OKAY? ARE YOU MAKING LOTS OF FRIENDS?
ONLY ONE.
I LIKE YOUR GLASSES. ARE YOU ENJOYING THEM?
NO. I MEAN, IT'S NICE TO SEE, BUT THEY MAKE ME LOOK LIKE A DORK.
ESO NO ES VERDAD. YOU LOOK VERY HANDSOME.
YEAH, RIGHT.

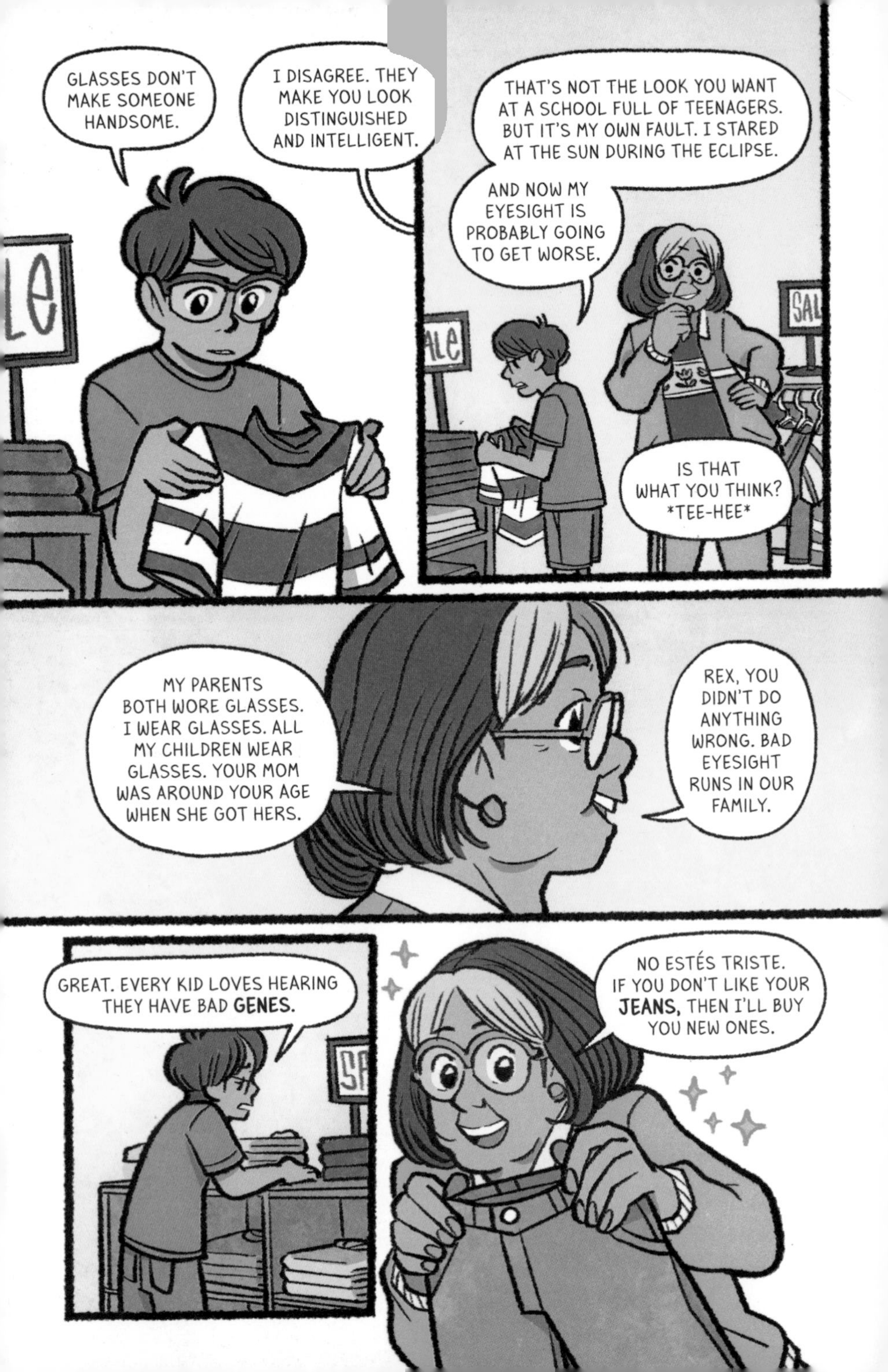
GLASSES DON'T MAKE SOMEONE HANDSOME.
I DISAGREE. THEY MAKE YOU LOOK DISTINGUISHED AND INTELLIGENT.
THAT'S NOT THE LOOK YOU WANT AT A SCHOOL FULL OF TEENAGERS. BUT IT'S MY OWN FAULT. I STARED AT THE SUN DURING THE ECLIPSE.
AND NOW MY EYESIGHT IS PROBABLY GOING TO GET WORSE.
IS THAT WHAT YOU THINK? *TEE-HEE*
REX, YOU DIDN'T DO ANYTHING WRONG. BAD EYESIGHT RUNS IN OUR FAMILY.
MY PARENTS BOTH WORE GLASSES. I WEAR GLASSES. ALL MY CHILDREN WEAR GLASSES. YOUR MOM WAS AROUND YOUR AGE WHEN SHE GOT HERS.
GREAT. EVERY KID LOVES HEARING THEY HAVE BAD **GENES.**
NO ESTÉS TRISTE. IF YOU DON'T LIKE YOUR **JEANS,** THEN I'LL BUY YOU NEW ONES.

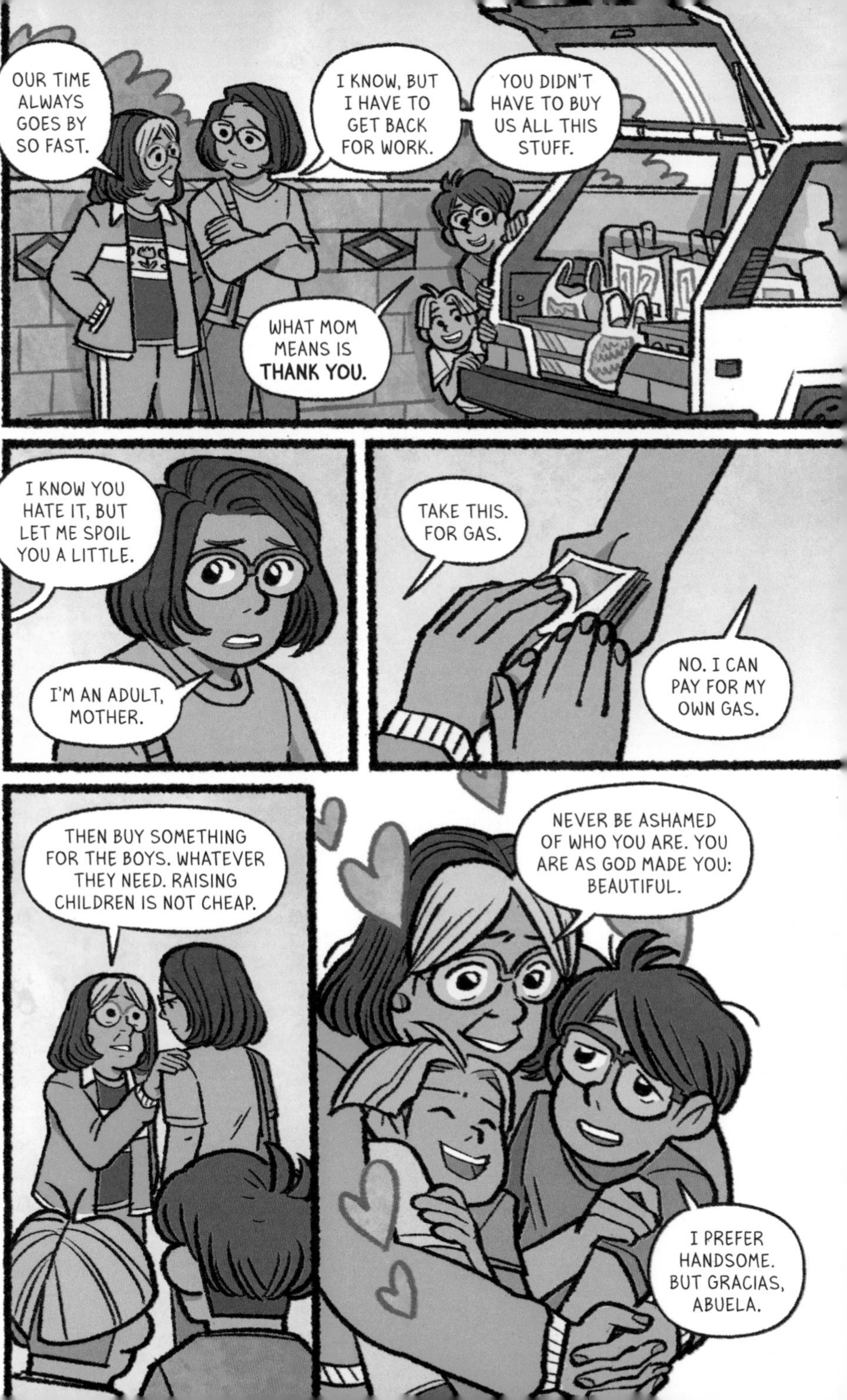
OUR TIME ALWAYS GOES BY SO FAST.
I KNOW, BUT I HAVE TO GET BACK FOR WORK.
YOU DIDN'T HAVE TO BUY US ALL THIS STUFF.
WHAT MOM MEANS IS **THANK YOU.**
I KNOW YOU HATE IT, BUT LET ME SPOIL YOU A LITTLE.
I'M AN ADULT, MOTHER.
TAKE THIS. FOR GAS.
NO. I CAN PAY FOR MY OWN GAS.
THEN BUY SOMETHING FOR THE BOYS. WHATEVER THEY NEED. RAISING CHILDREN IS NOT CHEAP.
NEVER BE ASHAMED OF WHO YOU ARE. YOU ARE AS GOD MADE YOU: BEAUTIFUL.
I PREFER HANDSOME. BUT GRACIAS, ABUELA.

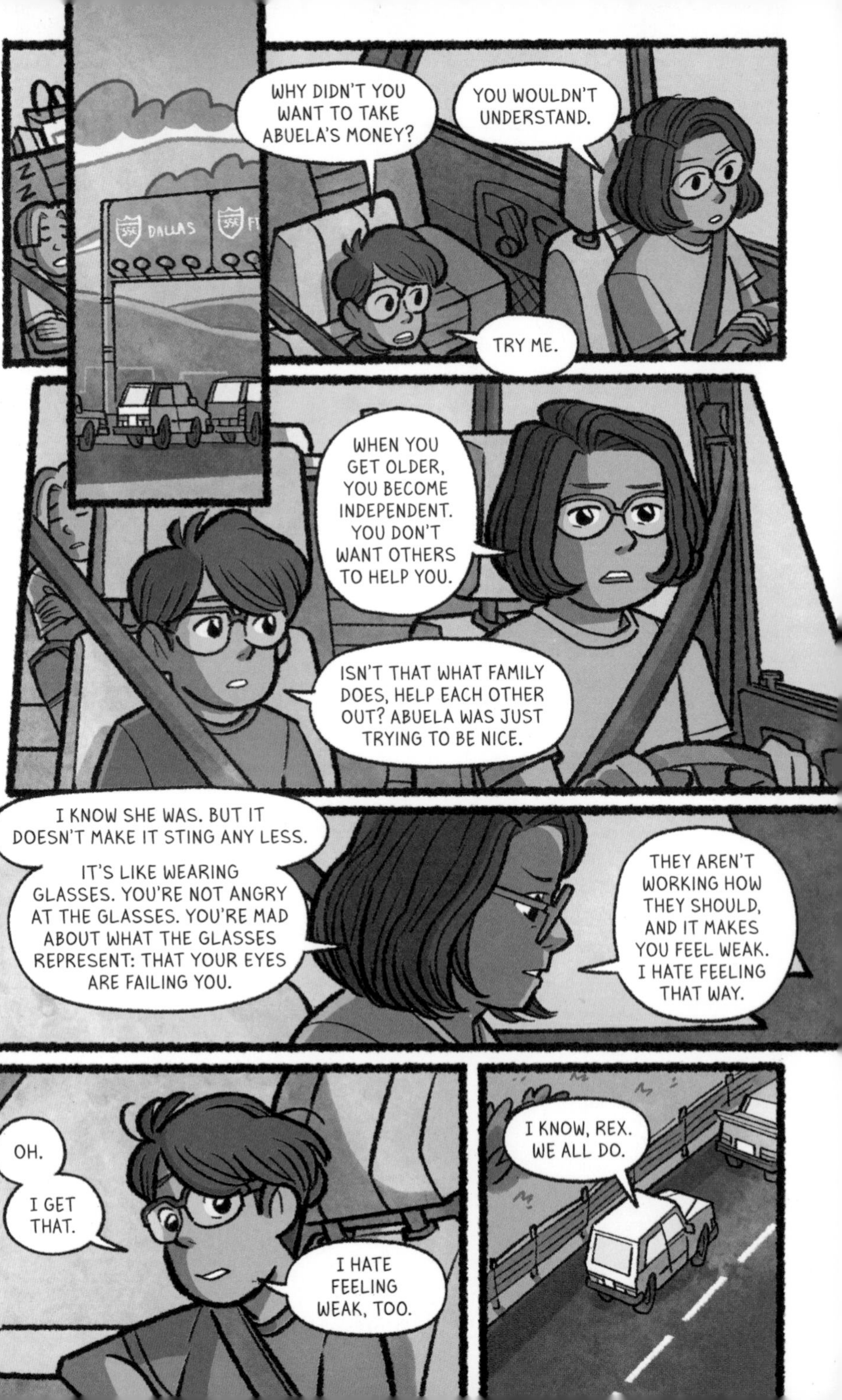

DALLAS
WHY DIDN'T YOU WANT TO TAKE ABUELA'S MONEY?
YOU WOULDN'T UNDERSTAND.
TRY ME.
WHEN YOU GET OLDER, YOU BECOME INDEPENDENT. YOU DON'T WANT OTHERS TO HELP YOU.
ISN'T THAT WHAT FAMILY DOES, HELP EACH OTHER OUT? ABUELA WAS JUST TRYING TO BE NICE.
I KNOW SHE WAS. BUT IT DOESN'T MAKE IT STING ANY LESS.
IT'S LIKE WEARING GLASSES. YOU'RE NOT ANGRY AT THE GLASSES. YOU'RE MAD ABOUT WHAT THE GLASSES REPRESENT: THAT YOUR EYES ARE FAILING YOU.
THEY AREN'T WORKING HOW THEY SHOULD, AND IT MAKES YOU FEEL WEAK. I HATE FEELING THAT WAY.
OH.
I GET THAT.
I HATE FEELING WEAK, TOO.
I KNOW, REX. WE ALL DO.

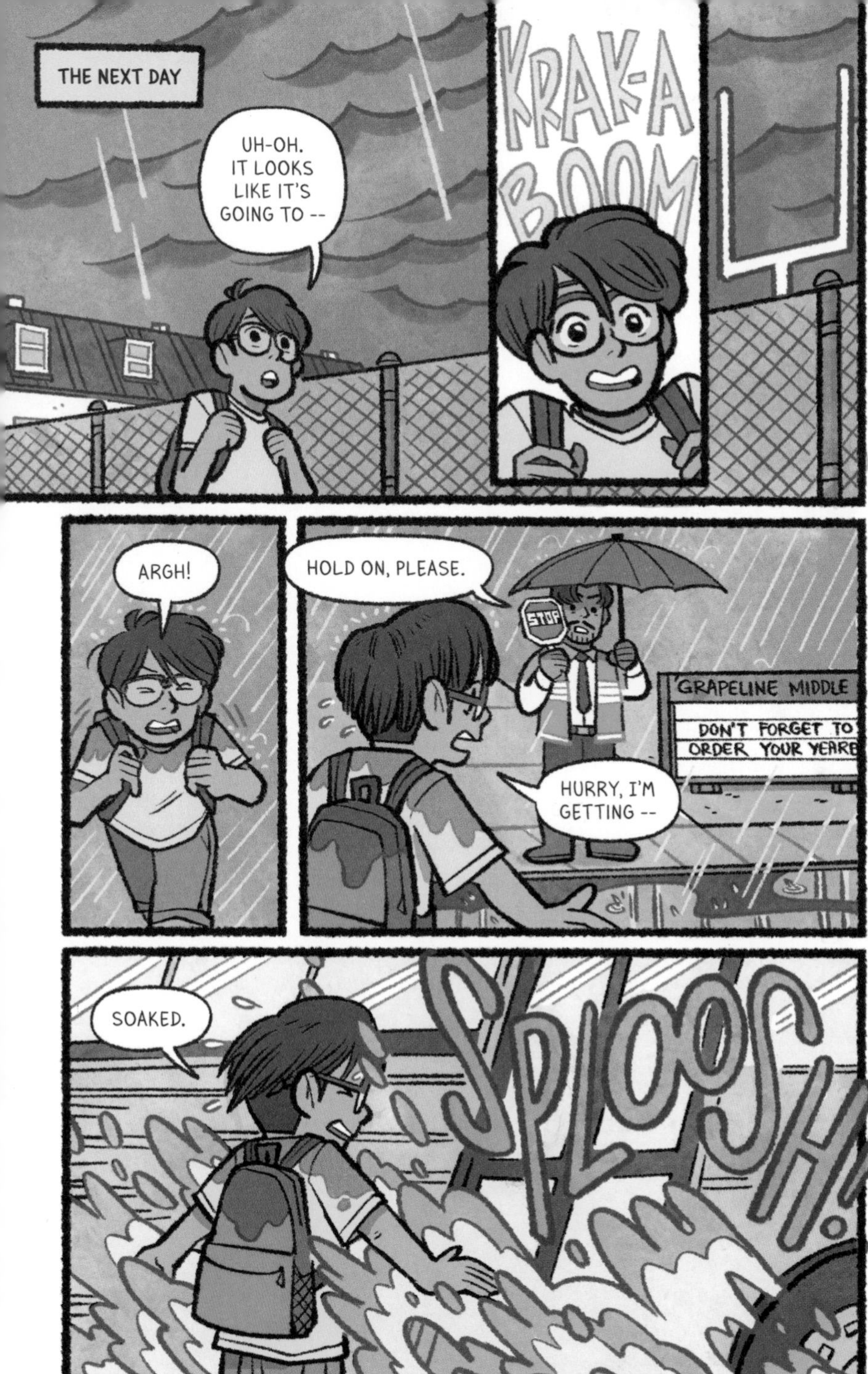
THE NEXT DAY
UH-OH. IT LOOKS LIKE IT'S GOING TO --
KRAK-A BOOM
ARGH!
HOLD ON, PLEASE.
STOP
GRAPELINE MIDDLE
DON'T FORGET TO
ORDER YOUR YEAR
HURRY, I'M GETTING --
SOAKED.
SPLOOSH!!

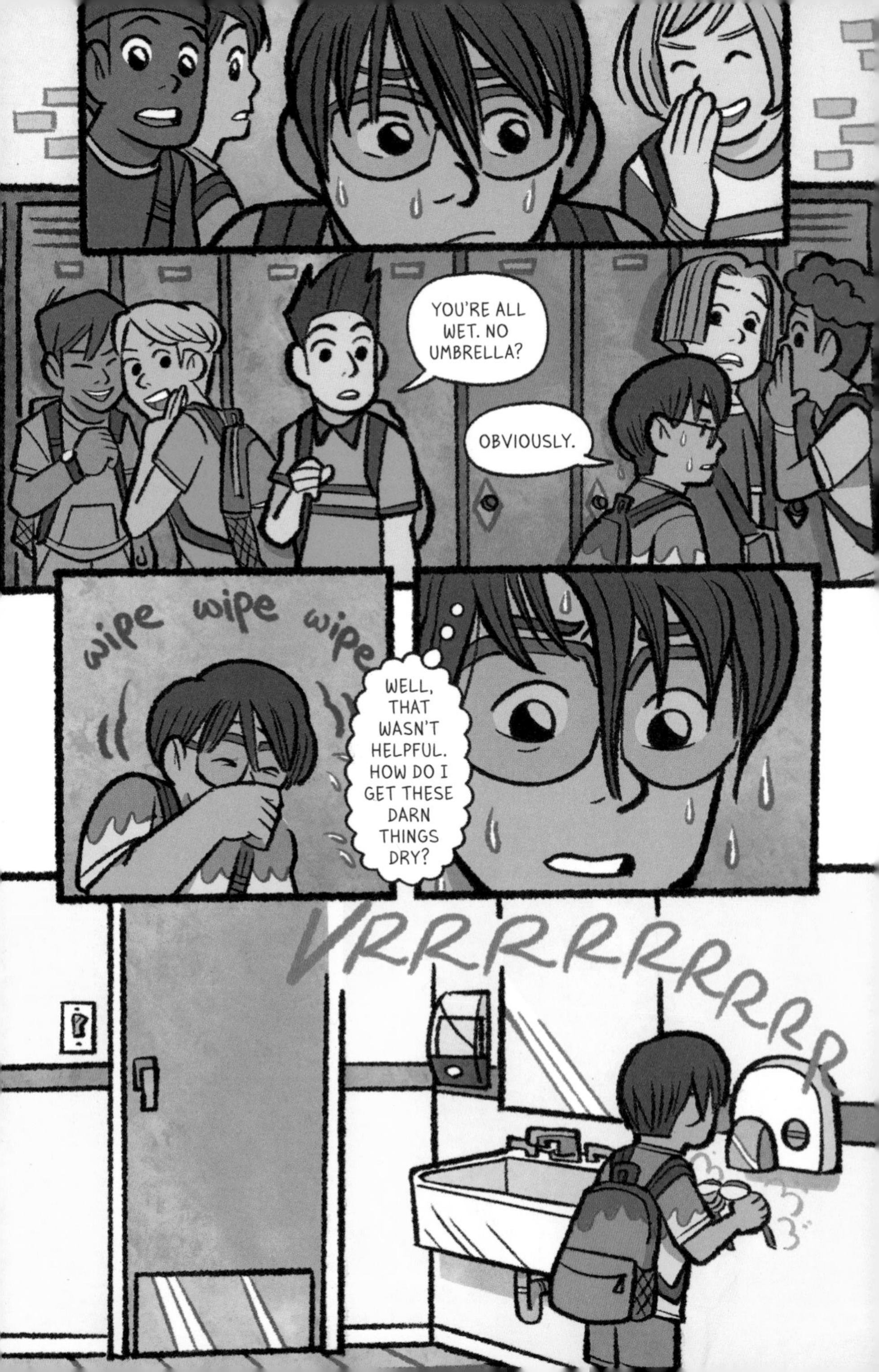
YOU'RE ALL WET. NO UMBRELLA?
OBVIOUSLY.
wipe wipe wipe
WELL, THAT WASN'T HELPFUL. HOW DO I GET THESE DARN THINGS DRY?
VRRRRRRRRRR

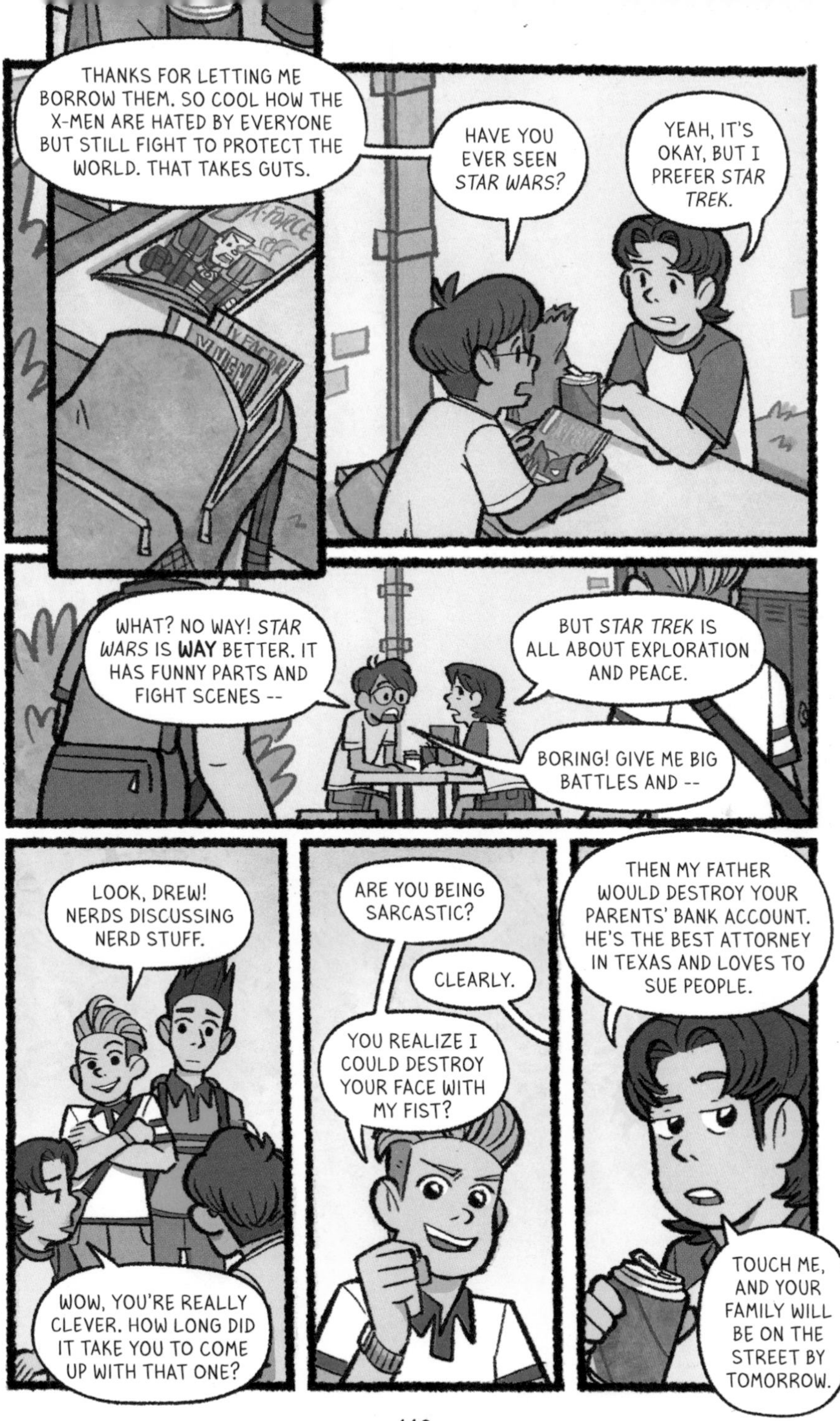
THANKS FOR LETTING ME BORROW THEM. SO COOL HOW THE X-MEN ARE HATED BY EVERYONE BUT STILL FIGHT TO PROTECT THE WORLD. THAT TAKES GUTS.
HAVE YOU EVER SEEN STAR WARS?
YEAH, IT'S OKAY, BUT I PREFER STAR TREK.
WHAT? NO WAY! STAR WARS IS WAY BETTER. IT HAS FUNNY PARTS AND FIGHT SCENES --
BUT STAR TREK IS ALL ABOUT EXPLORATION AND PEACE.
BORING! GIVE ME BIG BATTLES AND --
LOOK, DREW! NERDS DISCUSSING NERD STUFF.
WOW, YOU'RE REALLY CLEVER. HOW LONG DID IT TAKE YOU TO COME UP WITH THAT ONE?
ARE YOU BEING SARCASTIC?
CLEARLY.
YOU REALIZE I COULD DESTROY YOUR FACE WITH MY FIST?
THEN MY FATHER WOULD DESTROY YOUR PARENTS' BANK ACCOUNT. HE'S THE BEST ATTORNEY IN TEXAS AND LOVES TO SUE PEOPLE.
TOUCH ME, AND YOUR FAMILY WILL BE ON THE STREET BY TOMORROW.

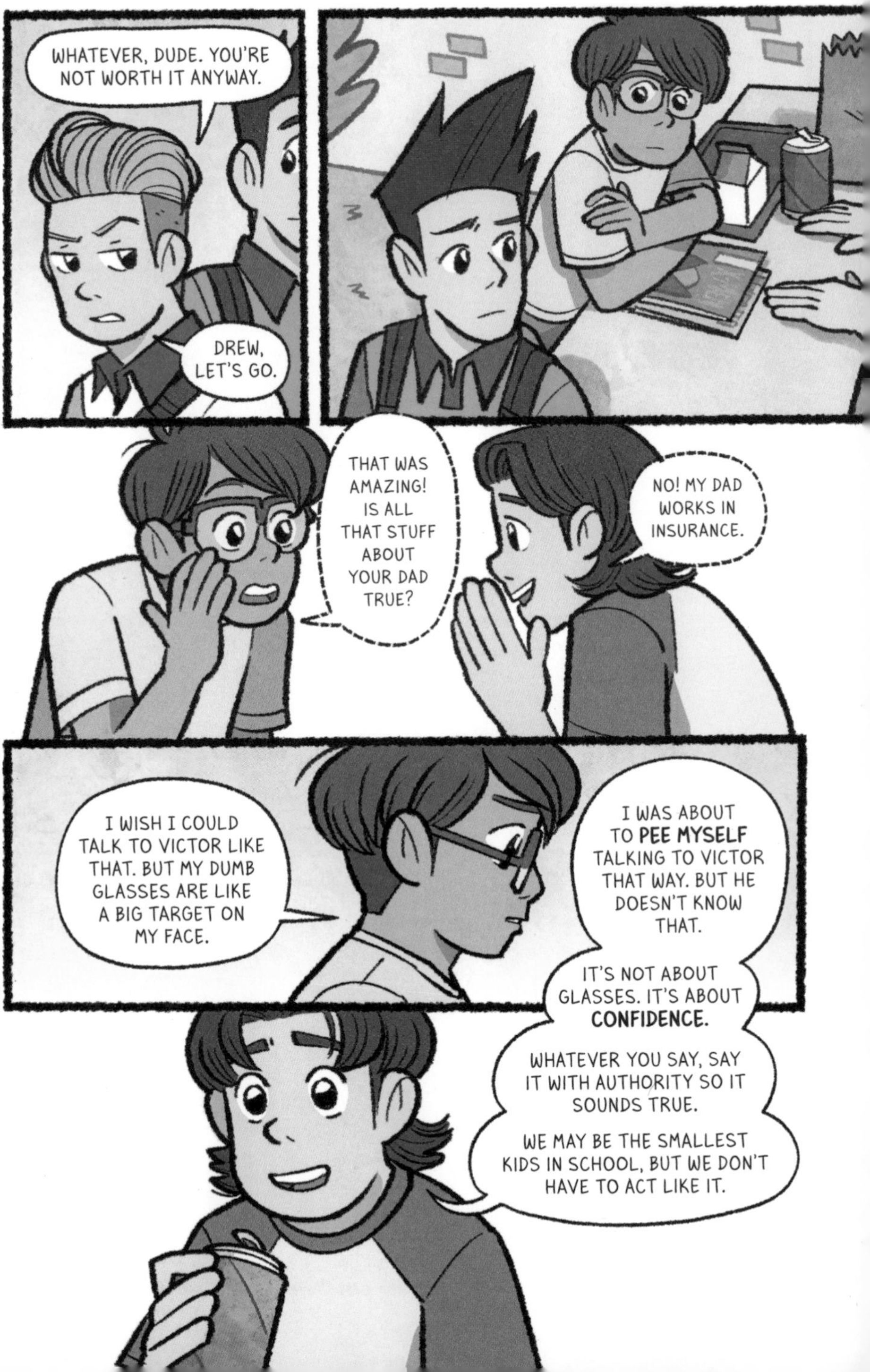
WHATEVER, DUDE. YOU'RE NOT WORTH IT ANYWAY.
DREW, LET'S GO.
THAT WAS AMAZING! IS ALL THAT STUFF ABOUT YOUR DAD TRUE?
NO! MY DAD WORKS IN INSURANCE.
I WISH I COULD TALK TO VICTOR LIKE THAT. BUT MY DUMB GLASSES ARE LIKE A BIG TARGET ON MY FACE.
I WAS ABOUT TO **PEE MYSELF** TALKING TO VICTOR THAT WAY. BUT HE DOESN'T KNOW THAT.
IT'S NOT ABOUT GLASSES. IT'S ABOUT **CONFIDENCE.**
WHATEVER YOU SAY, SAY IT WITH AUTHORITY SO IT SOUNDS TRUE.
WE MAY BE THE SMALLEST KIDS IN SCHOOL, BUT WE DON'T HAVE TO ACT LIKE IT.

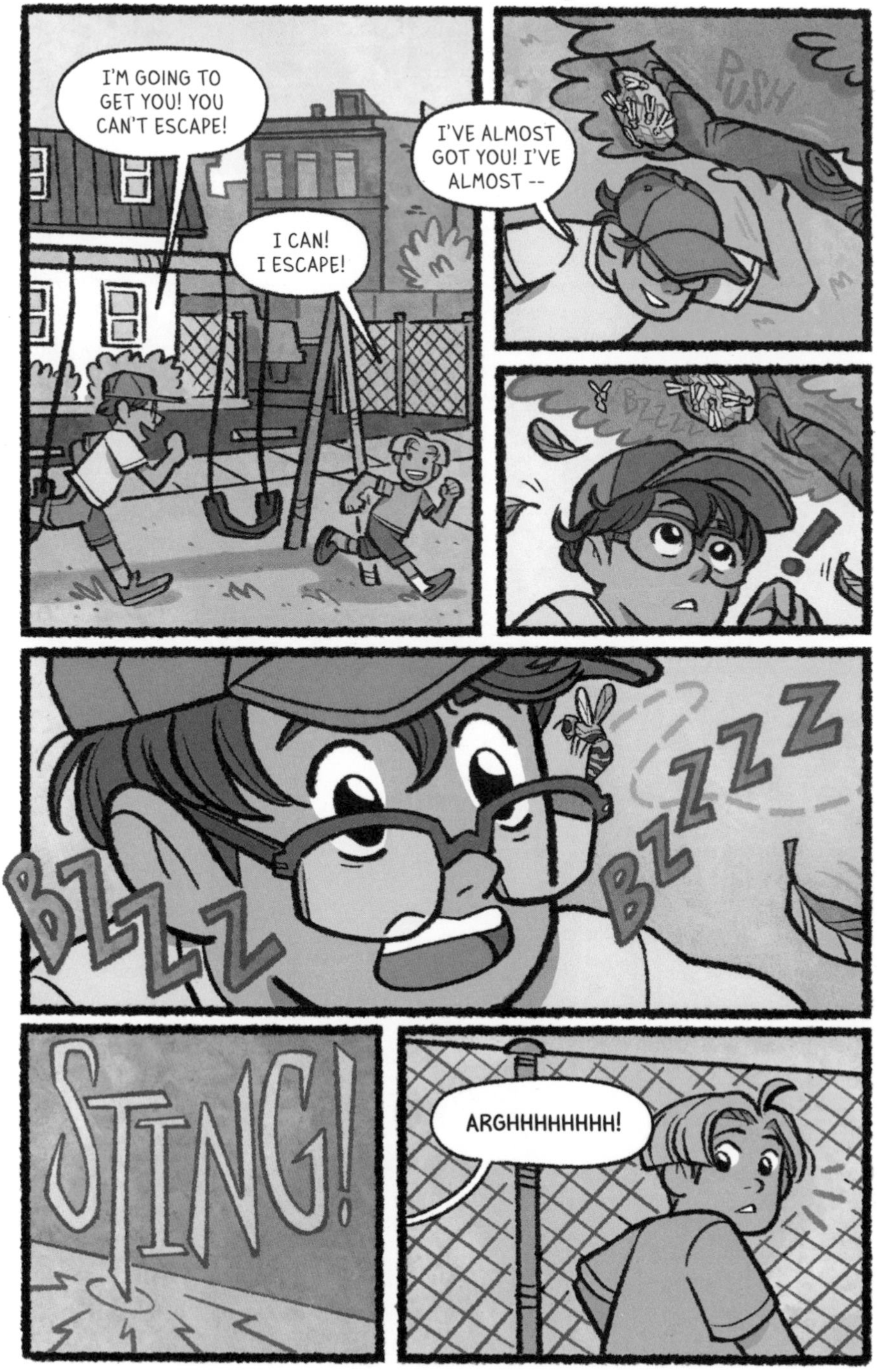
I'M GOING TO GET YOU! YOU CAN'T ESCAPE!
I CAN! I ESCAPE!
I'VE ALMOST GOT YOU! I'VE ALMOST --
PUSH
BZZZZ
!
BZZZZ
BZZZZZ
STING!
ARGHHHHHHHH!

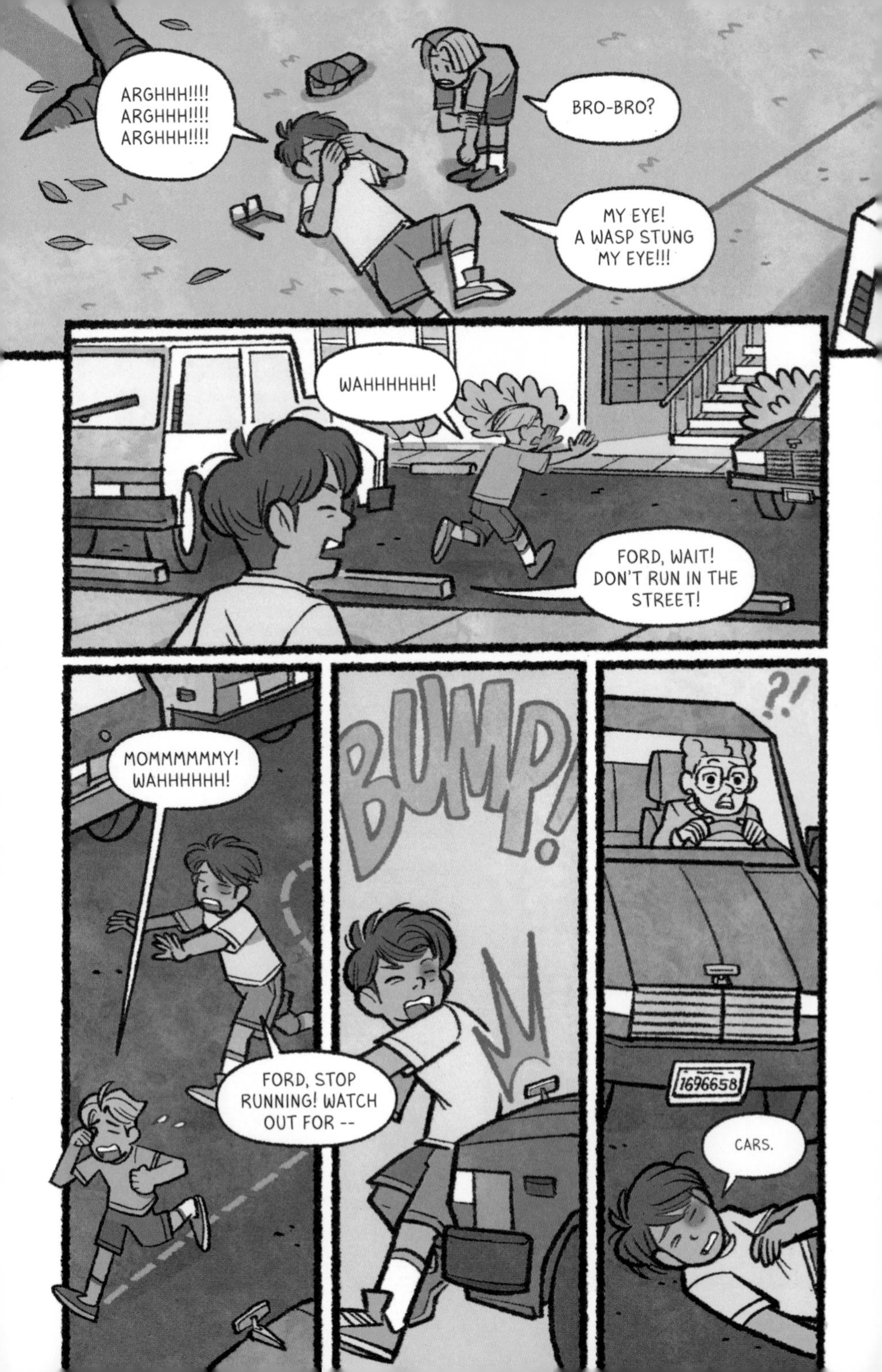
ARGHHH!!!! ARGHHH!!!! ARGHHH!!!!
BRO-BRO?
MY EYE! A WASP STUNG MY EYE!!!
WAHHHHHH!
FORD, WAIT! DON'T RUN IN THE STREET!
MOMMMMMMY! WAHHHHHH!
FORD, STOP RUNNING! WATCH OUT FOR --
BUMP!
?!
1696658
CARS.

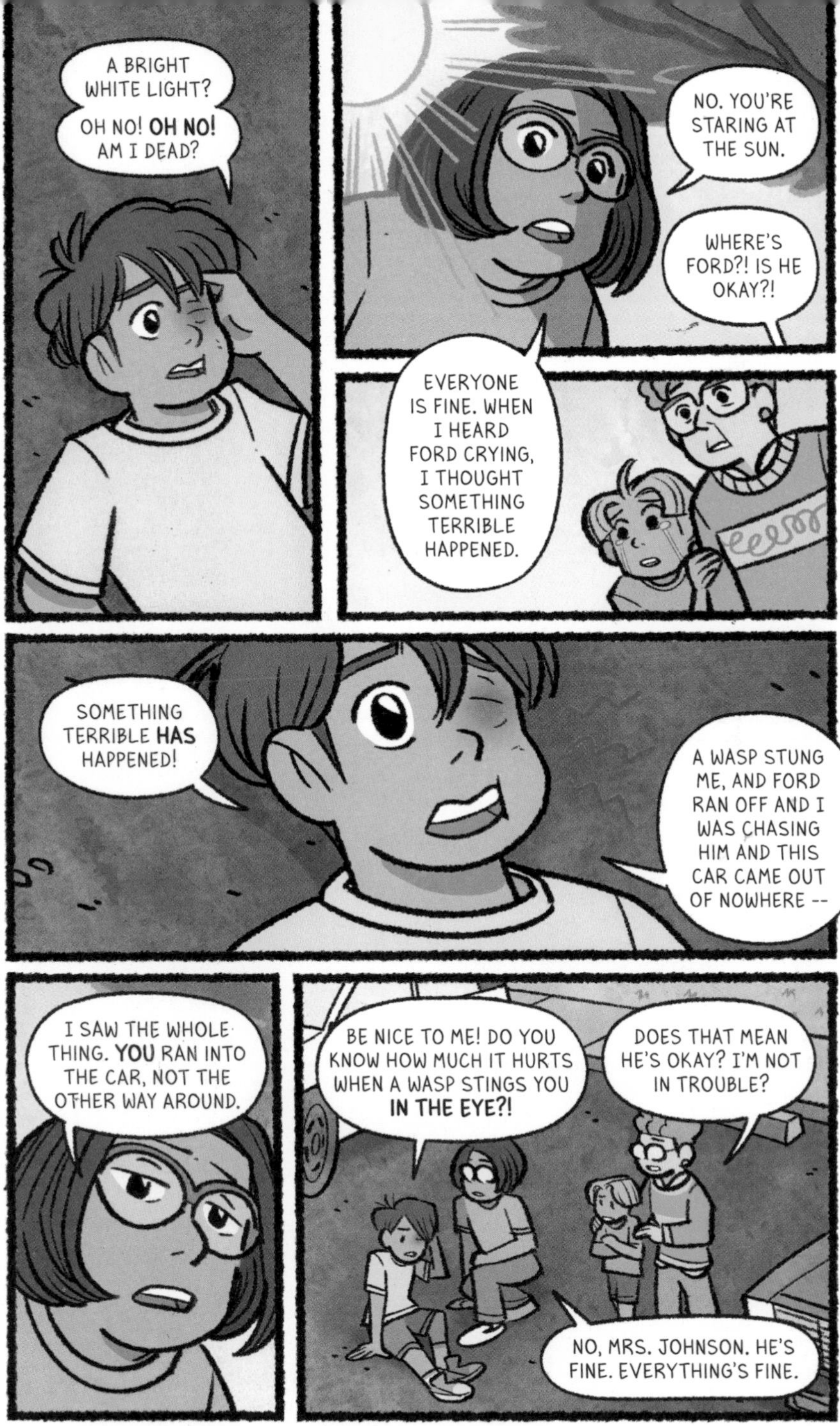

A BRIGHT WHITE LIGHT?
OH NO! **OH NO!** AM I DEAD?
NO. YOU'RE STARING AT THE SUN.
WHERE'S FORD?! IS HE OKAY?!
EVERYONE IS FINE. WHEN I HEARD FORD CRYING, I THOUGHT SOMETHING TERRIBLE HAPPENED.
SOMETHING TERRIBLE **HAS** HAPPENED!
A WASP STUNG ME, AND FORD RAN OFF AND I WAS CHASING HIM AND THIS CAR CAME OUT OF NOWHERE --
I SAW THE WHOLE THING. **YOU** RAN INTO THE CAR, NOT THE OTHER WAY AROUND.
BE NICE TO ME! DO YOU KNOW HOW MUCH IT HURTS WHEN A WASP STINGS YOU **IN THE EYE?!**
DOES THAT MEAN HE'S OKAY? I'M NOT IN TROUBLE?
NO, MRS. JOHNSON. HE'S FINE. EVERYTHING'S FINE.

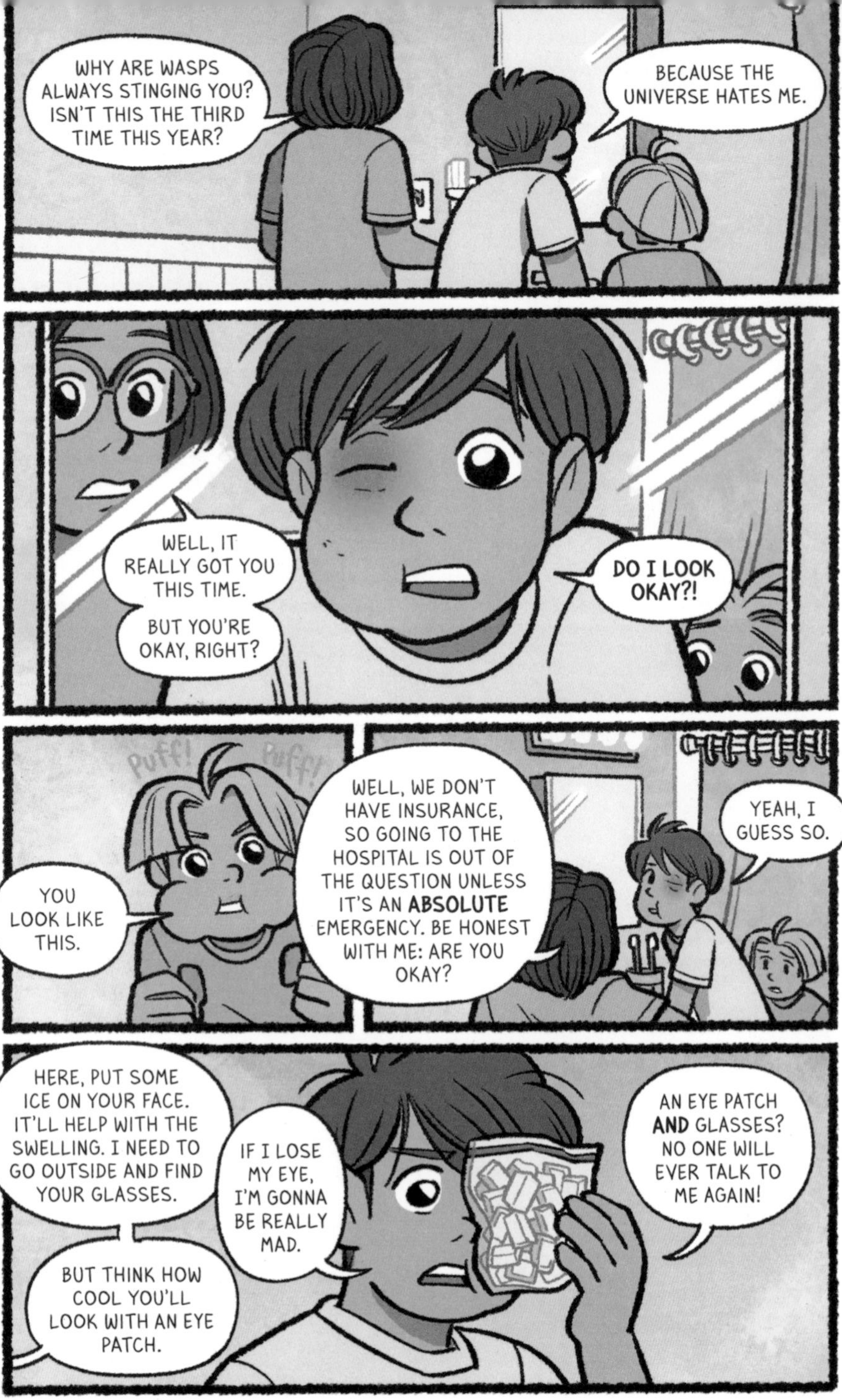
WHY ARE WASPS ALWAYS STINGING YOU? ISN'T THIS THE THIRD TIME THIS YEAR?
BECAUSE THE UNIVERSE HATES ME.
WELL, IT REALLY GOT YOU THIS TIME.
BUT YOU'RE OKAY, RIGHT?
DO I LOOK OKAY?!
Puff! Puff!
YOU LOOK LIKE THIS.
WELL, WE DON'T HAVE INSURANCE, SO GOING TO THE HOSPITAL IS OUT OF THE QUESTION UNLESS IT'S AN ABSOLUTE EMERGENCY. BE HONEST WITH ME: ARE YOU OKAY?
YEAH, I GUESS SO.
HERE, PUT SOME ICE ON YOUR FACE. IT'LL HELP WITH THE SWELLING. I NEED TO GO OUTSIDE AND FIND YOUR GLASSES.
BUT THINK HOW COOL YOU'LL LOOK WITH AN EYE PATCH.
IF I LOSE MY EYE, I'M GONNA BE REALLY MAD.
AN EYE PATCH AND GLASSES? NO ONE WILL EVER TALK TO ME AGAIN!

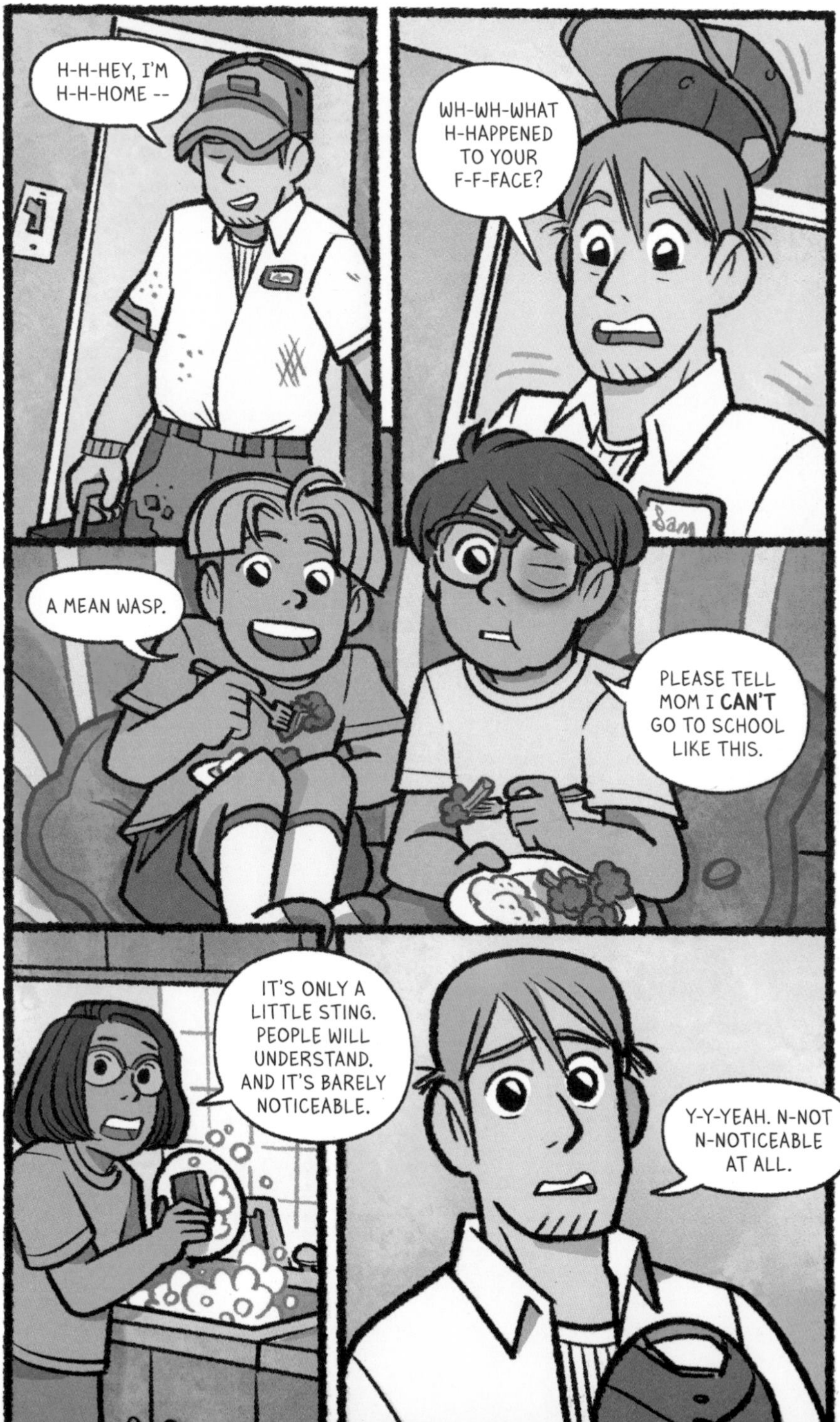
H-H-HEY, I'M H-H-HOME --
WH-WH-WHAT H-HAPPENED TO YOUR F-F-FACE?
Sam
A MEAN WASP.
PLEASE TELL MOM I **CAN'T** GO TO SCHOOL LIKE THIS.
IT'S ONLY A LITTLE STING. PEOPLE WILL UNDERSTAND. AND IT'S BARELY NOTICEABLE.
Y-Y-YEAH. N-NOT N-NOTICEABLE AT ALL.

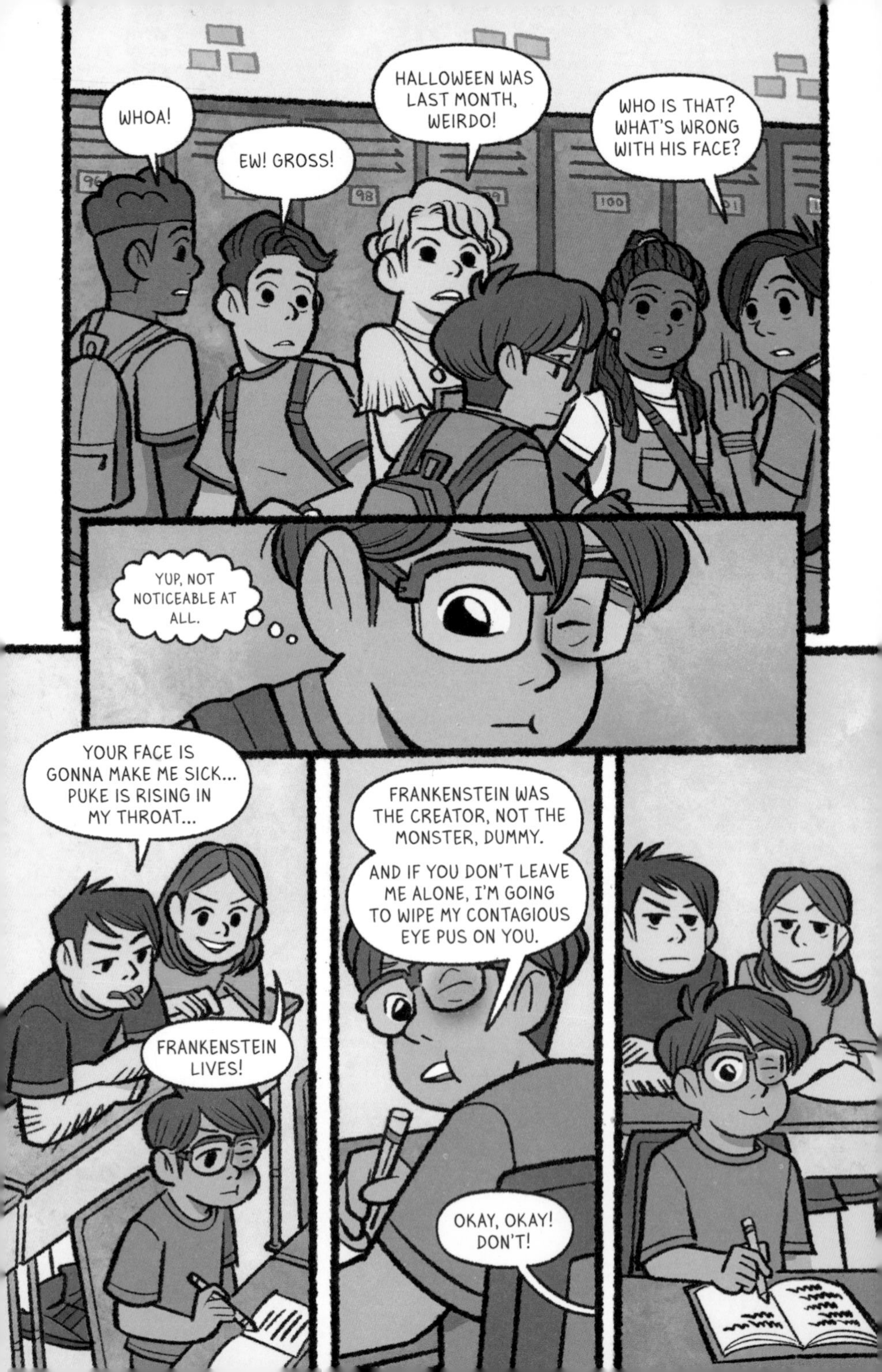
WHOA!
EW! GROSS!
HALLOWEEN WAS LAST MONTH, WEIRDO!
WHO IS THAT? WHAT'S WRONG WITH HIS FACE?
YUP, NOT NOTICEABLE AT ALL.
YOUR FACE IS GONNA MAKE ME SICK... PUKE IS RISING IN MY THROAT...
FRANKENSTEIN LIVES!
FRANKENSTEIN WAS THE CREATOR, NOT THE MONSTER, DUMMY.
AND IF YOU DON'T LEAVE ME ALONE, I'M GOING TO WIPE MY CONTAGIOUS EYE PUS ON YOU.
OKAY, OKAY! DON'T!

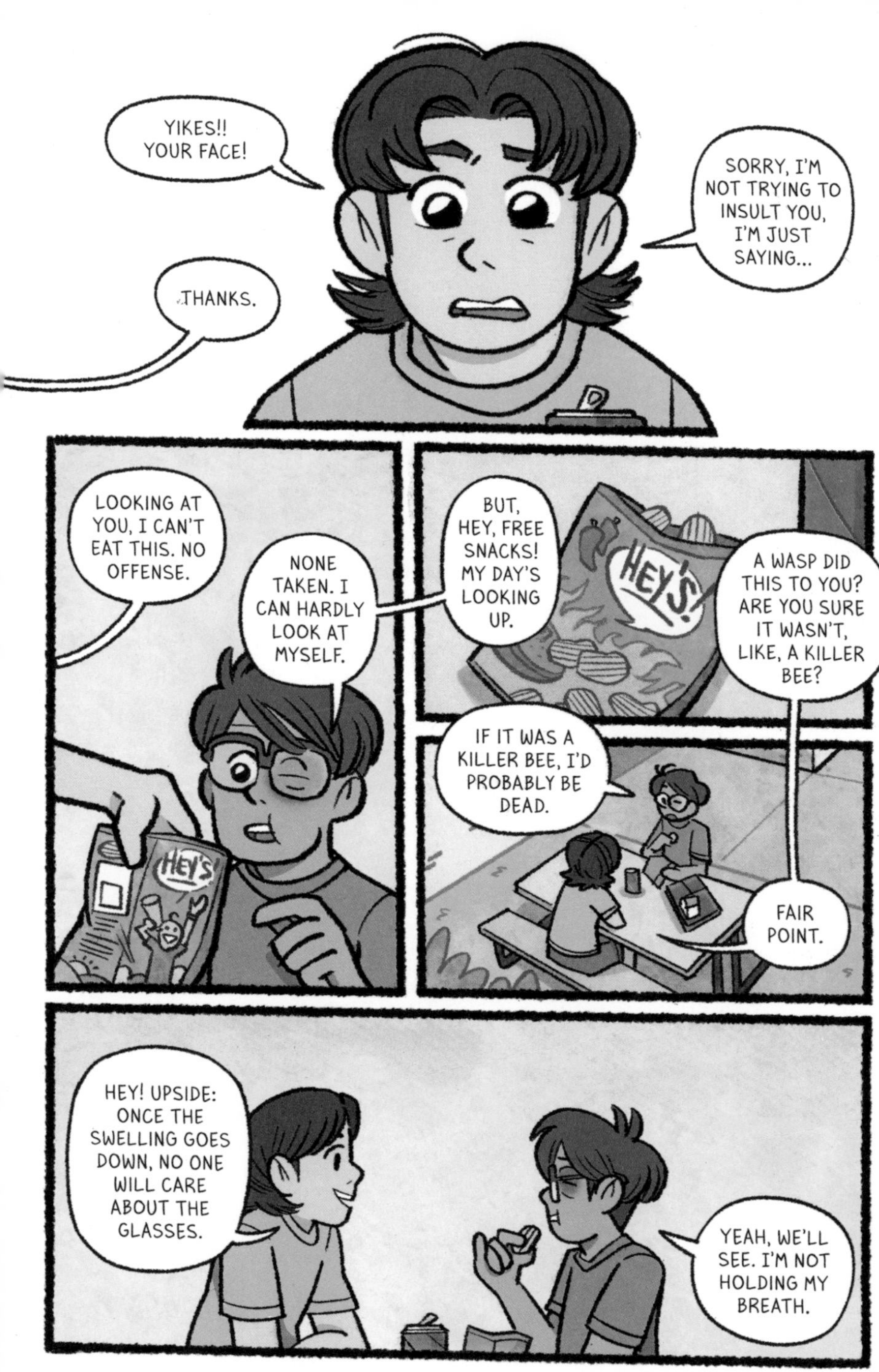
YIKES!! YOUR FACE!
SORRY, I'M NOT TRYING TO INSULT YOU, I'M JUST SAYING...
THANKS.
LOOKING AT YOU, I CAN'T EAT THIS. NO OFFENSE.
NONE TAKEN. I CAN HARDLY LOOK AT MYSELF.
HEY'S
BUT, HEY, FREE SNACKS! MY DAY'S LOOKING UP.
HEY'S!
A WASP DID THIS TO YOU? ARE YOU SURE IT WASN'T, LIKE, A KILLER BEE?
IF IT WAS A KILLER BEE, I'D PROBABLY BE DEAD.
FAIR POINT.
HEY! UPSIDE: ONCE THE SWELLING GOES DOWN, NO ONE WILL CARE ABOUT THE GLASSES.
YEAH, WE'LL SEE. I'M NOT HOLDING MY BREATH.

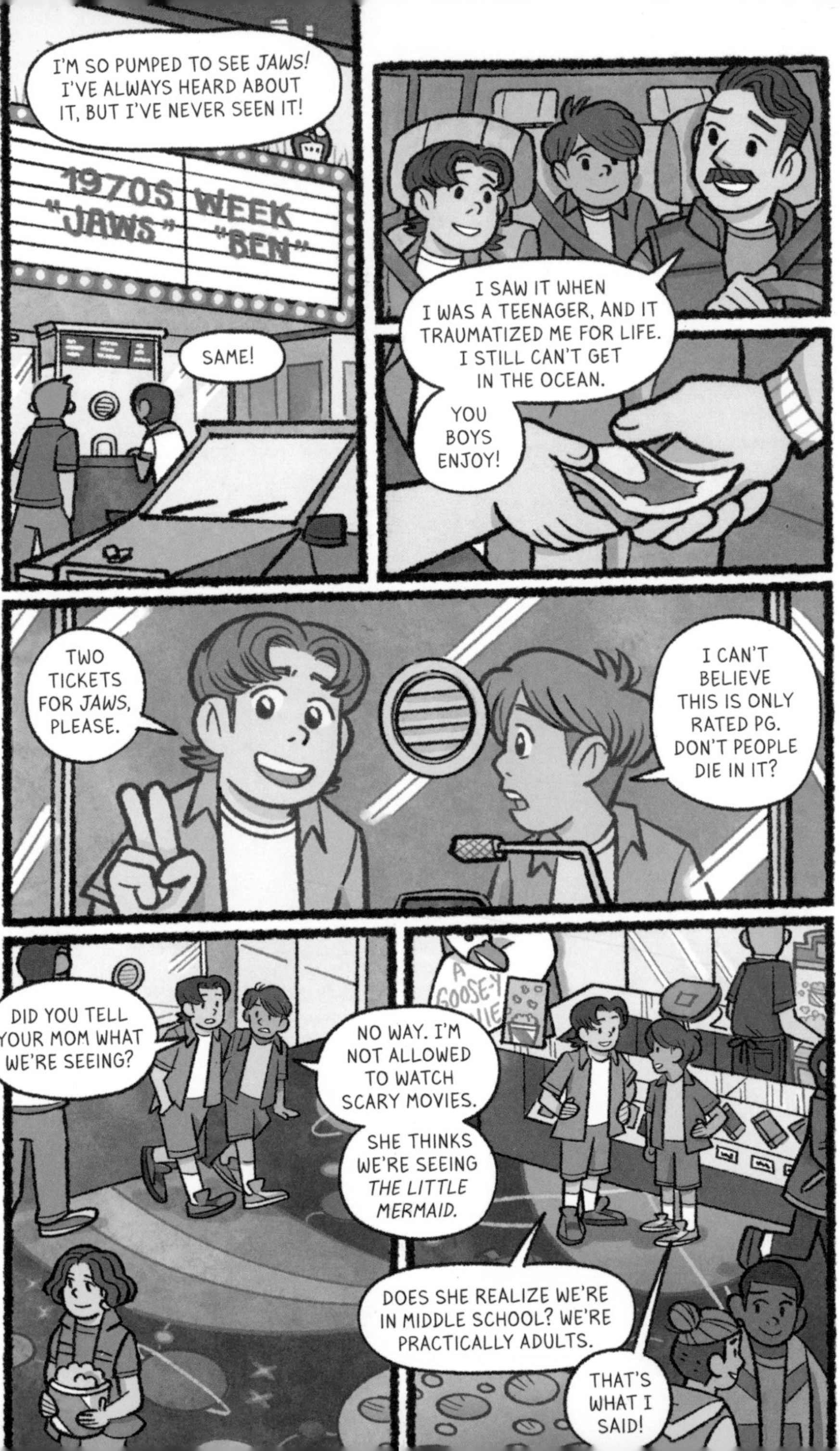
I'M SO PUMPED TO SEE *JAWS!* I'VE ALWAYS HEARD ABOUT IT, BUT I'VE NEVER SEEN IT!
1970S WEEK "JAWS" "BEN"
SAME!
I SAW IT WHEN I WAS A TEENAGER, AND IT TRAUMATIZED ME FOR LIFE. I STILL CAN'T GET IN THE OCEAN.
YOU BOYS ENJOY!
TWO TICKETS FOR *JAWS*, PLEASE.
I CAN'T BELIEVE THIS IS ONLY RATED PG. DON'T PEOPLE DIE IN IT?
DID YOU TELL YOUR MOM WHAT WE'RE SEEING?
NO WAY. I'M NOT ALLOWED TO WATCH SCARY MOVIES.
SHE THINKS WE'RE SEEING *THE LITTLE MERMAID.*
DOES SHE REALIZE WE'RE IN MIDDLE SCHOOL? WE'RE PRACTICALLY ADULTS.
THAT'S WHAT I SAID!

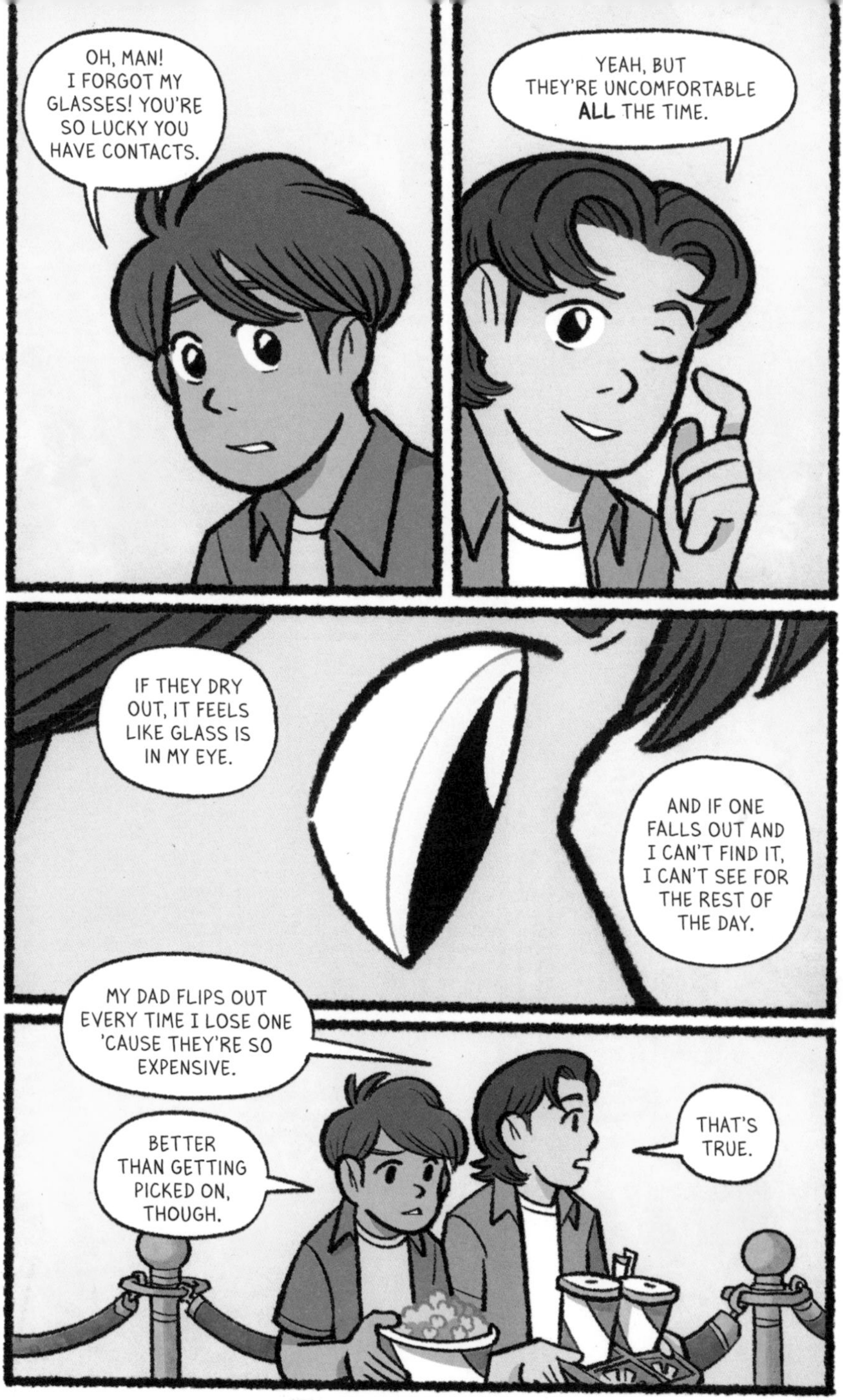
OH, MAN! I FORGOT MY GLASSES! YOU'RE SO LUCKY YOU HAVE CONTACTS.
YEAH, BUT THEY'RE UNCOMFORTABLE **ALL** THE TIME.
IF THEY DRY OUT, IT FEELS LIKE GLASS IS IN MY EYE.
AND IF ONE FALLS OUT AND I CAN'T FIND IT, I CAN'T SEE FOR THE REST OF THE DAY.
MY DAD FLIPS OUT EVERY TIME I LOSE ONE 'CAUSE THEY'RE SO EXPENSIVE.
BETTER THAN GETTING PICKED ON, THOUGH.
THAT'S TRUE.

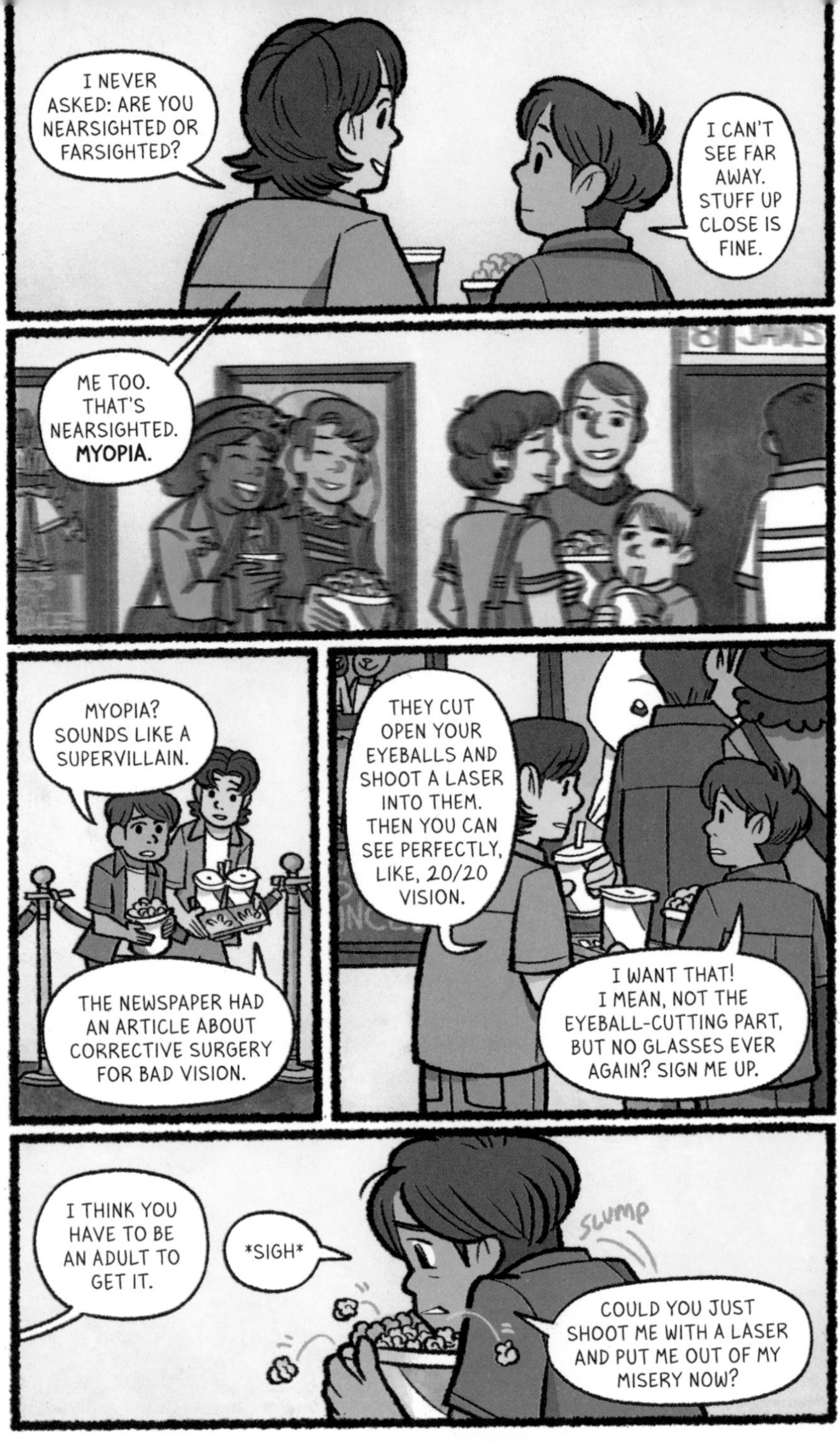
I NEVER ASKED: ARE YOU NEARSIGHTED OR FARSIGHTED?
I CAN'T SEE FAR AWAY. STUFF UP CLOSE IS FINE.
ME TOO. THAT'S NEARSIGHTED. MYOPIA.
MYOPIA? SOUNDS LIKE A SUPERVILLAIN.
THE NEWSPAPER HAD AN ARTICLE ABOUT CORRECTIVE SURGERY FOR BAD VISION.
THEY CUT OPEN YOUR EYEBALLS AND SHOOT A LASER INTO THEM. THEN YOU CAN SEE PERFECTLY, LIKE, 20/20 VISION.
I WANT THAT! I MEAN, NOT THE EYEBALL-CUTTING PART, BUT NO GLASSES EVER AGAIN? SIGN ME UP.
I THINK YOU HAVE TO BE AN ADULT TO GET IT.
SIGH
SLUMP
COULD YOU JUST SHOOT ME WITH A LASER AND PUT ME OUT OF MY MISERY NOW?

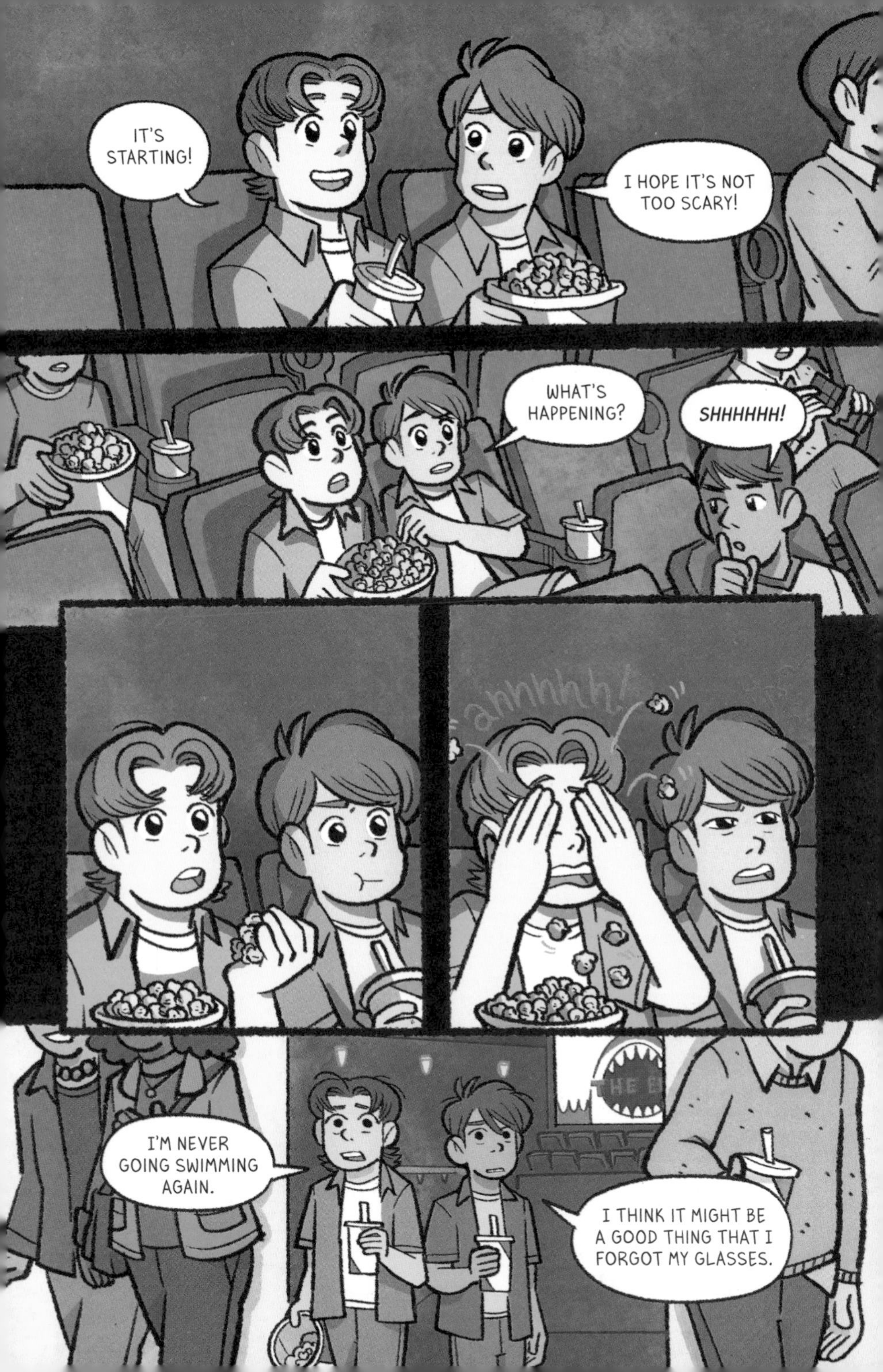
IT'S STARTING!
I HOPE IT'S NOT TOO SCARY!
WHAT'S HAPPENING?
SHHHHHH!
ahhhhh!
I'M NEVER GOING SWIMMING AGAIN.
I THINK IT MIGHT BE A GOOD THING THAT I FORGOT MY GLASSES.

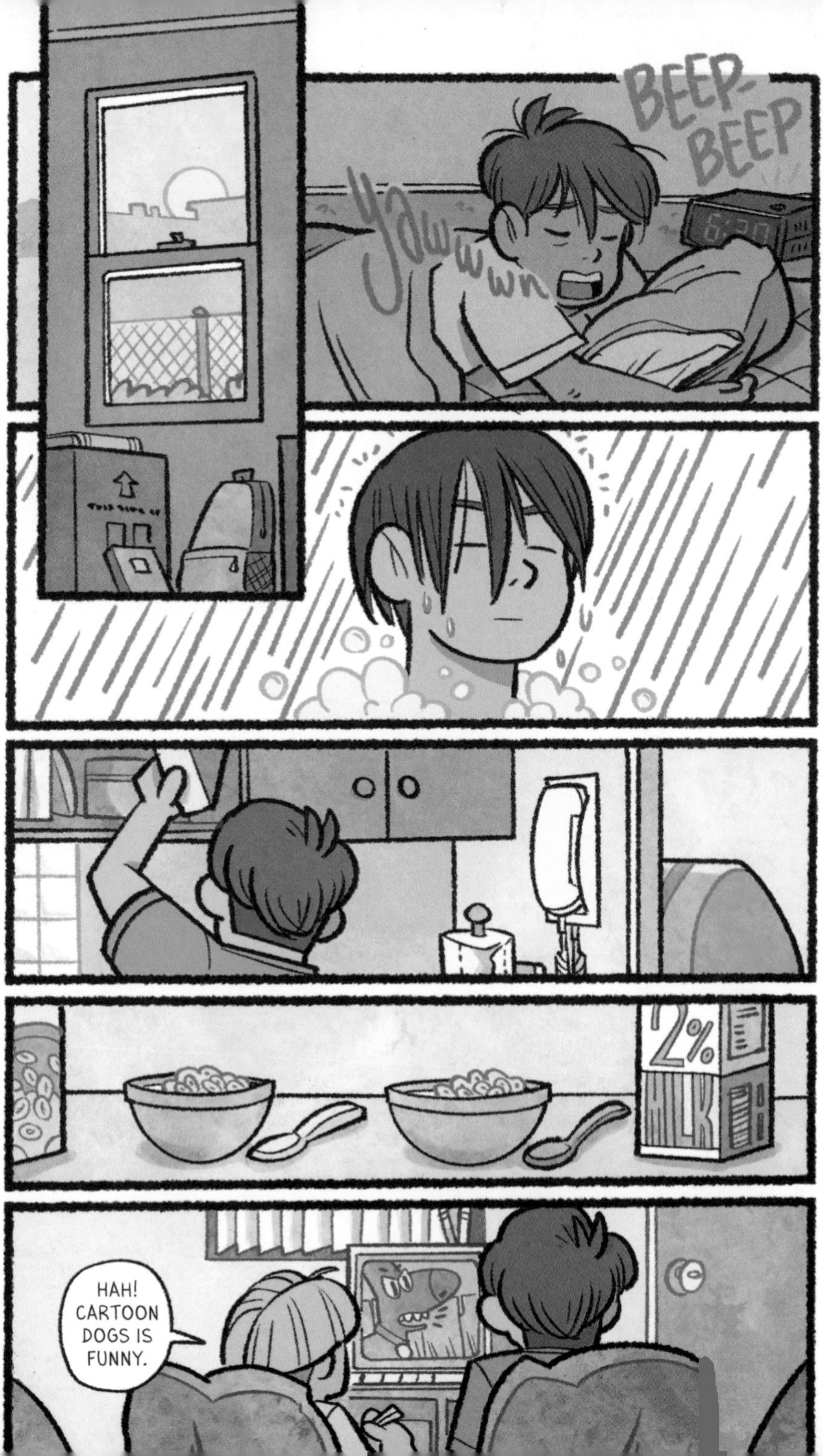
BEEP-
BEEP
YAWWWWN
2%
MILK
HAH! CARTOON DOGS IS FUNNY.

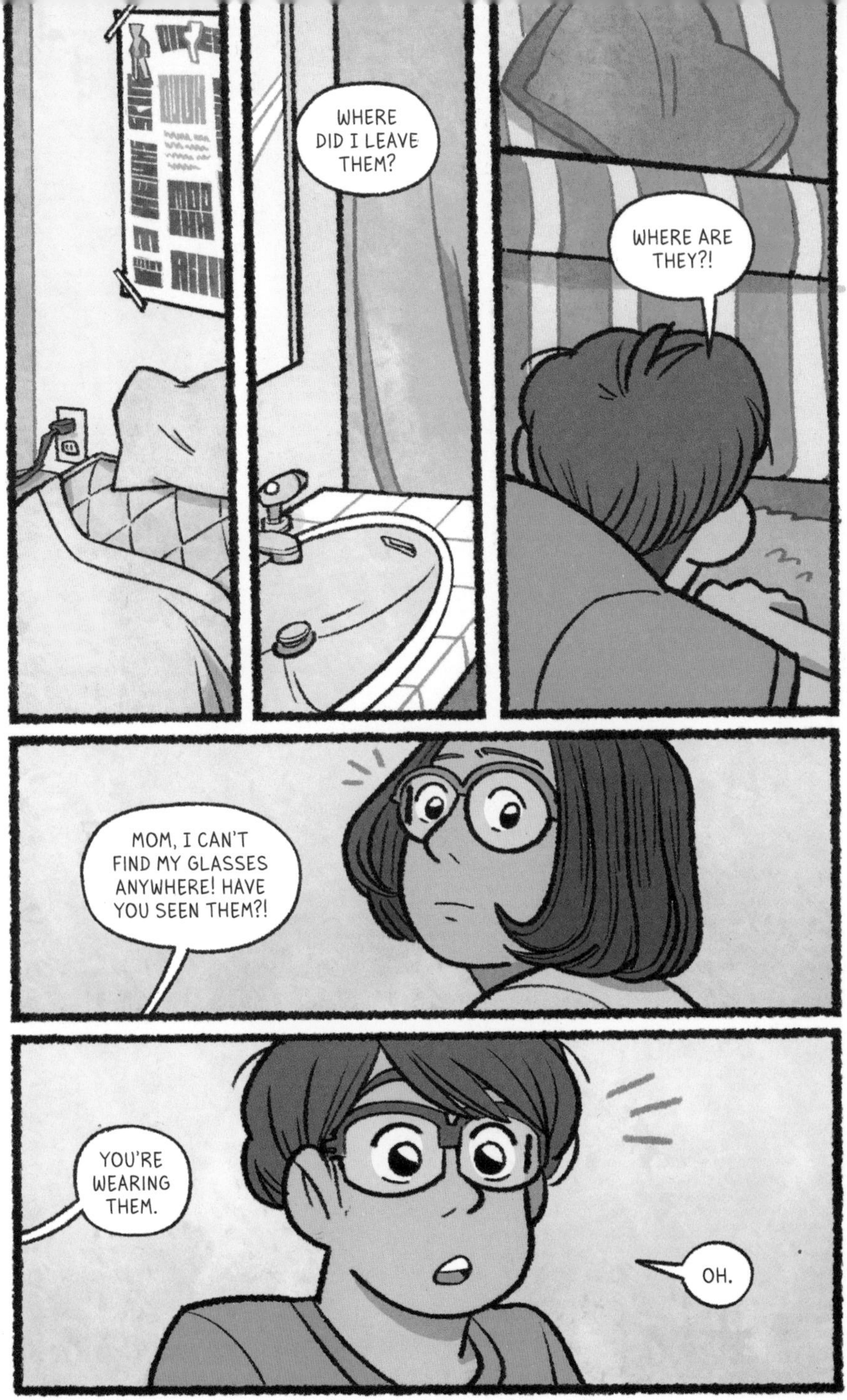
WHERE DID I LEAVE THEM?
WHERE ARE THEY?!
MOM, I CAN'T FIND MY GLASSES ANYWHERE! HAVE YOU SEEN THEM?!
YOU'RE WEARING THEM.
OH.

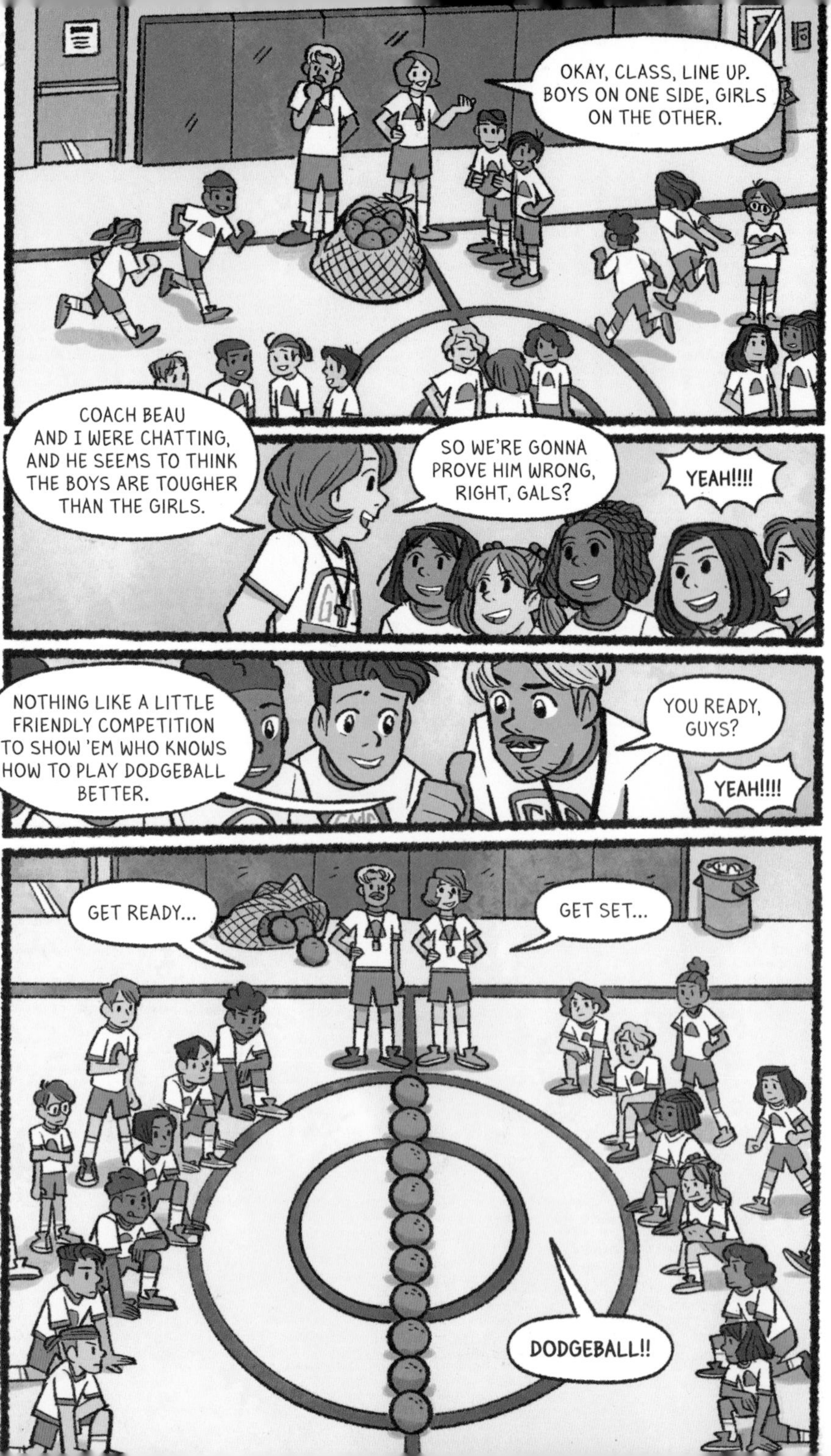
OKAY, CLASS, LINE UP. BOYS ON ONE SIDE, GIRLS ON THE OTHER.
COACH BEAU AND I WERE CHATTING, AND HE SEEMS TO THINK THE BOYS ARE TOUGHER THAN THE GIRLS.
SO WE'RE GONNA PROVE HIM WRONG, RIGHT, GALS?
YEAH!!!!
NOTHING LIKE A LITTLE FRIENDLY COMPETITION TO SHOW 'EM WHO KNOWS HOW TO PLAY DODGEBALL BETTER.
YOU READY, GUYS?
YEAH!!!!
GET READY...
GET SET...
DODGEBALL!!

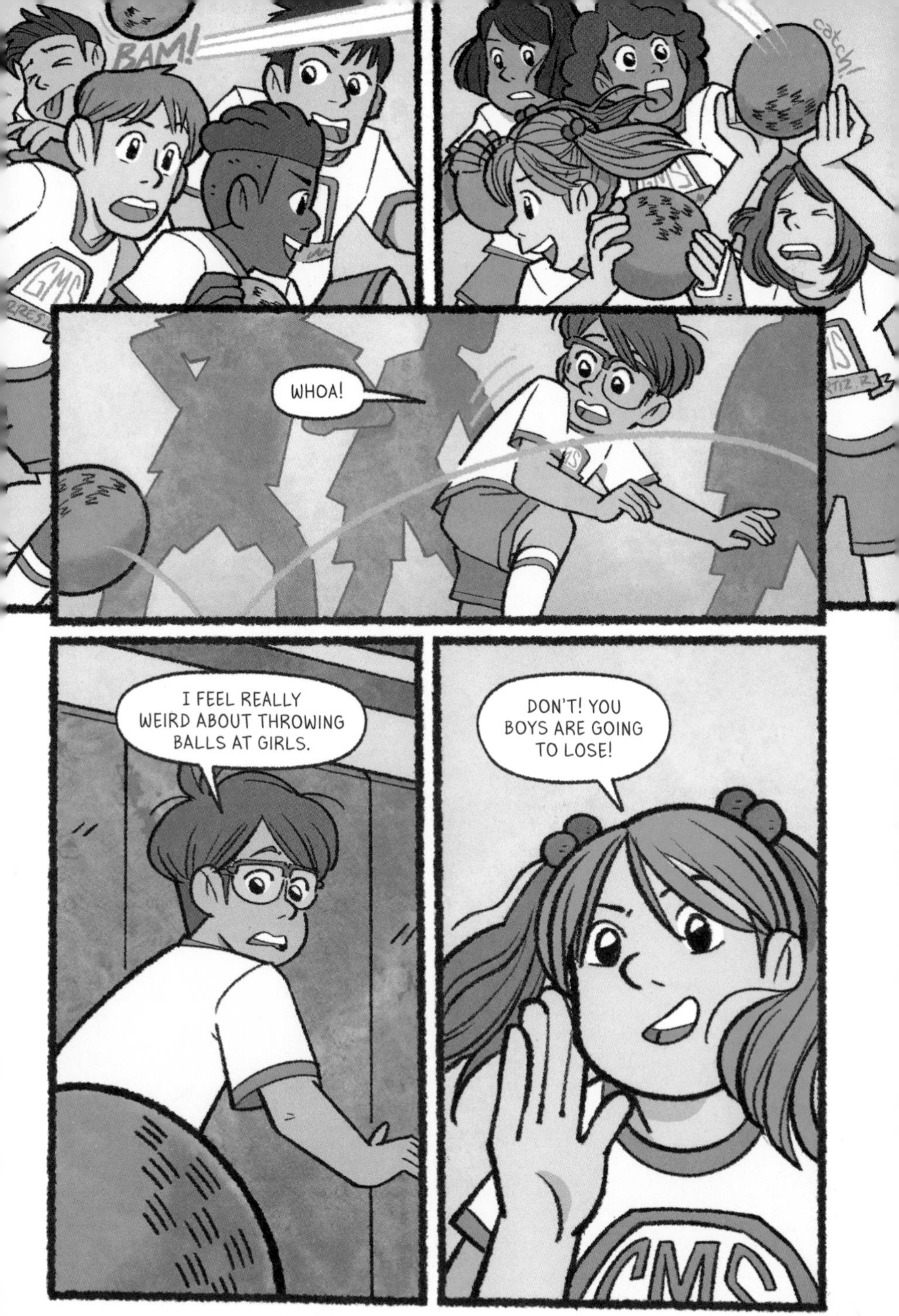
BAM!
catch!
WHOA!
I FEEL REALLY WEIRD ABOUT THROWING BALLS AT GIRLS.
DON'T! YOU BOYS ARE GOING TO LOSE!

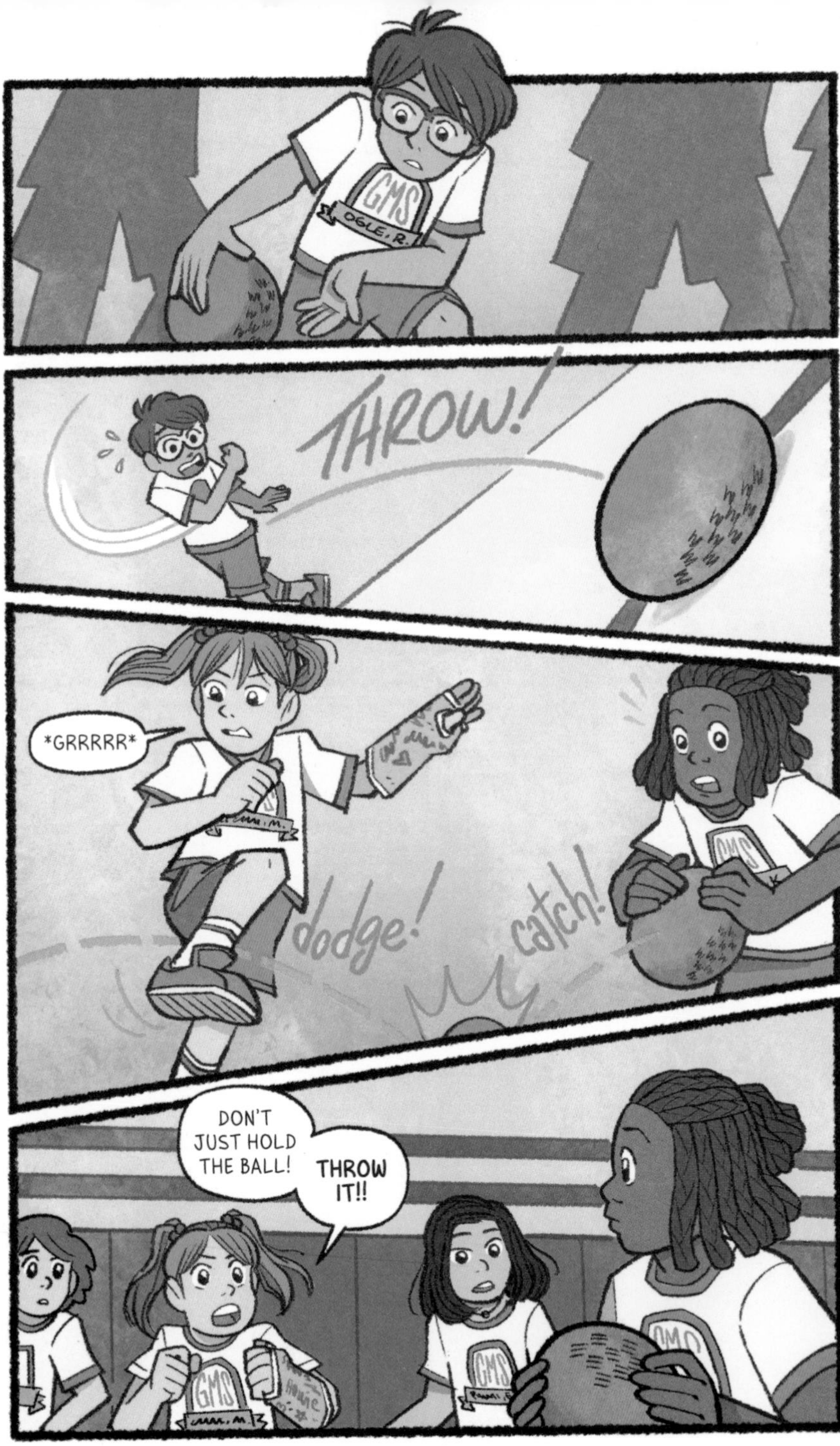
GMS
OGLE, R.
THROW!
GRRRRR
dodge!
catch!
GMS
DON'T JUST HOLD THE BALL!
THROW IT!!
GMS
GMS

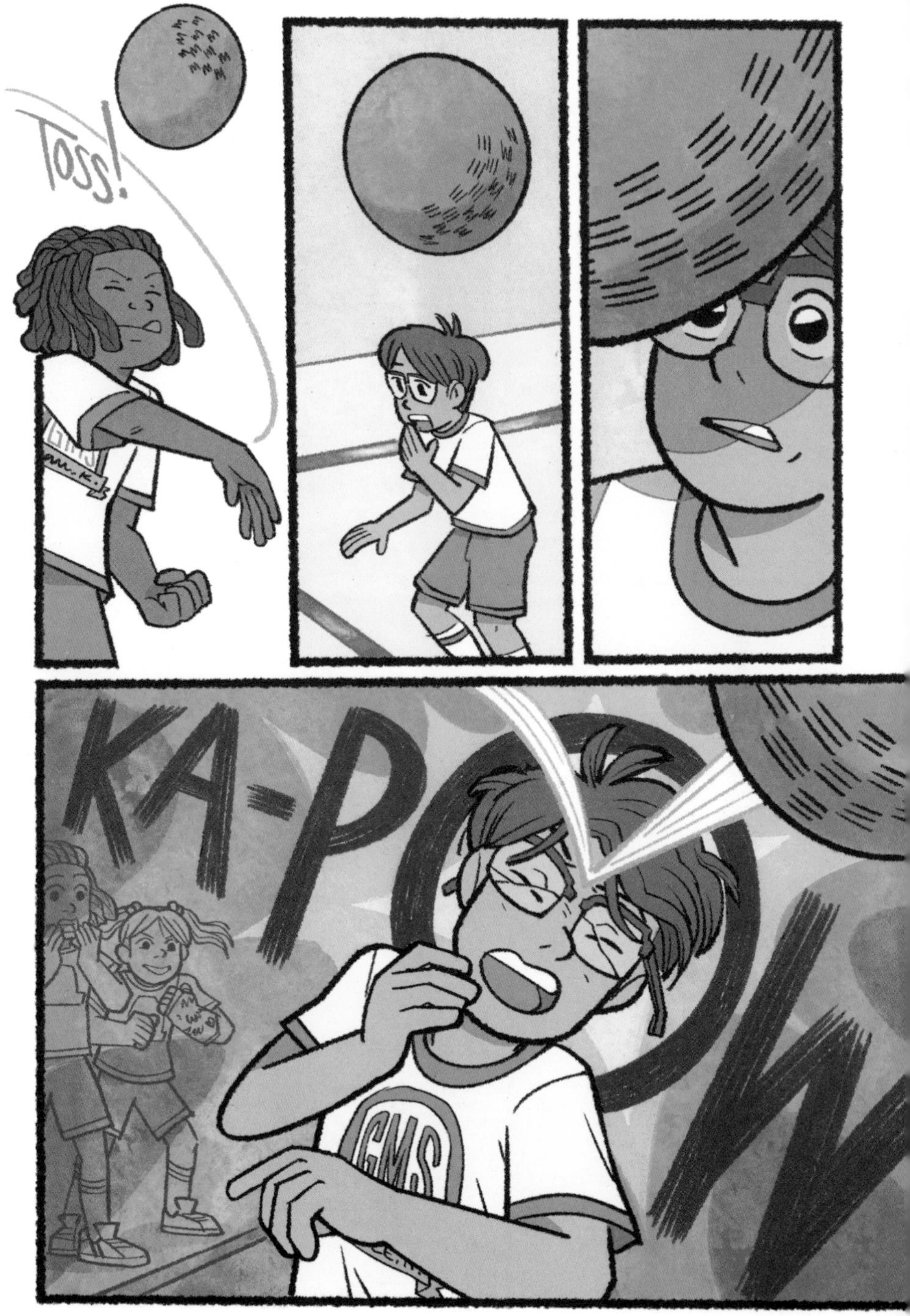
TOSS!
GMS
GMS
KA-POW

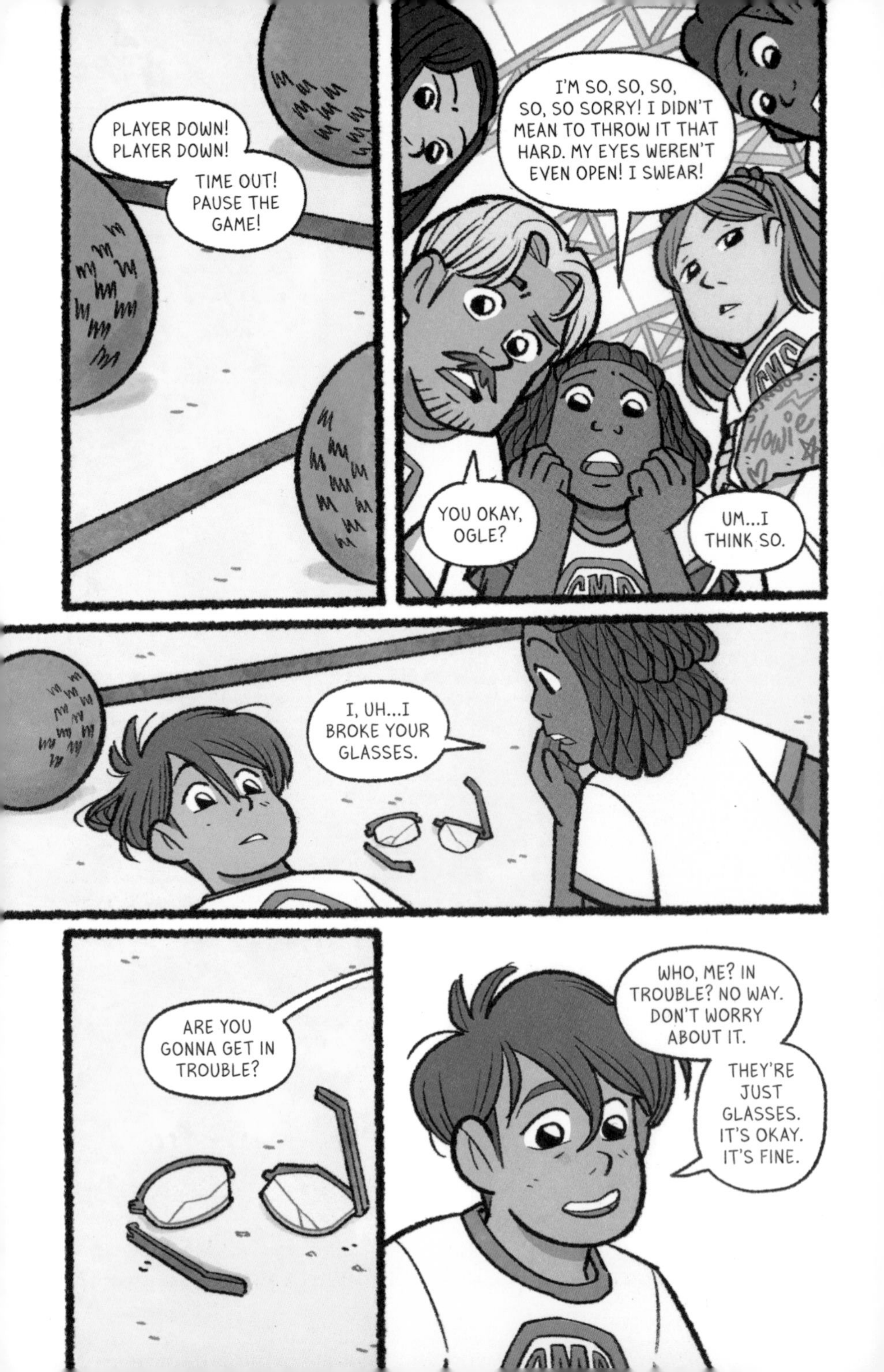
PLAYER DOWN! PLAYER DOWN!
TIME OUT! PAUSE THE GAME!
I'M SO, SO, SO, SO, SO SORRY! I DIDN'T MEAN TO THROW IT THAT HARD. MY EYES WEREN'T EVEN OPEN! I SWEAR!
YOU OKAY, OGLE?
UM...I THINK SO.
I, UH...I BROKE YOUR GLASSES.
ARE YOU GONNA GET IN TROUBLE?
WHO, ME? IN TROUBLE? NO WAY. DON'T WORRY ABOUT IT.
THEY'RE JUST GLASSES. IT'S OKAY. IT'S FINE.

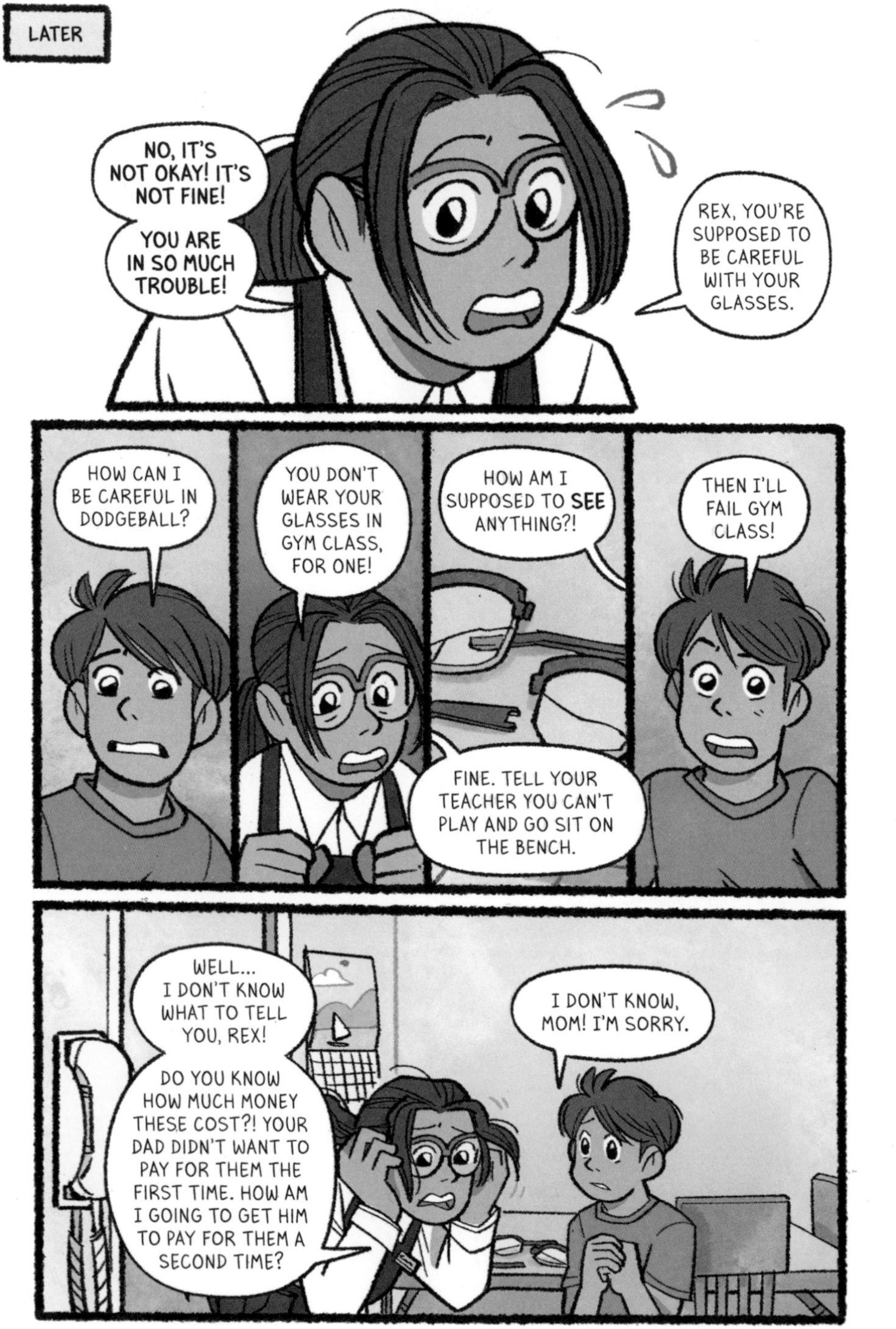
LATER
NO, IT'S NOT OKAY! IT'S NOT FINE!
YOU ARE IN SO MUCH TROUBLE!
REX, YOU'RE SUPPOSED TO BE CAREFUL WITH YOUR GLASSES.
HOW CAN I BE CAREFUL IN DODGEBALL?
YOU DON'T WEAR YOUR GLASSES IN GYM CLASS, FOR ONE!
HOW AM I SUPPOSED TO SEE ANYTHING?!
FINE. TELL YOUR TEACHER YOU CAN'T PLAY AND GO SIT ON THE BENCH.
THEN I'LL FAIL GYM CLASS!
WELL... I DON'T KNOW WHAT TO TELL YOU, REX!
DO YOU KNOW HOW MUCH MONEY THESE COST?! YOUR DAD DIDN'T WANT TO PAY FOR THEM THE FIRST TIME. HOW AM I GOING TO GET HIM TO PAY FOR THEM A SECOND TIME?
I DON'T KNOW, MOM! I'M SORRY.

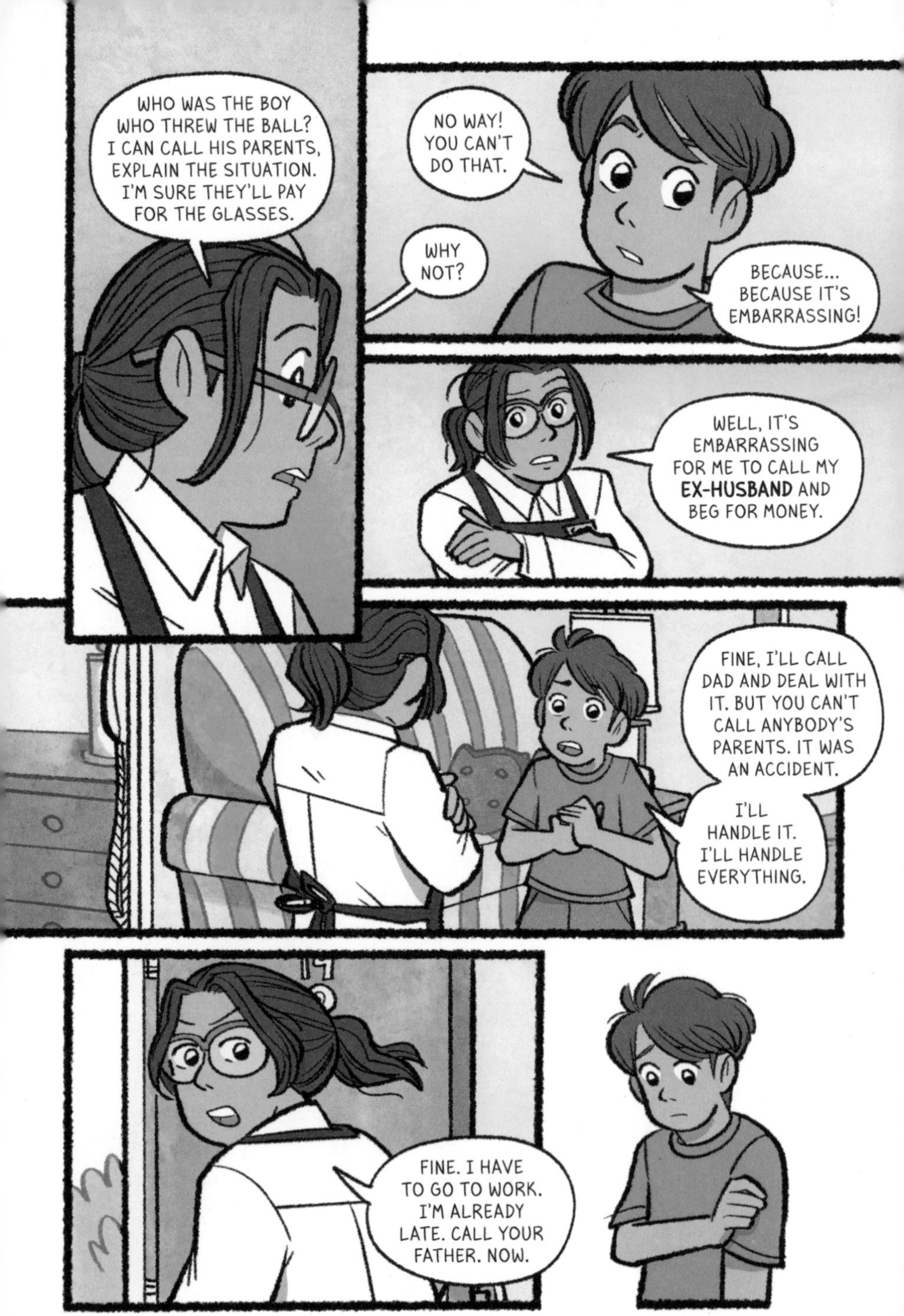
WHO WAS THE BOY WHO THREW THE BALL? I CAN CALL HIS PARENTS, EXPLAIN THE SITUATION. I'M SURE THEY'LL PAY FOR THE GLASSES.
NO WAY! YOU CAN'T DO THAT.
WHY NOT?
BECAUSE... BECAUSE IT'S EMBARRASSING!
WELL, IT'S EMBARRASSING FOR ME TO CALL MY **EX-HUSBAND** AND BEG FOR MONEY.
FINE, I'LL CALL DAD AND DEAL WITH IT. BUT YOU CAN'T CALL ANYBODY'S PARENTS. IT WAS AN ACCIDENT.
I'LL HANDLE IT. I'LL HANDLE EVERYTHING.
FINE. I HAVE TO GO TO WORK. I'M ALREADY LATE. CALL YOUR FATHER. NOW.

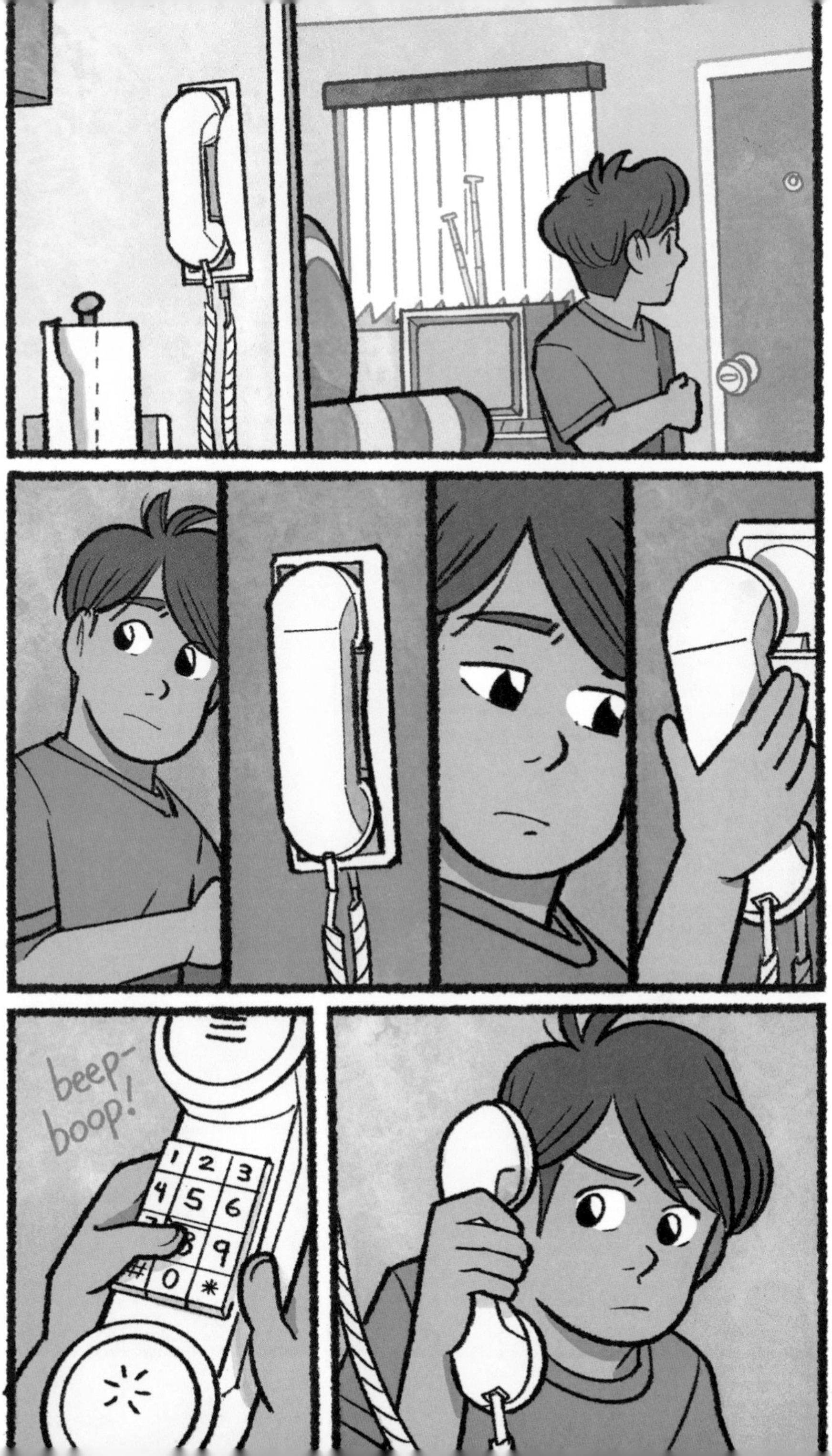
beep-
boop!

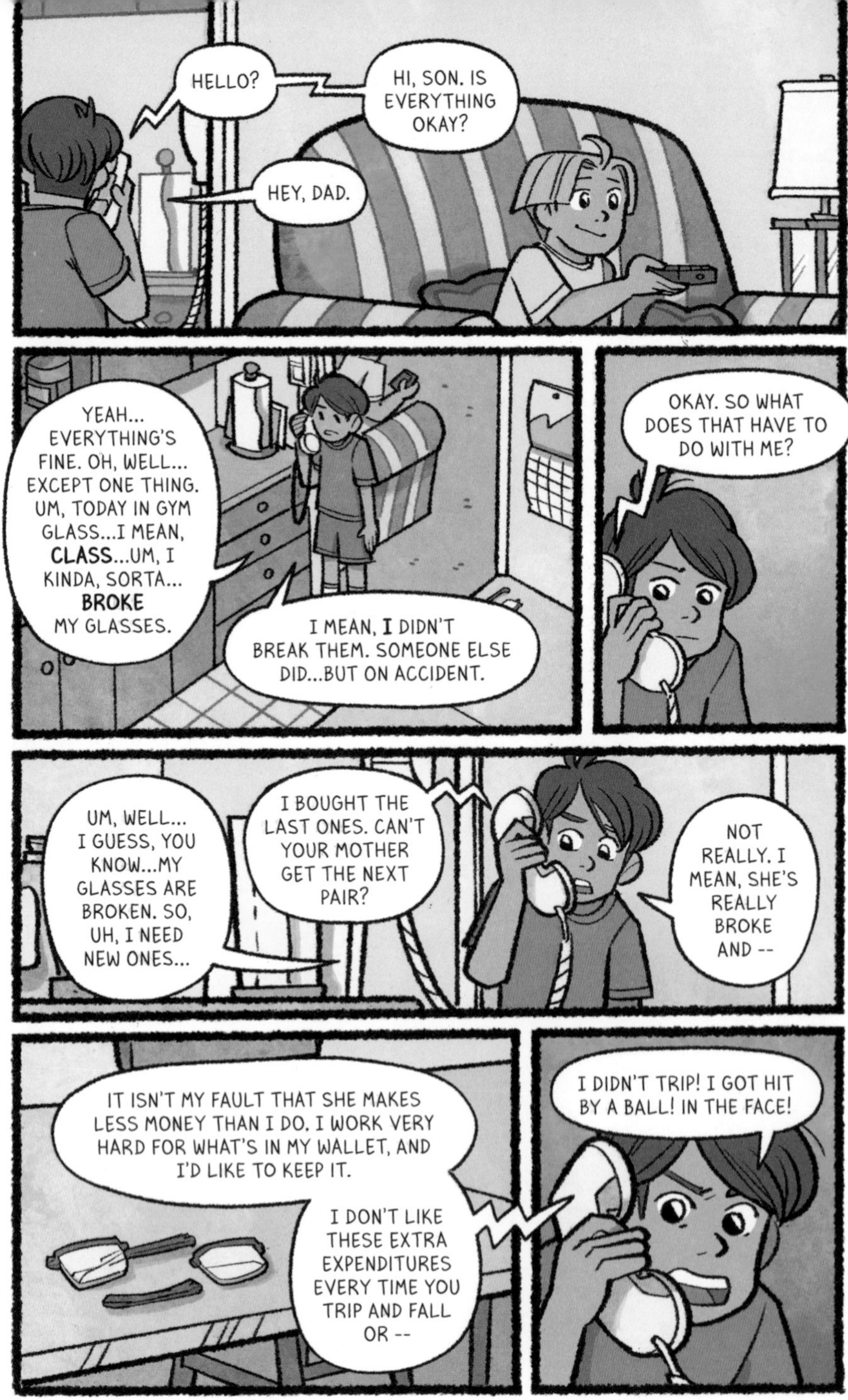
HELLO?
HI, SON. IS EVERYTHING OKAY?
HEY, DAD.
YEAH... EVERYTHING'S FINE. OH, WELL... EXCEPT ONE THING. UM, TODAY IN GYM GLASS...I MEAN, **CLASS**...UM, I KINDA, SORTA... **BROKE** MY GLASSES.
I MEAN, **I** DIDN'T BREAK THEM. SOMEONE ELSE DID...BUT ON ACCIDENT.
OKAY. SO WHAT DOES THAT HAVE TO DO WITH ME?
UM, WELL... I GUESS, YOU KNOW...MY GLASSES ARE BROKEN. SO, UH, I NEED NEW ONES...
I BOUGHT THE LAST ONES. CAN'T YOUR MOTHER GET THE NEXT PAIR?
NOT REALLY. I MEAN, SHE'S REALLY BROKE AND --
IT ISN'T MY FAULT THAT SHE MAKES LESS MONEY THAN I DO. I WORK VERY HARD FOR WHAT'S IN MY WALLET, AND I'D LIKE TO KEEP IT.
I DON'T LIKE THESE EXTRA EXPENDITURES EVERY TIME YOU TRIP AND FALL OR --
I DIDN'T TRIP! I GOT HIT BY A BALL! IN THE FACE!

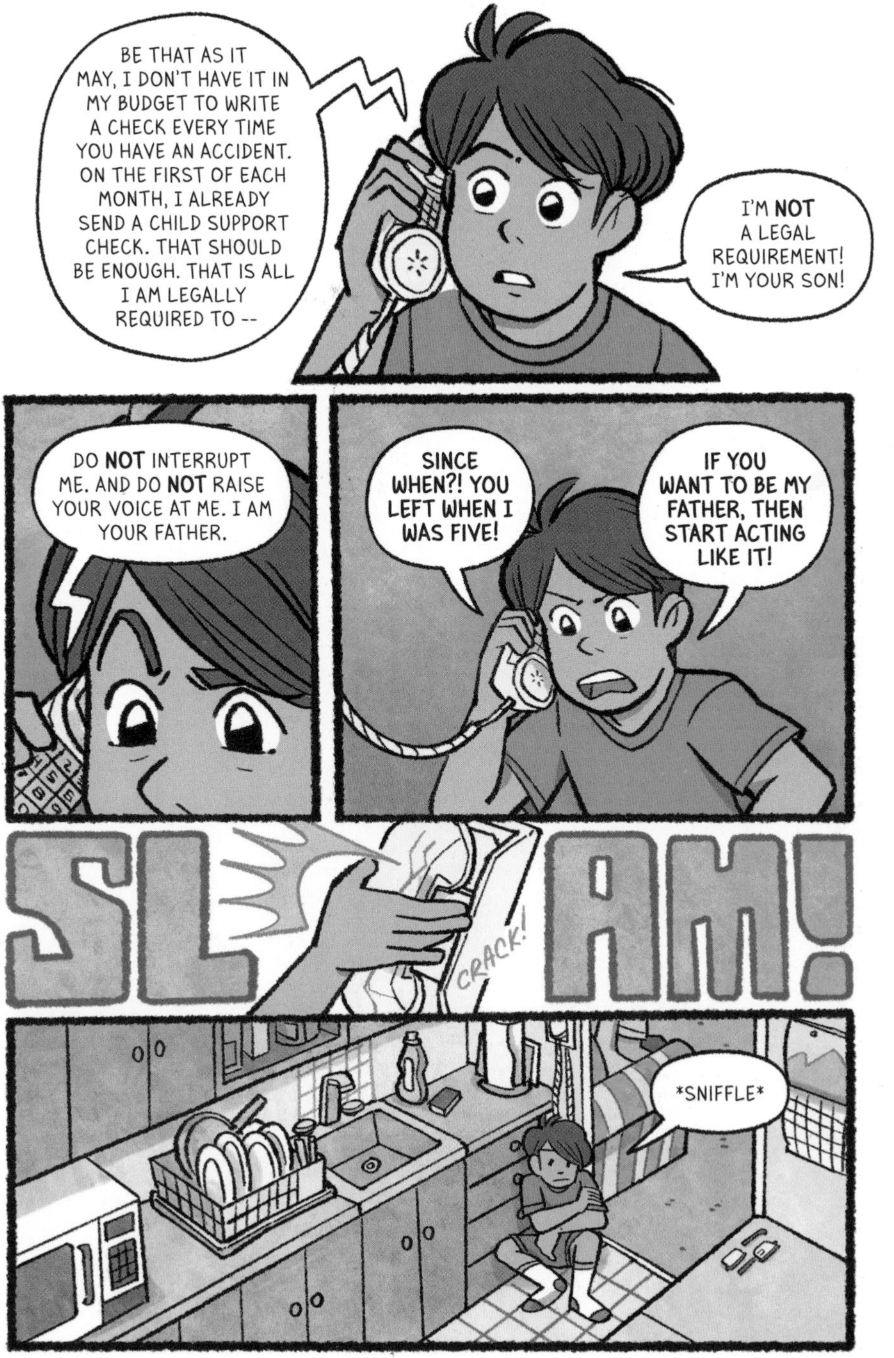
BE THAT AS IT MAY, I DON'T HAVE IT IN MY BUDGET TO WRITE A CHECK EVERY TIME YOU HAVE AN ACCIDENT. ON THE FIRST OF EACH MONTH, I ALREADY SEND A CHILD SUPPORT CHECK. THAT SHOULD BE ENOUGH. THAT IS ALL I AM LEGALLY REQUIRED TO --
I'M **NOT** A LEGAL REQUIREMENT! I'M YOUR SON!
DO **NOT** INTERRUPT ME. AND DO **NOT** RAISE YOUR VOICE AT ME. I AM YOUR FATHER.
SINCE WHEN?! YOU LEFT WHEN I WAS FIVE!
IF YOU WANT TO BE MY FATHER, THEN START ACTING LIKE IT!
SLAM!
CRACK!
SNIFFLE

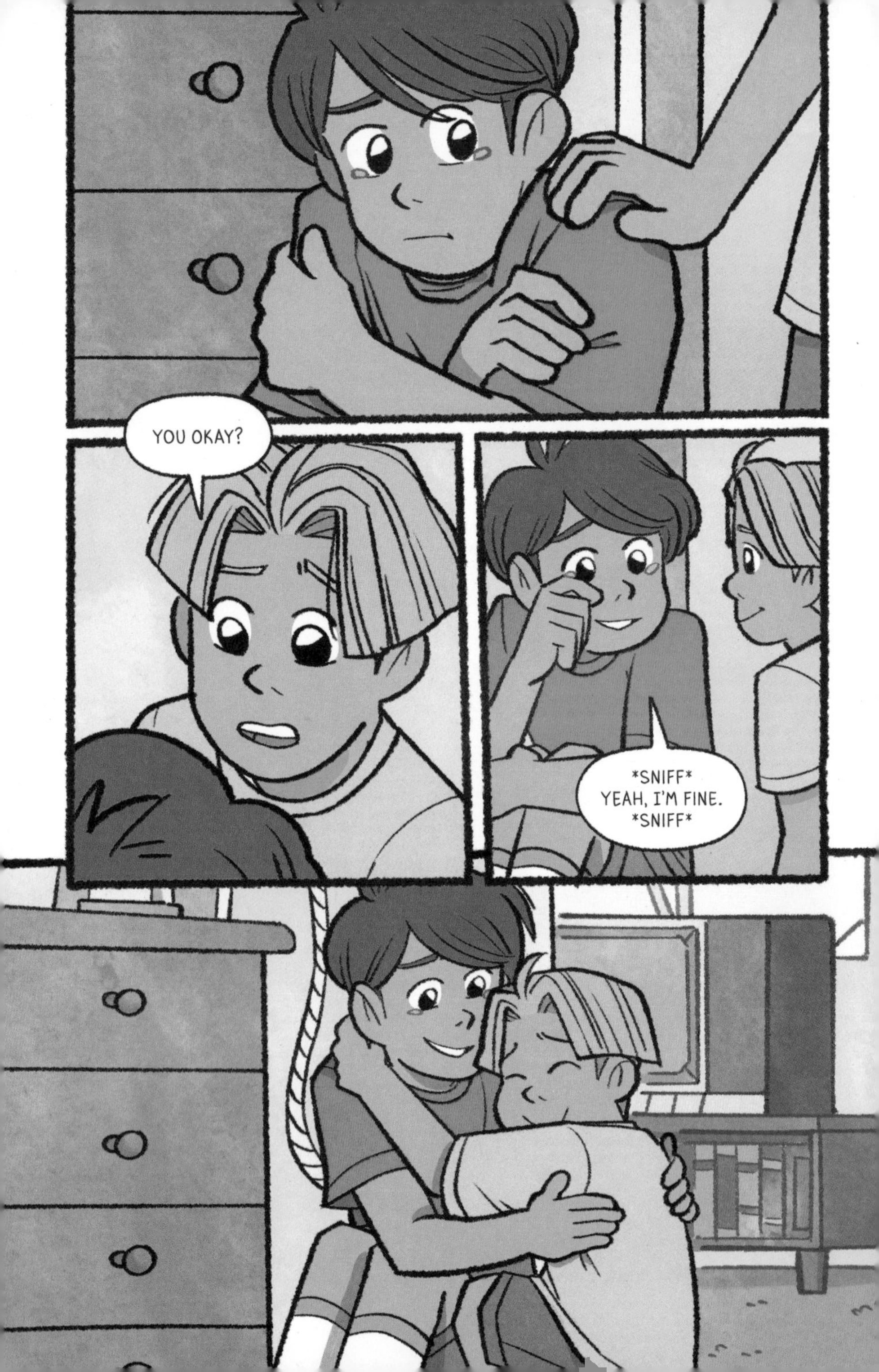
YOU OKAY?
SNIFF
YEAH, I'M FINE.
SNIFF

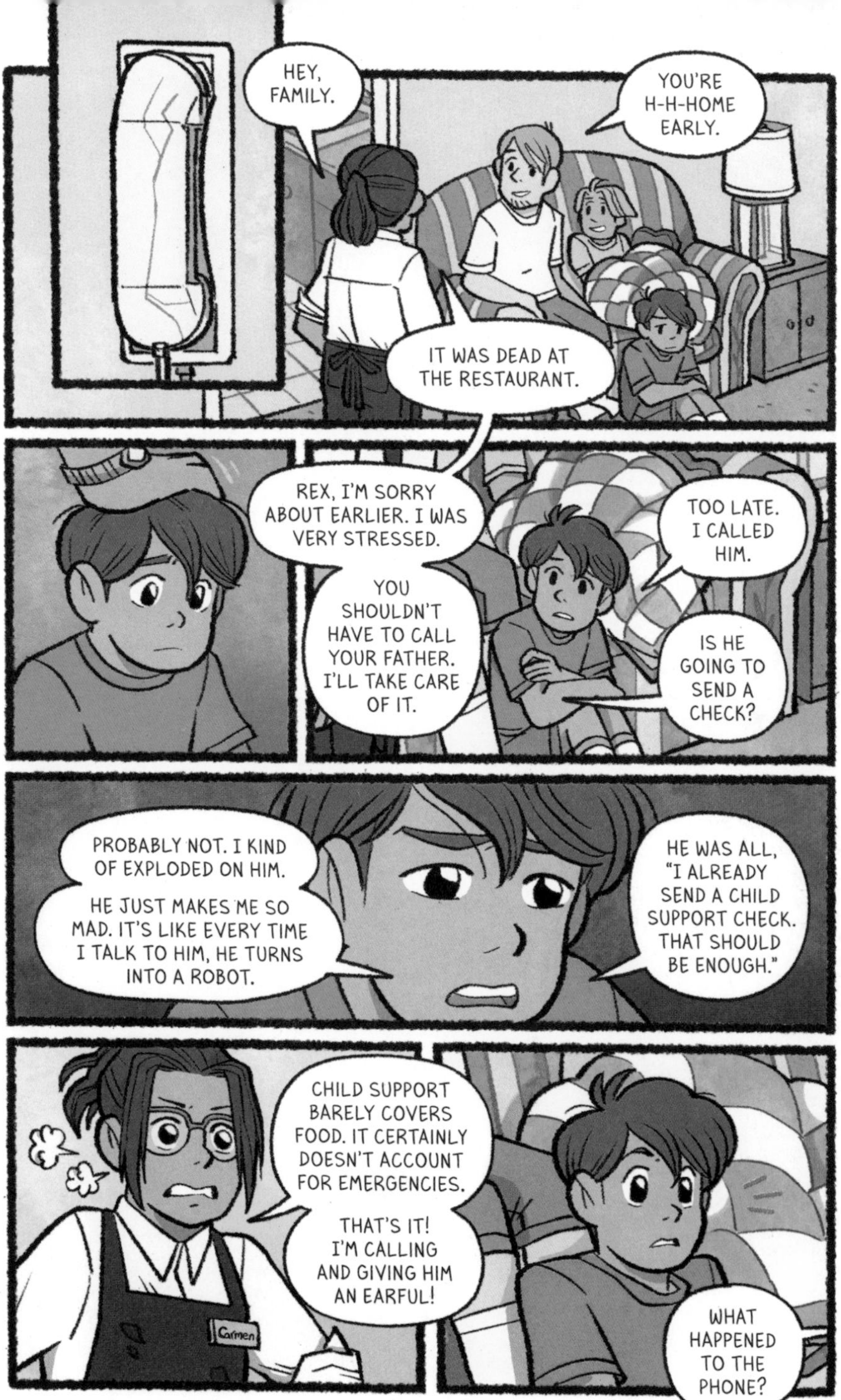
HEY, FAMILY.
YOU'RE H-H-HOME EARLY.
IT WAS DEAD AT THE RESTAURANT.
REX, I'M SORRY ABOUT EARLIER. I WAS VERY STRESSED.
YOU SHOULDN'T HAVE TO CALL YOUR FATHER. I'LL TAKE CARE OF IT.
TOO LATE. I CALLED HIM.
IS HE GOING TO SEND A CHECK?
PROBABLY NOT. I KIND OF EXPLODED ON HIM.
HE JUST MAKES ME SO MAD. IT'S LIKE EVERY TIME I TALK TO HIM, HE TURNS INTO A ROBOT.
HE WAS ALL, "I ALREADY SEND A CHILD SUPPORT CHECK. THAT SHOULD BE ENOUGH."
Carmen
CHILD SUPPORT BARELY COVERS FOOD. IT CERTAINLY DOESN'T ACCOUNT FOR EMERGENCIES.
THAT'S IT! I'M CALLING AND GIVING HIM AN EARFUL!
WHAT HAPPENED TO THE PHONE?

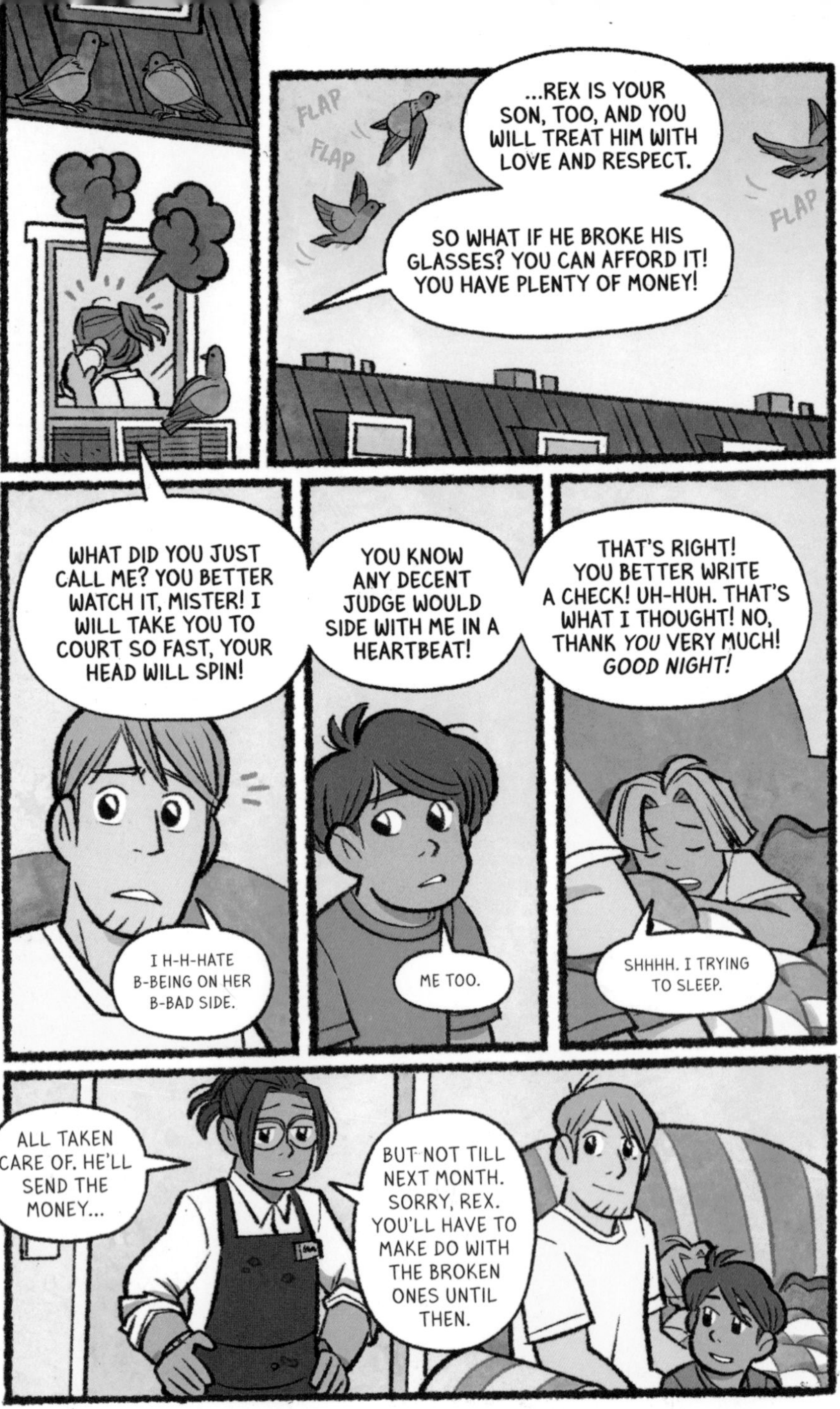
FLAP
FLAP
...REX IS YOUR SON, TOO, AND YOU WILL TREAT HIM WITH LOVE AND RESPECT.
SO WHAT IF HE BROKE HIS GLASSES? YOU CAN AFFORD IT! YOU HAVE PLENTY OF MONEY!
FLAP
WHAT DID YOU JUST CALL ME? YOU BETTER WATCH IT, MISTER! I WILL TAKE YOU TO COURT SO FAST, YOUR HEAD WILL SPIN!
I H-H-HATE B-BEING ON HER B-BAD SIDE.
YOU KNOW ANY DECENT JUDGE WOULD SIDE WITH ME IN A HEARTBEAT!
ME TOO.
THAT'S RIGHT! YOU BETTER WRITE A CHECK! UH-HUH. THAT'S WHAT I THOUGHT! NO, THANK *YOU* VERY MUCH! *GOOD NIGHT!*
SHHHH. I TRYING TO SLEEP.
ALL TAKEN CARE OF. HE'LL SEND THE MONEY...
BUT NOT TILL NEXT MONTH. SORRY, REX. YOU'LL HAVE TO MAKE DO WITH THE BROKEN ONES UNTIL THEN.

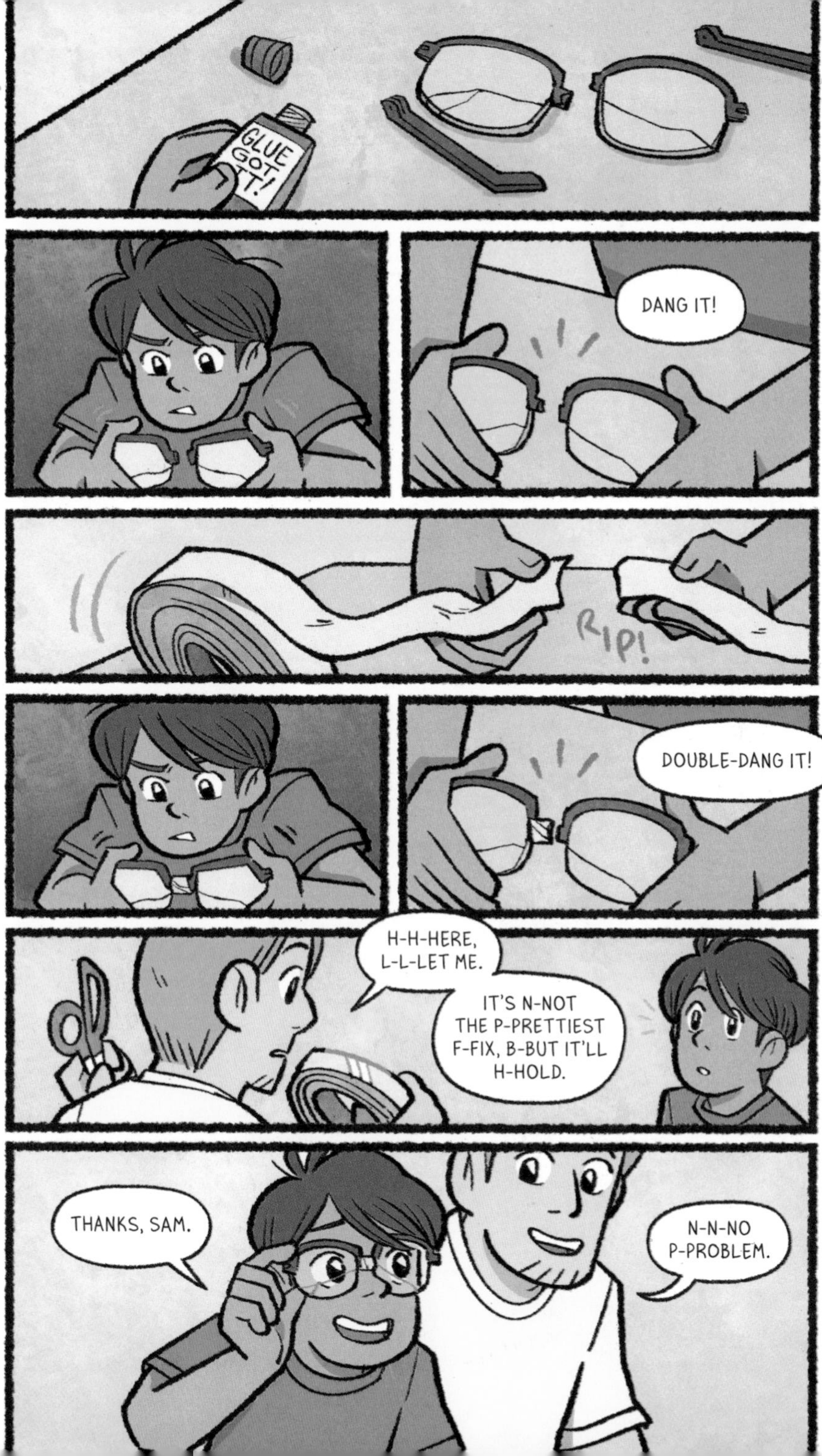
GLUE GOT IT!
DANG IT!
RIP!
DOUBLE-DANG IT!
H-H-HERE, L-L-LET ME.
IT'S N-NOT THE P-PRETTIEST F-FIX, B-BUT IT'LL H-HOLD.
THANKS, SAM.
N-N-NO P-PROBLEM.

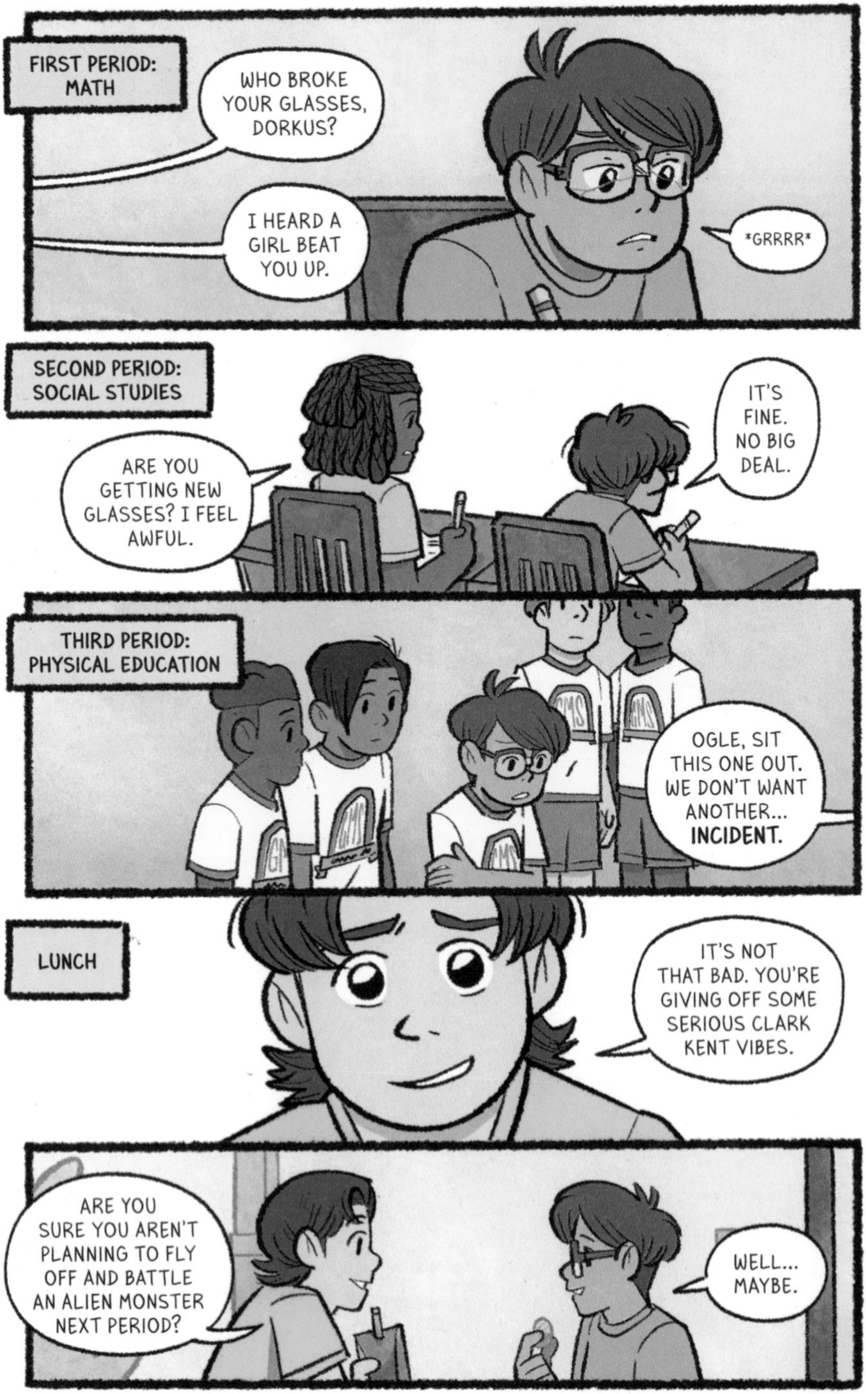
FIRST PERIOD: MATH
WHO BROKE YOUR GLASSES, DORKUS?
I HEARD A GIRL BEAT YOU UP.
GRRRR
SECOND PERIOD: SOCIAL STUDIES
ARE YOU GETTING NEW GLASSES? I FEEL AWFUL.
IT'S FINE. NO BIG DEAL.
THIRD PERIOD: PHYSICAL EDUCATION
OGLE, SIT THIS ONE OUT. WE DON'T WANT ANOTHER... **INCIDENT.**
LUNCH
IT'S NOT THAT BAD. YOU'RE GIVING OFF SOME SERIOUS CLARK KENT VIBES.
ARE YOU SURE YOU AREN'T PLANNING TO FLY OFF AND BATTLE AN ALIEN MONSTER NEXT PERIOD?
WELL... MAYBE.

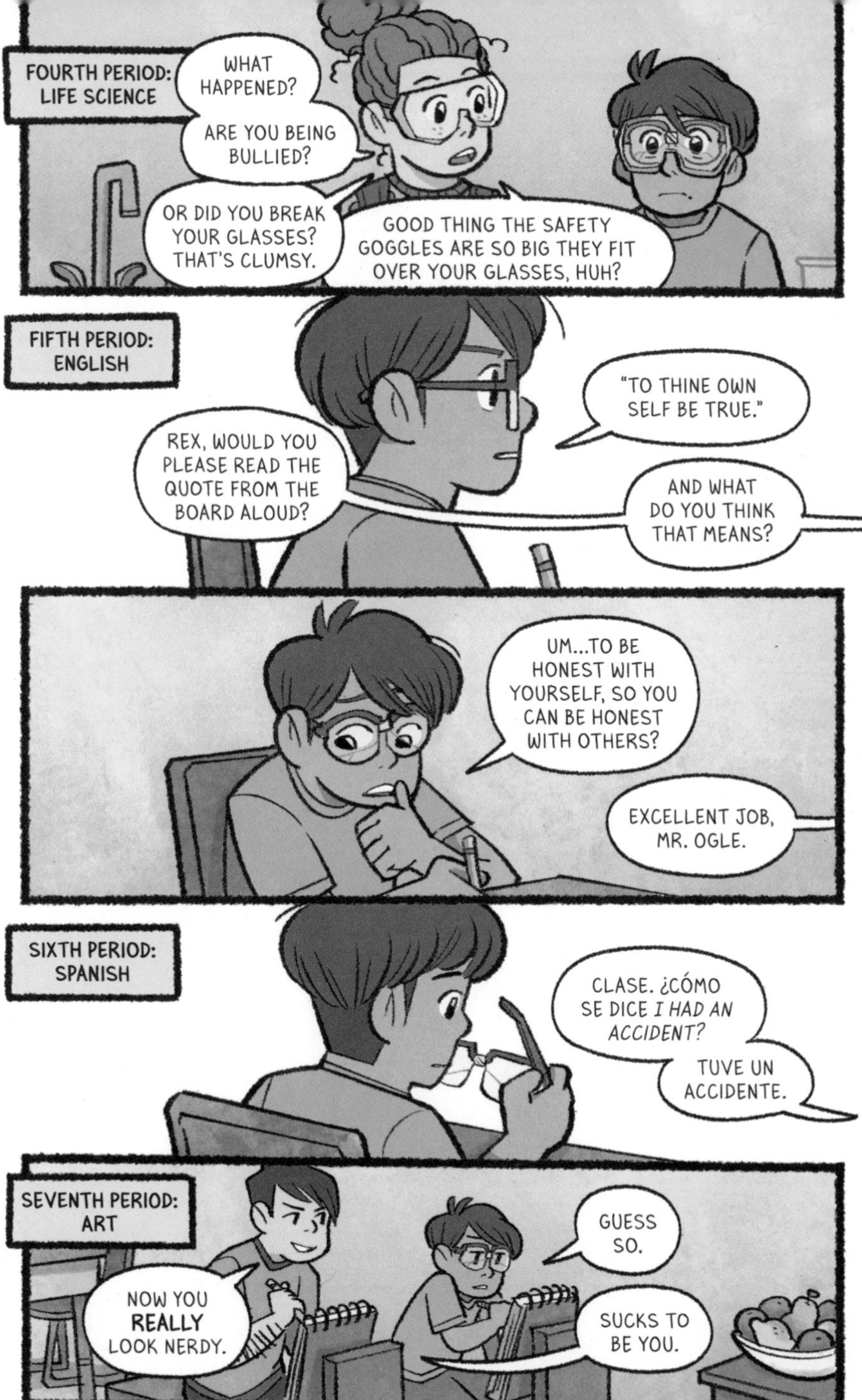
FOURTH PERIOD: LIFE SCIENCE
WHAT HAPPENED?
ARE YOU BEING BULLIED?
OR DID YOU BREAK YOUR GLASSES? THAT'S CLUMSY.
GOOD THING THE SAFETY GOGGLES ARE SO BIG THEY FIT OVER YOUR GLASSES, HUH?
FIFTH PERIOD: ENGLISH
REX, WOULD YOU PLEASE READ THE QUOTE FROM THE BOARD ALOUD?
"TO THINE OWN SELF BE TRUE."
AND WHAT DO YOU THINK THAT MEANS?
UM...TO BE HONEST WITH YOURSELF, SO YOU CAN BE HONEST WITH OTHERS?
EXCELLENT JOB, MR. OGLE.
SIXTH PERIOD: SPANISH
CLASE. ¿CÓMO SE DICE *I HAD AN ACCIDENT?*
TUVE UN ACCIDENTE.
SEVENTH PERIOD: ART
NOW YOU **REALLY** LOOK NERDY.
GUESS SO.
SUCKS TO BE YOU.

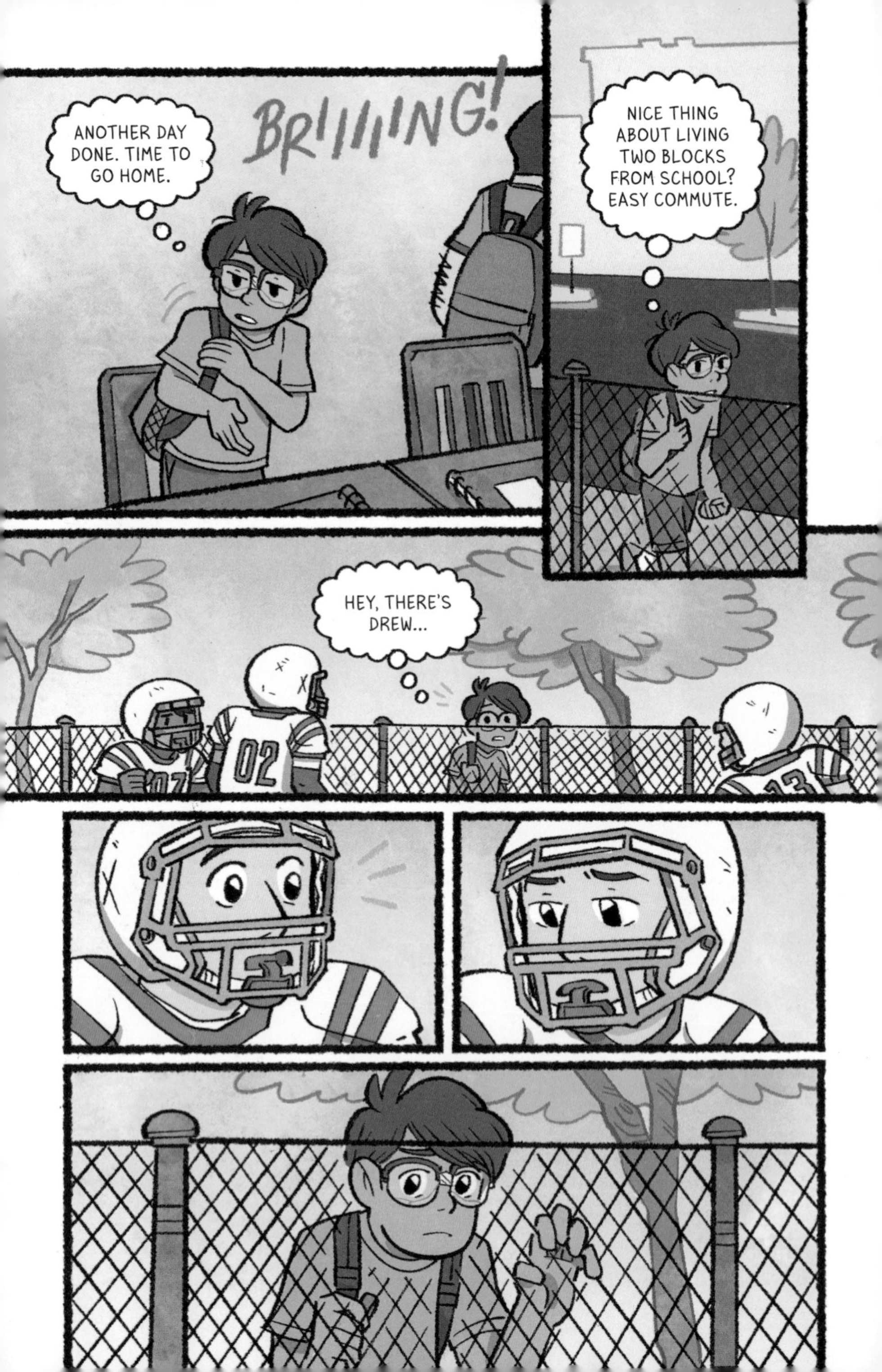
ANOTHER DAY DONE. TIME TO GO HOME.
BRIIIIING!
NICE THING ABOUT LIVING TWO BLOCKS FROM SCHOOL? EASY COMMUTE.
HEY, THERE'S DREW...
02

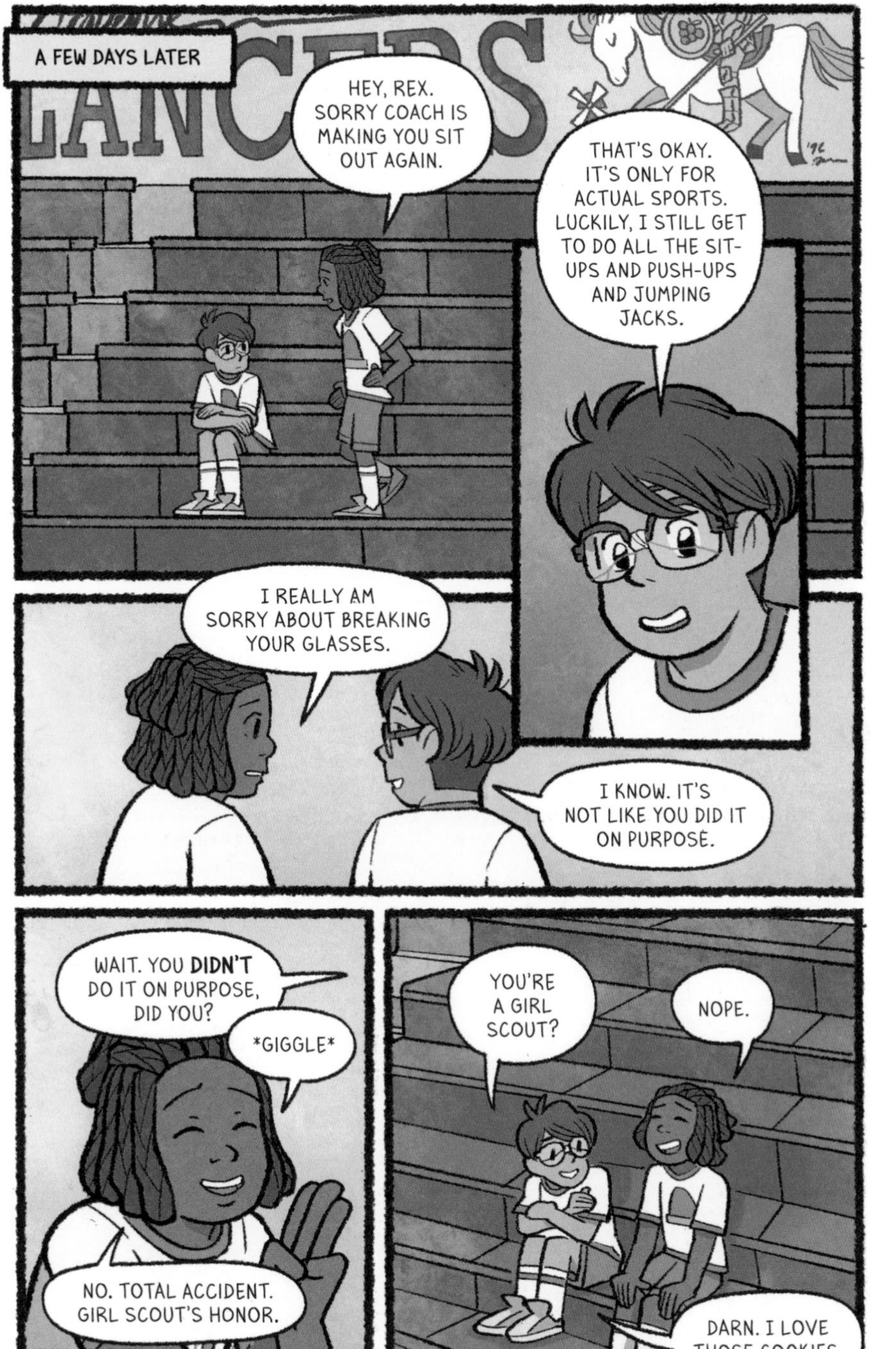
A FEW DAYS LATER
LANCERS
HEY, REX. SORRY COACH IS MAKING YOU SIT OUT AGAIN.
THAT'S OKAY. IT'S ONLY FOR ACTUAL SPORTS. LUCKILY, I STILL GET TO DO ALL THE SIT-UPS AND PUSH-UPS AND JUMPING JACKS.
I REALLY AM SORRY ABOUT BREAKING YOUR GLASSES.
I KNOW. IT'S NOT LIKE YOU DID IT ON PURPOSE.
WAIT. YOU **DIDN'T** DO IT ON PURPOSE, DID YOU?
GIGGLE
NO. TOTAL ACCIDENT. GIRL SCOUT'S HONOR.
YOU'RE A GIRL SCOUT?
NOPE.
DARN. I LOVE THOSE COOKIES.

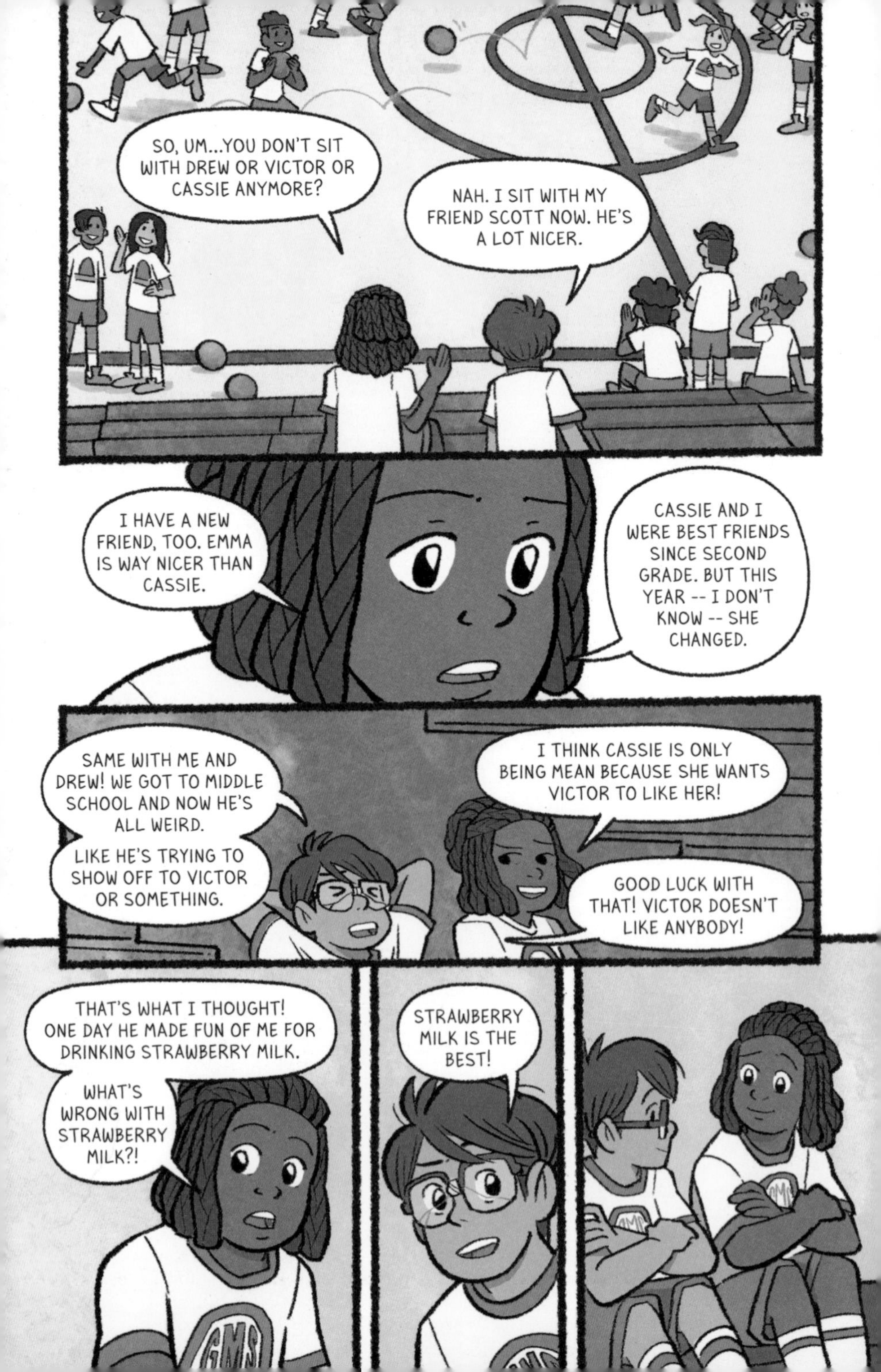
SO, UM...YOU DON'T SIT WITH DREW OR VICTOR OR CASSIE ANYMORE?
NAH. I SIT WITH MY FRIEND SCOTT NOW. HE'S A LOT NICER.
I HAVE A NEW FRIEND, TOO. EMMA IS WAY NICER THAN CASSIE.
CASSIE AND I WERE BEST FRIENDS SINCE SECOND GRADE. BUT THIS YEAR -- I DON'T KNOW -- SHE CHANGED.
SAME WITH ME AND DREW! WE GOT TO MIDDLE SCHOOL AND NOW HE'S ALL WEIRD.
LIKE HE'S TRYING TO SHOW OFF TO VICTOR OR SOMETHING.
I THINK CASSIE IS ONLY BEING MEAN BECAUSE SHE WANTS VICTOR TO LIKE HER!
GOOD LUCK WITH THAT! VICTOR DOESN'T LIKE ANYBODY!
THAT'S WHAT I THOUGHT! ONE DAY HE MADE FUN OF ME FOR DRINKING STRAWBERRY MILK.
WHAT'S WRONG WITH STRAWBERRY MILK?!
STRAWBERRY MILK IS THE BEST!

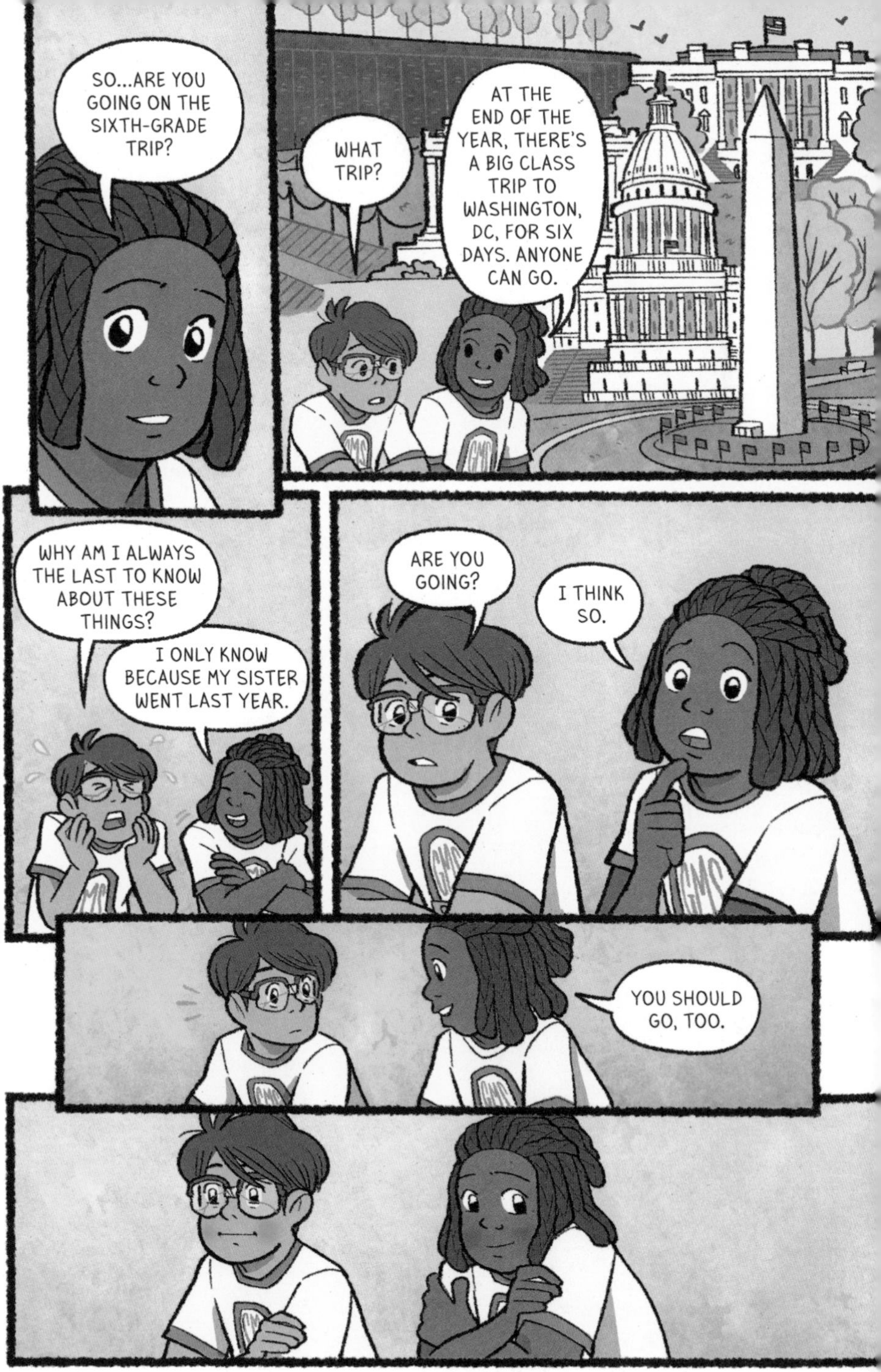
SO...ARE YOU GOING ON THE SIXTH-GRADE TRIP?
WHAT TRIP?
AT THE END OF THE YEAR, THERE'S A BIG CLASS TRIP TO WASHINGTON, DC, FOR SIX DAYS. ANYONE CAN GO.
WHY AM I ALWAYS THE LAST TO KNOW ABOUT THESE THINGS?
I ONLY KNOW BECAUSE MY SISTER WENT LAST YEAR.
ARE YOU GOING?
I THINK SO.
YOU SHOULD GO, TOO.

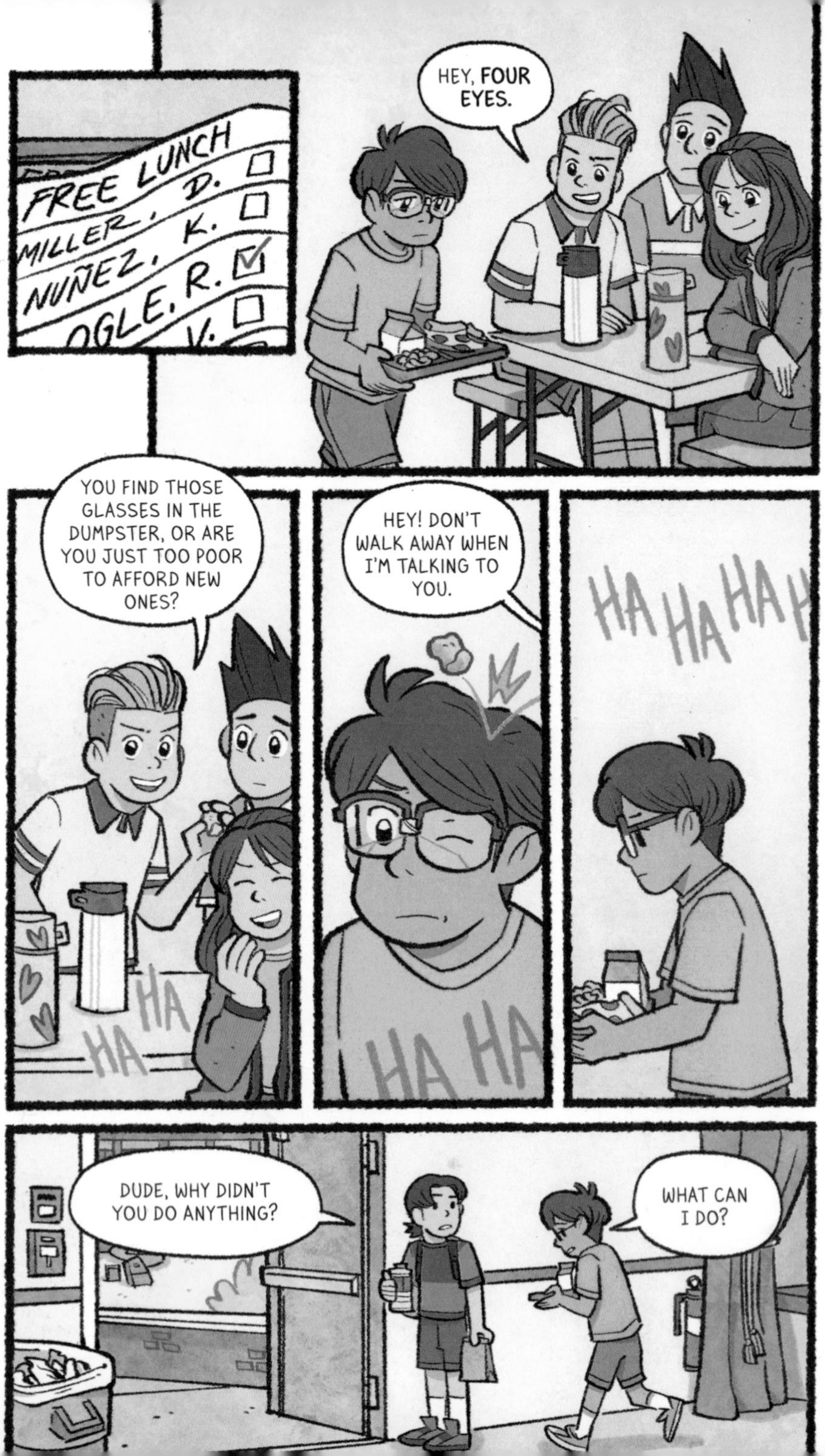
FREE LUNCH
MILLER, D.
NUÑEZ, K.
OGLE, R.
HEY, FOUR EYES.
YOU FIND THOSE GLASSES IN THE DUMPSTER, OR ARE YOU JUST TOO POOR TO AFFORD NEW ONES?
HA HA
HEY! DON'T WALK AWAY WHEN I'M TALKING TO YOU.
HA HA
HA HA HA
DUDE, WHY DIDN'T YOU DO ANYTHING?
WHAT CAN I DO?

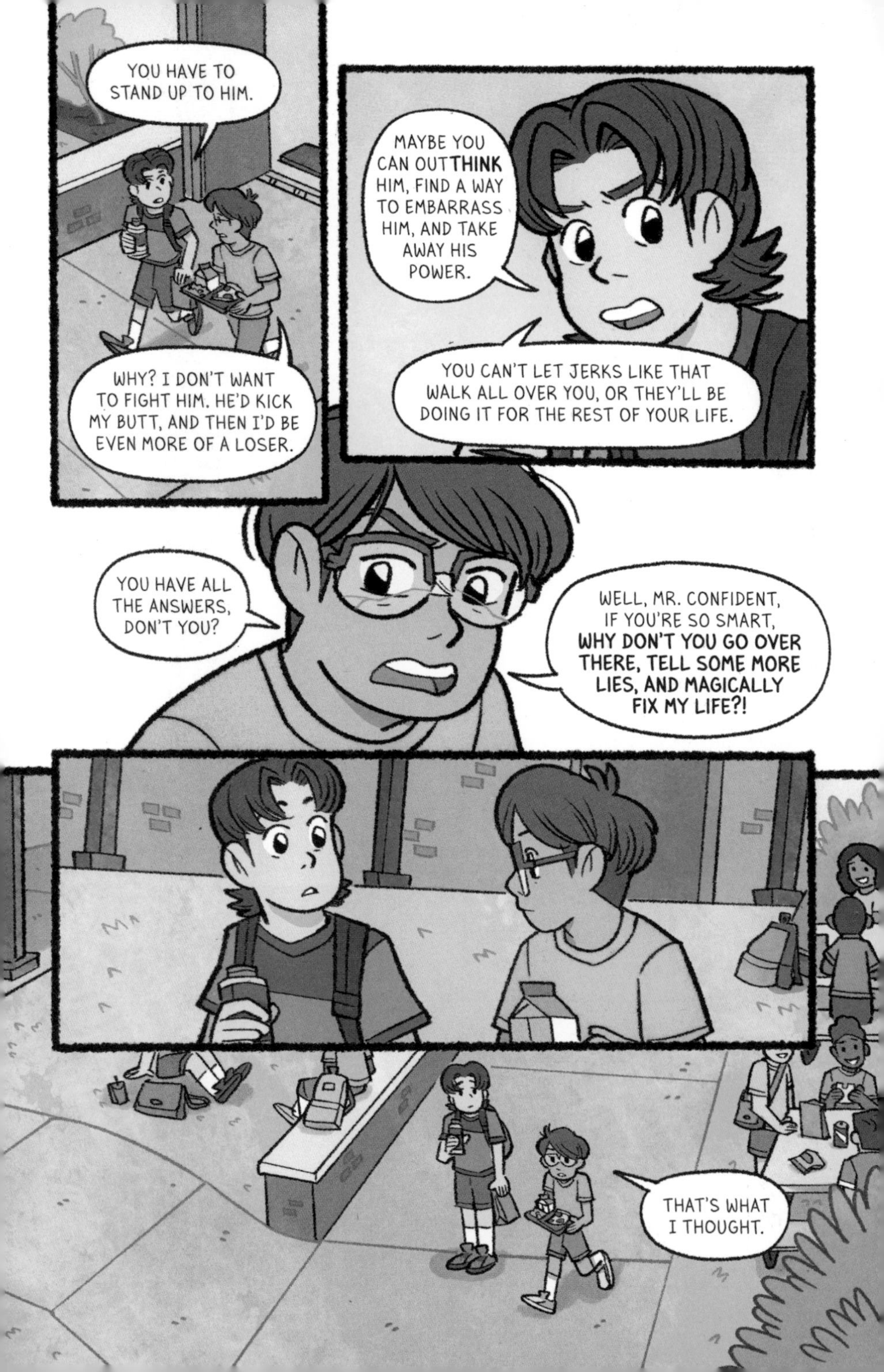
YOU HAVE TO STAND UP TO HIM.
WHY? I DON'T WANT TO FIGHT HIM. HE'D KICK MY BUTT, AND THEN I'D BE EVEN MORE OF A LOSER.
MAYBE YOU CAN OUT**THINK** HIM, FIND A WAY TO EMBARRASS HIM, AND TAKE AWAY HIS POWER.
YOU CAN'T LET JERKS LIKE THAT WALK ALL OVER YOU, OR THEY'LL BE DOING IT FOR THE REST OF YOUR LIFE.
YOU HAVE ALL THE ANSWERS, DON'T YOU?
WELL, MR. CONFIDENT, IF YOU'RE SO SMART, **WHY DON'T YOU GO OVER THERE, TELL SOME MORE LIES, AND MAGICALLY FIX MY LIFE?!**
THAT'S WHAT I THOUGHT.

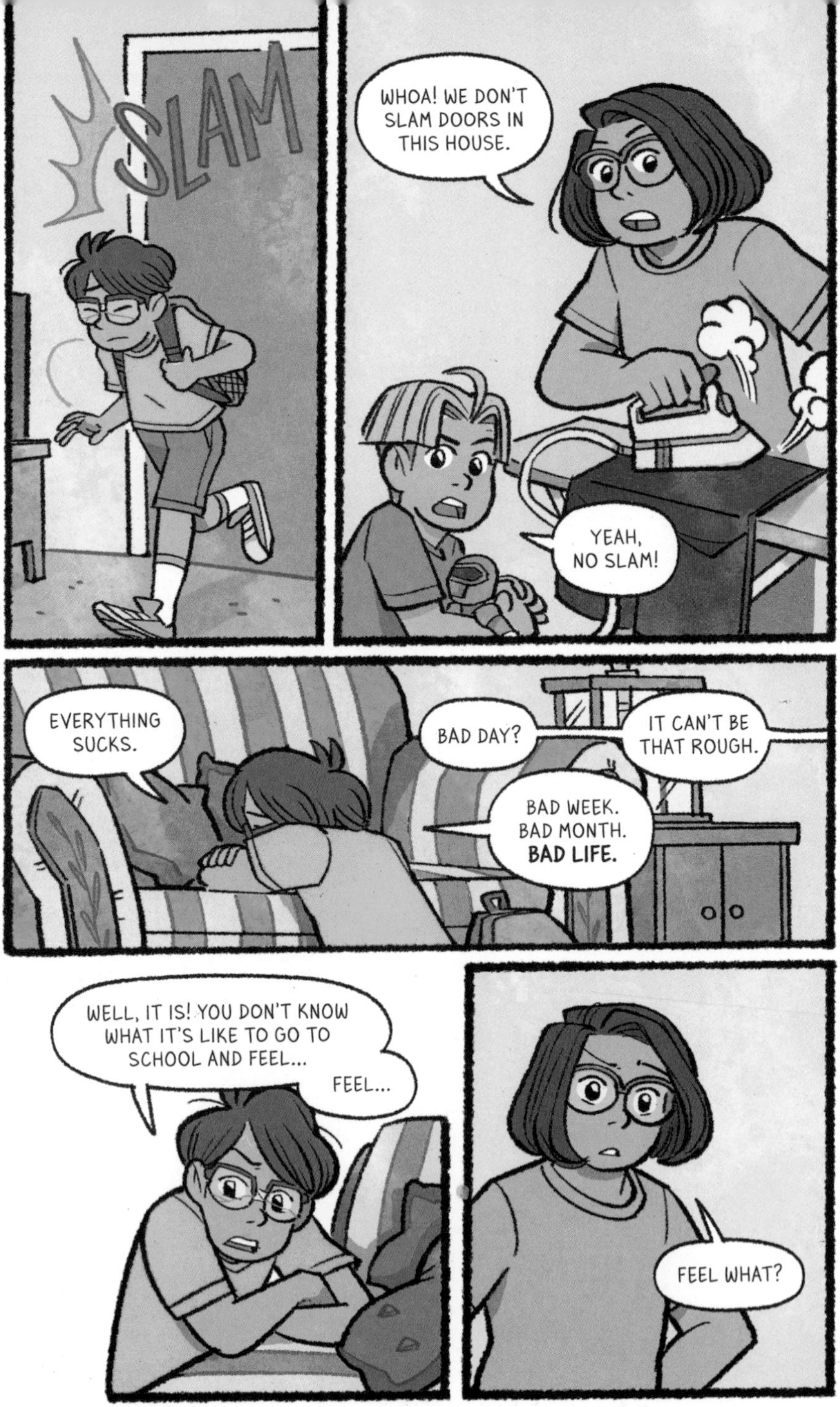
SLAM
WHOA! WE DON'T SLAM DOORS IN THIS HOUSE.
YEAH, NO SLAM!
EVERYTHING SUCKS.
BAD DAY?
IT CAN'T BE THAT ROUGH.
BAD WEEK. BAD MONTH. **BAD LIFE.**
WELL, IT IS! YOU DON'T KNOW WHAT IT'S LIKE TO GO TO SCHOOL AND FEEL... FEEL...
FEEL WHAT?

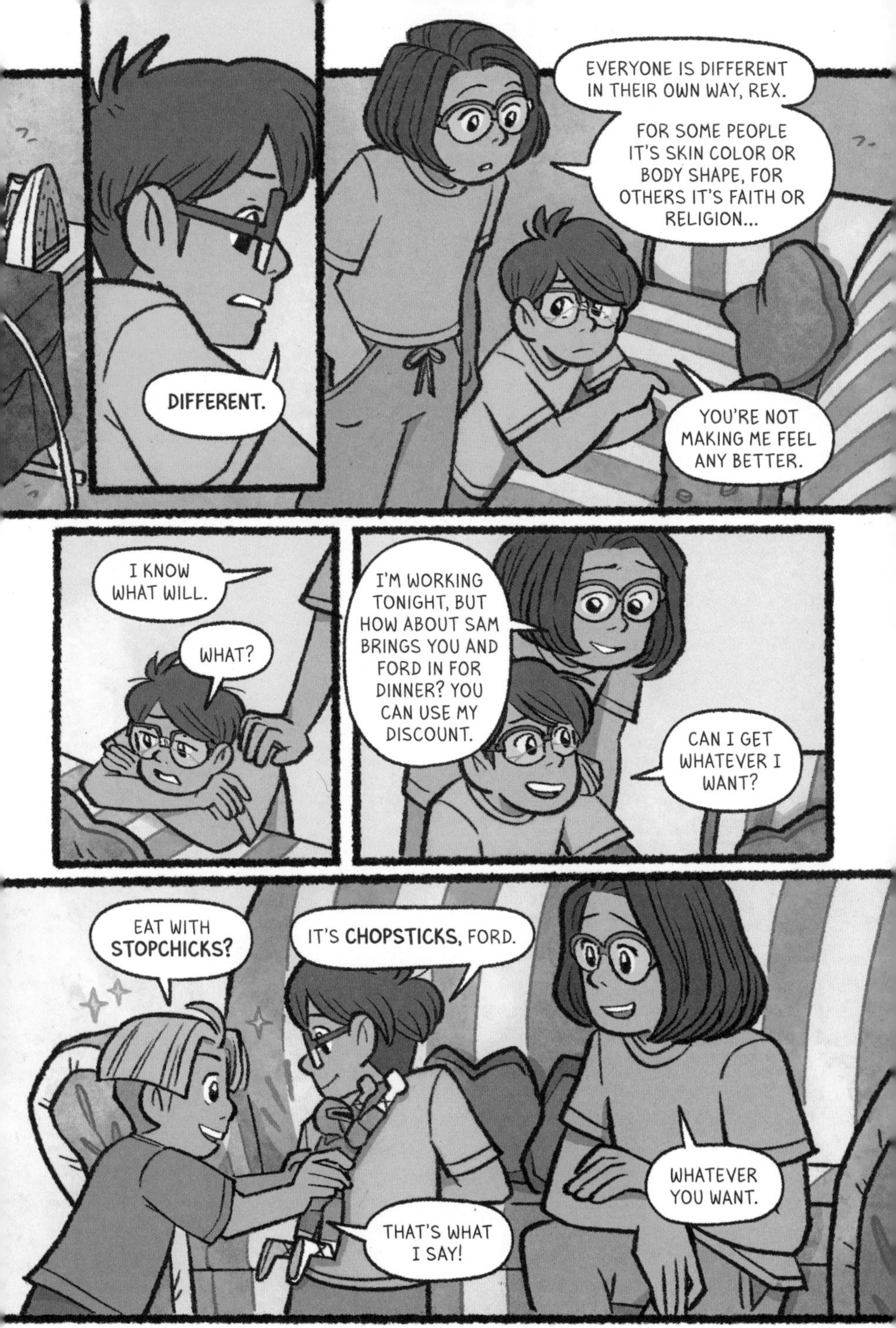
DIFFERENT.
EVERYONE IS DIFFERENT IN THEIR OWN WAY, REX.
FOR SOME PEOPLE IT'S SKIN COLOR OR BODY SHAPE, FOR OTHERS IT'S FAITH OR RELIGION...
YOU'RE NOT MAKING ME FEEL ANY BETTER.
I KNOW WHAT WILL.
WHAT?
I'M WORKING TONIGHT, BUT HOW ABOUT SAM BRINGS YOU AND FORD IN FOR DINNER? YOU CAN USE MY DISCOUNT.
CAN I GET WHATEVER I WANT?
EAT WITH **STOPCHICKS?**
IT'S **CHOPSTICKS,** FORD.
WHATEVER YOU WANT.
THAT'S WHAT I SAY!

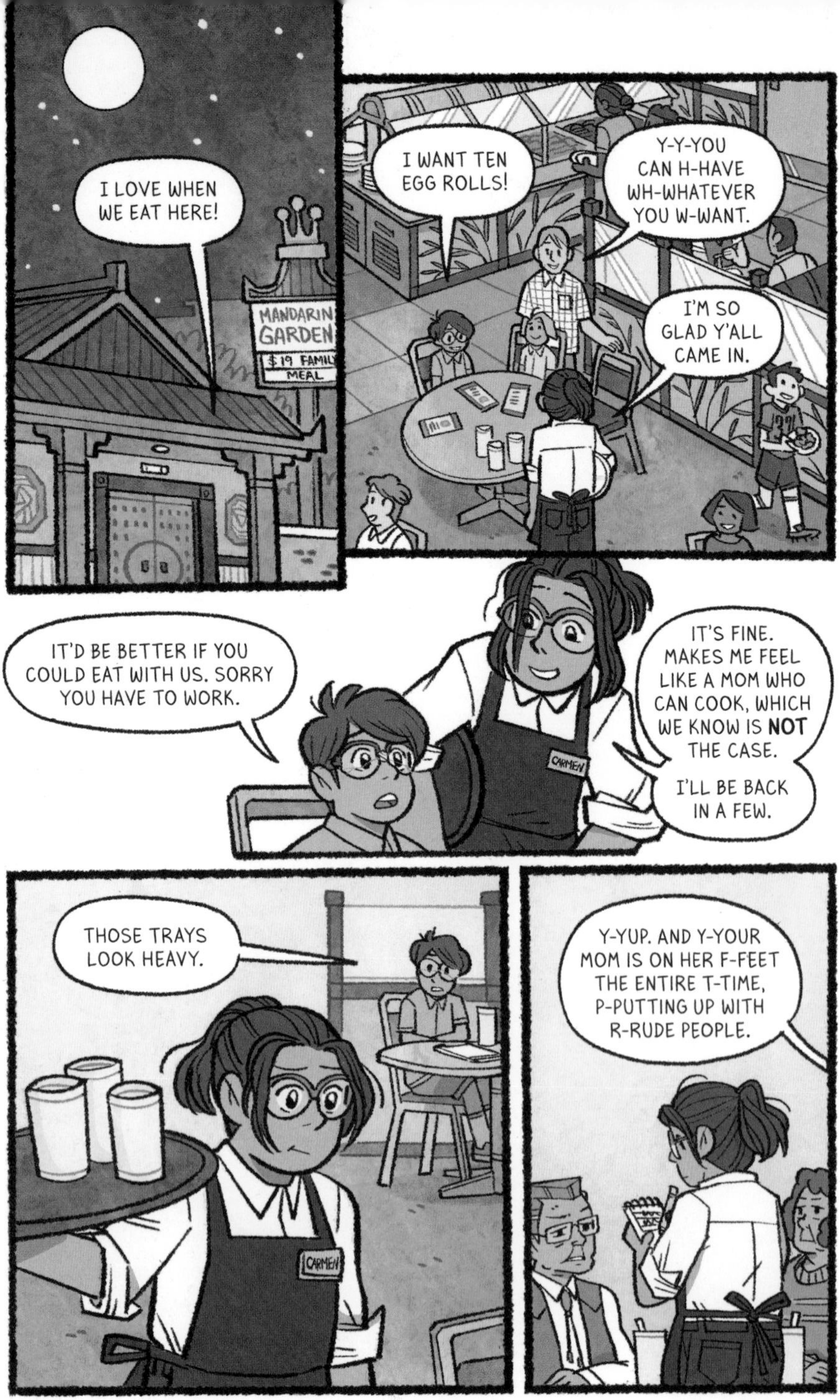
I LOVE WHEN WE EAT HERE!
MANDARIN GARDEN
$19 FAMILY MEAL
I WANT TEN EGG ROLLS!
Y-Y-YOU CAN H-HAVE WH-WHATEVER YOU W-WANT.
I'M SO GLAD Y'ALL CAME IN.
IT'D BE BETTER IF YOU COULD EAT WITH US. SORRY YOU HAVE TO WORK.
IT'S FINE. MAKES ME FEEL LIKE A MOM WHO CAN COOK, WHICH WE KNOW IS **NOT** THE CASE.
I'LL BE BACK IN A FEW.
CARMEN
THOSE TRAYS LOOK HEAVY.
CARMEN
Y-YUP. AND Y-YOUR MOM IS ON HER F-FEET THE ENTIRE T-TIME, P-PUTTING UP WITH R-RUDE PEOPLE.

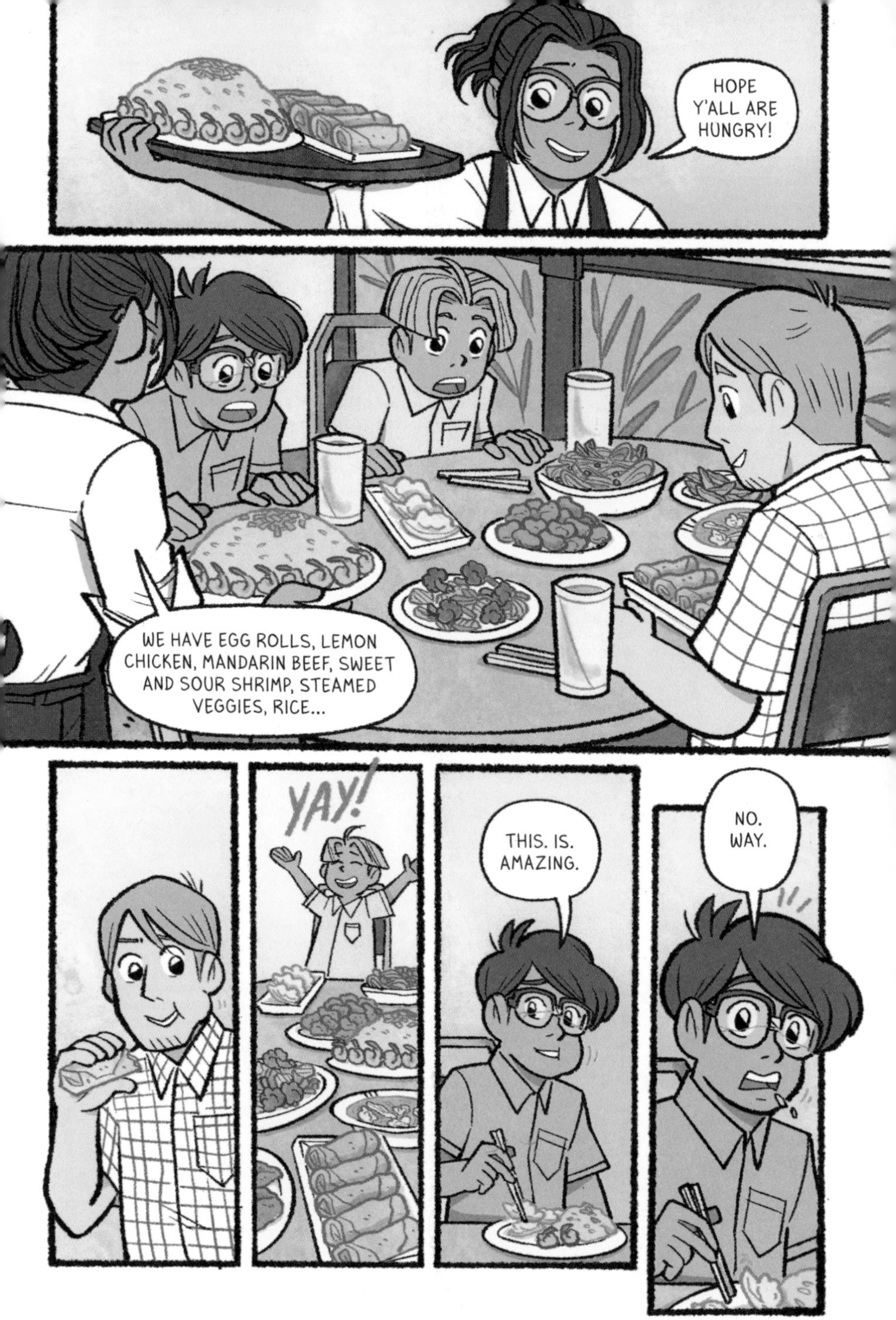
HOPE Y'ALL ARE HUNGRY!
WE HAVE EGG ROLLS, LEMON CHICKEN, MANDARIN BEEF, SWEET AND SOUR SHRIMP, STEAMED VEGGIES, RICE...
YAY!
THIS. IS. AMAZING.
NO. WAY.

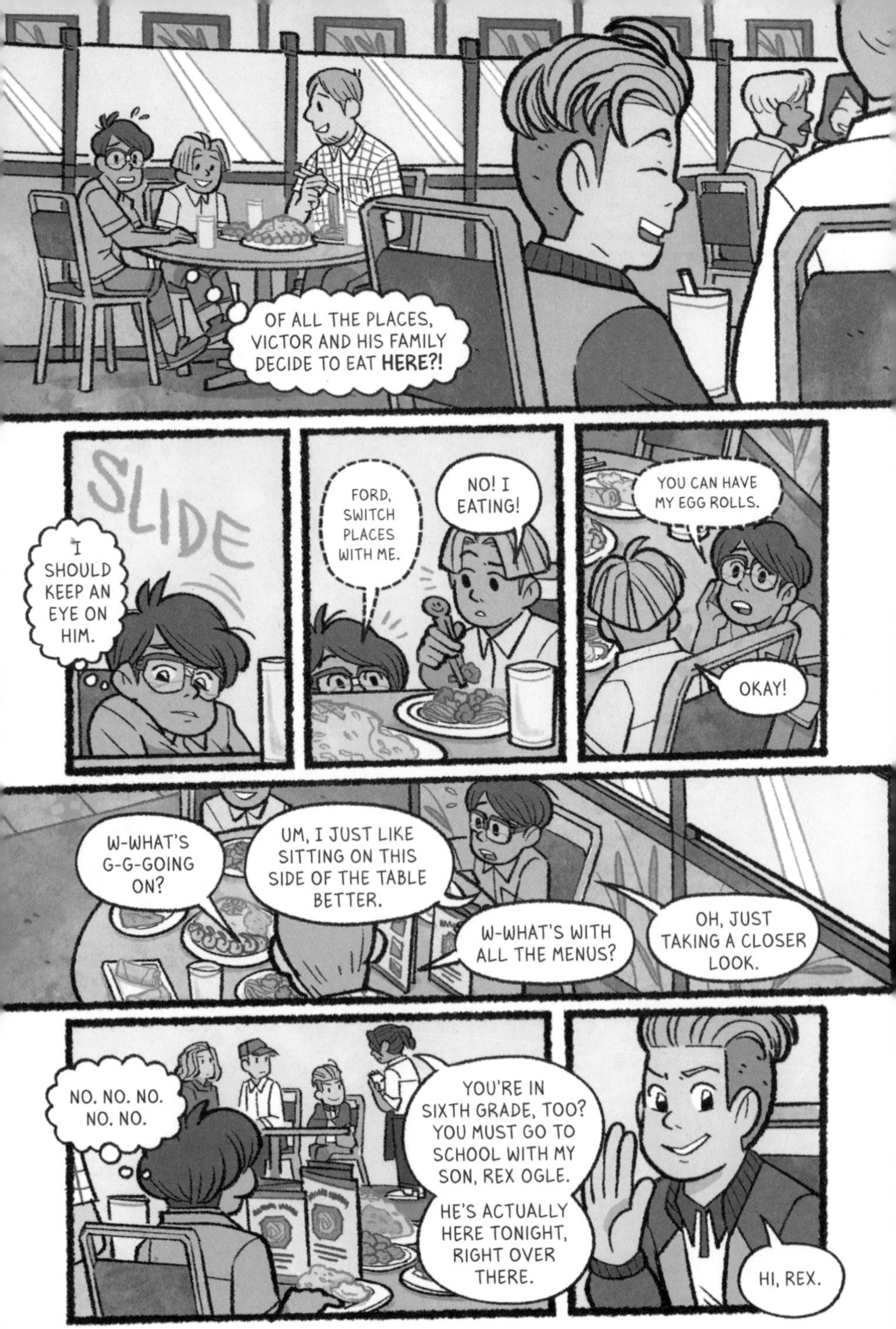
OF ALL THE PLACES, VICTOR AND HIS FAMILY DECIDE TO EAT **HERE?!**
SLIDE
I SHOULD KEEP AN EYE ON HIM.
FORD, SWITCH PLACES WITH ME.
NO! I EATING!
YOU CAN HAVE MY EGG ROLLS.
OKAY!
W-WHAT'S G-G-GOING ON?
UM, I JUST LIKE SITTING ON THIS SIDE OF THE TABLE BETTER.
W-WHAT'S WITH ALL THE MENUS?
OH, JUST TAKING A CLOSER LOOK.
NO. NO. NO. NO. NO.
YOU'RE IN SIXTH GRADE, TOO? YOU MUST GO TO SCHOOL WITH MY SON, REX OGLE.
HE'S ACTUALLY HERE TONIGHT, RIGHT OVER THERE.
HI, REX.

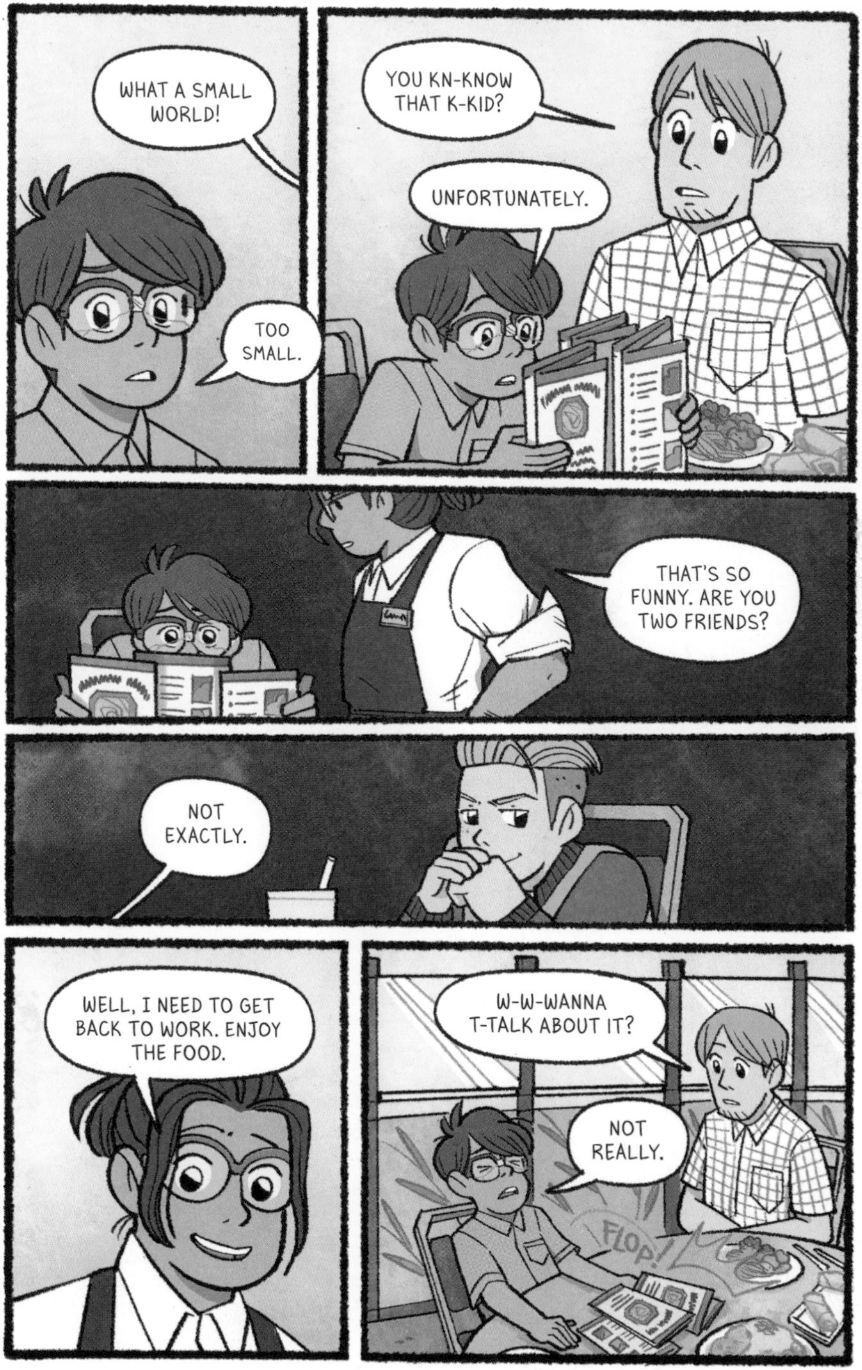
WHAT A SMALL WORLD!
TOO SMALL.
YOU KN-KNOW THAT K-KID?
UNFORTUNATELY.
THAT'S SO FUNNY. ARE YOU TWO FRIENDS?
NOT EXACTLY.
WELL, I NEED TO GET BACK TO WORK. ENJOY THE FOOD.
W-W-WANNA T-TALK ABOUT IT?
NOT REALLY.
FLOP!

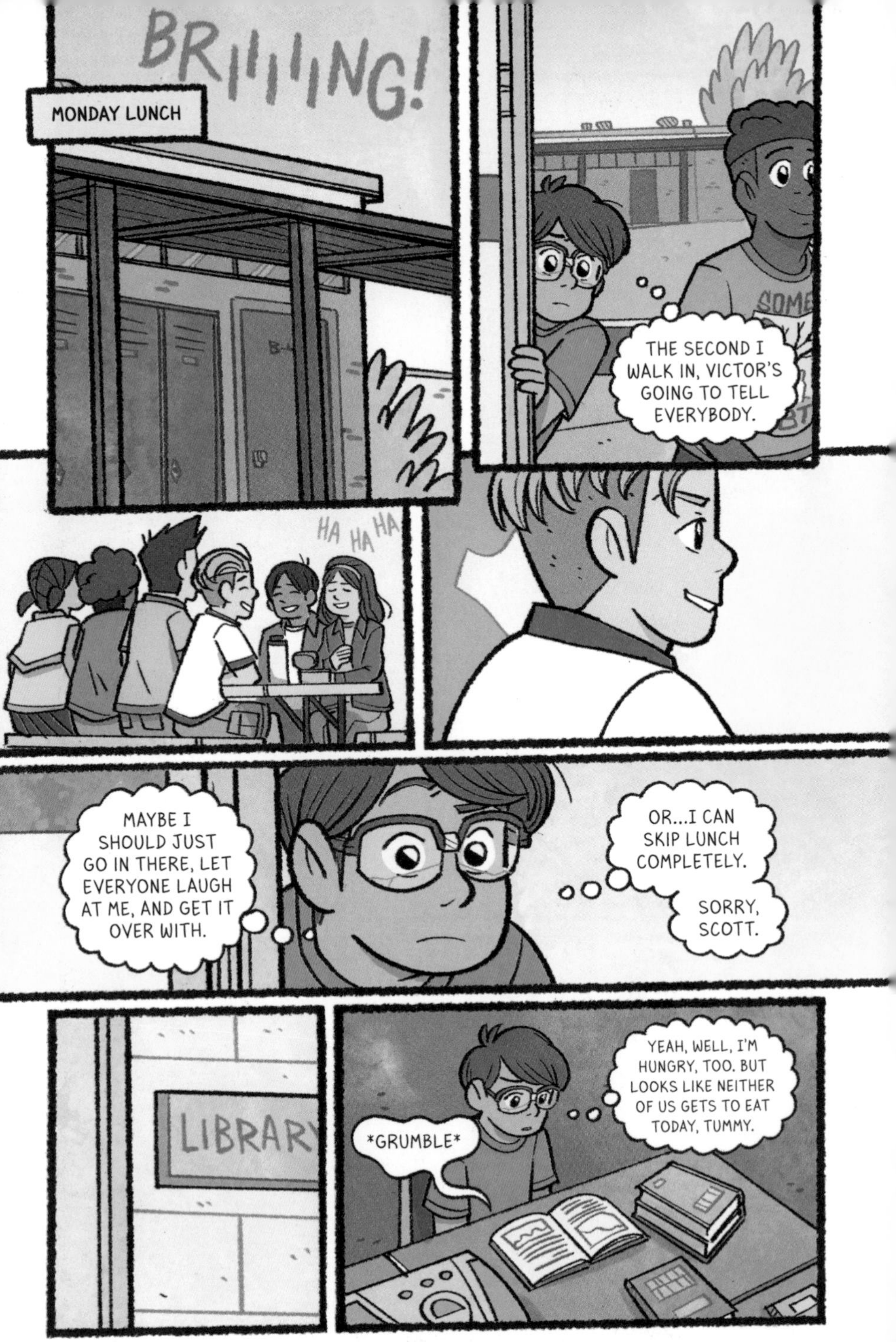
BRIIIING!
MONDAY LUNCH
THE SECOND I WALK IN, VICTOR'S GOING TO TELL EVERYBODY.
HA HA HA
MAYBE I SHOULD JUST GO IN THERE, LET EVERYONE LAUGH AT ME, AND GET IT OVER WITH.
OR...I CAN SKIP LUNCH COMPLETELY.
SORRY, SCOTT.
LIBRARY
GRUMBLE
YEAH, WELL, I'M HUNGRY, TOO. BUT LOOKS LIKE NEITHER OF US GETS TO EAT TODAY, TUMMY.

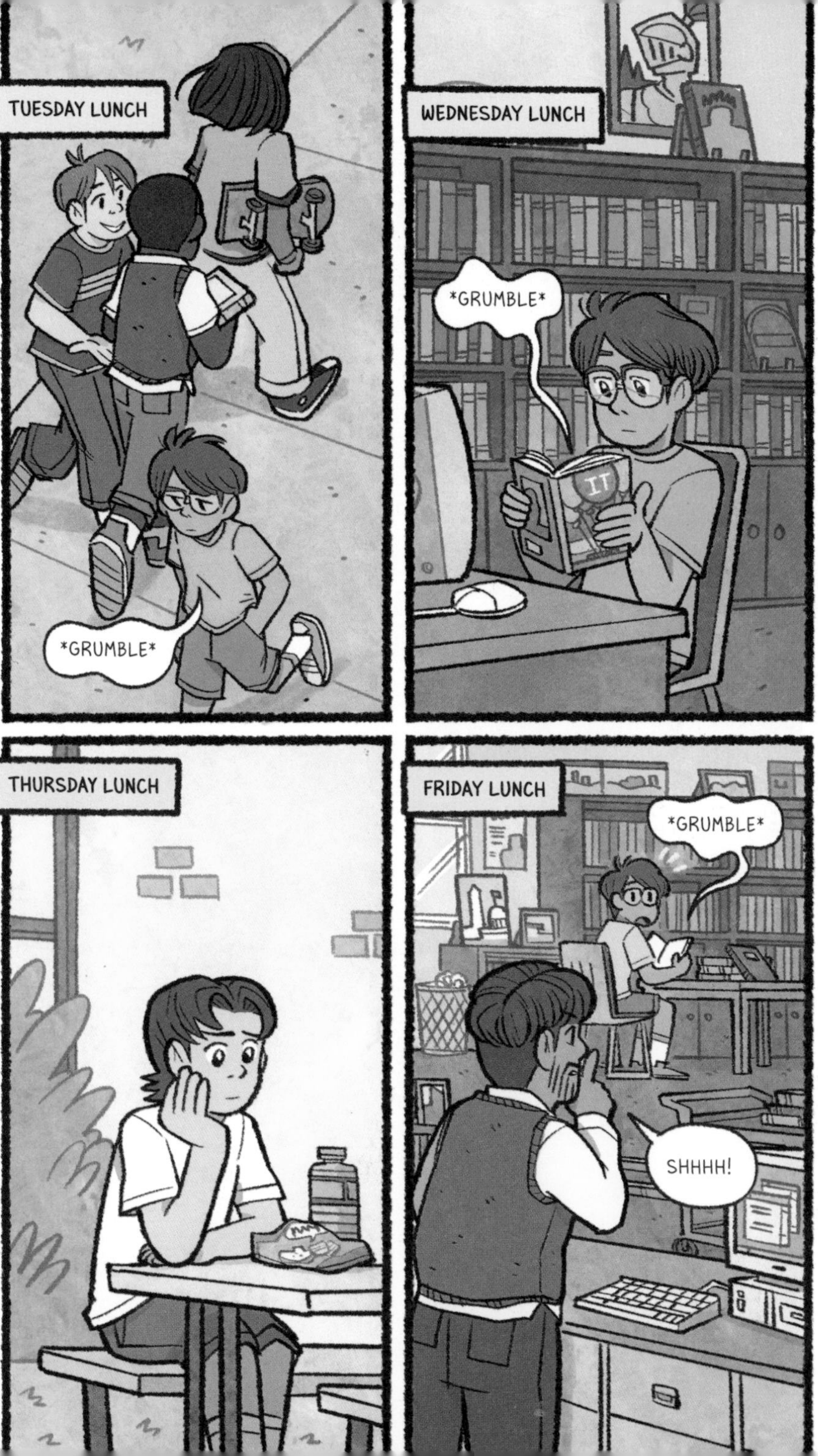
TUESDAY LUNCH
GRUMBLE
WEDNESDAY LUNCH
GRUMBLE
IT
THURSDAY LUNCH
FRIDAY LUNCH
GRUMBLE
SHHHH!

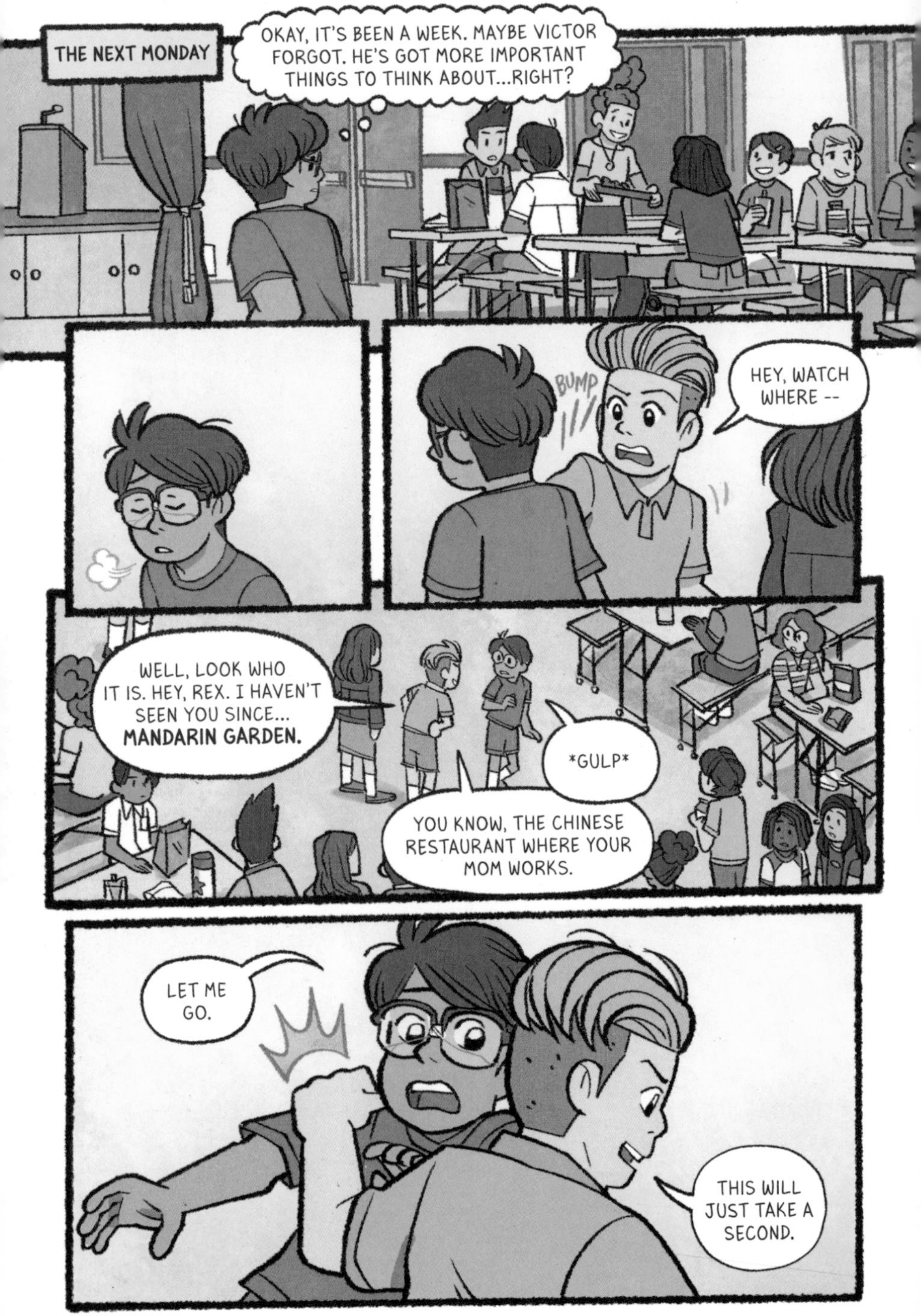
THE NEXT MONDAY
OKAY, IT'S BEEN A WEEK. MAYBE VICTOR FORGOT. HE'S GOT MORE IMPORTANT THINGS TO THINK ABOUT...RIGHT?
BUMP
HEY, WATCH WHERE --
WELL, LOOK WHO IT IS. HEY, REX. I HAVEN'T SEEN YOU SINCE... **MANDARIN GARDEN.**
GULP
YOU KNOW, THE CHINESE RESTAURANT WHERE YOUR MOM WORKS.
LET ME GO.
THIS WILL JUST TAKE A SECOND.

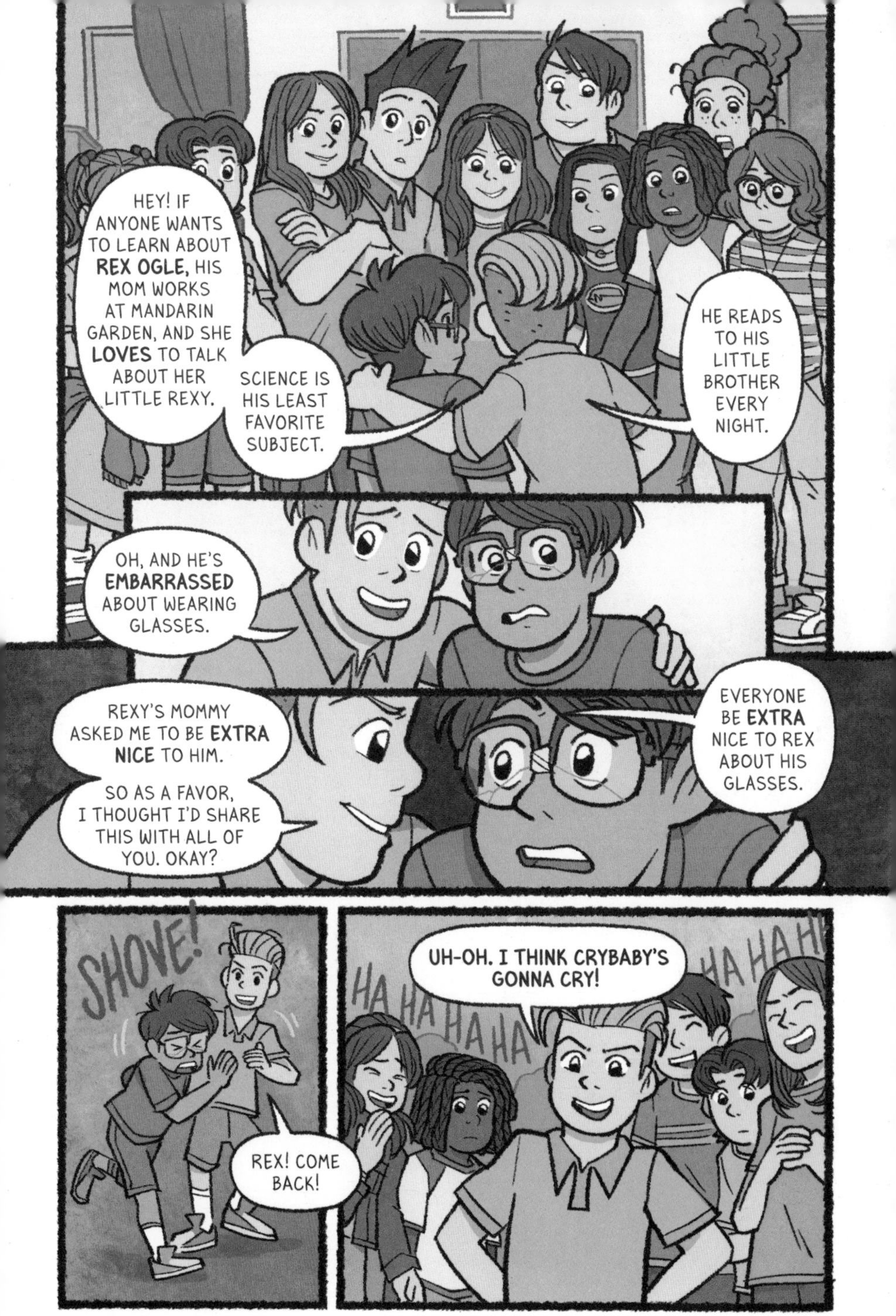
HEY! IF ANYONE WANTS TO LEARN ABOUT **REX OGLE,** HIS MOM WORKS AT MANDARIN GARDEN, AND SHE **LOVES** TO TALK ABOUT HER LITTLE REXY.
SCIENCE IS HIS LEAST FAVORITE SUBJECT.
HE READS TO HIS LITTLE BROTHER EVERY NIGHT.
OH, AND HE'S **EMBARRASSED** ABOUT WEARING GLASSES.
REXY'S MOMMY ASKED ME TO BE **EXTRA NICE** TO HIM.
SO AS A FAVOR, I THOUGHT I'D SHARE THIS WITH ALL OF YOU. OKAY?
EVERYONE BE **EXTRA** NICE TO REX ABOUT HIS GLASSES.
SHOVE!
REX! COME BACK!
UH-OH. I THINK CRYBABY'S GONNA CRY!
HA HA HA HA HA
HA HA HA

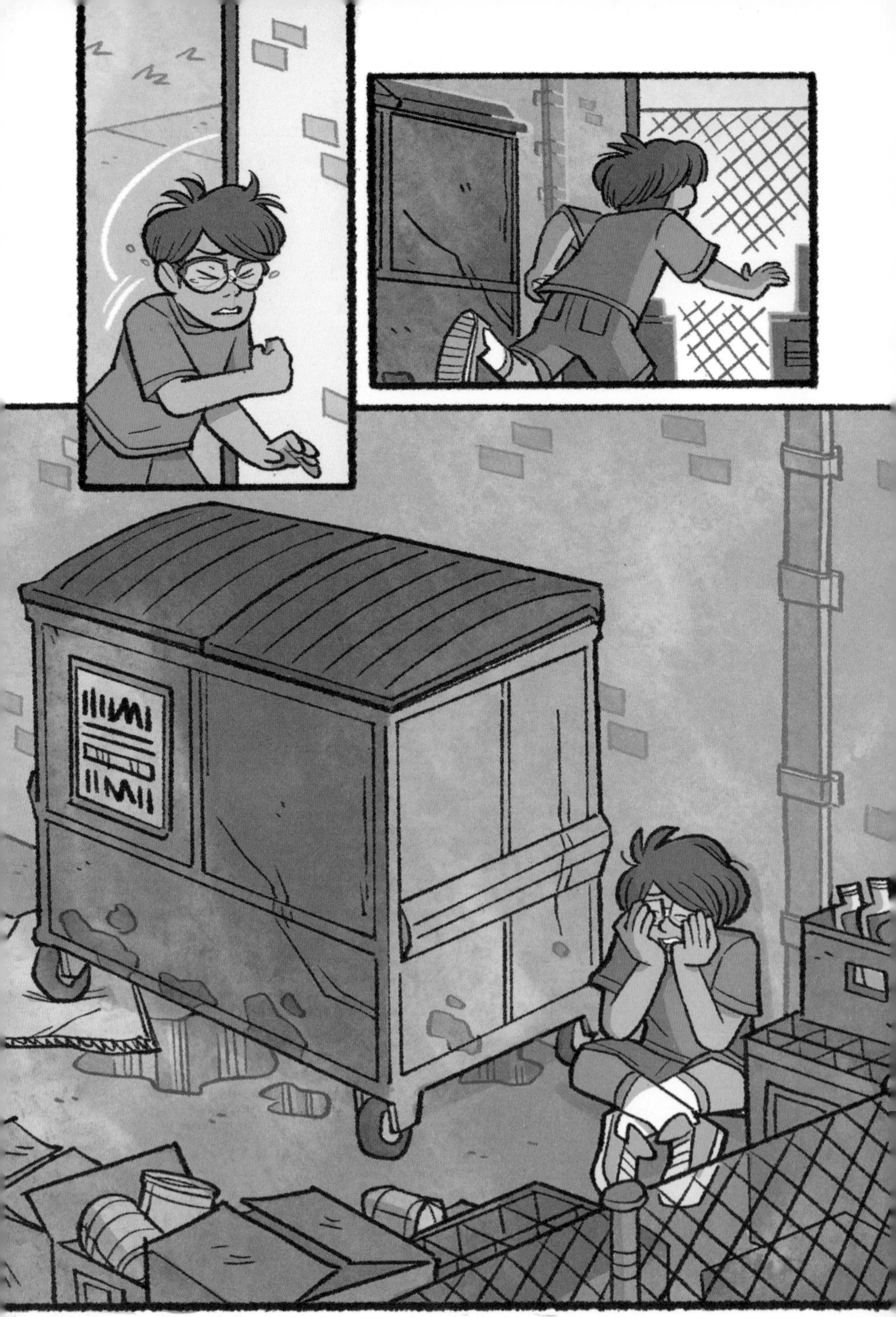

PART THREE

TRY AGAIN

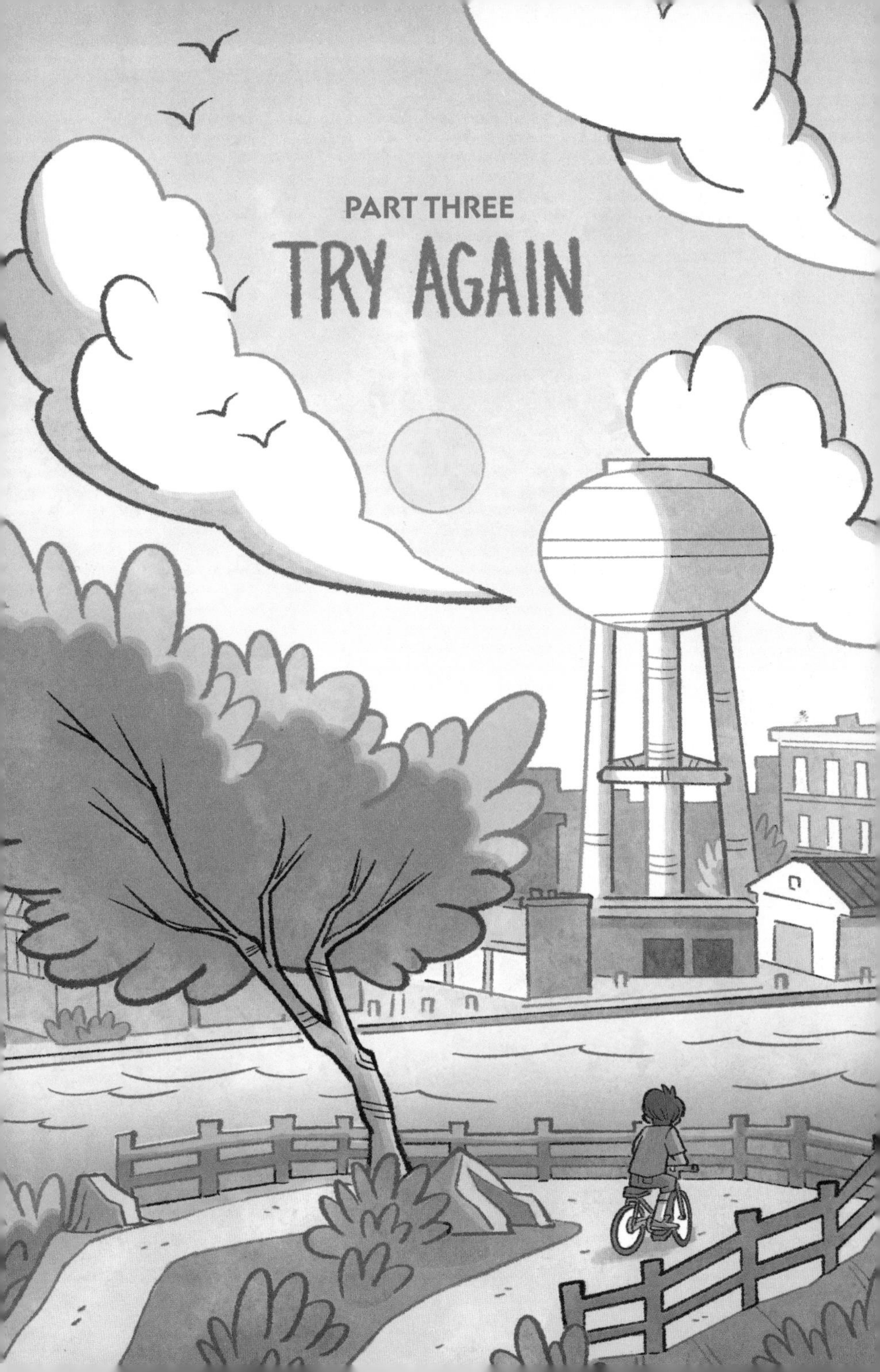

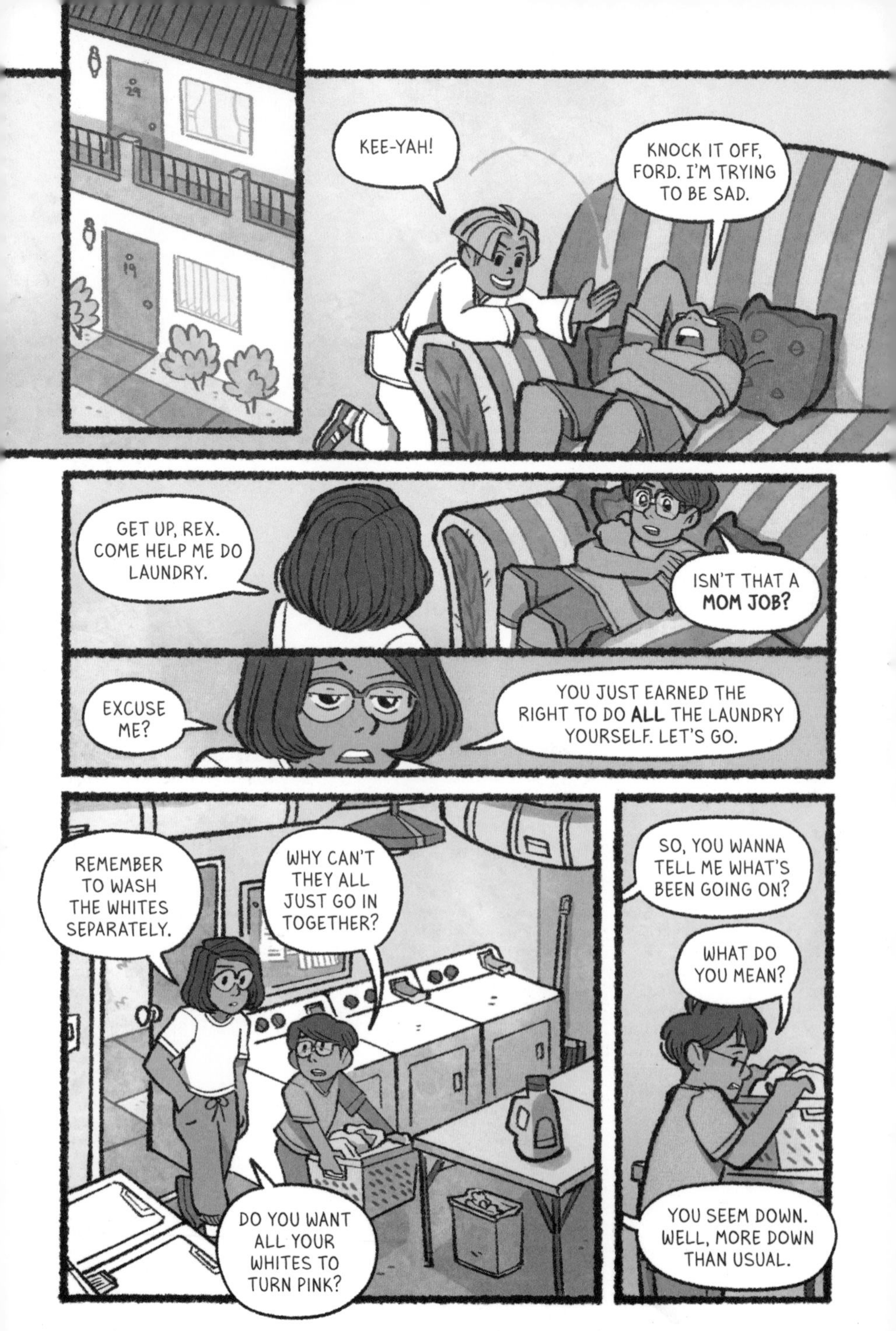
KEE-YAH!
KNOCK IT OFF, FORD. I'M TRYING TO BE SAD.
GET UP, REX. COME HELP ME DO LAUNDRY.
ISN'T THAT A MOM JOB?
EXCUSE ME?
YOU JUST EARNED THE RIGHT TO DO ALL THE LAUNDRY YOURSELF. LET'S GO.
REMEMBER TO WASH THE WHITES SEPARATELY.
WHY CAN'T THEY ALL JUST GO IN TOGETHER?
DO YOU WANT ALL YOUR WHITES TO TURN PINK?
SO, YOU WANNA TELL ME WHAT'S BEEN GOING ON?
WHAT DO YOU MEAN?
YOU SEEM DOWN. WELL, MORE DOWN THAN USUAL.

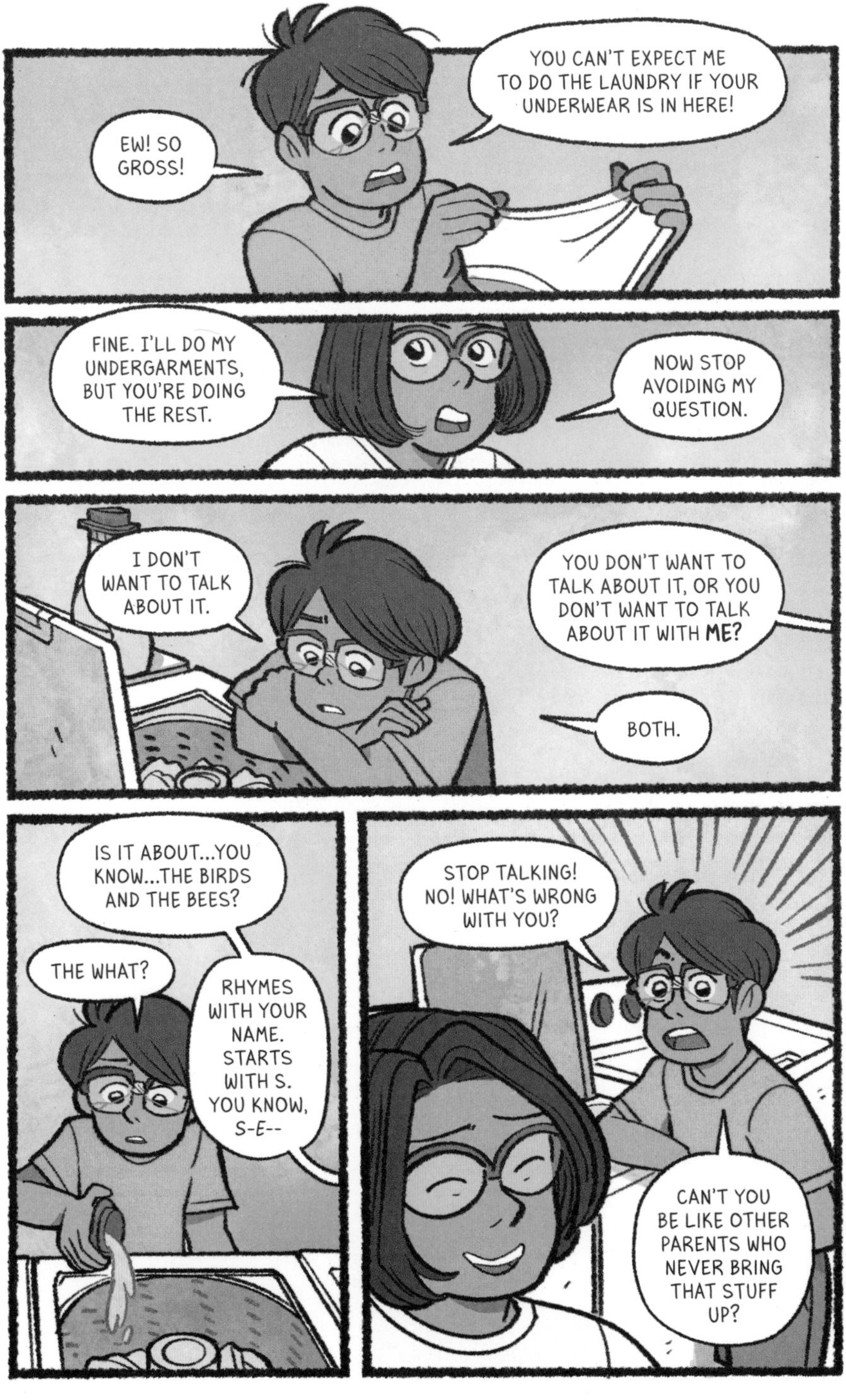
EW! SO GROSS!
YOU CAN'T EXPECT ME TO DO THE LAUNDRY IF YOUR UNDERWEAR IS IN HERE!
FINE. I'LL DO MY UNDERGARMENTS, BUT YOU'RE DOING THE REST.
NOW STOP AVOIDING MY QUESTION.
I DON'T WANT TO TALK ABOUT IT.
YOU DON'T WANT TO TALK ABOUT IT, OR YOU DON'T WANT TO TALK ABOUT IT WITH **ME?**
BOTH.
IS IT ABOUT...YOU KNOW...THE BIRDS AND THE BEES?
THE WHAT?
RHYMES WITH YOUR NAME. STARTS WITH S. YOU KNOW, S-E--
STOP TALKING! NO! WHAT'S WRONG WITH YOU?
CAN'T YOU BE LIKE OTHER PARENTS WHO NEVER BRING THAT STUFF UP?

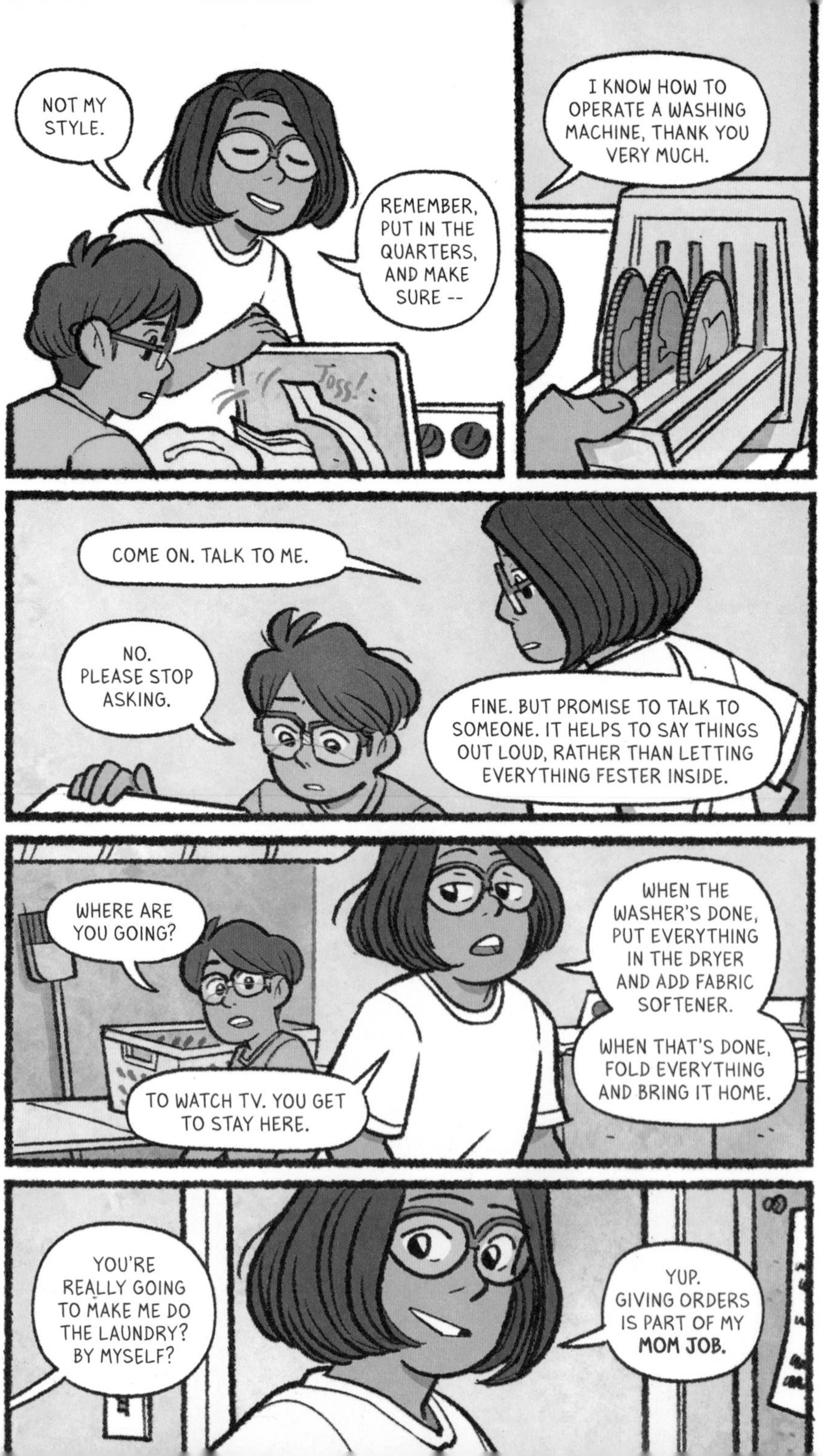
NOT MY STYLE.
REMEMBER, PUT IN THE QUARTERS, AND MAKE SURE --
TOSS!
I KNOW HOW TO OPERATE A WASHING MACHINE, THANK YOU VERY MUCH.
COME ON. TALK TO ME.
NO. PLEASE STOP ASKING.
FINE. BUT PROMISE TO TALK TO SOMEONE. IT HELPS TO SAY THINGS OUT LOUD, RATHER THAN LETTING EVERYTHING FESTER INSIDE.
WHERE ARE YOU GOING?
TO WATCH TV. YOU GET TO STAY HERE.
WHEN THE WASHER'S DONE, PUT EVERYTHING IN THE DRYER AND ADD FABRIC SOFTENER.
WHEN THAT'S DONE, FOLD EVERYTHING AND BRING IT HOME.
YOU'RE REALLY GOING TO MAKE ME DO THE LAUNDRY? BY MYSELF?
YUP. GIVING ORDERS IS PART OF MY **MOM JOB.**

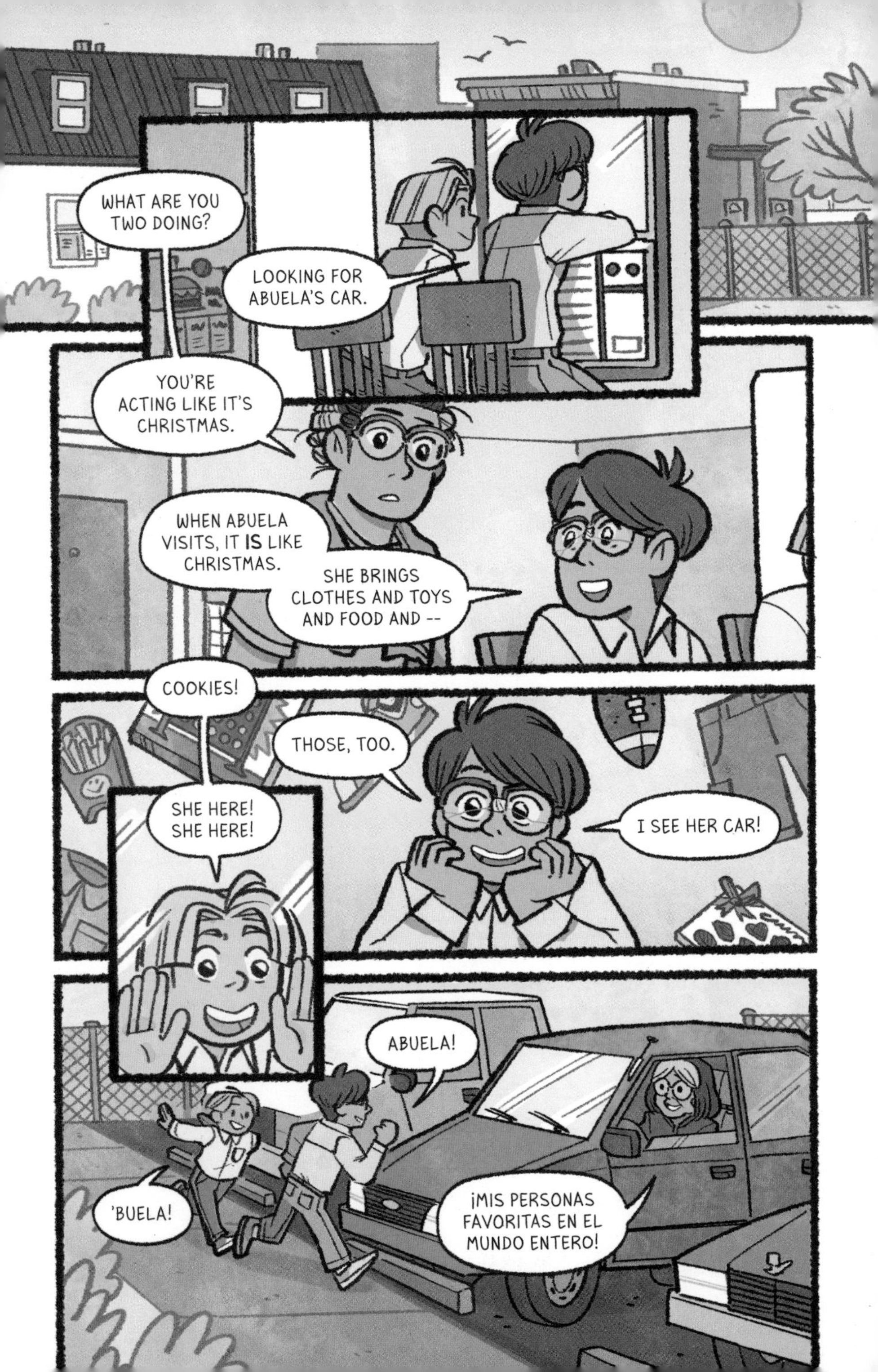
WHAT ARE YOU TWO DOING?
LOOKING FOR ABUELA'S CAR.
YOU'RE ACTING LIKE IT'S CHRISTMAS.
WHEN ABUELA VISITS, IT **IS** LIKE CHRISTMAS.
SHE BRINGS CLOTHES AND TOYS AND FOOD AND --
COOKIES!
THOSE, TOO.
SHE HERE! SHE HERE!
I SEE HER CAR!
ABUELA!
'BUELA!
¡MIS PERSONAS FAVORITAS EN EL MUNDO ENTERO!

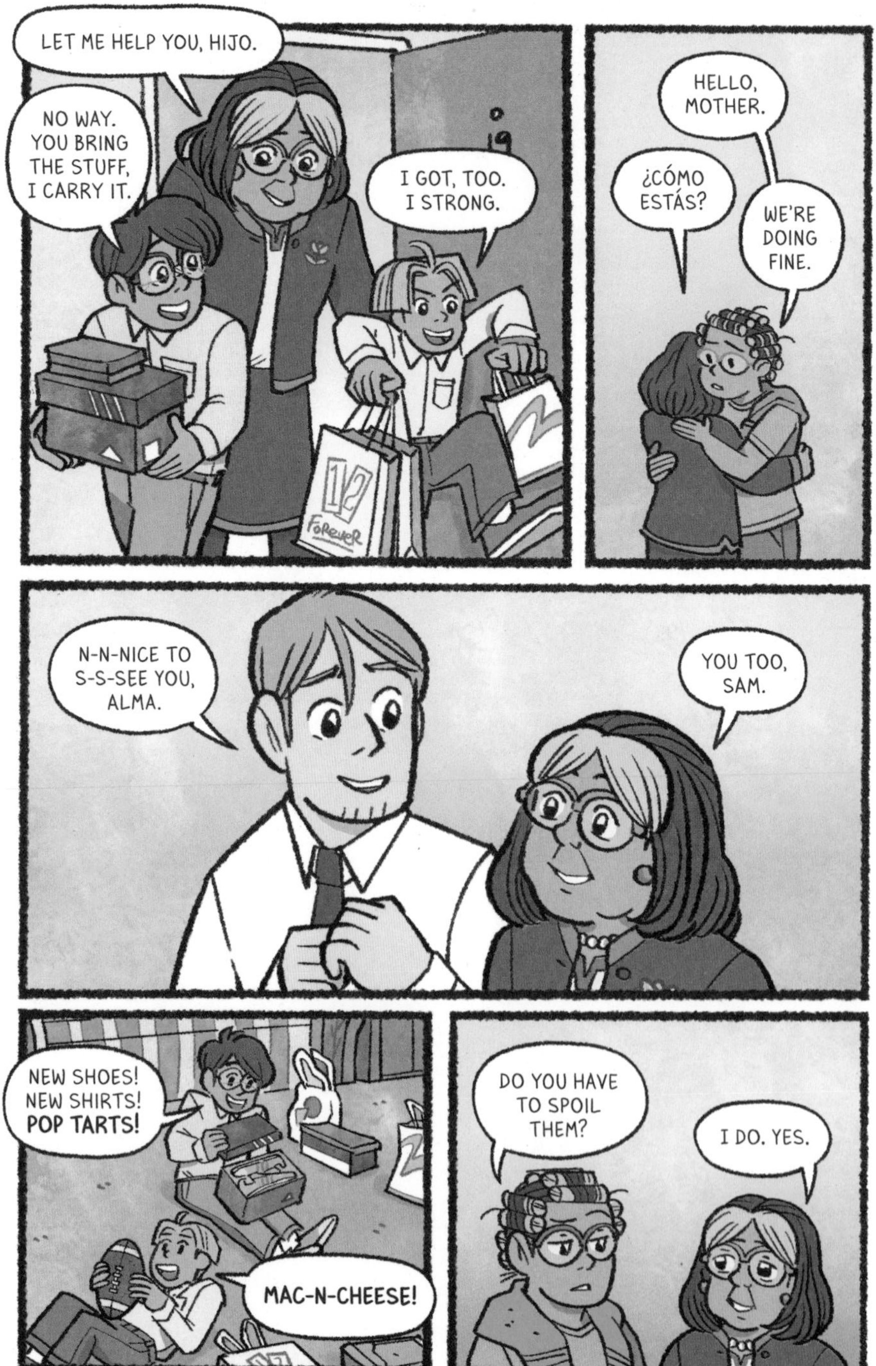
LET ME HELP YOU, HIJO.
NO WAY. YOU BRING THE STUFF, I CARRY IT.
I GOT, TOO. I STRONG.
HELLO, MOTHER.
¿CÓMO ESTÁS?
WE'RE DOING FINE.
N-N-NICE TO S-S-SEE YOU, ALMA.
YOU TOO, SAM.
NEW SHOES! NEW SHIRTS! POP TARTS!
MAC-N-CHEESE!
DO YOU HAVE TO SPOIL THEM?
I DO. YES.

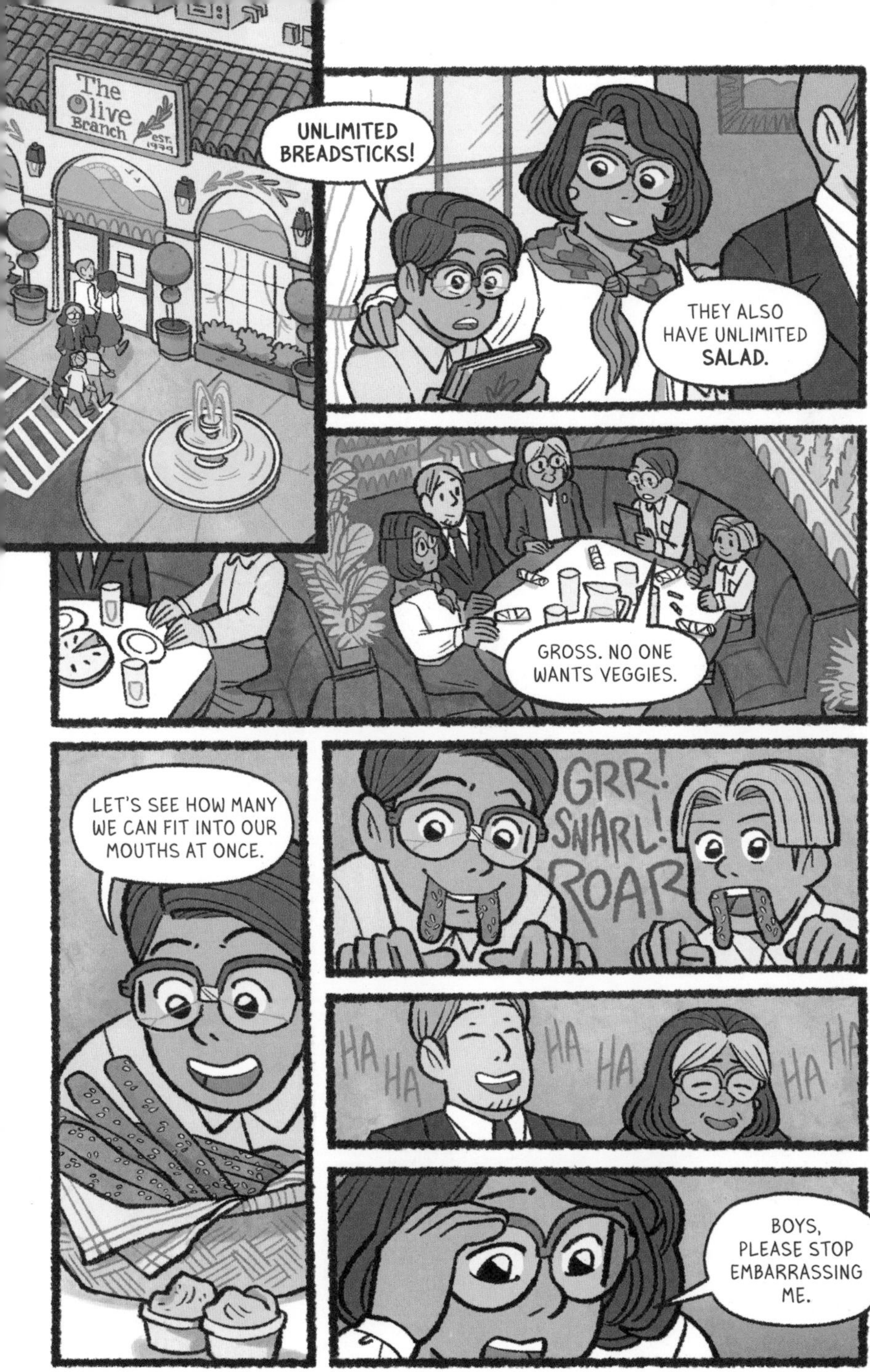
The Olive Branch est. 1979
UNLIMITED BREADSTICKS!
THEY ALSO HAVE UNLIMITED SALAD.
GROSS. NO ONE WANTS VEGGIES.
LET'S SEE HOW MANY WE CAN FIT INTO OUR MOUTHS AT ONCE.
GRR! SNARL! ROAR
HA HA HA HA HA HA
BOYS, PLEASE STOP EMBARRASSING ME.

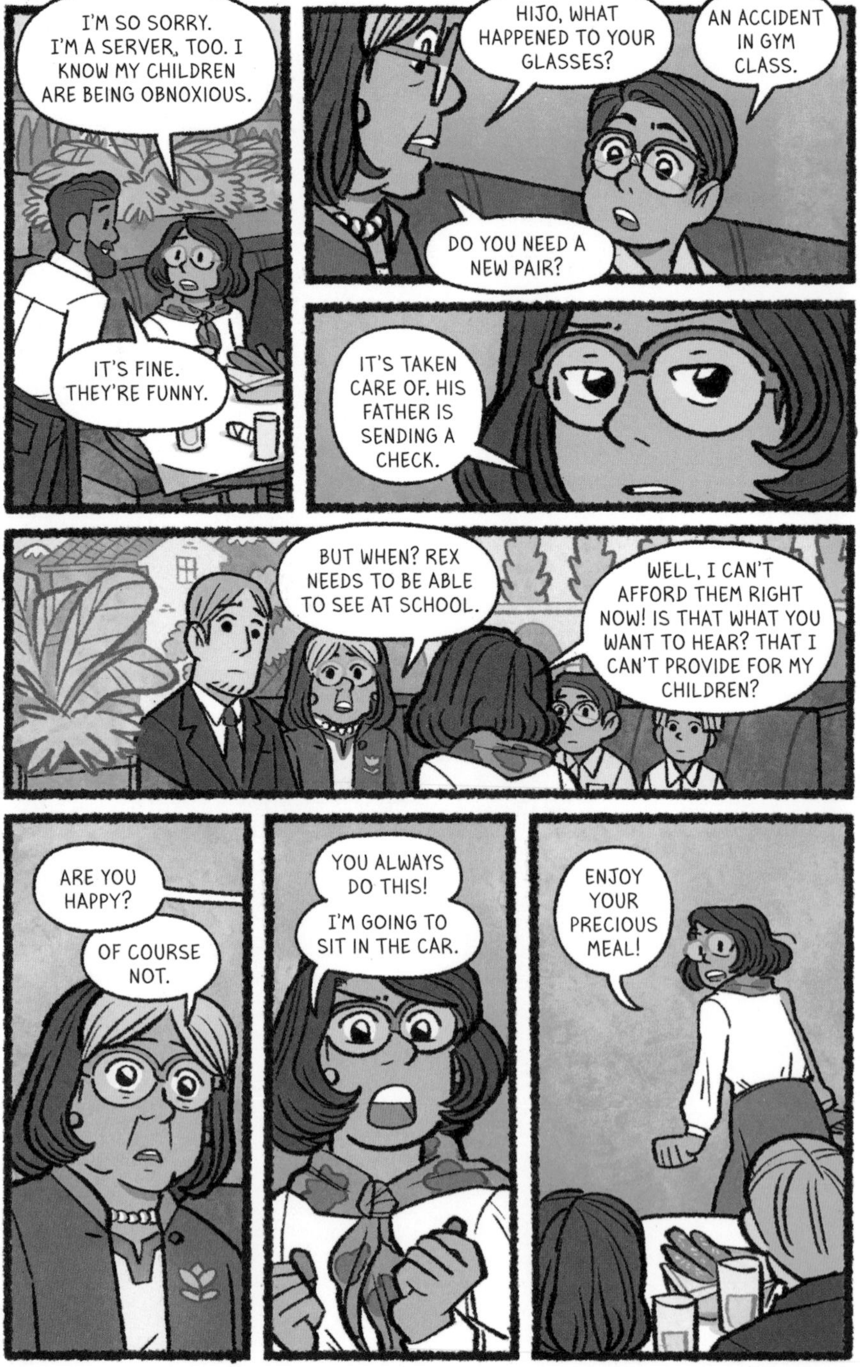
I'M SO SORRY. I'M A SERVER, TOO. I KNOW MY CHILDREN ARE BEING OBNOXIOUS.
IT'S FINE. THEY'RE FUNNY.
HIJO, WHAT HAPPENED TO YOUR GLASSES?
AN ACCIDENT IN GYM CLASS.
DO YOU NEED A NEW PAIR?
IT'S TAKEN CARE OF. HIS FATHER IS SENDING A CHECK.
BUT WHEN? REX NEEDS TO BE ABLE TO SEE AT SCHOOL.
WELL, I CAN'T AFFORD THEM RIGHT NOW! IS THAT WHAT YOU WANT TO HEAR? THAT I CAN'T PROVIDE FOR MY CHILDREN?
ARE YOU HAPPY?
OF COURSE NOT.
YOU ALWAYS DO THIS!
I'M GOING TO SIT IN THE CAR.
ENJOY YOUR PRECIOUS MEAL!

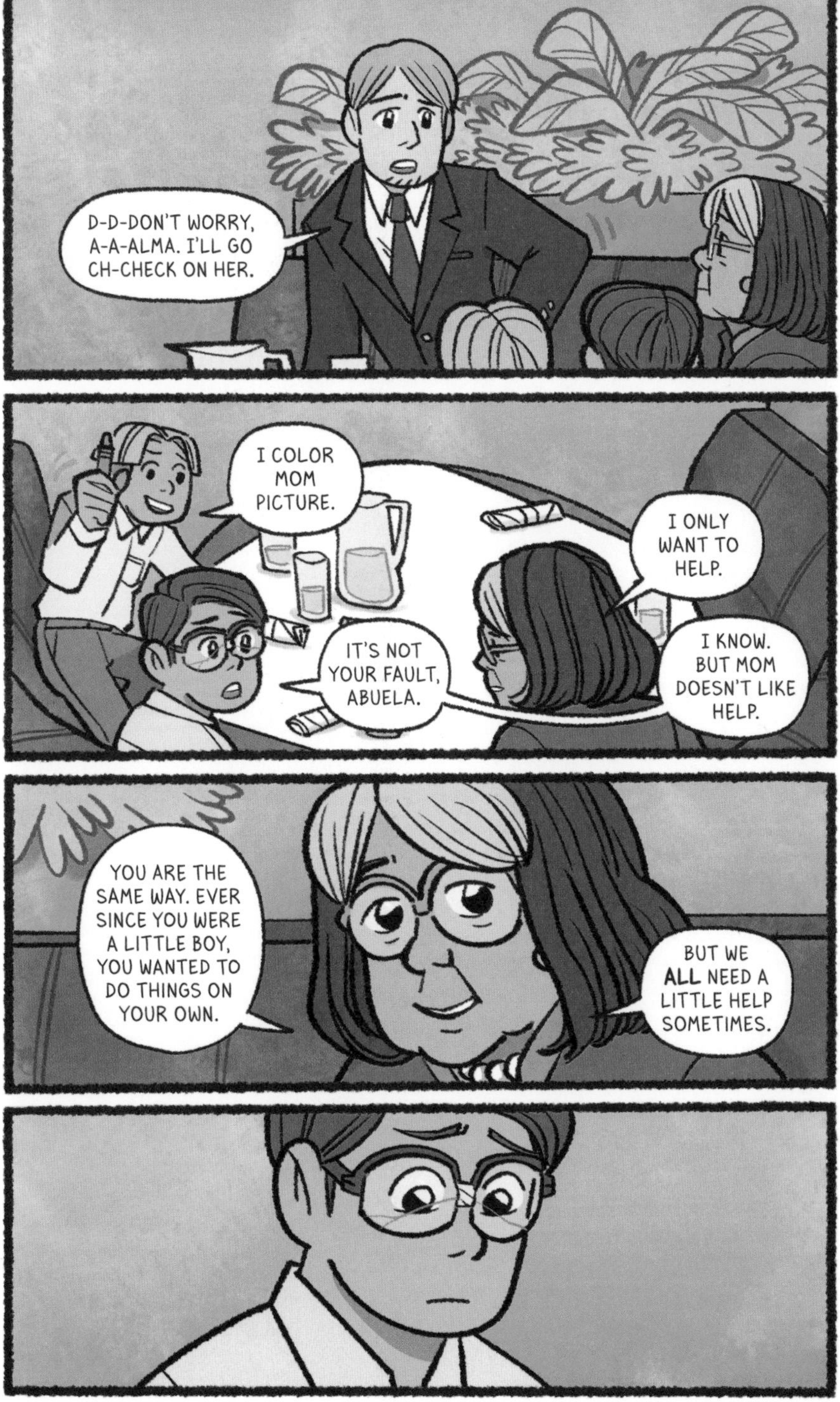
D-D-DON'T WORRY, A-A-ALMA. I'LL GO CH-CHECK ON HER.
I COLOR MOM PICTURE.
I ONLY WANT TO HELP.
IT'S NOT YOUR FAULT, ABUELA.
I KNOW. BUT MOM DOESN'T LIKE HELP.
YOU ARE THE SAME WAY. EVER SINCE YOU WERE A LITTLE BOY, YOU WANTED TO DO THINGS ON YOUR OWN.
BUT WE **ALL** NEED A LITTLE HELP SOMETIMES.

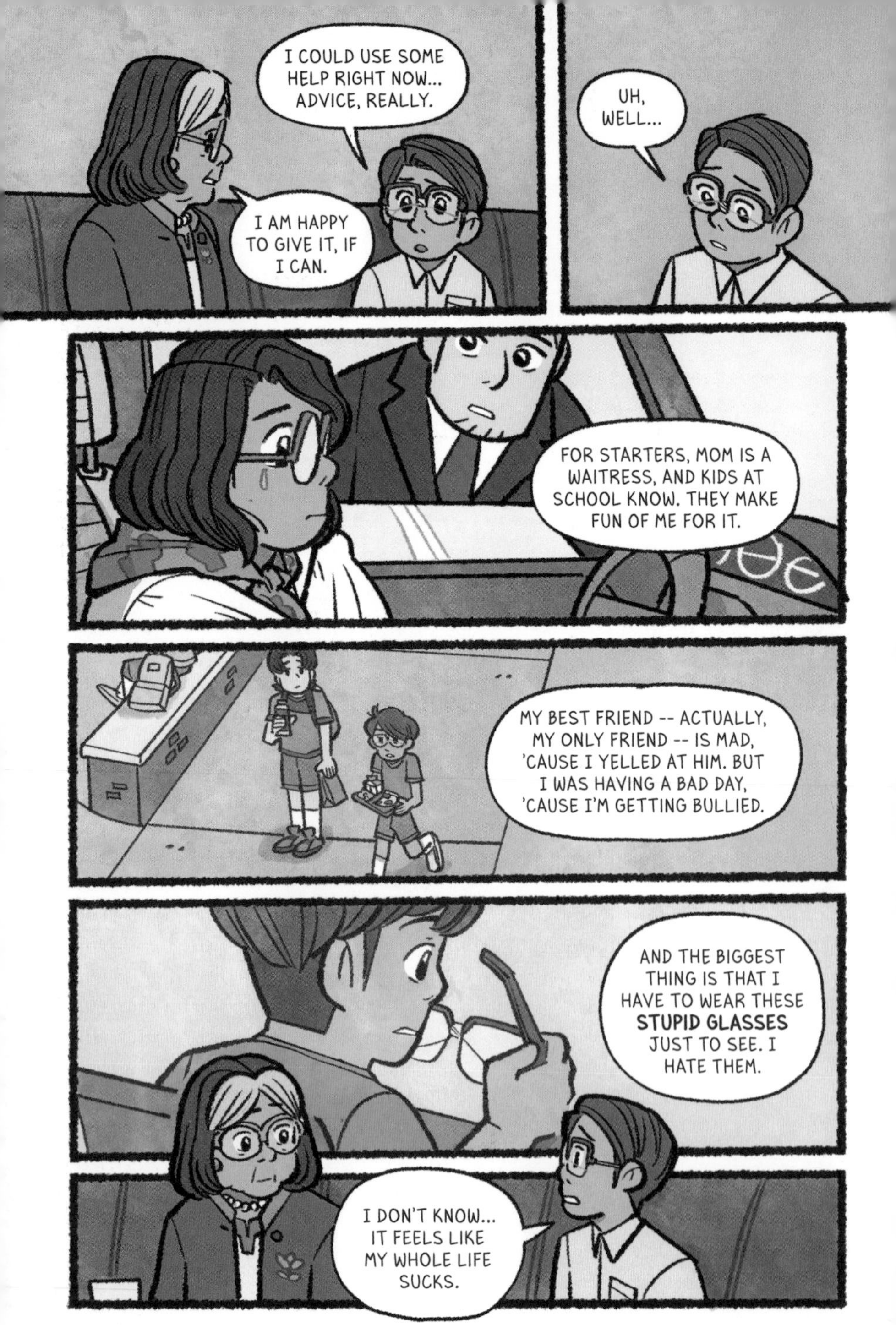
I COULD USE SOME HELP RIGHT NOW... ADVICE, REALLY.
I AM HAPPY TO GIVE IT, IF I CAN.
UH, WELL...
FOR STARTERS, MOM IS A WAITRESS, AND KIDS AT SCHOOL KNOW. THEY MAKE FUN OF ME FOR IT.
MY BEST FRIEND -- ACTUALLY, MY ONLY FRIEND -- IS MAD, 'CAUSE I YELLED AT HIM. BUT I WAS HAVING A BAD DAY, 'CAUSE I'M GETTING BULLIED.
AND THE BIGGEST THING IS THAT I HAVE TO WEAR THESE **STUPID GLASSES** JUST TO SEE. I HATE THEM.
I DON'T KNOW... IT FEELS LIKE MY WHOLE LIFE SUCKS.

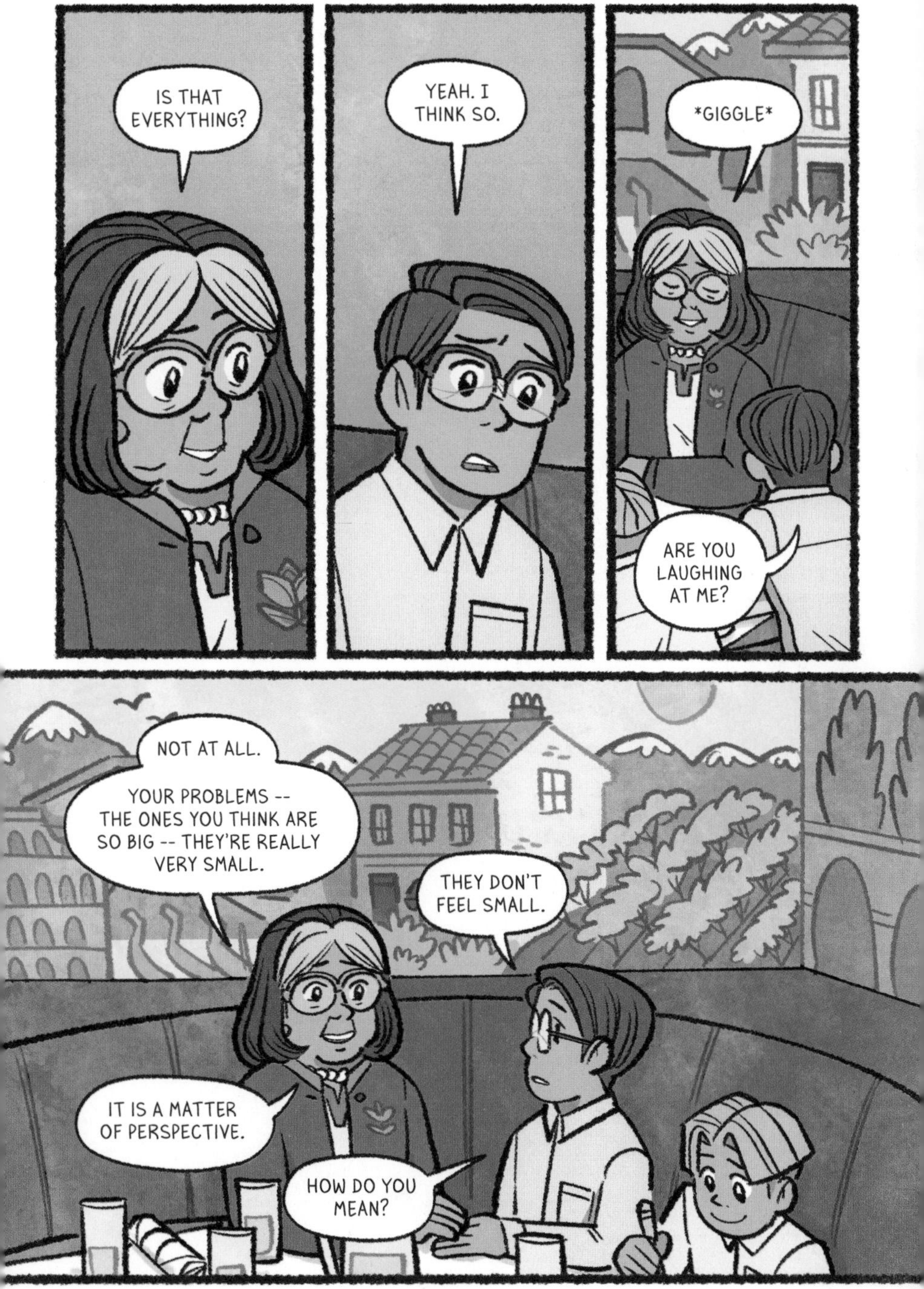
IS THAT EVERYTHING?
YEAH. I THINK SO.
GIGGLE
ARE YOU LAUGHING AT ME?
NOT AT ALL.
YOUR PROBLEMS -- THE ONES YOU THINK ARE SO BIG -- THEY'RE REALLY VERY SMALL.
THEY DON'T FEEL SMALL.
IT IS A MATTER OF PERSPECTIVE.
HOW DO YOU MEAN?

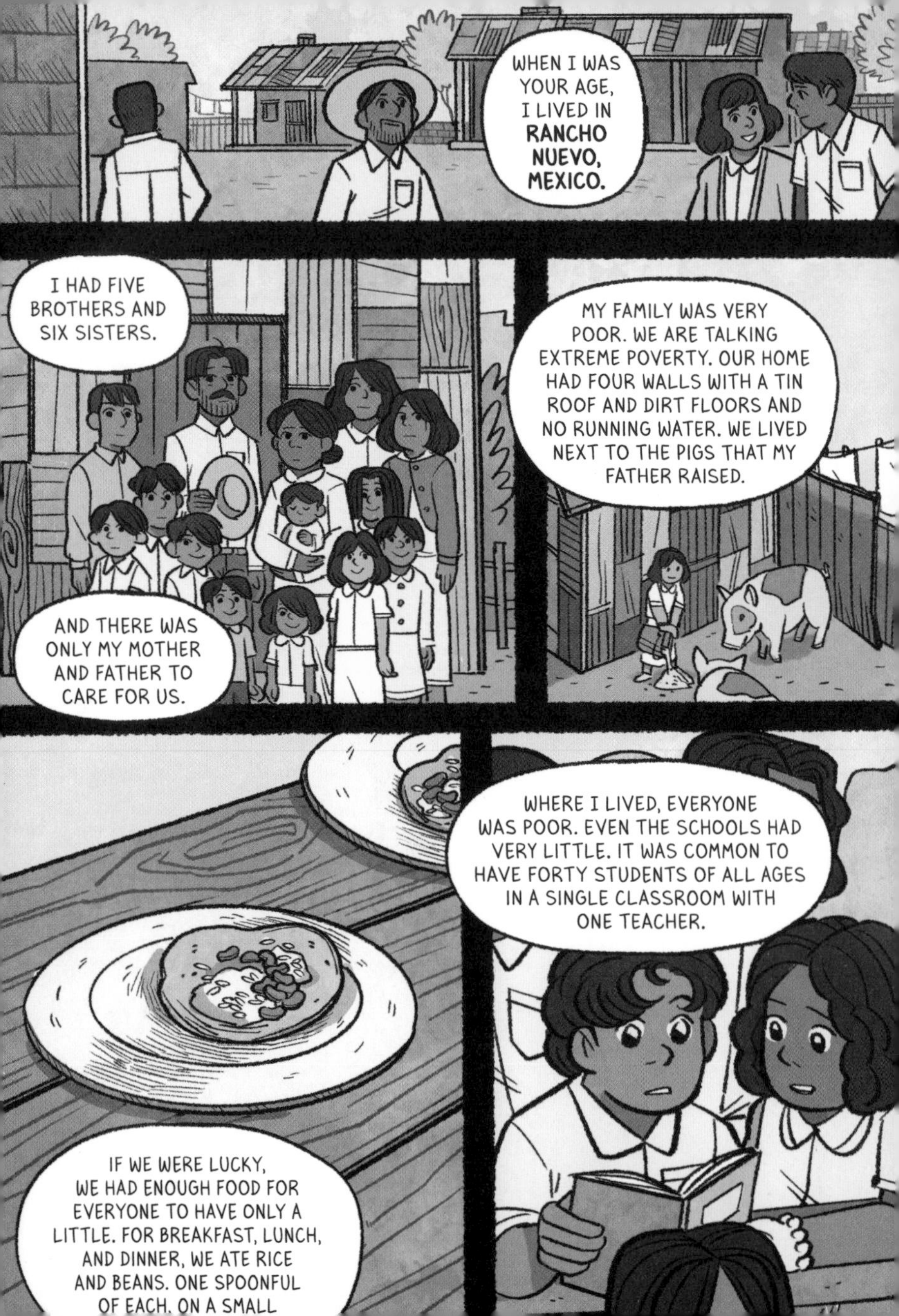
WHEN I WAS YOUR AGE, I LIVED IN **RANCHO NUEVO, MEXICO.**
I HAD FIVE BROTHERS AND SIX SISTERS.
AND THERE WAS ONLY MY MOTHER AND FATHER TO CARE FOR US.
MY FAMILY WAS VERY POOR. WE ARE TALKING EXTREME POVERTY. OUR HOME HAD FOUR WALLS WITH A TIN ROOF AND DIRT FLOORS AND NO RUNNING WATER. WE LIVED NEXT TO THE PIGS THAT MY FATHER RAISED.
IF WE WERE LUCKY, WE HAD ENOUGH FOOD FOR EVERYONE TO HAVE ONLY A LITTLE. FOR BREAKFAST, LUNCH, AND DINNER, WE ATE RICE AND BEANS. ONE SPOONFUL OF EACH, ON A SMALL
WHERE I LIVED, EVERYONE WAS POOR. EVEN THE SCHOOLS HAD VERY LITTLE. IT WAS COMMON TO HAVE FORTY STUDENTS OF ALL AGES IN A SINGLE CLASSROOM WITH ONE TEACHER.

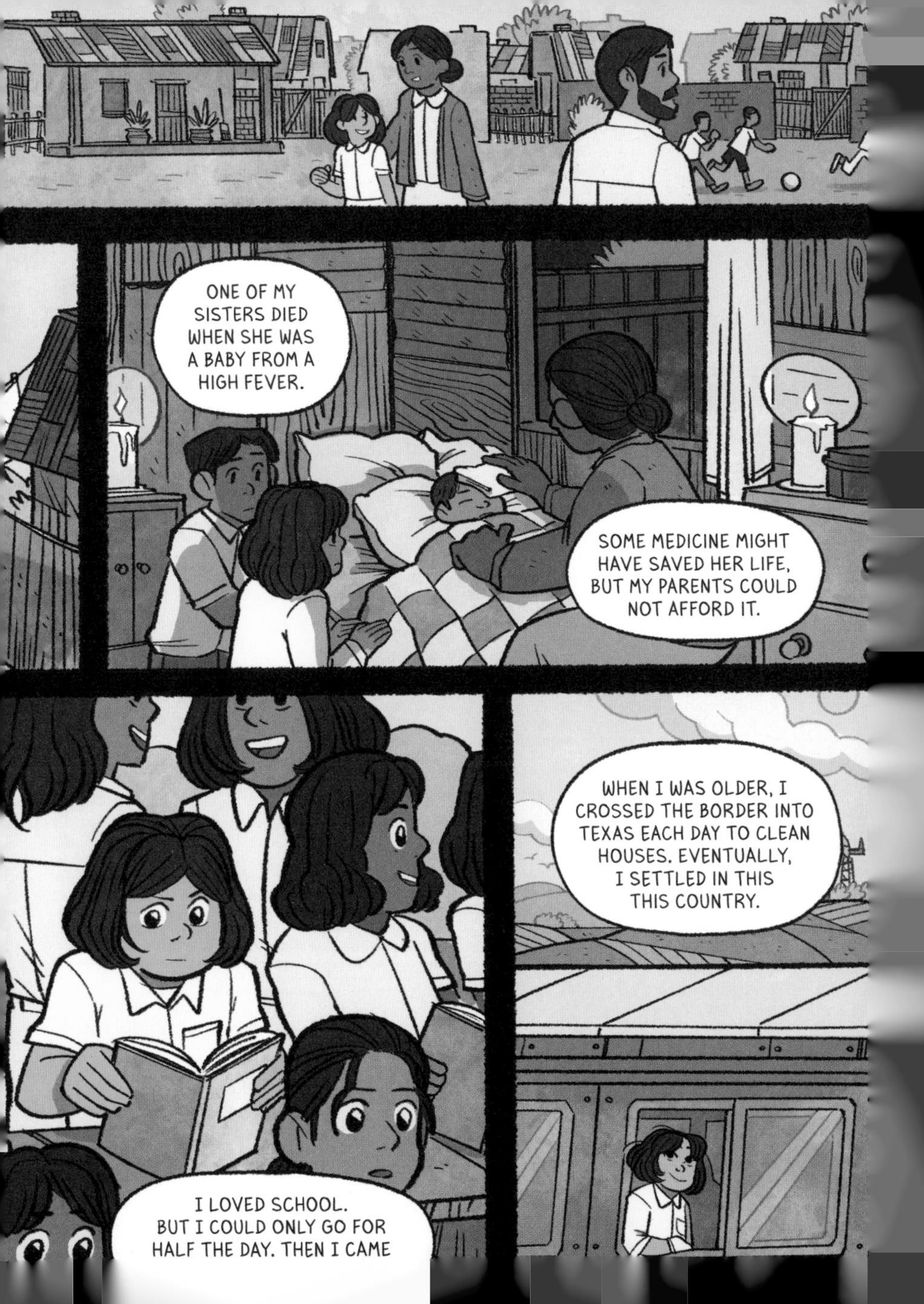
ONE OF MY SISTERS DIED WHEN SHE WAS A BABY FROM A HIGH FEVER.
SOME MEDICINE MIGHT HAVE SAVED HER LIFE, BUT MY PARENTS COULD NOT AFFORD IT.
I LOVED SCHOOL. BUT I COULD ONLY GO FOR HALF THE DAY. THEN I CAME
WHEN I WAS OLDER, I CROSSED THE BORDER INTO TEXAS EACH DAY TO CLEAN HOUSES. EVENTUALLY, I SETTLED IN THIS THIS COUNTRY.

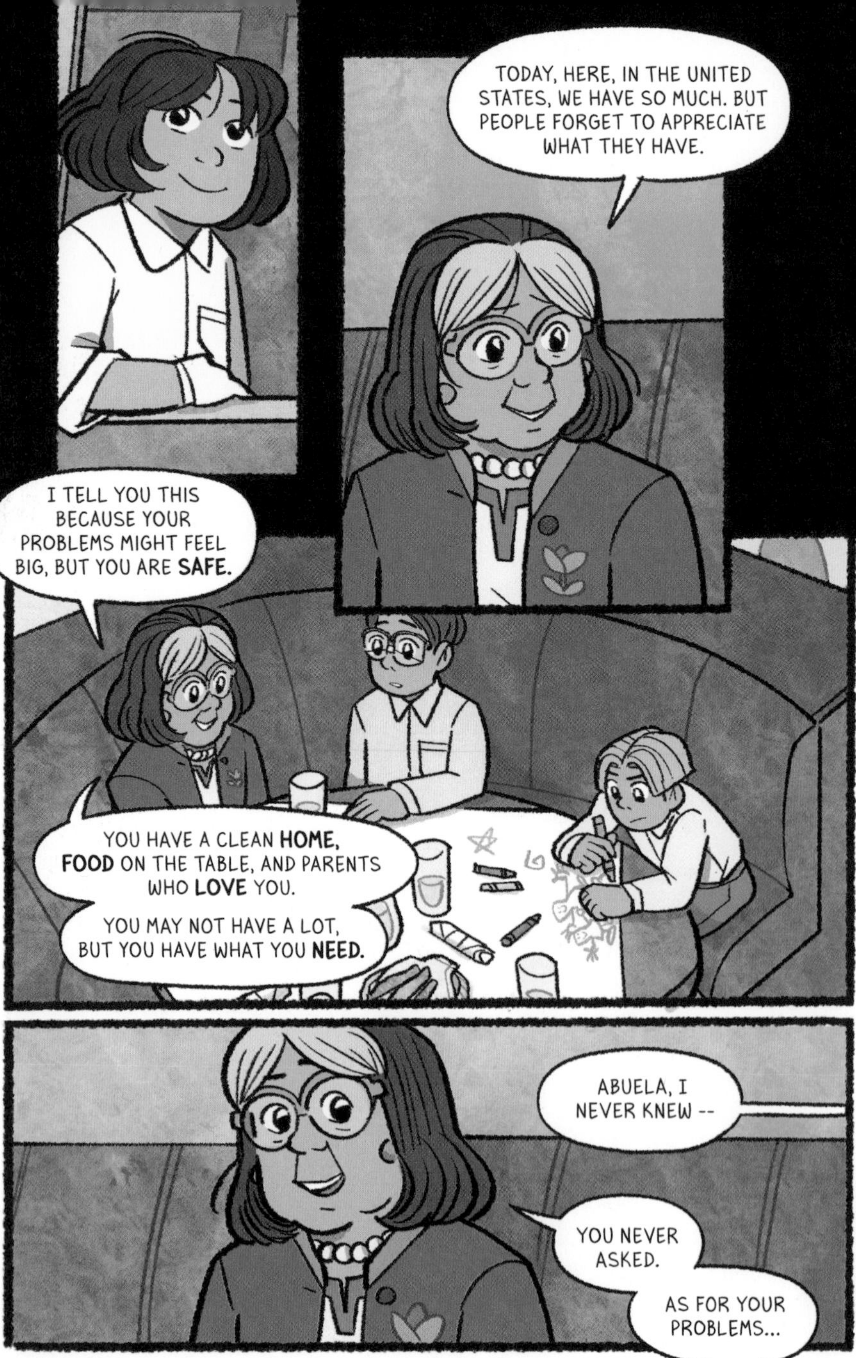
TODAY, HERE, IN THE UNITED STATES, WE HAVE SO MUCH. BUT PEOPLE FORGET TO APPRECIATE WHAT THEY HAVE.
I TELL YOU THIS BECAUSE YOUR PROBLEMS MIGHT FEEL BIG, BUT YOU ARE SAFE.
YOU HAVE A CLEAN HOME, FOOD ON THE TABLE, AND PARENTS WHO LOVE YOU.
YOU MAY NOT HAVE A LOT, BUT YOU HAVE WHAT YOU NEED.
ABUELA, I NEVER KNEW --
YOU NEVER ASKED.
AS FOR YOUR PROBLEMS...

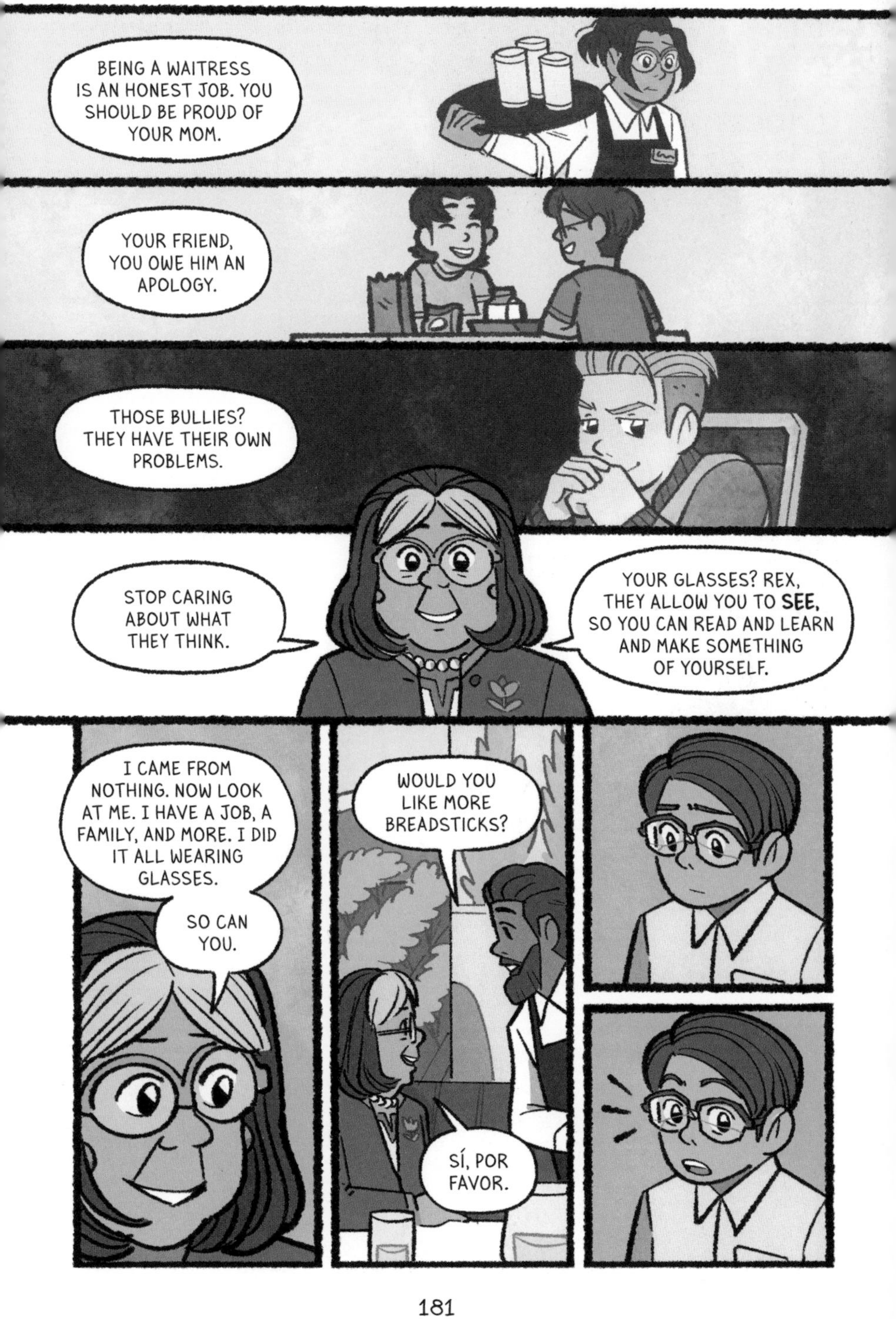
BEING A WAITRESS IS AN HONEST JOB. YOU SHOULD BE PROUD OF YOUR MOM.
YOUR FRIEND, YOU OWE HIM AN APOLOGY.
THOSE BULLIES? THEY HAVE THEIR OWN PROBLEMS.
STOP CARING ABOUT WHAT THEY THINK.
YOUR GLASSES? REX, THEY ALLOW YOU TO **SEE,** SO YOU CAN READ AND LEARN AND MAKE SOMETHING OF YOURSELF.
I CAME FROM NOTHING. NOW LOOK AT ME. I HAVE A JOB, A FAMILY, AND MORE. I DID IT ALL WEARING GLASSES.
SO CAN YOU.
WOULD YOU LIKE MORE BREADSTICKS?
SÍ, POR FAVOR.

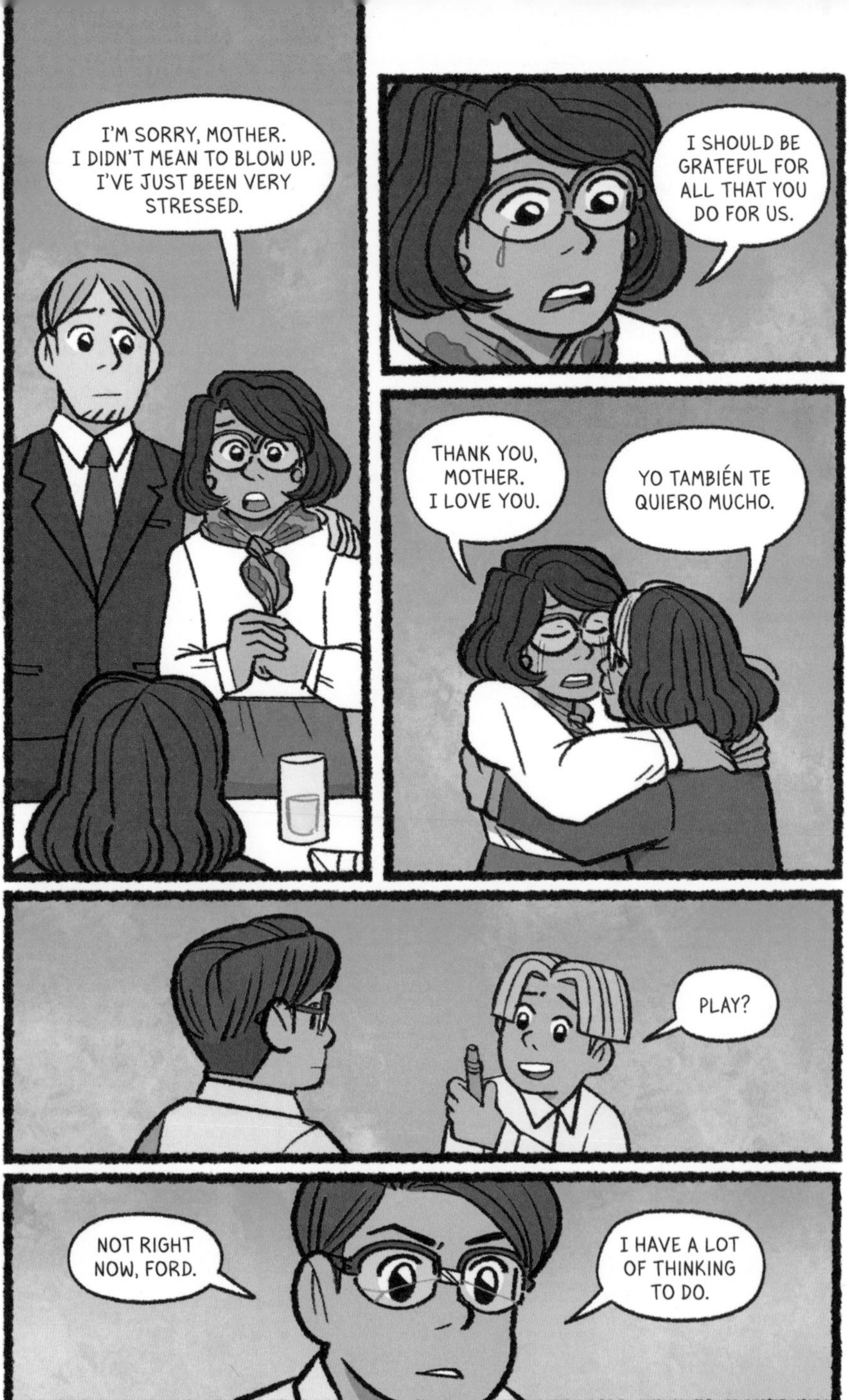
I'M SORRY, MOTHER. I DIDN'T MEAN TO BLOW UP. I'VE JUST BEEN VERY STRESSED.
I SHOULD BE GRATEFUL FOR ALL THAT YOU DO FOR US.
THANK YOU, MOTHER. I LOVE YOU.
YO TAMBIÉN TE QUIERO MUCHO.
PLAY?
NOT RIGHT NOW, FORD.
I HAVE A LOT OF THINKING TO DO.

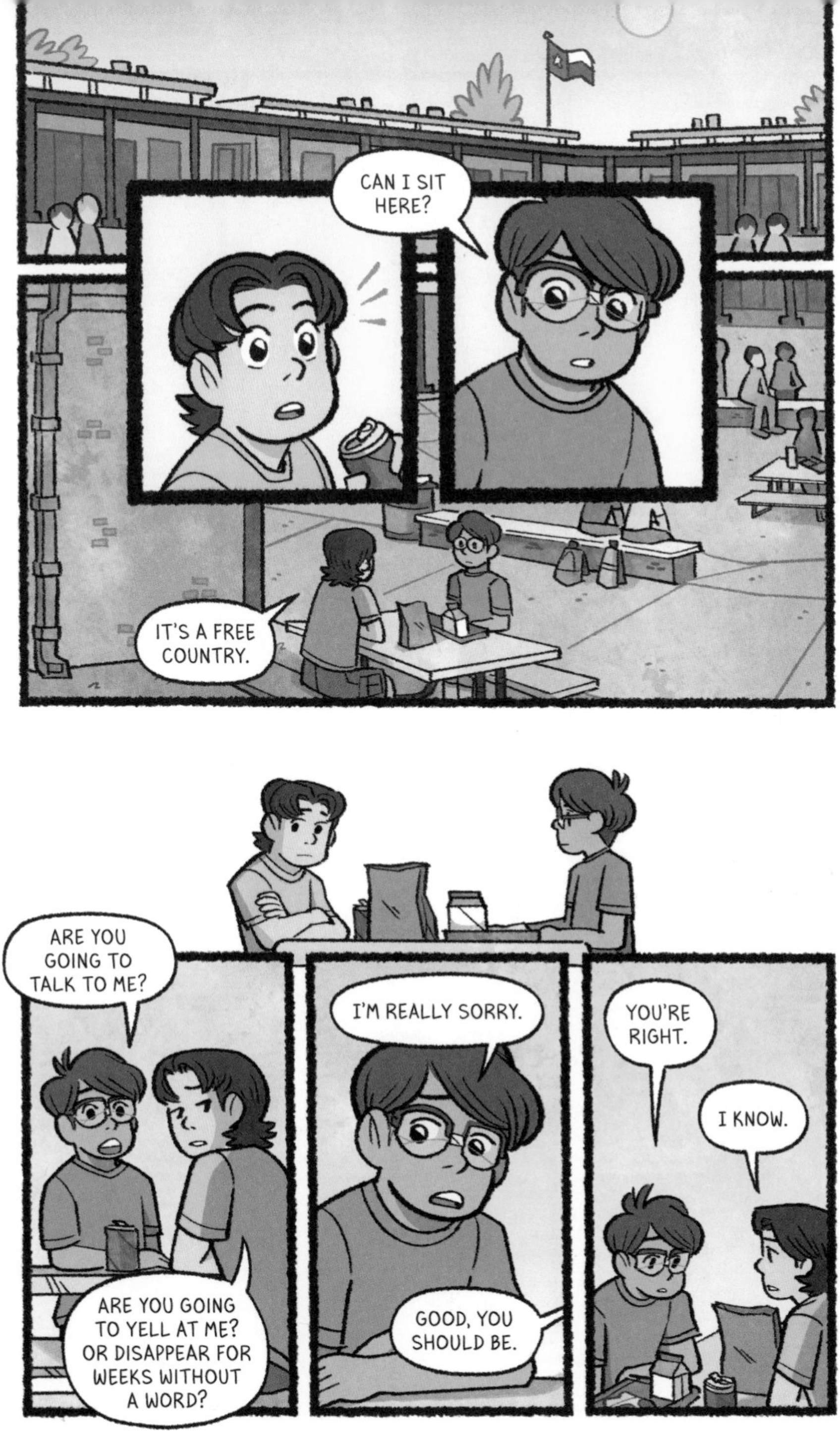
CAN I SIT HERE?
IT'S A FREE COUNTRY.
ARE YOU GOING TO TALK TO ME?
ARE YOU GOING TO YELL AT ME? OR DISAPPEAR FOR WEEKS WITHOUT A WORD?
I'M REALLY SORRY.
GOOD, YOU SHOULD BE.
YOU'RE RIGHT.
I KNOW.

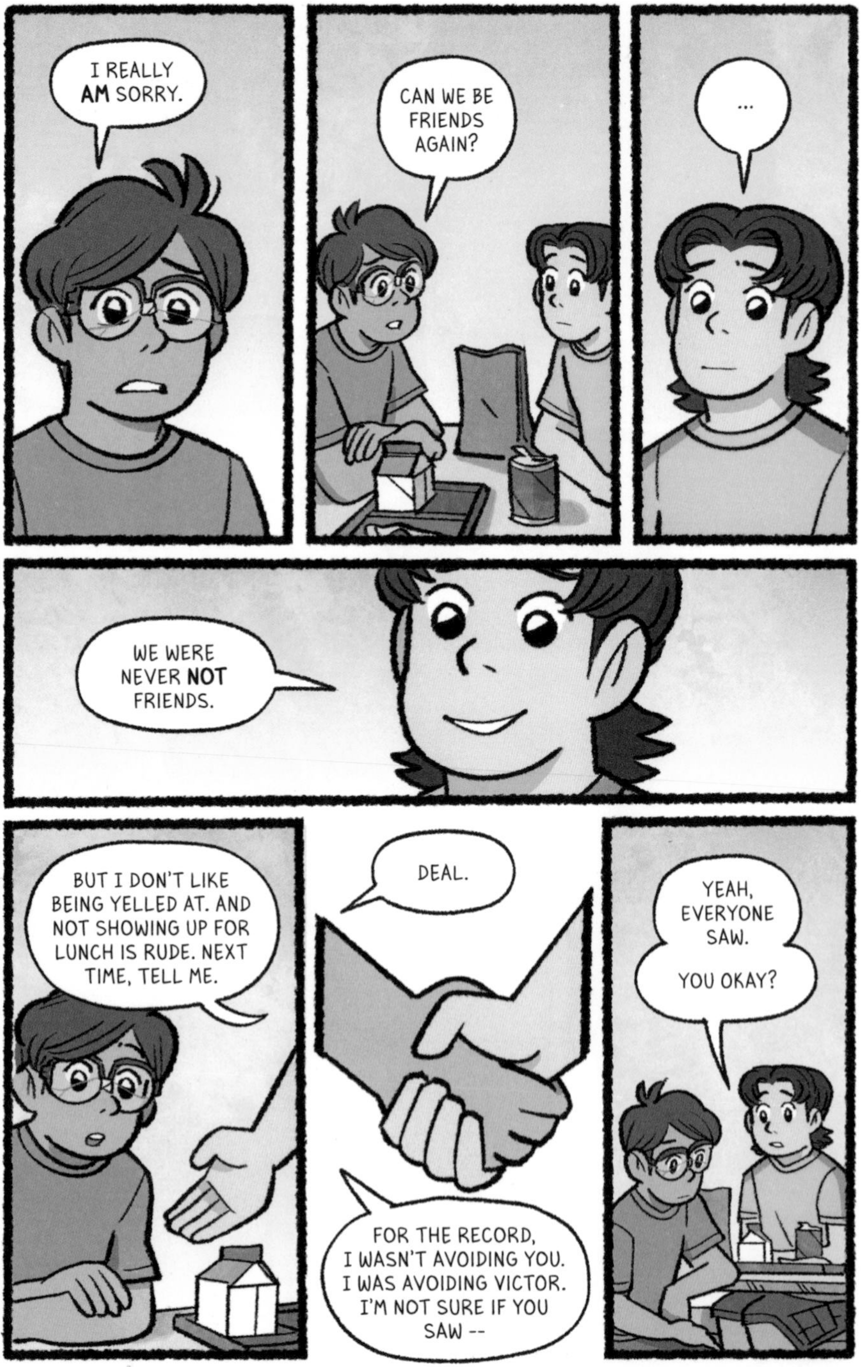
I REALLY **AM** SORRY.
CAN WE BE FRIENDS AGAIN?
...
WE WERE NEVER **NOT** FRIENDS.
BUT I DON'T LIKE BEING YELLED AT. AND NOT SHOWING UP FOR LUNCH IS RUDE. NEXT TIME, TELL ME.
DEAL.
FOR THE RECORD, I WASN'T AVOIDING YOU. I WAS AVOIDING VICTOR. I'M NOT SURE IF YOU SAW --
YEAH, EVERYONE SAW.
YOU OKAY?

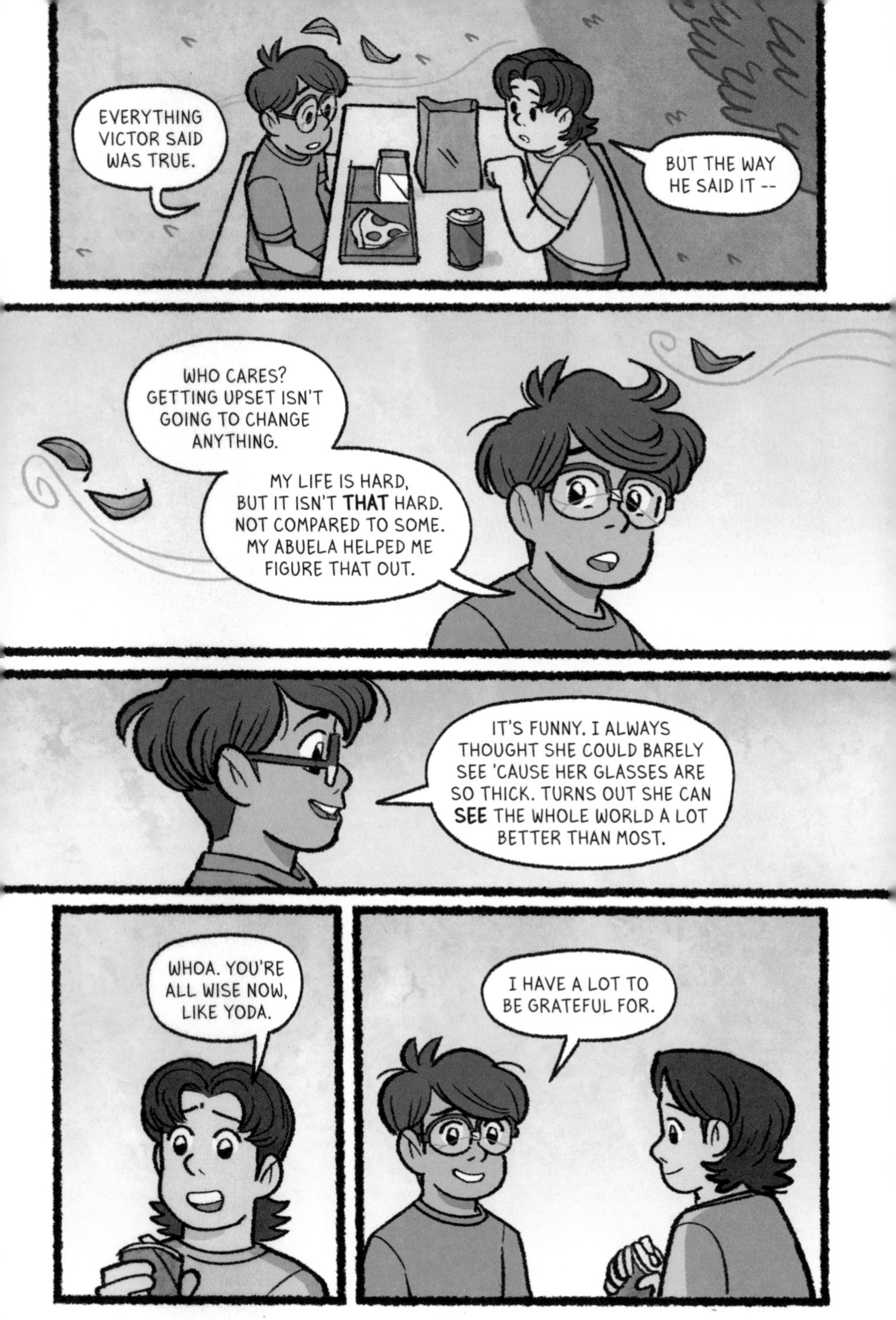
EVERYTHING VICTOR SAID WAS TRUE.
BUT THE WAY HE SAID IT --
WHO CARES? GETTING UPSET ISN'T GOING TO CHANGE ANYTHING.
MY LIFE IS HARD, BUT IT ISN'T **THAT** HARD. NOT COMPARED TO SOME. MY ABUELA HELPED ME FIGURE THAT OUT.
IT'S FUNNY. I ALWAYS THOUGHT SHE COULD BARELY SEE 'CAUSE HER GLASSES ARE SO THICK. TURNS OUT SHE CAN **SEE** THE WHOLE WORLD A LOT BETTER THAN MOST.
WHOA. YOU'RE ALL WISE NOW, LIKE YODA.
I HAVE A LOT TO BE GRATEFUL FOR.

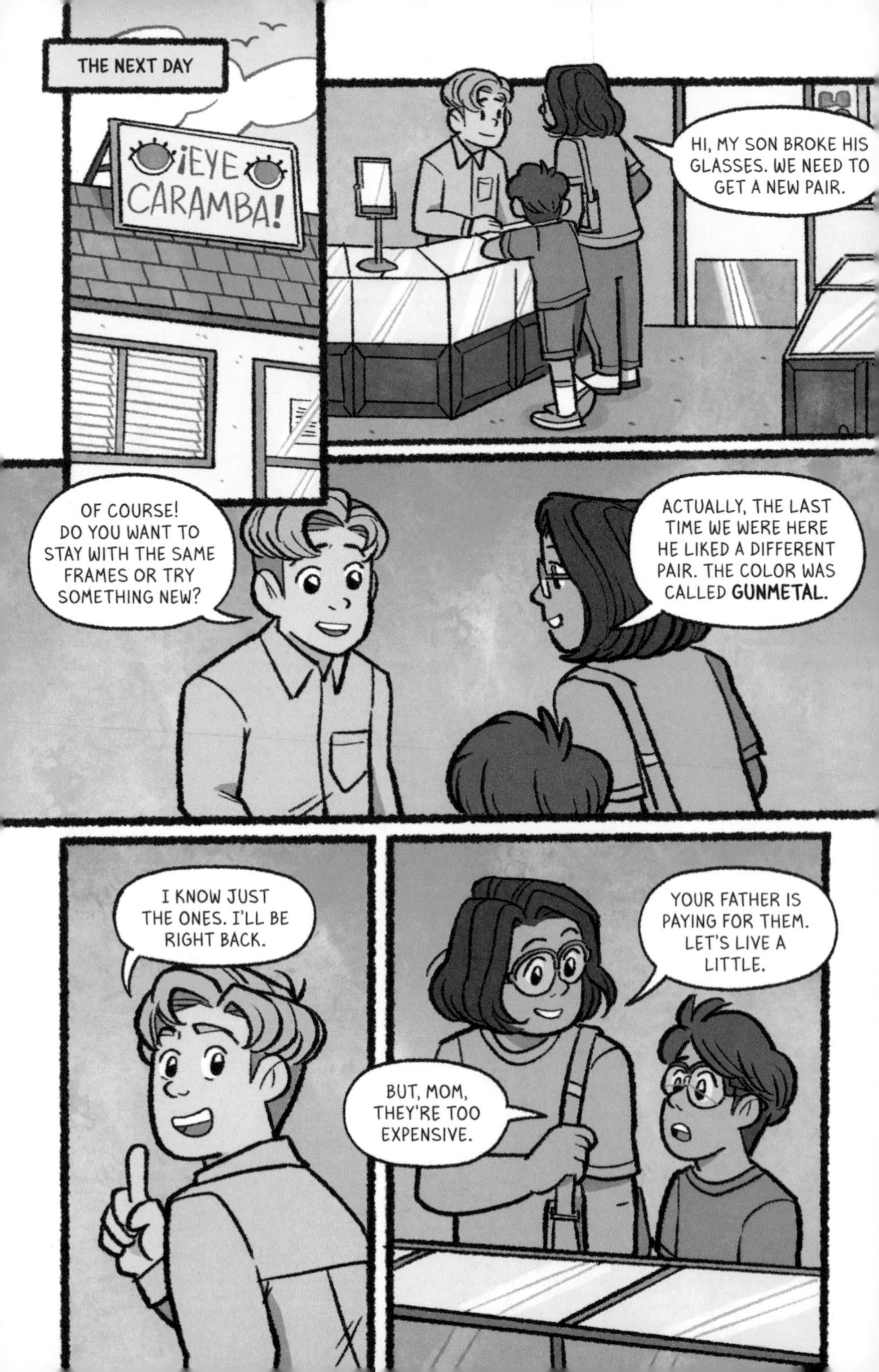
THE NEXT DAY
¡EYE CARAMBA!
HI, MY SON BROKE HIS GLASSES. WE NEED TO GET A NEW PAIR.
OF COURSE! DO YOU WANT TO STAY WITH THE SAME FRAMES OR TRY SOMETHING NEW?
ACTUALLY, THE LAST TIME WE WERE HERE HE LIKED A DIFFERENT PAIR. THE COLOR WAS CALLED **GUNMETAL.**
I KNOW JUST THE ONES. I'LL BE RIGHT BACK.
BUT, MOM, THEY'RE TOO EXPENSIVE.
YOUR FATHER IS PAYING FOR THEM. LET'S LIVE A LITTLE.

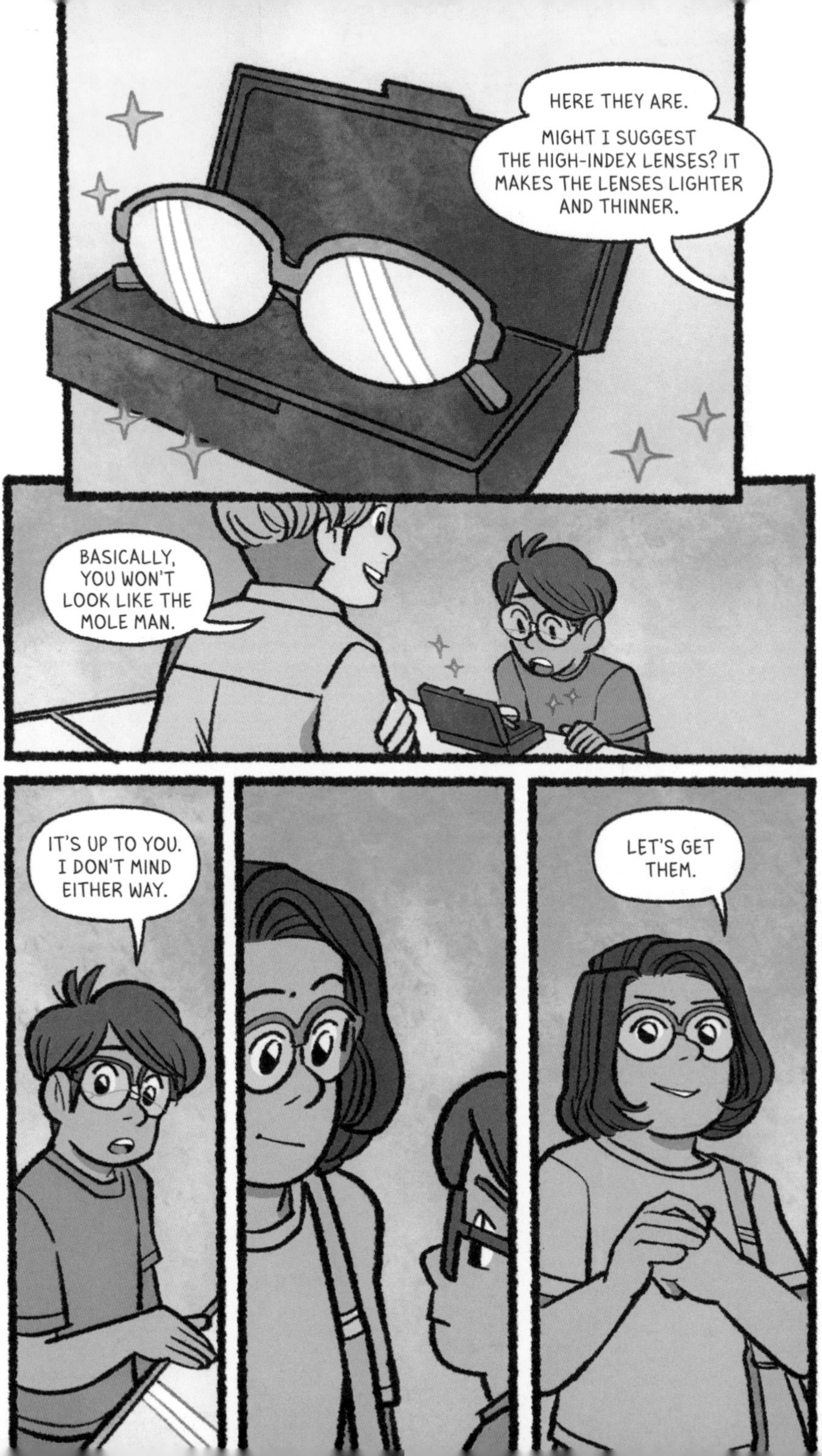
HERE THEY ARE.
MIGHT I SUGGEST THE HIGH-INDEX LENSES? IT MAKES THE LENSES LIGHTER AND THINNER.
BASICALLY, YOU WON'T LOOK LIKE THE MOLE MAN.
IT'S UP TO YOU. I DON'T MIND EITHER WAY.
LET'S GET THEM.

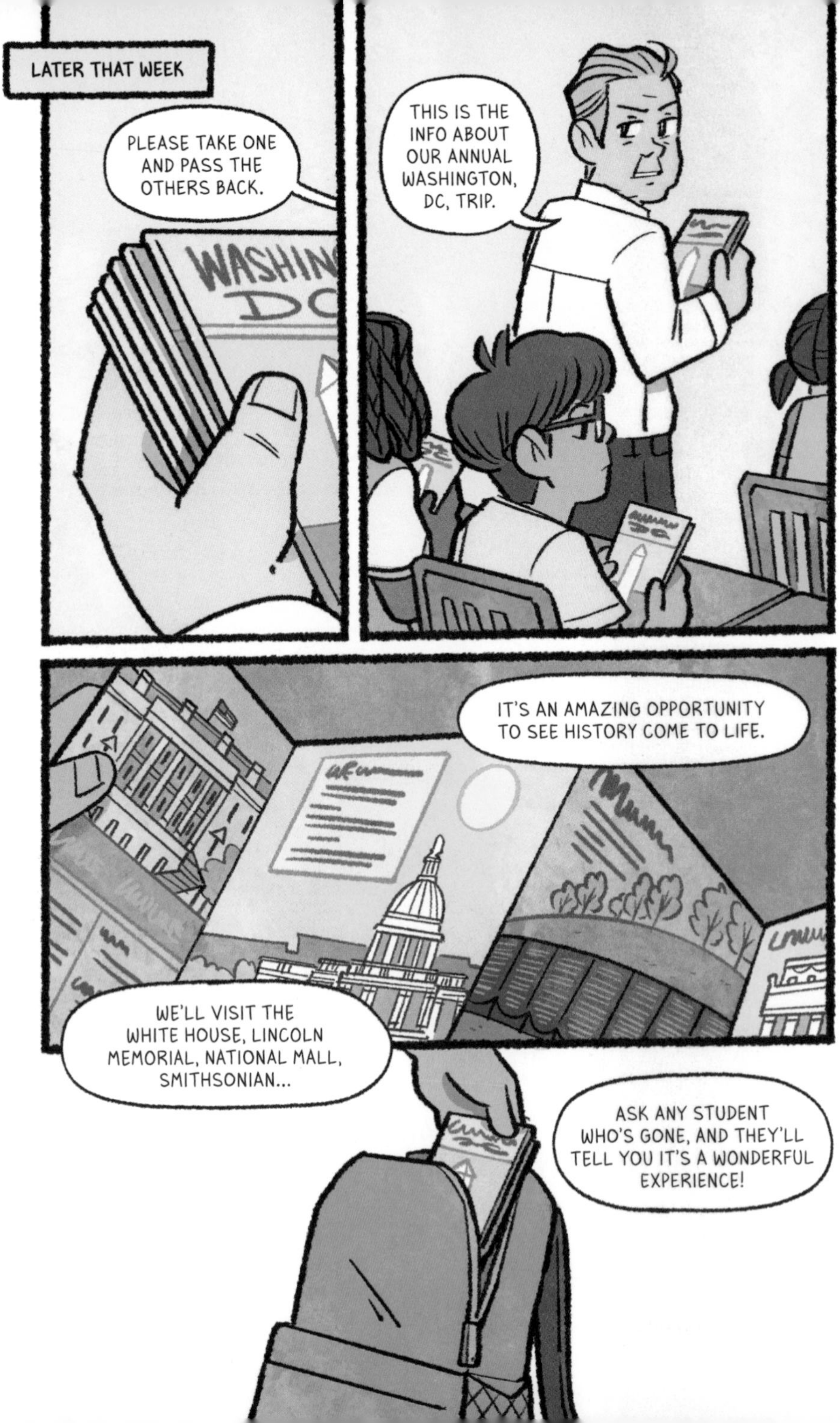
LATER THAT WEEK
PLEASE TAKE ONE AND PASS THE OTHERS BACK.
WASHIN
DC
THIS IS THE INFO ABOUT OUR ANNUAL WASHINGTON, DC, TRIP.
IT'S AN AMAZING OPPORTUNITY TO SEE HISTORY COME TO LIFE.
WE'LL VISIT THE WHITE HOUSE, LINCOLN MEMORIAL, NATIONAL MALL, SMITHSONIAN...
ASK ANY STUDENT WHO'S GONE, AND THEY'LL TELL YOU IT'S A WONDERFUL EXPERIENCE!

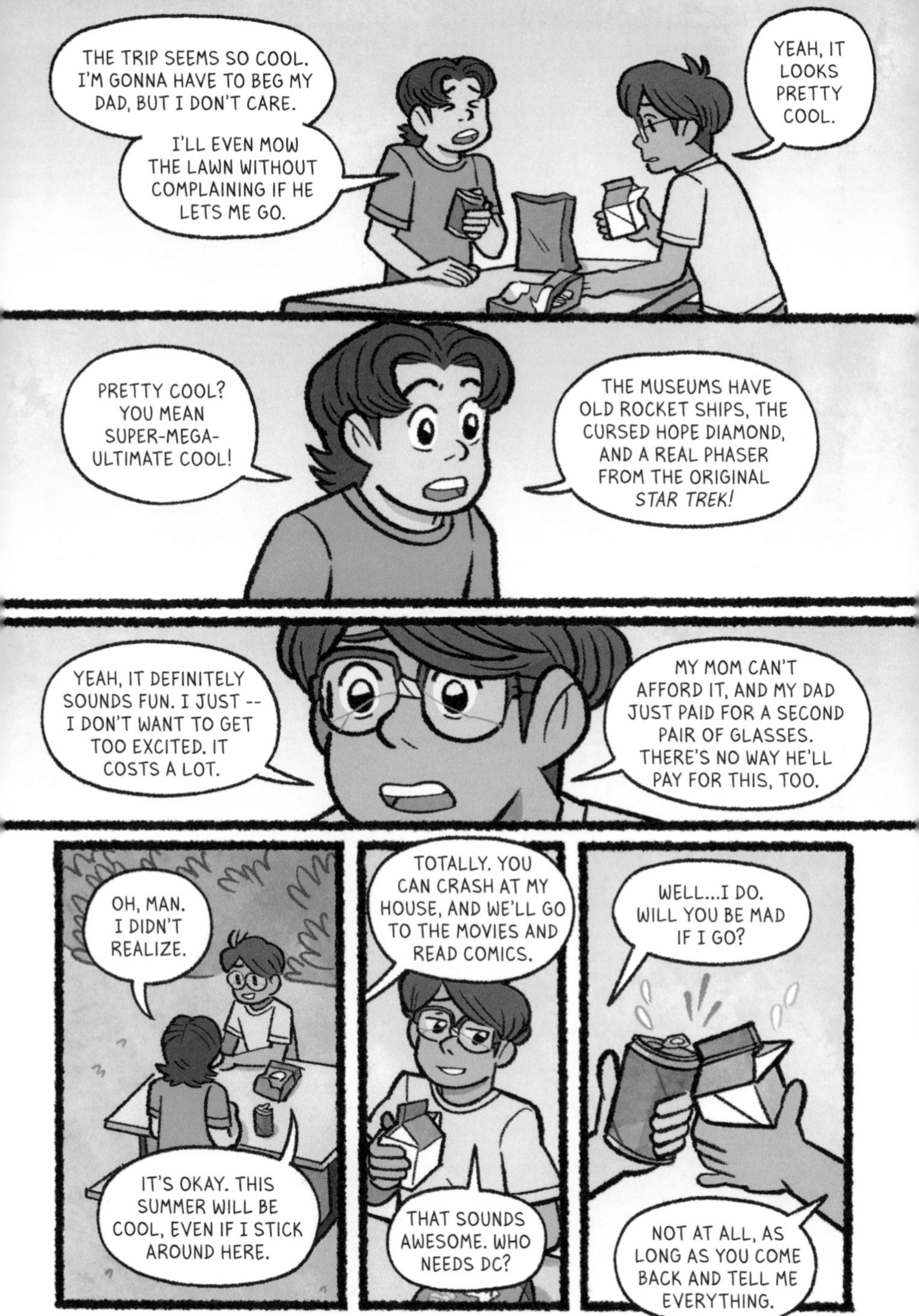
THE TRIP SEEMS SO COOL. I'M GONNA HAVE TO BEG MY DAD, BUT I DON'T CARE.
I'LL EVEN MOW THE LAWN WITHOUT COMPLAINING IF HE LETS ME GO.
YEAH, IT LOOKS PRETTY COOL.
PRETTY COOL? YOU MEAN SUPER-MEGA-ULTIMATE COOL!
THE MUSEUMS HAVE OLD ROCKET SHIPS, THE CURSED HOPE DIAMOND, AND A REAL PHASER FROM THE ORIGINAL *STAR TREK!*
YEAH, IT DEFINITELY SOUNDS FUN. I JUST -- I DON'T WANT TO GET TOO EXCITED. IT COSTS A LOT.
MY MOM CAN'T AFFORD IT, AND MY DAD JUST PAID FOR A SECOND PAIR OF GLASSES. THERE'S NO WAY HE'LL PAY FOR THIS, TOO.
OH, MAN. I DIDN'T REALIZE.
IT'S OKAY. THIS SUMMER WILL BE COOL, EVEN IF I STICK AROUND HERE.
TOTALLY. YOU CAN CRASH AT MY HOUSE, AND WE'LL GO TO THE MOVIES AND READ COMICS.
THAT SOUNDS AWESOME. WHO NEEDS DC?
WELL...I DO. WILL YOU BE MAD IF I GO?
NOT AT ALL, AS LONG AS YOU COME BACK AND TELL ME EVERYTHING.

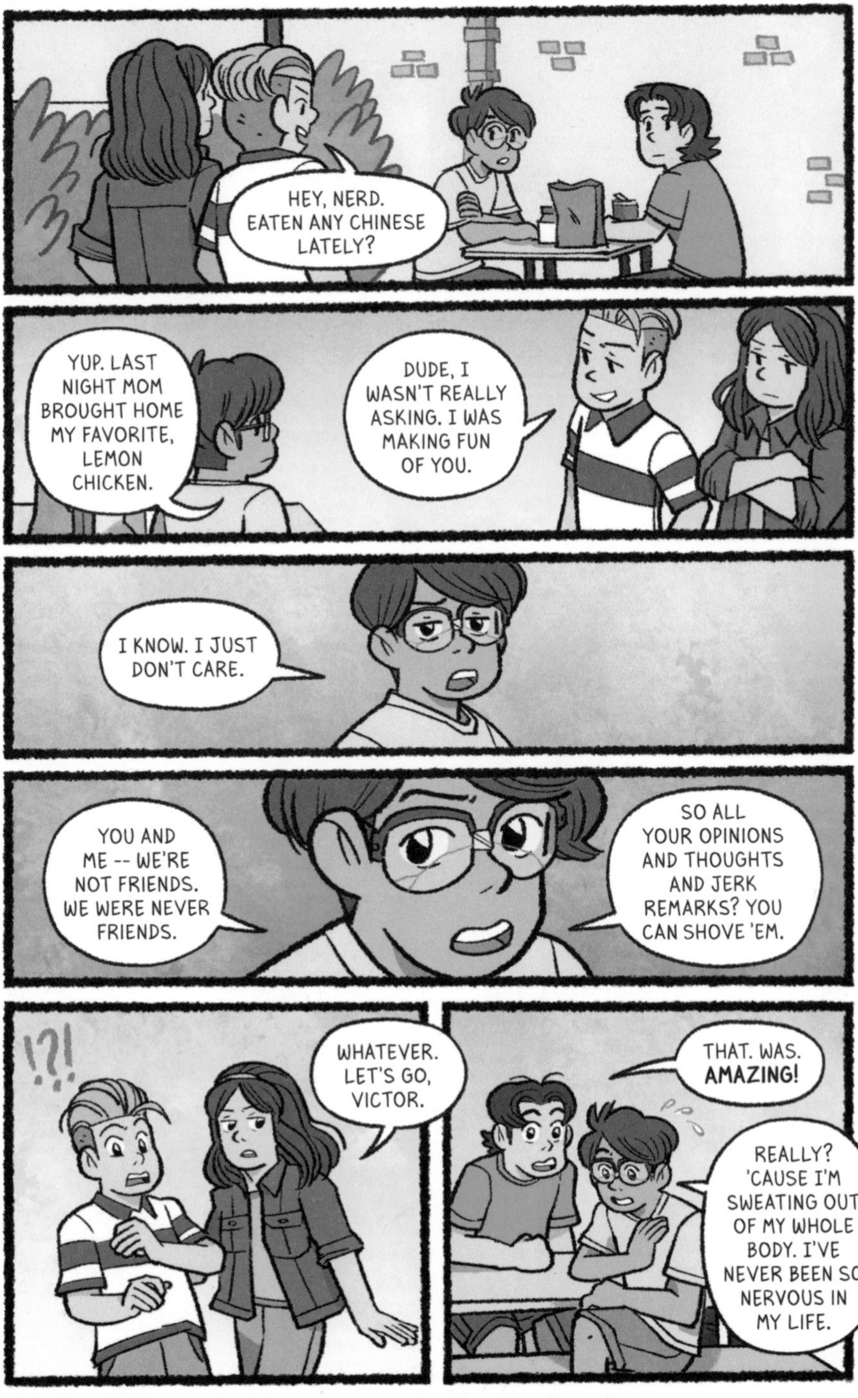
HEY, NERD. EATEN ANY CHINESE LATELY?
YUP. LAST NIGHT MOM BROUGHT HOME MY FAVORITE, LEMON CHICKEN.
DUDE, I WASN'T REALLY ASKING. I WAS MAKING FUN OF YOU.
I KNOW. I JUST DON'T CARE.
YOU AND ME -- WE'RE NOT FRIENDS. WE WERE NEVER FRIENDS.
SO ALL YOUR OPINIONS AND THOUGHTS AND JERK REMARKS? YOU CAN SHOVE 'EM.
!?!
WHATEVER. LET'S GO, VICTOR.
THAT. WAS. **AMAZING!**
REALLY? 'CAUSE I'M SWEATING OUT OF MY WHOLE BODY. I'VE NEVER BEEN SO NERVOUS IN MY LIFE.

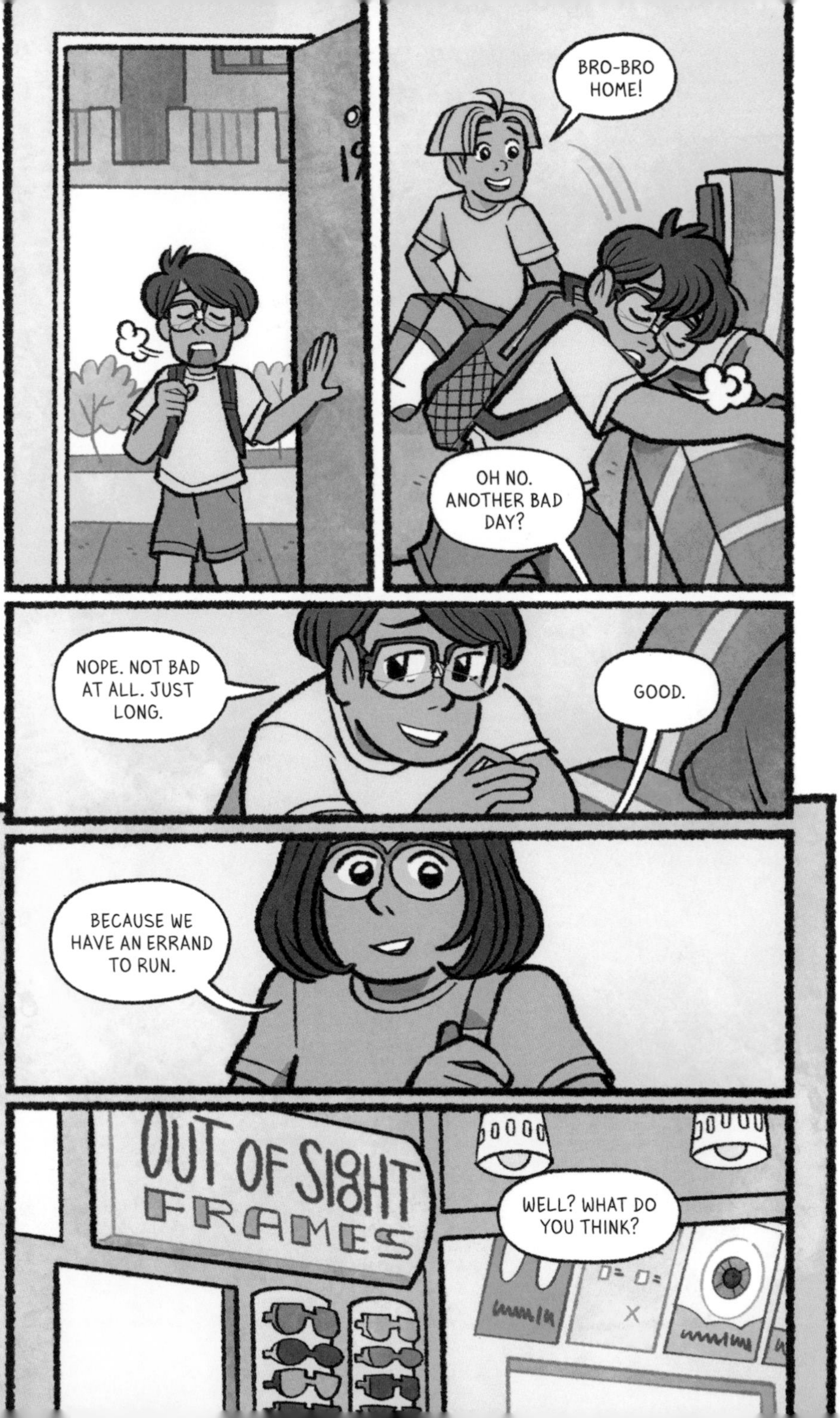
BRO-BRO HOME!
OH NO. ANOTHER BAD DAY?
NOPE. NOT BAD AT ALL. JUST LONG.
GOOD.
BECAUSE WE HAVE AN ERRAND TO RUN.
OUT OF SIGHT FRAMES
WELL? WHAT DO YOU THINK?

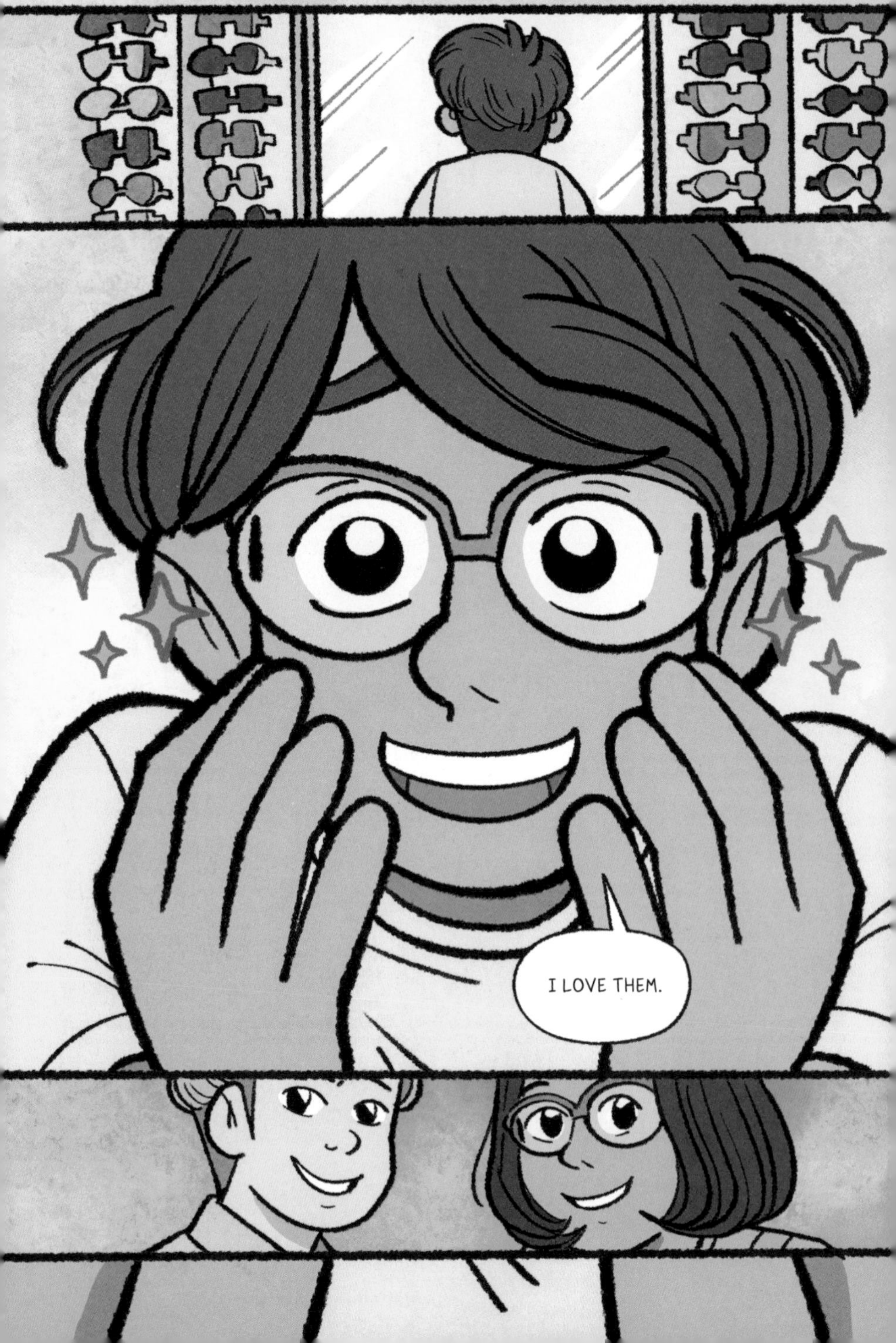
I LOVE THEM.

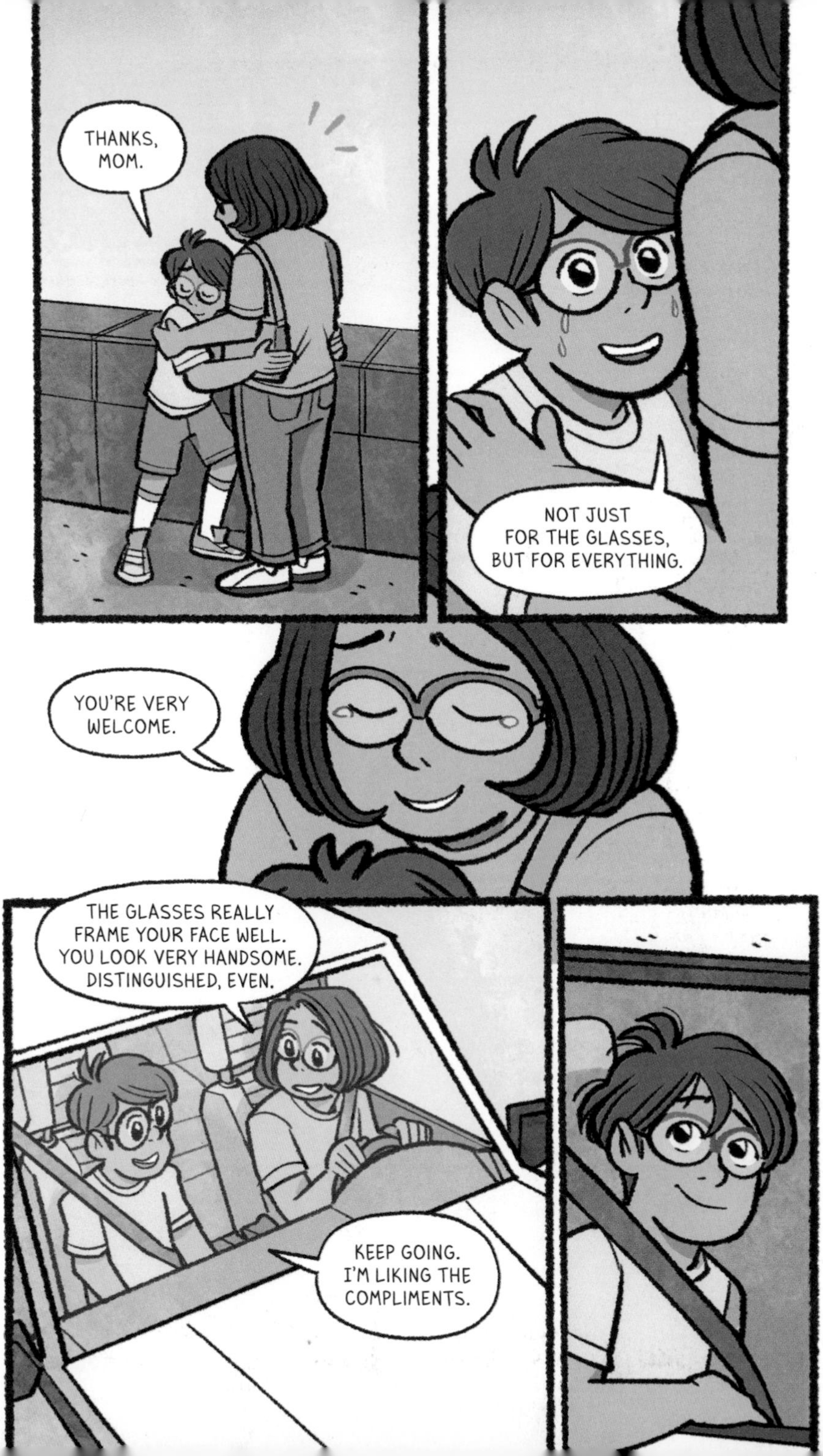
THANKS, MOM.
NOT JUST FOR THE GLASSES, BUT FOR EVERYTHING.
YOU'RE VERY WELCOME.
THE GLASSES REALLY FRAME YOUR FACE WELL. YOU LOOK VERY HANDSOME. DISTINGUISHED, EVEN.
KEEP GOING. I'M LIKING THE COMPLIMENTS.

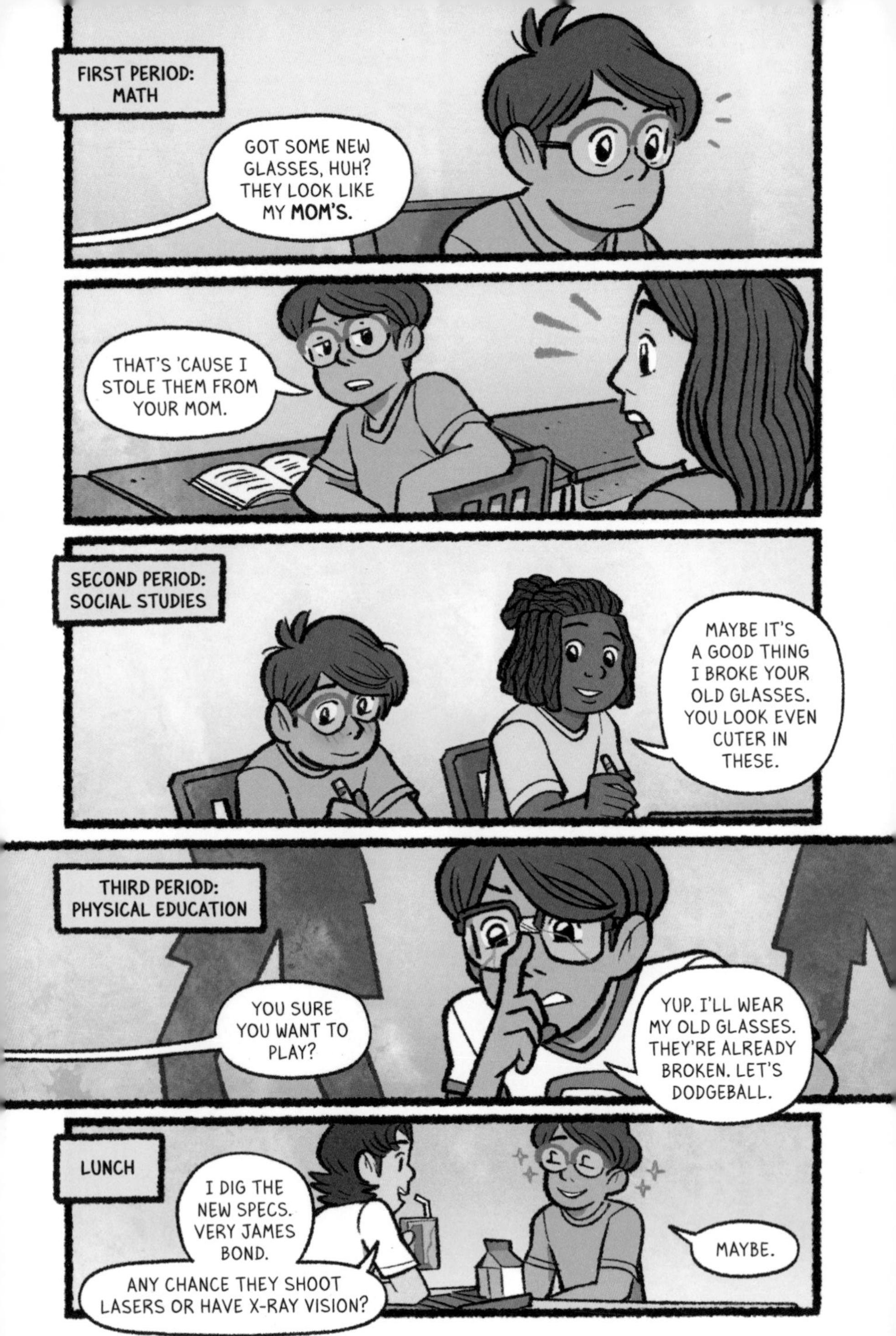
FIRST PERIOD: MATH
GOT SOME NEW GLASSES, HUH? THEY LOOK LIKE MY **MOM'S.**
THAT'S 'CAUSE I STOLE THEM FROM YOUR MOM.
SECOND PERIOD: SOCIAL STUDIES
MAYBE IT'S A GOOD THING I BROKE YOUR OLD GLASSES. YOU LOOK EVEN CUTER IN THESE.
THIRD PERIOD: PHYSICAL EDUCATION
YOU SURE YOU WANT TO PLAY?
YUP. I'LL WEAR MY OLD GLASSES. THEY'RE ALREADY BROKEN. LET'S DODGEBALL.
LUNCH
I DIG THE NEW SPECS. VERY JAMES BOND.
ANY CHANCE THEY SHOOT LASERS OR HAVE X-RAY VISION?
MAYBE.

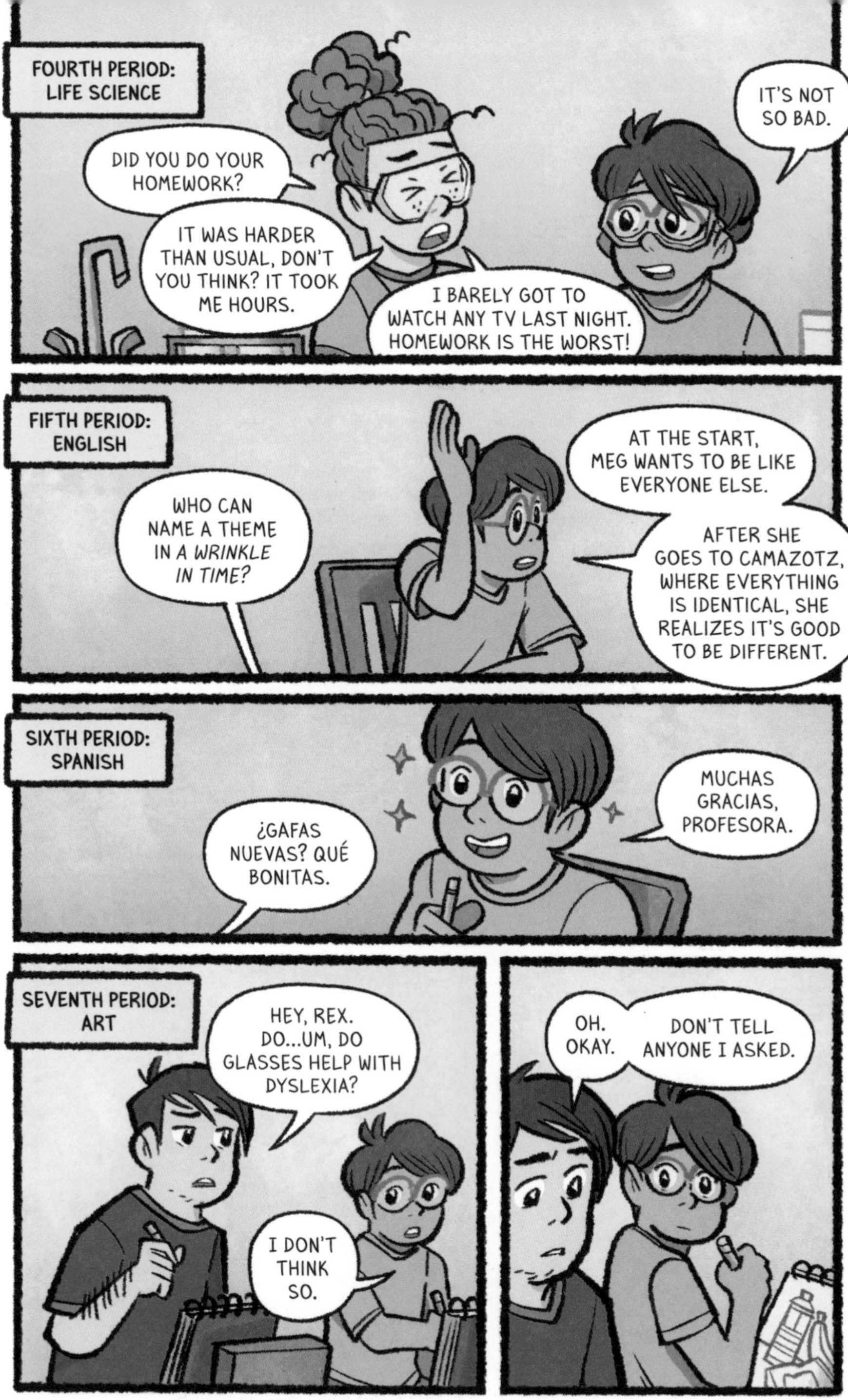
FOURTH PERIOD: LIFE SCIENCE
DID YOU DO YOUR HOMEWORK?
IT'S NOT SO BAD.
IT WAS HARDER THAN USUAL, DON'T YOU THINK? IT TOOK ME HOURS.
I BARELY GOT TO WATCH ANY TV LAST NIGHT. HOMEWORK IS THE WORST!
FIFTH PERIOD: ENGLISH
WHO CAN NAME A THEME IN *A WRINKLE IN TIME*?
AT THE START, MEG WANTS TO BE LIKE EVERYONE ELSE.
AFTER SHE GOES TO CAMAZOTZ, WHERE EVERYTHING IS IDENTICAL, SHE REALIZES IT'S GOOD TO BE DIFFERENT.
SIXTH PERIOD: SPANISH
¿GAFAS NUEVAS? QUÉ BONITAS.
MUCHAS GRACIAS, PROFESORA.
SEVENTH PERIOD: ART
HEY, REX. DO...UM, DO GLASSES HELP WITH DYSLEXIA?
I DON'T THINK SO.
OH. OKAY.
DON'T TELL ANYONE I ASKED.

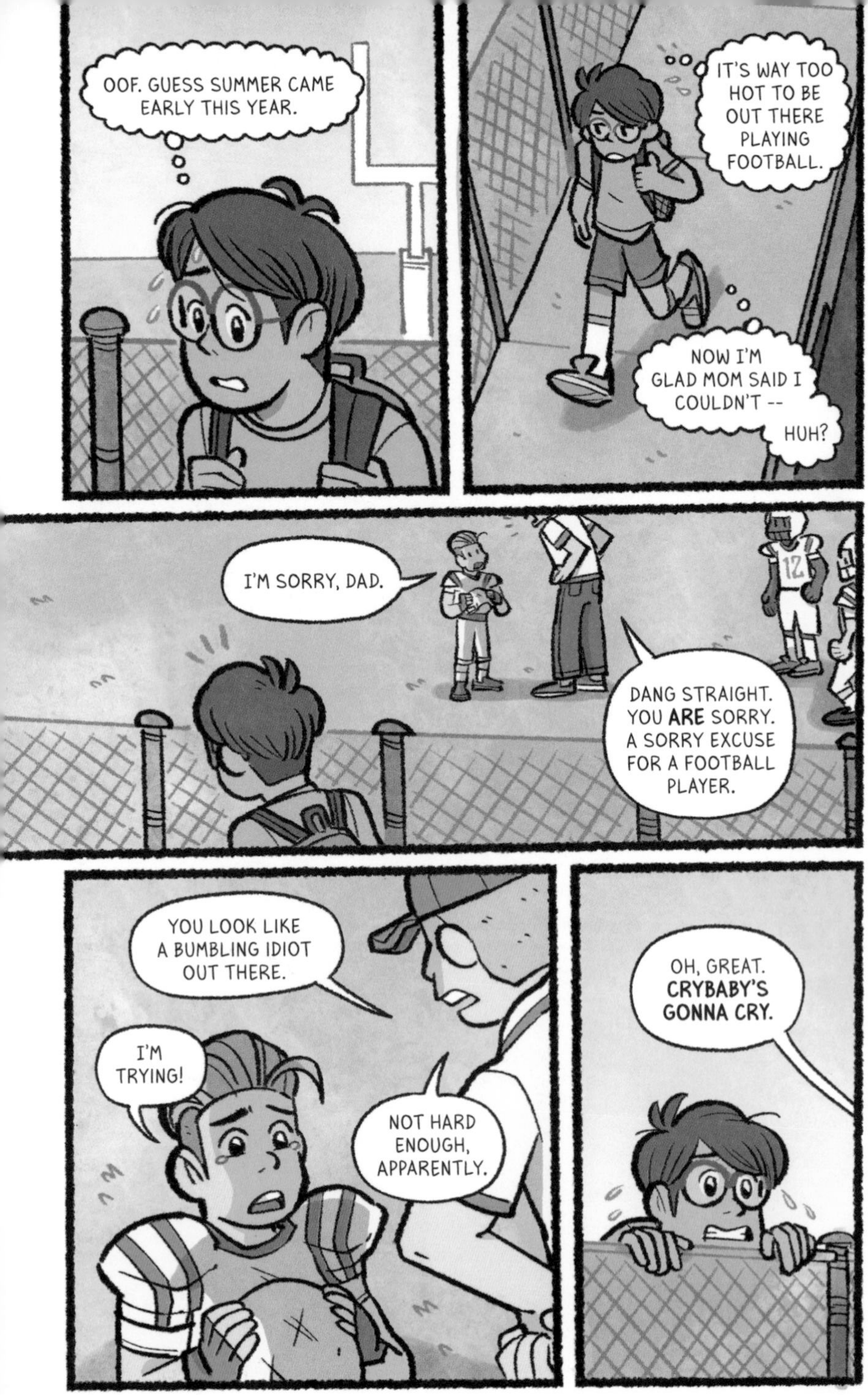
OOF. GUESS SUMMER CAME EARLY THIS YEAR.
IT'S WAY TOO HOT TO BE OUT THERE PLAYING FOOTBALL.
NOW I'M GLAD MOM SAID I COULDN'T --
HUH?
12
I'M SORRY, DAD.
DANG STRAIGHT. YOU **ARE** SORRY. A SORRY EXCUSE FOR A FOOTBALL PLAYER.
YOU LOOK LIKE A BUMBLING IDIOT OUT THERE.
I'M TRYING!
NOT HARD ENOUGH, APPARENTLY.
OH, GREAT. **CRYBABY'S GONNA CRY.**

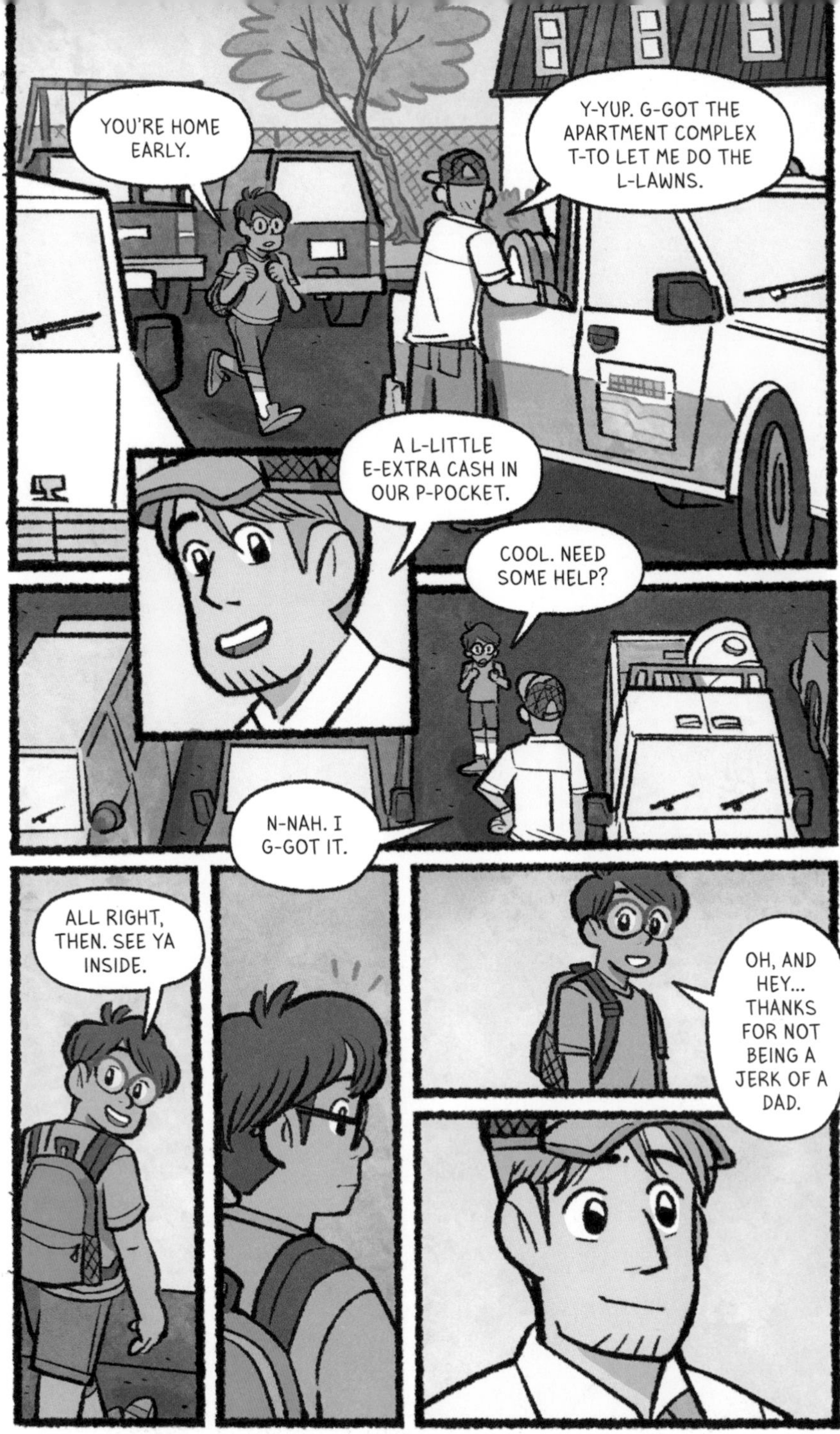
YOU'RE HOME EARLY.
Y-YUP. G-GOT THE APARTMENT COMPLEX T-TO LET ME DO THE L-LAWNS.
A L-LITTLE E-EXTRA CASH IN OUR P-POCKET.
COOL. NEED SOME HELP?
N-NAH. I G-GOT IT.
ALL RIGHT, THEN. SEE YA INSIDE.
OH, AND HEY... THANKS FOR NOT BEING A JERK OF A DAD.

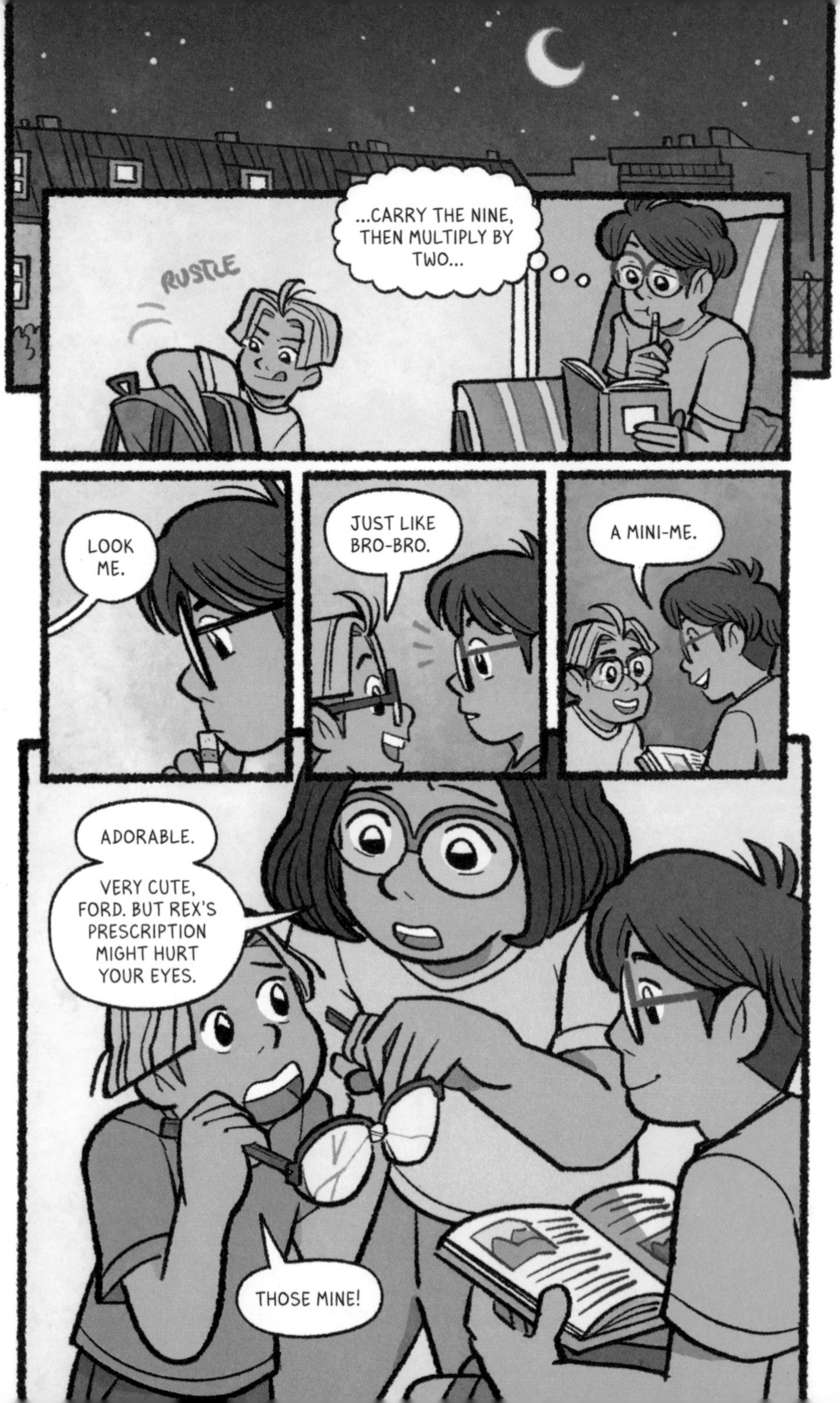
...CARRY THE NINE, THEN MULTIPLY BY TWO...
RUSTLE
LOOK ME.
JUST LIKE BRO-BRO.
A MINI-ME.
ADORABLE.
VERY CUTE, FORD. BUT REX'S PRESCRIPTION MIGHT HURT YOUR EYES.
THOSE MINE!

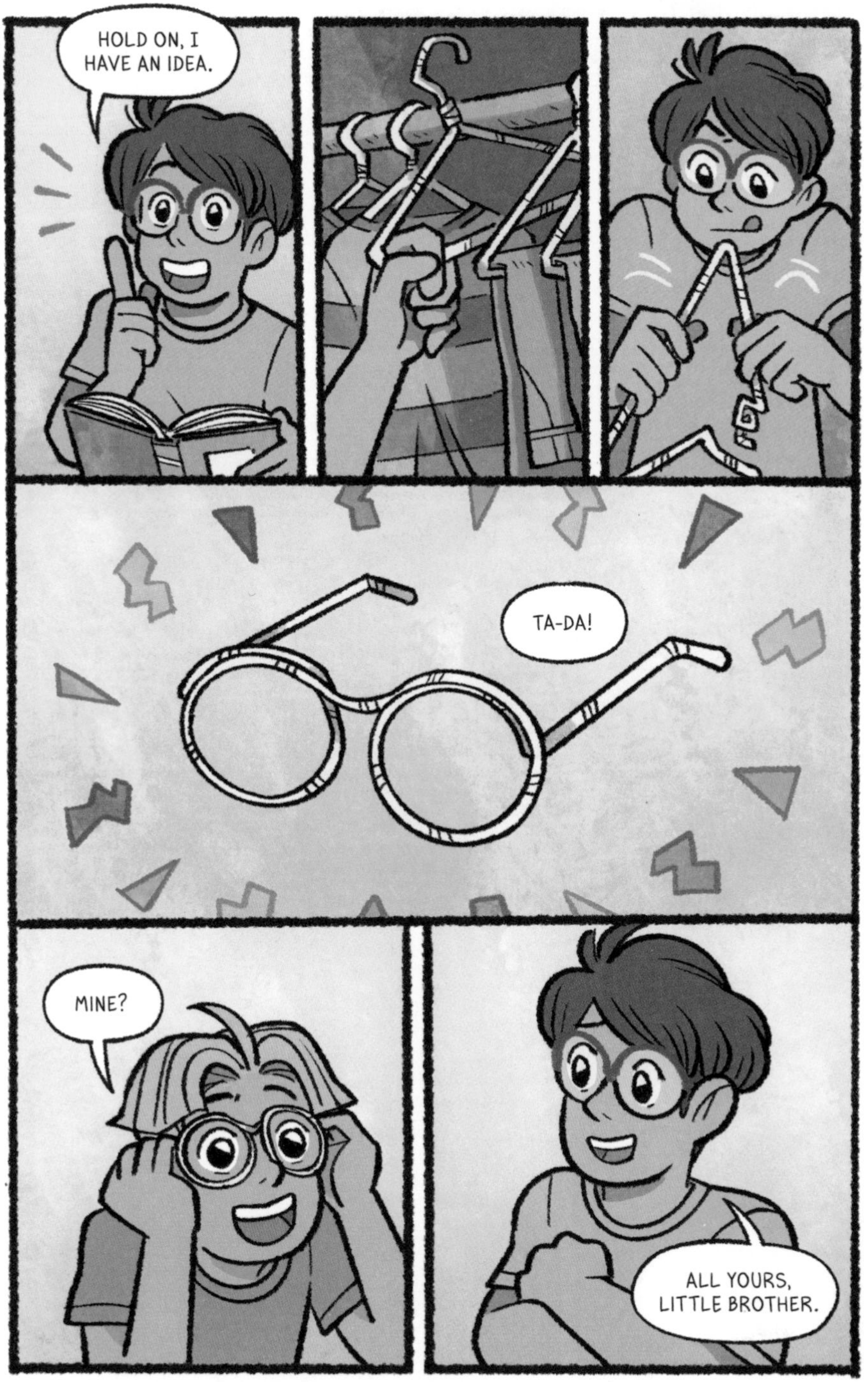
HOLD ON, I HAVE AN IDEA.
TA-DA!
MINE?
ALL YOURS, LITTLE BROTHER.

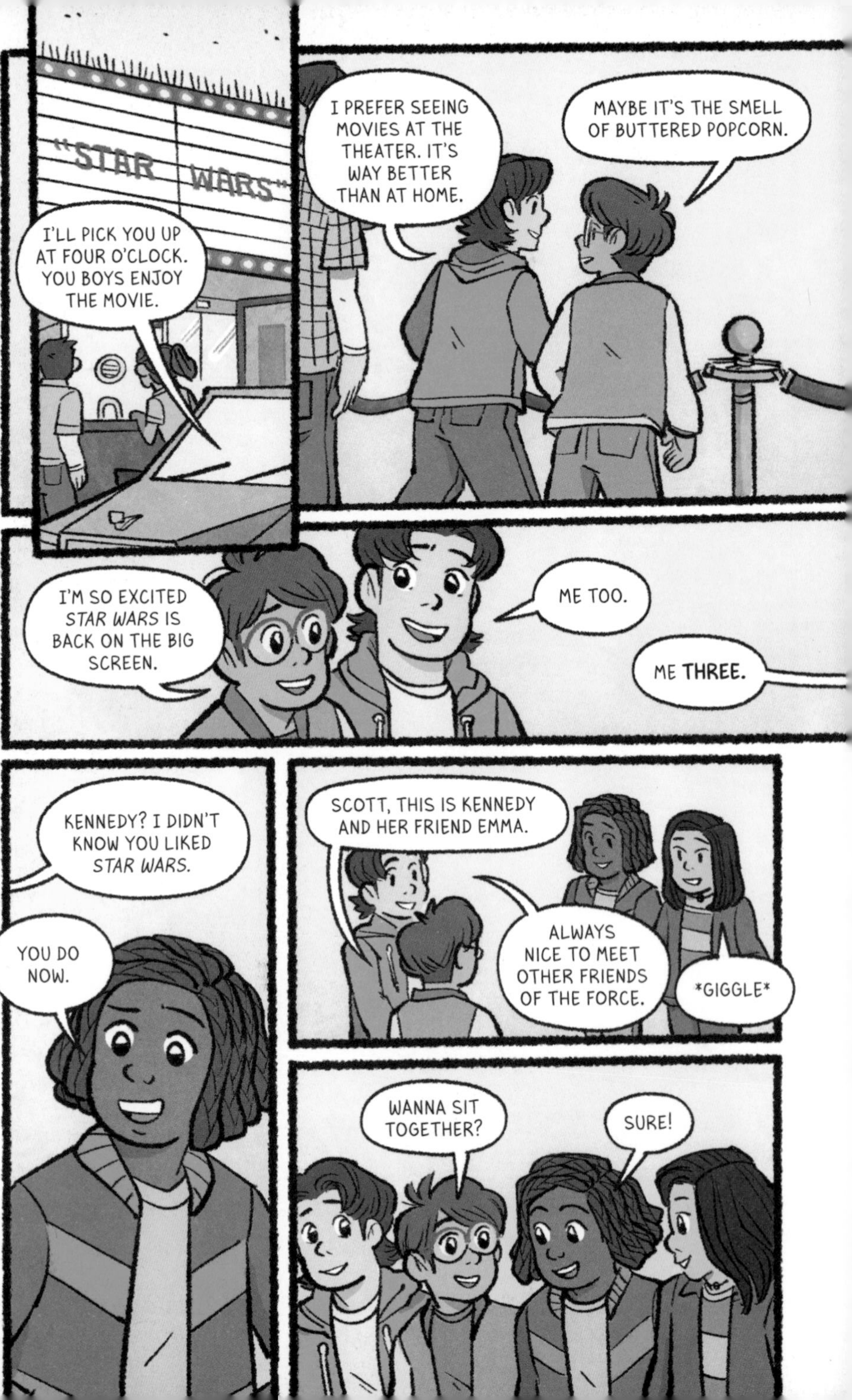
"STAR WARS"
I'LL PICK YOU UP AT FOUR O'CLOCK. YOU BOYS ENJOY THE MOVIE.
I PREFER SEEING MOVIES AT THE THEATER. IT'S WAY BETTER THAN AT HOME.
MAYBE IT'S THE SMELL OF BUTTERED POPCORN.
I'M SO EXCITED *STAR WARS* IS BACK ON THE BIG SCREEN.
ME TOO.
ME **THREE.**
KENNEDY? I DIDN'T KNOW YOU LIKED *STAR WARS.*
YOU DO NOW.
SCOTT, THIS IS KENNEDY AND HER FRIEND EMMA.
ALWAYS NICE TO MEET OTHER FRIENDS OF THE FORCE.
GIGGLE
WANNA SIT TOGETHER?
SURE!

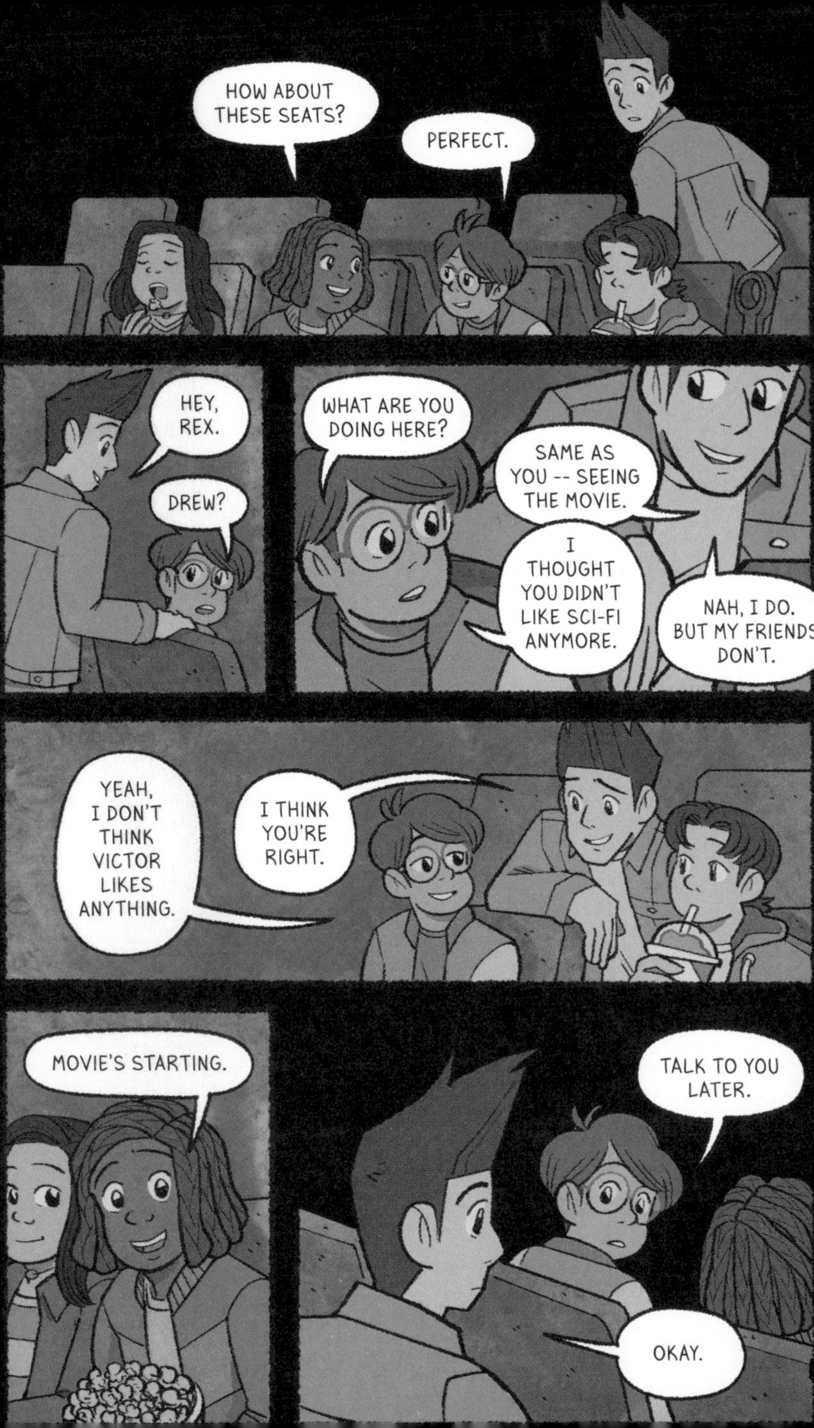
HOW ABOUT THESE SEATS?
PERFECT.
HEY, REX.
DREW?
WHAT ARE YOU DOING HERE?
SAME AS YOU -- SEEING THE MOVIE.
I THOUGHT YOU DIDN'T LIKE SCI-FI ANYMORE.
NAH, I DO. BUT MY FRIENDS DON'T.
I THINK YOU'RE RIGHT.
YEAH, I DON'T THINK VICTOR LIKES ANYTHING.
MOVIE'S STARTING.
TALK TO YOU LATER.
OKAY.

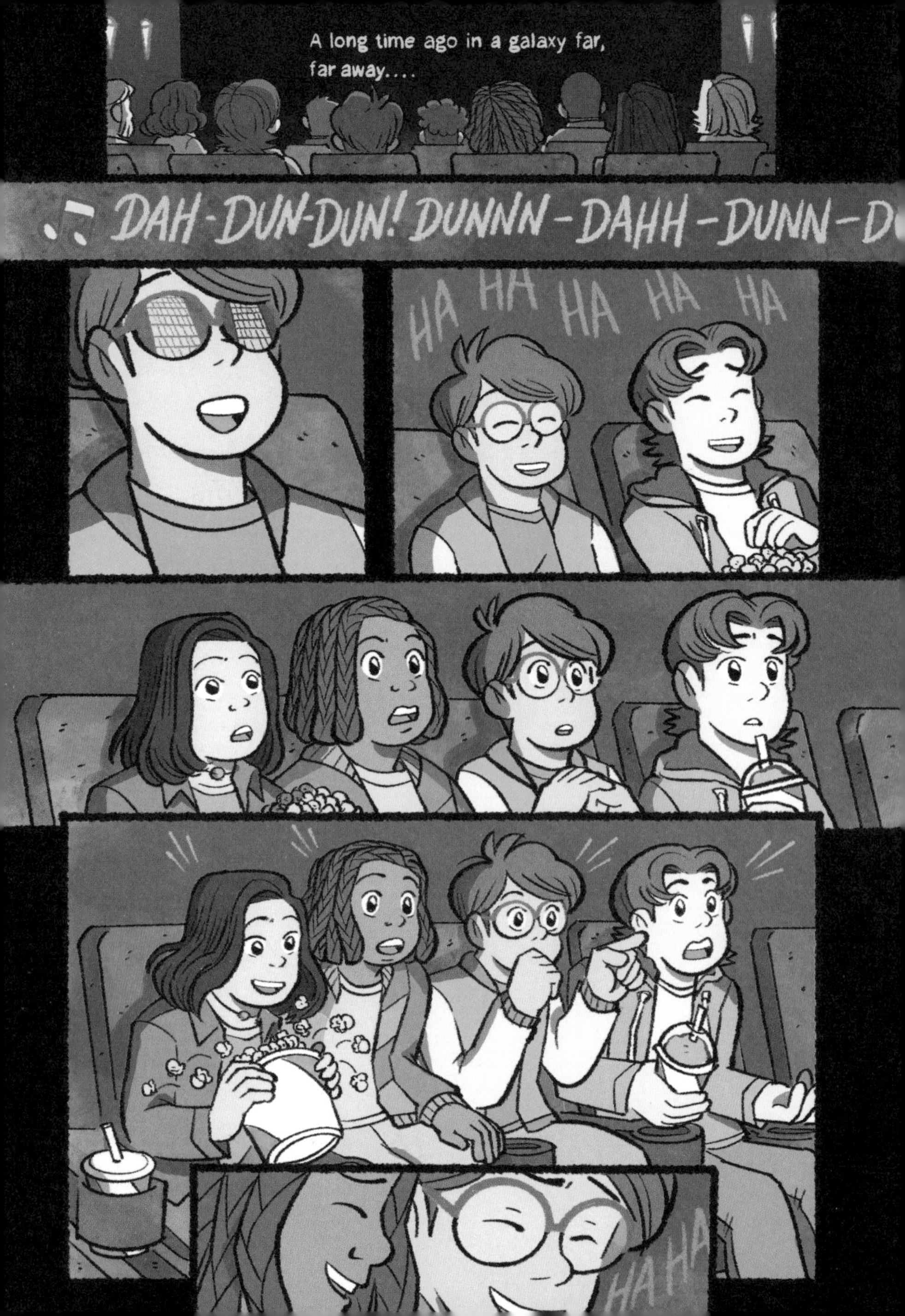
A long time ago in a galaxy far, far away....
DAH-DUN-DUN! DUNNN-DAHH-DUNN-D
HA HA HA HA HA
HA HA

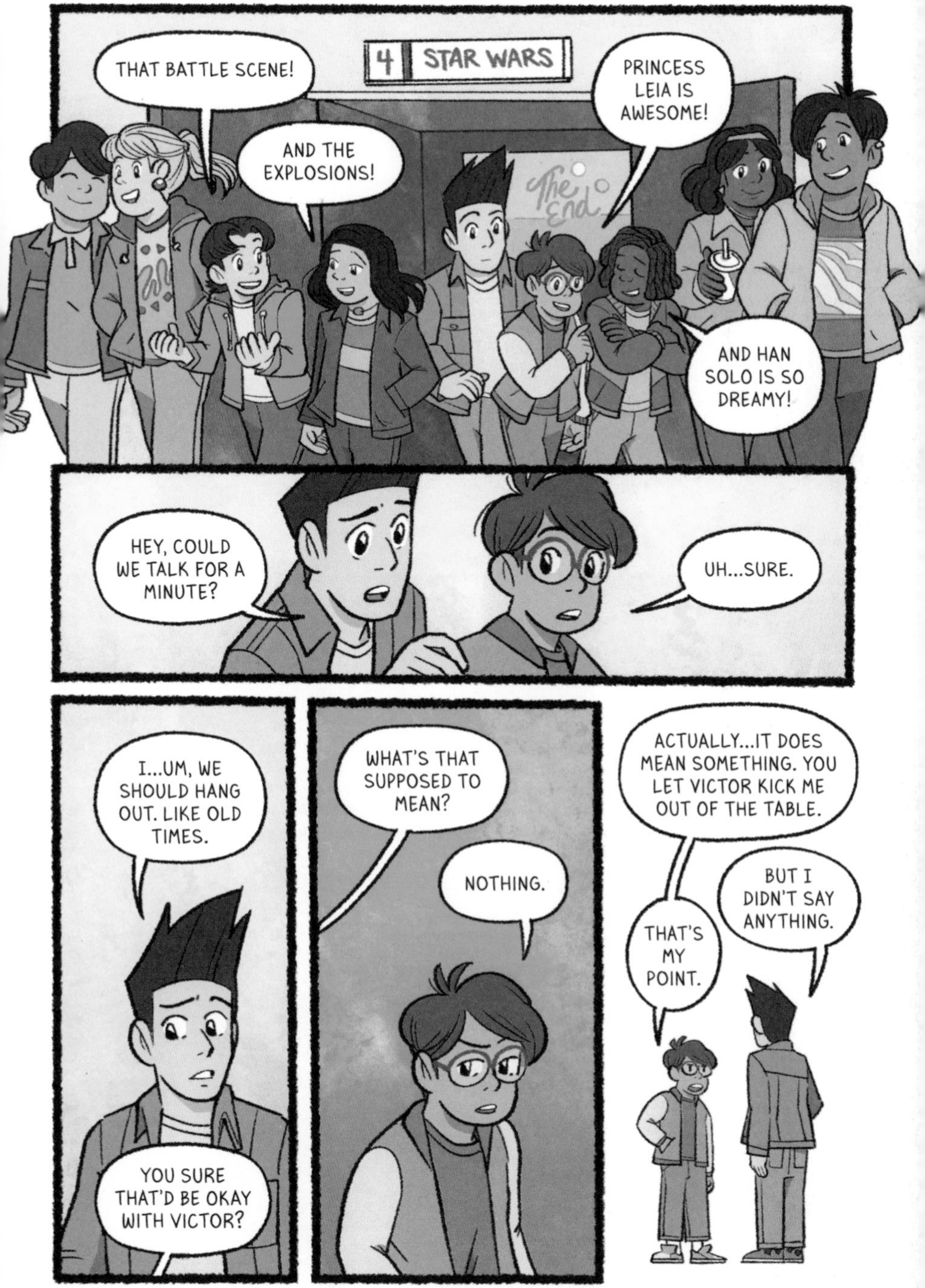
4 STAR WARS
THAT BATTLE SCENE!
AND THE EXPLOSIONS!
PRINCESS LEIA IS AWESOME!
The End
AND HAN SOLO IS SO DREAMY!
HEY, COULD WE TALK FOR A MINUTE?
UH...SURE.
I...UM, WE SHOULD HANG OUT. LIKE OLD TIMES.
YOU SURE THAT'D BE OKAY WITH VICTOR?
WHAT'S THAT SUPPOSED TO MEAN?
NOTHING.
ACTUALLY...IT DOES MEAN SOMETHING. YOU LET VICTOR KICK ME OUT OF THE TABLE.
BUT I DIDN'T SAY ANYTHING.
THAT'S MY POINT.

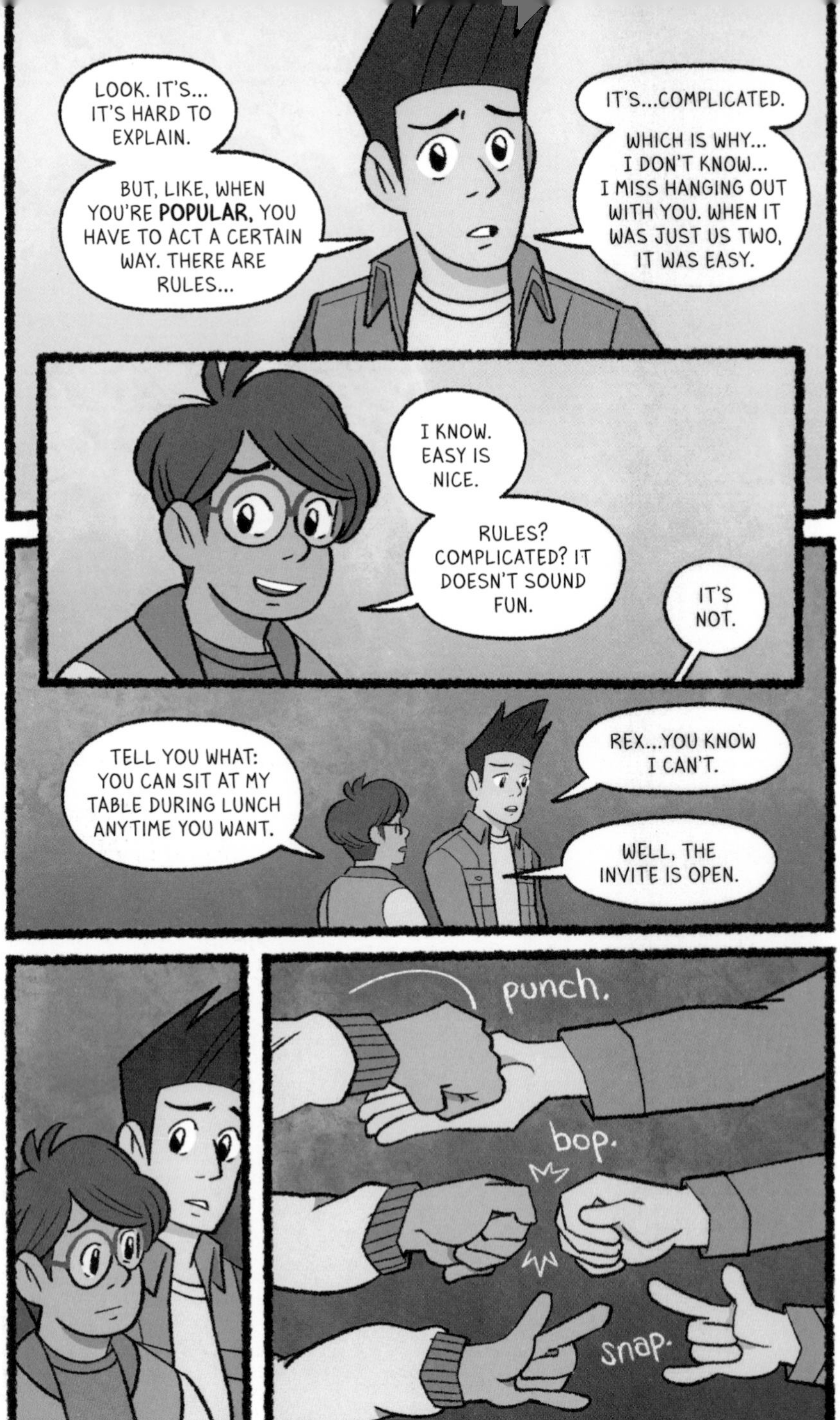

LOOK. IT'S... IT'S HARD TO EXPLAIN.
BUT, LIKE, WHEN YOU'RE **POPULAR,** YOU HAVE TO ACT A CERTAIN WAY. THERE ARE RULES...
IT'S...COMPLICATED.
WHICH IS WHY... I DON'T KNOW... I MISS HANGING OUT WITH YOU. WHEN IT WAS JUST US TWO, IT WAS EASY.
I KNOW. EASY IS NICE.
RULES? COMPLICATED? IT DOESN'T SOUND FUN.
IT'S NOT.
TELL YOU WHAT: YOU CAN SIT AT MY TABLE DURING LUNCH ANYTIME YOU WANT.
REX...YOU KNOW I CAN'T.
WELL, THE INVITE IS OPEN.
punch.
bop.
snap.

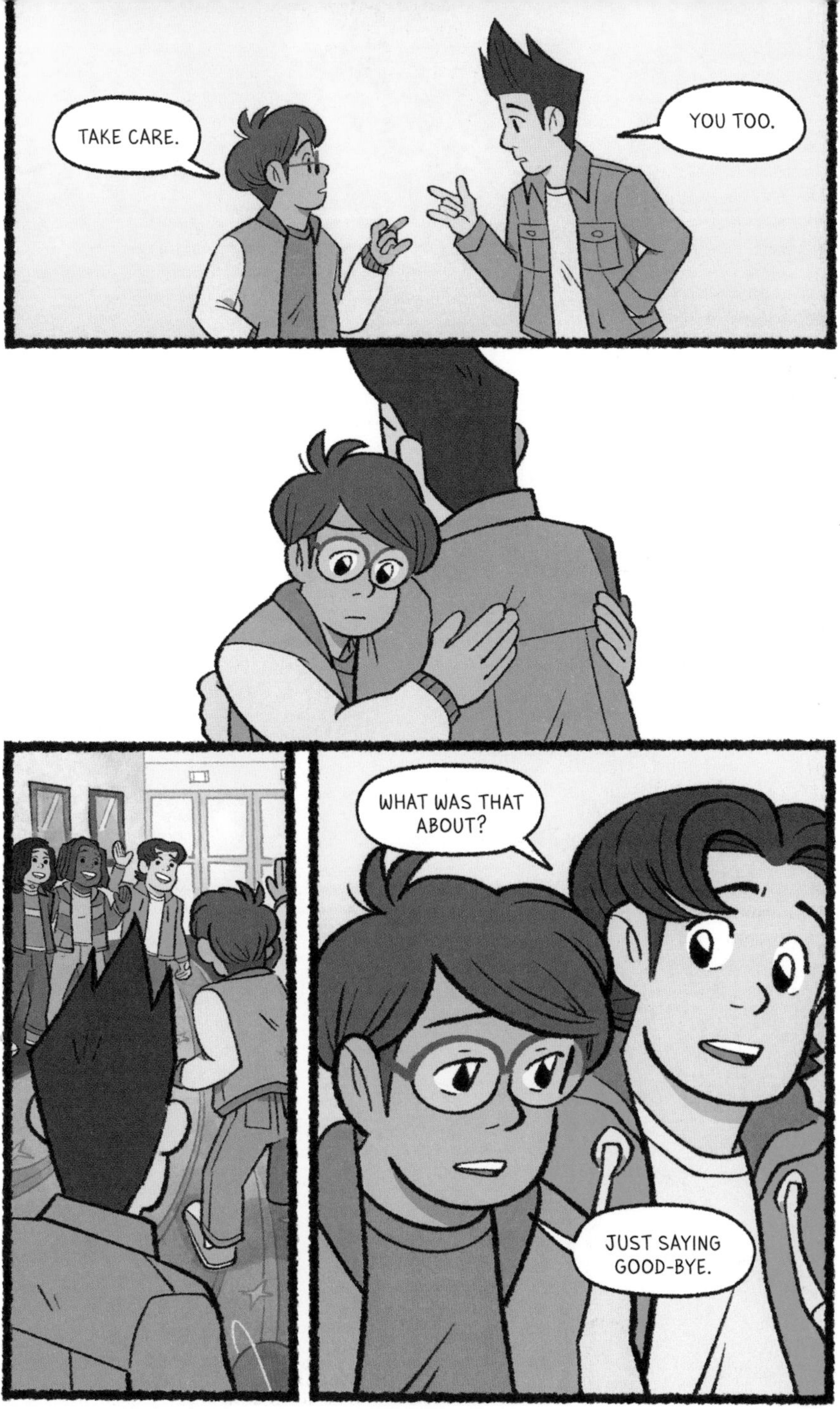
TAKE CARE.
YOU TOO.
WHAT WAS THAT ABOUT?
JUST SAYING GOOD-BYE.

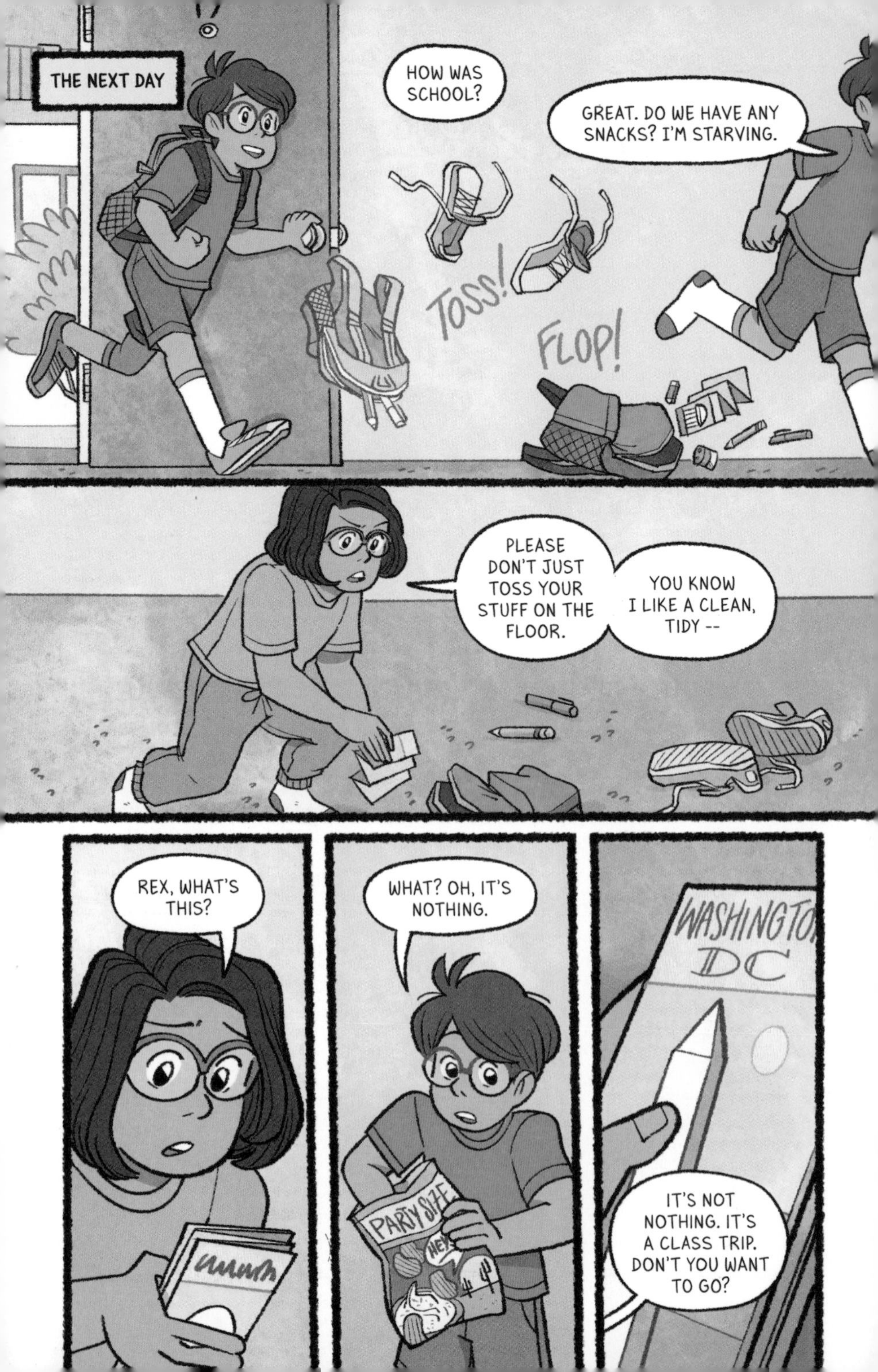
THE NEXT DAY
HOW WAS SCHOOL?
GREAT. DO WE HAVE ANY SNACKS? I'M STARVING.
TOSS!
FLOP!
PLEASE DON'T JUST TOSS YOUR STUFF ON THE FLOOR.
YOU KNOW I LIKE A CLEAN, TIDY --
REX, WHAT'S THIS?
WHAT? OH, IT'S NOTHING.
PARTY SIZE
WASHINGTON DC
IT'S NOT NOTHING. IT'S A CLASS TRIP. DON'T YOU WANT TO GO?

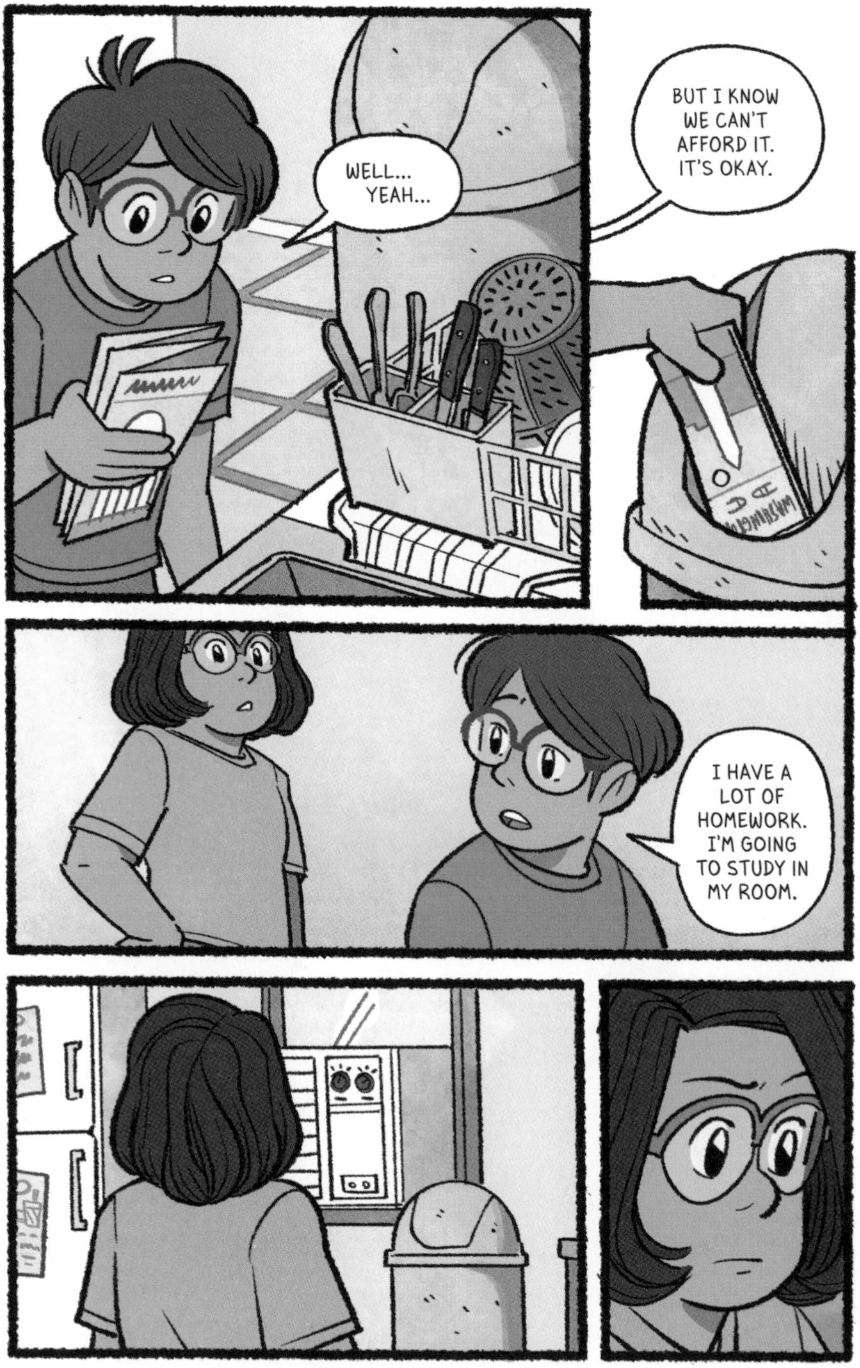
WELL... YEAH...
BUT I KNOW WE CAN'T AFFORD IT. IT'S OKAY.
I HAVE A LOT OF HOMEWORK. I'M GOING TO STUDY IN MY ROOM.

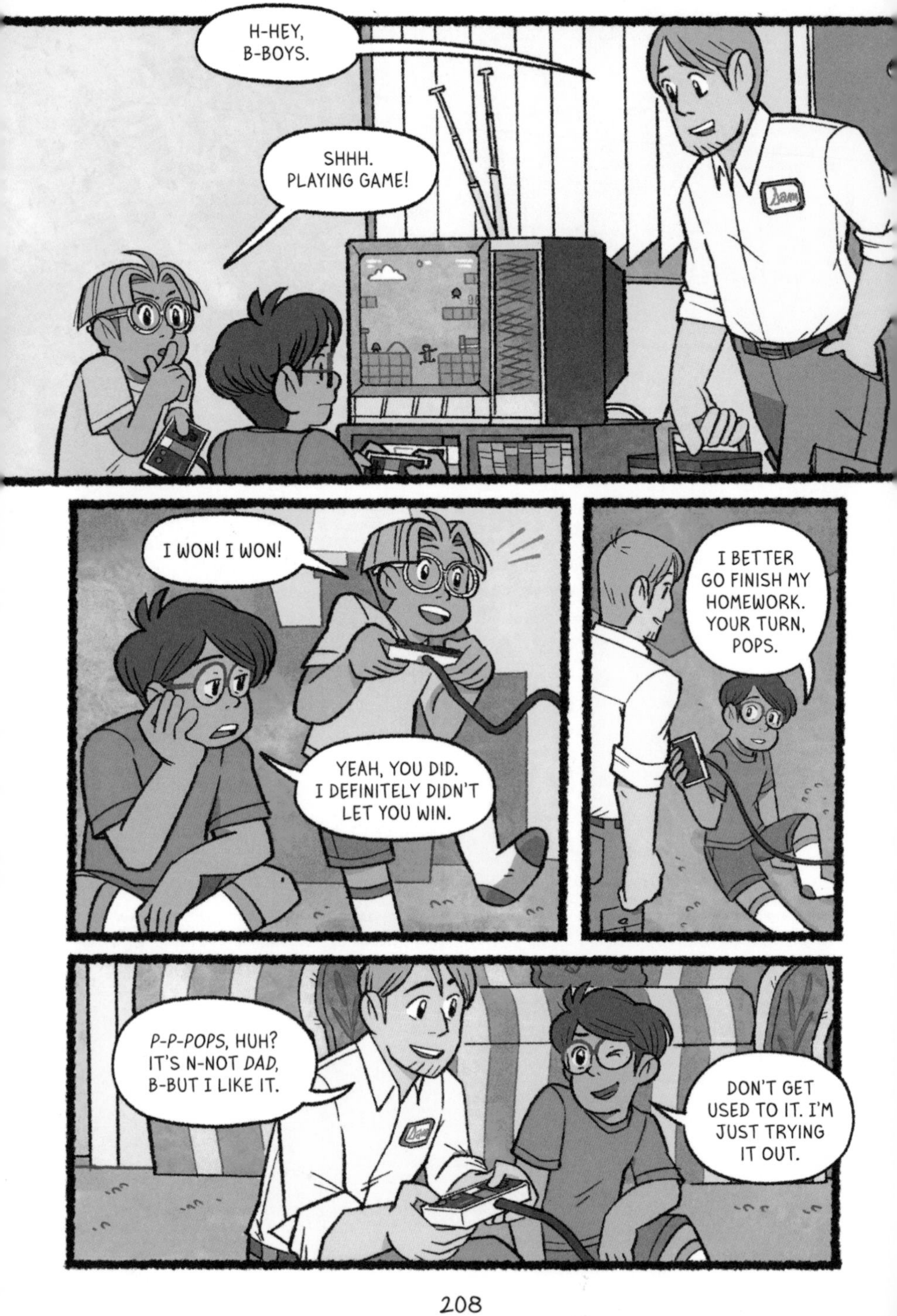

H-HEY, B-BOYS.
SHHH. PLAYING GAME!
I WON! I WON!
YEAH, YOU DID. I DEFINITELY DIDN'T LET YOU WIN.
I BETTER GO FINISH MY HOMEWORK. YOUR TURN, POPS.
P-P-POPS, HUH? IT'S N-NOT *DAD*, B-BUT I LIKE IT.
DON'T GET USED TO IT. I'M JUST TRYING IT OUT.

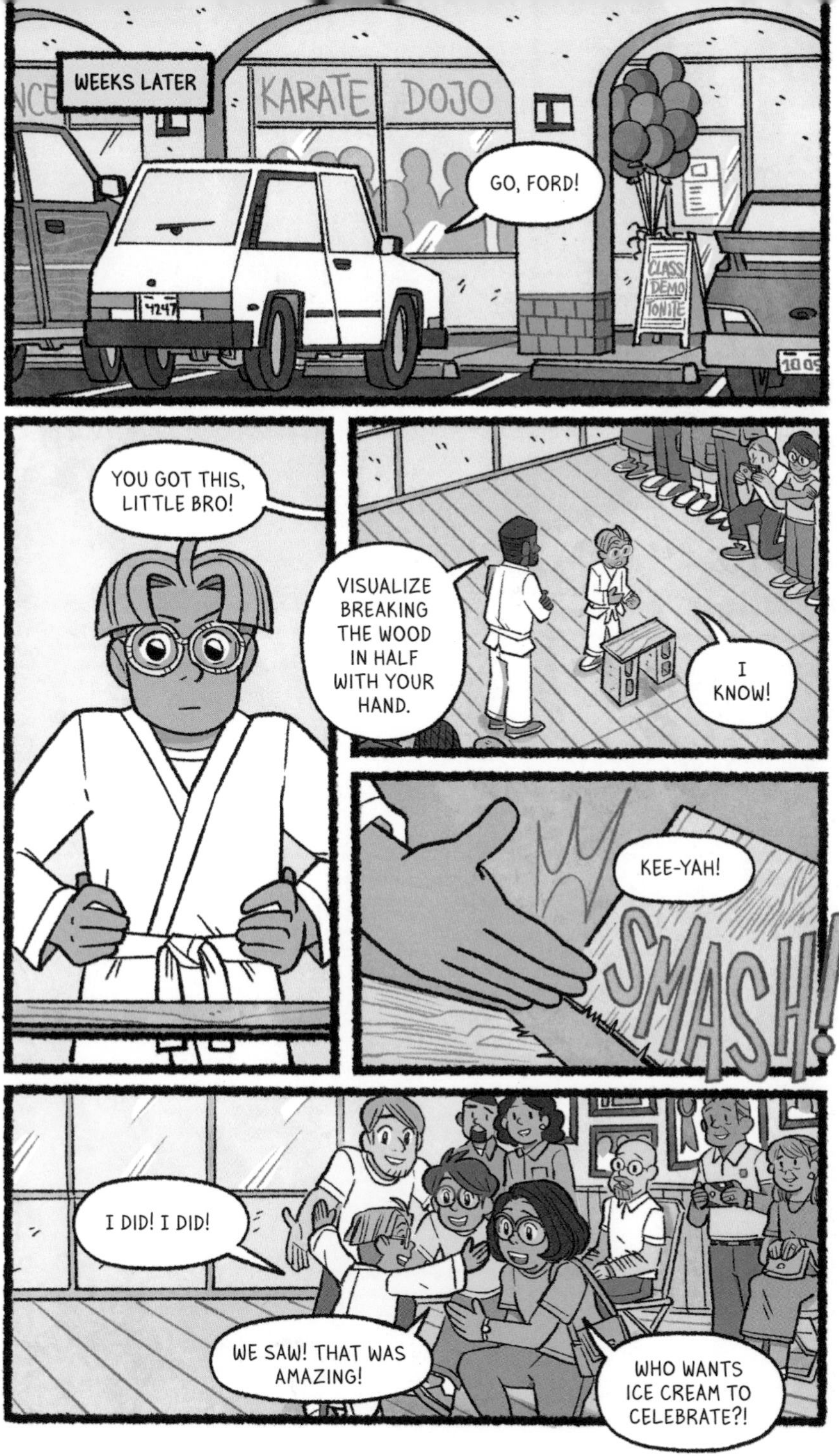
WEEKS LATER
KARATE DOJO
CLASS DEMO TONITE
GO, FORD!
YOU GOT THIS, LITTLE BRO!
VISUALIZE BREAKING THE WOOD IN HALF WITH YOUR HAND.
I KNOW!
KEE-YAH!
SMASH!
I DID! I DID!
WE SAW! THAT WAS AMAZING!
WHO WANTS ICE CREAM TO CELEBRATE?!

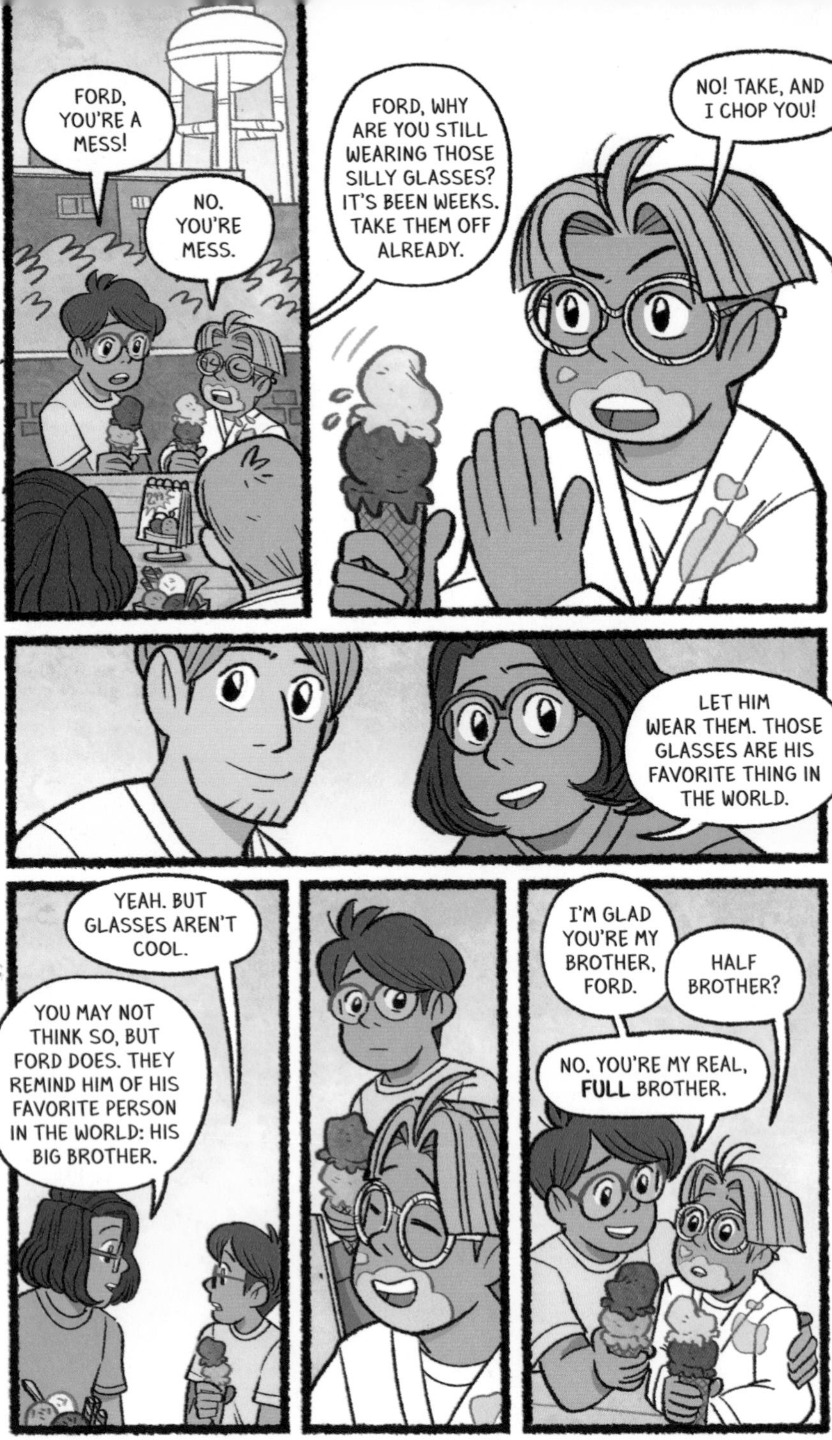

FORD, YOU'RE A MESS!
NO. YOU'RE MESS.
FORD, WHY ARE YOU STILL WEARING THOSE SILLY GLASSES? IT'S BEEN WEEKS. TAKE THEM OFF ALREADY.
NO! TAKE, AND I CHOP YOU!
LET HIM WEAR THEM. THOSE GLASSES ARE HIS FAVORITE THING IN THE WORLD.
YEAH. BUT GLASSES AREN'T COOL.
YOU MAY NOT THINK SO, BUT FORD DOES. THEY REMIND HIM OF HIS FAVORITE PERSON IN THE WORLD: HIS BIG BROTHER.
I'M GLAD YOU'RE MY BROTHER, FORD.
HALF BROTHER?
NO. YOU'RE MY REAL, **FULL** BROTHER.

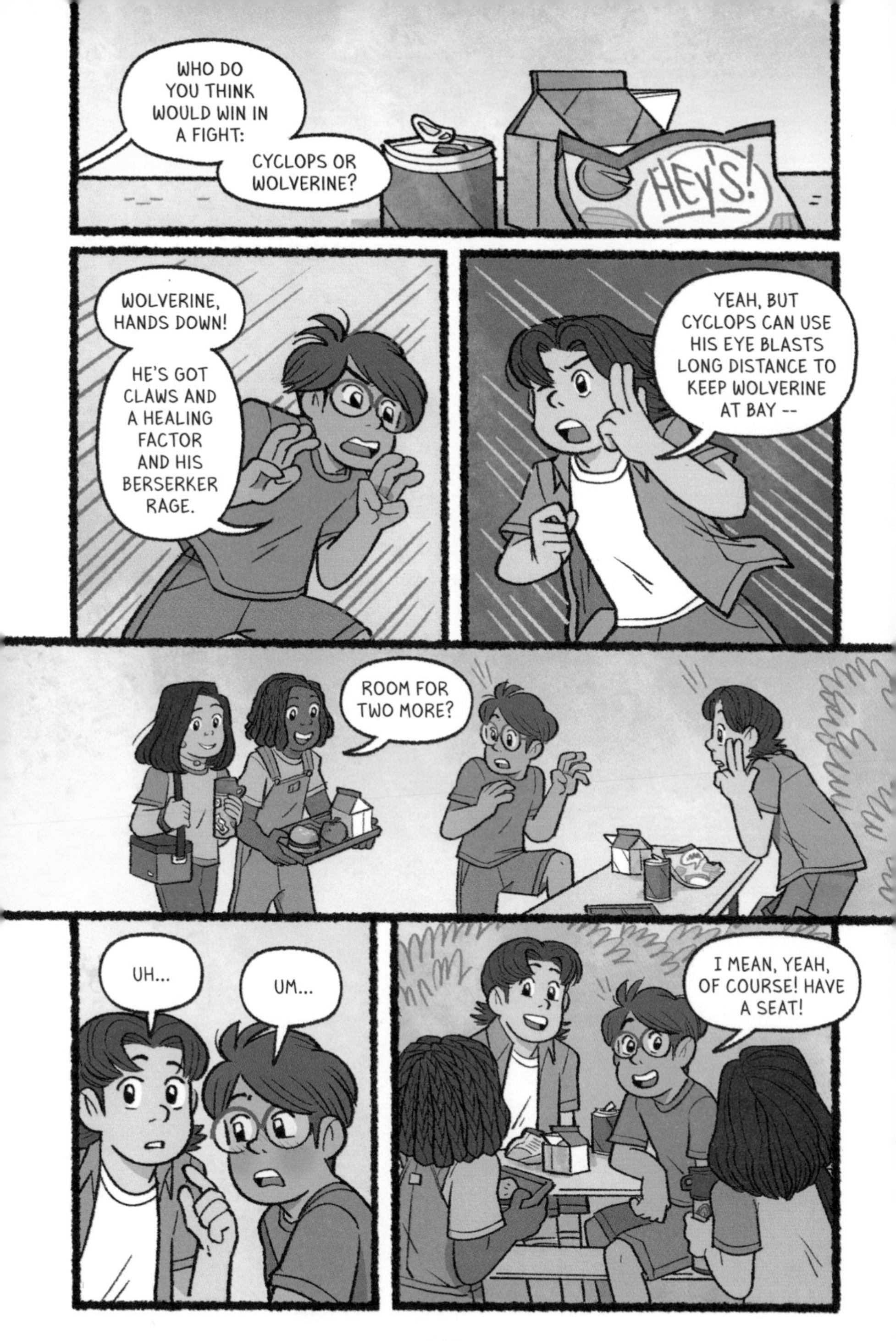
WHO DO YOU THINK WOULD WIN IN A FIGHT:
CYCLOPS OR WOLVERINE?
HEY'S!
WOLVERINE, HANDS DOWN!
HE'S GOT CLAWS AND A HEALING FACTOR AND HIS BERSERKER RAGE.
YEAH, BUT CYCLOPS CAN USE HIS EYE BLASTS LONG DISTANCE TO KEEP WOLVERINE AT BAY --
ROOM FOR TWO MORE?
UH...
UM...
I MEAN, YEAH, OF COURSE! HAVE A SEAT!

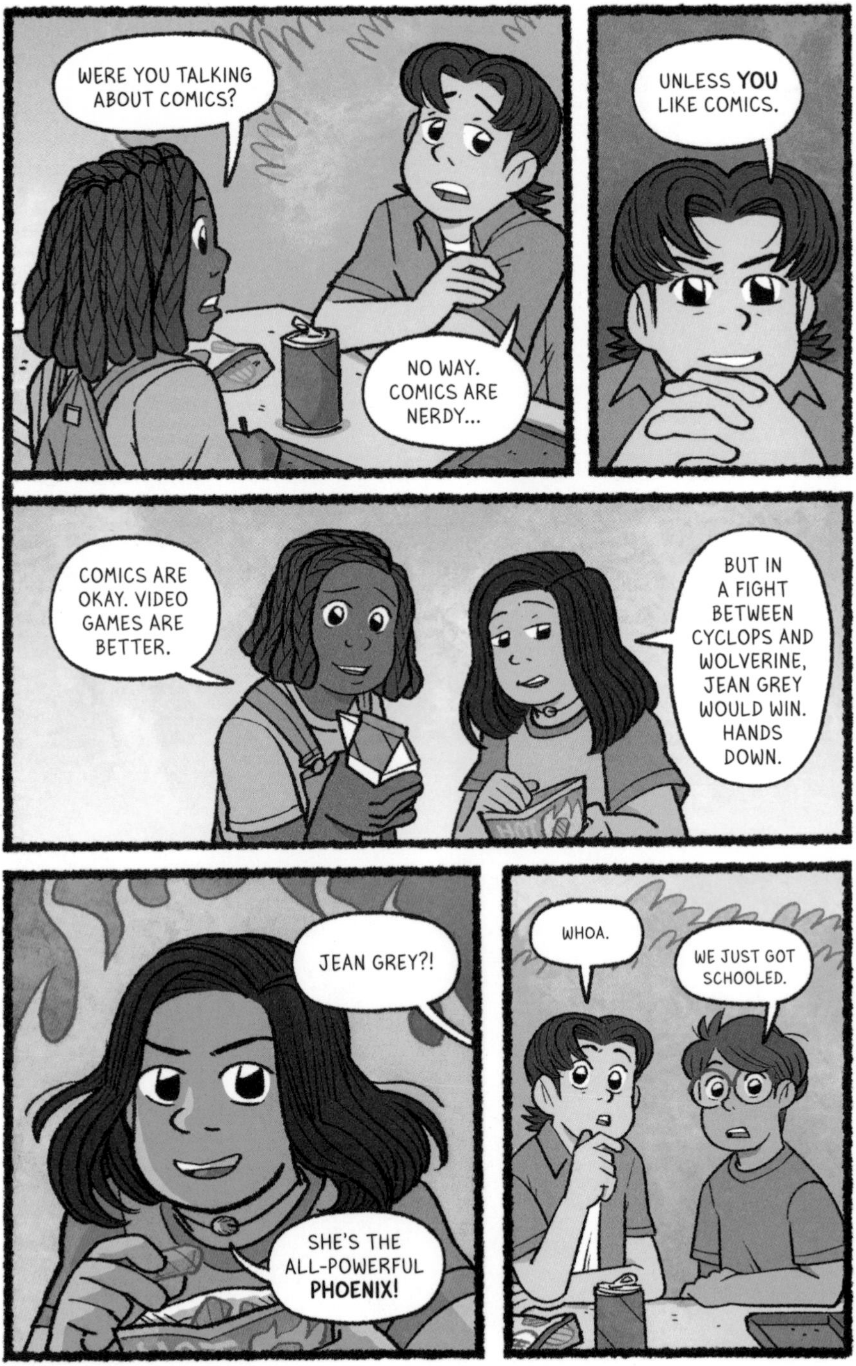
WERE YOU TALKING ABOUT COMICS?
NO WAY. COMICS ARE NERDY...
UNLESS **YOU** LIKE COMICS.
COMICS ARE OKAY. VIDEO GAMES ARE BETTER.
BUT IN A FIGHT BETWEEN CYCLOPS AND WOLVERINE, JEAN GREY WOULD WIN. HANDS DOWN.
JEAN GREY?!
SHE'S THE ALL-POWERFUL **PHOENIX!**
WHOA.
WE JUST GOT SCHOOLED.

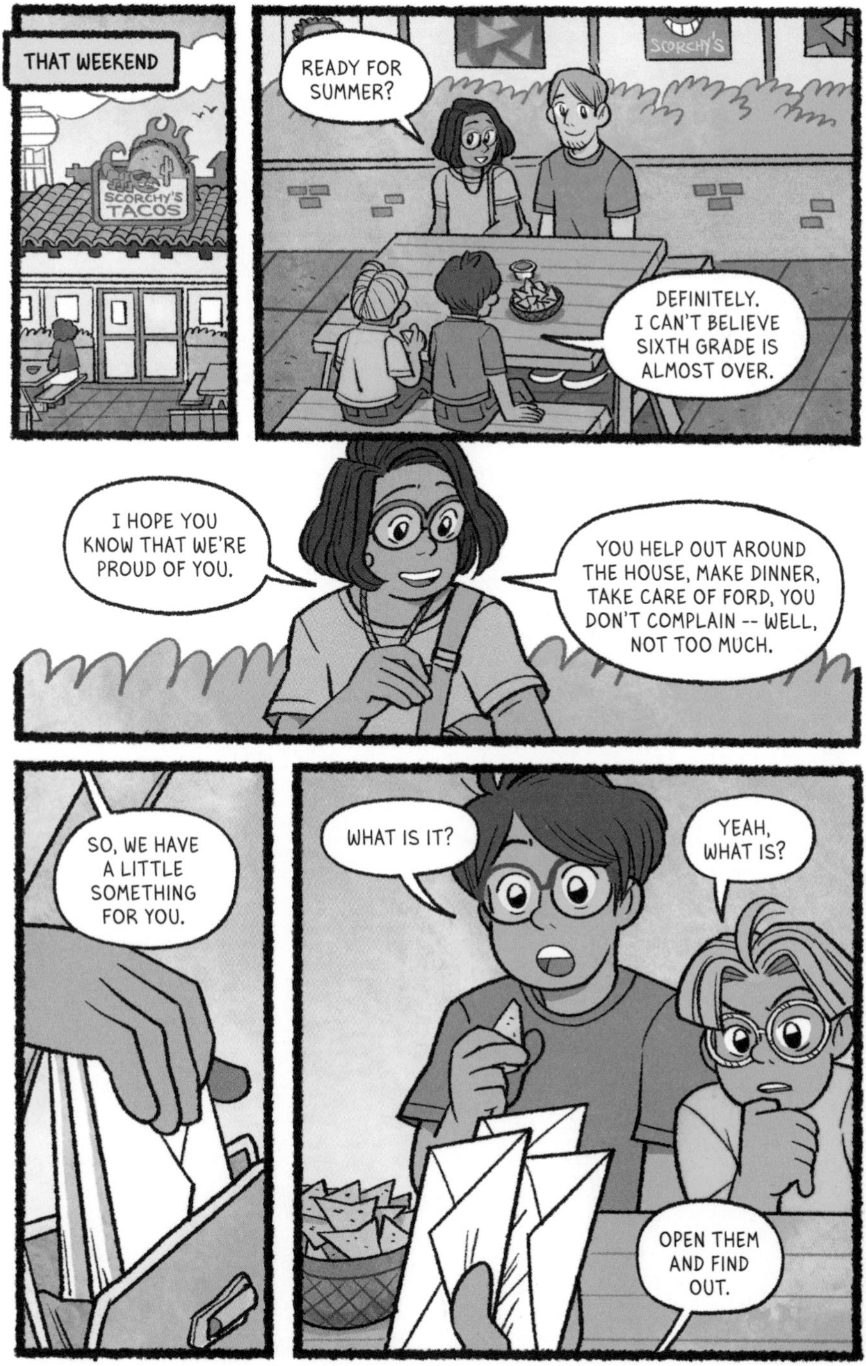
THAT WEEKEND
SCORCHY'S TACOS
SCORCHY'S
READY FOR SUMMER?
DEFINITELY. I CAN'T BELIEVE SIXTH GRADE IS ALMOST OVER.
I HOPE YOU KNOW THAT WE'RE PROUD OF YOU.
YOU HELP OUT AROUND THE HOUSE, MAKE DINNER, TAKE CARE OF FORD, YOU DON'T COMPLAIN -- WELL, NOT TOO MUCH.
SO, WE HAVE A LITTLE SOMETHING FOR YOU.
WHAT IS IT?
YEAH, WHAT IS?
OPEN THEM AND FIND OUT.

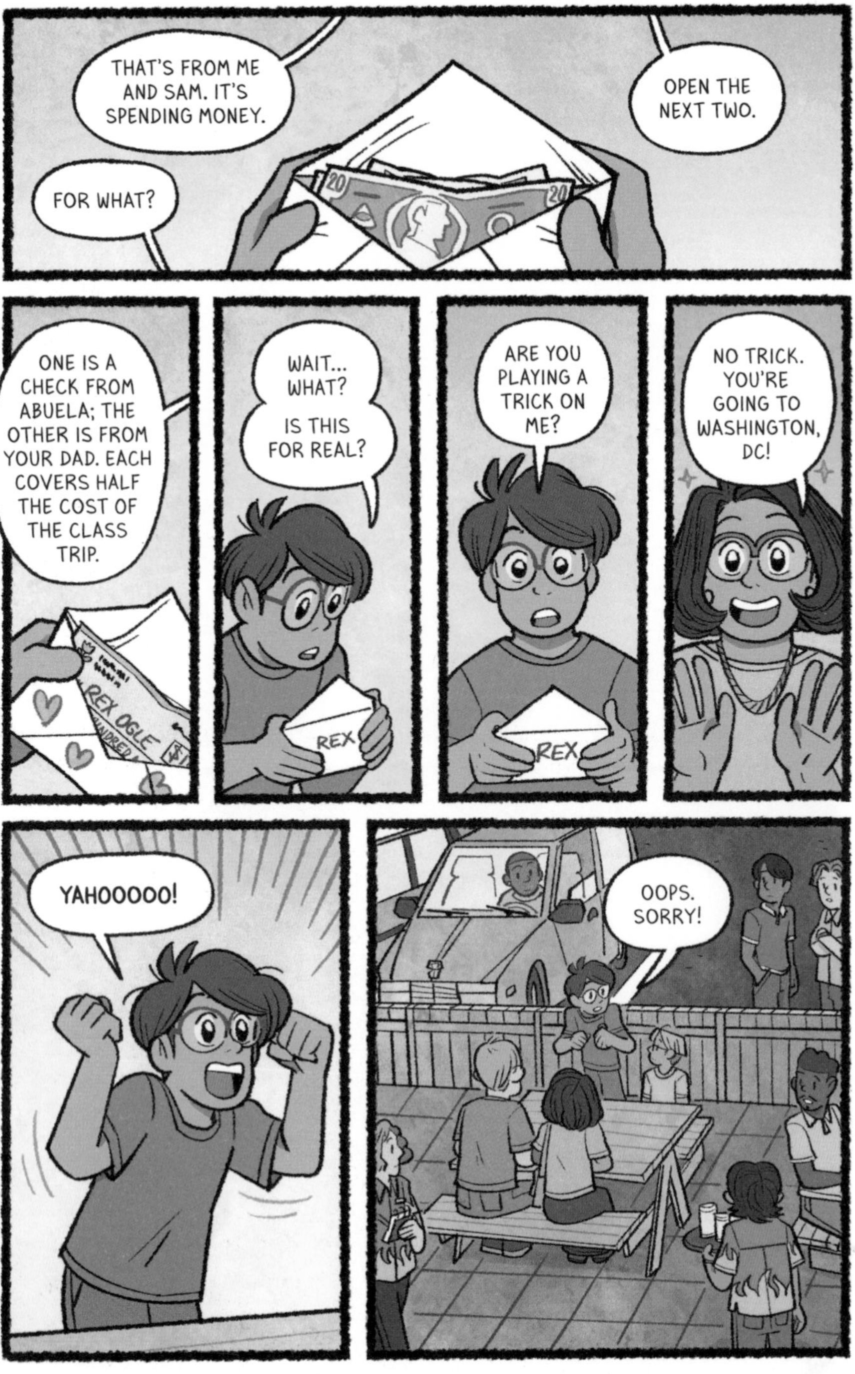
THAT'S FROM ME AND SAM. IT'S SPENDING MONEY.
FOR WHAT?
OPEN THE NEXT TWO.
ONE IS A CHECK FROM ABUELA; THE OTHER IS FROM YOUR DAD. EACH COVERS HALF THE COST OF THE CLASS TRIP.
REX OGLE
WAIT... WHAT?
IS THIS FOR REAL?
REX
ARE YOU PLAYING A TRICK ON ME?
REX
NO TRICK. YOU'RE GOING TO WASHINGTON, DC!
YAHOOOOO!
OOPS. SORRY!

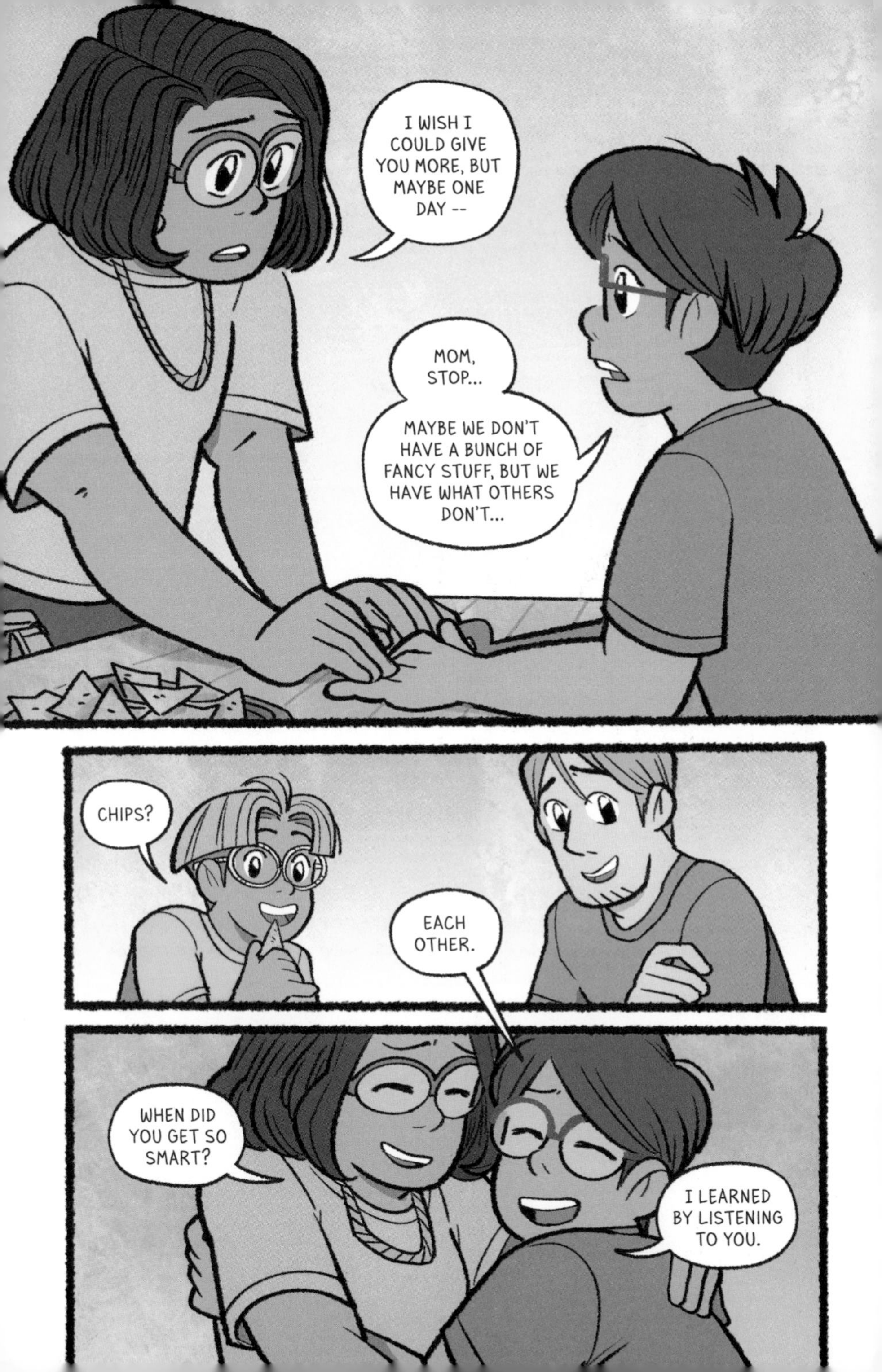
I WISH I COULD GIVE YOU MORE, BUT MAYBE ONE DAY --
MOM, STOP...
MAYBE WE DON'T HAVE A BUNCH OF FANCY STUFF, BUT WE HAVE WHAT OTHERS DON'T...
CHIPS?
EACH OTHER.
WHEN DID YOU GET SO SMART?
I LEARNED BY LISTENING TO YOU.

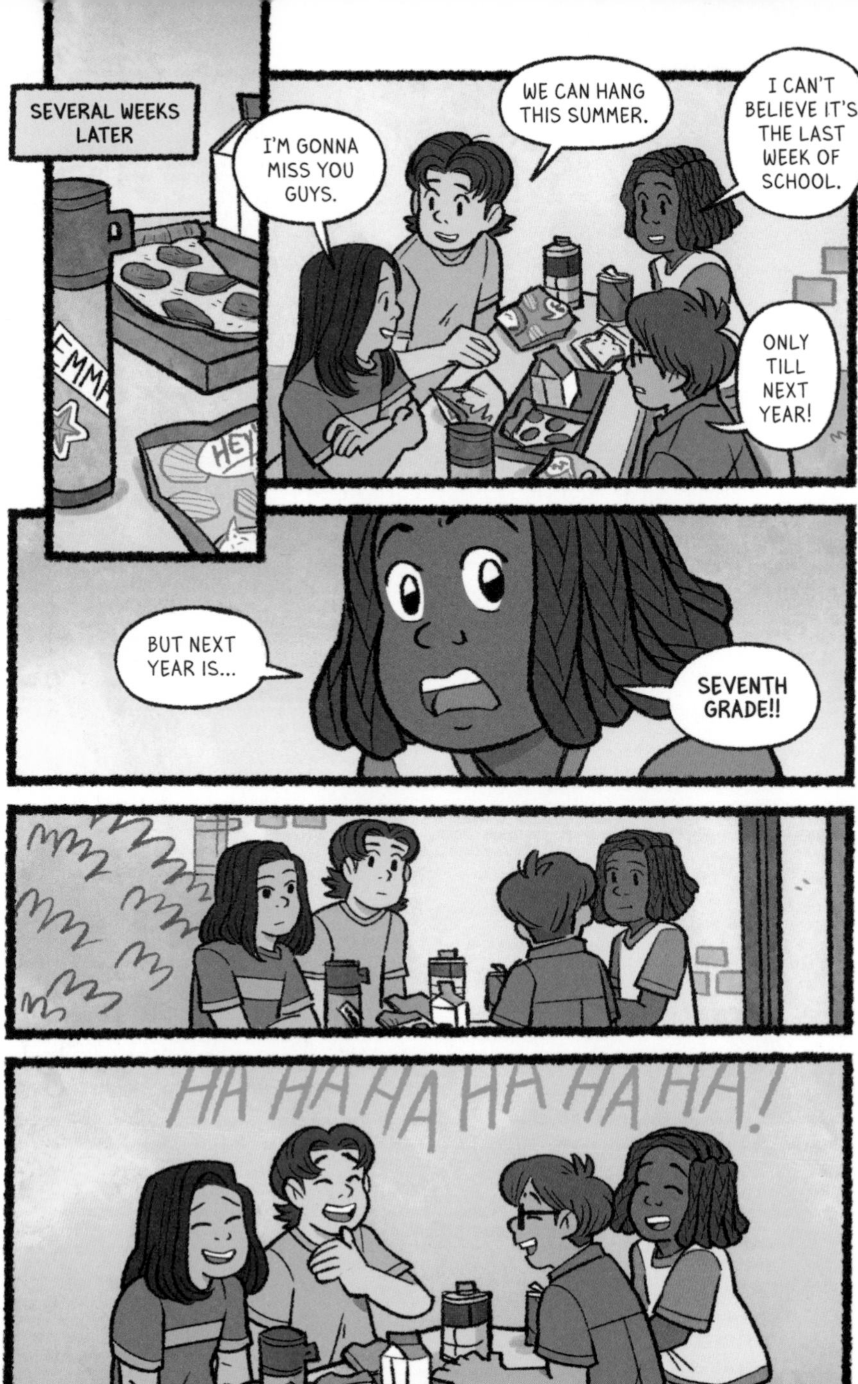
SEVERAL WEEKS LATER
EMMA
HEY
I'M GONNA MISS YOU GUYS.
WE CAN HANG THIS SUMMER.
I CAN'T BELIEVE IT'S THE LAST WEEK OF SCHOOL.
ONLY TILL NEXT YEAR!
BUT NEXT YEAR IS...
SEVENTH GRADE!!
HA HA HA HA HA HA HA HA!

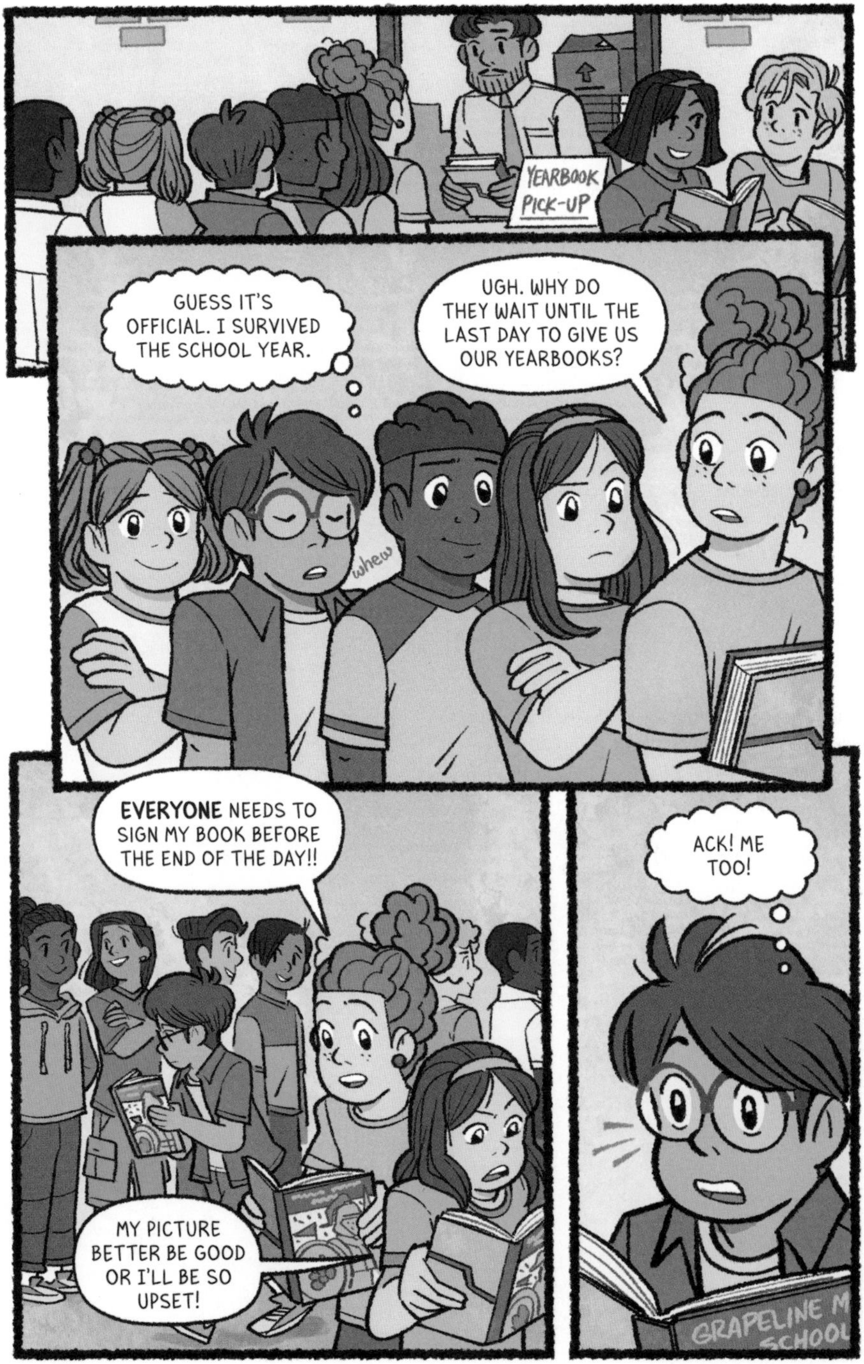
YEARBOOK PICK-UP
GUESS IT'S OFFICIAL. I SURVIVED THE SCHOOL YEAR.
UGH. WHY DO THEY WAIT UNTIL THE LAST DAY TO GIVE US OUR YEARBOOKS?
whew
EVERYONE NEEDS TO SIGN MY BOOK BEFORE THE END OF THE DAY!!
MY PICTURE BETTER BE GOOD OR I'LL BE SO UPSET!
ACK! ME TOO!
GRAPELINE M SCHOOL

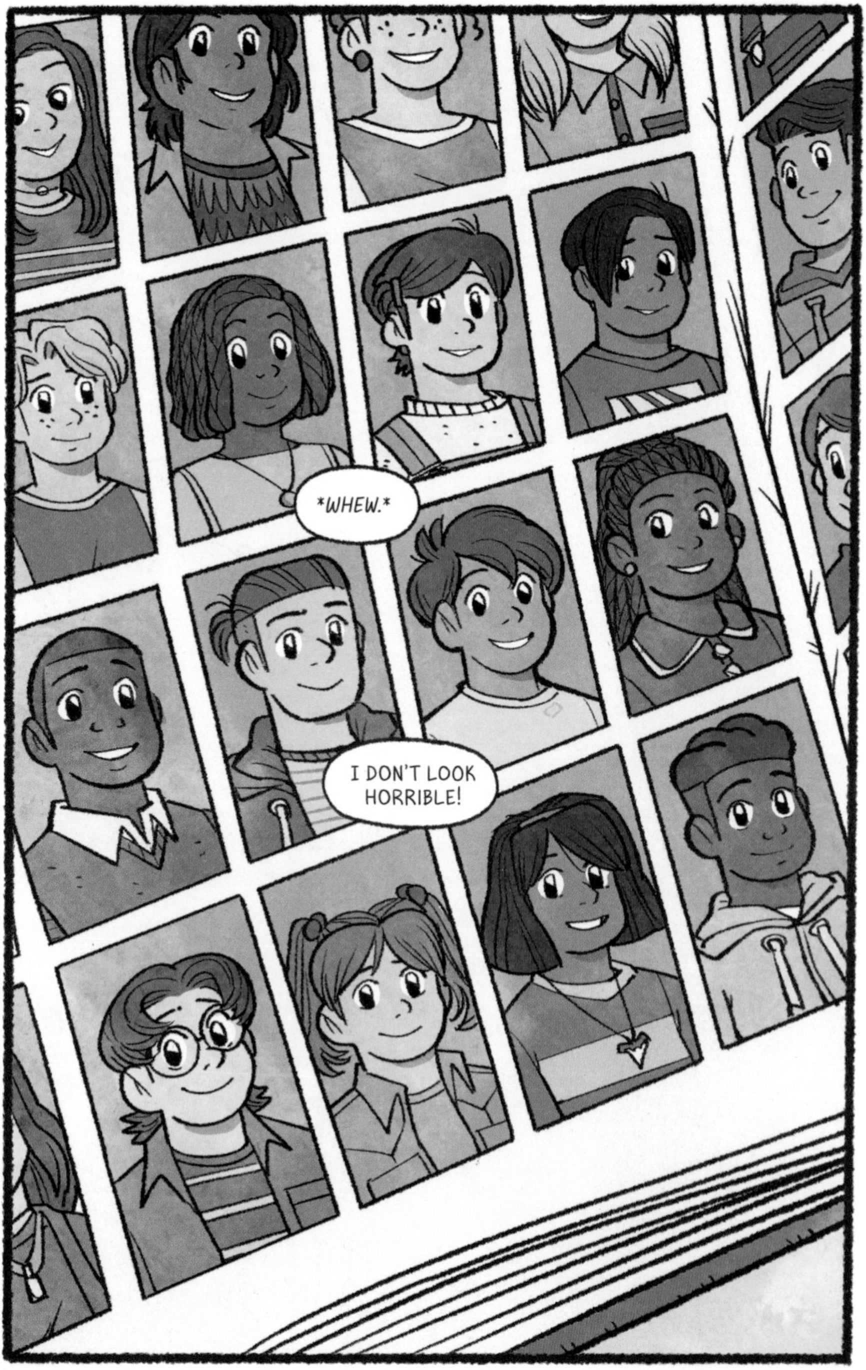
WHEW.
I DON'T LOOK HORRIBLE!

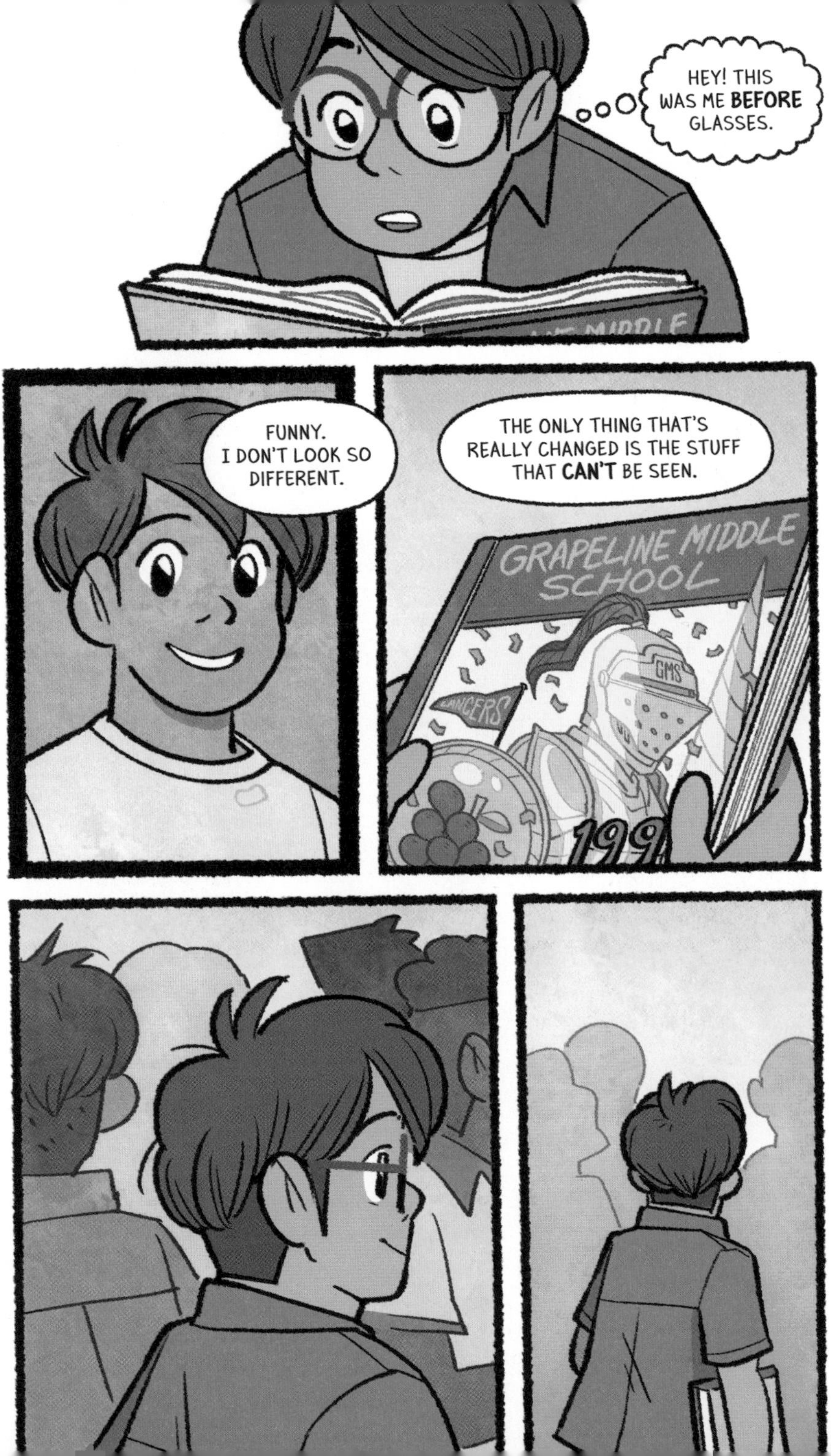
HEY! THIS WAS ME BEFORE GLASSES.
FUNNY. I DON'T LOOK SO DIFFERENT.
THE ONLY THING THAT'S REALLY CHANGED IS THE STUFF THAT CAN'T BE SEEN.
GRAPELINE MIDDLE SCHOOL
GMS
LANCERS

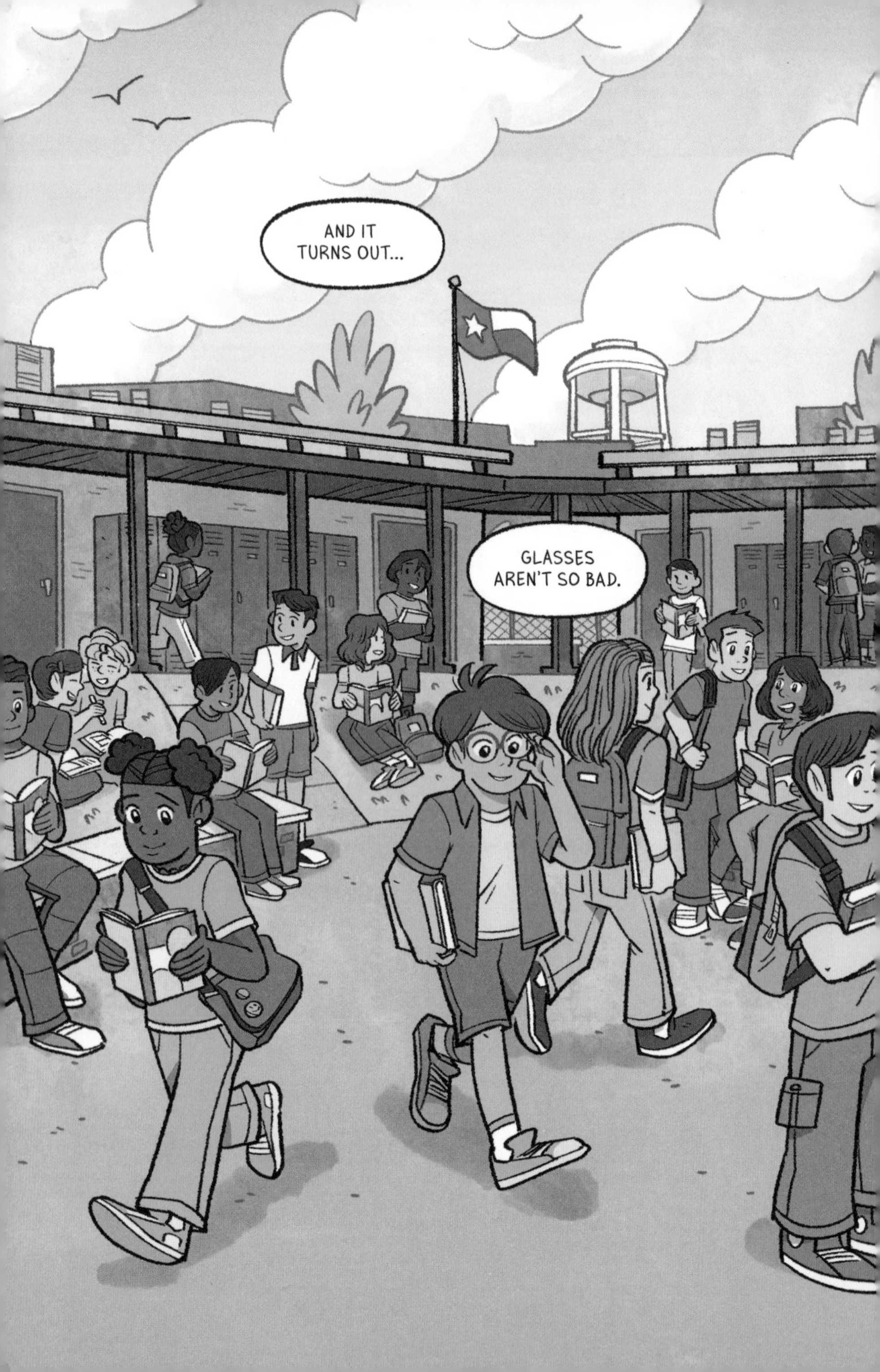
AND IT TURNS OUT...
GLASSES AREN'T SO BAD.